A MARSDEN ROMANCE COLLECTION

A MARSDEN ROMANCE COLLECTION

DAWN BROWER

MONARCHAL GLENN PRESS

CONTENTS

A FLAWED JEWEL

EXCERPT: ALL THE
LADIES LOVE
COVENTRY

Prologue 707

DAWN BROWER

A Flawed JEWEL

CHAPTER 1

March 3, 1861

"You need to suck in more, Miss Pieretta."

Tully, her maid prodded and pulled at the strings of Pieretta's corset to tighten it as much as possible. One of many torturous things a lady must endure to remain fashionable. It was her job to get Pieretta ready for the biggest voyage of her life. There was nothing Pieretta wanted more than to stay on the plantation where she grew up, but her presence was required at her grandpere's estate in France. She had no real desire to go anywhere. Everything she knew was in Charleston. She had no choice but to go live in a country she knew nothing about.

Tully yanked on the laces one last time squeezing Pieretta's ribs tightly inside her chest. She struggled to breathe. Pieretta squirmed in an effort to loosen the stays. "Miss Pieretta, please, we need to tighten this corset a little more, or you will never fit into that traveling dress you had the seamstress make for you. We all know you're only stalling so you don't have to leave the plantation. Your grandpere is expecting you, and you need to be on that ship."

"Oh be quiet, Tully. The laces are too tight. Fix them before I can no longer breathe." Stupid know-it-all maid thought she could order her around. It was bad enough that her entire life was about to change. Now she had to deal with Tully ordering her around. "The dress will fit and still allow air to enter my lungs. Mind your own business and do as you're told," Pieretta scolded her.

As a southern belle, she didn't have to do anything more than host parties and help her father manage the house. The most traveling she had ever done was to attend picnics and soirees at neighboring plantations. She had never traveled more than fifteen miles away from her home. The idea of sailing all the way to France—Pia hated to admit it, but it terrified her.

Pieretta had never boarded a ship, now she was expected to sale on a long voyage. She, at least, had seen one or two while they were in the Charleston harbor, but it had never crossed her mind ever to give one a closer look. It was not an experience she ever expected to have.

Her happiest moments were in Charleston, in the heart of the only home she had ever known.

Pieretta didn't want to leave everything behind. It was hard to comprehend why her grandpere insisted she come live with him in France. The fact she didn't have any living male relatives in Charleston shouldn't matter. She could look after the plantation and deal with the overseer. Her father made sure she understood every aspect of running the plantation. She had the best education possible. He believed females had a right to learn more than just how to run a household or proper etiquette.

Oh, Papa, I miss you so much...

A sting of pain hit her chest. She was reminded again of her father's death a month ago. Each day without her father was more unbearable than the one before it. Pieretta couldn't believe she had to live in a world where he no longer existed. His death had been so sudden—had suddenly just quit breathing. It had been so devastating to realize someone could die without any warning.

Pieretta was all alone in the world.

She had no brothers or sisters, and her only living relative was her grandpere. So it was with a heavy heart that she prepared to make the journey to live with him in France.

Her mother died when Pieretta was born, and her father

never remarried. He loved her mother too much to ever envision a life with someone else. The only females Pieretta spent time around on a regular basis were servants. Without the benefit of a maternal influence, Pieretta had more masculine ideas about her future. It would have been all right to stay and run the plantation if she had been a man, but as a woman, she had no real say in her life until she reached her majority.

Until then, her grandpere, Comte Renard Dubois, had the right to tell her how to live her life.

Because she had never been to France, she didn't know what to expect once she arrived. Grandpere had told her stories about his estate and how large it was, but she had never had the opportunity to visit. He outlined the many gardens and the different foliage that it encased. Pieretta looked forward to walking amongst the roses and counting the various shades his gardener cultivated.

She had never seen an actual rose, but her grandpere's description made them sound like the most beautiful flower on Earth. The blossoms were rumored to be filled with an aromatic scent that tantalized the nose. Rose buds bloomed in a variety of colors from the shade of a blushing bride's cheeks to the various hues of sunshine bouncing through the windows of her sitting room. Even with the allure of seeing roses for the first time, she still had no desire to travel such a long distance.

All of her trunks were packed and already aboard the ship. The only thing required of her now was to get herself ready, get in the carriage, and travel to the docks.

Pieretta wanted to throw a fit and stomp her feet, but that would be out of character for her. While her father often indulged her, Pieretta was not prone to temper tantrums. She did occasionally let her displeasure be known, but most of the time she was able to hold back the temptation to scream. Pieretta took a deep breath and exhaled slowly, preparing herself for whatever the journey might entail.

She stood up straight as Tully finished tying the corset's laces. She didn't want to stand still any longer than necessary and keeping still ensured the bows on her dress were tied evenly.

In her mind, fighting the inevitable would not help her situation. The servants needed to make sure she made it on the ship. Even though Pieretta didn't to move to France, she could make the best of the situation. Her life on the plantation had a repetitive quality to it—nothing ever changed.

Instead of harping on the negative, she could look at this forced trip as an adventure.

"Almost done, Miss Pieretta."

"It's taking forever," she groaned. Sometimes being female was a nuisance. Surely it didn't take this long for a man to get dressed.

"It'll be all done before you know it and then we will be boarding a ship to France."

Did Tully have to give her a reminder of it?

Tully finished lacing her stays, and the corset hugged every curve of her torso. She walked over and picked up Pieretta's traveling gown and opened it for Pieretta to step into. Once she was fully within the confines of the dress, Tully pulled it up and began the long process of latching all of the hooks up the side. She opted not to wear any petticoats or a hoop skirt, as it would be ridiculous to wear them in the small confines of the ship. Her traveling costume was made of the finest dyed black wool.

Black Wool was ever so dull and boring, but Pia didn't mind wearing it to honor her father. She'd miss him for the rest of her days. When she received the letter from her grandpere, Pieretta visited her favorite seamstress to have a few traveling costumes made for her crossing to France. She had no idea what the current fashion was and figured more gowns could be made upon her arrival at her grandpere's estate.

Besides only so much could be done to make a black gown look good...

She was trying to be practical, and Grandpere wouldn't mind. He would want his little princess to be happy. After all, one couldn't be happy if one wasn't fashionable. Grandpere believed she didn't have the brains for anything besides frivolous things such as fashion. He did not realize Pieretta had a lot of things on her mind, and fashion wasn't always at the forefront.

Soon he'd realize how mistaken he was about her character.

For instance, her love of mythology consumed her. Some of her favorite books housed stories of the gods and how they had fallen. She read everything from Norse to Greek mythology. Her favorite had always been Thor. Pieretta often wished she could visit Asgard and have the opportunity to meet him and Loki.

"Tully, please tell me you remembered to pack my favorite books."

"Yes, ma'am" Tully nodded. "You have more books packed than you do gowns."

"Books are more important."

"hmmph" Tully snorted. "I wouldn't know as I've never had the opportunity to learn to read."

"Maybe I will teach you on our voyage. Not like we have anything better to occupy our time with."

"I don't know how much use I'd have for learning." Tully frowned. "Why don't we just wait and see how the crossing goes. You might find something to entertain yourself with."

Pieretta sighed. No one truly understood her—especially her only living relative.

Grandpere knew next to nothing about what Pieretta actually liked. He assumed she was similar to her mother, Dominique Dubois Carlyle, who only thought of frivolous things such as the latest styles and idle gossip.

Her grandpere couldn't be more wrong.

He usually visited her at least twice a year, staying for a few weeks and then returning home. Her mother was his original princess. Grandpere had doted on her his whole life. When her mother died, he had been heartbroken. When he saw his new granddaughter with her mother's royal blue eyes and pale blond hair, he had decided that he had a new princess to coddle with affection. It had helped to ease the sting of his loss, finding a near carbon copy of his beloved daughter. He'd found a way to fill the empty hole in his heart with Pieretta.

Tully finished connecting all of the hooks on Pieretta's dress. She inspected her work, trailing her fingers over the dress to smooth the lines. Stepping away, Tully motioned for

Pieretta to sit down on the chair next to her vanity. "Miss Pieretta, you need to sit down so I can fix your hair."

She had no idea what Tully meant by fix her hair. She hadn't touched it. "What are you going to do to my hair, Tully?" Pieretta asked.

"Don't you worry any, Miss Pieretta. I am just going to pull it back a bit so it's out of your way. You're not going to want to deal with it on that there ship. It needs to be more manageable."

Pieretta sighed and sat in front of her vanity. Unfortunately, she had to deal with Tully even though she was a meddlesome nuisance. Tully had helped raise her, the servant believed she had a right to dictate how Pieretta should live her life. Tully's many lectures were a normal part of her day. In Pieretta's mind, Tully was overstepping her duties and trying to take the place of the mother she never knew. The maid was traveling with her only because a young unmarried lady could not travel alone. She was going to be the only person Pieretta would bring with her into this new life.

"I suppose you're right," Pieretta agreed. "It would be rather tiresome to constantly push my hair out of the way."

"Trust me, I know what I'm talking about."

Pieretta rolled her eyes. "Oh? And exactly how many ships have you sailed on?"

"I haven't always been on this plantation," Tully informed her. "I came over here on a ship when I was a tiny thing. Of course, my hair didn't have the opportunity to get blown around, but I do remember the howling winds."

"Howling winds?" Pieretta gulped. "What do you mean?"

"There was a nasty bit of storm for half the journey. The winds whipped right through the ship leaving an eerie whistling piercing our ears."

That didn't sound—appealing.

Tully pulled Pieretta's braid tighter and wrapped it around her head. Pieretta sighed, fighting tears as Tully continued to plait her hair. It was difficult to keep her emotions from welling up and spilling out of her. If she had one wish, it would be to find a way out of the situation her grandpere had forced her into. Her only option wasn't really an option in her mind. She could get married, but she didn't want any person to have that sort of power over her life. Relinquishing control meant fighting for the right to make any decisions for herself. Marriage was the one thing Pieretta had never wanted.

When she turned twenty-five, she would gain control of the plantation. It would be a long seven years living with her grandpere, but if anyone could do it, she could. Pieretta had to make sure her grandpere knew she was never going to get married. In Pieretta's mind, any woman had the capability to make her own decisions. It would be a cold day in hell before she allowed a man to have any kind of control over her life or her inheritance. Her father had made sure she was educated far beyond her station, and she had a working knowledge. She was intelligent and intended to use everything she learned to further her ambitions.

Tully finished fussing with her hair. Her pale blond locks were now securely wound around her head in a practical plait. Pieretta brushed a tear from the corner of her eye. Would she ever be happy again? She had serious doubts that happiness lay in her future. Pieretta stood and flattened her dress, smoothing the lines and wrinkles along the side of her skirt so it fell evenly as she moved. She glanced in the mirror. The dress wasn't designed to be flattering, but Pieretta believed she could make anything look good. She may be pale and sad, but she was still beautiful. She was curvy in all the right places with a small waist.

"All right, Tully, I guess now is as good a time as any," Pieretta said. "Go and have the carriage brought around. I'm ready for an adventure. That's how I'm choosing to see this change in my life."

Eerie winds and all...

Pieretta stood and looked around her bedroom one last time. Several years would pass before she could return and take control of the plantation. It was important that she store all of the good memories so the years in France would be easier to bear.

The fight to gain control over her life would be tough, but the things that mattered the most were worth fighting for. Even though at times she felt like she would never be happy again, Pieretta had hoped that she would find a reason to smile. Changes were always hard to make.

She wandered over to her bedroom door and pulled it open. She began the long trek down the stairs to the main hallway. At the bottom of the steps, she looked up as Tully made her way down the long staircase. No one ever promised life would be easy, and if Pieretta knew one thing, it was that she could get through any hurdle life put in her way. This was only one bump on a very long road ahead of her, but in the end, she knew she would get what she wanted. After all, Pieretta always did.

∾

THE DOCKS WERE NOT A PLEASANT PLACE TO WALK. THEY WERE filthy and smelled of unimaginable things. The scent of rotten fish and fresh salt water permeated the air. Pieretta needed to board the ship as quickly as possible, before she stepped in something disgusting.

The waterfront was booming with activity, and the noise was deafening. It was hard to ascertain the different sounds and locate where they might be coming from. The combination of the odors stung her nose and throat. The smoky air made her eyes water. Pieretta covered her nose with her hand in an effort to block out the stench but was forced to wipe the tears from her eyes as they started to stream down her face. Tully followed behind her as fast as she could. They both wanted off the docks as fast as they could manage it.

"Miss Pieretta, we need to move faster. I don't like it on these docks. Some of those men are making me uneasy. They're looking at us like we're a special treat they want to lap up."

"Don't be ridiculous Tully, they wouldn't dare harm us. We'll be fine. Just the same, there's our ship. Let's board quickly and be done with this area."

A lump formed in her throat. She gulped it down and refrained from looking at the men Tully referred to. They made her just as uneasy, but she refused to admit it.

They moved quickly to the gangplank so they could board

the clipper. The ship had three large masts each filled to the top with five sails. When they stepped on deck, the first mate and captain greeted them.

The captain folded one of his hands behind his back with the other one tucked in front just below his chest and bowed to Pieretta. "It's a pleasure to have you aboard, Miss Carlyle. I am Captain Devere, and this is my first mate, Cam. I know Comte Dubois is anxiously awaiting your arrival in France."

"Do you know my grandpere well then?"

"As this is one of his ships, I have had many occasions to spend time with him, discussing how his shipments are to be handled. You are one of our most important cargos. He made sure to have a meeting with me before I left France and gave me the strictest instructions regarding your safety on this crossing."

Did he? She shouldn't be surprised, and yet she was.

"Grandpere can be very protective. I'm surprised he didn't make the trip himself."

"He wanted to, but an emergency arose at the last minute on one of his estates. It was something that required his personal attention. It is why he gave me instructions as to your passage and care. I hope your crossing with us is pleasant."

Pleasant? As far as she was concerned, there really wasn't anything that could make this journey tolerable let alone pleasurable. It took every ounce of her will to not come back with a rude comment. The need to get to her cabin and rest was starting to become a top priority to Pieretta. She needed to vacate the captain's company with as much haste as possible.

With as much politeness as she could muster, she cleared her throat. "I certainly wouldn't want it to be unpleasant. Who is to show us to our cabin?"

"My first mate will gladly give you a brief tour of the ship and show you to your cabin. We would prefer you remain in your quarters for most of the trip. It is the safest option. We will have a tray brought to you for all of your meals."

Was the captain mad? How could he expect me to be confined to a small room for three weeks? She would have to make her needs known from the very beginning or be stifled inside of a cabin with Tully for the lengthy passage. Her throat closed up just at the thought of it—she hated being confined.

"I couldn't possibly stay locked inside a small room the entire journey, Captain. We are going to be on the ship for at least two weeks. I would go mad for sure. I must insist on daily walks above deck."

The captain studied her for several seconds before he nodded.

"Very well, but limit them to thirty minute intervals twice a day. Do not walk on deck once night falls for any reason. If I tell you to get below deck, you are not to argue. Just go. I wouldn't insist unless it was a matter of safety."

"I can agree to that."

"Very well, Cam will see you to your cabin now."

The first mate guided Tully and Pieretta below deck and escorted them to their accommodations. There wasn't a lot of free space aboard the ship. The captain gave his quarters to the two women for the trip. Pieretta wondered where the captain would stay during the crossing to France. It would be cramped for all those involved.

Pieretta sighed as she entered the cabin. The limited space didn't leave much room for her to share with her maid. The journey across the ocean stuck in such a tightly confined room with Tully constantly telling her what to do might drive her mad. Tully scrambled in behind her, scuffling her feet as she settled into the small room. If only Grandpere hadn't demanded she come live with him. Why must females be dependent on their male relations?

"Thank you, sir. I think we will be fine for now. How long until we set sail?"

"If all goes well, we should be on our way in an hour's time. Please remain here for the rest of the evening. It will be too dark to walk on deck, and it is easy to fall overboard when you can't see in front of you."

"I will heed your advice, sir. I have no desire to swim, or sink, any time soon." Pieretta shuddered.

As the first mate left the two women, Pieretta only had one thought. *It's going to be a very long and grueling excursion across the immense ocean.*

CHAPTER 2

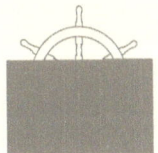

A week later...

"Captain Thor, sir. The ship has been spotted. The one you've been waiting for," bosun Cornelus informed him.

Thor lounged in his bunk. It had been an uneventful few days aboard the Sea Rover. He had waited patiently for the vessel leaving the American shore to cross paths with him. It carried a package he was desperate to get his hands on. That particular parcel held extreme importance to him—for one reason and one reason only. He needed it in order to finally get even with his former partner Renny Dubois.

The bloody man had organized Thor's early departure from this world.

If he hadn't been quick, he would instead reside in his eternal resting place. The bullet Renny had put into his shoulder would have entered his heart if he had not seen the glint of the pistol out of the corner of his eye. Since then, he had been patiently waiting for the opportunity to enact his revenge. As far as Renny knew, Thor died on that fateful night. The comte certainly hadn't bothered to check before he exited the docks as fast as his pudgy legs could carry him.

Thor had been twenty-four when his father died. At that time he inherited his father's business holdings along with the entailed property. Dubois-Marsden Shipping Firm was one of his more profitable business ventures. Thor had met with Comte Renard Dubois to learn more about the business side of the shipping company. He'd had a lot to learn before he could make sound business decisions. Renny took him under his wing and taught him everything. He trusted him completely. He'd been like a second father to him.

So it had come as a shock when Renny attempted to murder him. The brutal betrayal stung his pride and made it next to impossible to trust.

Thor had been on the docks in Paris overseeing the shipment of their latest cargo when everything changed. He'd looked up and saw Renny walking toward him. He turned to say something, and Renny pulled out a pistol, firing it at him. Thor had turned just enough preventing the bullet from hitting anything vital. His shoulder was nicked and he'd lost a lot of blood. With each wave of pain, he grew light-headed, causing him to lose his balance. His head had bounced off of the hard surface below him and knocked him unconscious. Renny, the bloody bastard, had left him for dead.

When he finally awoke, he had been surprised to find himself aboard a ship with his shoulder already doctored. Another captain had seen the whole thing and had Thor placed on his ship. It was on that ship, the Sea Rover, where he had made a life for himself.

It changed his life and from that moment on he became a new person, one that held no qualms about what must be done. Thor became an unscrupulous pirate—no bounty to small. Until the day would come when he'd become the Sea Rover's captain and his revenge became possible.

He worked his way up the ranks and, after a few years, he made first mate. When the old captain was killed in battle, Thor was promoted to captain as the laws of the ship dictated. He had been a pirate for five years now.

Snapping out of the distant memory, he looked up at his bosun with a smile on his lips. Thor had been planning his revenge against Renny Dubois for a very long time. All of his plans were finally going to become a reality. Today was going to be a very good day.

A cocky grin filled his face. "Corny, ol' man, that is the

best news I've heard all day. Make the call, all hands on deck. We're about to plunder us a ship."

Soon he'd have his hands on the means to take down the most evil man he knew. It didn't matter that Thor had to sink to his level to obtain it. In his mind the means more than justified the end.

If Pieretta Carlyle let him he'd try to make it up to her later—hell even if she wouldn't he'd find a way.

~

PIERETTA WAS ON THE DECK LOOKING OUT AT THE OCEAN. SHE had taken well to sea travel and enjoyed having the wind blow on her face. If only she was allowed more than thirty minutes on deck each day to enjoy it, her life on board the ship would be more ideal. The waves danced and rolled across the ship's hull, crashing into it and creating white crested waves atop the cerulean horizon. She looked across the indigo waves and saw a ship in the distance. In fact it looked like it was moving toward their ship, growing closer with each gust of wind. As the other clipper's sails brought them closer to her, Pieretta squeezed the guardrail of the ship tightly. She bit her lip, the sting of her teeth drawing a minuscule droplet of blood. Surely they could see the two vessels were going to cross paths. There was a commotion to her left so she turned to see what was going on.

"Captain! Captain!" the first mate called out.

She looked over as the first mate ran toward the captain. His face was flushed bright red from running across the windy deck. Once he arrived at his destination he stopped suddenly and with a high pitched voice delivered the imperative message to Captain Devere.

"Sir, there be a pirate ship drawing close. It's flying the red flag, we're about to be attacked."

"Hurry, all hands on deck. Make sure our important passenger gets below deck," he shouted as he ran off.

"Wait. What does it mean when it's waving a red flag?" Pieretta asked the first mate. By the way Captain Devere and his first mate acted, Pieretta knew it wasn't a good sign.

Her heart beat hard against her chest. Pirates? Surely they were mistaken.

"Don't you worry none about that, miss. Just get below deck like the captain said."

"No, I am not going below deck until you answer me."

The first mate kept shooing her, his hands waving wildly in front of her face. He made sure she turned around and started the trek back to her cabin. When she didn't move fast enough, he pushed lightly against her back in an attempt to get her to move faster. If Pieretta didn't start moving faster, it was very likely he would shove her all the way to her cabin. He clearly didn't have time to deal with the hysterics of a young girl. From the expression on his face, it was evident he was weighing his options. He kept lifting his eyebrows and looking back at the approaching ship. They continued their journey to Pieretta's cabin. The first mate needed to follow the captain's dictate to ensure her safe return to her cabin.

He turned back with a frown on his red face. "It means they're going to give no quarter." A tinge of fear colored each word he spoke.

The words didn't mean anything to Pieretta. The term was foreign to her. "I don't understand. What does give no quarter mean?" she asked him.

"They're not going to leave any survivors. They will kill us all if we allow them to board our ship. Go below deck as you were told." He scurried away. He had followed Captain Devere's orders and delivered her to her cabin—why should he care if Pieretta stayed inside. It was up to her to make sure she remained safely inside.

Pieretta's heart beat faster as the blood drained from her face. It frightened her, knowing that if the pirates boarded the ship they'd murder everyone. Pieretta quickly went inside the cabin and slammed the door shut. It was the only place she felt truly safe, but with each breath she took, she felt less and less protected on board the craft. She had never been more helpless than in that moment, thinking she was going to die. *What should I do?*

When she calmed down enough to look at her surroundings, she was surprised to see Tully paid no attention to her. Tully was unfolding one of her dresses and laying it across a table to smooth out the wrinkles, a complete waste of time in Pieretta's opinion. It wasn't as if she was going to wear it anytime soon. They were confined to the cabin.

Pieretta hadn't even considered this possibility when crossing the ocean. How could she have? She had lived a very sheltered life. It occurred to her in that moment— she really didn't know anything. She didn't want to have regrets, and more importantly, she wanted to live. She had never been given the chance to do any of the things she wanted with her life. More importantly, she had plans—beginning with an expansion to the plantation and making the lives of the slaves better. Pieretta didn't believe in slavery, but she didn't have the authority to make any changes until she had gained her majority. There were so many books she hadn't gotten a chance to read, and so much she still wanted to learn. Damn those pirates for making her fear for her life.

"Tully, we are going to be attacked by pirates," Pieretta shouted, frustration flowing through each word she enunciated. "Put those away, we need to take cover."

"You be a silly girl, Miss Pieretta. We are not under attack by no pirates." Doubt was evident in Tully's voice. Instead of heeding Pieretta's advice, she turned her back and resumed her work.

Pieretta gasped. Why wasn't she taking her seriously? She stormed over to her side and shook her.

"Tully, I was just on the deck. I heard the first mate and the captain. They are preparing for battle. Do not call me a silly girl!"

"Hmmph," Tully said, ignoring the warning. "Leave me be. I have work to finish." Tully turned around and resumed her task. Two seconds later she screamed when an earsplitting explosion hit the ship.

Pieretta jumped onto the bunk and covered her face in her skirts.

Tully joined Pieretta on their bunk, and they held on to each other. Tully squeezed her so tight it took everything Pieretta had to not push her away. They shook uncontrollably when another thunderous blast rattled the ship.

Pieretta closed her eyes, blocking out everything. She had

never been a truly religious person, but in that moment, it wasn't hard to remember some of the prayers her pastor said during church services. The Lord's Prayer popped in her head, and she could hear the words loud and clear as if she was attending mass. With a shaky voice she began to recite them aloud, hoping if she died, the Lord would grant her some absolution.

~

THOR MADE HIS WAY ONTO THE DECK OF THE SHIP. WITH EACH movement his stride became more of a swagger. Most of the ship's crew were already tied up and secured in the empty cargo hold. His men were pretty savage when they worked, but they kept the casualties to an absolute minimum. A laugh rumbled through his chest, echoing across the deck. This vessel had been much easier to capture than Thor had anticipated.

It was a grand day to be a pirate.

The captain would be required to answer a few questions before they vacated the vessel. Thor walked over to where the captain was tied to the center mast of the ship, blood dripping from his mouth and a resentful look in his eyes.

"Well sir, I commend you on a fine battle," Thor said. "You didn't make it too easy. However, your job isn't quite done. You have something I want. Now, Devere, be a good sport and tell me where I can locate it."

The captain spit blood at him in response, hitting him square in the face. Thor wiped it from his eyes with the sleeve of his jacket. If the captain was looking to make Thor angry, he was doing a tremendous job so far. Captain Devere had better start cooperating before Thor would have to do something he disliked. He did not enjoy killing people and avoided it whenever possible, but the captain might just force his hand.

"Now, mate, that's not the way to go about this. If it's death you are looking for, I would be happy to oblige, after you tell me what I want to know. Where is Pieretta Carlyle? Tell me where she is, and I will consider letting you live."

The captain looked up at him through swollen eyes, now

turning various shades of blue, black, and purple. "Why should I tell you anything? You are going to kill us anyway. I don't see the point of putting that girl through something that she doesn't deserve. I have no doubt that what you have in store for her is terrible. No one deserves to be tortured, even irritating females."

A cocky smile formed on his face. "Well that is no concern of yours."

The captain's face turned several shades of red at Thor's comment. "Go and bloody find her yourself." Each word uttered from his swollen lips was strained with barely contained rage.

"I know you work for that deplorable man Comte Dubois. I want to wring his neck more than yours. Don't be bloody stupid and save your own hide. Otherwise, I'll leave you for my men to torment. The choice is yours, mate. Now tell me where I can find her."

"You call him deplorable when you're a damned pirate. What makes you any better than him?"

Thor glanced at the captain's bloody and inflamed face, trying to decide how to best answer his question. He crossed his massive arms over his chest as he tilted his head up, looking at the billowing sails. After some careful internal deliberation, he chose the truth. "I keep my word."

The captain stared at Thor, disbelief clouding his eyes. His swollen lids folded down into tiny slits narrowing just enough to see the small specks of his black pupils shining through. "Why should I care about that?" he asked.

The man might just have a brain after all. He seemed to be considering his options.

"Well I guess that doesn't really matter, as your life is of little consequence to me. Whether or not you are still breathing depends on your willingness to help me locate Pieretta. Would you like to die now, or live to fight another day?"

Devere didn't take long to answer the question. He looked up at Thor. "She should be in my cabin with her negro maid. Good luck handling that one—she's a spitfire and stubborn as hell."

The Captain's head rolled back into unconsciousness. It

bounced off the tall mast and landed hard against his left shoulder. The man would surely wake up sore if he remained in that position overly long. Thor couldn't muster enough energy to care and left him where he was.

Being a pirate was bloody business.

He stopped letting his principles get to him years ago. It was a hard life at sea every day, plundering ships for supplies. It went against his nature to kill, but if he was forced to, he never thought twice about delivering a fatal blow. Because he didn't believe in murdering someone without cause, he decided to leave the captain and his crew alive.

Thor wanted to make them suffer. He hated anyone working for Comte Dubois. Renny was rotten to the core. His precious granddaughter was the key to his undoing. Pieretta Carlyle would ensure his vengeance. Joy burst through his heart at the idea of finally making the comte pay. No words could express his delight.

He walked away from the captain's slumbering body to make his way below deck. He had a lady to locate so he could properly kidnap her. This was the fun part about being a pirate. A huge smile formed on his lips making his eyes crinkle at the corners. Miss Carlyle would be the best prize he had ever plundered from a ship.

He couldn't wait to make her acquaintance.

The rest of the ship's occupants would be left tied up securely below the ship's deck, while the captain would remain tied to the ship's mast. It would depend on their will to survive if they managed to stay alive once the pirate ship left them to their own devises. If they were creative enough, one of them would come up with a way to free themselves and gain control of the ship. It would take some time for them to accomplish that task and would give Thor plenty of time to put some distance between them.

CHAPTER 3

She paced back and forth from one end of the cabin to the other. The quarters she shared with Tully were small so she didn't have much room to do it, but she couldn't stop herself. She twisted her fingers together in frustration, debating what could possibly be done. Pieretta stopped walking and wiped her hands on her skirt to remove the dampness building there. She continued her futile trek between the two bare walls of the tiny room. The cannons had stopped firing, and it was eerily quiet. Tully had passed out from fear hours ago, rendering her useless. Pieretta wondered if she should venture out to see what had happened. She feared the ship's crew was already dead. Pirates were surely all over the ship by now.

A loud racket shook the walls of her cabin. She jumped when her door crashed open. The doorframe swallowed up by a man, his body filling almost every inch of the opening.

She swallowed the lump building inside of her parched throat. She had never been intimidated by a man before, but his demeanor was imposing. His whole body was nothing but muscle. He walked into the cabin and approached Pieretta. Once he was inside, she got an even better look at him. The more she saw of him, the more she wanted to escape. The pirate was perhaps the largest man Pieretta had ever laid eyes on.

And he seemed solely focused on her...

As the pirate moved around the cabin, she saw that black clothing covered every inch of his body. His pants were tight over his thighs. The man's shirt hung loose and flowed over his chest. It was open at the navel, revealing a small trail of hair. His immense stature towered over her small frame.

He was so—huge.

The pirate had to be at least six feet tall. His dark black hair was pulled back with a leather tie. A light dusting of stubble covered his face and added to his appeal. He was terrifyingly gorgeous. The pirate was the type of man that made you want to simultaneously run from and toward. He was by far the most handsome man she had ever seen.

How scary is it the only man I had ever been attracted to was a damn pirate?

Once he stepped into the light from her small lantern, she was able to get a better look at all of his features. His cobalt eyes narrowed into tiny slits with a purpose she could only guess.

Pieretta scrambled back towards the bunk in an attempt to get away from him. In her haste, she tripped over the dress Tully had been working on earlier and fell onto the bed face first. He stalked toward her and pulled her to her feet.

Pieretta looked up at him and saw a smirk forming at the corner of his mouth. One side was upturned in a lazy half smile. Her meager attempts at getting away were thwarted by the stupid dress Tully had carelessly left laying on the floor.

Even if I managed to get away from him where would I go?

They were on a ship in the middle of the ocean. She resigned herself to being at this pirate's mercy, at least for the time being.

"Ah, I have found a fine jewel to add to my treasure." He pulled her firmly into his tight embrace.

A musky smell tinged with a hint of sandalwood and chocolate filled her senses.

Delicious...

"What?" Pieretta dumbly replied.

How am I going to survive when looking at him makes me brainless?

"What is your name, girl?"

Should I tell him my name? Why does it matter to him what it is? Pieretta didn't know much about pirates, but the little she was aware of told her they didn't care about the people they attacked. Her name shouldn't matter to him. Still locked in his arms, Pieretta was forced to tilt her head back to stare up at him. The look in his eyes told her all she needed to know. It was best to just answer his questions and pray for mercy.

With great reluctance, she told him her name. "Pia."

"Ah, Pia, you're coming with me." He yanked her toward the door.

"No, I don't think so—I think I would rather stay here," she replied.

She really didn't want to go with the pirate. If she had the choice, she would rather stay on the ship and die with the rest of its inhabitants. Pirates were not known for their mercy or for treating prisoners well. A female prisoner would suffer a fate worse than death.

Pieretta was horrified, and she did her best to fight her way out of his arms in an attempt to escape. She thrashed and pulled with all her might—only to have him laugh at her.

"The captain was right."

"About what?" She asked, stupidly. What else could she say?

"You're a feisty one. We're going to have a spot of fun." A cocky half smile filled his face. "Don't fight me. I promise you won't regret it."

Oh Lord. She started to pull again—harder this time. She had to do something—anything to escape.

Her efforts were futile as his grasp was so tight she could barely breathe. She squirmed in his arms with one last insufficient attempt to get away from him. She raised her small fists and pounded them with all of her might against his hard chest.

What is he going to do with me? I can't escape him. Where would I go?

Pieretta was at his mercy, on board a ship under his control in the middle of the ocean. She hadn't even told him her real name and had no idea why she did that. On further reflection, maybe she did know why. She had always hated her name, and Pia rolled off the tongue and sounded prettier than Pieretta. She decided right there from that moment on she would be Pia to everyone, including herself.

His amusement became evident as a rolling chuckle bubbled from between his full lips as he watched her struggle within the confines of his arms. It was the kind of laugh that rumbled through your soul. Once it started, Pia felt it all over her body, making her shiver with a need she didn't understand. She wanted to rub herself against him. Pia was suddenly aware of where she was. That little compulsion terrified her more than anything she had ever encountered. She needed to get away from him before she did something she would truly regret.

"Please don't take me with you," Pia begged again.

He stared down at her, disbelief clouding his eyes. "So you would rather die along with everyone else?" he asked her.

Pia felt the lump in her throat forming again. *He wouldn't kill me, would he?* Well if she was going to die, she would do her best to remain as brave as possible. There was no reason to give the man any enjoyment from her death. She wouldn't cry—would remain strong to the very end.

With a nod she said, "Yes, I think it would probably be better than whatever you have in store for me."

The pirate freed her long enough to grab her wrist and drag behind him. "Well it's good for you that I don't take orders, I give them. Come along, Pia. You're much more valuable to me alive than dead." He shook his head and frowned. "Lucky for you, my plans involve you still breathing, or I might have indulged your childish whims."

Good Lord, has the pirate captain claimed me as part of his treasure? If only there was some way to flee. She tried to pull away again, but he just laughed. Her attempt at escape had barely caused him to move an inch. Pia was doomed.

"You're a real bastard, aren't you?"

"I assure you, my father married my mother, and I'm legitimate." His amusement spread across his face as his lips curled into a smug smile.

Did he have to be so frustrating? He continued to chuckle at her attempts to pull out of his grasp. Pia had to restrain herself from using her free hand to slap him, for fear of what he might do to her if she gave in to the desire. He treated her like a bug that was easily ended with one stomp of his heavy boot. Perhaps the problem was the pirate could kill her without giving a second thought to what ending her life might mean. With her arm still firmly within his grasp, he continued to drag Pia along as they made their way topside.

"You know what I meant," Pia shouted.

"I don't read minds, and I don't assume to know what you mean."

Pia snorted. "How do people bear to be around your arrogance?"

"As long as they follow my orders, I don't care what they bear."

Her mind raced...the visual images almost made her fall over. What would this man look like bare? Pia had the sudden urge to fan her face with her free hand to alleviate the hot blush forming across her cheeks.

The sun hung low on the horizon, and she realized that she had been below deck for several hours. Tully had been passed out on the bunk for at least half of the—Wait a minute, what were they going to do with Tully? She should at least make an effort to save her. Tully had been her nurse since she was born. She may be bossy, but Pia would never wish her dead.

"I can't leave my maid. It isn't proper for me to travel alone."

"I could care less about your maid. My plans do not include carrying around any extra baggage. Your companion will remain here in your cabin."

Pia was at a loss for words. She opened and closed her mouth several times before she was able to convey her shock at his casual dismissal. "You mean you're going to leave her here to die? That's deplorable. You're a wicked man, and I hate you."

The damned pirate ignored her as they continued their journey across the deck. He made his way to what could only be part of his crew. The group consisted of some men Pia had never seen before. She was familiar with most of the crew on the ship from her daily walks on deck, and she didn't recognize one person standing before her. That could only mean one thing; these were the pirates who attacked her grandpere's ship.

The pirate captain approached an older man with snow white hair and dark brown eyes. "Bosun Cornelius, take this treasure to our ship. Put her in a secure spot so I can deal with her later. Pia and I have much to discuss."

"Aye aye, Captain," he said, as he took over the captain's grip on Pia's arm. There were several red marks forming on her already sore wrist. The bosun yanked her across the plank connecting the ships. Pia looked up at the sky and saw the red flag flying above her.

How can they live like this, taking the lives of the innocent? She could still see them plundering the ship, taking all the valuables. She wondered what they would do when they were done. The ship was badly damaged. Would they sink it?

"Where are you taking me?" Pia demanded.

The bosun acted like he didn't hear a word she said. Pia stomped her foot in frustration. She was strong and capable, and she would survive. The pirate could do his worst. She knew something he did not. She had a will stronger than most people, and she was a force to be reckoned with.

Cornelius marched her below deck, shoved her in a cabin, and then locked the door. Pia looked around the room. It appeared to be well kept. It was interesting to see the pirates were not slobs and took care of their belongings. The space was cramped, but it was not nearly as small as the cabin she had previously inhabited. The room held a large bunk and table. There was a trunk pushed up against the wall near the bed. Everything was bolted down to ensure it wouldn't move. The room was decorated in bland colors, everything a muted brown. Even the bedding was dark brown. As she finished surveying the room, she had a realization. Pia was in a room surrounded entirely by things the shades of dirt. Staring at everything in the place, it occurred to her she was probably in the pirate captain's cabin.

∽

THOR SUPERVISED AS THE REST OF THE CREW PLUNDERED ALL OF the bounty the ship had to offer. The cargo from Comte Dubois's ship would bring in a good price. It was just another reason Thor was happy with the results from attacking the ship. That ship had been fully stocked with Dubois goods. There were crates full of rum, brandy, and several bolts of silk. It was a double win for him. He now had the comte's precious granddaughter and his cargo.

Thor had made sure every crew member had been breathing before they sailed away. Enough food remained in their galley to ensure they didn't starve. That is, if they managed to get themselves untied. He left the maid passed out in the cabin where he'd found Pia. If she was brave enough, she would free the crew members so they could continue their voyage to France.

Anything that could be used aboard the pirate ship had been taken. As a token of good will, Thor made sure his crew retrieved Pia's trunks. He wouldn't give any of them to her right away. He would make her earn the contents. He was going to enjoy every aspect of it too. Thor had already thought of several ways she could receive some of the things encased within her many trunks.

Thor walked on deck and sought out his bosun. He located Corny near the quarterdeck where he was issuing orders to some of the crew. "Make sure these cases of liquor are stored in the ship's cargo hold. Take the food to the galley and give it to cook. We will be eating well for the next couple of weeks." The crew members quickly marched off to move the cargo to the areas he had designated.

Corny turned at Thor's approach. "Captain, I was just making sure the bounty was secured," he said.

"Good. Corny, is everything where it needs to be?" he asked.

"Aye, Captain. We are ready to set sail as soon as you give the order."

"And my personal treasure?"

"She is in your cabin, as you ordered Captain."

"Very well, tell Jamieson to set sail. Those tasked with cargo organization can finish that as we sail. Have all hands on deck to open the sails and hoist the anchor. I will be in my cabin. I do not want to be disturbed unless it is a dire emergency."

"Aye aye, Captain."

Thor turned and made his way to his cabin. It was time to get better acquainted with his precious jewel. She truly was beautiful. The lovely woman only had one flaw, her irritating and evil grandpere. It wouldn't be long before Thor erased that flaw from existence. The only way to ensure the man paid for his crimes was to take away the one thing he valued more than money, his granddaughter.

CHAPTER 4

The cabin walls were beginning to close in on Pia, suffocating her with the knowledge that she had no clue what she ought to do. It had been several hours since the pirate's bosun had shoved her in the cabin, and she was slowly going insane. She was both uneasy and excited at the prospect of facing him again. Did he really murder everyone on board grandpere's ship? If so, why would he spare me and kill everyone else?

The pirate was a devastatingly handsome man, but his arrogance knew no bounds. Against her better judgment, she found herself attracted to him. Pia chewed on her bottom lip, concerned about what his plans were for her. She couldn't let that attraction be her undoing. She knew it was unnatural to feel the way she did, because he was clearly an evil man.

From what little she knew about him he didn't think twice about murder. Her body reacted to him of its own accord. Pia's heart beat faster and her face flushed with heat when she was near him. If she had met him in any other way, she would have seriously reconsidered her no marriage policy. He was the only man who had ever made her think it might be worthwhile to sell herself on the marriage mart.

Yeah, like a pirate would marry anyone. She snorted at the silly idea.

More likely he would plunder every inch of the woman's depths, leaving her well satisfied and alone for the rest of her life.

Well, now that's an idea.

She could not have those kinds of thoughts. She was a virgin and a lady. Women of her station did not consider gifting their virginity to pirates.

No matter how delectable they smelled or how utterly gorgeous they were.

He was immoral and diabolical, giving her the impression he was capable of almost any vice known to man. Pia couldn't help wondering why he took her aboard his ship. There was something he wasn't telling her, and her mission was to discover that reason. The first order of business would be to gain more information and ascertain why the pirate kidnapped her.

Pia roamed aimlessly around the room growing more frustrated at the lack of things to do. The room was stifling, and she was starting to feel claustrophobic from being confined for so long . She was not used to such idle musings and desperately needed something to occupy her time. Pia wished she had access to her trunks. She had lots of books, and it would be spectacular if she could get her hands on one of her treasured tomes.

It was very easy for her to get lost in books because she thirsted for knowledge. Her current book involved her favorite mythological characters: Thor, Loki, and Balder. Pia found Thor's hammer, Mjölnir, the most fascinating part of Norse mythology. It was rumored to be able to crush anything and could only be wielded by Thor himself. She could read about Thor for hours.

Pia desperately needed something to do and wished— again—she at least had some reading material to help pass the time. Even if there was some sewing, at least it would occupy her mind. Normally sewing would have caused her to want to poke her eyes out. Taking the sewing needle and blinding herself would have been preferable to sitting for hours and pulling it through some cloth. Sewing or cross-stitching was such sleep inducing work. In the meantime, she was bored out of her mind with absolutely nothing to occupy her time while she was locked inside the cabin.

She refused to give in to her frustrations or worry over something she had no control over. Surely there had to be a way to convince the pirate captain to release her unharmed. Her grandpere was wealthy—she was wealthy—between the two of them they could surely buy her way out of this predicament.

Yes, that was a plan she would broach with the pirate when he deemed her worthy of his presence, the rat bastard.

The sinfully attractive rat bastard.

She heard footsteps nearing the cabin door. Maybe that was the dreadful, gorgeous man now. Goodness gracious, she had to stop thinking of him in those terms.

How am I going to negotiate if I am constantly salivating over him?

He may be one of the best looking men she had ever encountered, but he was also the same man who ordered the attack on her grandpere's ship and killed its occupants. Well, except for her. Poor Tully, she didn't deserve to die. She irritated Pia, but she would never have wished her harmed in any way. The door creaked open, and the man himself walked in. He looked her over like she was his favorite dessert, and he couldn't wait to lick the plate, alleviating it of every inch of its sweetness.

Heat filled her chicks at his unadulterated gaze. Where was a fan when she needed one?

"Oh good, I can see you have been anxiously awaiting my attention," he drawled. Amusement laced through every syllable.

She opened and closed her mouth several times like a fish out of water trying desperately to breathe. Pia couldn't tell how many times, because she stood there dumbfounded at his audacity.

I should be terrified right? Pfft.

She had let go of that useless emotion hours ago. She didn't have time to be frightened anymore, and it wouldn't do her any good to give the pirate anything to use against her. It was high time she did something to make things go the way she needed them to. She would buy herself out of this situation with any means at her disposal. It was a good thing she was a very wealthy heiress, because it might just come in handy in this particular situation.

"I assure you, Captain Pirate, I have not been anxiously awaiting anything. What I have been is bored silly. If you were trying to kill me with ennui, then by all means stay the course. If not, well I will surely expire before long. Maybe that is your intention? It's less messy, and it's a great means of torture. It is a miracle I haven't already gone insane from sheer boredom over the past several hours."

A rich throaty laugh echoed through the room.

The man dared to laugh at her. It was like he couldn't help himself, and it just burst out of him every time she tried to speak to him. It was the kind of laugh that made you weary and excited at the same time.

When she first heard it, it made her shiver from the inside out.

She was starting to realize it might always have that affect on her. It tickled down her spine and made her tremble.

His laugh was dangerous.

Oh Lord. A devilish smirk curved his lips. She was a goner for sure. Damn man, why must you have such an appealing face. She was so lost in her own thoughts she almost didn't hear him when he finally spoke.

"Thor," he replied.

"Excuse me?"

"I am Captain Thor, not Captain Pirate."

It was Pia's turn to laugh. Only moments ago, she had pondered her favorite book on Norse mythology, and here the blasted pirate was named after her favorite hammer wielding god.

"I suppose you carry a hammer only you can lift right?"

"Oh, I don't have a hammer per se..."

She sucked in a breath as he delivered the innuendo. Pia choked, finding it difficult to express the words flowing through her mind. Surely he didn't mean what his words implied...

Thor's face lit up with his roguish smile, and he crossed the short distance between them and whispered in her ear.

His hot breath caressed her neck as his words softly flowed through her eardrums. "I can assure you it will be my pleasure to share it with you."

Pia moved away quickly before she could take him up on his offer. Her heart beat faster. Its rhythm pounded through her ears and steadily gained pace with each breath she forced between her open lips. The more space she put between them the better off she would be. It was unfortunate the cabin was so tiny because it left her very few options. Pia needed to gain some distance between herself and the pirate. She took a deep breath and steadily exhaled with slow measures to gain some control over her body's reaction.

It was an attempt to remind herself she was supposed to be livid with him, not attracted to him.

Once her breathing was under control, she looked up into his blue eyes. "I am not interested in your over-inflated ego and images of grandeur."

Thor's lips upturned into a devilish half smile. There was once again a drop of mirth in each word he enunciated. "Oh, my ego is definitely not over inflated—or anything else. Trust me. It is well earned. However there is a part of me that is...inflated." He took a step toward her and asked, "Would you like me to show you?"

Thor's said the most outrageous things—Pia didn't know how to respond. Every sound and gesture he made was a form of seduction she was sorely unprepared for. Pia needed to steer the conversation on to another topic, one designed to ensure her virtue stayed intact. This one was taking her places she did not want to go—at least she didn't think she did.

Who was she kidding? A large part of her wanted to look him in the eyes and tell him exactly what she wanted him to show her. Her curiosity was going to get her into trouble.

What Pia needed to do was turn the conversation back on him. If she could make sure he didn't get any closer, she could remain relatively safe. "Pirate Thor?" she asked derision in her voice. "You imagine you are equal to a god?"

"I can't help what my parents named me, now can I?"

Disbelief coated her voice. "Your parents actually named you Thor?"

"Thor Williams, at your service," he said, making a

production of bowing, much like a gentlemen would before a lady.

He seriously went by that moniker? His parents named him after a Norse god? No wonder the man had an overinflated ego. If he lived up to her fantasies about the god of thunder, then this Thor would certainly be her undoing.

Pia cleared her throat. "Sooo—I am Pia Carlyle. I don't know why you decided my life was worth keeping. Not that I'm not glad that you did, but I've had a lot of time in this room all by myself to consider my options. I thought maybe we could strike a bargain."

The man had a perpetual smile on his face, as if everything she said was the most comical thing in the world. The real problem was his smile was so attractive she was having a hard time concentrating on her main purpose. If he kept doing that, she was going to climb all over him and beg him to show her his mythical hammer.

"Exactly what I came to discuss with you, Pia."

"Good. I am glad to see we are of the same mind."

He nodded. "I concur."

"I don't know if you are aware that my family has money. They will pay any ransom you demand."

"Oh, I am more than aware of who your family is, love," he replied.

"Good. So you will send notice of the ransom for my release?"

"I will do no such thing." He shook his head.

Pia's mouth hung open in frozen disbelief.

She recovered quickly while he continued to grin at her shocked disposition. In that moment, she realized this might not be something she could gain control over, but she still needed more information before she could assess what needed to be done.

"Why not?" she asked.

"I have other plans for you, dear. None of them involve extracting money from your grandpere."

Well that was a development she had not been expecting. She assumed because he was a pirate he could be easily bought off with her inheritance. Her limited knowledge of pirates suggested they were mercenaries. From what Thor had said though this very well could be a personal endeavor of his, and her grandpere was deeply involved. "You know my grandpere?"

"I know him better than you do. In fact, he and I have a debt that will not be easily settled with the exchange of money. You are going to help me to do that, and in the process, we will get to know each other very well." He wiggled his eyebrow suggestively. "We'll be as close as two people can possibly be when this is all said and done."

With each sentence Thor uttered, Pia felt the color drain from her face. "What do you have planned for me?"

"You will find out soon enough. For now, we are going to get some rest, you and I. We have a long journey ahead of us. No need to rush into it right now. Our more pleasurable pursuits will happen in due time."

He dragged her toward his bunk. It was fairly large for a ship, but not nearly big enough for two people. Especially if he was one of those two people. It would definitely be a cramped sleeping space.

"Surely you don't expect me to sleep there with you."

"Oh, I assure you, not only do I expect it, but you will do it."

"It isn't big enough for both of us."

Thor smirked, and a small chuckle echoed throughout the cabin. He shoved her over to the side that hugged the ship. Pia curled up against the wall in an attempt to make herself as small as possible. She watched as Thor sat and removed his boots, setting them next to the bed. After the task was complete, he rolled over and lay next to Pia on the bunk. He pulled his arms over his head and tucked both of his hands beneath his dark locks. Pia tried to find a comfortable spot on the small bunk, but his body engulfed more than half of it.

"We fit just fine. You fretted unnecessarily, love. Don't worry, you will soon be very used to having my arms wrapped around you, in sleep and in other things. For now just lie down and get some rest."

"I'd rather not."

"Well that is too damn bad, lie down and go to sleep. You

have no idea when you will have such a luxury again. I have many plans for you, and sleeping isn't exactly on my agenda."

Pia did what he asked, at least as much as she was able. What else could she do? He was right in some ways. Pia would need some sleep if she was going to be able to properly deal with her dastardly pirate. She needed to survive, and Pirate Thor wasn't going to take advantage of her, much. She was still fully clothed at least. From what little he shared with her, she knew nothing was going to happen on this night, getting a little sleep would only benefit her.

Pia lay her head down on the bed next to Thor. Once she was curled up next to him, he rolled over and wrapped his entire body around her. She could feel his hammer nestled against her rear. If she gave him the slightest encouragement, she was sure he would show her what he could do with it. With what little preservation Pia still had within her, she ignored what that meant. She did not want to find out what losing her virginity felt like any time soon.

~

ONCE PIA WAS ASLEEP, THOR LEFT THE CABIN AND LOCKED IT. He couldn't stay in the bed with her any longer. She was too much of a temptation. He had plans, and using her body wasn't on the list.

Yet.

She called herself Pia. He liked it much better than Pieretta. It rolled off of his tongue like a lover's caress, and they would be lovers. Every blush staining her cheeks told him how attracted she was to him. Her breathing became labored when he pulled her near, and he could feel her pulse racing beneath his fingers when he held her wrist in his hand. It was only a matter of time before she was completely his.

Thor hadn't known exactly what she looked like when he'd started this crusade. He had only been given a general description so he would know who to look for on board the ship.

She was stunning. He wanted undo her braid and run his

fingers through her pale blonde hair. He needed to spread it out across his bunk. Then he wanted to strip her luscious body of her drab mourning garb and lick her all over. He would start at her ankles, and work his way up to her pretty bosom. Her breasts were plump and just large enough to fill the palms of his hands. He loved how her waist curved into a nicely rounded derriere.

Thor had a fierce need to pull her on top of him and slide inside of her tight channel. Having her wantonly ride his shaft and find pleasure remained on top of his most desired fantasies. He wanted to get her naked so he could taste every inch of her and hear her scream with satisfaction. She was everything he had ever considered to be perfect, and he could not have dreamed up a more ideal woman to find pleasure with.

He had to snap out of this line of thought. It was too early for this part of the plan, but it would happen and soon. He needed her to be a willing participant in her own downfall. He had never forced anyone in his life, and he was not about to start with his jewel. She was far beyond anything he could have expected, and he found he wanted more from her than he had originally planned. He was beginning to think he just might want to keep her forever, something he had never considered with anyone else.

He made his way topside. He needed to talk to his first mate and bosun. They needed to set a new course. They were going to make a stop in southern France instead of Calais. When he had looked through the captain's logs, he had discovered the comte had traveled to his southern estate, and that was where they would see each other again for the last time.

He needed as much time with the feisty Pia as he could manage, before they had their final meeting with her grandpere. He needed her to fall in love with him. He would use every tool in his arsenal to make that happen.

What Pia didn't know was that their lives had been forever entwined before they ever laid eyes on each other. If not for her grandpere, they would never have met. The actions of the comte ensured they would forever be linked.

Thor had to admit he was actually looking forward to getting to know her better.

He intended to have his cake, and he would savor every sweet bite.

CHAPTER 5

Living the life of a lady had many perks and advantages. Pia had no qualms about using every one of those resources to ensure she came out on top. As an only child, Pia's father indulged all of her requests. Mr. Carlyle only had one rule he stood firm with concerning her. She could basically do anything she wanted, but if it was something he deemed dangerous, it was forbidden. Fortunately for Pia, his list of perilous things was not very long, so she pretty much ran wild on the plantation. As long as Pia was safe, her father did not object to any activity she wanted to experience.

Pia did have the benefit of a more formal education. The instructors her father hired taught her Latin, history, and math. When she wanted to learn about mythology, science, and, Greek, her father hired the best tutors he could find. She probably, in some ways, had a better education than some of the gentlemen in Charleston.

No one had a thirst for knowledge quite like Pia did. Getting lost inside the pages of a book was her favorite past time. The stories weaved lead her on adventures she couldn't have imagined herself. There were adventures to be found all from the safety of her library. As she studied with her tutors, she encountered Norse mythology and learned of the various gods. Thor had been her favorite, so it shouldn't surprise her that she was attracted to a man with the same moniker.

Her father even hired a fencing instructor when she expressed a desire to learn. He made sure the foils were dull and harmless before the lessons could commence. Pia was an apt student and excelled at everything she attempted. There was no one else more aware what her many flaws were than Pia, but she equally knew every one of her assets.

She had been locked inside his cabin for twelve days. Twelve days of doing nothing. She wanted to make sure the pirate felt at least a small amount of her frustration. Thor needed to feel it, but she had no way of accomplishing this daunting task. Pia had plenty of time and not a thing to do, except get lost inside her own mind. She could be patient, but after so long with only the pirate's occasional company, she started to slowly lose her mind. The ennui of her existence was torture only a strong person could survive. Pia questioned if she was capable of the kind of strength required to endure beyond this moment in her life.

It was beyond her comprehension why she couldn't bend Thor to her will. The pirate delivered innuendos and implied a lot, but he never acted on any of it. The more she knew about him, the less she understood what his intentions could possibly be. He made no secret that he hated her grandpere, but he failed to express how that information actually applied to her. The banter between her and Pirate Thor continued every time they were in each other's presence.

Thor remained stubborn in his desire to make her sleep next to him each night, and he absolutely refused to let her out of his cabin for any reason. Each night when he deemed it was time to rest, he made her lay down on the bunk. Once she was settled in, he would lay next to her so she could sleep inside the warmth of his embrace. It was beginning to feel safe locked in his arms as he hugged her close, her head resting above his heart. The one thing Pia knew for sure was she should not relax in his company, because it was the most dangerous place she could be.

Each night Pia experienced the same thing, and she grew more and more confused. *What exactly does he have in store for me?* She needed to find a way to make him talk. Well, she needed answers. He had no problem talking, but it was usually filled with innuendo. With each word he uttered, she became more confused. She wanted to hold on to her anger, but she also craved the companionship of another human being. All Thor offered her were baseless conversations leading nowhere. Pia was tired of only having him for company.

Pia was no stranger to the insinuations he alluded to every time he deigned to speak to her. She may be a woman, but she went unnoticed much growing up and had overheard men discussing their sexual exploits. Most of her knowledge was gained from books, and very few offered good illustrations of what they were talking about.

Pia had only been kissed once, when she was sixteen years old. There was a man on a neighboring plantation who thought she would be a suitable wife and had begun to court her. During a picnic at his home, he had lead her behind a tree and kissed her. It wasn't very notable, and Pia felt next to nothing, except wet and messy. What was enjoyable about a man leaving saliva all over your face? The sensation was disgusting, and his groping at her hadn't helped much. The man may have enjoyed it, but she never let him touch her again. She had doubts she would ever want to be kissed again, because the experience had been so distasteful.

She knew what desire was as she had inadvertently witnessed some clandestine meetings. Pia had just never really felt it before, and that was one of the reasons she didn't think she would ever get married. She just wasn't interested in what a man had to offer her.

That was until she came across a certain pirate. Why do I have to feel something for a dangerous pirate?

Losing herself in her own thought, she imagined the many things she would do to him if given the chance. They alternated between kissing him and strangling him, depending on the direction her thoughts wandered. The more she was reduced to keeping her own company, all Pia wanted to do was scream at or kill a certain pirate.

It was while she was doing her daily pacing the pirate did the unexpected and returned to the cabin in the middle of the day. He generally left her alone until it was time to settle in for the night. Apparently being the captain of a ship kept him busy, leaving little time to entertain her.

Pia hated to admit it, but she was excited. As her only source of company, she anticipated his arrival every night. At least with him around she had someone else's voice to listen to. His presence helped keep her sanity in place. If she were left alone any more than she was, she'd have gone stark raving mad by now. Pia had reached a pinnacle in her situation, suddenly willing to give anything a try in order to have a variation in their daily routine. He wouldn't tell her how he knew her grandpere, and she was hoping to goad him into doing so.

"Ah. I see you are as busy as usual, Pia."

She glared at him, but said nothing. Pia traipsed over to the bunk and sat on the edge.

"Are you attempting to give me the silent treatment? How novel of you."

Thor sauntered over to his desk and pulled out the chair. The stool was the only piece of furniture not bolted down in the cabin. Pia watched as he sat on it and pulled himself closer to the desk. Once seated, he pulled out a key and unlocked the cabinet attached to the side of the writing table. Thor slid open the cabinet and pulled out a piece of paper, followed by a quill, and then ink. It was sad that watching him sit at his desk was entertainment to her. He made a production of setting everything on the table in preparation to write.

Pia studied the back of his head. His sun-kissed black hair was pulled back in a leather tie. It was the only way she had ever seen him wear it. Her view was blocked from seeing what he was actually doing, but she was happy just watching his shoulders move as he scribbled something across the blank pages.

When he had entered the cabin, she had been determined to ignore him, but her eyes kept being drawn back. It was too easy to watch him with an unguarded gaze. Pia felt herself wishing they could have met differently. She wanted to give in to the urge to stroke her hands over his shoulders, and it wasn't long before she started to wonder what he would do if she licked his neck.

Pia let out a whoosh of air from her lungs, and a loud sigh emerged from between her lips. She couldn't help it. The cabin was beyond tedious. If she didn't stop these fantasies about the pirate, she was going to inadvertently act out one of them. By the time the actions took place, it would be too late to change her course.

Thor was too busy to pay her any attention. Pia wanted to know more about the pirate but was unsure how to go about getting her questions answered. I simply have to find a way to get him to open up to me. No matter how many questions she asked, he never gave her any personal information about himself. Any efforts on her part to gain insight into his persona were met with little success.

Pia had little recourse but to spend time with Thor. He became the only thing occupying her thoughts. Her days started with him next to her and ended the same way. The in-between hours were spent thinking of ways to extricate herself from the situation she was in. She saw no clear way out.

Pia lay down on the bunk and tapped her fingers together while daydreams of a dashing pirate floated through her imagination. In her mind, he was really a gentleman caller approved of by her father. The dashing man courted her and asked her to be his wife. Of course she said no. Couldn't they just have an affair instead? He was shocked, but agreed to her suggestion, leading him down a pathway to sin. He was willing to do anything for her as long as she was his. Pia was such an impious girl, if only she knew what to picture that wickedness to actually be. She could guess, but she was sheltered so she didn't know.

Pia had a one track mind and these days it involved her and the pirate in various compromising situations. She stopped being terrified of him. Pia was so used to his company even the fact he towered over her became completely natural to her. She didn't understand how she could have come to be so accepting of him in such a short time.

Lost in the world of her imagination, Pia didn't realize Thor had stopped writing and was watching her. He had placed his stuff back in the cabinet, and she hadn't heard a thing. Pia often got lost in her mind and drowned out the rest of the world. The only noise that existed was the music of her own daydreams.

"Is this what you do all day?"

The pictures running through her mind made it almost impossible to hear what he had said. Unfortunately for Pia, his voice was a huge part of her daydreams so it bled through, bringing her back to reality. Choosing to ignore his question, she kept the images dancing in her mind. *He was ruining my fantasy.*

Irritation corded into each word as Thor spoke. "I asked you a question."

She hummed her favorite song as she imagined dancing at a ball in his arms. *Why can't he say things I want to hear?* Things like: of course I will let you go, no I didn't kill everyone on board your grandpere's ship, or how about a kiss, Pia.

Wait, she didn't want him to really do that last part, did she?

"I think that this is quite enough, Pia. I am not going to tolerate your silent treatment for much longer."

What did he expect me to say?

Pia stuck her tongue out at him in defiance.

He laughed at her as he pulled her up and off the bunk. The sound echoed across the cabin walls, amusement filling the room with each chuckle that escaped his lips.

"I think you need a lesson on some things you can do with that tongue. If you stick it out at me again, you can expect this..."

The only thought Pia had as he pulled her toward him was: *be careful what you wish for.*

He plundered her mouth in ways she could never have imagined. Fantasy? What fantasy? Reality was much more exciting and fulfilling. If she was capable of thought, she would have started planning on ways they could do this again.

When his tongue intertwined with hers, they danced to a tune only they could create. Any thoughts of remembering how to breathe failed to find their way into her befuddled brain. Her hands wrapped around him, and she pulled him closer. Pia felt a strong need growing inside of her. She felt Thor's hands as they roamed across the back of her head, locating the braid secured at the nape of her neck. Once he had it securely in his palms, he pulled her tresses, tipping her chin up. With her head tilted back, he placed soft kisses along her décolletage. He kissed her neckline and stopped at the base of her ears. He trailed his lips across her cheek, placing little kisses along the way, and then plundered her mouth all over again. Their tongues entwined for what seemed like hours but were no more than mere minutes. Surely there wasn't anything better than this?

He whispered in her ear. "You taste so much better than I could have imagined."

Oh he did too—so so delectable.

She enjoyed kissing him just as much, but it had to stop before she did something irreversible. She began to pull her face away from his, but he still had his arms wrapped securely around her. Pia wasn't going anywhere just yet. Thor settled her firmly against the wall of the cabin and lifted her up so her bosom was level with his mouth. His tongue found the crevice between her breasts and licked upward. He brought his mouth to hers for one last mind blowing kiss as he eased her down the wall and swung her toward the bunk.

He stepped away from Pia, putting some much needed distance between them. Pia lost her balance and fell backward onto the bed. She sat there in silence and stared at him. Words escaped her, as she had no way of describing all of the emotions flowing through her body and soul. Her mouth was swollen from his attentions, and she felt a tingling in her lower regions. Her breasts were tight and heavy, and she knew what true desire was for the first time in her life. None of the books she had read had described it with any kind of accuracy. So this is why it was forbidden.

A wide grin spread across Thor's face as he gazed at her. She felt heat stinging her cheeks, and her heart raced wildly beneath her breasts. The mirth shining in his eyes told her all she needed to know about how she appeared to him. She had been well and truly pleasured by everything he had done with his mouth and hands. What that man did with his tongue should not be permissible.

"Do you still insist on giving me the silent treatment?"

Oh yes, absolutely if you kiss me as punishment. More please, oh I am quite certain, I want you to punish me more.

Pia was equally certain she had a lot of horrible ideas lately. She was a bad girl. She needed to talk to him before he did more than kiss her breath away. He finally was doing instead of implying. Maybe, just maybe, she could get some actual information out of him. So she decided to take a nonchalant approach to the whole situation.

She shrugged. "What is there possibly to talk about?"

"Perhaps you would like to know what I have planned for you."

"Oh, you think I have finally earned the right to know that?"

He shook his head. "No Pia, dear, you won't know exactly what my plans are for you until the very last second."

There was no other person alive who could frustrate her more than her pirate. Yes, he really was her pirate in her mind. He still needed to talk about things that mattered to her, or she wouldn't be held accountable for her actions. With as much indignation as she could muster, Pia looked up at him. "Then why are we discussing this?"

"Because your life is going to change forever in a short time."

What an asinine statement. Pia let out an unladylike snort. Hadn't it already changed forever?

"And that is different than the past week how? Why don't we talk about you instead? Like what a murdering fiend you are for what you did too everyone on that ship."

Thor folded his arms across his chest and leaned back against his writing table. "Because my plans for you will be irreversible once everything is in place."

Damn, that didn't sound good. Pia frowned. She had to try to get him to talk more. Her life depended on what he was going to do. So she needed to do something to get him to tell her what his plans actually were.

"Seems like that is also already true, what could be so different today? One thing is certain, you are very good at evading questions. Why don't you tell me why you needed to kill everyone aboard my grandpere's ship?"

"I never told you I killed everyone on that ship. You just assumed I did."

"An assumption that you never corrected. You wanted me to believe the worst in you."

Thor shrugged. "It suited my purposes at the time."

"So are you going to tell me anything else, since you are in such a sharing mood today?" Pia inquired.

"I grow weary of your persistent questioning. I have answered all you need to know for now."

"You answered nothing, you only implied you didn't kill anyone, much the same way that you insinuated you murdered a whole ship of people."

"Believe what you want Pia. The truth will be evident when it matters. I don't need to confirm or deny anything."

"Okay, I'm tired of your non-answers. Why did you come in here to bother me?"

"We will be making port in a couple of days. You will be able to come on deck. Once you are topside you will agree to everything I ask you to do. No matter what it is you will do it. If you don't, I will personally make sure that your only living family member dies."

"Are you saying you would murder my grandpere?"

Thor leaned down and looked her directly in her eyes his intentions crystal clear as he enunciated each syllable. "In a heartbeat."

Pia didn't want to think he would kill her grandpere. It just didn't make sense to her why he would do something so evil to someone she loved. "I don't believe you. Why not threaten my life?"

"Because it's clear you have no regard for your own life. I figured, if I threatened someone you love, then you would be more willing to follow my lead and do as I say. It also helps that I have a deep hatred for your grandpere. His death is nothing at all to me."

He had her there. She would die before she let him control her. Her grandpere though? Pia had to protect him.

"You are despicable."

"You enjoy it though, love. I could have done whatever I wanted to you earlier, and you would have followed me to hell and back. You were so hot, you seared my skin. Maybe talking with you isn't the best use of my time? In the future, I'll just show you what I want instead."

Without thinking, Pia slapped Thor across his left cheek.

Thor's amusement still hung in the air. His laugher echoed through the cabin as he sauntered out of the room.

Pia had a lot to think about. Would the pirate actually kill her grandpere? She believed he would. He made sure she knew he harbored no tender feelings for her grandpere. Oh yes, Pirate Thor would follow through with his threat to kill the comte. He left her little choice. If she wanted to ensure her only living family member remained alive, she would have to do everything he asked of her, even if she hated every minute of it. The only option Pia had was to pray she could actually follow through with whatever plans he had in store.

HE HAD ALMOST GONE TOO FAR WITH PIA. IF HE HAD STAYED there even a moment longer, he would have ravished her completely. He needed her, and as he got to know her, his plans changed course, moving in a completely different direction.

She was supposed to fall in love with him. He had blundered a bit there. He would have to make her forget he had threatened her grandpere's life somehow. Not that Comte Dubois didn't deserve to die. He was an evil man. If not for him, Thor would never have become a pirate. But that also meant he would never have met Pia. Thor's conundrum was his constant craving for Pia. It hadn't been in his plans to want her as much as he did.

He had intended to offer her some of the things from her trunks. It was clear to him she was restless. Thor would offer her a boon the next time he talked to her. Peace was important to have between them. It did not bode well with his plans to always be so overbearing and obnoxious with her. Although, she did appear to enjoy being kissed.

He walked up to the deck to check their progress. They should be in Bordeaux in less than two days. His plans would be in full motion once they were in port with the anchor dropped. When it was all done, he would be able to have what he wanted most. Revenge. Thor would also have something he was starting to desire almost more than that. Almost.

When he got topside, he located his first mate to make sure they were on schedule. Jamieson was at the bow of the ship with his sextant measuring the angles on the horizon.

"Are we on our scheduled course, Jamieson?"

"We are, Captain."

"Excellent work. Let me know if we run into any problems. I don't want to have anything spoil the plans I've made."

"Aye aye, Captain."

Thor walked away making his way to the galley. With his cabin occupied by a tempting beauty, he couldn't spend his leisure time there. He would make the cook get out his bottle of scotch and pour him a glass.

He was desperately in need of something to assist him while slumbering alongside Pia in their shared bunk. It would prove difficult to find any rest lying next to her later that night in his current state. Thor hoped the alcohol would help him pass out and prevent him from groping her...much.

CHAPTER 6

Thor started to speculate about life and the choices he made. A person's existence could become their own version of hell on Earth. Sadly he knew more about that than anyone else did. The choices he made often demanded every ounce of his blood, sweat, and tears. The very essence of his soul had been devoured whole, chewed, and spit out with nothing good remaining to maintain its life force. His soul remained on the brink of being lost, never to be retrieved again. At the same time life is inherently full of surprises at every turn, both good and bad depending on which path is chosen. The course he selected determined how much of his soul was beyond redemption or if it had one last chance to achieve salvation.

Watching the sun rise above the ocean announcing a new day, Thor thought of all of the reasons he set himself on this particular path. Revenge was the course of action he had taken, and he couldn't extricate himself from it even if he wanted to.

Pia was a revelation he had not anticipated. When he had heard she was traveling to live with Comte Dubois, all he could see was a way to enact his vengeance. The reality of it all was more of a shock than having his partner put a bullet through his shoulder. He was beginning to need her. He knew he had to alter his course before he crossed a line.

The port of Bordeaux beckoned him. Some plans already set in motion were irrevocable. Once the anchor dropped, he would need to make some quick alterations to his plans. In the missive he had written in front of Pia, those changes would be hastened. He just needed to send one of his crew to deliver the message of their arrival, and once it was done, everything should go smoothly.

His heart would never recover if he lost it all because he couldn't correct some of the mistakes he had already made. As it was, there was still a lot that was unforgivable. Sadly events to come might hamper any effort he made. Pia was still an essential part of his plan, but the difference was how she would be used in his revenge.

He still needed to make sure the comte paid for his treachery. The modification was in how much of it would destroy the humanity that remained of his soul. What he was doing to gain retribution wouldn't blacken him to the core. It was something he could, and would, happily live with. Some things were worth whatever price needed to be paid. This was one time there would be no regrets. There were times when he thought he would never be able to make Renny Dubois pay for his betrayal, and it was finally within his grasp. He just had to reach out and take it. He was so lost in thought he hadn't heard his bosun approach until he started to speak.

"Captain we are almost to the harbor of Bordeaux. I have Timmy getting ready to take a dinghy to shore. Is your message ready?"

Thor pulled out the missive. He had carefully written all of his instructions on the day he'd gotten his first taste of Pia. She had been so occupied with her own thoughts she hadn't even been curious about what he had been writing. At first that had disappointed him until he turned around and saw the expression on her face.

There had been such a look of longing in her eyes as she chewed her bottom lip. He lost control when her tongue slowly rolled over her lips leaving them a shiny invitation to be kissed. He couldn't restrain himself after that. He had to taste her. It was nice to see a lighter side of her personality emerge. If she had never stuck her tongue out at him, he may never have given in to his desire to kiss her.

He rolled the missive between his fingers remembering how much that day had transformed his outlook. His needs had altered so much because of that one moment of weakness. He wouldn't go back and change any part of that day, even knowing how much it would change him or what it forced him to admit about himself. After spending the past two weeks with Pia, he knew she was meant to be his. That day had sealed it for him. Thor turned to his bosun and handed him the message.

"Tell Timmy to wait for the reverend and bring all our guests back with him. The crew and I will await their arrival. Also, make sure he is aware I would like them here as quickly as possible. I want to have enough time to make sure Pia is back below deck before the sun sets tonight. It will be too dangerous to allow her to remain on deck after the ceremony."

"I will make sure that Timmy follows your directions, sir. After all it is a good night for a celebration."

Thor laughed. "It is indeed, Corny. It is indeed."

"The cook also wanted me to let you know that tonight's meal would be remembered for a long time to come. We got quite a haul from the galley of the ship we plundered, including a nice case of brandy and scotch. He wants to know if you'd like us to break it open for the celebration tonight."

"I think that's a fine plan, Corny. Also, any unnecessary crew can have shore leave for the night. Tell them they can go after tonight's celebration and remind them they need to be back on the ship before sunset tomorrow night. We will set sail after everyone's returned."

"Aye aye, Captain. I will take care of everything."

Thor found himself smiling in anticipation. Soon he would have everything he desired, including the alluring Pia. Her charms were something he ached to sample. After the blazing kisses they had shared, he knew her desire was equal to his. Pia was full of a fire that would consume with the right amount of fuel feeding her flames. It would be his honor and pleasure to share that bliss with her. After the ceremony just before dusk, she would be his in every way. Once the formalities were out of the way, they could explore what made each other burn.

~

IF PIA DIDN'T STOP WALKING BACK AND FORTH, SHE WAS BOUND to wear a hole in the cabin floor, clear through to the cargo hold. If that damn pirate showed his face today, she was going to pummel it with her fists. He needed to let her out of this cabin. He could at least have given her something to read. Then again, he did have that locked cabinet.

Staring at the cabinet as if seeing it for the first time, she analyzed it for weaknesses. Maybe it is possible to unlock it. With little to amuse herself, she was desperate enough to try anything. She scoured the room, looking for a tool that could help her pry it open. She turned the bunk inside out, throwing things on the floor. The blankets and pillows hit the ground with a soft thud. There was nothing there. She pulled the mattress up and pushed it against the wall. She looked beneath it. When she did not find anything of use, she let it flop back down haphazardly on top of its wooden frame. She turned and spotted the pirate's trunk. Rushing over to it, she tried to lift the top with her bare hands. The bloody thing was locked too, and she kicked it in frustration.

Nothing. There was nothing in the room. This was the worst torture ever imagined. She moved over to the cabinet to see if she could pry it open with her hands.

Pia kept trying to tear it open unaware that Thor had entered. He watched her for several seconds before he spoke. "Perhaps I could help you with that?"

Pia jumped back, startled by his voice next to her.

"Must you be so damned quiet?"

A chuckle rumbled out of his chest, developing into a full blown laugh. It was like a bolt of lightning striking the ground and spreading a light through a dark room.

"It was not my intention. I can see you have idle hands. Perhaps, I can give you something to keep them busy."

"Really? What? Do you have any books? I would love to have something to read. It would go a long way in curing the chronic boredom I've developed while being held captive."

"Sadly, pirates have little use for books. We don't have time for any leisurely pursuits. I might have a map or two you could entertain yourself with, but that wasn't exactly what I had in mind."

"I am almost afraid to ask. What exactly do you have in mind?"

"Well we could always continue where we left off the other day. That wall there was quiet handy in keeping you in place and what you were doing with your hands—purely inspirational."

Pia glared at him. Is he serious? Please let him be serious. She wanted to kiss him again and feel his hands roaming over her body. She wanted him to suck her nipples and squeeze her breasts. Wait, where did that idea come from? It was a fine idea indeed, and it needed to happen. I really, really need it to happen. She was about to make her demands when she remembered she was supposed to discourage such actions. She had to be sensible, and the pirate had already proven his kisses made her brainless.

"That is not what I had in mind and you know it."

"Pia, love, you are the most amusing woman I have ever encountered. I can see the conflicting emotions all over your face. No worries, my dear, I do have something else in mind. I thought perhaps you would enjoy a bath and a change of clothes."

She raised an eyebrow. "Is this some kind of trick? What's the catch?"

"No trick or catch. I want you to be comfortable and feel your best today. We are having a celebration tonight, and you will be able to come on deck."

"Really? I can leave the cabin now? I'd been starting to think you were lying about allowing me out of this blasted room."

"Yes, for an hour or so. Your attendance at the celebration is much desired."

"Then yes, absolutely, I would love a bath. But, I don't have any underclothes or another dress that I can put on when I'm done."

"Don't worry. I'll make sure you have something besides that drab dress you choose to wear."

"Are you serious? It isn't like you have given me a change of attire since I have been on your ship."

"I didn't have a reason to before. I was commenting more on your choice of attire, period. It's dreadful, and you need to wear something with more color. Black, my dear, does nothing for you."

"I'm in mourning, my father died. That's what you wear to honor the dead."

"I know. All the same, you will no longer wear black. I don't like it."

Pia pursed her lips together, letting her displeasure be known. She looked at Thor. "All right, Captain. As I have no choice but to follow your dictates, I guess I will have to agree if I want a bath and a change of clothes."

He smiled at her, and she felt her heart flutter faster. Damn him and his alluring smile. It should be illegal, not that it would stop him. He was a pirate after all. They never followed any laws, unless they were of their own making. If there was one thing Pia was more than aware of, it was that this particular pirate made his own rules. This ship was a nation of its own making. Any regulations were enforced by the one and only sovereign pirate, Thor.

"As always, Pia, you make things more interesting. I will send my cabin boy up with your hot water. Do not give him any trouble. If you try to leave the cabin before you are supposed to, you will regret it. Take this small peace offering and enjoy your bath."

Pia sighed. "I can't very well argue with your logic."

"Of course you can't, it won't take you long to realize that I am generally right in most situations. One more thing before I go, please clean up the mess you made before Gus comes with your bath. I know that you didn't have anything to do, but tearing the cabin apart isn't an acceptable form of entertainment. It wouldn't do very well for us to sleep on wet things tonight."

He turned and walked out the door, making sure it was secured behind him. Once it was closed, Pia stuck her tongue out at him. She didn't dare do it to his face any more. Even if she wanted him to kiss her again, she couldn't allow it to happen. They almost went too far the last time.

After reflecting on her situation, she didn't think it was wise to get too attached to the pirate. He was undoubtedly handsome and his kiss was an experience she would always treasure, but her heart would break if she allowed him to have it. She did not believe it was possible for her to have an affair without letting herself feel something for the other person. She had already begun to care about the pirate, and all they had done was kiss.

Pia sighed and looked at the room. She had made quite a mess of the small cabin. On this one occasion she conceded that Thor had a point. The room's current chaotic state needed to be set to rights. She had no idea how long it would be before her bath was brought to the cabin so she immediately began to clean up the room. It didn't take her long to put everything back where it belonged and decided she needed a break from the exertion.

Pia was lying on the bunk when the door opened. She turned to see a boy of no more than twelve come in carrying a wooden tub. He placed it near the bunk and walked out of the room. He wasn't much of a conversationalist.

Pia got up to inspect the tub. It wasn't very large. Looking at it, she wondered how anyone larger than her could possibly fit inside of it. She wondered where the captain got the tub, and if he had intended for her to bathe all along. Where did the rest of them bathe? Did they even bother?

It wasn't long before the boy returned. This time he was carrying two large buckets of steaming water. He quickly poured them into the tub. When he was done, he looked over at her and set the buckets down.

"Miss, I will be back with more hot water. Once the tub is half full, then a couple of pails with cooler water will be available so you can make it to your liking. I'm to bring you some soap and drying cloths as well. After I bring you everything, you are free to take your bath. I just wanted to let you know so that you can bathe in peace."

"Thank you, what's your name?"

"Gus, ma'am."

"Thank you, Gus. Are you bringing me a change of clothes too?"

"I don't rightly know, ma'am. I suspect the captain has

everything you need ready, and you will get it when he decides you need it."

"Hmm. Of course he does. Thank you again, Gus."

Odious man.

When Gus left, Pia silently fumed. Give it to her when he wants her to have it, will he. It was time to share her frustrations with him. Thor had no idea how much he drove her insane. The pirate would soon learn exactly what Pia's capabilities were. This was definitely going to be an amusing day.

Gus continued to fill her bath. He completed his task efficiently, working as fast as his small frame could manage. Once he was gone, she didn't waste any time because the water would cool and make her bath a miserable experience. She adjusted the water to her desired temperature. While she was finishing that task, Gus came in one last time with a couple stacks of dry cloths and a bar of soap.

"Here be your soap, ma'am. I will be by later to collect the water and tub. I will knock first so as to make sure you're decent."

Pia looked over as Gus left the room. The door shut with a quiet click. She heard the key turn, locking her inside once again. She began to undress, and it wasn't until he left that she realized she had a dilemma. *How the heck am I going to get my corset off?*

CHAPTER 7

Thor had decided he needed to give Pia something to occupy her time with. When he had walked in earlier and found the cabin a mess with her attempting to yank open his cabinet, he knew she was at her wit's end. So he dug through one of her trunks, locating some books for her. He had heard her expound at length about how much she loved every one of her damned books. Apparently, she really loved mythology. So it was with some amusement he picked up a book titled: Thor, God of Thunder. He couldn't wait to see the look on her face when he handed it to her. Yes, he was attempting to do her a favor, but that didn't mean he couldn't find humor in giving her that book just to get a reaction out of her.

When Thor walked into the cabin, he found Pia struggling to untie her corset. Thor leaned on the frame of the doorway and watched her with amusement. He let out a laugh that echoed throughout the cabin like a roll of thunder, much like the god he was named after. The boisterous sound succeeded in gaining her attention.

Pia glanced back at him briefly only to turn back around, still struggling to loosen her stays. "I'm glad I can amuse you. What are you doing here anyway? I thought I had privacy to bathe?" She waved her hands motioning him to come to her. "Never mind, make yourself useful and untie this blasted thing. I don't have a maid, as you left her on the other ship, so you can act in her place."

Her face was turned away as she stood quietly with her back to him. Thor took his packages and set them on the table. He walked over and pulled at the laces of her corset, loosening them. He leaned over her shoulder, his breath hot on her neck and whispered in her ear. "Oh, I assure you I have no problem acting as your maid. I have wanted to undress you for days."

"How crude, just unlace this thing. Then you can leave. Did you bring me a change of clothes? Forget the corset. I am not wearing it again. I don't have a maid to help with the blasted thing. It's far too much to deal with on my own."

Thor laughed as he listened to her ramble on without giving him a chance to respond. Pia talked so fast it was impossible to get a word in. Once she stopped to take a breath, Thor took the opportunity to speak.

"It was good of you to remember to straighten up the mess you made earlier. I did remember how agitated you were and thought perhaps you would like one of the books from your trunks. Yes, I did remember your clothes. They were especially made for you. I hope the dress pleases you."

"Wait, you have my trunks? Why didn't you tell me this sooner? There are things in there I could use. Why wouldn't you let me have my things?" she demanded. Her agitation showed as Pia swung her hands around in circular motion, emphasizing her disapproval through the movement.

"I didn't see any reason before now."

"I don't know why I'm surprised. Nothing you do shocks me anymore, just leave the stuff on the table and leave so I can bathe in peace."

"I have no intention of leaving."

"I beg your pardon?"

Thor raised an eyebrow, mocking her. It was clear he had her backed into a corner. She could not find a way to extricate herself from. He didn't budge on anything once he set his mind to it. Thor knew Pia would acquiesce to his demands.

"Well, love, it is as simple as this. I am going to go take a little nap over there on the bunk. I'm weary and want to rest before tonight's celebration. I won't bother you while you bathe. Go ahead and do as you planned."

Pia stared at him with her mouth gaping. Shock riddled her face, turning it a bright shade of red. It would be interesting to see what she would do. He was actually looking forward to it. He loved teasing her.

Thor watched as she reached down to check the temperature of the bath water. The water had a little steam billowing over the tub as she ran her fingers over it. Seeming to be satisfied with the temperature, she grabbed the soap and a dry cloth and set them near the tub. Her pantaloons and chemise hit the floor, leaving her completely naked before him. Her pert backside was in full view as she climbed into the tub keeping her back to him the entire time. It took everything he had not to walk over, pull her back out of the tub, and explore every inch of her body. Instead, he laid there in silence and watched as she scrubbed her body clean. Pia poured a bucket of water over her head to rinse herself off. When the water flowed over her head dousing every inch of her, Thor's eyes remained on her back as tiny droplets of water slowly trailed down the curve of her spine.

She was completely thorough in her bathing, washing every inch of herself. Thor was entranced as she slowly brought a washcloth across her neck and it disappeared from his view, down toward her bosom. He had never been so jealous of a piece of cloth in his life. He wanted to touch everything it brushed against. The longer he lay there watching her, the harder he got beneath his trousers. Siren's were fabled to tempt sailors to their doom. Pia could very well be one put on Earth to bring about his demise. The beautiful temptress scrubbing her skin pink in front of him was surely created to torture him with pleasure.

It took every ounce of his will not to strip his clothes off and pull her out of that blasted tub. His need for her grew with every breath he took. Thor assured himself he would have her soon. He could be patient and wait for the appropriate time. Thor gritted his teeth in frustration as he rubbed a hand over his aching member.

Yes, he was going to be inside her and soon. The little minx was begging him by bathing before him. No lady would have done so unless she secretly desired a man's attentions. In the evening, if all went as planned, Pia would have his complete attention. He just had to bide his time and survive this torturous experience. In the meantime, he intended to enjoy the show she provided for him.

"Pia, love, must you make so much noise splashing the water? I am trying to relax over here."

"Yes. If you have a problem with it, you can leave."

"I don't know. If you are going to be so loud, maybe I should just enjoy the scenery."

He was trying to goad her. It wasn't working. Pia just kept scrubbing her skin and removing the dirt. She was in the bath for thirty minutes before it became clear she was done. There was nothing left on her alabaster skin to scrub clean. She had cleansed her body so much that every inch had turned a delightful pink. Her skin glowed from all of her ministrations. If Thor were to hazard a guess, everything Pia did was for his benefit. He was certain she was trying her best to torture him, and he couldn't let her know it was working.

Pia slowly turned her head, impishness shining in her eyes as she looked over at Thor. "Was the scenery to your liking?"

"Immensely."

Her head turned slightly so he could see the outline of her profile. Pia's voice was husky as she replied. "Hmm. Well, I wonder if there is a way to improve on that."

"I'm sure you can think of something."

"Oh, I am intelligent enough. I'm sure I could be creative as well."

It was Thor's turn to smile. He had no doubt she could be creative. He couldn't wait to find out how resourceful she could be. "I have no doubt that you could do anything."

She gave him something to look at—and he lost his cocksure smile too.

With that, Pia stood and turned to face him. The droplets of water trailed between the valley of her breasts, creating a path toward her belly button. The small rivulet flowed even farther south. Thor's eyes tracked every inch of the course it made.

Thor got up and walked over to the table where the dry cloths were placed. He grabbed one and tossed it at her. If he didn't get away from her, he was going to lick every particle of water off of her body like a man desperate for a drink. Just looking at her made him salivate.

"Please be a dear, dry yourself off, and get dressed. The celebration is scheduled to start in an hour. I'll be back then to collect you."

He managed to remain cool and aloof as he walked toward the cabin door. Once outside, he quickly secured the lock. Thor rested his head on the door and took a deep breath. That was too close. He had almost given in and ruined all of his plans.

While she stood there dripping water all over the cabin floor, Thor had been struck dumb. The sneaky, sensual wench had effectively turned the tables on him. Thor had never been a betting man and wouldn't gamble his plans away at this juncture of the operation, at least at this stage when their relationship hadn't gone beyond a few kisses. He couldn't take any chances that his carefully laid plans might fall to pieces if he gave in to Pia's charms too early. She was every fantasy brought to life. The beautiful, wet witch had done something he'd never expected. If he wasn't already in deep, that little scene would've told him one thing. He'd willingly jump into shark infested waters to claim her as his own. He'd finally found a woman who was his equal in every way.

CHAPTER 8

Pia still held the drying cloth Thor had tossed at her. Her hand rose to grab it out of the air as he exited the room. Pia automatically began to dry herself with the towel. Could that have been any more embarrassing? He appeared to be upset with her. Why? She thought she had read the signs correctly. Thor wanted her. His body gave that away whenever he pressed himself against her.

She felt his hard shaft pressing against her derriere as they slept each night. Its length growing as he spooned against her, holding her in his tight embrace. While in her presence, it appeared as if the pirate was hard all the time. Why did he act like I just insulted him? She may be naïve, but she knew what a man's body did when he desired a woman. Pia didn't understand why Thor had damn near run out of the room. His desire was evident by the look in his eyes. So why did he feel the need to put distance between them?

She looked through the items he had brought for her. There was a clean chemise, pantaloons, a brush, and some blue hair ribbons. But the jewel in the treasure trove was the royal blue dress that matched her eyes. The bodice was lower than she would have liked, but it looked like it would hug her every curve. It was made of the softest silk and trimmed with the finest lace. He didn't bring her any matching slippers, so she would have to make do with her sensible travel shoes.

Why did he bring me something so fine and beautiful to wear?

She quickly put on her new chemise and pantaloons. Once she was partially dressed, she traipsed over and sat on the chair by the table. She grabbed the brush and untangled the knots already forming in her long blonde mane. Pia hummed a happy tune as her nimble fingers created a simple braid and laced one of the blue ribbons through it. After the braid was completed, she took another ribbon and tied it off at the end to make sure it stayed in place. After her hair was arranged to her liking, she pulled on her stockings.

Pia picked up her dress and stepped into it, pulling it up. Luckily the gown laced in the front, making it easier for her to put on without the assistance of a maid. All of her other ensembles hooked in the back. With her gown securely fastened, Pia walked over and grabbed her shoes off the floor. She sat on the edge of the bed so it would be easier to slip them onto her feet. Once she had them in place, Pia laced them firmly. She stood and smoothed the dress with her hands so it fell in even waves down to the floor.

The door opened, and Pia looked up as Thor entered the room. He had always been attractive, but in that instant, she was amazed at how good he really looked. To say he was handsome did not do him justice. He was breathtaking.

He had clearly taken the time to bathe. As usual, his beautiful onyx hair was pulled back in a leather tie. He was dressed in his finest pirate attire. He wore black leather pants that hugged his thighs, making it possible to see every inch of his body. His pearly white shirt billowed over his shoulders and was tucked into his trousers. His tan skin gleamed against the stark white of his tunic. Thor's eyes held a mischievous twinkle that made Pia a little nervous about this supposed celebration.

Thor took his time looking over Pia as he circled around her with an appreciative scrutiny. Once he had made a full circle, he stopped in front of her. "Ah good, you are ready."

"Well you did tell me I would be able to leave the cabin today. I wasn't going to delay that for any reason."

A small chuckle escaped him and reverberated through

the room. A roguish smile slowly formed on his lips. "Very true, love. Come along, I have a lot of surprises for you."

"Can I have a hint?"

"Only a small one. It is something you could never guess."

Pia stuck her tongue out at him. "You call that a hint?"

"Careful, Pia, you remember what happened the last time you stuck your tongue out at me."

Pia looked at Thor with an impish grin. "Oh, I remember that quite well. I just figured you must have gotten your needs taken care of elsewhere. You didn't seem interested in touching me earlier."

Thor raised an eyebrow at her, amusement shining in his eyes as he looked down at her. "Nothing could be further from the truth. I like to savor my treats, and make no mistake about it, you would be a treat. There wasn't enough time to enjoy you earlier."

It was Pia's turn to raise her eyebrow. As far as she was concerned, he already had his chance and blew it. She didn't believe in unwarranted second chances. So she told him the truth as she saw it. "Well, it was a onetime offer. One that has already expired, so it won't be an issue since you're not going to touch me again."

"Be careful about issuing me commands. You will soon realize that I'm the only one in charge."

"Right." Pia rolled her eyes. "Because you are the mighty Pirate Thor."

"Absolutely, it's best you don't forget that. Come. Our guests await us."

THOR ESCORTED PIA TO THE QUARTERDECK. IT WAS KIND OF NICE to stroll along with her. She looked ravishing in the blue dress, but he couldn't wait to get her out of it. They had been spending all of their time in his cabin. This was a different way to see her and enjoy her company. This celebration had been planned for weeks. As soon as the intel had come to him she would be crossing the ocean to live with her grandpere in France, he knew what he had to do. Comte Dubois was the one responsible for the life he now led. He would never have been a pirate if the man hadn't tried to execute him. This was his chance to pay the comte back in kind. He would have his precious granddaughter for his own, and the comte wouldn't be able to do anything to stop him. His plan was brilliant.

"Do you remember the conversation we had a few days ago?"

"You will have to clarify which conversation. We have had many."

Thor looked at her with delight shining in his eyes. Conversing with Pia was a game he would never tire of. His voice held a tinge of devilment. "Don't play coy Pia, you know what I'm talking about. I am referring to when we discussed the day you would be allowed to come on deck. Please don't disappoint me. I'm sure you'll enjoy some company other than mine, even if it's brief."

"Ah, the one where you said I had to follow all of your orders, or you would kill my grandpere."

"Yes, that one. If you do not do everything I ask of you, I will kill your grandpere."

With a petulant smile, Pia looked up at him. "I understand. You do not have to remind me of that."

"Excellent. I'm glad you're on board with the plan, because I have an extra special surprise for you. Well a couple of surprises, I hope they please you. Don't leave my side for any reason. I promise, you will regret it if you do."

Thor wished reminding her he would kill her grandpere wasn't a necessary evil, but he needed her to comply with everything he had planned. It was unfortunate they had to meet this way. She really was perfect for him. In a very short time, she had become the most important person in his life. He sincerely wished they could have met at a different time.

Life had sent him on a path, and he hadn't been given a choice. He had learned to embrace it as the tool that would eventually give him the revenge he sought.

His Pia was beautiful, but more importantly, she was also feisty and smart. He had a feeling she would always be able to surprise him. It was his deepest wish to have her with him all the time so she could continue to astonish him for the rest of their lives. So it was with a heavy heart he continued on his chosen path, hoping that one day she would be able to forgive him for what he felt must be done.

"I already told you I would do what you ask. You don't need to remind me again," Pia said as she stopped. "Is that my grandpere?"

Thor had been walking her toward where Comte Dubois was standing, guarded by several of his crew. He had been brought to the ship by one of the pirate crew. Comte Dubois was a man of average height, an olive complexion, and dark ebony hair dusted with grey. He was stout and had a small pouch of a belly, showing how comfortable he was getting as he aged. Everything was coming together nicely. Thor couldn't wait to see the reaction on the comte's face when he married his granddaughter.

"How did my grandpere get here, Thor?" Pia demanded.

"Thor? Pieretta you are mistaken. This man's name is not Thor." Comte Dubois told his granddaughter.

Pia stood looking at Thor in shocked silence. She tilted her head at him, confusion clouding her face. Thor knew she wanted to know what was going on, and the answers she needed from him would become apparent momentarily. His gaze was firmly on Comte Dubois as he responded to his statement. "Your grandpere would know exactly who I am, Pia. He did try to murder me after all."

"I did not try to murder you. I was trying to save you. Standing directly behind you was a pirate, and he was aiming his pistol straight at you. When I fired mine, I was aiming at him."

"Really, Renny, you expect me to believe you shot me while trying to save me? Then why did you leave me there to die?"

"I did no such thing. I went to get help. By the time I came back, you were gone."

Thor raised an eyebrow in disbelief. "So you took it as a sign I had died? You rushed to have me declared dead so you could gain control over our business. I'm actually amazed they took your word for it. There was very little evidence of my supposed demise."

Thor kept a close eye on Pia throughout his exchange with Comte Dubois. He saw the confusion spread over her features. She looked back and forth between the two of them, her face growing paler with each statement.

Looking directly into Thor's eyes, Pia asked. "Who are you really? Grandpere says your name is not Thor. I want your real name."

Thor shrugged his shoulders, dismissing what the comte had told her. The comte didn't really know him or the name his loved ones had known him by. He looked down at her. "Thor is my name."

"That's a lie. His name is William Thorston Marsden, Fifth Viscount Torrington," Comte Dubois shouted.

"He is correct. I go by a shortened version of my second name. Thor is short for Thorston. I was named after my father, and my mother wanted me to have my own identity. To my family and close friends I was always Thor. You wouldn't have known that, Renny. You always referred to me by my title. I was always Torrington to you. Did that make it easier to murder me? Was it more impersonal that way?"

"I told you I didn't try to kill you, Torrington," Comte Dubois insisted.

Thor had listened to enough of the comte's lies. It was time to end the charade and finish everything once and for all. He wanted the comte off of his ship and out of his life for good. He looked at the man with contempt, distaste filling his mouth from spending time in his malicious company. If his presence wasn't so important to fulfilling his vengeance, the comte would not be aboard, talking to them. He waved his hand at him dismissively. "No matter, I don't care. That is not why you're here."

"What do you want with me then?"

Thor looked at him. "I couldn't very well marry Pia without her only family being present to witness the union now could I?"

Thor heard Pia gasp. He knew it was a shock to her. He didn't think she would have agreed if he had outright asked her. They certainly didn't have a traditional relationship by any means.

When he had kidnapped her, his original plan had been to seduce her and return her to Renny as soiled goods. The more time he spent with her, the more apparent it became he couldn't do that to her. He knew he could never do that. This was the only choice he had if he was going to keep her safe with him. He needed to make her his wife. It was not in his makeup to just willingly hand her over to her grandpere and hope for the best. No, this is what must be done.

Comte Dubois started to spit and sputter at Thor's announcement. His voice filled with uncontrollable rage as he screamed. "You are not marrying my granddaughter, Torrington."

A wicked smile crossed Thor's lips. "I absolutely am. Pia consented to be with me for the rest of her life. I wanted to make sure she didn't have any regrets. It is part of the reason I made sure you were present. Ah, here is the priest now, it's time to begin."

~

THE CEREMONY WENT BY IN A BLUR. SHE DIDN'T EVEN REMEMBER saying I do. She couldn't believe Thor wanted to marry her. She was still confused by it all. He wouldn't let her go near her grandpere. He said her grandpere was too dangerous, and he wouldn't allow her to ever be around someone so evil. Here she was, married to a pirate viscount of all things, and she would never be allowed to see her family again.

This was why she never wanted to get married. Men had all of the control. Thor had threatened her grandpere's life. If she didn't marry him, he would have killed her grandpere. With the comte standing on the deck, the threat had seemed very real to her. He begged her to not marry Thor. Pia could tell he didn't understand why she was going through with it when he shook his head in confusion. Grandpere didn't know she was only marrying Thor to protect him. She couldn't be held responsible for his death.

Please let my grandpere be okay.

Her feelings for her pirate were complicated. They had spent only a short time together on board his ship, but Pia believed she had begun to understand him. In some ways, she felt she knew him more than she knew herself.

This whole situation felt wrong in so many ways. Marrying Thor turned her life even farther upside down. It sank deeper and deeper into a never-ending fiasco, one she could never escape. Why did he want to marry me? He attacked a ship and kidnapped me to make me his wife? Pia shook her head in confusion. Why would that matter?

Once it was all over, Thor had escorted Pia back to their cabin. Before he closed the door, he had informed her he would be back in an hour or so. He had some things to take care of on deck. Thor had looked at her directly in the eyes and said he was looking forward to spending the night with his new wife. When he left, she thought she'd be lucky if he actually gave her that much time.

She had done everything Thor had asked of her. One thing was for sure, Pia had a lot of questions, and Thor was going to answer them all. She had never wanted a husband. Thor had effectively tied her hands, making it the only decision she could make.

Pia had longed to be an independent woman. Thor took that away from her by forcing her to marry him. She wasn't exactly delighted to be his blushing bride. It didn't really matter because regardless of how she felt about the situation, Thor was her husband now. She wasn't going to back down. He would do what she wanted for once.

CHAPTER 9

Thor knew he had to face his bride sooner rather than later. Unfortunately, it was several hours before he was able to get away from the crew to seek her out. After he ensured Comte Dubois and the priest were back on shore, he could deal with the ramifications of the day's events. Some of his crew had been worried the comte might try and come back on board to harm him. So he had to assure them it was okay to go ahead with the shore leave he granted them. He wanted them to have some time to themselves before they set sail again.

Thor made his way to the cabin to deal with his new wife. He was prepared for a temper tantrum. In fact, he was looking forward to it. He liked when she got mad and feisty. It made things a lot more interesting.

He wasn't prepared to explain everything to her just yet. He wanted to show her everything he wanted from her first. He yearned to express all the bottled up desire and longing he had been holding back. Thor wasn't always good with words and often found actions were a much better way of getting his point across. They would have to talk eventually, but he was hoping to put it off for as long as possible. For now, Thor wanted her to feel everything he was feeling. He needed to experience what it was like to be inside of her. He patiently waited until he could love her the only way he knew how.

Pia was his wife, and he finally had the right to explore every inch of her luscious body. She had given him a very brazen invitation after her bath earlier that evening. It hadn't been the proper time to accept it, but he was more than ready now that they were legally wed.

He walked into the cabin and was surprised to find Pia asleep on the bunk. She had taken off her dress and draped it over the chair by the table. Thor stopped to stare at Pia for a while, admiring her beauty. Her chest rose and fell with an even pace. She was utterly and completely beautiful. To him she was perfect, but more importantly...she was his.

Thor removed his boots, and the rest of his clothes followed shortly after. He crawled onto the bunk with his wife. Her instinct made her curl next to him. She was used to sleeping with him and didn't rouse when he pulled her closer. He slowly caressed her, hoping she would awaken. He needed her conscious for every part of the loving he was going to give her.

~

Pia was having the best dream. It felt so real. She was almost afraid to open her eyes and discover it wasn't. She didn't want it to stop. Phantom hands wandered down her body. She felt light kisses across her cheek and trail down her neck. The warmth spread all over her body, increasing with each new sensation. Her body had never felt so amazing from such simple contact with another person. Wait, there really is someone's lips floating over my body, drowning it with kisses.

Her eyes flew open, and she found Thor staring into them.

"Good of you to wake up, love."

"What are you doing, Thor?"

"I'm loving my wife."

If Pia had been capable of snorting at that moment, she would have. He claimed her grandpere was the master of lies, and here falsehoods spilled from his lips. Both Thor and her grandpere expected her to believe them, but she didn't really know either one of them. She wanted a real conversation with her grandpere, but Thor would never allow that to happen. It was up to her to find a way.

In the meantime, she had to deal with Thor's amorous intentions. He said he was going to love her. She didn't believe he actually loved her in any way, shape, or form. But he did desire her, and as her husband, he would want to express it. Fortunately for him, she equally desired him, and she might as well get something out of this sham of a marriage. Her gaze drifted up to meet his. "You do not love me, Thor. I am just a pawn in your revenge against my grandpere."

"Nevertheless, we are going to find pleasure in each other."

Before Pia could get another word out, Thor kissed her. He peeled off her drawers and chemise. When she was completely nude, he caressed her body, placing soft kisses along her breasts. Pia moaned when he brought one of her rosy nipples into his mouth, savoring its taste. The man sure knew how to kiss, and Pia wanted him to put his lips all over her body. Wherever his mouth touched, her body blazed with need and pleasure.

Thor drifted down and kissed the inside of her thighs. He spread her legs wide as his face drifted to her very core. He used his hands to open her wider, and one of his fingers gently stroked her. She moaned when his tongue darted out and found her sensitive spot. He licked and sucked until Pia thrashed wildly on the bed. She felt the culmination of something grow inside of her. As his mouth caressed her, his fingers stroked her, pumping in and out, until she screamed out in ecstasy.

The pleasure was so intense she didn't know how much more she could possibly take. He kept moving his fingers in and out of her, while his thumb caressed the sensitive nub. Every sensation made her burn, and her flesh heated, turning a rosy pink as moans of pure bliss escaped her mouth. She bucked against him, needing something more, but she didn't understand what her body craved. All she knew was something was missing.

Once again she saw stars as the world exploded around

her. It was the most amazing feeling she had ever felt. It wasn't possible to feel this good. *What has Thor done to me?*

Before she finished the thought, Thor shifted her. He spread her legs wider and entered her slowly. He inched his way inside of her until he was fully seated within her quivering body. The pain caused her to bite her tongue and whimper. It hurt to take him inside of her. Everything had felt so good, and then he went and ruined it by pushing himself inside of her narrow passage.

"Shhh, it only hurts the first time, love. I promise the next time will be all pleasure."

He moved in and out of her, his pace steadily increasing. At first, she wanted to shove him off, but the more he moved, the better it felt. Pia's desire grew with each thrust. She wanted him deeper, harder, faster. She wrapped her legs around his waist, finding her own rhythm to match his movements. The sensations building up in her grew and Pia craved more. She couldn't get enough of him.

"Yes, like that, squeeze me, Pia. Good God, you feel so good. I can't hold out much longer. Come with me."

He kissed her again as he thrust deeper and faster. The movements brought Pia over the edge, and it was even better than the explosion she'd experienced earlier. This was a completion. It was just—right.

She screamed Thor's name as she came. He whispered her name as if it was a benediction. He soon followed and released himself inside her. He rolled to his side pulling her along with him. He curled his body around hers and held her as he fell asleep. Pia couldn't believe he was able to sleep after something so monumental, but she soon drifted off herself.

CHAPTER 10

Pia woke up in slow degrees, and Thor was still passed out next to her. She extricated herself from his embrace, getting out of the bunk as quietly as possible. She located her pantaloons and chemise lying on the floor where he had discarded them. Pia grabbed her dress and stepped into it, fastening the buttons as quickly and quietly as she could.

Now they were married, she hoped Thor would be more lenient in his desire to keep her confined in their cabin. Surely now he would start leaving the door unlocked. Pia was desperate to get off of the ship and go see her grandpere. She picked up her shoes and carried them out the door Thor had left unlocked. Thank the Lord. I can try to get away.

He must have felt secure in his ownership of her, because he hadn't bothered to ensure she couldn't escape. Finally, the pirate was getting sloppy. He would soon discover she was capable of taking care of herself. He may have just given her the greatest pleasure she had ever known, but he also had used her in the worst possible way. She didn't want to consider what other complications might arise from what they had just done. Pia was well aware they could have created a baby, but she didn't have time to think about it. She needed to get away, and this may be her only opportunity.

When she was far enough away from the cabin that she felt safe, she put her shoes on. It was difficult, but she managed to be as silent as possible as she crept on deck. Pia walked on her toes across the creaking timbers, cringing every time a small squeak emitted from underneath her feet.

She looked up realizing they were still anchored in the harbor at Bordeaux. The docks were in the distance, but it shouldn't take her long to get to shore. She scanned the sides of the ship and spotted two of the crew climbing up a ladder. They vacated a dinghy to board the ship, and the bosun greeted them as they walked onto the deck.

Pia's heart beat heavily in her chest as she hid from their view. She was terrified they would discover her hiding place. Standing as still as possible, she controlled her breathing so she wouldn't make any unnecessary noise. Pia took the time to still all of her movements, relaxing enough to listen to their exchange.

"Is everything taken care of?" the bosun asked.

"Yes, sir. We dropped the priest back at his parish and dumped the comte at his estate."

Estate? Grandpere had an estate in Bordeaux? Pia had thought he lived in Calais.

"Very good. You may retire for the night and give a full report to the captain in the morning. He is not to be disturbed tonight. The captain changed his mind, and we will set sail at dawn, please be prepared to lift anchor."

There were no crew members anywhere else on deck. The ship was almost like a ghost ship. That couldn't be how it was normally. Where did all of the crew go? Who was taking care of the ship? Pia had to try to get to the dinghy and row to shore. Then she could find her grandpere. Once she saw him, she would have the chance to explain everything. He would understand she really didn't have a choice.

As soon as the bosun was far enough away, Pia scrambled to the ladder and climbed down into the dinghy. She wasn't concerned for her own well-being, but she was desperate to see how her grandpere had fared. She may be the pirate's wife, but she could still make decisions for herself.

Her arms grew sore with each push of the oars through the water. Her strength was limited because of her small stature, but she managed to row herself to the nearest dock. Once the boat was next to the dock, Pia scrambled to the top and walked as fast as she could. Her breaths fell in pants from her mouth in the cold night air. She rubbed her hands together trying to warm them as she strolled across the docks.

The first thing she needed to do was find out where her grandpere's estate was. Pia didn't get very far before she was grabbed. She didn't even have time to scream before the unknown assailant dragged her away.

~

THOR WOKE UP AND STRETCHED. HE HAD NEVER FELT SO RELAXED in his entire life. He wanted to experience those sensations all over again. Thor was blissfully happy at the results of loving his new bride. He rolled over to pull Pia to his side.

He sat up with a start. His cheeks heated with anger. She wasn't in his bed. Where did the little minx go? She couldn't have gone far. Thor rolled off the bed and pulled on his clothing. He stormed up to the quarterdeck. Thor stomped his way to the cabin shared by his bosun and first mate and knocked on the door.

Thor waited for someone to come to the door. It opened to reveal his bosun, staring at him. "Corny, have you seen my wife?"

"No, Captain, I assumed she was with you."

"Well clearly she is not. Search the ship. Locate her at once." Thor watched as Corny woke the first mate.

The bosun and first mate rang the bell for all hands on deck. The crew searched everywhere, but Pia was nowhere to be found. It was only after several minutes of searching they realized the dinghy was gone. Pia had jumped ship.

Thor roared at them to get another dinghy ready. He was going to search for his wife and wring her little neck once he found her. She was his. How dare she leave him. He was blistering mad, his face heating with every word he shouted. Never before had he experienced a mixture of anger and fear. Thor required Pia be safely returned, but mostly he just needed her.

~

Pia was shoved into a carriage and quickly settled onto a seat. She didn't know who had grabbed her, but it couldn't be good. She slapped him. She was getting tired of people kidnapping her. Damn them all for thinking she was something they could throw around. What's wrong with people these days?

The man who had grabbed her rubbed his face to alleviate the sting. "Now, was that really necessary?"

Captain Devere sat across from her in the carriage. So, Thor hadn't killed him. She really did assume a lot about the man that was probably not true.

"Yes, you had no right to grab me and shove me in this carriage. I was frightened. It wasn't like I knew who was yanking me into this conveyance. It's a natural reaction for someone being kidnapped."

"I can assure you, I only have your best interests at heart," Captain Devere said.

Pia looked up at him. "Why did you take me?"

"I was asked to retrieve you by Comte Dubois. You made it a much easier task by rowing to shore. I must thank you for that. It made my job less dangerous."

"You are taking me to grandpere?"

"Yes, my dear, you may rest easy. You will be safe in his care in less than twenty minutes."

"When did you get here?" Pia asked. "I thought the pirate murdered everyone on board the ship. Is Tully alive? Thor had implied that he didn't kill anyone. Well he kind of told me that he hadn't killed everyone—but how was I to know if he was telling the truth or not. I'm relieved to see you are alive and well Captain."

"Yes, your maid is fine. She is at your grandpere's estate. He had her settled into the servants' quarters, and she will be there to assist you tomorrow."

Pia nodded her head. "Good. I know you mean well, Captain, but I don't know you. I want to look in on her myself as soon as possible."

Pia settled down on the seat, resting her head on the side of the carriage. One thing was certain. Her grandpere was alive. He wouldn't have been able to send someone to retrieve her if Thor had murdered him.

She needed to speak to her grandpere. There were a lot of questions she wanted to ask him. Pia hoped he was prepared to answer all of them, because she wanted the truth. Once she heard both sides of this sordid mess, she could decide the best course of action. She knew Thor would eventually come after her. Thor was tenacious and would not give up easily. Pia only hoped she had enough time to hear her grandpere's side before Thor caught up with her. She was grateful Thor hadn't murdered the ship's crew or Tully. It made it easier to accept her growing feelings for the wicked pirate.

CHAPTER 11

Thor needed to beat on something in the worst way, so he swung around and punched the nearest wall as hard as he could. The pain he felt pulsing through his fist helped him focus on the real issue. His needed to retrieve his wife and forget about his increasing fury. His rage was so great that if any of his crew members had gotten near him they would have encountered serious bodily harm. Before he had boarded the dinghy, he had bellowed at his crew to get the ship prepared to leave port. When he returned with Pia, he fully intended to set sail immediately.

They had been too slow getting the dinghy ready, and as a result, he had missed Pia by mere minutes. Thor arrived at the dock just in time to see Pia being shoved into a nearby carriage. Captain Devere quickly jumped into the conveyance after her.

Thor found a hack as soon as he was able and demanded the driver go to the comte's nearby estate. It was the only place Devere could possibly be taking his wife.

The journey to Comte Dubois's estate would be brief, but it gave him time to reflect quietly on the situation. He should have realized Renny would try to take his granddaughter back. Thor had gotten sloppy, thinking he had won. Damn the comte for being such an evil bastard. So it looked like he would have to kill the comte after all. Thor was not leaving his wife in that man's care. Pia had become his everything in a very short time. He would not leave her in the vindictive hands of the comte. Thor wouldn't put it past him to harm his own granddaughter if it suited his purposes.

Thor sat back, leaning his head against the side of the carriage combing his fingers through his disheveled hair. He wouldn't be able to live with himself if something bad happened to Pia. Thor tilted his head toward the sky praying he would get to the estate in time to get Pia out unharmed.

∽

PIA ANXIOUSLY CLUTCHED HER HANDS IN HER LAP AS THEIR conveyance navigated the narrow road. The carriage rattled, shaking the seats as it traveled down the lane to her grandpere's estate. Captain Devere had assured her it shouldn't take more than twenty minutes for them to journey there. She sincerely hoped he was correct because the carriage was becoming increasingly more uncomfortable with each bump it rolled over.

Pia was growing weary of all the drama surrounding her life over the past couple of weeks. She should have been able to mourn her father in peace. Instead, she had been forced to leave her home and then kidnapped.

As they traveled, Devere told her what happened on the ship after Thor had taken her. Tully had been the only one Thor's crew hadn't tied up. When she wandered on deck and found the captain tied to the mast, she quickly freed him. The captain then went down and released his crew out from the cargo hold. They raised the sails and sailed toward France with due haste. There had been minimal damage done to the ship when Thor had attacked it. The damage inflicted had been meant to intimidate more than harm anyone aboard the ship.

Once they had arrived in port, they traveled to the comte's estate. He had been too late to meet him before Thor's men had taken the comte aboard the Sea Rover. Once the comte was dropped off at his estate, he dispatched Captain Devere to retrieve her from Thor.

When they arrived at her grandpere's estate, the captain

escorted her into the house. It was a beautiful manor at the end of a long driveway lined with large trees. As impressive as it was in the dark, it had to be breathtaking during the day.

Devere lead Pia into her grandpere's drawing room where she found him lounging in a chair nursing a glass of brandy. He jumped up as she marched into the room and hugged her tightly in his arms. Pia felt safe snuggled deep in her grandpere's burly arms. She heard Captain Devere shut the door as he left the room.

Comte Dubois took a step back and looked at Pia. "Thank the Lord they were able to save you from that demon's clutches."

"Grandpere, did you really try to kill him?"

"Don't be ridiculous, Pieretta. I never tried to kill him. He was like the son I never had, and his father was one of my dear friends."

"Then why does he think you tried to murder him?"

"It is a misunderstanding, I assure you. I loved the boy. I would not have killed him. It is sad what he has turned into. I cannot abide the life he has chosen to live. I was trying to save him, as I tried to explain on the ship. Perhaps, if I had gotten to him sooner—he is just not the same man I knew. He is dangerous, and you should not have married him. I'm sorry, my dear, but that was very reckless of you. We will have it annulled as soon as possible."

"That would be difficult to get, considering the marriage was consummated," Thor said with a drawl as he sauntered into the room.

Pia gasped. How did he get to Grandpere's estate so fast? She was sure he had been fast asleep when she left the ship. She assumed she would have more time to get answers. *Why couldn't he have been a little slower in coming after me?*

Comte Dubois took one look at Thor and then shouted for Captain Devere to come back into the drawing room.

"If you are looking for the captain, he is indisposed at the moment," Thor said as he made his way over to Pia.

"Damn you, Torrington. You cannot have my granddaughter."

Thor ignored the comte and continued walking toward Pia.

"Why are you here, Thor?" Pia asked him.

"I thought that was clear, love. I missed my wife. I came to find her, because clearly she's lost. Wives are supposed to remain naked in bed next to their husbands awaiting another round of loving. We clearly have some miscommunication going on between us. You know where you belong, Pia. Get ready to leave now."

Pia looked at him with barely restrained belligerence. "No."

The shock and anger on Thor's face was palpable. His steely blue gaze was glued to her face as the lines of his mouth became tight from clenching his jaw. The muscles in his cheeks twitched, his face flushed with anger. He glared at Pia. "I must have heard you wrong, dear. You are my wife, and you will leave with me now. Did you forget our agreement?"

"No. I remember it quite clearly, and I want to make a new agreement."

"I must admit you have piqued my interest. What changes did you want to make, love?"

"I will not remain with a man that clearly does not love me and has no respect for my wishes. I want to be able to visit my family. My grandpere is all I have left."

Thor scoffed at her statement, his eyebrow raised with derision. His gaze locked with hers. "Your grandpere is a murderous villain, Pia. I will not tolerate you being in his presence. We will work through the rest of our issues once we take leave of this wretched place."

"Well that's too damn bad, because I will spend time with him."

"Enough," the comte shouted.

Pia and Thor turned to look at Comte Dubois. He was holding a pistol, and it was aimed at the both of them. Her grandpere had been lying to her. He had always meant for Thor to die. Her husband had been right for the pistol was clearly aimed at him.

"If the marriage can't be annulled, clearly Pieretta, dear, you need to be made a widow."

"But Grandpere you said you didn't try to kill him!"

"I lied. It's what I do. I couldn't afford for him to see that I was pocketing some of the funds from the company. I wasn't solvent and needed them to get by. The dowry I gave your mother was all I had left. It took me years to build my fortune back. I will not let this pirate take away everything I have built."

"You built it using my money, Renny. You had no right to help yourself to my funds. My life has been turned upside down by your greed, and I'll make sure you pay for that," Thor said.

Thor pushed Pia aside, diving for the gun. He struggled with Renny to gain control over the pistol, each trying to get a firm grasp on it. The two of them fell to the floor, rolling around. They wrestled for control of the pistol, trying to get it away from one another. As they struggled to gain control, the gun went off.

The sound of the gun echoed throughout the room. Everything started to move in slow motion. Pia's scream rattled the windows. Nothing was clear, and no one was moving quickly enough for her to know if either one of them had been hurt. With her heart pumping wildly in her chest, she ran over and fell beside the two motionless bodies. What should I do? Please let them be okay. Grandpere was a bad man, but she still didn't want him to die. Thor meant more to her than she wanted to admit.

A small movement caught her attention out of the corner of her eye, and she turned her head to see if it was real or not. Thor slowly turned over, and Pia immediately noticed a spot of blood near the top of his white shirt.

"Thor?" Pia asked hesitantly. Was he okay? In that moment, Pia realized how much he had come to mean to her. Without realizing it, the damned pirate had found a way into her heart.

"I'm okay, Pia. Your grandpere is bleeding all over me though. Send someone for a physician."

Pia ran out the door calling for a servant to come quickly. The butler arrived in response to her deafening screams for help. Pia grabbed his jacket, telling him to send for a physician. He pulled himself out of her grasp and retreated to find help.

Pia's attention immediately returned to her grandpere.

She felt faint. The comte's face was as white as a ghost, and Pia scrambled over to his side. She had to do something to help him. She looked across the room. Thor stood in the corner watching her.

"Don't just stand there, go get me something to hold on his wound. He's bleeding all over the carpet. Help me please, Thor. I know he is your enemy, but he will always be my grandpere."

Thor nodded at her and pulled a handkerchief from his pocket, handing it to her.

"It won't help, Pia, but it is yours to use as you wish."

"Thank you, Thor, I appreciate your help. I have to do everything possible to help him."

Pia knelt next to her grandpere, placing the handkerchief on the wound. His color wasn't improving. She turned his face in her hands and leaned over to see if he was still breathing. His breaths were shallow. Pia feared he wouldn't survive long enough for a physician to help, and tears welled in her eyes and rolled down her cheeks. She silently begged the Lord to save him.

As she wordlessly prayed, Tully ran into the room.

"Miss Pieretta, I heard you scream. Oh dear," Tully said, as her face grew pale at the sight of the comte bleeding all over her charge. "Is he dead?"

"Not yet, you fool. Don't just stand there, go in the hall and wait for the physician. Bring him in here immediately upon his arrival." Pia scolded her.

Tully ran out of the room. At least that was one less thing she had to worry about, she knew for sure Tully was well.

Pia watched as her grandpere opened his eyes. The pain glazed his expression. His voice broke with each word he tried speak, begging for her to understand.

"I'm sorry, Pia. Wanted what was best for you. I love you..." Those were the comte's final words as his last breath drifted away. Pia screamed in agony.

CHAPTER 12

L ife was full of decisions, and Pia had to make plenty in
her lifetime. She knew there were certain things thrust
upon a person in their lifetime which they had no control
over. Love and death were prominent reminders of this. Pia's
experience with love had been very limited. She knew one
thing for certain: love could bring her joy or unimaginable
sorrow, even if that love happened to be reciprocated. Death
on the other hand had its own judgment and resolution. Her
grandfather had paid for his actions with his life.

Pia prepared to bury her grandpere and say her final
goodbye. Several important thoughts floated through her
mind as the final preparations were made. Was Grandpere
really gone forever? What was going to happen with Thor,
now that he finally had his revenge? *How can I forgive him?*
Does he even care about me?

With the help of Grandpere's solicitor, she was able to get
through all of the funeral arrangements. Pia buried her
grandpere at his estate in Bordeaux. It was a small service.
The only people in attendance were a few of her grandpere's
servants, Tully, Pia, and of course, her husband. Thor stayed
by her side through it all, offering what little comfort she
would allow.

All she saw when she looked at him was his chest covered

in her grandpere's blood. She didn't know if she could stay with him. She still didn't believe he loved her. It was clear her feelings for him had changed during the time she had been his prisoner. She never believed she would ever fall in love.

When he kidnapped her, she had been so very afraid of what he would do to her, but, in the end, she had begun to trust him. At the very least she had come to believe he wouldn't truly harm her. It helped to see the evidence that he wasn't as dastardly as she'd believed. Tully alive and pestering her on a daily basis was enough of a reminder.

Pia was acquainted with all of Thor's faults and well aware he was capable of almost anything. After all, he did orchestrate her abduction. Pia knew she was a fool for letting herself fall in love with him. No matter how much she tried, she couldn't stop her foolish heart's devotion to him. How is it possible to fall in love so fast? She wanted him to return her love, and she desired him with an intense passion. But nothing would torture her more than staying in a loveless marriage. If he wasn't capable of caring for her, let alone loving her, she wouldn't stay with him. She needed more. If she couldn't have it, she would seek out someone to file for a divorce herself.

Still lost in her own thoughts, she didn't hear Thor walk into her grandpere's study. Pia had enclosed herself in the room, sitting on a comfortable divan to wallow in her misery. When she looked up and saw him standing so close, her heart skipped a beat.

He looked down at her with sympathy in the depths of his blue eyes. "Pia, the ship is ready to set sail whenever you're ready." His voice was interwoven with understanding.

With a petulant look firmly fixed on her face, she looked up at him. "I am not sailing away with you, Thor."

"Like hell you're not. You're my wife, and you belong with me."

"Do you honestly think I want to live like a pirate? What kind of life is that? What if we have children? Will they join the crew and plunder ships for bounty alongside you?"

"No. We will go back to England. I have responsibilities there that have neglected for far too long. I am a viscount, and

I have an estate to reclaim. Your grandfather had me declared dead, so I will have to fight to regain my title. I don't want to be a pirate, Pia. Please come with me so we can build a life together."

Pia nodded. She could see he needed to do that. He did not need her with him to accomplish it. There was no give and take. He took it all and gave nothing in return. He said nothing about loving and needing her. Once again, he selfishly planned on using her to gain something he felt was his due. The sad thing was he didn't even need her to reclaim his title. He could go back and live his life without ever seeing her again if he wished.

"You do not need me, Thor. You don't require me for anything. You should go back and claim your title. While you are there, file for divorce. I don't care on what grounds. We are better off without each other."

"No," Thor said with belligerence in his voice. "I will never be better off without you. How could I be? Please, Pia, don't fight me on this. You are my wife, and I want you to board the Sea Rover with me today."

"I'm not going to fight with you, Thor. I am not going with you, and I will not remain with a man who doesn't love and respect me."

"Who the hell told you I don't love or respect you?"

"Well you haven't exactly told me that you do. You fail to take my desires into consideration. You dictate to me and never ask if I am okay with your orders. I am not going to live with someone who is going to take me for granted. No, I would rather die. Because you no longer have anything to hold over me, that is the only option left."

Pia turned her back to him, deciding the conversation was over. She leaned her head against the back of the couch and closed her eyes. She assumed he had left because he ceased speaking. Pia's eyelids fluttered open, and she saw Thor's blue eyes staring directly into hers.

Thor cleared his throat and spoke, his voice shaking, overflowing with emotion. "Pia, I have loved you from the moment I saw you. I never intended to actually marry you. My original plan involved pretending to do it and then using you, but meeting you changed everything. No one ever plans to find love, and I certainly never planned on finding it with you. The thought of you leaving scares me more than anything. I cannot imagine a life without your fire to warm me each night. From the instant I met you, I planned on keeping you. I know I've blundered with everything I've done. Not respecting your wishes was only to protect you. Your grandpere was an evil man, and you didn't see it. With every part of my soul, I swear I never meant to make you feel less than you are. I could never hurt you."

Pia stared at him. She waited, wondering if she should believe him. There was nothing she wanted more than to believe what he was telling her.

His voice had faltered and became husky with emotion. Thor's expression showed remorse. His gaze implored hers as if pleading with her.

"If you don't love me, I will understand," he said. "Being without you could never make me happy, but I will let you go if that's what you truly want. I would rather take my dagger and push it through my own heart then ever knowingly hurt you again."

Pia stared at him in shock. She never expected that he would actually return her feelings. She looked down at her arm and pinched herself to make sure it wasn't a dream. Ouch, nope this is real. Thor always had a way of stealing her breath, surprising her at every turn. Her lips curled up into a sumptuous smile as happiness overtook her soul. Her heart pounded with excitement when she finally accepted his words.

It was imperative she heard him say it one more time to make sure she'd heard him right. "You really love me?"

"Yes, I love you. Do you love me, even a little? Can you stay with me? Please come back to England with me. I need my viscountess to help me reestablish my holdings, and I need her to hold each night. I want her to be the mother of my children. Without you, my life wouldn't be worth living. Please, Pia, come home with me."

"Yes. Yes, Thor, I love you too. I will come home with you. There isn't any place on this Earth I would rather be." She stood and rushed over to him, throwing herself into his arms.

Thor gathered her tightly against his chest wrapping his

arms around her as he hugged her close. Pia tilted her face up and met his eyes as his lips pressed down on hers. Thor plundered her in all the ways she loved most, and Pia enjoyed every minute of the passion they shared.

EPILOGUE

In the past, Thor had many demons hiding inside of his soul, and they soured certain aspects of his life. He had something miraculous happen to him that allowed him to exorcise those dark areas. An angel of mercy had taken pity on his possessed black core and helped to bring him back to the light. In those moments, his life changed as his heart started to feel again and the darkness bled from its depths.

When Thor found Pia, his soul was cleansed. She was the angel who showed him how love could change his life. His existence was forever altered when he fell in love with the spirited beauty. If someone had asked him before he met Pia if he believed in love, he would have laughed at their audacity. Love? No that was for fools. *Well color me a fool because I am blissfully in love with my wife, and I wouldn't change it for anyone.*

If he had never kidnapped her to get revenge on her grandpere, his soul would still be a dark carcass of unhappiness. Thor needed her light to balance the dark shadows that overtook his spirit. They were opposites, put on Earth to balance each other out. To have her love him as much as he loved her was a blessing he didn't feel he deserved. He would never make the mistake of hurting her again. He had made a promise he would never break. Pia was everything to him.

Sitting in his study on his main English estate, Thor was lost in thought, reminiscing about the day he met the love of his life. She wasn't perfect. Everyone had flaws. He loved every one of her imperfections, because to him, she was beyond perfection. She was more priceless than the most expensive jewel. Her flaws were what made her unique. Pia was irreplaceable. She was his flawed jewel.

Thor rested his chin in his hands as a contented half smile tugged at his lips. He had a good life with Pia and their two children. It wasn't long after they returned to England, they got the happy news that Pia was expecting their first child.

As with everything in their lives, it shouldn't have been a surprise that even their children refused to do things the easy way. Almost exactly nine months after their wedding, Pia gave birth to twins, a girl and a boy. Lilliana Rose was born five minutes before her brother, Liam Robert. Lily had dark hair and cobalt blue eyes similar to her father, where Liam favored his mother with pale blond hair and light blue eyes.

Nothing could make him happier than to spend the rest of his life watching his children grow. Thor wanted all of the experiences fatherhood had to offer. As long as he had Pia and the twins by his side, his happiness was assured.

Thor turned as a little girl with black curls toddled into the room. A short time later, she was followed by a petite blonde woman carrying a small boy in her arms.

Pia looked over at Thor, her face flushed red from chasing their bundles of joy. "It's your turn. They want daddy to tell them their favorite story. You know the one."

Thor knew exactly which story they wanted to hear. It was the best fairy tale in all creation. It was the story of a flawed jewel and her dastardly pirate. They wanted to hear about adventure, love, and how their parents found each other.

Thor sat on the sofa and beckoned them close. "I'm happy to tell it. Please, come sit down by daddy, Lily, Liam."

The three-year-old twins crawled up onto his lap and waited for him to begin. Pia took a seat on the corner of the sofa her gaze softening as he looked into his eyes.

He settled them against him and began his story.

"Once upon a time, a pirate set out on the high seas..."

**Read on for an excerpt from A Treasured Lily: A Marsden Romance Book **

A CRYSTAL ANGEL

DAWN BROWER

DAWN BROWER

A Crystal Angel

CHAPTER 1

December 1875

An emerald green vase flew across the room, hit the wall, and shattered into thousands of tiny shards. Quick reflexes allowed Thor, Viscount Torrington, to shift his head just in time to avoid it nearly connecting with his skull instead of the wall behind him.

"Pia, you really need to calm—"

This time a bronzed horse, crafted in mid-gallop, flew at him as he dodged to the right of his desk. He needed to subdue his wife before she permanently injured him. At the very least he wanted to stop her from breaking any other pieces of furniture or knickknacks lying about his study in her fit of rage. He didn't know what had brought on this impromptu temper tantrum, but he'd already had enough of it. The previous night's overindulgence hadn't left him feeling well. His stomach churned and his head ached something fierce. He'd been sitting at his desk the better part of the afternoon staring at the same business reports, unable to decipher the meaning of them.

"How dare you tell me to calm down. I know what you did, you bloody idiot." Pia stormed towards him, waving a rolled parchment within her tight grasp. She twirled it around in circles with each step closer to him, her face growing a deeper shade of red. "You have a lot of explaining to do. What made you think this bit of nonsense would ever be a good idea?"

Thor pinched the bridge of his nose as pain shot daggers through his skull. He'd been out playing cards with the Earl of Devon the night before, attempting to persuade him into doing a bit of business with him. The events of the night before were a bit sketchy in his throbbing head.

"I don't have a clue what you're talking about."

"Well, if you hadn't decided to get sloshed with the Earl of Devon last night maybe you'd recall agreeing to betroth your son to his only daughter."

"What? Of course I wouldn't."

Her eyebrows rose in derision, her pale blonde curls framing her red face. "Oh really? That's why the Earl sent over this document outlining it in fine details. He even signed it. His note says it has all of the items you discussed last night and he looks forward to doing business with you in the future. Just sign it and send it to his solicitors."

Some of it started to come back. Devon had mentioned something about tying their families together. His daughter, Gemma, was a couple of years younger than the twins, Lily and Liam. Though they never really had any opportunity to interact with each other, Thor wondered why Devon would think Liam and Gemma would make a good match.

"Let me see it."

Pia threw the paper on his desk and folded her arms across her chest. Her blue eyes glared at him as he opened up the document and read it. Thor scanned the contents and clenched his fists. Damn it, she was right. He was a bloody fool.

"You're right. It's a betrothal. In my defense, I don't recall agreeing to this."

"Well, you can just send Lord Devon an apology. We do not choose who our children decide to marry."

How to explain it wasn't going to be as easy as she thought. He didn't want to betroth Liam to the earl's daughter, but it might already be too late.

"Now Pia..."

"Don't even start, Thor. You messed up and you're going

to fix it. Unless you want this to be the birthday and Christmas present you give your son this year. The twins are going to be turning fourteen this Christmas. Liam just got home from Eton. Are you prepared to spoil the holiday with your foolishness?"

"I don't know if it's that easy." Apprehension filled him as he stared at his wife.

"Of course it is. Go over and tell him you're a drunken idiot and you made a mistake. Trust me, if you don't make this go away, I promise you'll regret it."

Thor ran his fingers through his hair and sighed in frustration. He didn't like it when Pia was angry with him. He had to repair this damage before his wife did some irreparable harm to an important appendage of his. No doubt it would be the most heinous of deeds.

"I assure you, I already do."

"Good. Don't bother touching me until you make sure the Earl of Devon understands you are not signing a betrothal contract. I don't want anything to do with a man who plans on forcing his son to marry someone he doesn't love. I love you, Thor, but I have to do what I think is best for our children."

"Pia—wait! Stop"

Pia spun on her heels, ignoring him, as she stormed out of the room. A few strands of her pale blonde hair had come loose and floated around her neck as she breezed out. Her feet stomped hard on the ground, echoing through his study in rhythm with the pounding in his head.

"Bloody hell, what a mess."

Thor stood up and walked out of his study. It looked like he would need to pay a call on the Earl of Devon. He had to clear up this mess if he ever wanted to bed his wife again.

~

LILLIANA BREEZED INTO THE ROOM, SMUGNESS OOZING OUT OF her. She couldn't wait to tease her brother with a bit of the information she just stumbled into.

"You are not going to believe what I just heard our parents arguing about."

Liam looked up from the chessboard, pale blond hair framing his face. "I don't really care. I'm trying to concentrate."

"On what?" Lily asked.

"Beating His Grace here in a game of chess."

"Don't let him fool you. He doesn't stand a chance. He has yet to beat me." Noah St. John, the Duke of Huntly and Liam's best friend, laughed as he watched him study the board.

"You should care, it was all about you after all."

Liam stopped staring at the chessboard and looked up at Lily. "I didn't do anything at school, I swear."

"Got a bit of a guilty conscience, do you?" Lily couldn't help asking him as a feeling of mischief rooted through her.

Noah's brown eyes widened with horror. "You don't think they heard about the incident, do you?"

"Of course not. No one knows it was us. They wouldn't have had time to send any notice to my parents." Liam paused and tilted his head in consideration. "Of course, anything is possible. At least you don't have parents they would send any notice to. Your guardian can barely be bothered to check up on you."

"I wouldn't call it luck."

Noah's face lost all color at the mention of his parents, his mouth forming a straight, grim line. They died the year before in a horrific carriage accident, leaving him alone in the world. He had no family to speak of and a solicitor for a guardian. Once he reached majority he would take over control of his lands and title, but for the moment he needed someone to do it for him. It was the reason he came home with Liam from Eton on every break since his parents died.

"You shouldn't pick on your friend, Liam."

Lily didn't have any friends of her own and sometimes found herself a bit jealous of Liam's relationship with Noah. She didn't have the luxury of going away to school, and many of the girls her age didn't like her. She longed for the day she would have a friend who understood her. Of course, she was also realistic and didn't expect it to happen.

"I have to ask"—Lily's curious nature took over—"what did you two do?"

"Nothing," both boys chimed in at once.

"I don't believe you."

"We can't tell you."

Noah nodded his head in agreement. "It would break the oath we took."

Lily stared at the boys, studying each of their faces. Both of them had carefully schooled features, not an ounce of emotion showing, equally determined not to reveal their secret. She decided it didn't matter what they did. Well to be more apt, it didn't matter in that moment. She'd still get the details out of them, but her other news would send Liam into fits.

"All right. I suppose I can let it go for now."

"Good, 'cause we didn't plan on telling you." Liam turned back to concentrate on the chessboard.

"Why'd you give in so easy?" Noah asked.

"Don't see the point. Besides I think we need to discuss what I overheard."

"If it isn't about school, I don't care."

"You should, Liam. I told you it would impact your life."

"Well, what is it then?"

"Father agreed on a betrothal contract."

"Failing to understand how this might concern me." Liam waved his hand dismissively and turned back to his game. "Who is he going to marry you off to?"

"Not me you, fool. The Earl of Devon sent one over for him to sign. He's going to marry you off to his daughter, Lady Gemma Kemsley."

Liam's face turned stark white and he swayed in his chair. He turned to look at Lily as the shock settled in. His blue eyes glazed over as the astonishment of her words became clear. "Pardon me, what did you say?"

"You're betrothed, as in when you both come of age, you're getting married. Congratulations, brother of mine."

"No. Why would he do that?"

"I don't know. Have to say I'm glad it's you and not me. If I marry I plan on doing it for love. I'm not making my marriage some kind of business contract."

Noah stood up and placed his hand on Liam's shoulder. "I'm sorry. What can I do?"

"Turn back time and make my father see how unwise this is."

"I would if I could. Maybe if you go talk to him..."

"Won't make a difference," Lily interrupted him. "If mother can't change his mind, no one can."

"I'm doomed." Liam crumpled in his chair, his head slumping over into his arms, resting on the table.

Lily rolled her eyes. "Oh, don't be so melodramatic. Maybe this Gemma girl is lovely."

"I don't care if she's the most beautiful docile chit in all of England. I'm going to hate her just on principle."

Lily shook her head. "How mean and rude of you. At least give her a chance. If you're going to marry her, you do realize you have to spend the rest of your life with her? It wouldn't be good to get off to such a horrible start."

"What do you care? You aren't the one he's making marry someone you've never met." Liam turned to glare at his sister.

Lily stared at the mulish expression on her brother's face and a wave of sympathy rolled through her. He was her only real friend and she wanted to help him if she could. She might have teased him, but she didn't want him to have an unhappy life. There had to be some way to undo what their father had done.

"Well, maybe we'll just have to come up with a plan to persuade him against it."

"You just said it was a futile endeavor!" Liam exclaimed.

"Don't give your sister a hard time for wanting to help you." Noah turned toward Lily and gave her his full attention. "What do you have in mind?"

"We could run away."

"What good would that do?" Liam scoffed at her idea.

"It would make him realize how dead set you are against it. If we leave, it would show him we would rather live alone than deal with such disrespect for our wishes."

"Where would we go?" Liam asked.

"We could go to Huntly. The servants would welcome someone to take care of."

Liam looked at Noah and appeared to think about his suggestion. He shrugged as a look of defeat crossed his features. "I suppose it's as good a plan as any. Maybe this can all be resolved before Christmas. If not, I don't want to be here anyway."

"Go pack a small bag that you can carry. We can walk over to my townhouse and hitch a carriage to take us all the way to Huntly."

"Why don't we just stay there?" Lily asked.

Liam shook his head and replied, "It'd be the first place they looked. It's too close. We need to get their attention. Going to Huntly will slow them down a bit. I think we should leave a note saying we took one of the Marsden ships to America."

"Good idea. Liam, you write the note and I'll go pack a quick bag for the both of us. Noah, you get whatever you need from your room and let's meet out front in thirty minutes."

Both boys nodded at Lily and they took off to complete their tasks. Lily went upstairs and packed a small reticule for her and one for Liam. She grabbed each bag and poked her head out her bedroom door. No one was around, so she quietly sneaked out to the front of the house to await the two boys. Soon they would be at Huntly and hopefully their father, Viscount Torrington, would realize the error of his ways.

CHAPTER 2

Pia walked into the sitting room and found an abandoned chessboard. Earlier when she checked on them, Liam and Noah had been deeply engrossed in the match. Now the room stood empty and the game unfinished.

"I wonder where the boys are?"

"Excuse me, ma'am."

Pia turned to see Tully directly behind her. "What is it?"

"I wondered if you realized the children all went out earlier."

"No, I didn't. Do you know where they were going?"

"No ma'am, but they each had a reticule."

What were her wayward children up to now?

"Why didn't you stop them?"

"I tried, ma'am. I saw them from the upper window. By the time I got it open they were long gone."

Tully could be so vexing. She didn't know why she put up with her childhood maid. She looked back at the chess set and saw a scrap of parchment sitting on one of the chairs. She picked it up and read Liam's note.

"Those bloody fools. They get this nonsense from their father. I'm going to wring their necks when I get hold of them."

Of course, she didn't mean to actually do any real harm to the twins, but the fright of their running away ran rapid through her head. She hoped nothing serious happened to them while they were out alone in the cold.

"What did the children do now?" Thor's voice bellowed from the open doorway.

"They ran away. It's your fault too."

"How's it my fault?"

"Your stupid contract with the Earl of Devon caused this." Pia flung the note at him. It fluttered in the air and floated to the ground at Thor's feet. He picked it up and scanned the contents.

"Bloody hell."

"Exactly. Now go get those children before someone kills them."

Thor pinched the bridge of his nose and shook his head. "Pia, I'm getting tired of your constant harping. You need to take a step back and think about what you're saying."

"Don't patronize me. I have every right to be worried about our children's welfare."

"I'm not disputing that, but you need to calm down—and before you start off into another temper tantrum, you'll see I'm right. If we're going to find our children we need to have clear heads. Acting out in anger isn't going to achieve anything good."

Pia glared at him and attempted to rein in her anger, as she could see his point. No matter how annoyed she was with Thor, attacking him wouldn't get any desirable results. She needed to focus on what was important—finding the twins and Noah.

"All right, I can see your point, but I'm still mad at you."

His lips tilted into a cocky grin and he winked at her. "Duly noted. Now let's go find the children. It says they are boarding a ship to America."

"Probably Lily's idea. She always asks to go back to Charleston."

"We don't have any ships going to America until after the New Year. I should be able to catch them at the docks," Thor explained.

Pia decided she didn't trust Thor to handle the children. They probably thought they could outmaneuver them and escape. It might be Christmas, and their birthdays, but they were still going to be punished for their behavior. They were not even fourteen yet and shouldn't be out on their own.

"Fine, I'll go with you."

"It's unnecessary, Pia. I can take care of this."

"Forgive me if I don't have faith in your abilities. You've ruined Christmas with your blundering already."

Thor sighed. "Are you going to continue to harp on me about this for the rest of the holiday?"

"Yes. You haven't made up for your mistake yet, but I'm willing to let it go for the moment. Did you talk to Devon?"

"I did. He said he wished I'd reconsider, but understood why I wouldn't sign the contract. He urged me to keep it in case I changed my mind."

"I hope you explained it wasn't likely."

"I did, but I kept the contract to make him happy. I still want to do business with him sometime in the future. I put it in one of the locked drawers."

"Fine. As long as you don't plan on signing it, I'm all right with that. Let's go get the twins and Noah."

Pia walked out of the sitting room and grabbed her pelisse. She donned it and turned toward her husband. "Well, what are you waiting for?"

Thor just shook his head and led her out the front door. The carriage still sat out front from when Thor had gone to see the Earl. The footman and driver looked surprised to see them out so soon.

"We need to go to the waterfront. Make it fast," Thor explained to the driver as he turned to help Pia inside. She shoved his hand away, lifted her skirts and stepped into the carriage unassisted. Thor pursed his lips in frustration and followed her.

The carriage ride was swift and bumpy as they traveled to the dockyard. Pia glared at Thor the entire journey, obviously still blaming him for the fiasco they were now dealing with. Once they arrived at the docks, Thor jumped out and helped Pia out of the carriage, and they began to search for signs of the three children.

"I don't think they are here."

"We need to go farther down the wharf to make sure,"

Thor replied. "The docks are extensive and they could be hiding behind something."

They continued down the pier, Pia trailing after Thor, holding her skirts so they didn't skim the dirty waterfront. Night had fallen, and the only light they had to guide their path was the moonlight streaming down from above, making it difficult for them to see anything clearly. They searched the entire area surrounding them without any luck locating the children.

"I don't see them," Thor exclaimed.

"Do you see them anywhere?" Pia asked at the same time Thor spoke.

"No, I don't see them. I'm beginning to think they're not here," Thor repeated his earlier conjecture.

Pia sighed as irritation set in; Thor could be so difficult.

"So, you're ready to give up on finding them. Leave them out here alone and cold."

"Of course not. I just think this was a diversion of theirs. They probably went someplace else. Liam knows more about Marsden Shipping than you realize."

"Have you started dragging him to business meetings already? I told you not to overwhelm him with all the inner workings of your many projects. He's too young to worry about these things."

Thor stopped in his tracks and pinned Pia with a furious glare. She sucked in a breath as rage flared across his features. She'd gone too far and now he'd finally snapped under her constant rants. "Enough, Pia, I'm not going to listen to you shriek the rest of the night. As far as Liam goes, I don't want him unprepared. It's why I was taken advantage of."

Pia knew Thor hated any reminders of her grandpère; the Comte had tried to murder him to gain control of their shared company. He failed, but it hadn't ended there. Thor kidnapped Pia to get revenge on him. It didn't turn out as planned; it had gone a whole lot better. If he hadn't wanted revenge, they would never have found each other. They both agreed everything ended the way it was supposed to. Of course, agreeing they belonged together didn't mean they always agreed on how to handle their children.

Pia forced herself to calm down and reply to him in an

even, neutral voice. "Liam isn't you. He doesn't have a business partner; he only has you. Give him time to grow up." This wasn't a new argument. Pia often berated her husband for trying to get Liam working at Marsden Shipping; hollering at him wouldn't make a lick of difference.

Thor scowled at her and explained, "I haven't been. It doesn't mean the lad isn't curious. He finds himself in my study all on his own. I'm not going to turn him away just because you think he's too young to learn it."

"Hmmph. Fine. I still think he's too young, but if he comes in on his own, I see your point."

She didn't see any reason to argue any further about it. Thor believed he needed to start learning and soon. It was his belief if he didn't start soon he would be at a loss when it was time for him to take over. Pia just wanted him to enjoy his childhood for as long as possible before taking on so much responsibility. When he gained his majority he could take his rightful place at Marsden Shipping and learn all he needed to know. Pia didn't think he would ever have a disadvantage, especially with Thor at his side each step of the way.

"Do you think someone may have kidnapped them?"

"What? No, of course not. No one would dare."

"You seem awfully certain of that," Pia whispered.

"They know what I used to be and an ex-pirate isn't someone to mess with. No one would hurt our children for fear of what I might do to him. No, the kids just ran away to prove a point."

"Which is your fault."

"Don't start again, Pia. I'm not going to make Liam marry someone. When he gets married, it will be his choice."

"Still, we wouldn't be out in this frigid weather if you hadn't gotten inebriated with your crony the earl last night."

Pia couldn't stop herself from berating him, her worry for the children clouding her judgment. She wanted to find them as soon as possible and Thor made a good target for her anxiety. His face was etched with worry barely visible in the moonlight. She bit her lip and tried to prevent another irate outburst from spilling out of her mouth.

"Pia, do you really want to sit out here and argue or do you want to look someplace else?"

She inhaled and exhaled, her breath visible in the darkness. "Where do you suggest we look?"

"Noah's townhouse. They're not stupid and would know they needed someplace warm to stay. Since Noah is our guest, naturally they would go to his home."

"Do you really think they went there?"

She studied him, her pale blonde hair escaping the tight chignon and framing her face. He reached over and cupped her face in the palm of his hand. She stared up into his eyes finding her own love reflected back at her. No matter what, she knew she could depend on him. Yes, he had made a mistake, but he was willing to rectify it. He had done as she asked and retracted the betrothal contract with the Earl of Devon. He would have done it regardless because it was the right thing to do. Pia realized how awful she had been acting toward him and wished she hadn't acted like a shrew. No one else, besides her, loved the twins more. She knew if he thought the children had gone to Noah's townhouse, then they had. She needed to trust him as her instincts screamed at her to do.

"Yes, I do."

"All right. I will trust your judgment. Let's go look."

Thor led her to the carriage and helped her back inside. Once she was snuggled under one of the carriage blankets, Thor told the driver to take them to the Duke of Huntly's townhouse. The carriage rattled along the uneven road and the clip-clop of horses' hooves lulled them with their even rhythm. After what seemed like hours, the carriage came to a stop. Thor looked out the carriage window. Pia could see an ornate townhouse from the open slot in the carriage. Thor opened the door and hopped out, turning to assist Pia.

"I thought we would never get here," she exclaimed.

They raced up to the front door and knocked. After an eternity, or what seemed like one, the door finally cracked open. A wrinkled man in his bedclothes answered the door. His eyes narrowed at them, and with a gruff voice he asked, "What can I do for you?"

"Pardon the late hour, but has the young Duke of Huntly been by with our children, Lily and Liam?" Thor asked.

"His Grace was here briefly about two hours past. He

ordered a carriage round to take him to the country estate. I didn't see any other children with him."

"Are you sure?" Pia bit her lip and wrung her hands together as worry nestled deep inside.

"I'm fairly certain I didn't see anyone else. His Grace came inside all alone. He awaited the carriage and after it arrived I only saw him enter it. I can't say if he picked anyone else up along the way."

"Well, there's nothing else we can do. Thank you for your time." Thor nodded at the older man and walked away from the door.

"What do you mean there isn't anything else we can do? We have to keep looking for our children."

"Of course we do, but they're not here."

"Clearly, but where are they?"

"That's easy enough; they are at the country estate of the Duke of Huntly."

"But the old man said he didn't see them." Pia's face scrunched up in puzzlement.

Thor leaned down and placed a quick kiss on her lips. "We have very intelligent children, Pia. They waited down the road and hopped in when no one else was paying attention. They tried to make it look like young Noah went home alone."

Pia bit her lip as she considered his words. She nodded her head, agreeing with his assessment. "So we're going to Huntly Manor?"

"Yes, we are. Get ready for a bit of a journey, love."

They both huddled into the carriage and sat back for the long ride to the country. The kids had a two-hour head start on them and would hopefully be safe inside by the time they arrived. There would be hell to pay once they caught up with their wayward children.

CHAPTER 3

The carriage traveled down a long, winding driveway flanked by large, barren trees, the branches towering above them. Moonlight illuminated the dark winter sky down the path toward Huntly Manor. Liam stretched his arms over his head to alleviate the kinks in his stiff muscles. Lily's head bobbed on the side of the carriage, her dark curls escaping from her long braid. Noah gazed out the window of the carriage, a solemn look on his face.

"So we finally made it?" Liam asked.

"Yes."

"Should we wake Lily?"

"Probably a good idea; we'll be at the front door soon enough."

"I know why we did this, but my parents are going to go crazy once they figure out we left."

"That's the point, isn't it?"

Liam looked over at his sleeping sister and back at his friend. He didn't like what his father had done, but what about their own actions? Were they any better? Did they have the right to worry their parents with their rash actions? Now, after hours of travel, he'd had time to think about the situation. They might have acted carelessly and should have talked to their mother first. She wouldn't have allowed him to be forced into a betrothal contract. His mother was dead-set against forcing either one of them into an unwanted marriage.

"It was. I'm not so sure about this anymore."

"There's no going back now. We're at my ancestral home now. All we can do is sit back and wait. They'll be here soon enough and it will be settled."

Liam nodded. "I suppose you're right."

"Are we at Huntly Manor?" Lily lifted her head, her blue eyes still droopy from sleep.

The carriage came to a full stop. Liam looked out the window at a large towering manor. There were at least forty tapered steps leading to the front door. Large sections of it resembled a medieval castle.

"Why didn't you tell me you lived in a castle?" Lily exclaimed, excitement filling her voice.

"Yeah, all you need is a moat and drawbridge and you'll be living in ancient times," Liam joked.

With a dry, humorless tone, Noah explained, "They were removed a century ago when the stairs were crafted. They've done a bit of remodeling, my ancestors, to make it into more of manor instead of a castle. A lot of the main structure still stands, but it is as modernized as they could make it."

"You don't like it here, do you?" Lily asked in a quiet tone.

"Not so much. It's never been much of a happy place. My parents hated each other. The best times I've had have been at your home. Sometimes I don't think you two know how good you have it."

"I'm sorry, Noah. You don't talk about your parents much. Why didn't you ever tell me?" Liam asked.

"I don't like talking about it and I've already said too much. Let's go inside and wait for your parents to come get us. I hope they still allow me to spend Christmas with you."

"Of course they will. They adore you and they'll know it's not your fault. We can be a bit—difficult—to say no to." An impish smile formed on Lily's face.

They all hopped down from the carriage and walked inside Huntly manor. They were greeted by a surprised housekeeper. "Your Grace." She curtsied. "We weren't expecting you."

"My apologies, Molly, this was a bit last-minute. Can you get some rooms ready?"

"Certainly. How many will you be needing?"

"Besides mine? I suggest getting four ready. We'll probably be getting some extra guests soon."

"Right away, Your Grace." Molly nodded her head. "Will you be requiring anything else? Perhaps some refreshments?"

"No, we're rather tired; just prepare the rooms."

"Very well, Your Grace. I will gather a few maids and have them organize the chambers for you and your guests."

Molly left to get the rooms ready. Noah led Lily and Liam into the library. The butler had lit a fire to keep them warm as they waited. They sat back and relaxed on the chaises until they could retire to nice warm beds.

"How long until you think they'll arrive?" Lily asked.

"Knowing Father, they are probably not too far behind us. With any luck we'll be asleep in a nice warm bed and they'll leave us there until morning."

"Do you think they will?"

"Not bloody likely."

Liam studied his sister and best friend. What were they thinking, running off in the middle of the night? They'd be lucky if their parents didn't murder them. He sighed and leaned his head on the chaise. Nothing to do about it now; they just had to sit back and wait for disaster to strike.

Pia's head rested on Thor's shoulder. She finally gave into her exhaustion and allowed herself to get some rest. Thoughts kept whirling through his head, not allowing him the same luxury. He couldn't help praying he was right and that the twins had coerced the young Duke of Huntly into going to his country estate. The carriage rattled along the roadway, the dark sky lightening as the sun rose in the distance. They had wasted a lot of time traipsing around London trying to locate them. At the rate things were going they wouldn't make it to Huntly Manor until dawn broke.

Pia lifted her head from his shoulder and yawned. "How much longer until we arrive?"

"I'm guessing an hour at least. The sun's beginning to rise."

"Did you get any sleep?"

"No, I have too much on my mind."

Pia's eyes pinned him. She stared at him for several seconds, biting her lip as if deep in thought. Thor didn't know what was rolling through her mind. A part of him was terrified of the answer; she hadn't been happy with his actions of late. He'd really messed up, his dealings with the Earl of Devon playing havoc on his family. At least he knew he'd taken care of it and could reassure Liam he was not betrothed to marry Lady Gemma Kemsley.

"As you should; they wouldn't have run away if not for your actions," Pia retorted.

"I've had enough of this." Thor smacked the side of the carriage with his fist, a sharp sting spreading through his fingers. "Can you just let it go?"

"I'd rather not." Pia glared. "It's all that is keeping me focused right now."

Thor nodded. "I make an easy target, love, but you know me. Just try and see it from my point of view."

"You're right. I know you better than anyone." Pia folded her hands in her lap. "They're going to be fine. I can't keep blaming you. The twins are headstrong and it's hard to predict what they may or may not do."

"I set us on this course and I do know what my actions caused. I'm responsible for their rash actions."

Pia placed her hand on his shoulder and stared into his eyes. "You're right; you did, but you didn't tell those two to run away. They did that all on their own. If they had bothered to think, they'd realize you wouldn't have gone through with that betrothal contract."

"I know, but I can't help feeling the guilt. It should never have existed. Drinking in excess is no excuse. We both feel the same way. We want our children to be happy and dictating who they choose to marry isn't going to give them any kind of joy."

"I love you, Thor."

"I love you, too."

Thor pulled Pia into his arms and placed his lips on hers. She opened her mouth, allowing him full access. His tongue rolled over hers with gentle swirls. His hand cupped her cheek as he deepened the kiss. Thor pulled back and stared into her blue eyes. He reached down and scooped her fully into his lap and began trailing kisses down her throat and across her shoulders. A soft moan escaped Pia's mouth. Thor could feel himself begin to harden as desire flooded him. He would never get enough of his wife. He always wanted her, and he needed to be inside of her. She reached down and undid his breeches as he lifted her skirts and settled them around his lap. Pia lowered herself on his length, engulfing him in her warm passage. Once he was deep inside her, she began to ride him, up and down in slow, agonizing strokes. Thor rested his hands on her hips, guiding her to go faster, until he could feel her channel start to ripple with the onslaught of her orgasm. He could feel his own orgasm begin to crest as her inner muscles gripped him. Soon it exploded through him, draining him of energy. He groaned as pleasure washed over him in waves. Pia's head fell forward, resting on his shoulder. He wrapped his arms around her and held on tightly, his member still buried inside of her.

"We haven't made love in a carriage in a very long time."

"We probably shouldn't be doing it now."

"Why not?" she asked. "I wanted you, and you clearly wanted me. I don't see anything wrong with what we just did."

"Our children are missing—"

"But not for long. We're almost to Huntly. We'll deal with our naughty children when we reach them."

A small weight lifted off his shoulders with his wife's reassuring embrace. They would find them and in the meantime they could enjoy each other for the remainder of the long journey to Huntly Manor.

"You're awfully sure about this, love." A warm, yet cocky smile formed on his face.

"Because nothing can go wrong now." She lifted her head and lightly touched her lips to his. "You're ready for another round, aren't you?"

"Well, we do have a little time..."

They began all over again, and Thor allowed himself to just enjoy loving his wife. Their children would feel their wrath when they caught up to them, but the worry dissipated with the assurance they were fine at the young Duke's estate.

CHAPTER 4

The sun began to stream through the windows of the bedroom Liam had been assigned at Huntly Manor, bright enough to wake him from a sound sleep. He sat up and rubbed the sleepy fog from his eyes. His gaze fell on the window.

"Should've remembered to close the curtains," he said to himself.

The bedroom door creaked open and Noah stepped inside. Tired from their journey, Liam noticed they both decided to sleep in their clothes, leaving them a rumpled mess. "I thought I might find you awake. I was so tired last night I forgot to close the curtains. As we were all exhausted, I thought perhaps you had forgotten to as well. I see your room is equally as bright as mine."

"Yeah, it sure is. Any chance we can get breakfast this early?"

Noah nodded his head. "Indeed, they are already preparing it. Should we retrieve Lily?"

"Yeah, we have a bit to discuss, though you should be prepared. Lily can sleep through anything and will be quite irritated at being awoken so early."

"I can handle it; I've grown accustomed to Lily's moods from visiting your house the past year."

Liam nodded and got up to follow Noah to Lily's room.

They opened the door to find her sound asleep on the bed, the room completely dark. Lily had remembered to close her curtains. She liked her sleep and apparently had enough forethought to remember the possibility of early sunshine streaming through the window. Liam walked across the room and spread the curtains wide to allow the bright light to cascade into the room. It fell in quick succession across Lily's face, illuminating her dark curls, and her wrinkled blue dress. In sleep, she appeared angelic, but Liam knew how devilish his sister could be. The brilliant glow of sunshine was not doing much to awaken her, so he walked over to her bed and began to push on her shoulder. Lily jolted upright, her eyes flying open as they landed on Liam.

"Why are you waking me up? Are Mother and Father here?"

Liam shook his head. "No. We are going down for breakfast and we need you to join us."

"How early is it? I feel like I haven't slept at all."

"It's still quite early, you probably only slept four hours or so." Noah's quiet voice entered the room from his place just inside the doorframe of Lily's room.

"Do we really need to get up this early?" Lily asked.

"Yes, I'm sure we will have visitors soon." Liam held his hand out to his sister to assist her from the bed. "Come on, let's go eat."

They followed Noah down to the small dining room and sat at the table. The servants began to serve them a light breakfast of poached eggs, bacon, and freshly baked bread. Liam picked up a slice of bread and spread creamy butter across it and set it on the plate of food the servant set in front of him. He no sooner picked up his fork to take a bite when the sound of voices interrupted him.

"Ah, there you three are. See, Thor, I told you they would be fine. I hope you had a nice adventure; it is going to be your last for several years to come."

His father glared at his mother and just shook his head back and forth in a slow motion. Liam watched his parents enter the room and take a seat at the dining table. Once they were both sitting, they turned their attention back to the three of them.

"So it looks like we have some things to discuss," his father said, folding his hands across his chest.

"Yes, sir." Liam nodded his head. "Indeed we do."

"You know you could have saved us all some time and just come to talk to me." Thor glowered at Liam.

"I didn't think of it at the time. I—we just reacted."

"Yes, have you had time to think about your actions and what they mean?" Pia asked them.

Liam could feel a well of emotions begin to roll through him. He still didn't want to marry some girl he'd never met. He could feel anger build up inside of him again. How could his father have done that to him? His arms folded across his chest defensively, he expressed his discontent. "You know why we left. I don't want to marry the Earl of Devon's daughter. I don't even know her. I'd like the chance to marry someone I love, if I marry at all."

"Liam, dear, you do know I wouldn't have allowed that to happen," his mother reassured him. "You shouldn't have run off."

Liam wouldn't regret his choices. He couldn't change them even if he wanted to. "I know that now, but I can't undo it." Anger and fury flowed through him as he stared his father in the eyes.

"There will be repercussions. We can't have you running off because you're scared. We need you to understand you can talk to us about anything, no matter how difficult the subject." Thor hammered home his point by pinning all three of them down with his gaze. "If you had bothered to ask, you would know I didn't sign the contract with the Earl of Devon. You are not going to be forced to marry anyone. It will always be your choice. I made a mistake and I apologize for it."

Liam lowered his head as the weight of his actions fell over him. He worried his parents and stressed over something that wouldn't have been an issue. He acted rashly. "I'm sorry, I promise I won't run away again. I will face whatever is bothering me. It is cowardly to think running will solve my problems."

The servants came in and set plates of breakfast in front of his parents, along with some silverware. His mother picked up her fork and began to cut her egg. His father continued to look across the table at them all.

"Liam isn't the only one at fault here." Lily began to play with her napkin, twisting it into a ball between her fingers. "I'm sorry too. Liam is right we shouldn't have run away."

Liam looked at his friend. He didn't say a word during the entire exchange. Noah didn't show an ounce of emotion. He continued to stare at Liam's father. When it mattered most to Noah, his emotions ran more deeply and he showed none. Liam learned his friend's biggest fear was losing those individuals he'd come to love most. They now included his entire family, and he didn't want to be cast off.

"Sir, I apologize for our actions. What do you plan to do?" Noah asked.

"I plan on eating some breakfast and then dragging you three back to London. Tomorrow is Christmas and we still have not decorated the tree. The servants should have it set up in the sitting room by now so we can direct our attention to it when we get home."

Surprise filled Noah's face. "You're going to allow me to come back with you?"

"Of course. Why would I punish you solely for all of your actions? However, there will be punishments meted out once I decide on the proper ones."

"Now, all of you eat. We have a long day ahead," Liam's mother ordered them.

Not long after they were done with breakfast, they grabbed their reticules, and all of them sat in a carriage for the long journey home. Fresh horses harnessed to the carriage had been swapped with those in Huntly's stable. They were exhausted, but anxious to return to London.

It was early afternoon when they arrived at Marsden House, and the kids went to their chambers to rest before dinner. The Christmas festivities would start after they had eaten the evening meal. Thor followed Pia up to her chamber and closed the door behind them. He wanted to spend some extra quality time with her alone. Their argument was well over with and set aside on their journey to retrieve the children. He pulled off his jacket, folded it, and placed it on a chair near the door.

A gamine smile on her face, Pia tilted her head and stared at him. "Do you need something?"

"Yes."

She raised an eyebrow and crossed her arms beneath her generous bosom. "What can I do for you?"

Thor began to undo his cravat, pulled it off his neck, and tossed it aside. "I need you, love." He pulled his shirt off next and tossed it in the opposite direction of the cravat. His breeches undone and hanging low on his hips, he stalked Pia.

Pia took a step back. "You're not tired?"

"I'm never too tired to make love to my beautiful wife."

Thor continued to move forward as Pia stepped back. She hit the bed and fell backward onto it. He kneeled beside her, towering over her small frame. Reaching up, she ran her hands over his bare, muscled torso and squeezed one of his erect nipples. Thor reacted by lifting her skirts and skimming his hands across her thighs.

"You have too many clothes on." Lifting Pia up, he pushed her bodice down, revealing her lush breasts resting on top of her corset. Thor licked her pink nipple and nipped at it, repeating the action with the other one. He hoisted her up off the bed and turned her around. His hands roamed across her back as he undid the laces of her dress and corset, pushing her chemise over her shoulders. Thor spun her back around and pushed all of her clothing down in one full sweep. He trailed his eyes over her naked flesh. Pia shivered and Thor could see her body begin to flush with desire. Thor picked her back up and placed her beside him on the bed. He continued to lick, nip, and kiss her whole body.

"Enough. I need you inside me," Pia demanded.

Thor stood and pushed his breeches off. He spread Pia's legs, pulled her forward, and pushed his thick member deep into her. Pia moaned as her channel rippled around his length. Pia squeezed him with her inner muscles. Thor bit his lip as the pleasure raked over his sensitive flesh. He had to rein in his control and ease into loving her. If she kept stroking him with the muscles in her tight channel he would ravage her. He set a slow pace, stroking himself in and out of her. Pia raked her nails across his chest and moaned. Thor began to push himself in and out of her with deep rapid strokes. Pia's breathing became shallow and rapid; Thor could feel her orgasm begin as she squeezed against him. She screamed when she went over the edge. Thor moaned and threw his head back as his seed emptied inside of her. Afterwards he pulled himself out of her warmth and stood up. Thor lifted her up into his arms so he could pull down the bed sheets, and placed her on the bed. He crawled in beside her and spread the sheets over top of them. Thor pulled Pia into his arms; she curled into him and rested her head on his shoulder.

"I think I can sleep now," he whispered in her ear.

"I should hope so." Pia's laugh was light and throaty.

"Remind me when we wake up I have a special present for you."

"What if I want it now?"

"I'm too exhausted, love. You undo me. It can wait."

A pout formed on her face at his words. "You can be awful sometimes."

"Me? Never, wicked, on the other hand..." Thor began to trail his fingers over her erect nipples.

"I thought you were too tired?" Pia gasped as his fingers trailed down her hips and began to play with the tiny sensitive nub near her entrance. She moaned while his fingers stroked over her heated flesh. He could feel her begin to squirm beneath him.

"I believe I said I'm never too tired to make love to my wife."

Thor kissed her, pushing his tongue inside her mouth, effectively distracting her from the conversation about her present. He began to stroke her center with his fingers, rubbing over the sensitive tip, causing Pia to gasp. Deciding to distract her further, he roamed down to kiss her center. He spread her thighs and replaced his fingers with his tongue. Pia wrapped her legs over his shoulders, bringing herself closer to his wicked tongue. He began to push his fingers inside of her, caressing her channel as his tongue massaged the sensitive area of her sex. Thor licked and sucked her until he could feel her explode around his fingers. He pushed her legs off his shoulders and spread them wide. Then he crawled on top of her, pushing himself deep inside her. He began to pound into her with furious thrusts, desperate for his own release. He hadn't lied to her; he would never have enough of her, and he was always ready to make love with her. He needed her like he needed air to breathe. If not for her, he would still be a pirate roaming the seas for treasure. Pia, his sexy, flawed, perfect jewel, the angel he never thought to find in life. His orgasm hit him as he reveled in her beauty. A few minutes later he rolled off her and wrapped her tightly in his embrace once again.

"Sleep, love, we have a busy evening planned."

Pia's eyes drifted closed. Thor watched her for several seconds before he began to feel his own eyes drift closed.

CHAPTER 5

Thor led Pia into the sitting room, where he found all three children sitting on the settee, patiently waiting for them to arrive.

"Oh good, you're finally here," Lily exclaimed.

Liam watched them with apprehensive eyes. Thor could tell his child didn't know what to expect from them. He still needed to punish them for their behavior, but hadn't thought of what would be the proper chastisement for their actions. The children needed to stew for a little while as he mulled over his options; once he decided on a proper punishment he would let them know.

"Are you in a hurry for your punishment?" Thor asked her.

"Um, no, I thought we were going to decorate the tree..." Fear filled Lily's eyes as she stared at him. Good, she needed to know he hadn't forgotten their rash behavior.

"Did you decide what you're going to do with us?" Liam asked.

Thor looked over at his son. Resignation filled his eyes. He was ready and willing to accept whatever punishment Thor planned on assigning them.

"I will get to it in a minute."

"We have a few other things to discuss with you first," Pia explained.

Thor and Pia walked fully into the room and sat on a settee opposite the children. All three of them stared back at them, their eyes wide and curious.

"As you can see the tree is set up and ready to decorate." Pia gestured towards the tree the servants had cut down and placed inside the sitting room. "We will get to it in a moment. First we want to discuss your birthday."

Liam's eyebrows rose as he looked over at Lily. "What about it?"

"We were planning a special surprise for you, but in light of your actions we have decided against it," Thor explained.

A glum expression formed on both of the twins' faces. Thor didn't want to disappoint them, but believed they hadn't earned the planned surprise.

"We were going to get you a carriage of your own to share. A little phaeton I was planning on teaching you both to drive; however, in light of your penchant for running away I've decided against it."

"But Father..." Lily began to say before Liam interrupted her.

"No, Lily. Father's right. I don't think we've earned the responsibility. Maybe in a couple of years, but we're too young."

Lily nodded her head at Liam and turned her attention back to Thor and Pia. "I understand. Liam's right, besides I'd probably only get in more trouble with my own carriage."

"So we will have to give you a less expensive birthday present."

Lily looked at them both expectantly. "We're still getting presents?"

"Yes and no," Pia explained.

"You still have your Christmas gifts," Thor offered.

Pia nodded. "Indeed. Our gift for your birthday is to allow you to even have a Christmas."

Both Liam and Lily groaned.

"We could cancel all of the festivities," Thor reminded them.

"No, please don't," Lily begged.

During the entire exchange Thor noticed how Noah watched and waited. He didn't know what to make of the young duke. His reserved demeanor made him feel sad. He had lost so much at a young age.

"What about you, Noah?"

"I don't understand, sir?"

"Do you still want to have the Christmas festivities?"

"I'm just glad you're allowing me to be a part of your family." Noah's voice was quiet and heavy with emotion.

"Son, you know you're welcome here anytime," Thor reminded him.

Pia held her hand over her heart, tears forming in the corners of her eyes. "Noah, don't ever feel like you're not welcome here."

Noah's head bobbed back and forth between the two of them. After several seconds he gave them a formal nod. "I won't."

Time ticked by while they talked and Thor considered how to discipline them. After they were well into the discussion, Thor decided the exact punishment to give them for their misbehaviors. He didn't want something too harsh; yet at the same time nothing equally too lenient.

"Now for your punishment," Thor began. "Each of you is going to help the maids clean for the next week. Expect to get up at dawn to assist them."

Another groan filled the room. "Unless you want more work..."

"No, Father, we'll help the maids," Liam offered before Thor could assign more tasks.

"Good, I will inform them of your duties and you're to listen to them. If even one maid comes to me with a bad report I'll make things infinitely worse. Do you all understand?"

Three heads nodded at him in agreement.

"All right. Lily and Liam, show Noah where the decorations are and we can begin trimming the tree," Pia ordered.

All three of the children hopped up and headed toward the box of decorations. With glee they began to hang up the various ornaments they collected over the past several years. Thor watched them as they hung each one up with care. Happiness radiating across their faces, they opened up each ornament and remembered when they picked it out.

"Don't you have a special gift for me?" Pia asked.

"Ah yes, I forgot."

"You did tell me to remind you."

"Indeed I did and then I got distracted."

A blush filled Pia's cheeks. "I remember how you became distracted."

His lips tilted into a smile filled with sin. "We'll have to become distracted in a similar fashion later."

"Yes, but now give me my present."

Thor looked over at his children and their friend. The tree was almost completely flowing with sparkling decorations as they continued to hang them on the green branches. Thor walked over and picked up a package near the box of decorations. It was adorned with the glittery dust of broken glass, ground down into fine grains and adhered to the sides of the box. It gave the impression of a thousand diamonds sparkling on the hard surface. A bright blue bow, matching the color of Pia's eyes, was wrapped around it. He picked it up, crossed back to his wife's side, and handed it to her.

She clapped her hands as joy spread across her face. "What is it?"

"Open it up and see."

Pia undid the ribbon with care and pulled it aside, letting it drift to the floor. She lifted the lid and gasped. Inside, against red plush velvet lay a crystal angel. A shiny gold halo floating above her head, gossamer wings spread high on her back, and her skirts hollow and fine, she shimmered much like the diamond sparkle on the package.

"Oh, Thor, she's beautiful."

"It's a special tree topper I had made for you. She's delicate, so we need to be careful when we place her on the tree. If she falls she could break rather easily."

"Will she stay in place?" Pia asked.

"Yes, there are a couple of hooks under her skirt to tie her down. When the children are done I'll help you place it on the highest branch. She's our own guardian angel to watch over us each Christmas."

"How lovely, thank you. I shall treasure her always."

Thor reached down and placed a soft kiss on Pia's lips. The children finished decorating the tree and turned their attention back on them.

"What's that?" Lily asked.

"A gift from your father," Pia explained as she turned toward Lily and Liam. "Are you ready to put it on the tree?"

"Yes," they both exclaimed.

Pia looked at Thor. "You're going to have to place it on the tree, as you're the only one tall enough to reach the top."

Thor nodded and followed her over to the tall, fragrant pine. They placed the crystal angel on top and anchored her to the branches surrounding it. She gleamed down on them from her vantage point. Thor turned to look at his family and happiness welled up inside of him. His life couldn't have been more perfect if he tried. He looked back up at the crystal angel and smiled. Now they had a guardian angel to watch over them, a protective shield against any danger. He pulled Pia into his arms and stroked her hair with his hand. She was his living, breathing angel, and the twins their beautiful blessing.

**Read on for an excerpt from A Treasured Lily: A Marsden Romance Book **

CHAPTER 6

"I just don't think it's a good idea."

"Nonsense." Lilliana Marsden looked up at her best friend, Lady Gemma Kemsley, and frowned. "It's a brilliant idea. My father is being unreasonable about allowing me to travel to America. The plantation in South Carolina is my inheritance. It's about time I claimed it."

"It's not going to work for you to just show up and claim it though. I don't get why you are in such a hurry. You know full well you won't inherit it until you marry." Gemma reached up and smoothed over her sanguine curls, tucking a loose strand behind her ear.

"Well, that's not entirely true." Lilliana's lips twitched into a cheeky smile; it helped to have a little insight into how her parents worked. Gemma didn't know how much she'd gotten away with over the years. Eavesdropping had become a habit of hers. A person could find out the most interesting things quite by accident. When she overheard her parent's most recent conversation she couldn't help the glee that filled her soul. Reining in her excitement had taken an enormous amount of restraint. She needed to leave England and start the life she envisioned for herself. One she had complete control over. Her parent's still hoped she would settle down and get married, but they didn't know her true reasons. "I stumbled across a bit of information that may help me to achieve my goal."

"I don't understand. Did you find a way to inherit it early?"

Lilliana got up, walked to the window of the sitting room, and pulled open the curtains. She stared out at the garden and pondered how to explain what she overheard, and exactly how it fit into her idea to get everything she wanted. Various shades of roses, red, orange, and white, scattered across the garden in a pattern that reminded Lilliana of a kaleidoscope. The garden remained one of the places that she turned to when she needed to reflect on what floated through her mind. It calmed her and made it possible for her to think rationally about any issue that arose in her life. Something about being surrounded by the plant life helped her to think and form her plans with a clear head. Lilliana needed to get Gemma to aid her in her quest to leave England. They worked their magic on her as she calmly let the curtain go and turned back towards her best friend.

"I don't *ever* plan on getting married. I told you that the day we met. My parents still insisted on a season or two. They believe everyone is capable of finding love. They don't understand they are a rarity."

A sting of pain stabbed through her heart, Lilliana rubbed her chest in an attempt to erase the phantom ache. After her disastrous first season, she knew quite well how unusual it was for a love match to exist within the ton. Her choices were lecherous old men and scheming vermin only after her money. There was one man though who made her want to believe he really loved her. She found out the hard way he only wanted to use her. She was thankful he didn't achieve his goal and Lilliana came out relatively unscathed, but the damage to her belief in love sat firmly in place.

"Most matches are made for business or political reasons. It's all about money and there is no way I'm handing over mine to a male to control."

Gemma tilted her head and crinkled her nose in confusion. Lilliana knew she didn't get it. Her friend wanted to get married and have children. The two years difference in their ages showed when they discussed the possibility of matrimony. In time, Lilliana believed Gemma would look back on this conversation with clarity. In the midst of starting her first season and barely seventeen years old, Gemma still approached life with rose-colored glasses on. For a brief moment in time Lilliana had worn that same veil of hope; her parent's love inspired her enough to want to find it herself.

Reality came crashing in like a bolt of lightning and shattered every ounce of optimism she held within her. Lilliana realized finding love at the various parties hosted within London society equaled finding a mythical creature. The chances of finding a unicorn would be an easier feat. So she gave up on love and formed a new plan for her life.

"I still think you are being preposterous. Why are you so against marriage?" Gemma folded her arms across her chest and stared at Lilliana. Her eyes pinning her in place as she spoke. "That's what a lady is expected to do after all. I just don't understand how you plan on claiming your inheritance without the benefit of a husband to help you get it."

Lilliana could feel her lips twitch into a smile. Her mother often commented on how Lilliana received all her father's traits, even his less than desirable ones. William Thorston Marsden, fifth Viscount Torrington, had a way of getting what he wanted out of people. She admired that characteristic in her father and sought to emulate it. Still, she wished she had been lucky enough to get her mother's pale blonde hair instead of her father's dark curls. In Lilliana's mind, her twin brother, Liam, was blessed because he inherited her mother's coloring.

"I suppose I should explain it so you won't be left in the dark. I'll need your assistance after all."

Gemma got up from her seat and crossed to the window where Lilliana still stood. "You're my best friend. I'll help if I can, but I'm going to be honest and say I don't like this. I don't want to lose you. Please reconsider."

"I will miss you, but I need to find my own way. Please understand this is the best thing for me."

Gemma sighed and then pulled Lilliana into her arms for a hug. Lilliana wrapped her arms around her best friend. She had been curious about Gemma once she realized who she was. Lady Gemma Kemsley had been the girl her father wanted her brother to marry when they were younger. She sought out an introduction to get her measure and hadn't been disappointed in the young woman. They had only been friends for a few months, but in all her nineteen years she had never been close to another female her age. It didn't matter that a couple years separated their age; they were a different kind of soul mate. They appreciated each other on a level that no one else ever could or would.

"I'll try to understand. I really will, but I'm never going to like it. You are my only friend. I will always wish for you to be near me..." Gemma pulled away from Lilliana and clasped their hands together. "Tell me what I can do to help."

Lilliana knew she could count on Gemma. Elation filled her as she could envision how it would all work out. Now all she needed to do was give her all the details so she could do her part in the plan.

"I overheard my parents talking. I had no intention of listening until I heard my name spoken. I found out some interesting things that I never knew. Not the least being that Mama never intended to get married and Father had blackmailed her into agreeing to be his wife."

Gemma gasped. "What?"

"Makes you stop and question the validity of their love and all that doesn't it?"

Gemma's mouth hung open with shock radiating from her eyes. After a small pause while the information sank in she asked, "Why would he do such a thing?"

"Once upon a time Papa sailed his ship, the *Sea Rover*, as its pirate captain. Apparently he had a little feud with Mama's grandpere and she became the leverage he needed to enact his revenge. They came out of it okay, clearly as they are still together." Lilliana flipped her hand dismissively as she spoke. "The point is that Mama said that by the time I'm twenty if I still don't wish to wed, she planned on giving me the deed to the plantation in South Carolina."

Lilliana tried over and over to explain to her parents how much marriage was distasteful to her, without going into too much detail. If her father knew exactly how her heart had been bruised, he would have murderous intentions. The real issue was she didn't want anyone to know how naïve she had been. Now, she knew she could get what she wanted and nothing made her happier. Anxiety filled with equal swirls of excitement tumbled through her belly.

"That's still too long for me to wait. I won't be twenty until December and that is nine months away. What I want to do is sail there now and use my family position to gain control. My plans are not going to change just because nine months pass by."

"What good will that do? Without the deed securely in your control will they allow you to oversee the plantation? Isn't someone already there taking care of the property?" Gemma asked.

"There is an overseer yes. I'm hoping to convince him that the letter giving him orders to give me control got lost on the mail packet before my arrival. Come let's sit down in comfort as we work out the details." Lilliana grabbed Gemma's hand and led her to the settee. After they were seated she poured them both tea and handed a cup to her friend. Lilliana took a sip of tea before continuing their conversation. "I've thought a lot about what needs to be done. Even if the overseer doesn't believe I have control of the plantation no one has the authority to throw me off the property because it is owned by my family. If I have to wait, I'd rather do it in South Carolina."

Gemma nodded. "Okay, I suppose that makes sense. What do you need me to do?"

"Well the tricky part is leaving without letting my parents know. First, I need to find a ship sailing to America. Once I book passage I'm going to need a way to get my trunks on board without raising suspicion. I'm not worried about funds. I've been saving all my pin money for months now." Lilliana gave Gemma a smile. Surely she would see how she thought of every possible issue in her plan.

"So how do you plan on getting your trunks on board the ship?"

"That is where you come in. Once I know what ship I'm on, I'd like you to invite me to come stay with you in the country for a week." Lilliana set her teacup down and gave Gemma her full attention. She really needed Gemma to help her. If she didn't, her whole plan would fall apart. Her eyes pleaded with Gemma as she spoke, "My family won't question it because they know that our schedule is relaxed at the moment. It will give me a reason to pack a trunk or two and have them loaded onto a carriage. The carriage with your family crest on it that is."

"Oh, I understand. You will have the carriage drop you off at the docks and our servants will unload your trunks to be delivered to the ship. They won't have a reason to let your family know that you're boarding the ship. The servants will assume they already know." Gemma nodded her head in understanding.

"I knew you'd get it." Excitement filled Lilliana's voice. "It's all coming together now. I only have one little facet to figure out before I can iron out the rest of the details. The first item I need to cross off my list is to figure out what ships are heading to America and if they are accepting passengers."

"However are you going to figure that out?"

"Oh, that's the easy part. I will just ask Liam," Lilliana proclaimed.

Gemma blinked several times before she asked, "Won't he find that suspicious?"

"Not at all," Lilliana said waving her hand. "He's constantly talking about the Marsden shipping line and its competitors. He just started to take over the business. Our father believes it's time for him to learn about his future inheritance."

"I see. When do you plan on getting the information out of him?"

"Tonight at the Silverton's ball. Father is making him escort me. I will make sure to have a friendly conversation with him in the carriage on our way."

"You have thought of everything. I'm sure it will work just the way you want it." A small smile grew on Gemma's face as she looked at Lilliana. "I just wish your plans didn't have to take you so far away from England. Why couldn't you have fallen in love with a nice earl or baron...or even a mere mister? Anything that might inspire you to stay where I have an actual possibility to visit you, chances are I'll never be able to travel to America to visit. Promise me you'll come back to see me."

"I promise to come back to see you. In the meantime, we'll

keep in touch with lots and lots of letters. I want to know everything about your life and when you find the man of your dreams."

"Good. I suppose I should go. I'll see you tonight at the ball."

Gemma stood up and grabbed her pelisse. After she donned it, she walked over and gave Lilliana a quick hug. She watched as Gemma left the room and got up to walk back to the window to look at the rose garden. All she could do at this point was hope all of her plans went off without a hitch. Doubts clouded her mind as she knew from experience nothing ever went exactly as planned, and naught could be done to alleviate her anxiety. Lilliana decided to try and let it go. She turned and left the sitting room to find some kind of diversion. Perhaps a book would work to distract her thoughts away from any possible problems—thinking, or over thinking in her case, had always been her worst enemy. With a smile on her lips Lilliana strolled to the library. Dark feelings would not sink through and ruin her good mood. Preparation was the key to success. No one planned and schemed better than Lilliana Marsden.

A TREASURED LILY

DAWN BROWER

Dawn Brower

A Treasured Lily

CHAPTER 1

"I just don't think it's a good idea."

"Nonsense." Lilliana Marsden looked up at her best friend, Lady Gemma Kemsley, and frowned. "It's a brilliant idea. My father is being unreasonable about allowing me to travel to America. The plantation in South Carolina is my inheritance. It's about time I claimed it."

"It's not going to work for you to just show up and claim it though. I don't get why you are in such a hurry. You know full well you won't inherit it until you marry." Gemma reached up and smoothed over her sanguine curls, tucking a loose strand behind her ear.

"Well, that's not entirely true." Lilliana's lips twitched into a cheeky smile; it helped to have a little insight into how her parents worked. Gemma didn't know how much she'd gotten away with over the years. Eavesdropping had become a habit of hers. A person could find out the most interesting things quite by accident. When she overheard her parent's most recent conversation she couldn't help the glee that filled her soul. Reining in her excitement had taken an enormous amount of restraint. She needed to leave England and start the life she envisioned for herself. One she had complete control over. Her parent's still hoped she would settle down and get married, but they didn't know her true reasons. "I stumbled across a bit of information that may help me to achieve my goal."

"I don't understand. Did you find a way to inherit it early?"

Lilliana got up, walked to the window of the sitting room, and pulled open the curtains. She stared out at the garden and pondered how to explain what she overheard, and exactly how it fit into her idea to get everything she wanted. Various shades of roses, red, orange, and white, scattered across the garden in a pattern that reminded Lilliana of a kaleidoscope. The garden remained one of the places that she turned to when she needed to reflect on what floated through her mind. It calmed her and made it possible for her to think rationally about any issue that arose in her life. Something about being surrounded by the plant life helped her to think and form her plans with a clear head. Lilliana needed to get Gemma to aid her in her quest to leave England. They worked their magic on her as she calmly let the curtain go and turned back towards her best friend.

"I don't *ever* plan on getting married. I told you that the day we met. My parents still insisted on a season or two. They believe everyone is capable of finding love. They don't understand they are a rarity."

A sting of pain stabbed through her heart, Lilliana rubbed her chest in an attempt to erase the phantom ache. After her disastrous first season, she knew quite well how unusual it was for a love match to exist within the ton. Her choices were lecherous old men and scheming vermin only after her money. There was one man though who made her want to believe he really loved her. She found out the hard way he only wanted to use her. She was thankful he didn't achieve his goal and Lilliana came out relatively unscathed, but the damage to her belief in love sat firmly in place.

"Most matches are made for business or political reasons. It's all about money and there is no way I'm handing over mine to a male to control."

Gemma tilted her head and crinkled her nose in confusion. Lilliana knew she didn't get it. Her friend wanted to get married and have children. The two years difference in their ages showed when they discussed the possibility of matrimony. In time, Lilliana believed Gemma would look back on this conversation with clarity. In the midst of starting her first season and barely seventeen years old, Gemma still approached life with rose-colored glasses on. For a brief moment in time Lilliana had worn that same veil of hope; her parent's love inspired her enough to want to find it herself.

Reality came crashing in like a bolt of lightning and shattered every ounce of optimism she held within her. Lilliana realized finding love at the various parties hosted within London society equaled finding a mythical creature. The chances of finding a unicorn would be an easier feat. So she gave up on love and formed a new plan for her life.

"I still think you are being preposterous. Why are you so against marriage?" Gemma folded her arms across her chest and stared at Lilliana. Her eyes pinning her in place as she spoke. "That's what a lady is expected to do after all. I just don't understand how you plan on claiming your inheritance without the benefit of a husband to help you get it."

Lilliana could feel her lips twitch into a smile. Her mother often commented on how Lilliana received all her father's traits, even his less than desirable ones. William Thorston Marsden, fifth Viscount Torrington, had a way of getting what he wanted out of people. She admired that characteristic in her father and sought to emulate it. Still, she wished she had been lucky enough to get her mother's pale blonde hair instead of her father's dark curls. In Lilliana's mind, her twin brother, Liam, was blessed because he inherited her mother's coloring.

"I suppose I should explain it so you won't be left in the dark. I'll need your assistance after all."

Gemma got up from her seat and crossed to the window where Lilliana still stood. "You're my best friend. I'll help if I can, but I'm going to be honest and say I don't like this. I don't want to lose you. Please reconsider."

"I will miss you, but I need to find my own way. Please understand this is the best thing for me."

Gemma sighed and then pulled Lilliana into her arms for a hug. Lilliana wrapped her arms around her best friend. She had been curious about Gemma once she realized who she was. Lady Gemma Kemsley had been the girl her father wanted her brother to marry when they were younger. She sought out an introduction to get her measure and hadn't been disappointed in the young woman. They had only been friends for a few months, but in all her nineteen years she had never been close to another female her age. It didn't matter that a couple years separated their age; they were a different kind of soul mate. They appreciated each other on a level that no one else ever could or would.

"I'll try to understand. I really will, but I'm never going to like it. You are my only friend. I will always wish for you to be near me..." Gemma pulled away from Lilliana and clasped their hands together. "Tell me what I can do to help."

Lilliana knew she could count on Gemma. Elation filled her as she could envision how it would all work out. Now all she needed to do was give her all the details so she could do her part in the plan.

"I overheard my parents talking. I had no intention of listening until I heard my name spoken. I found out some interesting things that I never knew. Not the least being that Mama never intended to get married and Father had blackmailed her into agreeing to be his wife."

Gemma gasped. "What?"

"Makes you stop and question the validity of their love and all that doesn't it?"

Gemma's mouth hung open with shock radiating from her eyes. After a small pause while the information sank in she asked, "Why would he do such a thing?"

"Once upon a time Papa sailed his ship, the *Sea Rover*, as its pirate captain. Apparently he had a little feud with Mama's grandpere and she became the leverage he needed to enact his revenge. They came out of it okay, clearly as they are still together." Lilliana flipped her hand dismissively as she spoke. "The point is that Mama said that by the time I'm twenty if I still don't wish to wed, she planned on giving me the deed to the plantation in South Carolina."

Lilliana tried over and over to explain to her parents how much marriage was distasteful to her, without going into too much detail. If her father knew exactly how her heart had been bruised, he would have murderous intentions. The real issue was she didn't want anyone to know how naïve she had been. Now, she knew she could get what she wanted and nothing made her happier. Anxiety filled with equal swirls of excitement tumbled through her belly.

"That's still too long for me to wait. I won't be twenty until December and that is nine months away. What I want to do is sail there now and use my family position to gain control. My plans are not going to change just because nine months pass by."

"What good will that do? Without the deed securely in your control will they allow you to oversee the plantation? Isn't someone already there taking care of the property?" Gemma asked.

"There is an overseer yes. I'm hoping to convince him that the letter giving him orders to give me control got lost on the mail packet before my arrival. Come let's sit down in comfort as we work out the details." Lilliana grabbed Gemma's hand and led her to the settee. After they were seated she poured them both tea and handed a cup to her friend. Lilliana took a sip of tea before continuing their conversation. "I've thought a lot about what needs to be done. Even if the overseer doesn't believe I have control of the plantation no one has the authority to throw me off the property because it is owned by my family. If I have to wait, I'd rather do it in South Carolina."

Gemma nodded. "Okay, I suppose that makes sense. What do you need me to do?"

"Well the tricky part is leaving without letting my parents know. First, I need to find a ship sailing to America. Once I book passage I'm going to need a way to get my trunks on board without raising suspicion. I'm not worried about funds. I've been saving all my pin money for months now." Lilliana gave Gemma a smile. Surely she would see how she thought of every possible issue in her plan.

"So how do you plan on getting your trunks on board the ship?"

"That is where you come in. Once I know what ship I'm on, I'd like you to invite me to come stay with you in the country for a week." Lilliana set her teacup down and gave Gemma her full attention. She really needed Gemma to help her. If she didn't, her whole plan would fall apart. Her eyes pleaded with Gemma as she spoke, "My family won't question it because they know that our schedule is relaxed at the moment. It will give me a reason to pack a trunk or two and have them loaded onto a carriage. The carriage with your family crest on it that is."

"Oh, I understand. You will have the carriage drop you off at the docks and our servants will unload your trunks to be delivered to the ship. They won't have a reason to let your family know that you're boarding the ship. The servants will assume they already know." Gemma nodded her head in understanding.

"I knew you'd get it." Excitement filled Lilliana's voice. "It's all coming together now. I only have one little facet to figure out before I can iron out the rest of the details. The first item I need to cross off my list is to figure out what ships are heading to America and if they are accepting passengers."

"However are you going to figure that out?"

"Oh, that's the easy part. I will just ask Liam," Lilliana proclaimed.

Gemma blinked several times before she asked, "Won't he find that suspicious?"

"Not at all," Lilliana said waving her hand. "He's constantly talking about the Marsden shipping line and its competitors. He just started to take over the business. Our father believes it's time for him to learn about his future inheritance."

"I see. When do you plan on getting the information out of him?"

"Tonight at the Silverton's ball. Father is making him escort me. I will make sure to have a friendly conversation with him in the carriage on our way."

"You have thought of everything. I'm sure it will work just the way you want it." A small smile grew on Gemma's face as she looked at Lilliana. "I just wish your plans didn't have to take you so far away from England. Why couldn't you have fallen in love with a nice earl or baron...or even a mere mister? Anything that might inspire you to stay where I have an actual possibility to visit you, chances are I'll never be able to travel to America to visit. Promise me you'll come back to see me."

"I promise to come back to see you. In the meantime, we'll

keep in touch with lots and lots of letters. I want to know everything about your life and when you find the man of your dreams."

"Good. I suppose I should go. I'll see you tonight at the ball."

Gemma stood up and grabbed her pelisse. After she donned it, she walked over and gave Lilliana a quick hug. She watched as Gemma left the room and got up to walk back to the window to look at the rose garden. All she could do at this point was hope all of her plans went off without a hitch. Doubts clouded her mind as she knew from experience nothing ever went exactly as planned, and naught could be done to alleviate her anxiety. Lilliana decided to try and let it go. She turned and left the sitting room to find some kind of diversion. Perhaps a book would work to distract her thoughts away from any possible problems—thinking, or over thinking in her case, had always been her worst enemy. With a smile on her lips Lilliana strolled to the library. Dark feelings would not sink through and ruin her good mood. Preparation was the key to success. No one planned and schemed better than Lilliana Marsden.

CHAPTER 2

R andall Collins stepped out of a black open carriage and followed the Earl of Devon into his gentleman's club, Whites. Devon wanted to discuss business in a more dignified setting, hence the journey to his favorite club. Rand didn't much like overly pompous aristocrats, but Devon had an interest in a possible investment with his shipping company. If the meeting went as planned Rand would have a new investor and could expand his business.

"Ah, here we are, have a seat Collins and we'll discuss what is next for RandCo Shipping," The Earl said as he sat down in the nearest seat at the table. "And whether or not I want to give you some of my money to invest."

It grated on his nerves he had to seek investors to expand his business. Rand had a lot of big ideas and hoped the earl liked them enough to continue to invest in shipping company. He took the seat across from the earl and settled into discussing the future of his shipping company. With a small fleet of clippers at his disposal he did well enough for himself, but wanted to branch out into steamships for larger cargos and more reliable speeds.

"Did you have a chance to look over the papers with my proposal?" Rand asked.

"I did, and I admit my knowledge of shipping is rather limited. I hope you don't mind I invited someone that knows a bit more than I do to help me decipher some of the details. Viscount Torrington and his son should arrive soon." The Earl of Devon raised his head and scanned the room. He appeared to be scanning the room, as if looking for someone he invited to join them.

Irritation filled Rand's gut as he let the earl's words absorb deep into his mind. He clenched his fists tightly under the table, not wanting the man to see how much his words bothered him. Hell yes he minded, Devon could consult anyone he chose, it was his right after all to make sure he was doing the right thing for himself. However, he could have at least let Rand know they'd be meeting with someone else prior to arriving at the club. It was hard to be prepared for a meeting when all of the details hadn't been presented in advance. Before he could voice objection, two men walked in and took a seat at the table. One was as dark as the other was light. They bore a striking resemblance, in spite of the opposite coloring, that made Rand believe them to be closely related.

"Ah Torrington glad you and Liam could make it," Devon said. "This here is Randall Collins. He has grand ideas for steamships. What are your thoughts on the matter?"

As they had not been introduced, Rand gathered the older gentleman Devon spoke to was Torrington, the man he previously mentioned would be joining them. The upper class tended to refer to each other by their titles or last names. Rand couldn't wait until he could sail back to America. The higher born in English society had a snobbish attitude that he had trouble stomaching. Torrington nodded his head at both Rand and Devon before he started to speak, "Liam knows a bit more about steamships than I do. He has been looking into them for a while now to determine if they are worth investing in. I'm a clipper man, but I realize their days are numbered."

"I like the idea of steamships, but even they have their pitfalls. The coal needed to keep them running can be expensive. The cargo needs to bring in a more than fair price if a profit is to be made. They have their advantages, faster and more reliable travel. I think it's more economical for most cargo to continue to be brought over by clipper. Steamships are great for passengers and mail." The light haired man nodded at them as he sat up straight and looked Rand directly in the eye as he delivered his viewpoint.

It was obvious that Liam's beliefs were in direct opposition to his own. Rand clenched his hands into tight fists underneath the table as anger and frustration permeated his whole body. The boy probably had a point, although minute, Rand however did not want to deal in passenger ships. People made things messy. They could be demanding and irritating on a good day and damn abusive any other time. The chances of him being willing to start a passenger line bordered on slim to none.

"Is that the only good thing you can think of for steamships? What about cargo that requires a faster delivery? I know you English favor your tea. Steamships travel at faster speeds and allows for a swifter arrival. This means what you deem to be important cargo will arrive to its destination much sooner." He had to gain control of the conversation before these idiots talked Devon out of investing in his shipping line.

Steamships did make great passenger ships. The mail packets arrived much faster when they were placed on a ship powered by steam, but Rand had grander ideas. There were plenty of reasons to start investing in steamships. Those that began to do it sooner would have profits much sooner than those waiting to see if it worked. Sometimes it was worth it to take on a risky venture; although Rand didn't think it was as chancy as they were making it sound.

A bit of color formed on Liam's face. He clearly didn't like pointing out flaws in his estimation of the value of steamships. "You make a valid point, sir. Some cargo could benefit from the faster steamship. There is a clipper design that has been noted to bypass even a faster steamship. The record for the ship surpassed the fourteen knots of the steamship. That clipper managed to snatch up some of the tea trade. We had a few ships built around that design and they have worked wonderfully with any cargo that requires a more speedy arrival." Liam continued to glare at him as he spoke. His eyes crunched up in disapproval and his lips pursed into a thin line.

"Okay, I admit I'm just getting more confused the more

these two gentlemen talk. Tell me straight Torrington, are steamships a good investment?" Devon asked.

"The short answer is yes, and no." Torrington grinned.

Torrington had an amused smile on his face as he watched his son sit back in displeasure. Apparently Liam's attitude entertained him or it could be the volley of their conversation back and forth, Rand didn't care to know what that something was though. He just wanted to derail them before they ruined his investment possibility. Damn them and their advice. If they kept talking about the negativities surrounding steamships they were going to talk the earl out of investing, and Rand would be right back where he started.

"That doesn't bloody help me." Devon threw his hands up in frustration.

"That's because there isn't an easy answer to your question. Any new venture is risky. All signs point to steamships eventually taking over. There are a few ships that are built to be powered by both steam and wind. We are having a few of those built to try out in our shipping line." Liam rested his hand on the table and tapped his forefinger on the polished wood as he explained, "The idea is that if coal runs out or becomes too expensive the option to use wind is still available and not all will be lost in the voyage. It will probably be a few years before we branch into a ship completely powered by steam."

"So you both do not believe steamships are the sound investment right now?" Heat began to dissipate through Rand as his anger reached a boiling point.

"In the future yes, but now it is still risky," Torrington said. "They are making a lot of progress in their designs, but they all have flaws. I'd go with what is a known quantity."

Rand unclenched his fists and wiped his sweaty palms over his thighs. His lips pursed in displeasure as he considered how to proceed. He couldn't erase the irritation from his voice as he spoke. "And yet you are still willing to try out a glorified clipper ship that could also be powered by steam?"

"Yes." Torrington continued with a bit of mockery in his voice, "I did say I leaned towards clippers at the beginning of the conversation."

Damned Englishman, and their perverse ways. The conversation was spiraling out of control. Rand tried to steer the conversation in the direction he wanted, but they were relentless in their opinions. He curled his fingers into fists underneath the table and refrained from smashing them against the polished wood.

"I'll admit there is a certain beauty about clippers, but let's be realistic. The popularity of the ship has faded a lot over the past twenty years. The ship isn't seen in quite the same light as it used to be."

"So do you recommend investing or not?" Devon asked as he turned his attention once more on Torrington. "I need to give the man an answer."

Torrington looked at Devon and shrugged his shoulders. He looked him directly in the eyes as he spoke. "Honestly, it's up to you and how much of a risk you are willing to take with your money. It isn't a bad investment. No matter what, eventually you will make money." Torrington picked up his drink and took a quick swig. He set his glass back on the table and scanned the table before his eyes landed on the Earl. "To put it simply, Devon, it depends on the market and how well the cargo is managed. I did look over his plan and RandCo has been steadily gaining in capital. It just hasn't been at a rapid pace. Expanding at this juncture requires more money and it's not gaining enough on its own."

The more they opened their mouths the more irritated Rand became. He couldn't believe the gall of these men. They were talking around him instead of including him in the conversation. He had to force his way into it in order to be heard. He built RandCo all on his own. Yes, the progress had crawled at the pace of a snail, but the growth remained true. It might take him longer than he wanted it to, but he could continue to do it on his own. He'd be damned if he remained sitting here taking their distain and disapproval.

Rand forced his way into the conversation. "Good of you to give the stamp of approval on my business, Ol' Chap. Why don't I save you all the time and just say that the offer is off the table. I don't especially like being discussed like I'm not here."

Liam began, "We didn't mean to imply—"

Rand interrupted, "Save it. You act like I don't know a lick about business. I built this company all on my own without your expert advice. I can continue to assemble it without your money too, Devon. I admit the boost probably would have made expanding easier. I just don't like the strings that extra help apparently comes with."

He looked over and found Torrington studying him as if trying to ascertain his origin. He must not have a lot of experience dealing with Americans. He knew he could be a bit brash and defensive at times, but he had no desire to change.

"A bit hot-headed, aren't you." Torrington raised his eyebrows at him and a quirky smile lifted at the corners of his mouth.

"A product of where I happened to be raised, I suppose." Rand shrugged.

Torrington laughed before saying, "In America? Yeah, I suppose that could be the explanation. From my experience most of you could take a bit of lessons on diplomacy."

"And you all could learn to be more accepting of the differences in all men," Rand retorted.

"Down puppy. I meant no offense. My wife happens to be American. She can be a bit...stubborn at times. Don't do anything rash," Torrington reasoned.

Rand had to admit that little tidbit amused him some. Torrington's wife must be an exceptional woman to put up with his arrogance on a daily basis. It would be interesting to meet her and get a more in depth look at her character. "Your wife's American? What state did she hail from? Maybe I know her family."

"Doubtful as they all died a number of years ago. Her plantation is being run by an overseer at present. It's located in Charleston, South Carolina."

"I never knew that," Devon stated.

"Yes, we're lucky it survived the War Between the States. She left shortly before the war broke out and sailed to France to live with her grandpere," Torrington explained.

"How ever did your plantation manage to survive the war?" Rand had to admit that he found it interesting that they had a plantation in Charleston that survived the war. A lot of the plantations had been burned to the ground by the Union army.

"Luck mostly." Torrington leaned back in his chair. "The union army decided to use it as a hospital. My wife, Pia, told her overseer to remain as neutral as possible and that allowed for a certain amount of leniency from both sides of the conflict."

"Well if we're done discussing business how about a bit of pleasure?" Devon asked.

"What do you have in mind?" Torrington questioned as he leaned forward and rested his hands on the table. "I have plans with my wife this evening and can't be drawn into anything too extensive."

"How about a game of whist?" Devon asked.

"I have to be back in a couple hours to take Lily to that ball." Liam looked at his father as he spoke.

Torrington nodded. "Good point. Lily has a temper and she isn't afraid to use it. Best if you're not late. Why don't you take the carriage home and send it back for me."

"I can always give you a lift back, Torrington," Devon offered. "Although I'm supposed to go to that blasted ball tonight too. Gemma is expecting me to escort her."

"As much as I hate to admit it, I think we'll have to attempt more amusing pursuits at a later date. Maybe tomorrow night?" Torrington looked to Devon for confirmation.

"Splendid idea." Devon nodded his affirmation. He turned towards Rand and asked, "Collins, you want to go to the ball?"

"Can't say I've ever been to a ball before. Sounds fun. I have a few days before I sail back home. It could be a nice diversion." Rand had been watching them discuss their options for entertainment. It resembled a pugilist in the ring; they volleyed shots back and forth at each other and danced around any real issues. If he hadn't been so irritated, he'd be a bit more fascinated by their way of speaking to each other. He never had any desire to go to a ball before, but he could add it to his once in a lifetime experiences.

"Good, good. Then just come with me to my townhouse.

My valet can help you get ready and you can help me escort my daughter, Gemma."

Rand got up to follow the earl out of his club. He nodded at Torrington and Liam. "Nice meeting you gentlemen. Perhaps we'll see more of each other before I depart."

Pompous jerks. His real wishes didn't even come close to wanting to see them ever again. He knew he'd see them at the ball later that evening, but hoped it would be the last time he ever laid eyes on them. They single-handedly made him restructure his whole plan for expanding his business. He didn't hold them in any high esteem. The meeting did not go as he intended it to. These men and their grand ideas, or lack thereof, had made sure of that. No, what he felt for them bordered on hate. He had to deal with uppity men who believed they were better than him his whole life. A person didn't grow up in an orphanage without having some lasting internal scars. The emotional distress the high class brought out was deep rooted and he couldn't let go of it easily. In his experience they didn't give a damn for anyone, but themselves. These individuals were not different. If he never saw them again he might be able to forget their existence.

CHAPTER 3

L illiana sat down at her vanity table and put the finishing touches on her hair. She did very well getting herself ready without a maid of her own. Having to depend on anyone for assistance went against all of her ideals. She had been ordering dresses that were easy to put on herself since before her come out ball three years prior. It had taken her a while to learn how to do her own hair, but like anything she put her mind to she excelled at it. Today, she wrapped her ebony curls partially up in a chignon with a few curls falling down to frame her face. Satisfied with her handiwork, Lilliana stood up and stepped into black satin shoes. She stopped wearing light colors when she decided never to marry. Young girls wore pastels. While they didn't have much choice in the matter, she certainly did.

Society dictated that if a lady remained unmarried they needed to appear more demure. One of the ways to convey that distinction to the world was in the color of their dresses. A year ago Lilliana decided she that she would no longer wear such hideous colors. White and pink did nothing for her complexion. She needed bolder colors that enhanced her looks. So she convinced her mother to allow her to wear something more suited for her. After a long heated debate she won and had more flattering colors for her wardrobe. She reached down and smoothed the skirt of her cobalt ball gown.

The blue gown enhanced the color of her eyes and enhanced their appeal. She had fallen in love with the color and fabric when she visited the modiste a few weeks ago. It made her happy to be able to finally show off the creation at a ball.

Lilliana loved to dress up and attend parties. It made her feel special and beautiful. Not to mention how fun it was to be able to dance and laugh with her friend, Gemma. She may not want a husband, but she still knew how to enjoy herself within the expectations set by the ton.

Lilliana grabbed her gloves and left the room. She walked down the stairs just as her brother walked in the door.

"Oh good, you're ready to go," Liam said.

"Did you doubt I would be?" Lilliana raised her eyebrows at her brother. "I'm always prompt and you know it."

They were twins, not that you could tell by looking at them. They each had very distinct features. Lilliana looked at Liam noting how much his coloring favored their mother. She couldn't help wishing once again she favored her mother instead of her father. They may each take after a different parent, but one thing remained true; a Marsden didn't take it well when someone ordered them around. Liam had a more diplomatic personality, but even he had bursts of temper. Liam managed to hold on and fight battles he believed were worth the energy needed to expend in order to win them. When he happened to be in a rage though, it was best to clear the room because he exploded when he couldn't hold his anger in.

"I'm aware of your tenacious attitude. I'm always prepared for a battle when I have to deal with you," Liam declared.

"Nonsense. I'm the epitome of graciousness." Lilliana flashed Liam a wholly wicked, gamine smile.

At her pronouncement Liam began to laugh. His chuckles bounced over the walls and boomed loudly throughout the entrance hall. The color of his face became bright red as he gasped for breath. Lilliana moved past him to wear her pelisse hung by the door. Early spring in London still held a chill, and she didn't want to be cold as they traveled to the ball. After she had the pelisse securely around her shoulders, she turned back to her brother. His laugher slowed down to a light gurgle as if he attempted to rein it in.

"I don't see what you find so funny, little brother."

"You are never gracious. You're a demanding wench, and you know it," Liam retorted.

Ignoring him, Lilliana strolled towards the entranceway. They walked out of the front door and into the awaiting carriage. Lilliana waited for her brother to be seated before she replied to his taunt. No reason not to be comfortable for the upcoming disagreement.

"No need to be mean, I can be nice. " Lilliana tilted her head. "If it serves my purpose."

"Lily dear, you don't do nice. You scheme and cajole your way into everything. No worries, I love you and wouldn't have you any other way. It's part of your charm." Liam flashed her a smile that mirrored hers. He could look positively wicked at times.

"You're just trying to suck up now for acting like a bird-wit."

"Awe, that's a bit harsh. I'm never thoughtless. You know that," Liam told her.

"Then explain your actions just now?" Lilliana raised her eyebrows in question."'Cause you generally don't act like an arse."

"I met an interesting American today. His comments grated on me a bit."

Lilliana's interest piqued at his comment. She couldn't tip her hand too much, or he'd latch on to her questioning and ask some relentless ones of his own. They were fairly close and often sensed things about each other. Liam knew her too well and probably would figure out before anyone else what her actual plans were. She couldn't allow that to happen for any reason. He would do everything he could to stop her from traveling to South Carolina.

Besides leaving Gemma, she would miss Liam a great deal. If anyone could persuade her to abandon her plans, it was her brother. So she began her questions remaining as neutral as possible.

"What did he do to irritate you so much?"

"I can't pinpoint it exactly. I think it was basically centered around his attitude. He had a penchant for rudeness."

"Sounds like an interesting chap. Any chance I can meet him?" Lilliana inquired.

"For what purpose? You aren't going to start some kind of feud with him because he was annoying, are you?" Liam questioned.

"Please." Lilliana raised her eyebrows. "What kind of person do you take me for?"

"The kind that enjoys trouble a bit too much."

Liam did have a point—she enjoyed getting people riled. She often said things just to see what kind of reaction she could get out to them. It amused her to no end how often they fell for it. This time though she really did want to meet the American. He must have arrived in England by way of ship and chances were he'd know the next ship sailing back home.

"You know me too well. I don't like people that aggravate my family in any way." Lilliana agreed.

"No worries, he didn't bother me that much," Liam replied, "but if you really want to meet him then you will have a chance tonight."

"Really? Why is that?"

This was going rather easy. Almost too effortless, and maybe she should take that into consideration, but Lilliana believed in taking risks. She needed to know why he was going to be at the ball. Any information about him would be useful in gaining his trust and help in obtaining the necessary sailing schedule.

"He is the guest of the Earl of Devon. He is attending the ball tonight with his family."

"Oh, poor Gemma."

"What the bloody hell does Gemma have to do with it?" Liam inquired.

"Well, isn't it obvious? As the guest of her father she'll have to put up with his rotten attitude more than we will." Lilliana explained.

"I'm sure your friend will be just fine. If not, you will come to her rescue like you always do."

"I don't get why you don't like her that much. She is the sweetest girl. You should try and get to know her a bit."

Lilliana could see Liam's frustration as he ran his hands over his face. No doubt learning the business had started to take its toll on him. She knew their father could be demanding and expected a lot out of his children. Perhaps she should go a bit easier on him. His stress levels had taken an all-time high when he started to take on more responsibility. He needed to learn it all so that one day he'd be in a position to take control.

Lilliana wanted to believe her parents were infallible, but she knew that someday they would no longer be with them. Their father realized it all too well. He lost his parents at a young age and hadn't been prepared to run the business on his own. So for that reason he started to teach Liam everything he needed to know as early as possible. Viscount Torrington didn't want his son to be taken by surprise with the responsibility of the estate and many businesses in his holdings.

"I'm sure she is delightful. I don't have time for her kind of amiable right now." Liam stared at her with derision in his eyes as the sarcastic reply left his lips. Something about Gemma bothered him, but Lilliana didn't know what. He always seemed to want to avoid her and he made every attempt to do so.

"What's that supposed to mean?" Lilliana asked. She sat up and stared at her brother anger simmering through her, making her cheeks feel heated. It offended her that he found Gemma so unworthy.

"Don't take that tone with me. Nothing against her, but you know she wants to get married. I see the stars in her eyes and I'm not that guy. I wish she'd quit looking at me like that. It will be a number of years before I even consider getting leg-shackled."

Oh, she got it all right. Her friend didn't compare to his expectations, and somehow he had gotten the notion she sought his attention. Maybe he saw something she didn't when looking at Gemma or it could be he was projecting his own ideas onto her friend. It might not have anything specifically to do with Gemma, but more what she represented to him. Liam had a lot on his mind and marriage didn't top his list of priorities. Lilliana didn't think that Gemma had set her sights on any one in particular. Sure, her brother exhibited a handsome face, but even Gemma had to realize his youth played a part in his reluctance to get married.

"I'm sure you're wrong about her. Yes, she does want to get married. She looks at everyone. You're around me a lot as my chaperone and she'd be a fool not to notice you. Nothing more than that." Lilliana flipped her hand nonchalantly. "I know you have your own resentments, but you have to remember she didn't have anything to do with what our two fathers originally planned. Besides, she hasn't settled on anyone just yet." Lilliana looked into his eyes pinning him with a glare. "Be nice."

The carriage stopped, and Lilliana looked up to see a footman holding the door open. They finally arrived at the Silverton ball. It was now time to start putting her plan in motion.

"I'm not going to argue with you, Lily. Let's try to have some fun at this function tonight," Liam suggested.

Lilliana smiled at his offer of peace. "I don't want to argue any more than you do. Let's go inside and see who's in town to enjoy this ball." She planned on having lots of fun at the social gathering. The first thing she wanted to do involved garnering an introduction to her brother's American foe.

They stepped out of the carriage and walked up the steps to enter the Silverton residence. Lady Silverton always hosted the best balls each season; Lilliana hoped that this one proved to be just as wonderful as the ones she had attended in the past. She knew at the very least she'd be a step further in her plans to go to America by the end of the ball. She hoped that the man she sought out could answer all of her questions.

"By the way what is the name of the American that you didn't like too much?" Lilliana asked.

"Why? I thought you decided to leave him be?" Liam asked.

"I never agreed to any such thing. I need to make sure he is an okay fellow to be around Gemma."

"Ah I see, I suppose that makes a bit of sense. His name is Randall Collins."

"Good to know. I like to have as much information as possible before I meet someone."

"I'm surprised you're not interrogating me for more details."

"Why? Is there something else I should know?"

"Nothing I can think of. I doubt you will have to worry very much though," Liam replied.

"Don't concern yourself with what I worry about, but why do you believe I won't have to?" she asked.

"He owns his own shipping line. He said he only planned on being in England a few more days before he set sail for home."

That had to be the best news that she'd hear that night. Lilliana carefully schooled her face to remain blank. She didn't want to give away how much his statement excited her. He owned his own ships! Surely she could talk him into allowing her passage on one of them. Lilliana wanted to rub her hands together with glee, but knew the action would only raise more questions. It took everything she had to physically restrain herself from making her hands do the motions.

"Oh good. Maybe I'll leave the man alone then."

"Somehow I doubt you will," Liam muttered.

"You have no faith in me."

"I have lots of confidence in you," Liam told her. "I just also happen to know you too well."

"I know." She sighed. "If you want you can go find one of your friends to talk to, I'll be fine. I'm going to probably be with Gemma all night anyway."

They walked into the ballroom after they were announced. Liam scanned the room and spotted someone he wanted to talk to. He nodded at them and strolled over to their side. Lilliana scoured the ballroom looking for her best friend. Drat, it looks like they haven't arrived yet. She'd have to bide her time and remain calm until she got her chance to accost Randall Collins for information. She walked to a chair and sat to await their arrival. She tapped her fingers on the arm of the chair. Many people believed that patience was a virtue, but the concept escaped Lilliana. She never did understand why she should be made to wait. Perhaps her actions could be construed as spoiled, but she liked to think of them as exacting and necessary. The night would be long if she had to sit here anxious for the Devon party to arrive. The American captain held the final detail to tie it all together. He needed to arrive and soon. If his ship held the capabilities to transport her to her desired destination, she'd unleash all her charm on the man. He wouldn't know what hit him. Lilliana always got what she wanted.

CHAPTER 4

"Ah we're here," the Earl of Devon said. "The worst part about these functions is waiting in line to get out of the carriage."

Rand agreed with the earl's assessment. Nothing compared to the atrocious confinement he'd been subjected to with the earl who talked too much and his daughter who could barely string two words together.

"Well at least we can finally get out of the carriage and stretch our legs," Rand said.

They each stepped out of the carriage and walked up the steps. Rand followed the earl and his daughter as they entered the residence. So far he believed the choice to attend the ball ranked near the top of his list of his worst decisions. He hoped his opinion of the situation proved to be wrong once he actually made it inside and experienced the event itself. After the announcement of their arrival, they walked down into the elaborate ballroom. It appeared as if anyone and everyone had shown up for the ball. The possibility they were amongst the last to arrive occurred to Rand as he tried to follow the earl and his daughter through the crowd. Once they got to the far side of the ballroom, they stopped walking and turned to look at the guests dancing on the ballroom floor.

"Quite the turnout, isn't it?" a voice asked from behind

Rand. He turned to see a beautiful woman with black curls floating around her heart-shaped face. Her full lips formed a crimson bow as they tilted up into a pleasant smile. For a brief moment he stood still, stunned at her appearance. In those brief moments he realized the lovely young woman came over to speak to the earl's daughter.

"Oh good, I thought it would prove impossible to find you in the crush of people here." Gemma gave the girl a quick hug.

A lighthearted laugh floated from within her and it seared Rand's soul. The night improved considerably with her appearance. Maybe the decision to come hadn't been the worst one he'd ever made after all...

"You doubt me?" she asked. "What is it with people doubting my abilities tonight, first my brother, and now you. Have faith in me please."

"Of course not! I would never doubt you. It just took us forever to arrive. I despaired at the idea I might not be able to spend any time with you. Have you danced yet?" Gemma inquired.

"Yes, I have danced. You know my card doesn't stay empty for very long, I have lots of names on my card. It's nearly full." She waved her card at Gemma with a triumphant grin on her face.

Rand stood there waiting for the forgetful chit to introduce him to her lovely friend. He hoped to add his name to her dance card before it filled up. By her last statement he believed he would be too late unless he acted fast, he prayed she would agree to add his name to her card. Her eyes glanced over and locked with his.

"Do I know you?" she asked.

"Oh how rude of me. I'm sorry I should have introduced you." Gemma apologized.

Yeah, she should have. Her youth exploded out of her every time she opened her mouth. Hopefully she matured as she got older. Otherwise her future husband may have an annoying female to deal with. She didn't matter to him though, his eyes remained glued on her friend.

"Mr. Randall Collins." Gemma gestured toward him. "Please meet Miss Lilliana Marsden."

Finally a name to go with the beautiful creature! It suited her perfectly. Her features rivaled any lily he had ever had the pleasure to see. Indeed, she was an elegant flower expertly cultivated and pleasing to be around. He really needed to hold her in his arms even for a brief moment. The introductions were made perhaps now he could entertain the possibility of dancing with her.

"Nice to meet you, Miss Marsden," he said.

"The pleasure is all mine, Mr. Collins," Lilliana replied. "You're not from around here are you?"

"No I'm not, I'm actually from America. South Carolina to be exact," Rand explained.

"Really? That's interesting. Lilliana has ties to South Carolina." Gemma jumped into the conversation as she relayed that interesting tidbit of information.

Rand turned his attention to Gemma and stared at her with little interest. He had forgotten the little mouse still stood by them. As soon as he had Lilliana's attention, Gemma became nonexistent. Her father had abandoned them both a while ago; Rand had no clue where the earl had disappeared too.

"I didn't know that, but of course we did just meet," Rand replied. "Where in South Carolina do you have ties?" Rand turned his attention back to the enchanting Lilliana.

"Charleston. Do you reside near there?" she responded.

"I actually reside in a nearby town, Beaufort."

"Oh, that's lovely. I have only visited South Carolina once. We sailed over when I was a child to check on the property held by my family. I'd like to see it again someday." Lilliana's voice had a whimsical tone as she spoke. A faraway expression clouded her eyes as she appeared deep in thought. After a few moments she shook her head and gave her attention back to Rand. "Are you sailing back soon?" she asked.

"In a few days I am heading home," he replied. "There hasn't been a whole lot in England to inspire me to stay."

"Nonsense." Lilliana smiled. "There's a lot in England that is absolutely stunning. You're just not inclined to give it a chance."

Rand found himself smiling back at her, absolutely

enchanted. A more charming female did not exist, at least one he had ever met. He must dance with her soon. Rand really needed to garner any chance he could to touch her, no matter how brief.

"I heard you say that your dance card had yet to be filled. Any chance I can add my name to it?" he requested.

"Oh." Lilliana looked at her card and chewed on her bottom lip. "I don't know I had hoped to spend some time with Gemma."

"Please." His eyes begged her to accept.

"Oh, all right, let's see. I suppose you can have the next dance. It's a waltz. Is that okay?"

"I have no problem with that," he agreed.

A half-smile formed on his face. He couldn't have been happier with the outcome if he tried, and a waltz would allow him to touch her more that he had hoped to. He couldn't wait to hold her in his arms and have her full attention.

"Gemma, you don't mind, do you?" she turned and asked her friend. "Maybe you can find a dance partner too."

As if on cue a male walked up behind Lilliana and said, "Are you staying out of trouble, imp?"

Rand looked up to see his nemesis from the earlier business meeting standing by Lilliana. He had no clue who Liam actually addressed with his statement until Lilliana spoke.

"Oh bother," Lilliana's annoyance came to the surface with her statement. "I'm being good. Go find someone else to interrogate." Lilliana grabbed his arm to prevent him from leaving. "No better yet stay. You can dance with Gemma. She needs a partner for the next dance."

Liam looked disturbed at the idea of dancing with Gemma. Not that Rand could blame him either. Given the choice he'd choose Lilliana every time. The little mouse seemed to become even more demure in his the presence of Liam Marsden. She withdrew and appeared both happy and frustrated to have him in her presence. If Rand had more time he would probably wonder why she was displaying such a huge contradiction, but at that particular moment he really didn't care.

"Uh...sure, I guess I can."

"You don't have to." Gemma leaped into the conversation to dismiss the idea. "I know you don't like to dance."

"No, it's okay. I want to," Liam said.

Rand didn't believe him for a minute. He concluded Liam only placated the girl. Not for a second did he think the young man actually *wanted* to dance with Lady Gemma. A look of fear crossed over Liam's features before he masked it with a more congenial expression. He didn't care though because he got what he wanted out of the situation. Lilliana Marsden would soon be in his arms. Rand only thing he cared about getting her there.

Lilliana stepped up and placed a kiss on Liam's cheek just as the sounds of the music of the current dance ended. She had a bright smile on her face and her eyes glowed with happiness. "Oh, that's fantastic. I knew I could count on you."

Rand felt irritation grow inside of him at the sight of Liam, but he let it go as soon as Lilliana turned towards him and held out her hand for him to take in his. This was what he had been waiting for since the moment he turned to see her for the first time.

"I suppose that means it's time for the next dance," Rand stated.

"You're going to dance with him?" Liam scowled. "I'm not sure that's a good idea."

"I don't care what your opinion is, Liam," Lilliana said. "I want to dance and Mr. Collins offered. Go dance with Gemma and quit being a brooding chaperone."

He glared at her, but then turned towards Gemma and took her hands. Rand still holding Lilliana's hand in the crook of his arm led her out to the dance floor. Gemma and Liam followed them, and they began the waltz. Lilliana danced beautifully in his arms. She had a light step and floated around the ballroom floor.

"Can I ask you a question?" Inquisitiveness reflected in her eyes as she stared directly into his. She mesmerized him and held his attention captive with her own.

"You can ask me anything."

"Is it possible for me to sail back to South Carolina with you?"

"Pardon me?" Rand stared at her with befuddlement.

"I want to go live on our plantation in Charleston. My father is being difficult about it. I decided I would have to take matters into my own hands," Lilliana explained.

In that moment he realized exactly who she happened to be related to. It all clicked into place as he saw Liam dance by with Gemma in his arms. Lilliana Marsden and Liam were brother and sister. So that made her the daughter of Viscount Torrington. Rand knew he would regret it if he allowed her on his ship. The little he garnered about the man while he sat before him in the business meeting earlier told him a lot about the man. He had very high expectations and little time for dimwits. No doubt he would kill him for taking his daughter away from him. Liam, her devoted brother, would help his father accomplish the task.

"I'm not so sure that is a good idea." He looked down at her with wariness in his eyes. "Your father is a force of nature and your brother isn't far behind him."

"I don't care. I'm capable of making my own decisions."

"And you expect me to take on their wrath?" Amusement laced his voice. "I'm not sure I'm up to these lofty expectations you have for me."

"Absolutely." She wrinkled her nose up at him. "I think you're more than up for what I'm asking of you."

"So you actually want me to help you run away from home?"

"Well, when you put it like that... Yes, I do."

He would be every kind of fool to go along with her idea, yet he wanted to. If he took her with him he might have a possibility of winning her over. In England he didn't stand a chance in hell of getting her to accept him as her own. As soon as he laid eyes on her he knew he wanted her. The more he talked with her the more he liked the idea of holding on to her forever. As foolish as her idea appeared to be Rand knew it also happened to be the only opportunity he may get of actually having her.

"I suppose you have all of the necessary details worked out," he replied. "I'm not likely to have your male relations storm my ship and demand you back before we depart am I?"

"Trust me. I'm good at strategies. You just happen to be the last detail I needed to make it all work the way I wanted."

"Trust has nothing to do with it." Rand laughed. "It has more to do with self-preservation. I happen to fancy breathing."

"Don't be ridiculous," Lilliana retorted. "There isn't any reason to be so dramatic. My father isn't likely to kill you."

"Right. Because he is the personification of civility."

He watched her blink several times as his words sank in. How bad of a temper did Viscount Torrington actually have? Rand watched as she mulled over his words. Perhaps he had misunderstood the viscount. His impression of the man suggested he had a violent side. One he had no problem showing to the world if he deemed it necessary.

"Father does have a temper, but I still believe you have nothing to worry about," Lilliana explained.

"You said I happened to be the final detail in your plans." Rand sighed. "Were you waiting for me to show up?"

What were the chances the chit new of his existence before their introduction? No, it wasn't likely as he hadn't been in England that long.

"Not exactly, I had no clue you existed before today," she told him. "These plans have been in the works for a few weeks now."

"And yet I'm the very thing you need to make it all work. How is that possible?"

"Simple really, I need someone with a ship that is willing to transport me. I am hoping that person is you."

He wondered how far he could push her. The decision to give into her and take her on his ship had already been made. Lilliana just didn't know he already decided to let her come back to America with him, but only because it worked in his own plans.

"What do I get for my trouble?" he asked. "I'd be risking quite a lot to assist you with your scheme."

"What do you want? Money? I certainly can afford to pay for my passage."

Rand's lips rose into a cocky smile. He desired a lot from her, but at this point only one thing would do as payment.

Would the lovely lady be willing to give it to him? He had nothing to lose and only one way to find out.

"How about a kiss?"

Lilliana looked stunned as she stared unblinkingly at him, and then just as suddenly she stopped dancing right in the middle of the dance floor. Her face flushed a pretty shade of pink as she began to move to the music again with him in the lead.

"How forward of you. I'm not sure I like your idea of compensation."

"It's a small thing, one little kiss. To be given to me at a time of my choosing." He leaned in close to her and whispered in her ear. "Are you afraid?"

Lilliana's breath sucked deep into her chest, and he could feel her slowly exhale it in little pants. Her pulse raced on her wrist beneath the palm of his hand and thrummed a small beat as he held it firmly in his grasp. A blush formed on her cheeks turning them a nice shade of pink, and her lips parted in anticipation. Her body's reactions suggested she had an interest in kissing him also. Would she take the bait and give him what he desired? He needed her to accept the proposal. Once she did he'd have her sailing with him in a few short days.

"All right, you have a deal," she agreed.

"Excellent. I will send information on where you can board the ship. I look forward to our voyage together."

He led her back to the side of the room when the dance ended and stopped next to her brother and Gemma. She looked up at him and smiled before turning her attention back to her friend. Rand nodded at Liam and sauntered away. He had some preparations to make before he could welcome her on his ship. Tonight, it looked like he was going to be preparing his ship to sail a tad earlier than he originally planned. Oh, but what an extraordinary reason to go through the hassle of making the trip a bit prematurely. He couldn't wait to have Lilliana Marsden on his ship, and in his world.

CHAPTER 5

Lilliana couldn't believe how easy everything started to fall into place. A note from Randall Collins arrived early that morning. His plans to leave had changed slightly. Instead of three days, his ship would sail back to North Carolina the next day. Excitement filled her as she realized it had all worked out as she planned. Randall Collins, with his unruly dark brown hair and mischievous hazel eyes, took her breath away. She didn't want to agree to a kiss as payment, but at the same time she anticipated it. He stirred feelings in her that she didn't know how to explain. So she decided to push it out of her mind. A lot needed to be done before she could leave with him.

She sent a note to Gemma to come visit her for tea so she could wrap up that little detail. Gemma needed to be made aware of when her invitation to visit happened to be taking place. She also needed to get permission from her parents to stay a week or two at the Earl of Devon's country estate. Her father would be the hardest to persuade, so he sat on the top of her list of things to accomplish that day. She left her bedroom and walked down the stairs to his study. No time like the present to get that little tidbit checked of her to do list.

"Are you busy?" She knocked on the side of the doorframe and walked into her father's study.

Viscount Torrington sat behind his desk with a bunch of

papers scattered across the top of it. His long dark hair tapered at the nape of his neck, but a riotous strand escaped and folded over the top of his forehead. His head rose at the sound of her voice and his blue eyes twinkled with delight.

"For my favorite daughter? Absolutely not." Her father rose to greet her.

"I'm your only daughter." A tiny giggle escaped her mouth as she crossed the room to give him a hug.

"That's a good thing too," he retorted. "I don't know if I could've handled two of you."

"Of course you could have." Lilliana gave him a mischievous grin. "I'm the essence of all that is good."

"Are you trying to trick me?" Viscount Torrington laughed. "I'm made of sterner stuff than those other fools you walk all over. What do I owe the pleasure of this visit?"

"Nothing much really, Gemma has to go back to her family's country estate for a week or two. She invited me to join her. It's my hope you'll allow me to go."

"I don't know if that's the best idea right now, Lily. Things are a bit busy around here at the moment," he explained.

"That's exactly why you should allow me to visit. Liam is busy learning the business. You can't expect him to keep escorting me to these functions. It's only the little season anyway. I don't need to go and it'll be nice to spend time with Gemma."

"What does your mother have to say?" he asked.

"I haven't spoken to her yet. I figured I'd approach you first. Please Daddy, let me go." Lilliana used her most coaxing voice on her father. She stuck her bottom lip out in a mock pout and batted her eyelashes at him expectantly.

"Thor, are you busy?" They turned as they heard a voice from behind them. "Oh, I didn't know you were in here Lily."

Her mother either had the worst timing or the best. Lady Torrington strolled into the room with a questioning look on her face. Her pale blonde hair was perfectly coifed without a hair out of place, and her emerald green gown rustled as she made her way across the room to join her husband and daughter. Lilliana took a moment to envy her mother's beauty and wished once again she had been blessed with her coloring. Sometimes she hated her brother for getting the

DAWN BROWER

lucky genes. She could very well deter her father from allowing her to go to Gemma's. If only she had more time to talk to him before her mother interrupted. She needed to convince her father to allow her to visit Gemma's country estate. Her mother's timing may have interrupted her plans, but maybe she could salvage it somehow.

"Hello Mama," Lilliana said. "I stopped in to ask Father's permission to visit with Gemma at her family's country estate for a week."

"Oh? And when were you going to ask me?" her mother asked.

"After I finished talking with Father," Lilliana said.

"Pia, I just asked her if she already spoke with you," her father said. "I think it would be okay for her to have a small visit. As long as she isn't gone more than a week."

Lilliana could feel elation soaring through her. She rocked on her heels and hugged herself with joy. Apparently that small amount of time had been enough to convince her father to allow her to go. Thank God for small favors. She needed to be on that ship in the morning.

"I suppose that would be fine," her mother said. "When will you be leaving?"

"Tomorrow morning. The earl's carriage is going to stop by and pick me up. It's short notice I know, it's why I'm asking now so I can get my trunks packed."

"All right, I don't like that you are leaving so fast, but I guess I'm find it to be acceptable. Our social functions are pretty slim right now anyway," her mother said.

Lilliana threw her arms around her mother in a fierce hug. She loved her parents dearly, but they tended to be a bit overprotective. It shamed her to know that her leaving would hurt them, but she had to leave, her happiness depended on it. She truly believed she belonged in South Carolina.

"Thank you, Mama. I need the break and some quiet time with Gemma."

"What I don't get a hug?" her father asked.

"You already got a hug," Lilliana teased.

"What I don't rate a second one?" He raised his eyebrows at her statement.

"Of course you do," Lilliana said as she turned to wrap her

arms around her father. "You deserve more hugs than I could ever give you, Daddy."

Her father squeezed her tightly in his embrace. Nothing compared to a hug from her father. It made her feel safe and loved. She meant what she told him. She could never give or receive enough hugs from him.

"Okay princess, I have work to do and some things to discuss with your mother. Go get packing or you'll never be ready to leave on time."

"I love you two, you really are the best parents, and you are right, I have a lot to do. Gemma is coming for tea soon as well."

Lilliana left the room with a huge smile on her face. The talk had gone a lot better than she hoped. Gemma would arrive any minute and she needed to pack. She doubted sleep would be easy tonight with all the excitement. As she entered the hall she heard the front door open and Gemma stepped inside. Gemma looked over at her and strolled to her side.

"Oh good, you're here," she said as she walked over to give her friend a hug. "Although I've already ordered tea and scones. Let's go into the sitting room and talk."

Gemma followed Lilliana into the sitting room, removed her pelisse and set it on a chair, and then sat on the settee. She turned and gave her full attention to her best friend.

"So what's the urgency?" she asked.

"He's leaving tomorrow. I need you to have the carriage bring me to the ship in the morning," Lilliana explained. "Everything will have to be stepped up a day. Can you manage it?"

"Of course," Gemma agreed. "It's a small thing to arrange to have one of our carriages pick you up in the morning. Are you sure you want to do this? I have to ask one final time."

"Yes, I do. I told you how much I needed to leave."

"I know, but Mr. Collins isn't exactly what I expected you to sail away with. He's a very handsome man. I don't want you to do anything you might regret later."

"Nonsense. I can handle Mr. Collins, besides I don't plan on getting married. Maybe a little fling is something I should consider."

"What?" Gemma's sanguine curls fell over her face as her emerald eyes widened in shock.

"Why shouldn't I know what passion is like? I don't need to save my virtue for my future husband if I don't plan on having one," Lilliana explained.

"There can be other ramifications of finding out what passion is besides losing your virtue, Lily."

"I'm aware of that. I didn't say I decided to experience yet, I'm only considering it. I need to make sure I'm okay with the possible complications first."

"Good, at least you are stopping to think about it first. I don't want you to make a mistake."

"I don't believe in mistakes. Everything we do is a life lesson. It is through those so-called mistakes that we learn and grow. If I decide to give myself to Mr. Collins, it will be a wonderful thing. I refuse to think of it as a possible error in judgment."

"I know you are going to do whatever you choose to do. I just hope that it's the right decision for your continued happiness. I only want what is best for you."

"I know you do." Lilliana acknowledged. "I'm truly going to miss you."

"I know, but you need to do this." Gemma's eyes held a hint of sadness in them as she gazed at her.

They turned when a maid brought in a tray with the tea and scones Lilliana had ordered. She carried the tray over to them and placed it on a table beside them.

"Do you need me to pour miss?" the maid asked.

"No, I can handle it. Thank you, Melly."

Melly curtsied and walked out of the room. Lilliana turned toward the tea and poured some into two cups and handed one to Gemma.

"Now that the details are settled, let's talk about a lighter subject." Lilliana said.

"What did you have in mind?"

"Oh, I don't know anything. What do you think of this weather we are having? Scorching hot one day and cold and rainy the next"

"That's England for you." Gemma said with a laugh.

The mood lightened and Lilliana sat back on the settee.

She needed to enjoy one last afternoon with Gemma before she no longer could. She needed the memory to take with her and hold tight. As much as she needed to leave, it also occurred to her that she'd be entirely alone in her new home. If she could take Gemma with her, she would have included it in her scheme. It's too bad it couldn't be done, because Gemma's friendship held a special place in her heart.

CHAPTER 6

After Rand had time to think about this foolhardy plan he realized the sooner he left the better. He trusted Lilliana to have all the details set, but he didn't hold a lot of conviction that her father would not get wind his daughter's plans. If it had any chance of working they needed to leave with all due haste. So after he left the ball he went to his ship and ordered the preparations to set sail. After that he only had one problem left, he had a whole day to kill and no idea what to do with himself.

The day had been excruciating for him. He found himself pacing the length of the ship most of the day in anticipation of her arrival. Sleep failed to arrive that night and made him cranky while he waited for the sun to rise. In his note he told her to arrive to set sail after the sun had risen in the sky. It made him happy to realize she knew the importance of punctuality as he watched the Earl of Devon's carriage arrive at the docks. As she stepped out of the carriage, she raised her hands block out the sun as she got a look at his ship. Rand turned and motioned two deck hands to follow him as he wandered down the gangplank to greet her.

"A couple crew members are going to load your trunks on the ship," he told her. "We set sail in less than an hour."

"Good. I don't want to wait to set sail. I'm glad we are leaving immediately."

"If you follow me I'll show you where you'll be staying during the voyage."

Lilliana followed him onto the ship and below deck to the cabin she'd be residing in the length of the journey to South Carolina. The cabin was small, but he hoped she'd make do with the sparse conditions. Especially, since it happened to be the only cabin available for her use. He watched her walk into the room and take off her pelisse. She set it on the table and turned toward him.

"Thank you for allowing me to sail with you, Mr. Collins."

"Please call me, Rand."

"I'm not sure that's wise. It's entirely too informal," Lilliana responded.

"My ship's a rather informal venue." With a smile he continued, "Trust me, it's easier if you acquiesce to my request."

He watched as she mulled over his words. Rand hoped she gave in and called him by his given name. He ached to hear his name pass through her lips. Little informalities had to start somewhere. Giving her permission to use his given name helped to ease her slowly into his strategy of lulling her to his will. He had a plan of his own and he intended to succeed.

"All right," she said with a sigh. "If you insist, I will call you Rand. I still think it's a bad idea though."

"Duly noted, but I'm glad you are willing to give it a try regardless."

"I suppose if I'm to call you Rand, you must call me Lily. Only my closest friends and family do."

"I'm honored to be amongst that small circle of people. If you'll excuse me, I have much to do before we depart," Rand replied.

"Rand wait; I have one question before you leave."

He turned back when he heard his name; a shudder rolled over him at the sound. The more she said it the easier it appeared to come out of her mouth. He loved hearing it and hoped to hear her say it for the rest of his life. It breathed life into him where none had previously existed.

"What do you need to know?"

"It's about the bargain we made."

He could see the hesitation in her words. Clearly she had been thinking about the payment that they agreed upon. Good, he wanted her to think about him kissing her and often, because he intended to do it more than she knew or expected him to.

"You mean the kiss you agreed to let me have," he responded.

"Yes. See I had more time to think about it..."

"I hope you are not going to go back on our bargain. It's not too late for you to go home."

"I have no intention of going back on our bargain. I'd like to modify it slightly, if you are willing."

"Okay, you have piqued my interest. How would you like to change our deal?" Rand asked.

"I make no excuses for my innocence. My upbringing demanded no less. What I'd like to do is rectify that with your help."

Surprised, he responded, "Are you asking me to take your innocence?" That couldn't be right, and yet he felt every inch of his body preparing to teach her everything she wanted to know. He hoped to God that she meant it because he wanted to be the only one she'd ever know. Lilliana belonged to him and in time she would realize it.

"I'm not sure exactly what I am asking of you. I just get this feeling when I'm close to you. I don't ever plan on getting married so..." her words trailed off. She started to pace in the small room her anxiety starting to show.

"You figure I'm as good as anyone in showing you what passion is all about," he finished for her.

Rand's stomach dropped as her words sank in. The pain, a sucker punch, he hadn't been expecting. At first he had no idea how to respond to her because her words were still floating through his brain. Never marry? He would work on changing her mind. As much as he wanted to teach her everything she desired. Rand knew if he did she'd never consider being his wife. There would be no reason to. She'd get all she wanted out of him and toss him aside in time. That didn't mean he couldn't seduce her to his way of thinking without actually sealing the deal.

"Yes," she said nodding in his direction. "I know its risqué, but I feel I can trust you."

"You shouldn't trust me Lily."

She stopped and stared at him as if she actually saw him for the first time. Her gaze rolled over him starting at his feet and resting at his eyes. With the intake of her breath he knew she saw the strength of desire in his eyes. She just didn't know the full extent of what he wanted to do with and to her. She'd find out one day, but not as soon as she liked.

"Regardless I do. Please consider what I'm asking."

"No."

"Why not?"

"Because you don't know what you are asking of me. I don't heel to commands," he countered.

"I don't understand. What do you want from me?"

"It's simple enough Lily." He crossed the short distance of the room, pulled her into his arms, and whispered in her ear. "I want everything."

"Then give me what I want." Lilliana's face was flushed, and her breaths came out in short pants.

"No. Things will go at a pace I set. I will not give into your demands."

"Why must you be so obstinate? You want me. Take what I'm offering you," she pleaded.

"Maybe I will, maybe I won't. In the meantime, I will take the kiss you owe me."

Rand tilted her head and leaned down capturing her lips with his. A small sound of surprise came out of her mouth, and he took advantage of its opening. He touched her tongue with his, and she innocently followed his lead. Their tongues intertwined as he gently glided his over hers. His lips caressed hers as he learned her taste. Her hands wound around his neck and her fingers ran with abandon through his hair. Rand lifted his lips and trailed them over her cheeks and chin in light kisses. He drew back and looked at her half closed eyes. When they fluttered open, he saw a hazy desire filling the blue depths, a need matching his. He placed a quick kiss on her forehead before he let her go. If he didn't put some distance between them, he wouldn't be able to stop.

He would need to move slowly, if he intended to win her forever.

"That's enough for now. I must go." With a half-smile on his face he said, "Think of me while I'm gone." He turned and left before she could answer him.

That had gone a lot better than he planned. He didn't have any doubts about winning her. When he wanted something bad enough, Rand never lost. Winning Lilliana would be an enormous battle, and he hoped her own nature would work against her belief that marriage didn't work for her. In the meantime, he had a ship to get ready to sail and no time to lose. He marched up on deck to get going before he lost something he treasured more than his own life. Lilliana Marsden now belonged to him. Damn anyone if they tried to take her away from him.

As he reached the top of the deck he saw Lilliana trunks ready to be taken below deck at a later time. Rand walked to the stern of the ship and located his bosun and first mate.

"Is the ship ready to set sail?"

"Yes, Captain," his bosun answered. "Sal and Jim are going to take the lady's trunks to her cabin. Do you want us to lift the anchor now?"

"Yes. It's time to go home," he told them. "The sooner we get there to better. Give the order."

"Aye, Aye Captain" the bosun said and left to follow Rand's orders.

"Do you need us to do anything else before we leave Captain?" the first mate asked.

"No, we don't have any cargo this trip. Just make sure the navigation goes well. We have a good wind and should be out to sea soon. I'll be in my cabin if you need me. You're in charge for the time being."

Rand walked back below deck to his cabin. He passed the closed door of Lily's cabin and for a brief moment considered knocking on it and kissing her senseless again. Deciding against it he continued on to his cabin. No reason to rock the boat just yet. A good seduction took time.

CHAPTER 7

Several hours later, Lilliana stood in the middle of her cabin and crossed her arms over her chest. A mere kiss left her with feelings she never experienced before with anyone else. Rand told her to think about him, and she thought about nothing else. Phantom tingles grazed across the tops of her lips and she could almost feel the slight pressure of Rand's as they caressed her. She ran her fingers across her lips, trying to understand the emotions swirling inside of her. In her first season, she had allowed one of her many beaus to kiss her. It hadn't stirred any emotions within her, and so she tossed it aside as something she didn't really care to experience again. Perhaps she had dismissed kissing too soon. Rand clearly knew what he was doing, and Lilliana realized with the right person doing the kissing it could be quite enjoyable. It now held an appeal it never had before.

Rand generated the most wonderful feelings, and she wanted to find out where they all would lead. Perhaps he had been right in denying her idea of a more clandestine affair right away. A challenge just made things a bit more interesting. After his kiss, Lilliana knew she wanted to explore all of her options, and she intended to get her way. Plans could be adjusted to reflect necessary changes.

Marriage and forever had never been on her agenda. That desire hadn't really changed, but she had a small thought that perhaps she wouldn't mind having Rand around long term. She now desired him in a way she hadn't needed anyone else. Lilliana started to scheme in her head how to make him hers. Her life would be exceedingly different with him by her side. Perhaps she could talk him into living with her permanently without the benefit of marriage.

Her ideals adapted to include him in every part of her life. Rand could help her run the plantation in South Carolina. So far he appeared to be a good man, when he hadn't jumped at her offer she learned what she needed to know about the depth of his character. He told her not to trust him, but clearly she could. The man hadn't wanted to take advantage of her and refused to take her innocence. She just needed to find a way to get him around to her way of thinking.

A knock on the door brought her out of her thoughts. She strolled to the door and opened it. She found Rand leaning against the doorframe with a cocky smile on his face.

"Did you miss me?"

He wore an overconfident smile on his handsome chiseled face. His brown hair looked a bit ruffled from working topside of the ship. It caused Lily to want to run her fingers through his hair and feel it for herself. He stood before her as if expecting her to give into the whims crossing through her mind. Cocky bastard believed he had won her over already. Okay he had, but he didn't need to know that just yet. If they had a chance, some boundaries had to be set up and established in advance. She garnered that much watching her parents over the years. Her father knew exactly how far he could push her mother before her she exploded with temper.

"Not at all." Lilliana brushed him aside. "I've been too busy to give you a second thought. Are you here for a reason?"

"Busy really? Doing what exactly?" he inquired.

"I started writing some correspondence I'll need to mail once I arrive in South Carolina. I'm going to have to let my parents know where I am eventually. I didn't dare leave anything at home to make them aware of my intentions."

"Probably a wise decision on your part. How will you explain to them your decision to leave?" Rand asked.

"I'll tell them the truth. They know I've wanted to live on

the plantation for over a year now. I loved it when we visited as a child. I grew up in England, but South Carolina calls to my soul."

"Then why all the subterfuge?" Rand raised his eyebrow questionably.

Lilliana raised her left eyebrow at his question. "I don't know what you mean."

"You know exactly what I mean. If you love the property as much as you say why deny you the opportunity to visit. What are you not telling me?"

"Ah I see your point. Technically I'm not supposed to visit without one of my parents with me. I didn't want to give them a chance to deny me the opportunity to go. I have the better part of a year until I'm old enough to gain the majority to go on my own. Father didn't want to let his only daughter go off to another country just yet. He was adamant about my staying home as long as possible. We had many arguments about the issue."

"I can't say I blame him. If I had a daughter I'd probably be a bit overprotective myself."

Lilliana shrugged her shoulders and turned away from him. "Yes, well there's overprotective and then there's smothering. Father tends to lean towards the latter."

"Most fathers are," he said. "At least the good ones."

Lilliana turned back around and face him. "Probably, I just know how my father is. I love him, but he can be a bit...relentless at times. Probably stems from his pirating days."

"Wait, what did you say?" Rand asked with a stunned expression on his face.

"Oh, I must have forgotten to mention that to you. My father used to sail his ship the *Sea Rover* as Pirate Thor Williams. It's how my parents met."

"But he's a viscount." Rand's bafflement at her pronouncement was evident in his words.

"And he used to be a pirate. What's your point?"

"That it just doesn't make sense. How can a member of the English aristocracy have been a pirate?" He raised his hands showcasing his frustration.

"I'm not sure on the details." Lilliana shrugged. "They are a bit sketchy. It had something to do with my mother's grandpere and attempted murder. Suffice to say he had a long road back to claiming his title."

Rand began to rub his temples. Lilliana knew she had to tell him about her father's past. The possibility of him getting his own ship ready and coming after them remained high in her concerns. As far as she knew a faster ship than the *Sea Rover* didn't exist. Her father had been excited to make the necessary modifications to make the ship faster than in his pirate days. She hoped they had a good head start before he realized she'd boarded a ship headed to America.

"You are going to be the death of me," he exclaimed. "How long do we have?"

"I don't know what you mean?" Lilliana faked innocence at his remark.

"I mean how long before your ex-pirate father comes after you?"

"Um, well, I'm not sure. I guess it depends on how long it takes him to realize I am not spending the week at the country estate of the Earl of Devon."

"I give it a day tops before he is getting his ship ready to set sail after us."

"I'm afraid you may be right," she agreed. "At some point they will see Gemma out in society and question my whereabouts. The only good news is that it'll take a while to get the *Sea Rover* ready to set sail. I happen to have overheard him say he planned to careen his ship. The rest of the fleet owned by Marsden Shipping is elsewhere earning their keep. We may have a while before he has access to a ship capable of coming after us."

"Really? How advantageous for you. No wonder you wanted to get on a ship heading for America as soon as possible," Rand retorted.

"I told you I had a plan."

"Indeed you did I just didn't realize how extensive the details were."

"I have always believed the details are what made the best schemes possible," Lilliana said. "I'm good at plotting and planning."

"I noticed," Rand said with a half-smile.

"You're not mad at me are you?" Lilliana leaned into him and attempted to cajole him into a more relaxed state.

Rand raised his eyebrow at her questioning her methods, but allowed her to lean her body farther into his. "Not at all, dear. I may have to readjust our course, but I think I can manage to evade your pirate father."

"He isn't a pirate anymore."

"My apologies, your *former* pirate father."

With a petulant smile she said, "You should apologize. He's reformed, mostly."

"Lilliana, dear I'll say one thing about you, things are never dull with you around."

So far things were going as planned. She adjusted the details to include winning over Rand, and he currently fell in line with each one. When she decided she needed him in her life, she realized she'd have to tell him all the family's dirty secrets. He'd taken the fact her father had been a pirate rather well in her estimation. Now to step up her plan to get what she wanted. She got a little taste of desire and craved more. She began to rub her hands across his broad chest and massaged her fingertips into his well-toned muscles. When she noticed his breathing change, she looked up into his eyes to get his full attention.

"Did you stop by for any particular reason?" she asked coyly.

He leaned down and his mouth grazed her ear. Lilliana shivered as his breath caressed her neck. He whispered, "I have many reasons for stopping in to see you."

"Name one," she replied.

"I'd like to kiss you again."

"What's stopping you?" Lilliana had trouble breathing. The pace of her heart quickened, and she became heated from being near him.

"The fact that you want it as much as I do." Rand took a step back. "I believe you are a closet wanton."

"I believe you just insulted me," Lilliana retorted.

"I would never do any such thing. I adore you. However, you are in a hurry to lose your innocence. I'm not sure you realize what you are ready to throw away. I'm trying to be a gentleman."

"Nonsense, I know exactly what I'm offering you. I never asked you to play the part of gentleman. Why not just give in? You want me as much as I want you."

"Your pirate father for one. If he catches up to us I'd like to say I left you unspoiled. It could very well preserve my life." Rand folded his hands over his chest as he looked at her.

"I don't believe you. My father has nothing to do with your intentions towards me."

"Maybe you're right, but what if you're wrong? Nevertheless, when or if I decide to make love to you it will be my decision. You've already given me consent to try. I'd rather it be at a moment of my choosing."

"I think you are being unreasonable." Lilliana pushed her bottom lip out into a pout at his refusal to give in to her demands.

"And I think you are acting like a spoiled brat."

Spoiled brat? How dare he? *That man doesn't know a lick about me and he referred to me as a brat and a wanton. Maybe I should just give him exactly what he believes me to be.* She stalked over to him and threw her arms around him, pulling his head down. Her lips crushed his breathing life into her frustrations. With each movement the constant turmoil of her emotions bled into the kiss, their tongues dueling for control. Lilliana pulled her tongue back in her mouth and bit down on his bottom lip. She kissed away the soreness with a gentle sweep of her lips to soothe the ache she created. Rand pulled her into his embrace, and her hands roamed through his hair to bring his head closer to hers. Rand groaned and put his arms around her so he could deepen the kiss. Finally, he was acting in a way that would lead to what she desired from him. After what seemed an eternity, Rand wrenched himself away from her and put some distance between them.

"Damn you woman. You drive me insane."

"Thank you, I do try." An impish smile formed on her face as desire flowed through her.

He laughed and continued to back away from her. It made her feel powerful to know the kiss had rattled him to the core. Yes, she believed that every one of her plans progressed nicely.

"I think I may have taken on more than I can handle," he said.

"Oh, you don't think you can handle little ol' me?"

"Not tonight imp. I only came down to invite you to dinner. You distracted me from my original purpose."

"Backing away in defeat then?"

"You can win this little skirmish love." He smiled. "But I promise you, I'll win the war."

"I guess we'll see about that." She gave him a searing look as she said, "I've never lost before and I don't intend to now."

"Well then its time you learned how to take defeat with graciousness."

"Grace is my middle name." She gave him a devilish smile. "I personify it."

"Touché my dear," he said. "I'll give you that much. Let's agree to disagree at this point. I need to eat, I'm famished."

"So am I, but not for food," she replied.

He groaned as he turned around and started to walk out of the cabin. After he crossed the threshold, he turned back around and looked at her. Her words had the desired outcome; Rand appeared to be struggling to get his emotions under control.

"If you decide you're hungry for real food, come up to the galley. I'm heading there now. Perhaps I'll see you later."

"Only if you choose to visit me in my cabin again." She threw the words at him to see what kind of reaction she could continue to garner from him. Battling with words was something she did rather well.

"I bid you goodnight," he said and walked away.

That little encounter had definitely gone in her favor, although he left a bit quicker than she would have liked. He called their battle of wills a war. When she told him she didn't intend to lose she meant it. If he wanted a war then he had one and he better be prepared for anything. In her limited experience she knew that everything happened to be fair involving desire and war. This confrontation of his included both and she planned on using everything in her arsenal to triumph. Lilliana liked nothing better than winning; after all she happened to be good at it.

CHAPTER 8

R and walked along the deck and took a deep breath. The more time he spent in the lovely imp's company the more power he lost over the situation. Stopping by to invite her to dinner a week ago had been a strain on his control. He needed to rein things in a bit. Never in his wildest dreams did he imagine a woman like her existed. Lilliana Marsden's reckless behavior stirred his own. The trip back home would be his undoing. He didn't believe he could resist the entire three weeks it would take to reach port. In order to keep his hands off of her he had done everything to avoid her. Retreat did not look good on him. Taking a step back made it possible for him to look at things with more clarity. He now had a plan of action and he intended to implement it soon.

"Have you been avoiding me?"

Rand could almost feel Lilliana standing behind him. He leaned on the ship railing to look out at the turquoise waves as they rolled across the ocean. He figured out she didn't really like being ignored and deliberately pretended he hadn't heard her. Keeping his gaze forward, he waited for her to explode.

"Damn you, answer me." The palm of her hand met his back with a resounding *thud*, leaving a trail of sharp tingles in its place.

He turned his head and looked over his shoulder. His gaze traveled over her from top to bottom. He noticed that she had not donned a gown, but had instead put on breeches and a tunic draped in a cuffed red jacket. He had to stop himself from growling in approval. In the sunlight, he could see the outline of her breasts beneath the white blouse. The breeches fit her perfectly, and he got a good view of her legs and hips. He ached to ask her to spin for him so he could also see how they fit her derriere. Instead he kept to his plan of indifference and acted like her presence didn't matter to him.

"Can I help you?" he asked.

"Yes, you can give me your attention."

"I didn't realize that attending to you had been made a requirement of allowing you to travel aboard my ship. I apologize if I am slacking in my duties," he said with a droll smile.

"Don't be absurd. I never demanded that you give me all of your attention. But I'm bored and I hoped you might want to spend some time with me." Her bottom lip lifted into a pout as she folder her arms across her pert breasts.

"I'm kind of busy right now. I doubt I'll be able to spend any time with you."

"Doing what? Ascertaining if the ocean might dry up this century?" Sarcasm dripped from every word.

"No need to get testy with me, dear," he said absentmindedly. "I am just taking a small break to enjoy the view. I love how the sun looks as it rises on the horizon."

"So what do you have to do that is taking all of your time?" she demanded.

"Oh little things, you know like sailing this ship. I'm to take over from the first mate in a few minutes," he explained. "Unless you'd rather I leave it to fate and let the ship roam wherever it wants to."

He couldn't help needling her. Her face flushed, and her eyes became a stormy blue; she was lovelier when anger overtook her features. He liked it almost as much as when her face glowed with passion. If he couldn't see his favorite expression on her face, he'd take the look of rage instead. At least it mirrored desire a little bit.

"Don't be ridiculous," she retorted. "I understand the necessity of steering the ship. I just didn't realize that you actually had a part in it."

Rand shrugged his shoulders at her response. "Well, I am the captain of the ship. It stands to reason I'd have something to do with how it is run."

"Oh, I thought you just owned the ship. You actually captain it as well?"

"I do on this one. The other ships in my line have captains I've hired to work with my company."

She walked past him to lean on the railing, stopping to look out at the wide expanse of the ocean. Rand got a chance to look at her from behind. He knew that he'd enjoy that particular view while she wore trousers, and the vision before Rand did not disappoint him. His hands itched to touch her, so he took a step back before he gave in to temptation. She turned around and looked up at him.

"So you leave often to sail your own ship?" she asked.

"I don't stay home that often. I haven't had a reason to," he replied.

"Do you even have a home of your own?"

"No, not really. I stay at a boarding house when I find myself in South Carolina. I didn't see the point of building a home when I'm rarely there. I make my living by sailing. I usually stick around long enough to do some accounting and once it's completed I order the ship ready to go out again."

"It sounds like a lonely existence," she said.

"I didn't notice it. I kept busy and I made money. It's all that mattered to me."

"You don't want a family of your own?"

"No. I didn't think I'd make a good husband. So I believed I made the right choice in devoting my life to building my shipping company," he responded.

"I don't believe you."

"What is there to doubt?" he asked. "My inability to make some woman happy or that I enjoyed my so called lonely existence?"

She stared at him as if trying to dissect his meaning. How could he explain to her that until he met her nothing else mattered? He found purpose in building his business. He had no family and no one that depended on him. That only left one thing for him to do with his life. He had plenty of ambition to spare, and he focused all of his energy creating something for him to believe in.

"I doubt both. I know you are capable of making a woman happy if you set your mind to it. No one enjoys a lonely existence. Why have you punished yourself with the belief you are better off alone?"

"I have no family. I don't know what it's like to be surrounded by people that love you. I'm not punishing myself. I'm living the only way I know how," Rand explained.

"How long have you been alone, Rand?"

"All my life. I never knew my parents. I grew up in an orphanage. I ran away when I turned ten and got a job on the first sailing vessel that would hire me. They told me my mother died giving birth to me and no one knew who my father could be. My mother named me before she took her last breath. No one could afford to keep me so they dropped me off at the nearest church. That is how I ended up in a home for boys."

"Have you ever considered finding your father?" she asked.

"No. I don't even know where to look. The only thing I have to go on is my mother's name. That doesn't exactly tell me who my father might have been."

"If you don't mind me asking, what is her name?"

"Emily Collins," he told her. "But as I said it doesn't help trace down my wayward father."

"I'm sorry," Lilliana replied. "I didn't mean to bring up something so sad. I'm glad you told me though. It explains why you are so comfortable being alone."

"You have no reason to be sorry, Lily. It is what it is. I don't have a problem talking about it. You are incredibly lucky to have parents who love you. Remember that when they come after you because you know they will."

"I do know it. No matter how much I don't want them to, they will. I know they worry about me. I only hope that once they see me they will let me stay," she said with resignation in her voice.

"Good. It will be easier if you realize that," he muttered. "I will leave you with that to think about. I need to relieve the first mate now."

"Can I come with you?" she asked. "I promise I won't bother you. Well at least too much. I'm just tired of my own company and you are the only person I know on this ship."

He thought about what her company would be like as he stood at the helm of his ship. Once the picture formed in his mind he couldn't let it go. He couldn't avoid her forever if he hoped to get her to want to stay with him. He figured he could fight his desire for her if he had something to keep his hands busy. There would be no harm in allowing her to keep him company as he kept the ship on course. His hands would remain damn near tied to the helm allowing him to refrain from giving into his baser instincts.

"Yeah," he murmured. "I don't mind if you keep me company. Follow me."

He turned away from her and began to stroll toward the wheel that steered the ship. As he approached, he saw the first mate keeping it steady and on course. He didn't know for sure if Lilliana followed him, but he figured she must have considering she asked to keep him company.

"I'm here to relieve you. Go get some sleep so you can take over later on this evening," he told his first mate.

"Aye, Aye Captain. I'm mighty tired. I'll see you later. Good day miss."

Rand turned and watched as the first mate bowed his head to Lilliana. She returned the gesture before joining him at the helm. She sat down on the deck, crossed the legs, and rested her back on the mast near the helm. Her hands rested on the deck as she leaned back to look at the sky.

"What is running through your mind?" he asked her.

"Have you ever looked at clouds and thought they reminded you of something?"

"No, I can't say I have."

"My brother and I used to play this game as children. We would lie down on the ground and watch as the big fluffy clouds floated by us. Sometimes they reminded of us of things in our lives: a bunny, a flower, or even a horse drawn carriage. It became one of our favorite games. When I looked up at the sky I remembered what a great childhood I had."

"Are you feeling a little homesick?"

"No not at all. I just wished you had even an ounce of what I had growing up. I had two adoring parents and you didn't even have one."

"I told you not to feel sorry for me, Lily. I'm content with how my life turned out."

"That doesn't mean that you shouldn't strive for more from life, Rand. You deserve everything, happiness included. You're a good man and you should have a little joy," she told him.

"I promise you I will," he said with a cocky smile. "It's just a work in progress."

"Good," she said with an impish smile. "In the meantime, I'll do my part in ensuring you continue to work on it."

He laughed and turned his attention back to keeping the ship on course. They sat in silence for an hour before she got up and stretched her legs. She walked over to him, wrapped her arms around his waist, and rested her head on his back. Rand enjoyed the feel of her arms wound around him. He could almost hear his heart drumming in his ears as it began to beat faster. He closed his eyes and absorbed the feeling. If he could he would turn around and hug her close to him, but he had to keep his attention on the helm of the ship.

In that moment he knew he loved her, because with her arms enveloping he let himself feel for the first time in his life. Rand had been alone his whole life. He didn't depend on anyone and didn't look to anyone else to fulfill any of his needs. Lilliana made him want things he never knew he wanted. With her he could feel himself lighten inside. He thought he didn't want anyone in his life until her. That need had been buried deep inside of him a long time ago.

"As fun as this has been I'm kind of tired. I'm going to go lay down in my cabin. If you want me you know where to find me," she told him.

Rand nodded in agreement. "That I do."

He watched for a moment as she traipsed across the deck. Enjoying the view of her derriere in breeches one last time, he hoped she continued to dress in a similar fashion the rest of the voyage. He let out a small breath of relief once he could no longer see her. He had managed to keep his hands to himself and have a pleasant conversation with her. He only had to make it another two weeks and get her safely tucked away at her family plantation.

CHAPTER 9

Lily walked out of her cabin and up to the deck. Rand hadn't openly admitted to it but she knew that he had been avoiding her. Once she tracked him down he at least allowed her to keep him company. She hoped to further her agenda and get him to see how an affair would benefit them both. To be honest, she wanted more than an affair—she wanted him to be her lover for life. Marriage still seemed too risky of an endeavor for her, but the more time she spent with Rand the more she knew she needed him in her life. Her plans now included him at her side. She just had to find a way to make that happen.

She roamed aimlessly along the deck and stared out into the ocean pondering what the next step in her plan should be. Seduction could hold the key to achieving her goal. Perhaps it was time to discover where the captain slept. She could ambush him in his cabin and let things take their natural course. Rand had said if he wanted her he would do it at a time of his choosing, but so far that time had not taken place. Lilliana was beginning to get restless waiting for him to make a move. She did not do well sitting idly by waiting for something to happen. Her nature leaned more towards taking action and seeing what happened afterward.

Not watching where her feet took her she ran into a deck hand and fell back on her derriere. She braced herself with her hands and looked up into a pair of brown eyes and a concerned frown.

"I'm sorry miss. I didn't mean to knock you down," he apologized.

"No it's not your fault..." She realized she didn't know his name. She stared at him a bit bewildered; Lilliana hadn't bothered to get to know anyone on board the ship. It gave her an idea on what to do to not only gain Rand's attention, but also help to alleviate some of her boredom.

"Sal," the deck hand told her.

"What?" Did he just say something about sailing?

"My name is Sal, miss."

"Oh. I feel silly now. I thought you were talking about the sails."

"I never thought about that actually. Sal is just a nickname."

"Really? What's your actual name?"

"Salvatorio," he said with a grimace. "It's a bit long, but it's a family name."

"I kind of like it." She smiled. "Sal perhaps you can help me with something."

"I will if I can, but first let me help you up."

He held out his hand and Lilliana gave him hers. Sal helped pull her up so she stood beside him.

"Thank you."

"You're welcome. What can I help you with?" he asked.

"I'm going a bit stir crazy. Do you happen to play any card games?"

"I'm fairly good at whist. I could get a couple of other men to play a game with you. A few of us have some free time right now," Sal replied.

"Oh splendid. I just need to retrieve my cards from my trunk. Where would you like to meet?"

"We can meet in the galley. We have a couple hours before the next meal. After that we are back on duty."

"Good. I shall see you soon then." Lilliana nodded and walked off.

When she reached her cabin she dug through the trunk for her cards. She didn't think Rand would like the idea of her playing cards and entertaining some of the crew. The only thing she had uncertainty about was how to get him to realize she was embroiled in a game of whist with some of his deck hands. She hoped that he would just stumble upon them, and she could get both of her agendas accomplished. Locating the cards, she put them in the pocket of her trousers and skipped up toward meet them in the galley. She sashayed as she made her way to the galley with a huge smile on her face. When she entered the room she saw three men sitting at the table. Sal she knew from her little accident on the deck.

"Good you are all here. Introduce me to your friends, Sal," she demanded.

"This guy here with the hook nose is Jimmy and the scary looking one is Georgie." Sal introduced her to his two shipmates.

She raised her eyebrows at him. "Scary?"

"I'm harmless, I can't help how big I am," Georgie explained.

"All right then. Let's get started. I'll cut the cards first to see who we partner up with." Lilliana began to shuffle the cards as she spoke. She cut the cars and drew a seven. The men followed suit and cut the deck to reveal a card. Sal drew an eight, Georgie a jack, and Jimmy a king.

"It looks like I'm partners with Sal. Do you mind if I deal first?" Lilliana asked.

"No, I don't see any reason why not." Georgie replied. The other two murmured their consent as well.

Lilliana sat down and began to shuffle the cards with dexterous hands. She placed them to her left to let Georgie cut them. She picked them back up and started to deal thirteen cards face down to each of them. After dealing all the cards, she flipped the top one over to reveal the trump.

"Hearts are trump gentlemen. Let's begin." She told them.

With a laugh they grabbed their cards and began to play in earnest. They played a grueling game for an hour before Rand found them. Sal and Lilliana were ahead, but barely. She was so engrossed in the game she hadn't realized he had walked in until he spoke.

"What are you up to?" Rand demanded.

She looked up into his eyes and smiled. "I think that's fairly obvious. We are playing Whist."

"Not a good idea. Time to break this game up. Sal, Jimmy, Georgie go see the bosun and report for duty."

"But we have an hour until..." Sal began to say.

Rand interrupted, "Don't argue. If you want to keep your position once we reach port you will follow my orders."

The three of them got up and walked away grumbling as they left the room.

"Was that necessary? We were having fun." Lilliana's voice filled with anger.

"Yes. I don't believe these men will over step any boundaries, but I happen to know that you want to lose that innocence of yours. I won't have you tempting them into doing something to jeopardize their livelihoods."

"Don't be ridiculous. I had no intention of propositioning any of them. I do have standards."

"Do you? You damn near accosted me the first day on the ship. How am I to know exactly what you will or will not do?"

"That's not fair. You are the only man I have ever asked that. I truly believed you would make a wonderful lover. Apparently I need to once again readjust my views. Clearly I was mistaken on your worthiness."

"Oh, so now I'm not good enough?" he asked. "Does that mean you are going to find another one of the men and ask them help you lose your innocence?"

Rand's face began to get red with each word he enunciated. His eyes shot daggers in her direction as he folded his arms across his chest.

"Maybe I should. You don't want me so what difference does it make who I give myself to?" Lilliana glared at him.

"I never said I didn't want you."

"Well, you sure fooled me. You keep avoiding me and definitely turn down every offer I make to you. You win, I give up."

Lilliana got up to storm away, but Rand grabbed her hand and spun her into his arms. She tilted her head to look up into his eyes. The lines of his mouth were tight as he pressed them together and stared at her.

"You can't give up. I won't allow it."

"It's not up to you to allow anything, Rand. You have no right to dictate to me."

He ignored her word and with tenderness lowered his lips to hers. This kiss was different as he coaxed her into yielding to him. Slow and gentle he caressed her in such a way her anger evaporated. A different kind of passion took its place. Heat spread through her and the kiss took on another level. It didn't take long before she ran her hands through his hair and pulled him closer to her. The kiss overtook them as they battled for control. Determined to win, Lilliana took a different strategy. In this war between them he had stepped back and took control of the situation. He always had the upper hand. That needed to change if she wanted to win. So much as she enjoyed the kiss she knew it needed to end. In order for her to get him where she wanted him he needed to chase her. This game needed to change, and she knew how to make that happen. She pulled away from him and took a step away to gain some distance.

"You don't get to do that whenever you want, Rand. I rescind my offer. I don't want to be your lover anymore." She licked her lips. "The kisses have been enjoyable, but this just isn't working for me. Maybe you're right; I need to look into finding someone else to introduce me to the art of love making."

She saw the dumbstruck look on his face before she turned and walked away. Maybe now things would go her way. She hoped she didn't miscalculate in her scheme and he didn't do the opposite; her intention was to present him with a challenge. All she could do now was sit back and wait to see if he took the bait.

CHAPTER 10

R and stood there and watched Lily walk away. Her beautiful derriere displayed nicely in her trousers. He wanted to cup her ass in his hands and pull her back into his arms. The more he saw her wearing men's attire the more he desired her. *Who am I kidding? I will want her no matter what she is wearing.* Damned if he didn't understand what the hell just happened between them? That kiss amped up things, and he wanted to strip all of her clothes off and just give in to her demands. He should be glad she halted things when she did, but all it did was leave him confused. No way in hell was he going to allow her to find another lover. If he had to give in to her demands first and convince her around to marriage he would. That plan didn't sit too well with him though. He wanted her to believe marriage between them was a good thing. Passion could be fleeting, and he wanted more than that with her. He needed her to love him as much as he had grown to love her.

He scrubbed his hands over his face and weighed his options. Perhaps avoiding her wasn't the best idea. Clearly she didn't want him to keep his hands off of her so he would just give her want she wanted. Short of the actual act that is, he still believed it was best to wait before making love to her. He believed they could be happy together and wanted Lilliana to be his wife. The best way to start changing her mind was to give her a little taste of what that future could hold. Once she started to crave him and what he could do for her it wouldn't take much for the rest of it to follow. With that idea in his head he decided to pay her a visit in her cabin. *Don't want me anymore? Well we will just see about that.*

Rand sauntered out of the galley and down to Lilliana's cabin. He rapped lightly on her door and waited for her to open it. When she did he couldn't help the slight intake of breath at the sight of her. Her hair was floating down her back in endless black waves. She still wore her trousers and tunic. Her blue eyes shined as she looked up at him.

"What do you want Rand? I thought we settled everything."

"You may have, but I'm not nearly done with you."

"Well that's a shame because as far as I'm concerned there isn't anything else between us. You can leave now."

She started to shut the door, but he stopped it with his hand. He pushed the door open and strode inside of her cabin. He shut the door with a quiet click behind him and turned the lock.

"What are you doing?" Lilliana asked.

"I believe we have a few things to discuss."

He stalked toward her. She took a few steps back to retreat from him. Tripping over her feet, she almost fell. Rand caught her, pulling her into his arms.

"This isn't a good idea." Lilliana said. Her breaths came out in small pants. A rosy glow started to form on her cheeks, and her eyes became glassy. All he did was hold her and rub her back gently with his fingers. He wanted her to become accustomed to his arms wrapped around her. They did need to talk before he demonstrated what he came to her cabin for.

"I'm tired of good ideas. I think it's time I did something I wanted for a change. Starting with how much I want you. I refuse to let you give up on me...on us."

"I already told you..."

"You will not find another lover. You're mine."

"I belong to no one. You best realize that now," Lilliana said with conviction.

"No. You do. You belong to me. And I will tell you exactly why."

"Oh do tell this should be interesting," her reply scathing.

"Because no one else will ever be your equal and because I also belong to you. We are a pair and we belong together. No one else will do for me anymore than any other man will be for you. Stop fighting it."

"Right. Cause I'm the one that's been hiding and avoiding you."

"I'm done. I give up. You said I won, how could I have won, if I don't have you? I'm here and I will show you what it can be like between us."

"You're going to make love to me now?"

He could hear the surprise in her voice and he smiled. "Not exactly. We are going to take this slow. Passion done right is savored. I plan on enjoying every inch of you until you beg for mercy."

"I don't beg."

"You will," he promised.

Pushing her hair aside he caressed her cheek with his lips. Light kisses feathered across her forehead and nose to finally rest on her lips. He tasted her lips with his. Lilliana moaned and pressed her body against him and rubbed her breasts against his chest. He could feel himself harden as her hands roamed across his back. Reaching under her shirt his hand found her breast, and he pinched her nipple between his thumb and finger. He wanted to feel her everywhere. Spinning them around he pressed her against the door and lifted her up.

"Wrap your legs around my waist," he ordered.

Once he had her in the position he wanted, he lifted her shirt and placed his mouth on one of her rosy nipples, and Lilliana groaned with pleasure. He licked and raked his teeth over them until they were pebbled like tiny red berries. He started to rain kisses along her neck and then nibbled on her ear lobe. Her hands pulled at his hair and yanked the silky strands back so she could place her mouth on his. He swung her around, walked her over to the bed, and laid her down. Taking a step back he could see her face flushed with desire and heavy pants leaving her mouth. She sat there staring at him.

"What are you waiting for? Join me."

"No. This is all we are doing tonight. I told you I'm taking my time."

She picked up the nearest object and hurled it at him. It happened to be a heavy book, and he barely dodged before it smacked him in the head instead hitting the wall behind him with a loud bang.

"You are the most frustrating man. Just go before I cause you bodily harm. I hate you."

"No you don't," he said with a laugh. "That's why you're so frustrated. We will continue this at a later time. There are a few things I want from you before we take that final step."

"Too bad. You're not getting them"

"Oh I will. You will gladly give them to me too."

"No, not a chance in hell," she shouted.

"Oh yes, love. I will leave you now. We will table this discussion for when we make port. We should be arriving in South Carolina sometime tomorrow. Good night."

Rand turned and left her to think about his parting words. He would get her to agree to marry him when they arrived. She might not love him yet, but she would. He was willing to settle on passion for now.

CHAPTER 11

The afternoon sun shined brightly in the sky and beamed down on top of her with brilliance and warmth. Lilliana looked out at the approaching land mass from the deck of the ship. When she decided to shirk her parent's mandates and travel to South Carolina she had never envisioned a journey quite like the one experienced for the past three weeks. Spending time with Rand and getting to know him had been a torturous experience. The man made her feel things she never wanted to feel before. She didn't believe loving any man was a good choice, but here she was letting that unwanted emotion wash over her. Still she didn't want anything of a permanent nature from him. She may have foolishly fallen in love with him, but her views on anything long term hadn't changed. Marriage was still out of the picture for her.

Rand's visit to her cabin the night before had left her hot and needy. She did everything she could think of to get him to succumb to her way of thinking. Nothing in her arsenal had worked in her favor and it might be time to concede defeat. Rand had an agenda of his own and it didn't mesh with hers. Now they were approaching the port of Charleston. Soon she'd be separated from him, never to see his handsome features again. He hadn't given in and become her lover, but perhaps there was a way to still make that happen.

He said he wanted to discuss something with her once they docked at port. There had to be a way to get him to agree to an affair, but she hadn't thought of a means of accomplishing that feat. So with a heavy heart she sighed the closer the ship came to port. No, this journey hadn't gone has she planned at all.

"Why do you look so sad?" she heard Rand say from behind her. "You're almost to your desired destination."

"I don't know what's bothering me. I feel like something good has ended." She wrapped her arms around herself as if to ward off a chill. "There's this feeling of dread that has taken root deep down in my soul."

"It doesn't have to," he whispered in her ear.

She turned around to look into his eyes. Lilliana could see the same anxiety reflected back at her. Rand wanted her, and it appeared like he had some idea on how to make that happen.

"I suppose not," she said.

"I've been meaning to ask you something."

"What's that?"

She had always been a very curious person. Rand needed to get on with whatever he wanted to discuss with her. This hot and cold nonsense was starting to get on her nerves. He needed to just give in already or let her go.

"How do you plan on getting yourself and your trunks to the plantation?"

That's all he had to ask her? Disappointment flowed through her as she let his words crash through her heart. He hadn't wanted to find a way to spend time together. That didn't mean she couldn't find a way to make it happen. Lilliana had a strong will and determination that rivaled any army general. Never had she failed to achieve a goal she set for herself, yet she couldn't help feeling rejected.

"Oh that," she said without enthusiasm. "I sent a letter on the mail packet before we left, letting them know of my arrival. If everything went as it should the overseer will have a carriage waiting to transport me."

"What will you do if the letter didn't arrive in time?" he asked.

"I don't know, I'm sure I'll think of something."

"Because you always do," he said with sarcasm in his voice.

"Precisely. I can take care of myself."

She watched as he rubbed his temples in frustration. Lilliana knew that she could be a bit vexing and understood his actions. Being aware of her faults did not endear her to his dilemma though; she had her own issues to deal with. Her nature did not allow her to give him any relief. He would need to find a way to work through his aggravation all on his own.

"All right," he finally said. "Let me know if the carriages arrives or not."

"Fine."

"I mean it Lily. I want to know either way so I can see you off."

"Because you care so much about my welfare," she said sarcastically.

"Are you trying to make me angry?" he asked. "I do care about you and you know that. I also want to have a discussion with you before you run off, but I have a few things to take care of before I can have a proper conversation."

"I am just in a mood." Lilliana explained, "I won't run off without talking to you before I leave."

"I need to get back to my crew and help them with the ship. Do you need anything before I leave?" he asked. "Will you be all right if I leave you alone here?"

"Of course, don't be silly. I already told you I could take care of myself. It's not like I'm about to jump ship or something. Go do what needs to be done to dock the ship. I have a plantation to get to later today."

"Okay. I will find you later. Do not leave without seeing me first, promise me."

"I won't, I promise."

If she truly had to say goodbye, she wanted something to remember him by. A kiss she would never forget. They had already kissed a few times but, Lilliana knew she would never tire of kissing Rand. After the first one it had become her favorite activity. If another man kissed her, she knew it would not inspire the same feelings that Rand's did. No man would make her feel quite the same way.

Lilliana enjoyed watching Rand stroll along deck giving orders to his crew members. He had an authoritative tone in his voice, and they all jumped at his commands. She missed him already and their separation hadn't happened yet. However would she get by knowing she wouldn't see him each morning? A sting of pain hit her chest at the thought of never seeing him again. She couldn't explain the feeling in her chest. Could it be love? Did she go and allow herself to fall in love with Rand? Surely she hadn't been that stupid.

The ship docked at the port in Charleston, and they dropped the anchor. Once they secured the vessel Lilliana only had to wait for them to bring her chests from below. She had already meticulously packed her belongings securely in her trunks. Lilliana scanned the dock to see if anyone from the plantation had arrived to retrieve her. She wanted to get to her new home as soon as possible. No carriages appeared to be anywhere near the wharf. Her heart sank with the realization that she would need to find another mode of transportation to her family's plantation.

Either the letter hadn't made it to the plantation or they didn't have any real idea when the ship was expected to dock. She had only given them an estimation of when her arrival would be. Depending on the wind available ship speeds varied making it difficult to determine an exact time a ship might dock at port. Still even with only a broad idea of when to expect her they should still be waiting for her. The overseer would know to account for the variations and make the necessary adjustments. It might be an inconvenience to come and check each day, but that was one of his duties. That must mean the missive she sent got lost or delayed somewhere along the way.

"Did your transport arrive?"

She turned to see Rand standing behind her. Sometimes she thought he had the worst timing, or perhaps the best. He always seemed to appear when she needed his assistance most. After all she wouldn't have been able to sail to

Charleston without his aid. It looked like she would now need him to help her find a way to her plantation.

"No. It looks like my message may have been waylaid," she replied.

"Don't worry about it. I had a feeling that this might happen. I will ensure you make it to your destination. It just might take a bit longer than you planned."

"How much longer?" she asked.

"A night perhaps, I will have to arrange for a carriage to take you to your plantation. In order to do that, I'll have to go to shore and hire one for the journey. I'm unsure how long that will take and I still have a few things to do on board the ship. You are welcome to stay aboard in your cabin or I can escort you to a local inn. If it's possible to take you this evening I will make sure you get there."

"No, don't rush on my account. I can handle one more night on board the ship if you don't mind. I think I'd prefer to stay in my cabin. At least I know what to expect from the accommodations."

It also might give her another opportunity to have Rand as a lover. He wanted to discuss something with her perhaps that was his plan all along.

"Good." He nodded in approval. "I would feel better knowing you are safely on board the ship. You never know what you will find in an inn."

"Thank you for helping me. I know you don't have to."

"Yes, I do. I would never forgive myself if something happened to you, Lily. Your well-being is very important to me."

"I suppose I should make myself comfortable in my cabin. I had hoped to go on land and see a little more of the country I am to call home," she said whimsically.

"If you are willing to stand my company I can take you on a small tour of Charleston when I go to arrange for a carriage. We will have to walk and will only be able to see the downtown area, but I think you will enjoy it. There is nothing like Southern hospitality."

"I'd like that very much," Lilliana said with a small smile on her face.

"Good be ready in an hour and we will go to shore. While

we are out we can stop some place for a meal and finally have that conversation. There's something I want to ask you."

"What?"

"Not now Lily, later will come soon enough."

"All right. Come get me in my cabin when you are ready to depart," she told him.

He nodded in assent and walked off to finish whatever a captain needed to once they docked at a port. She admired his handsome face and commanding presence and couldn't wait to spend the afternoon with him strolling along Charleston's streets. Maybe somewhere along the way she would figure out how to spend more time with him. Of course that could be the very thing he wished to discuss with her. She had no idea what his plans included. Hopefully he had something in mind that would allow them to see each other again. Rand may be planning to sail again very soon. Lilliana wanted him to stay with her long enough for them to become lovers, finding a way to make that happen eluded her. No time to worry about what may or may not happen. Lilliana did have one thing to look forward to and focusing on the positive had always been instinctive for her. For now she would go down to her cabin and rest for the upcoming adventure. She had a new town to learn and fall in love with.

CHAPTER 12

The culmination of Rand's life summed up to one thing, loneliness. That realization hit him hard when he discussed it with Lilliana while they were out at sea. Before Lily he had been blind to the reality his life had become. She breathed life into him. He hoped the journey from England to North Carolina had endeared her to him. He believed she wanted him, but was that enough for her to agree to be with him forever? She was an intrinsic part of what he wanted for his life. She held all of his wishes and dreams in the palm of her hands. He knew she wanted to live on the plantation, and he would do whatever it took to make that desire a certainty for her. So with nervousness coursing through his veins he approached her cabin door and knocked on it.

"Come in," she called from behind the door.

Rand walked inside at her bidding. She was sitting on her bed reading a book. Her black curls were falling loosely around her shoulders. Lilliana looked up at him, her blue eyes beaming with questions.

"It could have been anyone knocking. You should have at least gotten up to see who decided to rap at your door," he scolded her.

"It only could've been you. I didn't have expectations for anyone else to call on me." Lilliana shrugged and set the book down next to her. "You didn't have to knock you know. You have an open invitation to visit me any time you like."

Did she still believe that propositioning him would work? He would seriously like to take her up on her offer of just a liaison, but he wanted so much more. He hadn't planned on discussing what he wanted until later. She needed to understand that a love affair would never happen between them. Lilliana deserved everything he had to offer her. He just needed her to accept what he proposed for their future.

"Yeah, I believe you said something similar before," he replied.

"I've been waiting for you for what seems like forever," Lilliana exclaimed. "Why do you keep resisting? We are friends, right? I think that will make us the best lovers because we understand each other."

"No, becoming your lover will make us more than friends. I doubt we could remain anything resembling friendship once the affair ended. If you want to be just friends I suggest you forego the idea we become lovers. It's not something that can be separated. That kind of relationship changes things. I'd want more and you would too. You just don't realize it because of your innocence. Make up your mind one or the other because I refuse to only be your friend. I want a hell of a lot more than that from you."

"Perhaps you could define what constitutes more for you? I don't know how much I'm willing to give."

"More means everything a man could want from a woman. Probably more than even that. I want you to belong to me in every possible way."

Lilliana stood up and walked over to him. She placed her hand on his chest and looked up into his eyes. Her eyes pleaded with him, and it broke his heart that he couldn't be what she wanted him to be. She must understand how it needed to be in order for them to have any chance of a decent relationship. He offered her all of himself and he desired the same from her.

"That may be a bit more than I want. What you are asking of me scares me more than I can express with mere words. I don't give control over easy. If there is a person I could do that with, it would be you. I'm just not so sure I am capable of allowing you to have that much power over me." Lilliana took a few steps away from him putting some distance between them as she spoke.

"I need you Lily. I don't want to change you. I happen to like you the way you are. If you want me, even a little, I need you to take a chance. There is no maybe in this situation. It's all or nothing."

"So I either agree to go along with your plan or you leave me to what? Forget I ever existed? Are you capable of doing that? I don't know if I could ever erase you from my memories. I like you, Rand. A lot more that I thought I could possibly ever like a man. Generally they are worthless to me. Most of them see dollar signs when they look at me."

"And you think I'm like them?" he asked bewildered. "First off, they are all fools if they only see you as a way to gain extra funds. You are the most beautiful woman I've ever met. I see you as a woman not a way to pad my finances."

"Don't act so offended, I meant what I said. I'm very fond of you. I didn't mean to imply you only saw money when you looked at me. I'm just stating how my beaus of the past have viewed me. You are the only male outside of my father and brother that I respect," she told him. "I want you to understand that you are the only male, outside of my family, I could ever possibly trust."

"I see."

"No, I don't think that you do. You mean an awful lot to me Randall Collins. I really do want to attempt more with you. I just don't see that we need to go beyond what I am offering you."

The conversation had derailed, and it looked like he needed to put it back on track.

"I had hoped to convince you that being with me would be not only the best thing for me, but also for you," he replied.

"What do you mean?"

He could hear the anxiety in her voice as the words left her mouth. Lilliana paced through the room and wrung her fingers together. She frowned, and her forehead crinkled up with confusion. Even though this escalated his plans he knew that he had to lay everything out for her—a decision had to be made. If they had a chance of moving forward, he needed her to agree to everything.

"I want to ask you something. I have been thinking about it for a while now," he began. "I know that we both had a different idea of what our future would hold, but I like to think that all changed on our journey."

Lilliana's forehead creased with uncertainty. She remained silent for several seconds before she responded.

"I suppose on some level that is true. What is it that you want to ask me?"

"I think we both have a certain amount of affection for each other. I believe we work well together and could potentially make each other very happy. What I mean is...what I want to ask you..." Rand said his voice shaking and cracked with emotion.

Why did he find it so hard to get the words out? Could he make it any harder on himself? She just stood there in front of him patiently waiting and he stumbled over his words. He just needed to say them and believe she would give him the answer he desired.

"Will you please marry me?" He breathed a sigh of relief as he finally managed to get the words out.

"You want me to be your wife?"

"With all my heart."

Lilliana crossed the distance of the room and stopped directly in front of him. She looked into his eyes and searched for something. He didn't know what, he just knew she was trying to figure him out and appeared to think the answer might reveal itself on his face.

"Why?" she finally asked.

"I thought I explained about the fondness I have for you and how well we are together. We have a spark between us that is dying to ignite. Please consent to be my wife, Lily. I can't just be your lover or your friend. I need all of you."

"You really believe we can make it work?" Lilliana asked. "Because I never intended on getting married. I explained that to you. Why would I have changed my mind? I wanted a lover not a husband."

"I honestly do. I think that we have a better chance than most at making a marriage work," he replied.

"I need more convincing. I don't believe marriage is for me. I need a reason that will make me want to tie myself to you."

She needed more convincing? How did she expect him to convince her? Rand stared at her for several minutes as he weighed his options. He reached down and picked up her hand and pulled her closer to him. With her hand still encased in his, he placed it over his heart and wrapped his free arm around her waist. His heart beat rapidly as he stared into the depths of her blue eyes. Her tongue darted out, and she licked her pink lips, wetting them in expectation. Rand placed his lips on hers and began to kiss her, coaxing her mouth open with fine tuned passion. Lily's free hand began to roam through his hair, tousling it with eager frenzy. He put a small amount of distance between them and began a trail of feather light kisses over her cheeks and down the arch of her neck. A soft moan vibrated against her throat as he caressed it with his lips. Her pulse raced beneath his fingers, and he couldn't tell the difference between the beats of her heart against his drumming rapidly in his ears. Passion ignited fast between them. Their shared ecstasy was never in doubt, only whether or not they would share it for a lifetime.

Rand needed her to agree to be his wife. He hoped that by giving her a small taste she would see that they were meant to be. That this thing between them wouldn't go away after a few times of loving each other. They needed forever to explore each other and the desire that built each time they came together. He released her and backed up a little bit to look her directly in the eyes. They were still flushed with unspoken yearning. He took a deep breath and told her his view on their situation.

"It's time to make a decision. I already explained I require everything from you. I want to wake up each morning by your side and know that you're mine. I want the privilege of making love to you whenever I want and knowing you want that too. If you don't agree to marriage we won't have that. Do you really only want one night? Wouldn't it be so much better to have every night in each other's arms?"

"That does hold some appeal but why would we need to

get married to have that. We can still do that without marriage."

"And what if we have children? Do you want them to grow up with that stigma? No. I want it all. Please agree to marry me."

"What about your ships? You said I'd have every night but not if you go off sailing for months at a time."

"I don't plan on sailing again once we are married. There are plenty of men who would love to earn a decent wage and captain my ships for me. I can run the business from here in Charleston and stay with you." Rand caressed her back with his hand. "I used to think the business was all I wanted. Everything I believed about myself changed when I met you. Together we could do anything."

"All right," she said. "You do have a point."

"So, is that a yes?"

"Yes, I will marry you."

Rand pulled her into his arms and held her for a long moment before he felt he could let her go. Leaning down he kissed her forehead and again lightly on her lips as relief pour through his veins. Now that she agreed to marry him, he needed to make it official.

"Good, I'm glad you agree. While we are out we can get married."

"Are you in some kind of hurry? Why do we need to get married so fast?" she asked.

"I don't want to give you a chance to change your mind. Plus I'd like to arrive at your plantation as your husband. Once we get there I want to start our lives together and build something worth keeping forever. I don't see any reason not to begin to make that happen immediately."

"I suppose that makes sense," she said.

"Good, come with me and let's make it official."

Rand grabbed her hand in his and pulled her out of the cabin. They walked up to the deck of the ship and strolled down the gangplank onto the dock. As they roamed the streets of downtown Charleston, Rand couldn't help thinking about the happiness filling him to the brim. She had actually agreed to marry him. For a brief moment, he believed she might say no. That moment of apprehension had made him react with a bit of spontaneity. When he asked her to be his wife his original intention centered around waiting and doing everything right. He panicked and demanded an immediate ceremony for fear she might change her mind. He didn't want to take any chances that she might, with Lily anything was possible. Rand had one goal and it was to make Lily his wife. He didn't have time to worry about anything else, including how her parents would react to their sudden marriage. Viscount Torrington would put him through hell for marrying his daughter without prior permission to do so.

It didn't take them long to find the local church. The church had four long white columns in front of tall burnt red doors. The inside of the chapel had simple designs. It lacked decorations, but had detailed stained glass windows. A man with white hair dressed in the robes of a clergy knelt at the altar lost in prayer. Rand didn't want to disturb him so he led Lily toward a pew and waiting for him to finish his worship. After several minutes he stood up and realized they sat in the pews. He walked over to them and nodded to both of them.

"I am Reverend Thomas," he said. "How can I help you two?"

"We were hoping that you would be willing to marry us," Rand said.

"Certainly," the man agreed. "Did you have a special time in mind?"

"Actually we want to get married right now," Lilliana murmured.

"Really? Is there a reason you two are in a hurry?" he asked.

"Just want to start our lives together. We don't see any reason to wait," Rand responded.

"I guess I can accommodate you. We will need two witnesses," the reverend said. "Do you have anyone in mind?"

"We don't know anyone here in Charleston. We only arrived on my ship this afternoon," Rand explained.

"Well a couple of my parishioners are due to arrive any minute. We can ask them if they would be willing to stand as witnesses," he said.

"That would be lovely," Lilliana said with a smile.

"In the meantime, why don't you tell me a bit about yourselves? What are your names?"

After Rand gave the reverend their names, they heard a couple walk into the church. They all turned their attention to the new arrivals. An older couple walked up the aisle and stopped by the pew that Rand and Lily were sitting in.

"Jamieson, Eliza glad to see the two of you," the reverend said with a nod.

"We're glad to see you as well Reverend Thomas." Jamieson nodded at him. "Eliza and I are here for our monthly meeting to help the less fortunate in our community."

"Yes, before we begin I'd appreciate your assistance with another matter," the reverend told him.

"What can we do to help?" Eliza asked.

"These two young people wish to get married," the reverend responded. "Would you be willing to stand as witnesses while I perform the ceremony?"

"Oh, how wonderful. I'd be happy to," Eliza smiled.

"I will as well," Jamieson agreed.

"Perfect we have everything we need to begin if the two of you are ready." The reverend looked at Lilliana and Rand.

"We are more than ready." Rand folded Lilliana's hand within his own. "Please begin the ceremony Reverend Thomas."

"Follow me to the altar," he told them.

Lilliana and Rand got out of the pew and walked, still holding hands, up to where the reverend stood. He opened the Bible and began the ceremony to make them husband and wife. The simple wedding appealed to Rand. He liked that they were about to start their lives together without any more complications. They would still have to deal with Lilliana's family at some point, but he wouldn't have changed anything.

"You may kiss your bride," the reverend said to close the ceremony.

Rand pulled Lily into his arms and pressed his lips to hers. The kiss was simple and sweet—nothing like he wanted to do. He had a fierce desire for his beautiful bride, but he knew he couldn't give into those temptations yet. As soon as he got her back to his ship he could have her in every way he wanted. Rand had waited this long, surely he could wait a few more hours to make her completely his. He lifted his lips off of hers and raised his face to look into her eyes. A smile of happiness showed across her extraordinary face. In that moment any doubts he had fell away.

"Are you ready to leave Mrs. Collins?" he asked.

"I am more than ready Mr. Collins."

Rand turned towards Jamieson, Eliza, and Reverend Thomas.

"Thank you all for making sure we were able to have a wedding today. We are forever in your debt." He nodded in their general direction as he spoke.

"Think nothing of it young man. It's nice to see two young people in love and ready to take on the world," the reverend said.

"Nevertheless we appreciate your willingness to perform the ceremony on such short notice. Perhaps we will see you on Sundays for mass." Lilliana smiled at him.

"You are more than welcome to join our congregation," the reverend told them.

"Good day to everyone my wife and I are going to find someplace for a nice dinner."

"Best of luck to you both," the reverend said.

Rand and Lily turned and walked out of the church. Never once did they let go of each other's hands. They found a quiet place to have dinner and patiently waited for to take the next step in their growing relationship. They were now man and wife, and Rand couldn't have planned it all better if he had tried. Lilliana glowed, and he felt himself basking in it as they spent a few quiet moments just enjoying each other's company.

CHAPTER 13

A beautiful and enormous feeling swept over Lilliana as she looked at her husband. She shouldn't be surprised by how he made her feel, but every time she looked into his eyes a new thrill rolled through her. She should have expected him to want marriage, but it hadn't really crossed her mind. The more they discussed it the more it had made sense to her. It had taken her a while to admit it to herself, but Lilliana knew she loved Rand. As wonderful as the emotions coursing through her were they didn't compare to the fear of rejection. He hadn't once mentioned his own feelings. Telling him would be a risk, but surely it was worth it.

No matter how many times she let that thought roll through her mind she still had trouble believing it. A husband, she actually had willingly tied herself to someone else forever. For a person that never intended to be anyone's wife so far she found it incredibly easy to be Rand's. Admittedly they had only been husband and wife less than two hours, but everything between them had a natural and oh so right feel to it. Rand hadn't said anything about love in his proposal, and it bothered a small part of her. She needed to know that he loved her, but she would wait until he knew it as much as she did. Forcing him to say the words would take away the joy of them. They wed and for now that had to be enough.

They finished eating their meal and left to procure a coach to take them to the plantation the next day. A small bubble of excitement continued to well inside of her at the thought of them being together in every way possible. She wanted him so much. Nothing could ever change how much she loved him.

"Ah if it isn't the two newlyweds themselves," a male voice said from directly behind them said with a laugh.

Rand and Lily turned to see the witnesses from their wedding directly behind them.

"Jamieson, Eliza," Rand nodded. "We didn't expect to see you two again so soon."

"We just finished our meeting with Reverend Thomas," Eliza smiled.

"It went well, I expect," Lilliana said.

"It did indeed, "Jamieson agreed. "If I am not being to forward, can I ask you a question?"

"Of course," Rand said. "What do you want to know?"

"Well your wife looks mighty familiar to me. Where to you hail from?" Jamieson asked.

"Lily is late of London, England. She's traveling to live at her mother's plantation," Rand replied.

"Actually now it's mine." Lilliana grinned.

"What?" Rand looked surprised.

"It's my dowry. Didn't I mention that?"

"No dear, you failed to inform me of that little bit of knowledge."

"Well now you know," she said with a shrug.

"Oh, I see the resemblance, now," Jamieson said. "You are the daughter of the Viscount Torrington."

Lilliana looked up at him with shock on her face. She didn't think anyone would make the connection from her to her parents. Somehow this man knew not only them, but her relationship with them.

"You know my parents?" she asked.

"I would think so. I am the overseer of the plantation after all. I've worked for your father for years," he replied.

"How serendipitous and quite convenient," Rand said. "We were just looking to hire a carriage to take us to the plantation. Perhaps you can assist us."

"We did get a letter in the post today that Miss Marsden would be arriving shortly. It didn't mention a husband," he said.

"Well as you know that bit was last minute. You did witness the wedding after all. Its Mrs. Collins now," Lilliana told him.

"Indeed we did." Jamieson nodded. "Eliza is the housekeeper at the plantation and also my wife."

"It will be wonderful to have someone living in that big house again," Eliza beamed. "When are you planning on arriving at the plantation?"

"As soon as possible," Lilliana said. "As my husband said, we're looking for a carriage. I have a couple trunks that need to be transported from Rand's ship."

"We can help you with that. We brought a carriage to town. We can meet you at your ship. If you are ready to come tonight you can travel back with us," Jamieson said.

"Oh, that's wonderful. We thought we would have to sleep on the ship again tonight. I'd much prefer a bed that didn't rock quite so much," Lilliana said looking pleased. A joyous smile lit up her face.

"My ship is docked at the port. We can walk back there now and meet you to load the trunks onto your carriage."

"A solid plan young man. We will meet you there shortly," Jamieson answered.

Lilliana and Rand started to walk back to his ship. Once there, Rand began to order a couple of his deck hands to get Lily's trunks ready to be taken to the awaiting carriage. Lilliana leaned on the railing of the ship and surveyed her surroundings. Nothing about the day had gone as she imagined it. She found herself wed and heading off to her plantation to start her life anew.

"Are you ready to go see your plantation, dear," Rand said from behind her.

Lilliana smiled as she turned and wrapped her arms around him. She rested her head on his shoulder and for a brief moment just enjoyed the feel of his arms wrapped around her.

"Yes," she told him. "I feel like I've been waiting forever to get to where I am right now."

"We haven't arrived just yet."

"I know, but we will soon. This journey has been about more than reaching the plantation. It's also about me and what I want out of life. Thanks to you I'm realizing all of my dreams. I owe you so much."

"You don't owe me anything," he said with a shake of his head. "You have it all mixed up. It's I that owes you."

"We will have to agree to disagree," she responded.

"I have a feeling we will be doing that a lot in our lifetime."

"You may have a point," she said with a laugh. "But for now let's go to the plantation. I would like to arrive before nightfall."

"I would as well."

"Which reminds me. Did something about Jamieson seem familiar to you?" Lilliana said.

"Not particularly," Rand said.

"I don't know what it is just yet, but he reminds me of someone. I'll figure it out when I've had more time to think about. With all the excitement of the day my mind can't stay focused on one thing."

"I'm sure you will." He leaned down and placed a soft kiss on her forehead. "Let's go join them in their carriage."

"All right," she said.

Lilliana walked down to meet Jamieson and Eliza at the carriage. Once they arrived Lilliana took a moment to observe them. They were an older couple around her parent's age. "Have you been taking care of the plantation the entire time that my parents have been married?" Lilliana asked them.

"I took over shortly after your parents were married," Jamieson told her. "I used to work with your father."

"Please tell me you didn't sail with him in his pirate days," Rand exclaimed.

"Actually I used to be his first mate," Jamieson said.

Lilliana heard Rand groan at Jamieson's admission. She really didn't see why. So what if Jamieson used to be the first mate on her father's ship. That didn't make him a bad person, but perhaps she was a bit biased. She adored her father and didn't think that the fact he used to be a pirate detracted from his lovable nature.

"Oh that's wonderful. You will have to tell me some stories from when you two sailed together." Lilliana asserted.

"Well, I must admit the most interesting one involved your mother." Jamieson explained.

"I know he kidnapped her. Father used to tell us the story of how they met as a bedtime story."

"Are you serious?" Rand asked baffled.

"Of course I am. I wouldn't joke about such a thing. Their story had a very romantic element to it," Lilliana told him.

"He kidnapped her!" Rand shouted.

"What's your point?" Lilliana asked. "It led to them falling in love. You do realize I wouldn't exist if that hadn't happened."

"I do." He sighed. "That doesn't make what he did right."

"Perhaps not, but my father would never hurt my mother." She folded her hands over her chest, staring into his eyes. "Everyone is human Rand. We are all capable of making mistakes. He owned up to his and my mother forgave him. It isn't our place to judge."

"You're right, of course. I just can't wrap my head around it."

The carriage rattled along the narrow road as they talked. The journey toward the plantation amounted to a few miles outside of Charleston. Talking as they traveled helped the journey go faster, making it seem like it only took minutes to arrive.

"Well lad, the little lady is right. Thor loves Pia. That fact became evident pretty fast to the crew. If you take out the things you find atrocious it did have a romantic feel to it," Jamieson told him.

"I will have to take your word for it," Rand replied.

"Jamieson, have we met before?" Lillian asked.

"Only once, when you were about five or six years old. Your parents traveled to make sure that the plantation's assets were okay after the end of the war. You all stayed for a few months. Your mother was a bit reluctant to leave. You liked it so much that was when she declared it would be part of your dowry."

"I didn't know that. My parents never told me why they made it part of my dowry," Lilliana said. "You seem so familiar to me though, I don't think that brief meeting would have left an impression."

"No ma'am I doubt it would have. I barely saw you on that visit. I spent most of my time with your parents making sure they had all the information they sought."

She couldn't put her finger on what was so familiar about him. Lilliana was determined to figure it all out. Spending time with Jamieson and Eliza on the plantation would help her ferret out the mystery. She had time to figure out why he was so recognizable to her. Perhaps it was just because she had met him before, but she doubted it.

CHAPTER 14

The carriage pulled to a stop in front of a large plantation house with four large white columns encasing the entranceway. The house was entirely white with large windows and two large green front doors. A wide staircase led to the porch and entranceway. Rand could see why his wife wanted to live in the plantation home. It was a piece of beautiful architecture with a rich history. The fact that it had survived the war was an amazing feat. He couldn't wait to start his new life in this home with Lilliana.

Jamieson hopped down from the carriage once it was at a complete stop. First he helped Eliza down from the carriage, and then he began to reach for the trunks strapped down to the back of the carriage. Rand helped Lily from the carriage and turned to speak to Jamieson.

"I can help you with those," Rand said.

"If you are willing to help me get these up to your room I'll be much obliged."

"Most of this stuff does belong to my wife. I'd be an awful cur to leave it for you to do alone."

"I'd understand if you wanted to get settled in right away. I'm sure the journey here was quite lengthy. I appreciate your help." Jamieson nodded at Rand in appreciation.

"The faster we get these unloaded to sooner we can all relax. I'm sure you'll appreciate a little extra time to unwind."

"I do indeed. Let's get these trunks inside," Jamieson proposed. "It'll be dark soon."

Jamieson reached over and pulled the straps off of the trunks and began drag it over so it would be easier to lift. Rand stepped over by the other side. They each stood by their chosen side, lifted, and walked the trunk indoors. Rand let Jamieson lead him up the stairs to the room he would share with his wife. Once they reached the room they set the trunk by bed and went to retrieve the other trunk.

"Those trunks are a lot heavier than they look," Jamieson said once the trunks were delivered to their room.

"I have no idea what she has in any of them." Rand laughed and wiped a bead of sweat off his brow. "I am not sure I want to know either."

"Can't say I blame you. Sometimes it's best to be left in the dark."

Rand laughed again. "You may be right there."

"I am, trust me. I've been married twice and I learned the hard way not to question certain things in a woman's boudoir."

"What happened to your first wife?" Rand asked. "If I'm not being too personal that is."

"No, no it's okay. It's been a lot of years since my first wife died. I gave up on the domestic side of things after I lost her and our child. It took a lot for me to get back on my feet. Thor played a huge part in making me want to live again. Meeting Eliza made me realize I could allow myself to be happy. My wife, I loved her dearly, and I know she wouldn't have wanted me to throw my life away because she died."

"I'm so sorry. That had to be very difficult for you. I'm sorry I made you relive it even for a small moment. I couldn't imagine what I'd do if I lost Lily."

"I hope it doesn't come to that." Jamieson's face became solemn. His eyes took on a darker hue as he frowned.

Rand hoped speaking of his deceased wife and child wouldn't leave him in a melancholy mood for the rest of the night. He hated that he may have caused him any misery. Unfortunately he could relate on a small level. Growing up as an orphan gave him firsthand knowledge to the wretchedness of losing a family member. He never wanted to experience that heartache ever again. At the sound of Jamieson's voice he snapped back to the present. He couldn't let the despair of the past wrap its way around his heart again.

"Let's go downstairs. It's time for dinner and I'm sure Eliza has a wonderful meal prepared for us," Jamieson said.

The two of them left the bedroom and strolled down the stairs. Rand followed Jamieson to the dining room. They went inside the room to find Lily laughing at something Eliza had said. She looked up at him and her smile grew brighter. She motioned for him to come closer and take the seat next to her.

"Is everything all taken care of?"

"Yes. The trunks are stored up in our room."

"Good. I can unpack tomorrow," she said.

"That's a scary thought. Those trunks were quite heavy."

"I had to take what I deemed important. I don't plan on returning to England anytime soon." She shrugged.

"Yes. I can see why taking things that you needed and deemed important would top your list. If there is anything you need that you didn't bring with you please let me know."

"I don't need you to provide for me, Rand. I can take care of myself."

"I know you can, but you're my wife now. It's my privilege to see to your wants and needs. I look forward to it all."

"It feels a bit controlling to me." Lily's left eyebrow lifted widening it so the blue of her eye was more noticeable. Her cheeks flushed a pretty shade of pink as she pressed her lips together forming an appealing pucker.

"I didn't mean it to be. Forgive me?"

"You're forgiven." Lilliana leaned over and wrapped her arms around him to give him a quick hug. "I know you didn't mean it the way it sounded. Sit down and eat something. I'd like to start our first night as husband and wife on a good note."

He intended to have a beautiful wedding night with her. He had an idea on how he could make it both beautiful and wonderful. With a firm plan set in his head he sat back to enjoy the meal.

"It looks like you have prepared a lovely meal, Eliza," Rand said.

"It does indeed," Lilliana said. "If you don't mind me asking what do you call all of this?"

"We eat a light meal in the evenings. Our big meals are usually served at noon. This is just a simple meal of corn bread, frizzled beef, stewed fruits, and oyster pie." Eliza replied.

"It all looks delicious," Lilliana said. "I can't wait to sample everything."

"We also have tea or milk if you'd like," Eliza offered.

"I'll have some tea please. I haven't had a decent cup in ages."

Rand laughed. "She acts like the crossing over on my ship deprived her of the niceties in life."

"Nonsense, I had a lovely time aboard your ship. I just haven't had tea since the morning we left England," Lilliana replied. "I'm quite looking forward to a nice cup of it. If it's not too much trouble that is."

"You should know Mrs. Collins..." Jamieson began to say.

"Lily, please," she interrupted. "You've worked with my father. You can call me by my given name. My closest friends and family call me Lily. I insist you do as well."

"Lily," Jamieson began, "I received a letter from your father. I just got a chance to look over today's post."

Rand stopped eating and looked up as Jamieson spoke. It couldn't be good news he had to impart. Viscount Torrington had to be out for blood since Lilliana ran away from home. He would be in his crosshairs for assisting her in her act of defiance. Something he was not looking forward to, but knew it would be a necessary evil if he wanted to make peace with the man.

"That doesn't surprise me," Lilliana said. "What did he say?"

"He is coming for a visit. He mentioned that you might show up before him and I needed to make sure you didn't leave before he arrived."

Lilliana laughed before saying, "Why ever would he think I'd leave? I told him in the letter I left for him and mother I planned on residing here."

"Wait a minute you left them a letter? You didn't tell me that," Rand exclaimed.

"I didn't?" Lilliana answered. "I swear I mentioned it."

Rand rubbed his temples as he let her words wash over him. How could she have forgotten to mention that little tidbit to him? Didn't she believe he had a right to know something so important? "No dear, I'd have remembered you telling me that you left your ex-pirate father a letter telling him you had run away from home. In fact, you said earlier that you intended to write them once you arrived at the plantation."

"Hmmm...well I guess I do remember saying that. I didn't know how you would take it. It's not important really. I gave it to Gemma to give them once they realized I hadn't gone to stay at her country estate." Lilliana paused and looked him in the eye. "I had to do it, you know that."

"Yes, I do. I'd have just preferred knowing that you had." Rand sighed.

"Oh I see, you think I deliberately left you in the dark? Which I suppose you are right about. I had intended on letting you know at some point though. It slipped my mind. Whenever you are around me I tend to forget important matters, for more desirable ones. In my defense you never once asked for any details on what I had in the works."

"You are right once again, I didn't ask, because I really didn't care at the time," Rand agreed.

Lilliana flashed him a brilliant smile.

"I did say we would have to deal with your parents at some point."

"Indeed you did," Lilliana looked over and asked, "Jamieson, did my father give you any idea when they might arrive?"

"I'd give it a rough estimate of within a day of your arrival to a week depending on the weather for their crossing."

A day? That wasn't nearly enough time to prepare for the arrival of his wife's parents. "So it's a possibility for them to show up sometime tomorrow." Rand sat back in his chair and awaited a response to his question.

"It is," Jamieson agreed.

"We will just have to make sure we are ready for their arrival. I'm sure Torrington will want my head when he arrives," Rand replied. He folded his hands under the table and began clenching and unclenching them. He didn't want her parents to dislike him, but he didn't regret marrying Lily.

"I'm not likely to let him kill you, lad," Jamison replied.

"Nor I, as I rather like your head where it is," Lilliana agreed. "I really don't think you need to worry though, they will be happy I decided to get married. They have been pushing me towards matrimony for a while now."

"I have to agree with you. I'm rather attached to my head myself." Rand nodded at his wife. "I have to disagree with you though; we have plenty to be worried about. I know if my daughter married some random man I'd be out for blood. Just be prepared for the worst."

"I'd rather not dwell on it to much. Let's make plans for something fun instead." Lilliana said changing the subject.

He didn't want to cause Lily any stress so for her sake he would attempt to let it go. He knew she was being too nonchalant about it though.

"You could go horseback riding and learn the land you inherited," Eliza suggested.

"That's a lovely idea. Do you have horses here that we can ride tomorrow?" Lilliana asked.

"Yes, there are a few in the stable suitable for riding. I can help you when you are ready to leave," Jamieson replied.

"After breakfast we can go for a ride. Does that work for you Rand?"

"I think it's a fine idea."

"Wonderful. It will be nice to be able to ride a horse again."

"There you go picking on my ship again," Rand said with a laugh.

Lilliana stuck her tongue out at him with a playful laugh in return.

"I have fond memories of your ship. I am not the one picking on it."

"I know, dear. I'm just giving you a hard time." Rand moved to get up. "If you will excuse me, I'm tired and going to go rest in my room."

"I can come up with you," Lilliana said.

Rand stiffened at her offer to join him, but he didn't want her to come along with him just yet. He had plans for their special night. He would welcome her willingly later on, eagerly.

"No, finish your meal. Join me later. I'm not going anywhere, I promise."

Rand left them in the dining room and bounced up the stairs to the room he shared with Lily. He had an idea on how to make their first night together as husband and wife unforgettable. He needed a few things and everything would be perfect. Lilliana deserved the best and he intended to make sure she had it.

CHAPTER 15

Lilliana sat as long as she could with Jamieson and Eliza, trying her best to enjoy the food before her. It all tasted like grains of sand. What she wanted was to join her husband in their room. The food did nothing to quench her needs. Only Rand would be able to accomplish that. She had no idea what Rand was up to, but she intended to find out.

"If you will excuse me, it's time I retired. It has been a long day." Her patience had its limitations and she found herself at the edge of them as she looked over her supper companions.

"Of course, have a good night. We'll see you at breakfast," Eliza said.

Lilliana nodded at both of them as she got up from the table. She walked out of the room and with a slow gait strolled up the stairs. The staircase was wide and open with plush red velvet cascading down each step. The baluster and newels were burnt mahogany, polished to a perfect shine. The hallway wove down an intricate path that led to several bedrooms. She remembered where hers was because she loved it so much. It was located at the end of the hall on the left. The room was decorated in a mint green and browns. It reminded her of a decadent forest.

When she reached her destination she opened the door and gasped in surprise. The illumination from all of the candles bathed the room with a soft glow. Lilliana looked up and saw her husband's desire filled gaze. He had removed some of his clothing and sauntered to her side in his bare feet. Lilliana stared into his eyes as he reached up and caressed her face with one of his hand. His other arm wound around her waist and pulled her toward him.

"I've been waiting for you."

"I'm here now," she said as she licked her lips. "If you had given me a clue I'd have been here sooner."

"I don't mind. The best things are worth waiting for."

"You say the sweetest things," she whispered.

"I don't. I say what I mean." He placed a small kiss on her neck. "I feel like I've been waiting for you my whole life."

"You don't need to wait anymore. I'm here, take everything you want."

"I intend to. Now that I have you exactly where I want you, I am going to take my time...and savor every inch of you."

He leaned down and pressed his lips over hers in a light kiss. Lilliana released a small breath filled with anticipation; Rand pressed his lips more firmly to hers. He tasted wonderful, like honey and cinnamon. She let her tongue duel with his for control. Their passion escalated the longer they kissed. Lilliana raised her arms and wrapped them around his neck and pulled him closer to her.

He pulled away and looked down at her. Lilliana bit down on her swollen lip and moaned. If he didn't start giving her what she needed she had no problem forcing him to her way of thinking.

"Take it easy, love," he whispered as his lips caressed her ear. "We have all night to explore each other."

"I need so much..."

"So do I, but it will be so much better if we take our time."

"I don't want to. Please Rand."

She ran her hands through his hair and pulled his head towards hers. Their passion ignited full force. Lips, tongues, and teeth battled to get the upper hand. He turned her around and pressed her against the wall; Rand unlatched every hook of her dress and pulled it down. She didn't wear a corset so she stood before him in only her chemise and pantalettes. She could feel his body towering over her as his hands roamed her body. He continued to place little kisses along her neck and shoulders.

"I'm going to take every last stitch of clothing off of you now, Lily." His breath hot on her ears as he whispered, "Then I'm going to taste you everywhere."

She felt herself grow wet between her legs at his words. His words evoked so many different tumultuous emotions inside of her. Her skin was sensitive to his touch; every place his hands roamed she grew hotter, needier, and more desperate to see what he would do next. Rand peeled the rest of her clothing of as fast as possible and turned her back around to face him. He took a step back and let his gaze roam over her nude body. Lilliana's body heated to a scorching flame under his direct scrutiny. Looking boldly into his eyes she reached up and cupped both of her breasts in her own hands and pinched her nipples. She saw him gasp with a sharp intake of breath and slowly release it. Her desire escalated the longer he watched her.

She wanted to reach out and touch him; more importantly she wanted him to remove the rest of his clothing so she could look at his gorgeous body.

"You are stunning and you're mine."

He took a step closer to her and reached out to touch her naked body. His hands roamed over her naked breasts and plumped her nipples between his fingers. They became stiff from his ministrations, and he drew one of the nipples inside of his mouth. His tongue roamed over it and brought a long drawn out moan from her mouth.

"Please Rand, I need you."

"And I will give it to you, love. Together we will do and feel so much tonight."

He pulled her with him to the bed and laid her down with gentleness on the soft mattress. His gaze caressed her again before he lay down next to her on the bed. His hands trailed over her belly and brushed over the curls between her legs. His nimble fingers found her center as they rubbed her tender flesh. Lilliana ached so much and needed him to be inside of her. She didn't understand why he didn't make her his. He seemed to be moving too slow for her and, she had no clue how to make him go any faster. She didn't know what to expect having never made love to man before, but Rand made her want and need everything he did with her. Every sensation trailing over her body made her ache for him in so many ways.

He changed positions and crawled over top of her. He lowered his face between her legs and pushed her legs further apart. She didn't know what he intended until his lips kissed the nub between her legs. She would have squeezed his head with her legs if he hadn't been holding them in place. His tongue rolled over her sensitive flesh and she screamed.

"So beautiful," he said before he lowered his head again and started to lick her core.

The more he licked the tighter her body got in anticipation. Rand's gaze held hers for a moment as he watched something wonderful build within of her, a pressure so deep that at any moment an explosion would occur. She couldn't help being frightened by the intensity while secretly hoping for something more. He continued his relentless strokes of his tongue on her hypersensitive center. She didn't know what happened inside of her but she knew if he didn't stop she'd burst from all of the sensations. Her intuition proved right as she ruptured from the inside out. Her body quaked with uncontrollable spasms, and she screamed with each new ripple of pleasure outpouring from her body. Nothing had ever compared to what he just made her feel. She wanted to feel it again.

She looked up through hazy eyes as he undressed. Finally she would be able to see his beautiful body. Once all of his clothes were removed, he joined her on the bed again. His shoulders, chest, and arms were rippling with well-defined muscle. Light patches of hair dusted his chest and trailed down to his stomach. She looked at his thick manhood and wanted to wrap her hands around it. She couldn't help but wonder how it would fit inside of her. Every inch of him appeared too large, and she feared her body wouldn't be able to accommodate him. She really wanted to try though because she had a need building up inside of her. One she knew only he could fill.

"I think you are ready for me now," he said.

"I've always been ready for you."

"I know and we're going to do things a little differently," he whispered. "Do you trust me?"

"Always."

He rolled her on her side with her derriere facing him. He lifted her leg, pulled it over his hip and with slow thrusts started to enter her from behind. Her tight channel didn't want to let him in, but she desperately needed to feel all of him inside of her. She leaned back as he slid himself inside of her one slow inch at a time. When he reached her barrier he stopped for a moment to allow her body time to adjust, and then pushed fully inside of her. Lily's heart filled with so much love to have him joined with her. Even the brief sting of pain was worth it to know how it would feel to have him deep inside of her. She never thought she could feel so much emotion welling up inside of her. A small tear formed in the corner of her eye as her own happiness overwhelmed her. Rand waited for as she became accustomed to being filled by him, and once the ache left she started to move against him. Having him inside of her was beyond her wildest imagination. The completeness made her feel whole and part of him.

"Easy love. There is no need to rush."

"Please, Rand. Love me."

"I do, I am."

He continued to push himself in to her until he filled her completely. The completeness of his filling her had been amazing, but it didn't compare to his strokes caressing her channel. The different feelings he caused as he thrust himself in an out of her couldn't be explained. As he rocked himself inside of her, he also caressed her with his hands and lips. He pinched her nipples and rubbed them with the palm of his hands. A thousand tiny sensations roared through her body, and she knew she would explode at any minute. Just before her body detonated he leaned down and absorbed her scream with his mouth. Her core squeezed him, and she felt his seed burst within her. He wrapped his arms around her and groaned as he kissed her wild abandon.

"Lily, you undo me," he said as he trailed light kisses over her forehead and cheek.

"No more than you do me."

He slowly pulled himself out of her. Emptiness overcame her at the loss of him. She wanted more and as soon as possible. The reality of loving him had far surpassed anything in her wildest dreams. Rand got out of bed and blew out any candles still lit then crawled back in bed tugging the covers over top of them. He left a lantern lit on the bedside table to extinguish itself as the fuel burned out. He pulled Lily into his arms and held onto her as if his life depended on it.

Lilliana couldn't sleep. Emotions filled her to the brim in a turbulent fashion. She had trouble stilling them long enough to relax and fall to sleep. She could hear Rand's even breaths as he slept beside her. She wondered how he could remain so calm as her own emotions jumped all over the place. Lilliana needed him to know how much he meant to her.

"Rand, are you asleep?" she asked quietly.

No answer came from him. She found it incredulous he could sleep at a time like this.

"I guess you are," she said as she snuggled closer to him. "If you were awake I'd tell you how much you mean to me. I'd let you know that you changed me. I know that you don't love me yet, but I can love you enough for the both of us. In time I know you will love me too. You just need to allow yourself to feel it. I can wait for you."

She closed her eyes and took a deep breath.

"I can wait because you are worth waiting for. I just wish you stayed awake to allow me to say this all to you. I'm going to do it again when you will actually hear me." She caressed his cheeks lightly with the tip of her fingers. "I don't mind telling you I love you a million times."

With a smile on her lips she opened her eyes to gaze at his handsome face. Yes, she could and would do whatever it took to make him feel how much she loved him. For now she would lose herself in some much needed sleep. The morning would arrive soon enough and she could tell him that fact over breakfast if needed.

CHAPTER 16

R and held Lilliana tight. He heard every word she said the night before. He just hadn't known how to respond to them. Rand no longer had a lonely feeling roaming through his soul. Lilliana's confession had meant so much to him. She had given him a gift he didn't think he could ever return. He didn't feel worthy of her love, but he was selfish and would not refuse it. He needed her and would never let her go. Lilliana fit into his life perfectly—in a way he never knew he needed. She gave him a new purpose, and he intended to make sure she never regretted gifting him with her love. After she fell asleep, he watched her all night. A more beautiful sight didn't exist for him. His wife had sneaked into his heart and seized it when he let his guard down. She owned his soul.

While his gaze remained on her she rolled over and opened her eyes. "Good morning," she said and rubbed her eyes with her hands.

"Good morning to you beautiful." He gave her a quick kiss. "Are you ready to start your day?"

"Can't we just stay in bed all day, I can think of a few things we can do," she said coyly.

"Well I never said we had to get out of bed just yet." Rand kissed her again.

She wound her arms around his neck as he deepened the

kiss. When he lifted her leg around his hip, he could feel her wetness stroke his shaft. The need to be inside her grew as his cock hardened. He trailed kisses down her neck and he pushed himself inside of her. She moaned with pleasure. With slow strokes, he slid in and out of her tight channel until her breaths became heavy on his shoulder. She bit his ear and licked away the pain.

"You feel so wonderful inside of me," she said with a groan. "Give me more Rand. I need it."

At her words he began to move harder and faster inside of her. A squeal of pleasure filled the room as he rolled Lily on her back and raised her hips under his hands. She wrapped her legs around his waist and held him tight against her. He rode her hard until she screamed as her orgasm rolled over her. He followed her into bliss a short time after her.

Rand held her tight in his arms when each wave of pleasure reached in and grabbed a hold of his soul. He rolled them onto their sides with heavy breaths coming out of his mouth. His breathing started to slow down and even out as his body became more relaxed. He didn't think loving her could get any better, but this time the pleasure had been even more intense than the first time.

"Darling, I do believe you have found your calling."

"And what's that?" she asked with boldness in her voice. Her fingers trailed lightly down his back.

"Loving me," he said and kissed her forehead.

"Always."

"I hate to say it, but I do believe we need to start moving now."

"Must we?"

"Yes, Jamieson and Eliza are expecting us for breakfast and we did make plans to go horseback riding. Unless you have changed your mind about getting a look at this land you inherited."

"I do want to go horseback riding. So let's start the day."

"Good. Let's get moving. I'm famished."

"So am I," she said with a laugh. "And yes, for food."

They got up and quickly got dressed. Rand grabbed Lily's hand as they strolled down the stairs into the dining room. Eliza and Jamieson were already seated at the table. Jamieson had a paper spread out in his arms as he read it. Eliza sipped from her cup as she gazed at nothing in front of her.

"Good morning," Lilliana said them both.

Jamieson closed his paper and looked over at the two of them as they sat down at the table. Rand nodded to him.

"I trust you both slept well," Jamieson said.

"Indeed we did," Lilliana said as a small blush grew on her cheeks.

It did his heart good to see that his wife could be embarrassed. He believed her brazen attitude overflowed every aspect of her life.

"Can I get you two any coffee or tea?" Eliza asked. "We have a small breakfast bar and we serve ourselves. There are hard-boiled eggs, sausages, and toast. A variety of jams as well as some scones if you like."

"I'd like some tea," Lilliana answered.

"What about you, Mr. Collins?"

"Coffee, and please call me Rand. I don't see why we should remain formal."

"Thank you," she said with kindness. "I don't see any reason either. I will get your drinks and be back soon."

He watched as she left the room. Eliza was a kind woman. He liked to think his mother would have been like her.

"Would you like me to make a plate for you?" he asked Lilliana.

"Oh, that would be lovely, thank you."

"Anything in particular you want?"

"A bit of everything," she said with a laugh. "I did tell you I'm famished remember."

Rand got up to make a plate for himself and Lilliana. As she requested he put a little bit of everything on her plate before he set it in front of her. He decided he would do the same for himself as he finished filling up his own plate. He sat down at the table and took a bite of toast as he looked over at his wife.

"Are you still planning on taking a couple of horses out today?" Jamieson asked.

"Yes we are. After we finish breakfast if that's still all right." Lily said.

"Of course it is. Technically you do own them after all."

"I guess I do. I hadn't thought of that," she answered.

"When you are finished, I will walk out to the stable with you and show you which horses are good for riding," Jamieson said.

They ate in silence as Rand watched Lilliana eat everything he had put on her plate. She really had worked up an appetite. Once she finished eating she dabbed her mouth with her napkin and looked over at him.

"What?" she asked.

"Nothing, just admiring my wife."

"We'll I'm done eating and want to go riding. Are you finished?"

"Eating? Absolutely."

"Well I guess we are ready to go investigate that stable of horses," Lilliana proclaimed.

"If you'll follow me I will show them to you," Jamieson replied.

A door slammed and a loud noise rumbled through the house followed by an equally thunderous bellow.

"Lilliana Marsden, where are you!"

"I think your parents have arrived." Jamieson said with a tilt of his head. "I believe that bellow was your father."

They looked up as they saw Viscount Torrington storm into the room followed by a woman that Rand assumed was his wife and Lily's mother. Viscount Torrington's face was so red it bordered on being purple. If Rand were a coward he would try to slink out the door, and out of harm's way. He didn't back down from anyone and he planned on staying married to Lily for the rest of his life. If he had one hope it would be a very long life. He could have gone a while without dealing with her father, but it looked as if he didn't have much choice in the matter.

"Young lady we have some things to discuss." Torrington glared at Lily as the words roared from within him.

"Are you hungry father? We were just enjoying breakfast. Please have a seat," Lily replied with a cajoling voice.

Rand suppressed the urge to roll his eyes at Lily and her father. Did she really believe treating him like a child in the throes of a temper tantrum would work?

"Don't try to placate me young lady. You deliberately

disobeyed and lied to us. You will answer for your indiscretions." Torrington practically bellowed the words at her.

Rand's lips formed a thin line of displeasure. He understood Torrington's irritation, but he couldn't and wouldn't allow him to lay a hand on her. Lily was his to protect now. "Well, I can't allow you to punish her. Please have a seat Viscount Torrington so we can discuss the situation like civilized people." Maybe if he reasoned with her father they could handle the situation as peacefully as possible.

Torrington turned and glared at Rand. Up until that point his attention had been solely focused on Lilliana. He knew that he would have to face him eventually, and it looked like it was time to do so. Rand had no regrets even if it looked like the man intended to beat him to a bloody pulp.

"I think I understand now." Torrington stormed over to Rand's side of the table and leaned on one of the chairs. "You are the one I need to hold responsible. Why did you kidnap my daughter, Mr. Collins? Did my interpretation of your business make you that mad? I don't take those actions lightly."

Rand should have known that the viscount was entirely too calm as he stood there talking to him. He believed the man capable of reasoning, but he should have factored in Lilliana's importance to him. If he had a daughter he would have been capable of murdering the poor sot that ran away with her. He didn't blame the man for his feelings on the matter. However the fist that planted in his face and knocking him out he did find fault with. *The blasted man hadn't even let me explain anything* was his last thought before blackness took over and he fell unconscious.

Lilliana jumped out of her chair and ran around the table to kneel before Rand's crumpled body sprawled out on the floor. At first she had remained rooted in her seat in horror watching her father's fist meet Rand's face. It was only after her mind could process the scene before her she was able to act. A scream to match her dismay erupted from her mouth before she rushed to her husband's side. Now she patted his cheek lightly to see if she could get him to wake up without any success.

"Jamieson, we need to get him upstairs." Lilliana gasped. "I don't know how long he is going to be out."

"I can certainly help. Thor, you are going to need to help me, he isn't a small lad."

"Damned if I do. I think he's exactly where he belongs."

Lilliana turned and glared at her father. His only reaction was to shrug without care. Her father may believe Rand belonged on the floor, but it was only because he didn't really know him. In his mind he kidnapped her forcing her to accompany him to South Carolina.

"Don't be an arse. He likely deserved to be pummeled a bit for running off with your daughter, but he is now her husband. You need to respect that." Jamieson spoke up to her father.

"In fact, I don't. I plan on murdering the thieving bastard

as soon as he wakes up. He clearly had a death wish and I'm happy to oblige," Torrington replied.

Lilliana could see from the expression on her father's face he meant every word he said. She had to find a way to reason with him. The blame belonged squarely on her shoulders, not Rand's. The decision to run away had been made long before she had met him. She needed to make him understand how much she loved Rand. She adored her father, but she was not going to allow him to harm her husband. No matter what it took she would make sure her father understood he couldn't come between her and the man she loved.

"Daddy, I can't allow you to hurt him any more than you have. Please understand this decision was mine to make, not yours. I belong here with my husband." She walked over to him and placed her hands in his. She looked up into his eyes and showed every ounce of emotion rolling through her in one look. Lilliana pleaded and demanded with her eyes for her father to understand what she wanted from him. If he couldn't hear her words she wanted him to see what his actions would do to her. "I need your help. Can you try to recognize that and assist Jamieson to take him up to the bedroom?"

"Fine. I will help him, but then you and I are going to have a long overdue talk."

Lilliana turned to Jamieson and said, "Can I trust you to make sure no harm comes to him while you both take him upstairs?"

"You have my word, the lad will arrive safely. " Jamieson nodded at her father. "I will make sure he comes back down with me after we settle him in your room."

"I'm not going to do him any harm." He glared down at Rand's unconscious body. "Not until he is awake at least."

He walked over and grabbed Rand's head and heaved upward as Jamieson grabbed his feet. She noticed that even though her father had agreed to help carry Rand he didn't do it with any kind of care to his well-being. It irritated Lilliana to watch him be so disrespectful to her new husband. She would just have to take Jamieson at his word. He would make sure her father didn't hurt him. Once they came back down she would make sure her father understood what would happen if he did anything at all to her husband. She would never speak to him again if he marred him in any way.

"I think we need to talk before your father comes back down."

Lilliana turned to look at her mother. She had barely noticed her arrival after her father forced his way into the dining room. Breakfast was completely ruined. She had lost her appetite anyway when she watched Rand fall from his chair and hit the ground with a loud thud.

"I think you may be right. I've made a mess of things," Lilliana said with a sigh.

"Darling, that is the understatement of the year." Her mother rolled her eyes as she pushed a strand of her pale blonde hair behind her ear. "You didn't have to deal with your father for the past three weeks. I don't think I've seen him this mad since my grandpere tried to murder him."

"Your grandpere actually did that? I thought that was just something you made up to make the story sound more daring."

"Yes, he did and don't change the subject. You need to explain yourself. Why did you run off? Did meeting that man cause you to lose your mind?" her mother asked.

"No of course not. Don't be ridiculous. I didn't leave because of Rand. He just made it possible for me to get what I wanted."

"Then explain this all to me. Why did you marry him? I know you were against marriage."

"I'm not allowed to fall in love? I didn't leave because of him. I left because I wanted to live here. You were just not listening to me. So I made the necessary arrangements to get what I wanted. Rand just agreed to transport me." Lilliana walked over to her mother and grasped her hands within in her own. "He's an amazing man, Mama. I'm not saying that just because I love him. He protected me and made sure I had everything I needed. Even when I threw myself at him he refused me. He's a good choice and I stand by it."

"Well you don't have to convince me. It's your father that isn't likely to believe you. It might take a little bit to make him understand, but I will try to help you."

"Thank you. I am sorry that I worried you. I tried to alleviate that."

"When you have children of your own someday you will realize a mere letter isn't reassuring enough. Parents always worry about their children. It's a responsibility that never goes away."

"I need to check up on him," Lilliana said.

"Your father isn't likely to let you near him until he has words with you. I've never seen him so irate and scared at the same time. Thor always seems to have things under control. Let him have his say first. I'm sure your husband will be fine in the meantime."

"I suppose you're right. I will wait." Lilliana looked over at the open doorway. "However, I'm not going to let him scream at me while my husband needs me. I will give him a moment of time to say his piece, but if I think Rand needs me the conversation is over."

Right after those words left her mouth Thor breezed in followed by Jamieson. He still wore a thunderous expression on his face. His lips pursed in displeasure, and his eyes narrowed to tiny slits as he focused his attention on her once again.

"Now that I've tossed the rubbish into another room, you and I are going to have a little discussion on mistruths and nearly giving your parents heart palpitations."

"I already apologized to mom. I'm extending it to you as well. You know I didn't mean to make you worry about me. This is where I want to be. I'm sorry, Daddy, but this is where I belong."

"You wouldn't be here if not for that upstart American. I can't believe you married him. We can rectify that when we get home."

"Are you listening to me at all? I'm not going back to England. Not now and probably not for a long time. I married Rand of my own free will. Nothing you say will make me want to leave him. I love him and I'm staying here as his wife."

"I'll tell you how I will rectify it. I will make sure the bloody bastard is no longer breathing."

Lilliana flinched as those words left her father's mouth.

How could he threaten the man she loved? Didn't he want her to fall in love and get married? Both her parents kept pushing her toward that end, and now he doesn't like the result? No, her father would understand he couldn't dictate to her any longer, and he would never lay a hand on her husband again.

"You will do no such thing. Rand hasn't had an easy life. You are not going to make it any more miserable. He grew up alone in an orphanage. His mother died giving birth to him. He told me he knows next to nothing about his parents. I know it pains him that he didn't know anything about her except her name."

"Your daughter has a point, Thor. You need..."

Her father interrupted Jamieson, "I don't need to do a bloody thing. You have no idea what I went through when I found out she hopped a ship with him. I've never been so scared in my life."

"I think I understand that kind of pain better than anyone," Jamieson replied quietly.

She heard her father groan so she turned her attention back to him. He had a perplexed look on his face as he watched Jamieson.

"I'm so sorry—I wasn't thinking. I know you experienced a loss that would cripple even the strongest man."

Lilliana bobbed her head back and forth between the two of them. "I don't understand what you are talking about."

"I lost my first wife, Emily, and our child. She died giving birth to him. The poor boy wasn't breathing when he came out. I lost everything in one moment and wasn't even there to see them both through it."

"Emily? How interesting, that's Rand's mother's name," Lily replied deep in thought. She couldn't help wondering if there was a connection. Could there be? No, Jamieson said they both died. She grabbed Jamieson's arm and gained his full attention. "I don't mean to pry, but is there maybe a possibility—"

Her father turned toward Jamieson and asked, "Do you know what she is talking about?"

"Are you suggesting what I think you are? How could that even be possible?"

Lilliana wasn't sure if she hoped she was right, or if she prayed she was wrong. She could see pain in every inch of Jamieson's features. "What was your Emily's full name?"

"Before we married it was Emily—" Jamieson paused for a second and rubbed his hand over his face, "Good God, how did I not see it?"

"See what?" her father asked.

"Her name was Emily Collins...they both share the same name. Do you think they did it on purpose? Gave him her family name to hide him from me?"

Her father shook his head and shrugged. "I'm not sure, Jamieson. I don't have the answers you seek, but surely this is a good thing. You have a son."

"Only a few decades too late," bitterness laced Jamieson's voice.

All this information was a little too much for her to take in. Jamieson was Rand's father. No wonder he seemed so familiar to her. Lilliana stared at him for several moments. She took in all of his features and mannerisms. The more she looked at him the clarity of it all became firmer inside of her head. She knew why Jamieson seemed so familiar to her. It should have been obvious from the start. He reminded her of her own husband. It all made sense now that she had all of the information. How was she going to tell her husband about this? It was all so—extraordinary.

"Who do you think hid him from you?" Lilliana asked.

Her father placed a hand on Jamison's shoulder, giving him support. Her father knew something she didn't. He must have been privy to this story. They were close; they sailed on a ship together. Jamieson must have shared the details with him.

"Her damn family. When they found out she was pregnant they disowned her. I arrived after she had given birth to him. They told me she died and that the baby never even had its first breath. How could they have lied to me?" Jamieson crinkled up as pain poured out of his eyes. A small sound of pain fell from his lips before he spoke again. "I grieved so much that it led me to signing on to work with Thor on his ship. Nothing could have kept me in Beaufort after that. No one knew she was really my wife and wouldn't tell me anything. Told me it was a family affair. I didn't much see the point in fighting them. I believed I had nothing left to live for."

"Rand is your son. Why would they do that to their own grandchild? They may have hated you, but Emily was still their daughter," Lilliana said bewildered.

"Not everyone sees things in the same way. She ruined herself by getting involved with me. They believed her soiled goods. I don't know why they lied about my son dying. I would ask them if they were still alive. That is if I could stop myself from strangling them."

"I get why this information is interesting to Jamieson, but explain to me why you even care Father."

Lilliana understood why Jamieson was a bit emotional at the news, but her father seemed equally overwhelmed. Not too long ago he was out to murder her husband. Something that still irked her.

"I can't very well murder my friend's only child. Especially as he just found out he existed, now can I?"

"Oh, I see how you are. You can murder my husband, but not your friend's son. That is some convoluted logic." Lilliana's blood boiled at his statement. She clenched her hands into tight fists and restrained herself from hitting her own father.

"I have to agree with her there, Thor. That doesn't make much sense to me," her mother interjected as she walked into the room.

Lilliana turned to look at her mother. At least she had one reasonable person on her side. "Thanks Mother, though I could have used your support a lot sooner."

Her mother waved her hand in dismissal. "I came in when I was needed. Have you settled everything?"

"Father was just going to explain why it made a difference that Rand is now Jamieson's son, not just my lowly husband." Lilliana glared at her father. "I'm not so sure we've settled anything."

"You didn't watch him suffer when he believed they both had died. It's personal and I also understand what it's like to be a father now." Her father folded his arms over his chest.

"Although I can't kill him, it doesn't mean I can't maim him a bit. He did abduct my daughter."

Jamieson frowned and said, "Well from what I understand of the situation she left rather willingly. You can't harass the lad for helping her out. Besides it isn't like you didn't do a little kidnapping in your day."

"He does have a point dear," Pia agreed.

If the situation wasn't completely ludicrous Lilliana would laugh. How had things gotten so far out of hand? She hoped Rand took the news all right that he had a father. It probably wouldn't help having to deal with her father as well. It would be some pretty difficult news to swallow on top of all the chaos already in their lives. At least her father wouldn't murder him now. She still thought it was absurd he only decided against that action because Jamieson believed Rand to be his son.

"Well, you two keep discussing this nonsense. I'm going to go check on my husband."

With those words Lilliana stormed out of the room to go check on Rand. Maybe he was awake now and she could spend some time with him. He did say he would take her horseback riding around the plantation. Of course that might be asking a bit too much, she would let him decide what he was capable of doing. If all he wanted was to go for a sedate walk she'd do it. She was just grateful to have him in her life. Maybe that would be a good way for them to get away from the madness that had overtaken everyone.

CHAPTER 18

R and woke up in his room with a splitting headache courtesy of his new father-in-law. When his head cleared he walked down the stairs to confront him. No way did he intend to leave Lilliana to fight his battles for him. When he reached the doorway he overheard them discussing his mother. Everyone always said you never heard anything good when you eavesdropped. He learned that lesson the hard way. Rand tromped away from his wife—and his father.

With the earth-shattering news—Jamieson being his father—dropped on him, he needed to get away and think. Rand practically ran out the front door to gain some distance between him and his newfound family. The only thing he thought about as he strolled away from the house was how much his life changed in such a short period of time. He didn't notice where his feet led him; he just kept prodding along until he couldn't take another step. When he finally took notice of his surroundings he saw a large oak tree looming in front of him. Its branches blew in the breeze as the leaves whistled with each movement.

His breaths became shallow as he swallowed that truth with a heavy reluctance. He never expected to find the man who helped create him. So many emotions rushed through him he couldn't pinpoint which one to hold onto. He needed to get back to the house and be there for his wife. He knew he acted like a coward by walking away. Closing himself off and not dealing with the issue wouldn't solve anything. He should have stayed and faced his demons instead of running at the first sign of adversity.

Jamieson seemed like a good man, aside from working as a pirate's right hand man. If what he said held true then he didn't know of his existence. Rand couldn't hold him accountable for the actions of someone else. He should give him a chance to be the father he never had. Easier said than done, in his opinion at least, years of believed abandonment were hard to let go of. He knew Jamieson said he thought he died. Rand heard all of the details; it was just hard for him to process. He wanted to believe everything he heard, but it all had a surreal feeling to it.

He had more than himself to think of now. With a heavy heart he started back toward the house. Lilliana depended on him, and he couldn't let his own inner turmoil get the best of him. As he walked back up the plantation steps, Lilliana exited the house and stopped with the door open. She stared at him for several minutes before she stepped forward and wrapped her arms around him.

"I'm so sorry. My father shouldn't have hit you."

"I don't blame him, Lily, he should be protective of his daughter."

"Still. He could have at least listened first before reacting." Lilliana frowned.

"I don't want to talk about it. I just want to hold you for a little while."

"There is something I should tell you..."

"I already know."

She was going to tell him about Jamieson. He didn't want to discuss his newfound father with her. He wanted to forget he had overheard the conversation.

"You do? How?"

"I overheard part of the conversation. It was a little bit to take in. It's why I'm outside. I needed the fresh air. To think," he said in a quiet tone.

"I see. I'm at a loss on how to respond. I thought you were out here because of me and my father. Instead it has to do with the news about yours. How does it make you feel?"

"I don't feel like talking about it. Why don't we go for a ride instead. It is what we planned before your father rudely interrupted us."

"Shouldn't we ask Jamieson..."

"Ask me what?"

They turned to see Jamieson standing in the open doorway. Rand wanted to walk away again. He didn't want to deal with him and what the man could mean for him. He did want to make his wife happy so he tried to put a smile on his face just for her, even though smiling made his face hurt.

"We are looking to go horseback riding." Rand said.

"Ah, I'd hoped to talk to you. I went looking and you were not in your room."

He wanted to give him a chance, but he hadn't had enough time to process it all. Jamieson may mean well—he just couldn't handle his well meaning emotional responses at the moment ."I'm not much in the mood to talk right now."

"It's kind of important, son."

"Don't call me that. I'm not your son," Rand replied scathingly.

"Rand!" Lilliana's shock evident on her face. "I don't think you need to be so rude to Jamieson. He is only trying to reach out to you and talk."

"You know?" Jamieson asked.

"That you believe you are my father? Yes. It doesn't make it true," Rand said.

"If your mother is—was Emily Collins, then yes, I am your father," Jamieson said with conviction.

Rand stood and looked at the man for the first time and took him in. Jamieson's features resembled his in a lot of ways, and he carried himself with an air of authority. Looking him over it didn't surprise him as much to realize that the man claimed to be his father.

"I know you think this is some kind of miracle. I'm not so blind to the ramifications of this mess. I'm not going to hug you and say I'm glad you are my long lost dad. I'm not made like that. I can't just accept you and be okay with years of perceived abandonment."

"No one is expecting you to... Just give it some time." Lilliana wrapped him in a tight embrace.

"Just show us the horses. I can't deal with this right now."

"I can do that," Jamieson agreed.

They strolled to the barn, and Jamieson led them to two horses in stalls next to each other. They were beautiful well-mannered animals.

"The chestnut is named Max and the white filly we call Sally. They are both good horses and are great for riding. Do you require a side saddle?"

"No, I don't ride side saddle," Lilly told him. "I have a skirt made just for riding astride, it splits down the middle. I made sure to wear it when I got dressed this morning anticipating going horseback riding."

"Good, I don't much care for the side saddle, it's dangerous," Jamieson replied.

"My father agrees and never allowed me to learn how to ride with one."

"I'll help you two get the horses saddled so you can be on your way."

Jamieson opened the stall and threw a saddle up on one of the horses. Lilliana stood to the side as Rand put the saddle on the other horse. Once both horses were prepared, they mounted them and rode them out of the barn. Lilliana's laugh of delight filled the air as she brought the horse to a light canter. Rand caught up to her quickly and kept up with the pace she set.

"I think we should talk about what happened," Lilliana said.

"I'm not ready to think of him as my father, Lily. Don't push it."

"You really need to give him a chance, but it's your decision I won't push."

"Thank you for supporting me."

"I'm your wife. It's what I'm supposed to do." She smiled. "How about a race?"

He started to tell her to no, but she took off at a fast gallop before he could get the words out. He knew she was only trying to lighten his mood, but he deemed a horse race too dangerous. No way would he put her life at risk by galloping their horses at full speed.

"Slow down Lily," Rand called.

His heart thundered in his chest as she sped in front of him. He wanted to reach out and stop her, but it was physically impossible. Rand could feel the color draining from his face with each bit of distance that grew between them.

She didn't hear him call out to her. Lilliana kept her horse's pace at a fast gallop. Rand raced to catch up to her, but she had gained a terrifying lead. She turned her head to look back at him, and with her attention divided she didn't see the tree branch directly in her path. She turned a moment too late, and Rand screamed as she flew from the horse. Her body hit the ground with a loud *thud*. He stopped his horse and jumped off of it racing to her side. Fear like he never knew before spread though his body. He couldn't lose her, not when he just found her, not ever. A tear began to form in his eye and fell down his cheek as he knelt beside her still body. Pain began to seep into his heart at the thought of losing her.

"Oh Lily, please be okay," he said pulling her into his arms. "I love you, I can't lose you when I just found you."

He stood and carried her back to the house trying not to jostle her. His fear was palpable and deep rooted inside of him. He had never been so afraid in his life. When he saw her flying from the horse all of his worst nightmares came to life.

"Quick someone help me, Lily took a nasty fall from her horse," Rand yelled.

Just as the words left his mouth he heard a voice bellow, "What the bloody hell did you do to my daughter?"

"I didn't do a damned thing to her, she fell from her horse. Help me take care of her."

Torrington reached to take Lilliana out of his arms, but Rand refused to relinquish her over to him.

"I'm not handing her over to you, she's fine where she is and I'm taking her upstairs until a physician can look at her."

Rand could hear them discussing the situation as he walked with huge steps toward their bedroom.

"Thor leave the man be, can't you see how distraught he is?" He heard Lilliana's mother say, stopping Viscount Torrington from going after Rand.

"He's manhandling my little girl."

"Sorry Thor, but I have to disagree with you again," Jamieson said.

"On which part, ol' friend, the manhandling or the fact that she's my little girl?" Thor asked.

"Well both actually. What I see is a man looking out for his wife."

"I fail to see your point." Thor's angry voice bellowed through the plantation walls.

"Rand and Lily are married. Sorry, Thor, but I believe that trumps your rights a bit."

"Bloody hell, I need a drink," Thor cursed. "What the hell are you waiting for, my daughter needs a physician. Send for one already."

Even though Rand had fear coursing through his body a small smile formed on his face. He heard Thor storm into the sitting room. At least Jamieson had his back. Maybe he could accept him in his life if the man willingly stood up to an ex-pirate.

Pain crashed through her skull as someone poked at her body. Tiny shards of agony filled her head with every touch. A constant thrum of torment beat against the back of her head, and every inch of her body was stiff with soreness. Whoever thought it a good idea to add to the throbbing burrowing its way inside of her would soon find the error of their ways. She didn't do well with any kind of discomfort, and the idiot kept adding to it with each poke and prod he made. If only she could open her eyes to tell him to stop stabbing her with his fingers. Her eyes refused to open, but she could hear everyone around her.

"She's just unconscious," she heard someone say. "I expect she'll be in a lot of pain once she wakes up. Her body is one huge bruise."

"But she will be okay?" a familiar voice asked.

Rand. He wanted to make sure she would be okay. *Of course I will be*, she wanted to scream the words at him. He shouldn't be made to worry about her.

"She better be all right, boy," another familiar voice roared. "Or I'll make sure you take your last breath."

Her father threatened her husband again. When would he stop tormenting Rand? Her mother had to be nearby; she wouldn't leave knowing Lilliana was hurt. Why hadn't she said something? Lily needed to hear her mother's voice.

"You won't be murdering my son, Thor. Back off."

Ah, yes, Jamieson would be there to help support Rand. Happiness filled her at the sound of Jamieson's voice. Rand had someone in his corner. He needed someone on his side. He often let the weight of the world hold him down. Jamieson would make sure he didn't give into his darker side.

"He's right, Thor. You are only making things worse by threatening him. Be happy that Lily chose him. You know we thought she'd never get married. I'm happy she found someone to give her heart to."

Oh yes Mama, I did. He's wonderful! I can't wait for you to know him as I do. She needed to wake up and tell them everything. The pain in her skull throbbed harder and faster as it tried to beat her from the inside out. *Please stop I can't take the pain anymore.*

"There are too many of you in the room," a man she assumed was the doctor told everyone. "Only two visitors at a time or she'll never get enough rest to heal."

"Fine. Everyone can leave. I want to spend some time alone with my wife."

Good for you Rand. Tell them all to leave. It should just be you and me for a while. My head hurts and I can't think with all of them hovering over me.

She heard some rustling as a door opened and closed. She believed that all of them left the room without arguing with Rand. That made things easier on both of them. The silence was blissful and the pain began to ease a bit as it washed over Lilliana. She could feel a head lay down on her waist and grabbed a hold of her hands. It must be Rand. He wouldn't have left her. He must have found a chair to set by the bed so he could keep vigil. She needed to wake up and help ease his pain.

"I will keep you company," Jamieson said.

So she was wrong. Not everyone left the room. Jamieson stayed behind to be with Rand.

"I'm fine. I don't need you."

"Yes son. I believe you do. You don't have to do everything alone."

"I've done it alone all my life. I don't see why I should change that now," Rand said in a bitter voice.

"Right now I'll remind you that you are not alone. You have me and Eliza if you want us, but more importantly you have a wife," Jamieson said. "I'm so sorry son; I wouldn't have abandoned you if I'd known you lived."

"It couldn't be helped. You didn't know. And you're right. Lily needs me. I can't let this eat up inside of me."

"I would never hurt you intentionally."

"In my head I understand that, but my hearts been bruised beyond recognition. I didn't allow myself to feel anything for anyone until I met Lily," Rand said.

"If you give me a chance, I'd like to get to know you."

"I don't know. Give me some time to let it all sink in."

"I can respect that. I hope you give me a chance. Eliza and I were never blessed with children. Since I missed out on raising you, I'd like to have a chance at being a grandfather."

"I can't make any promises. Right now I'd like to be alone with my wife."

"All right. I will leave you be for now. She will get better Rand."

Lilliana heard the door open and close again. Jamieson had left. The only ones in the room were her and Rand. She needed to open her eyes and let him know she would be okay.

"Lily, love, please wake up," he pleaded.

I'm trying! I would if I could.

"I love you, I should have told you sooner I know. I just couldn't get the words out. Last night I heard everything you said. I wish I could have spoken then. Please hear me now. I need you to know how I feel. I have never had these strong feelings before."

I knew you loved me! I hear you Rand, I hear everything you are saying to me. I just can't seem to open my eyes. It hurts too much. Give me some time. I can do it I know I can.

"You are also right about my father. I do need to give him a chance. It's just so hard for me to accept anyone in my life. I've been alone for so long. I can't be alone anymore. Wake up Lily. Please don't leave me."

"I love you," Lilliana said with a hoarse whisper.

"Did you say something?" he asked with desperation.

"You heard me," she barely got out the words before he pulled her into his arms with a fierce hug.

"Can you open your eyes, love?"

"Hurts...too...much."

"That's okay, you should rest."

"My parents..."

"I can get them for you, if you want," he said.

"Yes, please. Need to speak to them." Lilliana croaked out, her voice hoarse from being so tight and dry. She struggled to get them out and let her Rand know what she wanted.

"I'll get them now. Just relax as I retrieve them."

Lilliana heard him leave the room in a rush. It seemed like hours before they finally came up the stairs. She must have drifted off again because when she opened her eyes only her mother sat at her side.

"Where's Daddy?" she asked with a hitch in her voice.

"I'm over here, princess."

Lilliana turned her head slightly to see her father standing by the window in her room. The afternoon sun streamed through the glass. Her father had a troubled look on his face.

"So happy to see you both," she said.

"You gave us quite a scare, young lady," her mother said. Her blue eyes held an enormous amount of concern and warmth. Her forehead crinkled up as she spoke. Her pale blonde hair was in disarray, as she must have run her hands through it with worry. "What were you thinking?"

"I wanted to make Rand smile. He looked so sad when he found out Jamieson was his father. Instead I ended up with a cracked head. That'll teach me for galloping at such fast speeds."

"I'm glad you are okay. I've never been so scared in my life." Her mother leaned down to hug her. "That doesn't make what you did right. Don't ever do something so foolish again."

"I know and I'm sorry, forgive me."

"Always, princess, we can never stay mad at you, but did you really have to go and marry Jamieson's only son? Right now I'd really like to murder him for putting you in danger," her father said.

"Be kind Daddy. I love him."

"I'll try. I'm not happy about it."

"I know, I promise you'll get used to the idea in time."

"I will make sure he plays nice," Pia said and kissed Lily on the cheek. "In the meantime you need your rest."

"Rand..."

"Is not so patiently waiting for us to leave." Pia smiled. "There isn't supposed to be more than two of us in the room at a time. Rand said you wanted to see us both which left him standing in the hallway."

"I did. I heard you talking. I had to make it right." She could barely keep her eyes open, and they were tiny slits as she looked at him. She fought the struggle her body demanded of her. She refused to succumb to the sleep her body required to heal. She needed to talk to them and make them understand. If she let herself doze back off she wouldn't be able to take care of her immediate concerns.

"You did, princess." Her father leaned over and kissed her cheek. "Don't worry about us. Just concentrate on getting better."

She watched her parents walk to the door to leave.

"I love you both. Thank you for being such wonderful parents."

"The pleasure, princess, belongs to us, you were one of our blessings. We couldn't have asked for a better daughter."

Rand entered the room immediately after they left and sat down by her side. He lifted her hand to his mouth and placed a quick kiss in her palm. Her husband had been put through a lot in a very short time, and she didn't have a clue how to help him through it all.

His hazel eyes had held so much pain as he looked at her. She would have done anything in her power to ease it, but he hadn't given her a chance. Rand had done a good job of acting like he would be okay, but she knew him better than that. He may have laughed a little and acted untroubled, but she knew inside it shredded him. If he needed a little bit of time to himself to ease the hurt within, then she would ensure he had it.

"Did you say everything you needed to them?"

"Yes, I believe I did."

"I'm glad."

"What about you?"

"I don't know what you mean," he said.

"Have you talked with your father?"

"I had a small talk with him while you talked with your parents. We have a long way to go, but he knows I'm willing to try and build a relationship with him. I talked with Eliza as well. She cried a little bit and hugged me. It turns out she isn't capable of having children of her own. She wants to consider me her son. It's not a huge step, but it's a start. It's all I can offer them right now."

"Well that's good for you. You now have two wonderful people to call your parents," Lilliana said.

"I know it is, but it's still not going to be easy for me. I don't know what I'm doing here. It's all new territory for me."

Lilliana looked into Rand's eyes and just enjoyed gazing into their depths for a few minutes. He had such a sensitive nature, but didn't know how to express it.

"You will be fine. Besides you will have me every step of the way."

"I know. If I didn't have you by my side I wouldn't be able to do all of this. I wouldn't even be here to know who my father was. I owe everything to you. Thank you for agreeing to be my wife, Lily."

Lilliana needed to lighten the mood a bit. It had taken a turn she didn't want to go down just yet. She didn't need his gratitude, but she'd gladly take any love he'd willingly bestow upon her.

"I had my own selfish reasons for marrying you, you know."

"Oh yeah? What were they?" he asked with a smile.

"I knew you wouldn't be able to keep you hands off of me if I happened to be your wife." A hushed chuckle filled the room.

"I knew you were a wanton from the moment I met you."

"Really, do tell, what gave me away?" she asked with coyness.

"You had a devilish smile and you knew how to lure in your prey."

"So you are now my prey? I didn't know I had such power."

"You hold all the power, Lily. You are my life. I'd be lost without you. Do not ever do anything like you did earlier today. I thought I died a million times seeing you lying on the ground."

She could imagine how that scared him. If it had been in reverse and he lay on the ground hurt, she'd have been frantic. If she had a way of doing it all over again she'd never get on the horse.

"I didn't mean for that to happen, I'd never hurt you."

"You can be a bit reckless at times. Its part of why I love you so much, but it scares me at the same time."

"Is that all you love about me?" she asked.

"No, I love everything about you. I adore how your eyes fill with that devilishness I spoke of earlier, I admire your tenacity to get what you want, cherish the way you fight for those you care about, I worship the ground you walk on, but mostly I just love you with every beat of my heart."

"Oh Rand, I love you too. You have a great capacity for love. I knew it from the moment I looked into your eyes. It's why I knew you were the right man, not only to take me to Charleston, but to welcome into my life forever." Lilliana reached up and caressed his cheek with the palm of her hand. "You are the reason I changed my views on marriage. Because of you I started to believe love existed again." Lilliana paused, and looked down at her lap. A lump of emotion welled up inside of her. Once she regained control she looked up into Rand's eyes. "When I first started to socialize in society the men hadn't inspired me to believe in it. None of the ton marriages had been based on love. They only married for some kind of gain, either financial or power. I never wanted a marriage based on such low expectations. I always knew I wanted more. I thought my parents' marriage was a rarity and love only found the lucky few. I'm glad I'm among those blessed with it."

Rand leaned down and brushed her lips with his. At that moment she wished she hadn't cracked her head so hard on the tree branch and on the ground. She wanted to show him exactly how much she loved him, but her body hurt too much.

"I wish we could make love, but it would be too painful," she said with a bit of whimsy.

"We have the rest of our lives to express our love to each other, it can wait for you to heal. I want to be able to love you over and over. As soon as you are ready we are going to spend a whole day in bed doing just that. In the mean time you will have to settle for a few brief kisses and caresses."

"You're going to torture me, aren't you? That will be your revenge for me scaring you so badly. Admit it."

"You know me so well, love. I have to get my kicks in somewhere." He laughed.

Lilliana stuck her tongue out at him.

"I will get even if you do."

"Promise?"

"Always."

With that, Rand got up and lay down next to her in the bed. Lilliana curled up next to him and rested her head on his shoulder. A small sigh escaped from her at how good it felt to be in his arms. They had come a long way in a few short weeks. They loved each other and had a long happy life ahead of them. Rand treasured her as much as she did him. Lilliana belonged with Rand, their love made them stronger. They could face anything as long as they did it by each other's side. Lilliana couldn't have asked for a better beginning to their story. More importantly, Lily couldn't wait to have children of her own. It would be her turn to craft a fairytale. She would tell her children a tale of true love, much as her father had with her and Liam. It would start with, *Once upon a time a lady asked a gentleman to help her run away...*

READ ON FOR AN EXCERPT FROM A SANGUINE GEM: A Marsden Romance 3

CHAPTER 20

Liam Marsden had a lot of things on his mind. However, he couldn't dwell on what was beyond his control. He had more pressing issues to deal with, starting with a meeting his father demanded. He had never let him down before, and he had no intention of starting at this juncture of his life.

He walked into his family home and strolled down the hallway towards the study. As he opened the door, he got a brief look at his father engrossed in his own work. The viscount had his dark hair pulled back at the nape of his neck; loose strands fell over his forehead as he tilted his head to read the paper in front of him. Liam had always admired his tenacity and willingness to do anything to accomplish any task. He didn't give up easily and believed the world belonged to him to take what he wanted from it.

"Ah good you're here," He glanced up at Liam and set his work aside. "I have a few things I need to discuss with you."

"I came as soon as I received your missive. What's so urgent?"

"A good number of things that I didn't foresee."

On closer scrutiny, Liam could see stress lines forming on his father's face. His eyes filled with worry as he rubbed his temples. What could have happened to make him appear so concerned? Liam didn't think this meeting would be a jovial one. His father didn't often worry about things. No, Viscount Torrington took action and left the fretting to others.

"This is serious?" Liam asked as he raised an eyebrow.

"I received a letter from your sister. Some of it is good news. Most of it is actually."

"It's the part that isn't good news that concerns you." Liam sat down and leaned forward, giving his father his full attention. "What has happened?"

"First, I should tell you that you are the proud uncle of a strapping baby boy. You sister had her child a month ago. They named him William Jamieson after his two grandfathers. Poor boy has a lot to live up to with that name." He laughed.

"If I'm an uncle that means you are a grandfather. How does that make you feel old man" Liam grinned. He couldn't resist an opportunity to tease his father.

"Bite your tongue, boy. It'll be a long time before I'm an old man," With a devilish grin on his face, his father sat back in his chair and studied Liam. "This is good for you because I don't think you are quite ready to fill my shoes."

Liam hoped his father lived a very long life. He couldn't imagine a life without the man's robust personality filling a room wherever he went. Like most children, he believed his parents infallible. He knew they were mere human beings, but he liked to believe they would live forever.

"No, I can't say I'm in a hurry to take the reins from you. I pray you're here for many years to come. For more reasons than one," Liam said. "But regardless of how I feel about your possible demise that isn't why you summoned me here. Nor is it the news about my new nephew. Grateful as I am to hear about it, something else weighs on your mind. I think it's time to dispense with the pleasantries."

"That isn't all your sister wrote about," he said with a heavy sigh. "She has some concerns that she asked me to look into."

"Is it about the merger of Marsden Shipping with RandCo? There isn't an issue with its completion, is there?" He needed to dispense with that bit of concern first because it was at the forefront of his mind. "If so, I'd like to take care of it immediately."

"No, that at least is going well. We should have considered a merger as soon as Lily and Rand married." Viscount Torrington sighed and stood up. He strolled over to a nearby shelf and pulled out a decanter of brandy along with two glasses. "This is something entirely different and I'm not sure how to proceed."

"What's Lily worried about?" Liam's concern rose. What could be so dreadful?

Viscount Torrington handed Liam a brandy filled snifter. He took a sip of his own and set it down. He stared past Liam, his eyes unfocused. "The Earl of Devon was a pretty good friend of mine."

"I remember." Liam nodded.

"At one time I'd hope to have a merger with him," his father paused and stared down at his drink. "It was the reason we attempted to betroth you and Gemma."

Liam would rather forget about that time in his life. He grimaced and stared up at his father. "Right, that was several years ago." What was his father getting at?

"The business merger and familial one fell through at the same time. We never found a reason to revisit either." He downed the rest of his drink in his glass. "I have to admit a part of me is glad it didn't. As much as I liked the man I abhor the gentleman who inherited his estate."

Liam rubbed his temple; a pain throbbed through his head listening to his father rattle on. "What does Alfie have to do with this?"

"Lady Gemma is my concern."

She wasn't his, so Liam had no clue why he brought her into the conversation. In fact, everything he'd said so far hadn't made any sense to him.

"Father, what exactly is the problem?" Frustration built to the boiling point deep inside him. "I don't understand what Lady Gemma has to do with all of this."

"Lady Gemma keeps in touch with Lily. She wrote your sister about some disturbing news."The viscount sat back and studied Liam. He steepled his hands together as he spoke. "She thinks I might have a solution to the problem. I can think of a couple of ways we could assist her, but you would have to be willing."

"What it is you would like me to do?" Liam replied, a horrible feeling sinking to the bottom of his gut.

Viscount Torrington leaned forward and set his hands on his desk. His eyes bore into Liam's as he appeared to weigh over the issue that troubled him.

"You know I'd never force you to do anything, but I think in this you believe as I do."

"I'm at a loss as you haven't explained anything to me," Liam reminded him. "How am I to know if I agree or not if you don't?" He silently hoped his father wasn't about to ask what he thought he was. After he mentioned the botched attempt to betroth him to Lady Gemma, Liam couldn't help but wonder—he couldn't possibly want him to marry Gemma. *Could he?*

"First, you should be aware of the circumstances regarding Lady Gemma and why Lily is so concerned," his father told him. "Then I will explain my idea and the two possible solutions to it. One is a better option, and the other should only be considered if you are against the first."

"And what is happening with her?" Liam stood up and paced around the room. He stopped a few steps away and pinned his father with a stare. "Quit stalling and tell me what's going on."

"Alfie is—being difficult."

"In what way?"

If his father didn't tell him what was going on soon. Liam wouldn't be held responsible for his actions. Their conversation was driving him mad.

"He has squandered the entire inheritance. If the estate weren't entailed, he'd sell it to pay off his enormous debts. That leaves him in a bit of a bind. He needs money and as fast as possible."

Liam nodded. "I think I see the correlation. Lady Gemma still has an inheritance, and he wants to get his hands on it."

Viscount Torrington stood up and joined him in front of the desk. His eyes had an angry edge to them. Liam knew his father well enough to realize he wanted to do some damage to the new Earl of Devon. Whatever Alfie was doing enraged him. Liam had a bad feeling about what was going on with Lily's friend.

"In a manner of speaking yes and he is willing to use whatever is at his disposal to get it. Lady Gemma is afraid he might force the situation to get his way."

"I see." Liam scowled. "Does she have reason to believe he will act so dishonorably?"

"This is old news." His father frowned and crossed his arms over his chest. "I got the letter today from your sister. It might already be a foregone conclusion. I'm afraid we may be too late with how slow mail travels between England and America. I don't know what we'll find if we go to the Earl of Devon's estate."

Not good news, in fact, they were quite horrid. Liam might have issues with Lady Gemma, but he'd never wanted anyone to hurt her. He'd willingly help her deal with her cousin if he could find a good solution to her problem.

"I hadn't even considered that. We are wasting time. What are your solutions?" Liam asked.

"Lady Gemma needs a husband. She doesn't gain majority and control over her funds for five more years. She only has one solution that will effectively work for her."

With those words, Liam's fears were realized. His heart beat faster in his chest and the pounding in his head intensified.

His father wanted him to marry Lady Gemma.

Liam should be appalled at the suggestion, especially as he'd already tried to betroth them when they were younger. He had never denied that Lady Gemma had beauty in spades. She had luxurious crimson hair and eyes the color of jade. His mouth watered thinking about her beautiful complexion and soft curves. That was until she open her mouth to speak. Listening to her droll on and on for what seemed like forever, he invariably forgot how exquisite her body and face appeared and wanted to put some much needed distance between them.

Why should he sacrifice his life for her?

The brazen redhead had been the bane of his existence for several years now. It took the death of her father for her to back away. Admittedly he admired her tenacity and willingness to make her wishes known, but that didn't mean he ever desired to tie himself to her forever. Perhaps his father's other solution would be easier for him to stomach.

"You are not suggesting what I think you are." Appalled, Liam sat back down in his chair. Shock filled him to the brink. He had to be reading the situation wrong.

"I had hoped that you had some tender feelings for the chit. You are constantly arguing with her." His father sat back down in his chair, a slight knowing smirk resting on his face. "That is a form of passion. Trust me I know a bit about denial in that area."

"Well, you're incorrect in your assumption." Liam glared. He didn't have any feelings for Gemma. She was a nuisance nothing more. "There aren't any tender feelings on either side. The girl irritates me to no end. I never did understand what Lily saw in her."

"That's too bad. I still have the betrothal contract I signed with Lady Gemma's father. We could have used it to our advantage."

Liam stared at his father with a blank expression. He'd actually signed the contract? How could he have done that? His father had reassured him he'd never force him to marry anyone.

"Excuse me could you repeat that? I don't think I heard you correctly." Liam hoped he'd heard wrong. Sadly he doubted he had. "You informed me the betrothal hadn't been finalized."

"That's correct," His father grinned. "However Devon hoped I'd change my mind and told me to keep the contract. All I have to do to make it legal is sign my name to it."

Liam blanched. His father was losing his mind. There wasn't a chance in hell he'd make him marry Lady Gemma. "But you're not going to, right

"So you are not willing to help?"

"I didn't say that." Liam shook his head. "I'm willing to hear the other plan you have. I'm hoping it is preferable to the latter."

"The other plan involves you basically kidnapping the girl and taking her to your sister in South Carolina."

Relief flooded him at his father's words. Calm now that the storm of anxiety fled his stomach, Liam took a deep breath and considered his father's other idea. He had to agree that the second plan held more appeal. It was preferable, but not that much better in the grand scheme of things. He would still be forced to spend a considerable amount of time in Lady Gemma's company. How would he be able to get through a voyage with her? They would have to take the Sea Rover for the crossing. No other ships were available, and their steamships were only in the planning stages of being built. If he had any luck, it wouldn't take more than three weeks to complete.

The bonus, of course, would be to see his sister and his new nephew. He sincerely wished to see them so that no price was too high for him to be able to spend time in their company. He would even be willing to get to know his brother-in-law as well. Maybe he would find a way to like the rat bastard. His father may have forgiven him for stealing Lily, but Liam didn't feel like he deserved such absolution. The man had a lot of audacity to run away with the daughter of Viscount Torrington—a former pirate. Liam would give him that much.

"That plan is more conceivable to accomplish," Liam said. "But is kidnapping really necessary? Do you believe Lady Gemma will be unwilling to go to live with Lily?"

"I honestly do not know," his father sighed. "I hate to tell you this, but I think you're going to need ammunition to get her out."

"Explain," Liam demanded.

"If you go in prepared Alfie won't have anything to argue about."

"How do you suggest I do that?"

His father grinned. It almost had a wicked tinge to it. "I'm going to sign this betrothal. Go to the bishop and demand a special license. With the right amount of money and the betrothal as evidence, he won't deny you."

"I fail to see why I need to go to such lengths."

"Alfie won't let Gemma go willingly. You're going to have to force his hand." His father paused and looked him in the eye. "I'm not telling you to marry the girl. Just use the tools I'm giving you to save her."

"All right I will go see the bishop now. Afterward, I will

retrieve Gemma and bring her back here to plan our next move." Liam said.

"Good. I'd hate to disappoint your sister. I hope we are not too late to help Lady Gemma."

With those words, Liam got up and walked out of the study. He had never been a fan of Lady Gemma Kemsley, but he had never wished her ill will either. If she had more trouble than she could handle, Liam had no choice but to help her. His sister depended on him, and he had never let her down before—he certainly didn't plan on starting with Lady Gemma.

The chit had better be prepared to do everything necessary to leave her home. Liam didn't suffer fools and luckily for him he knew that she didn't either. No matter what he believed, her to be he had always been able to see the keen intelligence in her eyes. Perhaps with age she had also gained some maturity to go along with it.

CHAPTER 21

Gemma Kemsley couldn't believe her rotten luck as she strolled into the sitting room on her father's—her cousin's estate. She still had trouble wrapping her mind around the fact that her father passed away eighteen months ago. Her cousin, Alfie, inherited the title and the entailed estates upon his death. He also became her guardian. A reality that Gemma loathed for many reasons, the biggest being he had lecherous intentions towards her.

He said in no uncertain terms she would be his wife whether she liked it or not. Well, Gemma didn't like it and vowed to find a way to escape his plans for her. She took a page out of her best friend Lily's book and started to scheme her way out of the situation. The only option for her would be to run away and live in America. Lily would welcome her into her home. She just needed to find a way to leave without Alfie knowing what she had in mind.

"Ah, there you are Gemma, dear. We have some things to discuss."

Disgust filled her at the sight of her cousin invading her space. He smelled just as foul, like a night of overindulging in cheap liquor. Bloody hell, why couldn't he be in London at one of his clubs? They probably wouldn't admit him anymore. No doubt the whole ton had begun to realize the new Earl of Devon was headed to debtors' prison. It couldn't happen soon enough to satisfy her. The horrid man continued to harass her on a daily basis. She didn't know how much longer she could stand to put up with his unwanted advances.

Why did her father have to die and leave her in Alfie's care? She missed him every day. Living without him was hard enough, but to constantly have to defend herself rattled her to her very core.

"As far as I'm concerned we have talked more than I have ever liked. Go away Alfie I am not in the mood to fend off your licentious advances today," Gemma told him.

"I don't care what you want, dear. I came to inform you that your time is up. At the end of the week, we will wed. Just as soon as I can obtain a special license." His eyes leered over her bosom as he delivered the awful news. "You look especially lovely today. How about we seal the deal with a kiss?"

Lovely? Like that was going to work on her. She'd rather stand outside in a lightning storm and beg to be struck dead than marry her cousin. Kiss him? Not bloody going to happen.

Alfie reached for her. Gemma took a step back to prevent being held in his embrace. She knew it wouldn't stop at a kiss. No, her cousin wanted to do more than press his lips on hers. He wanted to ravish her until she no longer retained any shred of innocence.

Alfie believed she owed him because he allowed her to live with him after he moved in. As her guardian, he got a stipend to provide for her living expenses. He couldn't touch the majority of her inheritance without a valid reason.

Thankfully her mother had left her a large sum of money upon her death. Only marriage or reaching her majority would allow her access to it though.

It took her a while, but she finally understood why her best friend, Lily, had been so against marriage. It was unbelievably ironic that she succumbed to it as soon as she left England, but that didn't make her argument against matrimony any less valid.

"I'd rather kiss a dead fish than allow you anywhere near me." She gave him a scathing look and frowned at him.

Heat filled her cheeks at the idea of him touching her. Not in a good way either. She didn't desire him; rather she wanted never to lay eyes on him ever again. Alfie was the exact opposite of the man she truly wanted—or rather used to long for.

"No reason to be so vicious. You'll like it once I warm you up a bit," he said, an evil grin on his lips.

In her haste to get away from him she tripped and fell backward on the settee. She tried to get up before he could take advantage of the situation, but her efforts were futile. He pounced on her after her misfortunate collapse. His lips pressed hard against hers. When she tried to open her mouth to scream he pushed his tongue inside her mouth and squeezed her breast in the palm of his hand.

Pain shot through her and continued to spread through her nipple. Alfie pulled her onto him and grinded himself against her stomach. She could feel his hardness as he rubbed himself on her. She'd lose the contents of her stomach soon if she couldn't get him to let her go.

What could she do? Not a lot of options were making themselves known to her and she was fast running out of time. An idea came to her as Alfie pushed his tongue into her mouth again. Gemma bit down on his lip and drew blood. She could taste it as a small drop fell on her tongue, it was bitter and disgusting.

"You little bitch," he shouted with rage. "You're going to pay for that."

He yanked Gemma's dress and tore the side of her bodice. He reached forward and pinched her nipple between his forefinger and thumb. She screamed out as his nails dug into the sensitive tip. She had to put some distance between them before something she couldn't escape from happened. It was clear Alfie planned on claiming her against her will.

Gemma grabbed his arm, her nails digging in and leaving half-moon imprints into his flesh. She yanked his arm away from her, ripping his hand off her bruised breast. She fought to get away from him, but it was a struggle she was losing. Her cousin was too strong, and she didn't have the ability to fight him. Tears started to fall from the corner of her eyes.

This was wrong, so very wrong, and Gemma couldn't stop it from happening to her.

"Alfie, Ole' Chap, I do hope you are not doing what I think you are."

That voice—Gemma knew that voice. Her heart raced in her chest and tingles of fire danced across her stomach. It haunted her dreams and made her want things she knew she'd never have. Alfie let her go, and she fell back on the settee. She jerked her bodice over her exposed breast, embarrassment settling in the bottom of her stomach like a dead weight.

Gemma looked over and straight into the stormy blue eyes of the only man she had ever wanted—ever allowed herself to love. His pale blond hair hung loosely over his collar making her want to run her fingers through it. She knew that the fine blond strands would be silky if she'd were to touch them.

At one time, she believed he would be her everything, the one person she was meant to spend the rest of her life with.

Too bad he didn't return her feelings.

No man had ever compared to him—no one ever would. This man standing in front of her, glaring at her cousin, filled her with desire and longing. Liam Marsden had ruined her for anyone else.

"I don't know why you feel comfortable waltzing in, but Gemma and I were in the middle of something. You can show yourself out the same way you came in," Alfie said.

Fool. Liam Marsden didn't take orders.

Gemma didn't know why her cousin even thought that nonsense had a possibility of working. She was simultaneously irritated and relieved Liam had showed up. She didn't know why he came out to the country, but he had saved her from ruin. She might be perpetually angry with him—but now, she'd have to set that annoyance aside to thank him. Gemma owed him a debt she didn't think she'd ever be able to repay.

"Well, I came to see my fiancée. I have to say I don't like that I walked into you getting rough with her. Explain yourself, man, before I commit murder."

Fiancée? She stood up her gaze whipping toward Liam's.

A blaze of longing rushed through her with that one word. What the bloody hell was Liam talking about? The only place he had ever asked her to marry him had been in her dreams.

Sadly, in reality he ignored her whenever she came near him.

So this little announcement of his baffled her. What was the man up to? Did he know something about her situation and decided to come and save her? It wouldn't work as much as she wanted it to. Claiming to be her fiancé wouldn't make Alfie let go of her. He'd fight Liam every step of the way unless there was proof of his prior claim.

"Gemma is not your fiancée," Alfie said. He sneered, evil apparent in his gaze. "I think I'd know if I had approved of someone for her to marry."

"That's because you didn't approve it." Liam folded his arms across his chest. He oozed smugness as he looked Alfie in the eye.

Gemma hid a smile. That had to goad her cousin a bit.

"Then you can leave. I'm the only one who can approve who Gemma marries." Alfie waved his hand attempting to dismiss Liam.

Liam ignored him and stalked forward. "Her father signed the contract before he died." He turned and gave her a glance that scorched her from the inside out. Gemma only barely restrained from fanning herself. "I have waited patiently for her mourning to end so we can be married. I think it's time that we proceeded with our plans."

"What contract? Why wasn't I made aware of this?" Alfie asked as he glared at Gemma.

Gemma just shrugged her shoulders in his general direction. She didn't have the answers he sought. She didn't have any idea what Liam was talking about. Surely her father would have told her if he had signed a contract for her to marry someone. This had to be some ruse on Liam's part. Whatever he planned she had every intention of following along with it. Anything to help her get away from her cousin would be very much preferable to submitting to his licentious groping.

"I have it right here," Liam said as he shoved the contract at Alfie. "The old earl's signature is at the bottom giving permission for me to marry his daughter, Lady Gemma Kemsley."

"I don't understand. Why didn't the solicitors tell me about this?" Alfie asked, his face turning three different shades of red.

Liam had the contract in his hands and Alfie attempted to snatch it from him. Liam just shook his head and folded it back up, placing it back in the safety of his inside pocket. Cool, calm, and collected—that was Liam.

"Possibly because they didn't know. This document has been in my father's keeping since I was fourteen years old. They decided to betroth us several years ago." Confidence intertwined with each word he spoke. "Good for business you know. We had no idea Gemma's father would die so tragically before he could tell her about it. It's sad, but well I think it's time we move on."

"I don't care." Alfie stomped his foot like a small child. "I don't approve and Gemma isn't going to marry you."

Gemma had to restrain herself from laughing at the ridiculous situation she found herself in. The only man she had ever loved demanded she marry him and her libertine cousin thought he had a chance of denying it. Not for a minute did she believe the contract had any validity to it. Lily had to have put Liam up to the scheme to help her escape. Gemma knew that Liam didn't want her. She'd learned it the hard way two years ago. It didn't matter though; he was here to save her. She knew Liam would do anything his twin sister asked him. They'd always been close. If she demanded he save her best friend he'd do it without blinking. Liam wouldn't be in her ancestral home stepping in between her and Alfie otherwise.

"Seems like you don't have any say in the matter, Alfie," Gemma said solemnly. "Papa signed the contract. That supersedes your wishes. I have no choice, but to marry Liam Marsden."

This was surely a dream. Marry him? A flutter of hope started to ignite within her. She squashed it before it could take root. Liam wasn't going to marry her. Gemma refused to give in to something surely destined to destroy her. Hope was an evil four letter word, designed to bring a person to their knees and wrap them up in despair.

"You could refuse him."

"I don't want to." Gemma laughed.

Alfie clenched his fists at his side. His hand flew up and stopped in midair as if he rethought the action he'd been about to take. He glanced over at Liam and Gemma did as well. He was in a position to strike. Alfie would never have gotten the slap across Gemma's cheek.

Gemma grinned with relief. Alfie would have to find some other heiress to get him out of debt. She had no intention of letting him touch her or her money.

"Good. Go pack a small bag, whatever you deem necessary to take today. We can send for your other belongings later," Liam instructed her. "Oh and Gemma, change your gown too. Something pretty, perhaps green to match your eyes."

"I'm to leave today? Isn't that sudden?"

Assuagement filled her at the idea of escaping Alfie. Her hand flew to her chest as she allowed herself to believe it was going to happen. Liam worked fast, not that she was complaining, but she thought it'd take more time for him to extract her from her cousin's clutches.

"Yes. I have a special license. We're to be married today."

"Give me fifteen minutes. I don't have a lot that needs to be packed immediately. I will instruct the housekeeper to pack the rest of my trunks for delivery to Marsden House."

"I will wait for you here. I need to have a private word with Alfie on how a woman in his care should be treated."

Liam's mouth crunched up into a firm line. Displeasure filled his eyes as he turned to pin Alfie with his gaze. They darkened to a stormy blue, one Gemma had never seen before. She wanted to tell Liam not to hurt her cousin for altruistic reasons, but if she were honest she wanted him beaten.

He would have forced himself on her if Liam hadn't walked in. Her skin still crawled with revulsion from the places he'd put his hands. She shuddered at the memory, disgusted she'd had to endure his groping. Gemma loathed the man as much as she adored Liam. They were two different men and each invoked a different feeling in her. Sadly, she wasn't at all happy with either emotion.

Living with unrequited love was horrible—dealing with Alfie's nasty disposition, however, was a far worse ordeal.

"Liam, don't hurt him—much." Gemma paused and waved her hand dismissively. "I'd hate for this to come back to haunt us."

He looked at her with a devilish smile. That carefree smile so full of sin had always been her undoing. Her heart skipped a beat, and her stomach started to tingle.

"Darling, I promise you he'll be hurting far more than it will show on the outside. He'll feel a pain that will haunt him long after we are gone from his life. Now scoot so I can inflict all those deep seated wounds he fully deserves."

Gemma nodded and ran out of the room. She skipped the steps and walked into her bedroom. She grabbed a valise and put a change of clothes in it. Then she took her jewelry case and a stack of letters. She placed them inside and tied it closed. Gemma didn't need much and everything necessary had been enclosed in the satchel. She found a green gown in her armoire and changed as fast as she could. Thankfully she followed Lily's advice and had had gowns made she could put on herself. She picked up the bag and with much haste went back to the sitting room.

She paused inside the doorway. Her eyes flew to Liam as he lounged on a nearby chair. His legs were crossed in an easy manner as he tapped restlessly on the arm. Alfie sat stiffly on the settee and held his stomach in a tight embrace. Not a mark showed anywhere on him as Liam had promised.

"I'm ready to go."

Liam turned and looked at her. He nodded in her direction and started to walk over to her side.

"You're both going to regret you've crossed me," Alfie spat out.

Liam stopped and turned back to Alfie before they exited the room.

"Alfie, don't do anything stupid." His voice was hard and commanding as he issued the reminder. "As long as you leave us be we will leave you alone. Make one wrong move towards me or Gemma and you will regret it. That isn't a threat. It's a promise. I take care of what's mine."

Gemma snorted. Liam had claimed her. She didn't believe he meant it. Whatever his reasons for helping her, it had nothing to do with wanting her. Still, a part of her couldn't help wishing it were true. When she'd first heard the words, her whole body lit up with an uncontrollable longing.

Liam turned back to Gemma and placed her hand in the crook of his arm.

"Ready to go, love?" he asked, his tone softening just for her ears.

"Oh yes. Let's go and never look back."

She let him lead her out the door and to his awaiting carriage. Liam helped her as she entered the carriage and followed her inside. He took her bag and placed it under one of the seats and then sat across from her. The carriage started to move, and it jerked her forward causing her to collapse into his arms. She hadn't been prepared for it to depart.

"You always did fall into my arms." Liam laughed as he set her next to him on the seat.

"Don't go ruining a good rescue by turning into an arse," Gemma scolded him. "I know that was a farce. Did Lily put you up to it?"

"Not at all. Well, not entirely. She did ask for my father to help you out of the situation. He placed the particulars in my hands."

"And this is the solution you came up with?" Gemma paused with a sigh. "I'm sorry. I should be thanking you. Instead, I'm harping on how you did it." She stared at him. "I don't mind really. It worked to get Alfie to let me go without a fight—well not much of one anyway. I truly do appreciate your assistance. I don't want to think about what he'd have done if you hadn't arrived in time." Gemma shuddered at the memory of her cousin's hands on her bosom. "I take it you are going to help me get to America so I can stay with your sister until I reach my majority?"

"No."

"What do you mean no?" she asked. "How am I going to escape from Alfie if I don't leave the country?"

"I thought that had already been settled. You're marrying me. Today. Nothing else is going to deter him."

"I don't want to marry you. I'd much rather go to South Carolina."

"We will do that. It is probably best we leave for a short period anyway. On our wedding trip can go visit Lily," he said.

"Why are you being obstinate? I am not going to marry you."

"Yes, you are." Liam emphasized each word as he looked her directly in the eyes. Gemma's lips pursed, disbelief filling her as he spoke. "Your father gave his permission. You are stuck with me. You just told Alfie you didn't want to refuse me."

Were they actually getting married? The infernal flutter of hope sprung to life. Gemma didn't know if she could eradicate it again. Did her father truly want her to marry Liam? She bit her lip and once again wished he was still around to ask. He'd know what to do. But if the contract Liam had was legit, it was clear her father had wanted her to marry him. She already had her answer.

Warmth pooled in her cheeks. She clenched her fists in her lap.

Gemma wanted to scream with outrage. Damn her rotten luck. She knew Liam didn't love her, and she didn't want to find herself stuck in a loveless marriage. Worse yet he knew she loved him once; maybe he counted on her still having those feelings for him. No matter what she said, she was far from over him. A one-sided love—married to him for the rest of her life—would be hell. She had to make him see that it wouldn't work.

"Can't we just pretend?" Gemma asked. "You don't want to marry me, Liam. Don't make me hate you."

"You are not going to talk me out of this, Gemma. It's decided. I've accepted it, and now you need to as well."

"Like hell I do,"

Gemma pushed him back and scooted across to the other side of the carriage. She didn't need to sit next to him while he dictated to her.

"No need to make things interesting, love. I'm already

willing. Now sit back and relax. The rector is expecting us to arrive shortly."

"What rector?"

"The one in the next town. I've made all the arrangements. I already told you I had a special license, didn't I," he said. "In less than an hour you will be my wife. Don't worry you'll get used to the idea.

If Gemma had something to throw at him, it would have already bounced off his head. Liam Marsden had to be the most stubborn male in existence.

"Bloody hell, you are irritating."

"Welcome to my world," he said with a droll smile. "It's all part of the plan, love. Makes life more… intriguing."

Gemma sat back in her seat and fumed. Winning an argument with Liam was akin to dreams becoming reality. No way would he allow her to get ahead. Just like the real world never compared to the bliss of dreams.

Neither one had a chance of happening for her right now. She gave up on her fantasies a long time ago; just as she now gave up on convincing Liam to forego marrying her. It would amount to wasted energy and useless hope.

Gemma knew when to sit back and lick her wounds to fight another day. If she had to be Liam's wife, she'd need a new plan of attack. She had learned from the best and Lily had taught her well. Her fiancé didn't know what he had in store for him.

Gemma didn't give up anything that belonged to her.

Liam would love her or at the very least desire her as much as she did him. With a plan forming in her head, she relaxed, and her lips lifted into a half smile.

A SANGUINE GEM

DAWN BROWER

USA TODAY BESTSELLING AUTHOR

Dawn Brower

A Sanguine Gem

CHAPTER 1

L iam Marsden had a lot of things on his mind. However, he couldn't dwell on what was beyond his control. He had more pressing issues to deal with, starting with a meeting his father demanded. He had never let him down before, and he had no intention of starting at this juncture of his life.

He walked into his family home and strolled down the hallway towards the study. As he opened the door, he got a brief look at his father engrossed in his own work. The viscount had his dark hair pulled back at the nape of his neck; loose strands fell over his forehead as he tilted his head to read the paper in front of him. Liam had always admired his tenacity and willingness to do anything to accomplish any task. He didn't give up easily and believed the world belonged to him to take what he wanted from it.

"Ah good you're here," He glanced up at Liam and set his work aside. "I have a few things I need to discuss with you."

"I came as soon as I received your missive. What's so urgent?"

"A good number of things that I didn't foresee."

On closer scrutiny, Liam could see stress lines forming on his father's face. His eyes filled with worry as he rubbed his temples. What could have happened to make him appear so concerned? Liam didn't think this meeting would be a jovial one. His father didn't often worry about things. No, Viscount Torrington took action and left the fretting to others.

"This is serious?" Liam asked as he raised an eyebrow.

"I received a letter from your sister. Some of it is good news. Most of it is actually."

"It's the part that isn't good news that concerns you." Liam sat down and leaned forward, giving his father his full attention. "What has happened?"

"First, I should tell you that you are the proud uncle of a strapping baby boy. You sister had her child a month ago. They named him William Jamieson after his two grandfathers. Poor boy has a lot to live up to with that name." He laughed.

"If I'm an uncle that means you are a grandfather. How does that make you feel old man" Liam grinned. He couldn't resist an opportunity to tease his father.

"Bite your tongue, boy. It'll be a long time before I'm an old man," With a devilish grin on his face, his father sat back in his chair and studied Liam. "This is good for you because I don't think you are quite ready to fill my shoes."

Liam hoped his father lived a very long life. He couldn't imagine a life without the man's robust personality filling a room wherever he went. Like most children, he believed his parents infallible. He knew they were mere human beings, but he liked to believe they would live forever.

"No, I can't say I'm in a hurry to take the reins from you. I pray you're here for many years to come. For more reasons than one," Liam said. "But regardless of how I feel about your possible demise that isn't why you summoned me here. Nor is it the news about my new nephew. Grateful as I am to hear about it, something else weighs on your mind. I think it's time to dispense with the pleasantries."

"That isn't all your sister wrote about," he said with a heavy sigh. "She has some concerns that she asked me to look into."

"Is it about the merger of Marsden Shipping with RandCo? There isn't an issue with its completion, is there?" He needed to dispense with that bit of concern first because it was at the forefront of his mind. "If so, I'd like to take care of it immediately."

"No, that at least is going well. We should have considered a merger as soon as Lily and Rand married." Viscount Torrington sighed and stood up. He strolled over to a nearby shelf and pulled out a decanter of brandy along with two glasses. "This is something entirely different and I'm not sure how to proceed."

"What's Lily worried about?" Liam's concern rose. What could be so dreadful?

Viscount Torrington handed Liam a brandy filled snifter. He took a sip of his own and set it down. He stared past Liam, his eyes unfocused. "The Earl of Devon was a pretty good friend of mine."

"I remember." Liam nodded.

"At one time I'd hope to have a merger with him," his father paused and stared down at his drink. "It was the reason we attempted to betroth you and Gemma."

Liam would rather forget about that time in his life. He grimaced and stared up at his father. "Right, that was several years ago." What was his father getting at?

"The business merger and familial one fell through at the same time. We never found a reason to revisit either." He downed the rest of his drink in his glass. "I have to admit a part of me is glad it didn't. As much as I liked the man I abhor the gentleman who inherited his estate."

Liam rubbed his temple; a pain throbbed through his head listening to his father rattle on. "What does Alfie have to do with this?"

"Lady Gemma is my concern."

She wasn't his, so Liam had no clue why he brought her into the conversation. In fact, everything he'd said so far hadn't made any sense to him.

"Father, what exactly is the problem?" Frustration built to the boiling point deep inside him. "I don't understand what Lady Gemma has to do with all of this."

"Lady Gemma keeps in touch with Lily. She wrote your sister about some disturbing news." The viscount sat back and studied Liam. He steepled his hands together as he spoke. "She thinks I might have a solution to the problem. I can think of a couple of ways we could assist her, but you would have to be willing."

"What it is you would like me to do?" Liam replied, a horrible feeling sinking to the bottom of his gut.

Viscount Torrington leaned forward and set his hands on his desk. His eyes bore into Liam's as he appeared to weigh over the issue that troubled him.

"You know I'd never force you to do anything, but I think in this you believe as I do."

"I'm at a loss as you haven't explained anything to me," Liam reminded him. "How am I to know if I agree or not if you don't?" He silently hoped his father wasn't about to ask what he thought he was. After he mentioned the botched attempt to betroth him to Lady Gemma, Liam couldn't help but wonder—he couldn't possibly want him to marry Gemma. *Could he?*

"First, you should be aware of the circumstances regarding Lady Gemma and why Lily is so concerned," his father told him. "Then I will explain my idea and the two possible solutions to it. One is a better option, and the other should only be considered if you are against the first."

"And what is happening with her?" Liam stood up and paced around the room. He stopped a few steps away and pinned his father with a stare. "Quit stalling and tell me what's going on."

"Alfie is—being difficult."

"In what way?"

If his father didn't tell him what was going on soon. Liam wouldn't be held responsible for his actions. Their conversation was driving him mad.

"He has squandered the entire inheritance. If the estate weren't entailed, he'd sell it to pay off his enormous debts. That leaves him in a bit of a bind. He needs money and as fast as possible."

Liam nodded. "I think I see the correlation. Lady Gemma still has an inheritance, and he wants to get his hands on it."

Viscount Torrington stood up and joined him in front of the desk. His eyes had an angry edge to them. Liam knew his father well enough to realize he wanted to do some damage to the new Earl of Devon. Whatever Alfie was doing enraged him. Liam had a bad feeling about what was going on with Lily's friend.

"In a manner of speaking yes and he is willing to use whatever is at his disposal to get it. Lady Gemma is afraid he might force the situation to get his way."

"I see." Liam scowled. "Does she have reason to believe he will act so dishonorably?"

"This is old news." His father frowned and crossed his arms over his chest. "I got the letter today from your sister. It might already be a foregone conclusion. I'm afraid we may be too late with how slow mail travels between England and America. I don't know what we'll find if we go to the Earl of Devon's estate."

Not good news, in fact, they were quite horrid. Liam might have issues with Lady Gemma, but he'd never wanted anyone to hurt her. He'd willingly help her deal with her cousin if he could find a good solution to her problem.

"I hadn't even considered that. We are wasting time. What are your solutions?" Liam asked.

"Lady Gemma needs a husband. She doesn't gain majority and control over her funds for five more years. She only has one solution that will effectively work for her."

With those words, Liam's fears were realized. His heart beat faster in his chest and the pounding in his head intensified.

His father wanted him to marry Lady Gemma.

Liam should be appalled at the suggestion, especially as he'd already tried to betroth them when they were younger. He had never denied that Lady Gemma had beauty in spades. She had luxurious crimson hair and eyes the color of jade. His mouth watered thinking about her beautiful complexion and soft curves. That was until she open her mouth to speak. Listening to her droll on and on for what seemed like forever, he invariably forgot how exquisite her body and face appeared and wanted to put some much needed distance between them.

Why should he sacrifice his life for her?

The brazen redhead had been the bane of his existence for several years now. It took the death of her father for her to back away. Admittedly he admired her tenacity and willingness to make her wishes known, but that didn't mean he ever desired to tie himself to her forever. Perhaps his father's other solution would be easier for him to stomach.

"You are not suggesting what I think you are." Appalled, Liam sat back down in his chair. Shock filled him to the brink. He had to be reading the situation wrong.

"I had hoped that you had some tender feelings for the chit. You are constantly arguing with her." His father sat back down in his chair, a slight knowing smirk resting on his face. "That is a form of passion. Trust me I know a bit about denial in that area."

"Well, you're incorrect in your assumption." Liam glared. He didn't have any feelings for Gemma. She was a nuisance nothing more. "There aren't any tender feelings on either side. The girl irritates me to no end. I never did understand what Lily saw in her."

"That's too bad. I still have the betrothal contract I signed with Lady Gemma's father. We could have used it to our advantage."

Liam stared at his father with a blank expression. He'd actually signed the contract? How could he have done that? His father had reassured him he'd never force him to marry anyone.

"Excuse me could you repeat that? I don't think I heard you correctly." Liam hoped he'd heard wrong. Sadly he doubted he had. "You informed me the betrothal hadn't been finalized."

"That's correct," His father grinned. "However Devon hoped I'd change my mind and told me to keep the contract. All I have to do to make it legal is sign my name to it."

Liam blanched. His father was losing his mind. There wasn't a chance in hell he'd make him marry Lady Gemma. "But you're not going to, right

"So you are not willing to help?"

"I didn't say that." Liam shook his head. "I'm willing to hear the other plan you have. I'm hoping it is preferable to the latter."

"The other plan involves you basically kidnapping the girl and taking her to your sister in South Carolina."

Relief flooded him at his father's words. Calm now that the storm of anxiety fled his stomach, Liam took a deep breath and considered his father's other idea. He had to agree that the second plan held more appeal. It was preferable, but not that much better in the grand scheme of things. He would still be forced to spend a considerable amount of time in Lady Gemma's company. How would he be able to get through a voyage with her? They would have to take the Sea Rover for the crossing. No other ships were available, and their steamships were only in the planning stages of being built. If he had any luck, it wouldn't take more than three weeks to complete.

The bonus, of course, would be to see his sister and his new nephew. He sincerely wished to see them so that no price was too high for him to be able to spend time in their company. He would even be willing to get to know his brother-in-law as well. Maybe he would find a way to like the rat bastard. His father may have forgiven him for stealing Lily, but Liam didn't feel like he deserved such absolution. The man had a lot of audacity to run away with the daughter of Viscount Torrington—a former pirate. Liam would give him that much.

"That plan is more conceivable to accomplish," Liam said. "But is kidnapping really necessary? Do you believe Lady Gemma will be unwilling to go to live with Lily?"

"I honestly do not know," his father sighed. "I hate to tell you this, but I think you're going to need ammunition to get her out."

"Explain," Liam demanded.

"If you go in prepared Alfie won't have anything to argue about."

"How do you suggest I do that?"

His father grinned. It almost had a wicked tinge to it. "I'm going to sign this betrothal. Go to the bishop and demand a special license. With the right amount of money and the betrothal as evidence, he won't deny you."

"I fail to see why I need to go to such lengths."

"Alfie won't let Gemma go willingly. You're going to have to force his hand." His father paused and looked him in the eye. "I'm not telling you to marry the girl. Just use the tools I'm giving you to save her."

"All right I will go see the bishop now. Afterward, I will

retrieve Gemma and bring her back here to plan our next move." Liam said.

"Good. I'd hate to disappoint your sister. I hope we are not too late to help Lady Gemma."

With those words, Liam got up and walked out of the study. He had never been a fan of Lady Gemma Kemsley, but he had never wished her ill will either. If she had more trouble than she could handle, Liam had no choice but to help her. His sister depended on him, and he had never let her down before—he certainly didn't plan on starting with Lady Gemma.

The chit had better be prepared to do everything necessary to leave her home. Liam didn't suffer fools and luckily for him he knew that she didn't either. No matter what he believed, her to be he had always been able to see the keen intelligence in her eyes. Perhaps with age she had also gained some maturity to go along with it.

CHAPTER 2

Gemma Kemsley couldn't believe her rotten luck as she strolled into the sitting room on her father's—her cousin's estate. She still had trouble wrapping her mind around the fact that her father passed away eighteen months ago. Her cousin, Alfie, inherited the title and the entailed estates upon his death. He also became her guardian. A reality that Gemma loathed for many reasons, the biggest being he had lecherous intentions towards her.

He said in no uncertain terms she would be his wife whether she liked it or not. Well, Gemma didn't like it and vowed to find a way to escape his plans for her. She took a page out of her best friend Lily's book and started to scheme her way out of the situation. The only option for her would be to run away and live in America. Lily would welcome her into her home. She just needed to find a way to leave without Alfie knowing what she had in mind.

"Ah, there you are Gemma, dear. We have some things to discuss."

Disgust filled her at the sight of her cousin invading her space. He smelled just as foul, like a night of overindulging in cheap liquor. Bloody hell, why couldn't he be in London at one of his clubs? They probably wouldn't admit him anymore. No doubt the whole ton had begun to realize the new Earl of Devon was headed to debtors' prison. It couldn't happen soon enough to satisfy her. The horrid man continued to harass her on a daily basis. She didn't know how much longer she could stand to put up with his unwanted advances.

Why did her father have to die and leave her in Alfie's care? She missed him every day. Living without him was hard enough, but to constantly have to defend herself rattled her to her very core.

"As far as I'm concerned we have talked more than I have ever liked. Go away Alfie I am not in the mood to fend off your licentious advances today," Gemma told him.

"I don't care what you want, dear. I came to inform you that your time is up. At the end of the week, we will wed. Just as soon as I can obtain a special license." His eyes leered over her bosom as he delivered the awful news. "You look especially lovely today. How about we seal the deal with a kiss?"

Lovely? Like that was going to work on her. She'd rather stand outside in a lightning storm and beg to be struck dead than marry her cousin. Kiss him? Not bloody going to happen.

Alfie reached for her. Gemma took a step back to prevent being held in his embrace. She knew it wouldn't stop at a kiss. No, her cousin wanted to do more than press his lips on hers. He wanted to ravish her until she no longer retained any shred of innocence.

Alfie believed she owed him because he allowed her to live with him after he moved in. As her guardian, he got a stipend to provide for her living expenses. He couldn't touch the majority of her inheritance without a valid reason.

Thankfully her mother had left her a large sum of money upon her death. Only marriage or reaching her majority would allow her access to it though.

It took her a while, but she finally understood why her best friend, Lily, had been so against marriage. It was unbelievably ironic that she succumbed to it as soon as she left England, but that didn't make her argument against matrimony any less valid.

"I'd rather kiss a dead fish than allow you anywhere near me." She gave him a scathing look and frowned at him.

Heat filled her cheeks at the idea of him touching her. Not in a good way either. She didn't desire him; rather she wanted never to lay eyes on him ever again. Alfie was the exact opposite of the man she truly wanted—or rather used to long for.

"No reason to be so vicious. You'll like it once I warm you up a bit," he said, an evil grin on his lips.

In her haste to get away from him she tripped and fell backward on the settee. She tried to get up before he could take advantage of the situation, but her efforts were futile. He pounced on her after her misfortunate collapse. His lips pressed hard against hers. When she tried to open her mouth to scream he pushed his tongue inside her mouth and squeezed her breast in the palm of his hand.

Pain shot through her and continued to spread through her nipple. Alfie pulled her onto him and grinded himself against her stomach. She could feel his hardness as he rubbed himself on her. She'd lose the contents of her stomach soon if she couldn't get him to let her go.

What could she do? Not a lot of options were making themselves known to her and she was fast running out of time. An idea came to her as Alfie pushed his tongue into her mouth again. Gemma bit down on his lip and drew blood. She could taste it as a small drop fell on her tongue, it was bitter and disgusting.

"You little bitch," he shouted with rage. "You're going to pay for that."

He yanked Gemma's dress and tore the side of her bodice. He reached forward and pinched her nipple between his forefinger and thumb. She screamed out as his nails dug into the sensitive tip. She had to put some distance between them before something she couldn't escape from happened. It was clear Alfie planned on claiming her against her will.

Gemma grabbed his arm, her nails digging in and leaving half-moon imprints into his flesh. She yanked his arm away from her, ripping his hand off her bruised breast. She fought to get away from him, but it was a struggle she was losing. Her cousin was too strong, and she didn't have the ability to fight him. Tears started to fall from the corner of her eyes.

This was wrong, so very wrong, and Gemma couldn't stop it from happening to her.

"Alfie, Ole' Chap, I do hope you are not doing what I think you are."

That voice—Gemma knew that voice. Her heart raced in her chest and tingles of fire danced across her stomach. It haunted her dreams and made her want things she knew she'd never have. Alfie let her go, and she fell back on the settee. She jerked her bodice over her exposed breast, embarrassment settling in the bottom of her stomach like a dead weight.

Gemma looked over and straight into the stormy blue eyes of the only man she had ever wanted—ever allowed herself to love. His pale blond hair hung loosely over his collar making her want to run her fingers through it. She knew that the fine blond strands would be silky if she'd were to touch them.

At one time, she believed he would be her everything, the one person she was meant to spend the rest of her life with.

Too bad he didn't return her feelings.

No man had ever compared to him—no one ever would. This man standing in front of her, glaring at her cousin, filled her with desire and longing. Liam Marsden had ruined her for anyone else.

"I don't know why you feel comfortable waltzing in, but Gemma and I were in the middle of something. You can show yourself out the same way you came in," Alfie said.

Fool. Liam Marsden didn't take orders.

Gemma didn't know why her cousin even thought that nonsense had a possibility of working. She was simultaneously irritated and relieved Liam had showed up. She didn't know why he came out to the country, but he had saved her from ruin. She might be perpetually angry with him—but now, she'd have to set that annoyance aside to thank him. Gemma owed him a debt she didn't think she'd ever be able to repay.

"Well, I came to see my fiancée. I have to say I don't like that I walked into you getting rough with her. Explain yourself, man, before I commit murder."

Fiancée? She stood up her gaze whipping toward Liam's.

A blaze of longing rushed through her with that one word. What the bloody hell was Liam talking about? The only place he had ever asked her to marry him had been in her dreams.

Sadly, in reality he ignored her whenever she came near him.

So this little announcement of his baffled her. What was the man up to? Did he know something about her situation and decided to come and save her? It wouldn't work as much as she wanted it to. Claiming to be her fiancé wouldn't make Alfie let go of her. He'd fight Liam every step of the way unless there was proof of his prior claim.

"Gemma is not your fiancée," Alfie said. He sneered, evil apparent in his gaze. "I think I'd know if I had approved of someone for her to marry."

"That's because you didn't approve it." Liam folded his arms across his chest. He oozed smugness as he looked Alfie in the eye.

Gemma hid a smile. That had to goad her cousin a bit.

"Then you can leave. I'm the only one who can approve who Gemma marries." Alfie waved his hand attempting to dismiss Liam.

Liam ignored him and stalked forward. "Her father signed the contract before he died." He turned and gave her a glance that scorched her from the inside out. Gemma only barely restrained from fanning herself. "I have waited patiently for her mourning to end so we can be married. I think it's time that we proceeded with our plans."

"What contract? Why wasn't I made aware of this?" Alfie asked as he glared at Gemma.

Gemma just shrugged her shoulders in his general direction. She didn't have the answers he sought. She didn't have any idea what Liam was talking about. Surely her father would have told her if he had signed a contract for her to marry someone. This had to be some ruse on Liam's part. Whatever he planned she had every intention of following along with it. Anything to help her get away from her cousin would be very much preferable to submitting to his licentious groping.

"I have it right here," Liam said as he shoved the contract at Alfie. "The old earl's signature is at the bottom giving permission for me to marry his daughter, Lady Gemma Kemsley."

"I don't understand. Why didn't the solicitors tell me about this?" Alfie asked, his face turning three different shades of red.

Liam had the contract in his hands and Alfie attempted to snatch it from him. Liam just shook his head and folded it back up, placing it back in the safety of his inside pocket. Cool, calm, and collected—that was Liam.

"Possibly because they didn't know. This document has been in my father's keeping since I was fourteen years old. They decided to betroth us several years ago." Confidence intertwined with each word he spoke. "Good for business you know. We had no idea Gemma's father would die so tragically before he could tell her about it. It's sad, but well I think it's time we move on."

"I don't care." Alfie stomped his foot like a small child. "I don't approve and Gemma isn't going to marry you."

Gemma had to restrain herself from laughing at the ridiculous situation she found herself in. The only man she had ever loved demanded she marry him and her libertine cousin thought he had a chance of denying it. Not for a minute did she believe the contract had any validity to it. Lily had to have put Liam up to the scheme to help her escape. Gemma knew that Liam didn't want her. She'd learned it the hard way two years ago. It didn't matter though; he was here to save her. She knew Liam would do anything his twin sister asked him. They'd always been close. If she demanded he save her best friend he'd do it without blinking. Liam wouldn't be in her ancestral home stepping in between her and Alfie otherwise.

"Seems like you don't have any say in the matter, Alfie," Gemma said solemnly. "Papa signed the contract. That supersedes your wishes. I have no choice, but to marry Liam Marsden."

This was surely a dream. Marry him? A flutter of hope started to ignite within her. She squashed it before it could take root. Liam wasn't going to marry her. Gemma refused to give in to something surely destined to destroy her. Hope was an evil four letter word, designed to bring a person to their knees and wrap them up in despair.

"You could refuse him."

"I don't want to." Gemma laughed.

Alfie clenched his fists at his side. His hand flew up and stopped in midair as if he rethought the action he'd been about to take. He glanced over at Liam and Gemma did as well. He was in a position to strike. Alfie would never have gotten the slap across Gemma's cheek.

Gemma grinned with relief. Alfie would have to find some other heiress to get him out of debt. She had no intention of letting him touch her or her money.

"Good. Go pack a small bag, whatever you deem necessary to take today. We can send for your other belongings later," Liam instructed her. "Oh and Gemma, change your gown too. Something pretty, perhaps green to match your eyes."

"I'm to leave today? Isn't that sudden?"

Assuagement filled her at the idea of escaping Alfie. Her hand flew to her chest as she allowed herself to believe it was going to happen. Liam worked fast, not that she was complaining, but she thought it'd take more time for him to extract her from her cousin's clutches.

"Yes. I have a special license. We're to be married today."

"Give me fifteen minutes. I don't have a lot that needs to be packed immediately. I will instruct the housekeeper to pack the rest of my trunks for delivery to Marsden House."

"I will wait for you here. I need to have a private word with Alfie on how a woman in his care should be treated."

Liam's mouth crunched up into a firm line. Displeasure filled his eyes as he turned to pin Alfie with his gaze. They darkened to a stormy blue, one Gemma had never seen before. She wanted to tell Liam not to hurt her cousin for altruistic reasons, but if she were honest she wanted him beaten.

He would have forced himself on her if Liam hadn't walked in. Her skin still crawled with revulsion from the places he'd put his hands. She shuddered at the memory, disgusted she'd had to endure his groping. Gemma loathed the man as much as she adored Liam. They were two different men and each invoked a different feeling in her. Sadly, she wasn't at all happy with either emotion.

Living with unrequited love was horrible—dealing with Alfie's nasty disposition, however, was a far worse ordeal.

"Liam, don't hurt him—much." Gemma paused and waved her hand dismissively. "I'd hate for this to come back to haunt us."

He looked at her with a devilish smile. That carefree smile so full of sin had always been her undoing. Her heart skipped a beat, and her stomach started to tingle.

"Darling, I promise you he'll be hurting far more than it will show on the outside. He'll feel a pain that will haunt him long after we are gone from his life. Now scoot so I can inflict all those deep seated wounds he fully deserves."

Gemma nodded and ran out of the room. She skipped the steps and walked into her bedroom. She grabbed a valise and put a change of clothes in it. Then she took her jewelry case and a stack of letters. She placed them inside and tied it closed. Gemma didn't need much and everything necessary had been enclosed in the satchel. She found a green gown in her armoire and changed as fast as she could. Thankfully she followed Lily's advice and had had gowns made she could put on herself. She picked up the bag and with much haste went back to the sitting room.

She paused inside the doorway. Her eyes flew to Liam as he lounged on a nearby chair. His legs were crossed in an easy manner as he tapped restlessly on the arm. Alfie sat stiffly on the settee and held his stomach in a tight embrace. Not a mark showed anywhere on him as Liam had promised.

"I'm ready to go."

Liam turned and looked at her. He nodded in her direction and started to walk over to her side.

"You're both going to regret you've crossed me," Alfie spat out.

Liam stopped and turned back to Alfie before they exited the room.

"Alfie, don't do anything stupid." His voice was hard and commanding as he issued the reminder. "As long as you leave us be we will leave you alone. Make one wrong move towards me or Gemma and you will regret it. That isn't a threat. It's a promise. I take care of what's mine."

Gemma snorted. Liam had claimed her. She didn't believe he meant it. Whatever his reasons for helping her, it had nothing to do with wanting her. Still, a part of her couldn't help wishing it were true. When she'd first heard the words, her whole body lit up with an uncontrollable longing.

Liam turned back to Gemma and placed her hand in the crook of his arm.

"Ready to go, love?" he asked, his tone softening just for her ears.

"Oh yes. Let's go and never look back."

She let him lead her out the door and to his awaiting carriage. Liam helped her as she entered the carriage and followed her inside. He took her bag and placed it under one of the seats and then sat across from her. The carriage started to move, and it jerked her forward causing her to collapse into his arms. She hadn't been prepared for it to depart.

"You always did fall into my arms." Liam laughed as he set her next to him on the seat.

"Don't go ruining a good rescue by turning into an arse," Gemma scolded him. "I know that was a farce. Did Lily put you up to it?"

"Not at all. Well, not entirely. She did ask for my father to help you out of the situation. He placed the particulars in my hands."

"And this is the solution you came up with?" Gemma paused with a sigh. "I'm sorry. I should be thanking you. Instead, I'm harping on how you did it." She stared at him. "I don't mind really. It worked to get Alfie to let me go without a fight—well not much of one anyway. I truly do appreciate your assistance. I don't want to think about what he'd have done if you hadn't arrived in time." Gemma shuddered at the memory of her cousin's hands on her bosom. "I take it you are going to help me get to America so I can stay with your sister until I reach my majority?"

"No."

"What do you mean no?" she asked. "How am I going to escape from Alfie if I don't leave the country?"

"I thought that had already been settled. You're marrying me. Today. Nothing else is going to deter him."

"I don't want to marry you. I'd much rather go to South Carolina."

"We will do that. It is probably best we leave for a short period anyway. On our wedding trip can go visit Lily," he said.

"Why are you being obstinate? I am not going to marry you."

"Yes, you are." Liam emphasized each word as he looked her directly in the eyes. Gemma's lips pursed, disbelief filling her as he spoke. "Your father gave his permission. You are stuck with me. You just told Alfie you didn't want to refuse me."

Were they actually getting married? The infernal flutter of hope sprung to life. Gemma didn't know if she could eradicate it again. Did her father truly want her to marry Liam? She bit her lip and once again wished he was still around to ask. He'd know what to do. But if the contract Liam had was legit, it was clear her father had wanted her to marry him. She already had her answer.

Warmth pooled in her cheeks. She clenched her fists in her lap.

Gemma wanted to scream with outrage. Damn her rotten luck. She knew Liam didn't love her, and she didn't want to find herself stuck in a loveless marriage. Worse yet he knew she loved him once; maybe he counted on her still having those feelings for him. No matter what she said, she was far from over him. A one-sided love—married to him for the rest of her life—would be hell. She had to make him see that it wouldn't work.

"Can't we just pretend?" Gemma asked. "You don't want to marry me, Liam. Don't make me hate you."

"You are not going to talk me out of this, Gemma. It's decided. I've accepted it, and now you need to as well."

"Like hell I do,"

Gemma pushed him back and scooted across to the other side of the carriage. She didn't need to sit next to him while he dictated to her.

"No need to make things interesting, love. I'm already

willing. Now sit back and relax. The rector is expecting us to arrive shortly."

"What rector?"

"The one in the next town. I've made all the arrangements. I already told you I had a special license, didn't I," he said. "In less than an hour you will be my wife. Don't worry you'll get used to the idea.

If Gemma had something to throw at him, it would have already bounced off his head. Liam Marsden had to be the most stubborn male in existence.

"Bloody hell, you are irritating."

"Welcome to my world," he said with a droll smile. "It's all part of the plan, love. Makes life more… intriguing."

Gemma sat back in her seat and fumed. Winning an argument with Liam was akin to dreams becoming reality. No way would he allow her to get ahead. Just like the real world never compared to the bliss of dreams.

Neither one had a chance of happening for her right now. She gave up on her fantasies a long time ago; just as she now gave up on convincing Liam to forego marrying her. It would amount to wasted energy and useless hope.

Gemma knew when to sit back and lick her wounds to fight another day. If she had to be Liam's wife, she'd need a new plan of attack. She had learned from the best and Lily had taught her well. Her fiancé didn't know what he had in store for him.

Gemma didn't give up anything that belonged to her.

Liam would love her or at the very least desire her as much as she did him. With a plan forming in her head, she relaxed, and her lips lifted into a half smile.

CHAPTER 3

Things hadn't gone quite as Liam had planned it. The situation had gotten out of control when he walked in and saw Alfie's hands all over Gemma. Rage filled him as he fought to restrain himself from murdering the rotten bastard.

How dare he force himself on a woman!

Seeing Gemma fighting off his unwanted attentions had changed his approach to the situation. He had come in prepared for anything, but hoping for the best. Marriage to Gemma was only to be utilized as a last resort. She had been right in assuming the contract was a means to extricate her from her cousins clutches. Liam never thought he'd be grateful for his father's foresight. For once the unwanted betrothal with Lord Devon appeared to be a good thing.

When he'd first heard about it years ago, he'd been angry and disillusioned. So much so he'd listened to his sister's scheme and along with her and his best friend, Noah, he had run away. How serendipitous his father still had the original contract. If Lord Devon hadn't insisted on his father keeping it, they wouldn't have had the means to extricate Lady Gemma from Alfie's clutches.

Now he found himself on the way to his own wedding.

Sweat beaded on his forehead. He wiped it away with the back of his hand. A flutter of energy dissipated throughout his stomach. Oh hell, he was getting married and soon. What had he gotten himself into?

Liam originally had no intention of going through with the ceremony. Tying himself to one woman was the last thing he wanted at that point in his life. He was too bloody young to even consider the idea. He couldn't back out of the situation now. Fate had decided on a new path for him, and it included Gemma as his wife.

The carriage rolled to a stop in front of a vicarage. Liam leaned forward and looked out the window. He glanced at his bride-to-be and found her to be sitting calming across from him. At least she had stopped arguing with him. Thank goodness for small favors, he didn't want to drag an unwilling bride into the vicarage. What would the vicar think then? How would he explain it? Gemma had to be willing, or it wouldn't work.

"Wait here. I'm going to see if they are ready for us. I will retrieve you once it's time to start the ceremony," he told her.

"Fine."

"You're not going to argue with me?" he asked.

Thank God. The last thing he needed was to fight with Gemma before the wedding. The one he hadn't set up yet. He didn't want her to realize how much he'd been bluffing since he'd walked into the sitting room and found Alfie attacking her.

The urge to protect Gemma became ingrained in his soul in an instant.

Gemma always bickered with him and now wouldn't be a good time for her to unleash her inner wrath. He had come to accept it as second nature for her, but for this to work she needed to project a calm demeanor.

"No point."

Gemma had to be plotting something. Liam knew her too well to believe anything else. His twin sister, Lily, happened to be the queen of devious plans. No doubt she had taught her best friend how to create the most intricate ones. He needed to be at his best if he hoped to thwart whatever rambled through her brain.

"All right. I will be back shortly," he told her as he stepped out of the carriage.

He ambled inside the vicarage and found the clergyman sitting at one of the pews near the altar, his head bent down in prayer. The man obviously hadn't heard Liam walk inside as he only looked up once he stood in next to him.

"Sorry to disturb you," Liam said. "I had hoped you could perform a wedding today."

"Yours I assume?" the vicar asked.

"Yes. I'd like to get married immediately. My fiancée awaits your decision in the carriage."

"I presume you have a special license as the bans have not been read in this vicarage."

"Indeed I do. Will you perform the ceremony?" Liam asked.

"I will as long as you are both willing."

He hoped Gemma wouldn't make a fuss. This was for her own good. If he was willing, she better damn well be too.

"We are."

"Very well, retrieve your young woman. I will perform the ceremony."

Liam nodded and strolled out of the vicarage. Now to get Gemma inside so they could get married without any unforeseen interruptions. He hadn't planned on a wedding that day, but at least everything seemed to be falling into place. She didn't need to know exactly what his original intentions were though. Liam hadn't wanted to marry her, but he'd been left with no choice. Alfie would never leave her alone if she remained unwed.

He'd always stand by her, and that's all the information Gemma would need to know. That included tying them together forever. He just accepted them as a fact. Gemma needed him therefore he gave her the only thing that would help… himself and everything it entailed.

"It's time Gemma. Follow me inside," he said as he opened the carriage door.

"Do we really need to take it this far?"

"We are not going to go over this again, Gemma. Come inside."

She reached out and grabbed onto his hand for support as she exited the carriage. Her gloved hand slid across his palm leaving a trail of heat. Once her feet hit the ground, she looked back up into his eyes, her jade green eyes staring back at him in defiance.

Liam sighed. She didn't appear too happy at the prospect of being his wife. Too bloody bad—this wasn't an ideal situation in his eyes either.

"If this is my only choice I will make the best of it. Rest assured I do know when to give in and fight another day. I just wanted to make sure that you are positive you want to tie yourself to me forever. I know how you feel about me," she said.

"You have no idea what I feel for you Gemma. You never did. Let's go attend our wedding now. The vicar is patiently waiting for us."

Gemma followed him inside making small steps ensuring a slow progress. Liam could feel his pulse start to race with anticipation. Heat spread through him. Desire he'd never experienced before. A thousand sensations traveled over him leaving him breathless. Soon he would be her husband, but something even more surprising became evident to him.

In a short time, Gemma would be his.

It was simultaneously enlightening and terrifying. He started to shake with the sudden realization—Gemma would soon be his wife. This was truly and utterly happening. She would belong solely to him and no one else. He would have a claim on her that he never realized he wanted. Somehow that made all the difference to him as he turned and waited with extreme patience for her to join him in front of the vicar.

"I know it's been a taxing day love, but we have an even longer journey back to London," he said with an amused smile. "But I'm a patient man. I'm willing to wait forever to make you mine."

"I know exactly how patient you are Liam. Trust me when I say my fervor matches yours."

"Good. Then we can proceed at a quicker pace. Vicar whenever you wish to begin we are ready," Liam said.

"I am ready now. Please join me here," the vicar said.

They ambled over to join him. The vicar started the ceremony and for Liam it went by in a blur. He barely remembered saying the vows which joined him and Gemma together. Through the entire ceremony, he stared into her green eyes and lost himself in their depths. Something lurked there, something that he hadn't noticed before. He couldn't explain it, but he felt he had missed an important detail. A facet that made Gemma essential to him, but he couldn't pinpoint the exact element that had changed. Maybe the only real change resided deep inside him. Perhaps Gemma had not changed at all, but how he saw her had.

"You are now man and wife," the vicar said. "You may now kiss your bride."

Liam looked up at the vicar startled at his pronouncement. "What?"

"Never mind Liam," Gemma said with a disgusted voice. "You don't need to kiss me. We have a long journey ahead. We should go. Thank you again, vicar for marrying us."

Gemma started to leave, but Liam stopped her. He turned her to face him, and he could see how much he had disappointed her. She wanted to kiss him, and he had ruined the moment by being lost in his own thoughts. How could he be so foolish? The least he could do was make this day as happy as possible for her. It wasn't and ideal situation. They should get some enjoyment from their wedding. His heart thrummed hard in his chest and sweat dripped down his neck.

In that instant he realized he wanted to kiss her too.

"I want to kiss my wife."

He leaned down and pressed his lips against hers. With as much gentleness as he could muster Liam placed a soft kiss on her lips; with a slow pace he caressed them with his own over and over again. He pulled her into his arms and with gentle hands stroked her back. She let out a small breath of satisfaction.

Liam wanted more, and he promised himself he would have it later. The first taste of her lips left him with a craving like none before. He pulled back and saw his own need reflected in her eyes. They had that at least. An equal desire for each other, but Liam knew he couldn't press her just yet.

If their marriage was to have any chance of becoming anything good, they had to take their time with each other. They had the rest of their lives together. He wasn't sure if it was a good thing or a bad thing, but he looked forward to learning everything he could about his new wife.

"Let's go home, Lady Marsden."

"I don't think I'll get used to that anytime soon," she said.

"You will. Sooner than you realize."

"What's next Liam?"

"Other than going home? We will plan a trip to visit my sister in America. I want to meet my new nephew, and she will want to make sure you are all right. We won't leave right away though. I have some things to take care of before we can make the trip."

Liam nodded at the vicar as they walked out faster than they had come in. They really did have a long journey ahead of them. It would be at least an hour before they made it back to London. He didn't want to waste any time lingering in the church. He helped Gemma back into the carriage, and he settled once again across from her.

"How long do you think before we leave?"

"Two weeks at least, if I can manage to get everything in place that quick. A month at most," he said. "Are you in a hurry to share a small space with me?"

"Not at all. My urgency is a deep desire to see Lily again. It has been three years since she left. I miss her terribly. I too want to meet her new son."

"And you shall. I promise."

"Because you always keep your promises?" she asked with sarcasm as she leaned her head against the side of the carriage.

She might not believe he did, but she'd learn soon enough. Liam was as good on his word. Once given, he made sure he didn't disappoint the person he'd given it to.

"I do indeed, Gemma. Every last one of them," he said with desire in his eyes. "One day you will know exactly how good I am at keeping a promise."

"I think I already know," her voice just above a whisper. "I don't need any demonstrations."

"Don't worry, love. I don't plan on giving one anytime soon. Relax we have a while before we arrive home."

She looked at him and turned her head to look out the window. Her choice not to answer him told him everything she tried to hide. He knew her desire as well as he knew his own. Two years ago she had let him know exactly how much she wanted him. He had turned her away then. A mistake, he knew it now. She didn't fully trust him, but he would rectify that with time. Soon she would see that she could rely on him for anything.

CHAPTER 4

Gemma sat in silence for the rest of the trip to London. She still had trouble wrapping her mind around the fact that she had just married Liam Marsden. Saying yes had really only been a token effort on her part; marrying him had always been her secret wish. Perhaps not the wisest choice she had ever made, but she knew that she couldn't turn back and change it. Marriages were not as easily undone as they were to enter into. She only hoped that she wouldn't come to regret her choice. No matter what Liam said, she knew he wouldn't have forced her into the marriage if she had truly been adamant against it. She looked out the window of the carriage and saw the outskirts of London coming into view.

"Not much longer and we will be at our destination."

Liam looked over at her. He had been quiet for the rest of the journey as well. Gemma couldn't help but wonder what he had rolling through his mind. She wished she knew why he insisted marriage was their only option.

"True enough, I'm sure you are as ready to get out of this carriage as I am," he said.

"Probably more so, on your part. You did travel more than I have today."

"More than you know."

"What do you mean?" she asked.

Maybe if she got him to talk a little bit she'd figure out

what his plan was. Liam had a way of being closed mouthed. Gemma didn't understand what was going on, but at least she could be thankful to be out of her cousin's clutches. Even if Liam irritated her, Gemma knew she owed him more than she could ever pay back.

"It's nothing. Suffice to say I had a lot to accomplish in a short time."

"You're not going to tell me are you?" Gemma pursed her lips in displeasure.

"I don't see the point," he said, frustrated. "I'm tired Gemma. Just leave it be."

Liam wouldn't discuss it with her even if he didn't have the excuse of being tired. She wouldn't push the issue... yet. She knew when to let something go and bring it back up at a later time. He may not want to answer her questions now, but he would when she was ready to force him to.

"Fine."

"You're not going to try to make me talk? That's a refreshing change," Liam said.

"I'm in a semi-good mood. Don't ruin it by being an imbecile." Gemma glared at him.

"I'm never without wit, love."

"Truly?" she raised her eyebrow in question. "You could have fooled me."

"Now who's being the difficult one?" he asked with an amused laugh.

"I call it as I see it, *love*." She emphasized the last word with sarcasm. Gemma believed he mocked her by saying it so offhanded when talking to her. He didn't love her, and she didn't see the point of the charade.

"Do you now?" he asked. A cocky grin filled his handsome face."Should make our lives inherently more interesting."

"Absolutely." Wickedness filled her, and she grinned up at him, letting it shine through.

Maybe she should look at this as an opportunity. One she could use to her advantage. She'd have more freedom as a married woman. As she studied Liam, she realized something else.

He was her husband.

By marrying her, he'd give her the right to take certain

liberties—with him. Part of her was rather excited at the prospect. A tingle of energy fluttered inside of her. Yes, maybe this marriage thing wouldn't be so bad.

"I don't like that look on you. Whatever idea you just formed I'd advise against it."

Liam had no idea. Gemma wasn't the meek wallflower he first met. She'd had to grow up and fast. Her father's death changed everything for her. Losing him—dealing with her awful cousin—it gave her the backbone she'd been lacking before. Her husband had no idea how much courage it had taken her to tell him how she felt about him two years ago. Loving Liam made her brave. Too bad he never returned her feelings. Now he was hers and she'd find a way to make him pay for that slight, without losing her heart to him again.

"Of course you would. I happen to think it's a rather genius idea."

"Gemma..."

"What?" Innocence resonated through her voice.

"Nothing. I'm not going to humor you with a response. I'm going back to my own corner and enjoy the peace and quiet."

"Coward." Gemma ground her bottom lip between her teeth and raised an eyebrow. She licked the sting from her lip and then asked, "Are you afraid of little ole' me?"

He gave her a scathing look. Some things just didn't change. Liam had always been so easy for her to goad into a response. He failed to realize she only wanted his attention. Something he didn't usually deign to give her. Which is why the marriage had come as a shock to her, Liam usually avoided her. The carriage came to a stop and surprised Gemma. She looked out and saw a townhouse she didn't recognize.

"This isn't Marsden House."

"Of course not, Marsden's my parents' home," Liam said.

"I didn't realize you had your own townhouse."

"No reason you would. I haven't had it that long, and we haven't socialized in a while," he said. "Come let's go inside. They are expecting us."

He'd certainly thought of everything. The staff probably had everything arranged for his new wife's arrival. Too bad she'd not been given the luxury of being prepared.

Liam stepped out of the carriage and turned to help her down. She took his hand and jumped down. He continued to hold onto her as he escorted her inside her new home where the staff greeted them.

"This is the butler, Pemberly and the housekeeper, Janie." Liam introduced them. "This is my wife, Lady Marsden."

"Welcome home," they both said in unison.

"Is Lady Marsden's room ready?" Liam asked.

"Yes, sir it is," Janie said.

"Good. Can you show her around the house and where her room will be?" Liam asked.

"You're not going to show me around?" Gemma asked.

"No, I have some things to do."

She couldn't believe he was leaving her. Alone. In a new home she'd never laid eyes on before. How inconsiderate...

"I thought you just said you were tired," Gemma said with a petulant voice.

"I am," Liam rubbed his temples in frustration. "Don't be difficult Gemma."

Her husband was an arse. How dare he tell her not to be difficult? She had every right to be as demanding as she wanted. Her whole life had been uprooted, and while it was a good thing it was still rather drastic. Why couldn't he understand how unsettled it all had made her? Did the blasted man every really look at anything around him? Gemma didn't see the point in arguing with him. If he wanted to abandon her she'd let him. This was her life now. She'd just have to find a way to get through her husband's tough shell. It would just take time. For now, though, she didn't want to lay eyes on him. His actions disgusted her and she had more pride than to beg.

"I see. So you are going to run away already. I'm not surprised. Will I see you later?"

"No. I will be out."

"Ah. I get it. Go run to your club, Liam. I'll be fine here with Janie and Pemberly. I don't need you." Gemma turned to walk towards Janie.

Damn her infernal heart—why did she allow herself to start to hope. She *knew* better.

"Gemma, wait..."

No doubt he had a list of reasons why he needed to leave. She didn't have the energy or inclination to listen to him droll on about them. She'd rather he go and save herself the aggravation.

"Go, Liam. I see you have more pressing—issues." She turned her attention to the butler and housekeeper.

"Now, Janie, I'd love a tour. Please show me around my new home," Gemma said with as much enthusiasm she could muster. She'd been taking care of herself for a while now—since her father passed away. A sharp pain stabbed through her chest as she remembered the loss. "Pemberly, could you please see to it that my satchel is taken to my room. I believe it's still in the carriage."

"Yes, Lady Marsden," Pemberly said and turned to leave the room.

Gemma turned to see Liam still standing in the entryway. His lips were twitching downward. Eyes narrowed to tiny slits he observed her with the staff. His arms were folded across his chest, his head slightly tilted, as he tapped his foot. If Gemma were to hazard a guess, he seemed to be contemplating what his next move would be.

"Why are you still here?" she asked. "I thought you had something better to do."

"It isn't like that, Gemma."

"It never is, is it?"

"I don't understand why you are so damned angry, but I'm not going to sit here and have a disagreement with you in front of the servants. We will discuss this later."

"Fine by me."

Gemma watched as Liam stormed out of the house. She fought tears from falling down her face. None of it should surprise her. He only married her to protect her from her awful cousin. He never promised or claimed to love her. She couldn't hold him responsible for her broken heart. No, she knew where to place the blame; it belonged squarely on her shoulders.

She foolishly still loved Liam Marsden. Stupid of her to hope he might return those feelings... No time to cry, there were other more pressing matters at hand. She had a household to get familiar with and servants waiting for her direction.

"Janie, please show me around the house."

"It would be my pleasure, Lady Marsden," Janie said.

Janie led her around and showed her every nook and cranny. The townhouse was lovely and bright. It would be a wonderful place to live and raise a family. If only she thought a family might be in her future. Maybe someday, if her husband ever touched her again. That kiss in the church had to be an anomaly.

"This here is your room. It was prepared for you earlier today."

"And where is my husband's room?"

"Right next door."

"Thank you, Janie," Gemma said. "I think I am going to retire to the sitting room. Can you have tea sent there?"

"Absolutely madam. Would you like something to eat as well?"

"Yes, something light. It's been a long day, and I don't want a heavy meal. I don't want supper tonight."

"Very well, I will have it prepared."

Janie left her standing in her bedroom. The coloring matched her eyes. The draperies and bedspread were both a nice shade of green. She had to wonder if Liam had ordered the room made up in that color or if it had already been decorated in that shade. He had asked her to change into a green gown earlier. It made her wonder how much he noticed about her.

How silly of her to consider he'd made the room up in a color to match her eyes. He wouldn't have gone that far. It would imply he'd been planning this for a while. Gemma knew that couldn't have been possible. It was only her wishful thinking that Liam might have feelings for her beyond protecting her from Alfie.

Speculating about the possible motivations of her husband wouldn't get her anywhere. She already had a sharp sting in her chest. No need to add to the pain. She walked out of the room and down the stairs. She weaved her way through the hallway until she located the sitting room. She sat down and waited for her tea to arrive.

"Excuse me, Lady Marsden," Pemberly said. "I know you just arrived, but we have a caller."

"We do? Who?"

"That would be me," a male voice said.

Gemma looked up into the eyes of a very handsome man. She had never seen him before, but if she had he might have given Liam a rival for her attention. Never before had she seen such a good-looking man. His features were as dark as Liam's were light. The shade of his hair held the hue of a black midnight sky and his eyes a deep rich brown, like chocolate. His countenance screamed power and authority. This man was not someone to toil with.

"I don't know you," she said. "I'm sorry, that's rather rude of me."

"No apologies necessary," he said smoothly. "I don't socialize so you wouldn't know me on sight. You probably recognize my name though. I am Noah St. John, Duke of Huntly."

"Oh, now I certainly feel more foolish, Your Grace. I have to ask though why are you here?"

"I came to see your husband, Liam."

"Oh, Pemberly probably told you he isn't in. He left rather suddenly."

"He did indeed, but when he said Lady Marsden was in I had to meet you."

"Oh, and why?"

"Because I didn't believe my dear friend had succumbed to marriage when he vowed he wouldn't for many years to come. His new wife had to be an enchantress of some sort. It's my duty as his friend to see for myself that he made a good choice." He grinned. "You're quite beautiful, Lady Marsden. Liam is a lucky man. You sure you want to stay with him?"

Gemma didn't know if she should be flattered or appalled. Did Liam put him up to this nonsense? She didn't think he had a cruel bone in his body, but she had been wrong before.

"What are you after, Your Grace?"

"I don't know what you mean."

"Why are you throwing flattery at me and asking me so blatantly if I want to leave my husband... of less than five hours."

"So the newness hasn't worn off yet?" The duke raised his eyebrow, mocking her.

Ah, she understood now. The duke was a rake and ascertaining her intentions. She didn't believe in being unfaithful and wouldn't find a lover to replace her husband. Liam was the only one she ever truly wanted. Besides, she had no clue what true passion entailed. She didn't know what she missed by denying herself the joys of intimacy.

The Duke of Huntly wouldn't be getting anywhere with her. Even if Liam never truly loved her, nothing would get her to be untrue to herself. When she made a vow, she meant it and had every intention of keeping it. Even in the face of such a handsome, enticing male, she would stay true to her beliefs.

"You're cynical. That's your problem. You don't believe anyone can be faithful to each other. I get it now. You're testing me. Rest assured, Your Grace, I don't plan on having an affair with anyone." Moisture formed on her palms. Gemma wiped them across her skirts. "If that is all you came to ascertain, you can turn around and leave. It's been a trying day, and I'd rather not deal with anymore... difficulties."

"No one ever does, dear. Look at you. Liam left you all alone on your wedding night, no less. It won't take long for your bed to be too cold, and you'll want someone to warm it up for you." His lips tilted up into a cocky smile. "Let me know if you change your mind and I'll be happy to show you what true pleasure is."

An unladylike snort erupted from her mouth. She tilted her head and looked closely at the duke. His eyes had narrowed into tiny slits, and his lips curled into a sensuous smile. His arms were folded across his chest. True pleasure he said. Gemma didn't doubt he could deliver on that promise. If only Liam had been the one to offer it to her, then she'd have been already leaping into his arms. This man would never do though.

"How kind of you to offer yourself to service my needs," she said with derision in her voice. "I'm going to have to decline your very generous offer, Your Grace. I'm not into inflicting pain on myself. Besides, I respect myself too much.

I'm sure you won't have any trouble finding a different candidate."

"Indeed I won't. I'm not used to getting turned down," he said. His lips tilted into a half smile filled with cockiness.

"You proposition the wives' of your friends' often?" Gemma asked, sarcasm laced through her voice.

"No." The Duke of Huntly laughed. "Only you hold that distinction. I had to be sure, you see."

"So you wouldn't have become my lover if I jumped at the chance?" Gemma raised her eyebrow questioningly.

She could see the play of emotions on his face. This man before her was a conundrum. She didn't understand him completely. Gemma wasn't even sure how close his relationship was to her husband. Why did he come in and immediately proposition her? What kind of game was he playing with her? Gemma didn't like playing the fool and didn't appreciate this man making her look and feel silly.

"On the contrary, I would have, if only to prove to Liam exactly what kind of woman he married," he said quietly.

"I see, so you did this all for purely altruistic intentions," she said with skepticism in her voice. "Somehow I doubt that."

"Very astute of you. I promise I won't ever offer again. I honestly am only looking out for Liam."

"A little late don't you think? We *are* already married."

"Nothing is ever too late." He shook his head. "Something could have been done to correct the mistake."

"Really? What possible solutions would you have for it?" she asked.

"Annulment, if possible... divorce, if not. Death is usually final."Her mouth hung open for several seconds as she processed his word. Once she got control over her thoughts, she stared up into his brown depths. "Death? Really? That's a bit extreme, isn't it?" Surely he didn't mean what he insinuated.

"Yes. Quite so. Sometimes it doesn't give us much of a choice." A solemn glint in his eyes as grief filled his voice. "Death waits for no one."

Noah St. John had some dark stains on his soul. She could see shadows in his eyes telling her he had ingrained demons buried inside him compounded by unearthly pain. Gemma didn't want to dig too deep for fear of what she'd find. It also became clear that he had no idea how to relate to anyone. Someone had hurt him, and he carried the wounds around for the world to see. She didn't know what happened to him, but her heart hurt just looking at the grave look in his chocolate-brown eyes.

"I don't think I want to know why you feel that way, Your Grace. It's been a long day, and I'm going to retire soon. Do you wish to leave a message for my husband?"

"No. I will stop by again another day and catch up with him." He nodded and added, "You're different. I think I like you. Someday I will figure out where you got that backbone of steel. For now I bid you goodnight."

The duke turned to leave. Gemma watched him walk out the door. After he left, Janie pushed in a cart with tea and a light repast. She sat down on the settee and poured a cup of tea. Absentminded she sipped it as she pondered the odd conversation she had with the duke. Then, she shook her head. She didn't see the point in worrying about the Duke of Huntly. She had more pressing concerns, like how to deal with her husband.

CHAPTER 5

Liam had intended to visit his father to give him an update on the situation. Gemma's attitude had him going to his club instead, exactly as she had suggested. Her claws had come out, and she had assumed the worst in him. He tried to explain to her that he needed to see his father, but she kept pushing him away. No one could drive him mad faster than Gemma. She had always been able to make him angrier than anyone else. He took a swig of brandy and set the glass down on the table. What he should do is go home and make love to his new wife, but he had already decided he needed to wait. They didn't have a normal romance or courtship. Liam believed they needed time to adjust before taking that step.

"Met your wife earlier this evening."

Liam looked up at his best friend, Noah, and smiled.

"I see you survived relatively intact, Gemma must be having an off night." The smile left Liam's face to be replaced with a grimace as he regarded his friend. He picked up his glass of brandy and downed the remaining liquid. It burned as it traveled down his throat. His head shook in several involuntary rapid successions.

"That bad?" Noah let out a loud whistle and sat down. He grinned down at Liam and raised his eyebrow. "I found her rather charming."

"She has her moments." Liam ran his finger around the rim of his empty glass. He needed more brandy."Unfortunately I don't get to see them very often."

"Why the hell did you marry her if she's such a harridan?"

"I don't know. I didn't plan it. I just needed to." How do you explain the loss of your mind? That was the only explanation for marrying Gemma. He was only supposed to use the contract as a means of extricating her. Instead, he'd been compelled to marry her. Damned if he understood why. Deep down he believed he'd made the right decision, even if it didn't feel like it was. "I know that doesn't make sense. I can't wrap my head around it myself."

"I admit I was a bit confused to find her in your house. The same chit your father attempted to betroth you to when we were still at Eton. It boggled my mind—thought there might be something nefarious afoot. What gives?"

"Yeah, I never thought I'd marry her either." Liam paused, tilted his head, and considered how to explain it to his best friend. "When I saw her, Alfie had his hand down her dress— I saw red. She drives me insane, but no woman should have to put up with something so bloody awful."

"Bloody hell. You're in love with her," Noah said, shock filling his voice.

Liam's breath seized inside his chest. No, he didn't— couldn't love Gemma. He only married her to protect her. Nothing more...

"Of course not. Don't be absurd. I don't love her. I..."

Noah raised his eyebrow at him with a questioning look in his eyes. No way, no how. Liam did not love Gemma, did he? He had strong feelings for her whenever he found himself in her company. He had simply chalked that up to them disliking each other. What had his father said about it being a different form of passion? Could both his father and Noah be right?

"No, I don't love her," he reiterated. "I'm not sure I even like her."

"Is that why you are here getting drunk?"

Liam nodded. "She got all mad because I had to leave. Acted like I was abandoning her. I was only going to go see my father. He needed to know what happened."

"So you left your blushing bride to go visit your father?" Noah asked. "It couldn't have waited until the next day?"

Put like that, Liam could see why Gemma had reacted the way she had. He shouldn't have even planned to leave her alone. No reason his father couldn't have waited until the next day to hear the news.

Liam wondered if he'd be surprised that he married Gemma after all.

His father seemed to believe that strong feelings existed between him and his new wife. The blasted man probably would laugh, thinking he was right.Liam would have to disabuse him of that notion rather quickly. The last thing he needed to hear was his father's gloating. He would make sure not to mention how he blundered when he brought her home. His father had a strange sense of humor and would find his predicament hilarious.

"You're right. I messed up. Clearly I've lost my mind and I'm not thinking straight," Liam said in a remorseful voice.

"Damn right, I am." Noah picked up his glass of brandy and took a drink."By and by. She's a spitfire that wife of yours."

"Why do you say that? Did you do something to make her even more livid?" Liam asked. "I've already got to atone for my own blunder, please tell me you didn't make it worse."

"I may have." Noah nodded, guilt filling his eyes. "I couldn't understand why you got married so fast. I expected a cloying manipulative female. Your wife didn't appreciate my methods of determining her worth."

"Oh hell, what did you do?"

If Noah messed things up even worse... Liam would be paying for a long time. He already blundered all on his own. He didn't need his friends adding onto the situation. Gemma wasn't likely to forgive him for some time. Bloody hell.

"Not much. Not nearly as much as I could have done," Noah explained. "I only propositioned her a bit. She didn't take the bait though. I'm not sure she likes me after my blatant innuendos."

If Liam hadn't already downed a bottle of brandy, he'd consider starting another one. No, what he should do is punch Noah in the face for even thinking of issuing his wife an unsavory invitation. Liam fumbled forward and almost fell out of his chair. Gripping the table he pushed himself back and leaned against his chair. He clenched his fists together as heat traveled up the back of his neck. Noah's idiotic actions were sure to cause him more trouble once he got home.

"Damn it, Noah. Gemma isn't like the females you know. She is innocent."

"I know that now." He shrugged his shoulders. "I didn't then, nothing to do about it now. I'm glad she's one of the good ones. You deserve to be happy."

Time would tell—Liam had his doubts about happiness with Gemma. They might find a certain level of it, but they'd probably fall short of finding true bliss.

"So do you. Don't discount finding someone to love again."

"Marriage isn't for me. I've already tried that route, and it left me devastated. I'm not about to open myself to that kind of pain again."

"I know you feel that no other female can compare to Rubina. You loved her, but she's gone. Don't let her death ruin your life."

"It's not as simple as that. I never told you how we argued that day." Noah's face grew dark, and sadness permeated his eyes. His eyes scanned the room never fully looking at Liam. "She left because she needed a break from me. She told me that I was too intense for her, and she couldn't be my everything. I needed to find a way to live without her. She got her bloody wish. The only problem is I'm merely surviving, without her I've always been a little lost. I don't want another wife. There's no way I'll put a female through the tragedy of getting too close to me."

"You might change your mind someday," Liam said, "I hope you do. I'd like my friend to be happy again."

"I doubt it. I'm not meant to have a family. You get rather used to being alone when your parents die when you're still a child." Noah said. "But that isn't the issue right now. We need to figure out how to get back into your wife's good graces."

"Gemma doesn't hold a grudge. She'll forgive you." Liam shook his head, disgusted with himself. "Me, on the other hand, she will make grovel. This isn't the first time we've had a disagreement. We tend to quarrel a lot."

"That's another form of heat between you. Just channel it in another way. She'll forgive you."

"Of course she will, eventually," Liam said. "I'm not sure she'll accept me in her bed just yet. We had a rather unusual courtship. By that I mean we haven't had one at all."

"How did you end up married to Lady Gemma of all women? Last I knew you didn't intend to get married any time soon."

"That I didn't. It's Lily's fault."

"What does your sister have to do with it?" Noah asked baffled.

"Gemma is her friend. Lily wrote Father asking him to help her. Gemma's cousin, Alfie, intended to force her to marry him so he could get his hands on her money."

"So your father made you marry her?"

"No, he'd never insist on that. He learned his lesson about forcing one of us to marry against our will a long time ago, as you know." Liam took another swig of his brandy. "He suggested two options. Marriage only if I cared for the girl. I had every intention of going through with the other plan until I saw Alfie attacking Gemma. I jumped in and claimed her before I knew what I was doing."

"Marrying her was your first instinct?" Noah asked.

"Yes, and pummeling my fists into Alfie as soon as she left the room."

"Now that makes a bit more sense. That's the Liam I know." Noah's laugh echoed through the room.

"He deserved it. When I walked in, I found him groping her, and the bodice of her dress ripped."

"I'm sure he did deserve it. I'm not arguing with you. I applaud your restraint. I may have murdered him myself."

"If he ever comes near Gemma again I might do that."

Liam didn't like the idea of anyone ever touching his wife. He would commit murder in order to protect her. She didn't know exactly what he was capable of, but she should. When he told her he took care of what belonged to him, he meant it.

Someone came by and refilled his glass. He picked it up and swished the contents around. The aroma filled his nose, enticing him; he tipped it back and drank it in one swig. This time the burn made him feel good as it traveled down his throat. He set the empty tumbler down on the table and stood up. The room spun around a bit, and he grabbed onto his chair for support.

"You should go home to your wife. It's getting late. Do you need help getting home?"

"I'm only slightly foxed. I think I can manage to get home on my own." Liam tilted backward a bit. He held out his arms to steady himself. Who the hell made the room spin?

"Right. I can see how capable you are. Come on, I'll give you a lift in my carriage."

"All right. I think that perhaps you're right."

"I'm always right." Noah reminded him as he helped him up.

Noah stood up next to Liam, and they left the club. Liam's stumbled forward in a haze as he followed his friend to his carriage. He climbed inside and fell in a clumsy heap on one of the seats. Noah motioned for the driver to start moving, and the slow rock of the carriage made Liam's stomach churned with each rotation.

"You're not going to be sick, are you?"

"I must be looking pretty green for you to be asking me that," Liam said. "I'm fine. Just a little dizzy."

He could see the skepticism in Noah's eyes, but he told the truth. He didn't feel sick at all. Simply disoriented.

"You do look like hell. I haven't seen you drink this much in a very long time. I suppose you picked a good time to get seriously inebriated. Marriage does that to a man. Throws us all off balance."

"Right. Probably shouldn't have married her. Thanks for pointing that out to me," Liam said with a lot of sarcasm. "Don't really regret it though, don't know why."

"Maybe you should figure out why. It might be an important detail you're suppressing."

Gemma once told him she loved him. What were the chances she still did? How would that play a part in their marriage? Liam's heart beat hard inside his chest. His breathing became more rapid. He rubbed his hand over the ache beneath his ribs—something was wrong with him.

Did he want Gemma to still be in love with him?

Surely she'd have given up on that girlish wish. What would he do if she hadn't stopped loving him? Could he learn to love her? Perhaps he could...

Liam knew one thing for certain, he needed to court his wife. Not tonight though, his drunken state was less than desirable. He had one final thought right before he passed out cold. It's a good thing he didn't intend on making love to Gemma once he made it home. He would be a dismal failure as a lover, and she deserved a special night.

Liam couldn't give it to her, so they would have to put off their wedding night—he was a bloody fool.

CHAPTER 6

Gemma had heard her husband come in late. The constant fumbling and failed attempt at a quiet murmur woke her up. She didn't know who had helped him to his bed and did not care.

The fact that someone had to assist him told her all she needed to know.

Liam had decided to carouse with friends and get inebriated instead of spending time with her. His actions caused a feeling of deep hurt and betrayal; the pain threatened to swallow her whole.

After a short time, the door next to hers opened and closed with a muffled thud. Soft footsteps could be heard in the hallway as they passed by her bedroom door, indicating that her husband's rescuer had left. Gemma had no desire to see who had aided Liam, but she did have an overwhelming need to talk with her foolish husband.

She got up out of bed and donned her wrapper. Crossing the room she opened the door and took slow, silent steps towards the bedroom next to hers. Stopping in front of the closed door she started to doubt the wisdom of visiting her husband's room.

Did she really want to go in there?

Yes, she did—Liam needed to know what a nitwit he was. She opened the door and walked inside before she changed her mind. Light from the moon streamed through the room and gave it an eerie glow. On tiptoes, she moved with as much stealth as she could manage over to the bed where she saw Liam's body spread in a haphazard fashion across its vast space.

The bed, a rumpled mess, much like the clothes still hanging on Liam's lax body, gave the impression of chaos. The person who had brought him home had simply dumped him on the bed. One boot stood on the floor next to the bed, the other on its side in front of the bedside table.

"Liam," she whispered. When he didn't answer she said in a louder more firm voice, "Liam, wake up."

"Hmm—what—Gemma?"

"Good, you're awake I want to discuss something with you."

"Not a good time." His voice still held the remnants of his drunken escapade. He slurred over his words, but Gemma didn't care. She had something to say and intended to say it whether he liked it or not.

"I'm not happy, Liam. I don't think we should have gotten married. If you hadn't been so adamant, I wouldn't have done it. I love you, but I don't want to be married to a man who doesn't feel the same. I think we should have our marriage annulled."

Gemma looked over at her husband and saw that his eyes had fallen closed again. Dratted man, he hadn't been listening to a word she'd said.

"Liam!" she shouted at him.

His eyes flew open and scoured her face. With a slow lazy he smile his gaze fell on hers with an intensity she didn't quite understand. He sat up and reached for her.

"Ah, lovely Gemma. Come here."

Seriously? Apparently alcohol consumption had turned her husband into an idiot. No way did she intend to get any closer to him.

"No. You're not listening to me. I don't think that's a good idea." She scrambled backward and out of his reach.

"You're wrong, love. It's the best idea I've had in a long time."

Liam leaned forward, grabbed her hand and pulled her

towards him. She fell forward and placed her hands on his shoulders to brace herself. He wrapped his arms around her and captured her lips with his. Heat filled her as he kissed her with an urgency she didn't understand. She opened her mouth in a gasp, and he took advantage by pushing his tongue inside. His tongue danced with hers and coaxed her into pressing deeper into his arms. She reached up and ran her hands through his light blond hair and pulled the strands firmly through her fingers.

He groaned and started to place light kisses on her cheeks and down her neck. He stopped to untie her wrapper and pushed it off her shoulders. She watched as it pooled at her feet. Liam slipped her nightgown over her shoulder so that her bosom gleamed brightly in the moonlight.

"Perfect." He caressed each breast with his hands and licked one of her tight nipples. A thousand sensations traveled down her body and merged into a bundle of energy between her thighs. Gemma's emotions were all over the place with each new feeling Liam brought out of her. He made her feel too much, but she wanted more from him than passion. She had to stop before it went too far. They needed to get the marriage annulled. If they consummated their marriage that option would no longer be available to them.

Gemma could feel him start to push her gown further down her body and trail kisses across her stomach as she stood before him. She held her breath and let herself get lost in his touch. For a brief moment, it was everything she wanted. She could pretend Liam loved her. Until reality snapped her back to the present—giving her a good look at what this would all mean. She couldn't give into her desire. As much as she'd like to be with Liam in every way possible it would only lead to a devastating heartbreak. She had to stop him… and soon, before it was too late. Everything he did to her had an amazing effect on her body, and she would kill to know how it all would feel, but the price was too high.

"Liam, we shouldn't be doing this," Gemma whispered.

He kept going as if deaf to the sounds around him. Completely engrossed in the task at hand, he ran the palm of his hand across her hips and with innate slowness trailed his fingers across her buttocks. As he explored, Gemma's body lit up into a tight, overwhelming tangle of need. He left a trail of heat with each caress. A long drawn out moan escaped her mouth as an unrelenting pressure built up inside her.

"That's right, love. Feel it, let go," Liam whispered in her ear. He continued to stroke her flesh as he spread kisses all over her neck and bosom.

She looked into her husband's eyes, and they reflected her own desire. They hadn't gone too far, yet. She could still stop this. But, she didn't want to. Liam made her feel so amazing. He played her body as adeptly as a violist plucked the strings of their instrument. Her body wanted him to keep going—to see where it all might lead. Gemma couldn't give into those base instincts. Her first instinct should be to protect her fragile heart. It thrummed so loud inside her chest it almost deafened her, as if it pleaded with her for mercy. This couldn't happen… she had to end it. Stepping back she pulled her gown back up and picked her wrapper up. Putting it back on, she tied it tightly across her breasts.

"What are you doing, Gemma?"

"This isn't why I came here, Liam. I don't want this."

"You could have fooled me, love. You were just moaning with pleasure."

"Pleasure is an empty feeling when there is no love to sustain it. I don't want this with you. I tried to tell you that, but you got lost in *your* wants," Gemma said with a wobbly voice.

"You're saying you don't want me."

She could hear the anger in Liam's tone. Rage laced with confusion and pain. She hadn't handled this well, but she had to protect her heart. Only he had the power to destroy her emotionally.

"Want is a relative term. I'm sure you could make me want you a whole lot. You demonstrated that rather well a few moments ago. I'm asking you to leave me be. I can't be intimate with someone when love is absent. I'd rather we didn't visit that aspect of our marriage."

"It's a mistake," Liam said.

"I don't believe so. I think it's the only way I can ensure neither one of us does something we will regret."

"It's already too late for that. Just go, Gemma. I'm still a little drunk, and I'm afraid I'll say something that will come back to haunt me later." Liam sat on the bed with his head bowed. He scrubbed his face with his hands.

"We should discuss..."

"I told you to leave. Please don't make me repeat myself, unless you're willing to stay and finish what we've already started." Derision filled his voice. "You've left me in quite a state of unrest. I might be willing to allow you to pleasure me in another way if you're so eager to stay."

Gemma could see a large bulge filling his breeches. It appeared to grow under her direct scrutiny. One day her curiosity would be her undoing, but today would not be that day. She would not allow herself to explore any part of Liam's gorgeous body.

"No need to be crude. I told you I hadn't come in here for that. It's not my fault you assumed I had."

"And yet you didn't mind it all that much when I touched you, did you?" He raised his eyebrows in question.

"Well, I can't deny it had a certain pleasantness to it. It doesn't mean I wish to repeat it. I will take your leave now."

She turned to go with as much dignity as she could muster. The sight of his growing manhood caused tingles to crawl up the base of her spine as nerves pooled in her belly. Part of her itched to reach out and touch him, to learn everything she could, but she couldn't give into that desire. She still had a deep-rooted need inside her. One she knew that only he could sate, and yet she also realized it could never happen. Not for the sake of her sanity.

"You can run, Gemma, but you can't hide. This thing between us can't be ignored." Liam laughed.

Gemma reached the door and turned to look at him. He still sat before her with his trousers now open and leaning his arms back against the bed. His gaze held every temptation she tried to escape from. Liam had always been her undoing. Too bad he also couldn't prove to be her salvation.

"Who said anything about hiding? I don't plan on going anywhere. Good night."

Gemma's heart raced and pounded against her chest. Things hadn't gone at all how she thought it would. Nothing ever did where Liam was concerned. He drove her mad, and she couldn't help how he made her feel. She had always loved him and no matter what,she knew she always would.

Her love had never been in question.

Gemma's position had already been laid out and stomped on. His feelings toward her were the reason she held back. She didn't lie to him. She needed more than pleasure, no matter how wonderful it made her feel. What she desired above anything else in the world was for her husband to love her. If she could make that a reality then her marriage would no longer be a sham. Nothing else could make her life any more perfect.

CHAPTER 7

A constant drum of pain beat with a steady and consistent rhythm against Liam's skull. The afternoon sun streamed through the window, and he could feel its blinding intensity skimming across his eyelids. The very idea of opening his eyes made him want to turn over and cover his head with his pillow. Liam might consider it except a cold draft had settled over his body, and he struggled to get warm.

Why had he gone to bed without covering himself with a blanket?

Lifting one eyelid into a small slit to canvass the situation, it all came crashing back to him at the sight of his tousled bed. Gemma had come to see him, in his bedroom, and he'd made a fool of himself. For one glorious moment, the experience held every fantasy that played through his mind. The pure bliss of holding her, tasting her, and hearing her soft moans filled him with an unsurpassable desire—until it all crashed and burned.

Liam remembered Noah had helped him up to his room and torn the bedsheets down his bed before finally pushing him onto it in a disorderly manner. Then, he had closed his eyes, oblivious to the world around him. That was until Gemma wandered into his room. Somehow his boots had been removed, but the particulars escaped his brain. The rest of his clothing, although messy and wrinkled, remained on his body as he lay on the bed. No doubt he should at least thank his friend for getting him this far; he'd probably have passed out at his club if not for his assistance.

His actions with his wife had been deplorable. He should apologize. Liam had decided not to explore that side of their marriage until they knew each other better. He'd blundered rather badly at the sight of her in her night clothes. When he opened his eyes and got a good look at her need shot straight through him. All reason left him. Liam wanted her and he bloody hell wouldn't deny himself.

Perhaps she'd be in a forgiving mood. She'd come into his room after all—not the other way around. He would talk to her and assess the situation. Maybe he still had a chance to win her over; to make her see that being with him was the best possible option for her.

With slow and deliberate movements, Liam pulled himself into a sitting position on the bed. Every muscle in his body ached, and his eyes were dry and gritty. He rubbed his face in an attempt to remove all the remnants of sleep from his mind and body. It didn't do much to help. He needed a bath and a shave. He reached up and pulled the bell to alert his valet he needed help. He didn't move an inch while he waited for Grady to arrive.

"You need assistance, sir?"

"Yes, Grady, I feel bloody awful. Please get a bath prepared."

"Very good, sir. I will see to it immediately. Would you like a tray brought up? You missed breakfast."

"Is it really afternoon? I was hoping that the sun was just especially bright and high this morning."

"Luncheon is in an hour, sir. It's now very late morning."

"No tray then. I will eat in an hour. Maybe by then I can tolerate food." His stomach rolled at the idea of eating. How much did he drink last night? "Where is my wife?"

"Lady Marsden is in the sitting room having tea. His Grace, the Duke of Huntly just arrived. She is entertaining him."

"Is she now? Skip the bath, Grady, help me shave and get dressed. I will probably have to go intervene. Noah made a mess of things with her yesterday."

Grady nodded and started to prepare everything to aid Liam. It didn't take long to get him ready to go downstairs. Less than twenty minutes later he was dressed, shaved, and at least on the outside, ready to face the world. The nauseous feeling still sat like a heavy brick inside him, but his outward appearance gave him a sense of confidence. The only thing left for him to do was go face his wife and best friend. He hoped he could make it through the whole meeting without falling over.

Liam strolled down the stairs and walked down the hallway to the sitting room. He could hear Gemma's melodious laughter resonate through the room. He stopped outside the doorway and leaned against the wall. The room began to spin, and he needed to get his bearings before he ambled his way into the room. While he stood there, he listened to their conversation.

"I assure you, Your Grace, you have nothing to apologize for," Gemma explained.

"I disagree, but let's just say we are at an impasse and move on. As long as you don't hold it against me."

"I don't see any reason I would. You were just looking out for your friend. I can't fault you for that. I kind of like that you were willing to go to such lengthy measures. It shows how loyal you are." Gemma grinned. "Although in hindsight it may have been amusing to see how far you would have taken it. You don't strike me as someone who would betray his best friend. If I had been in my right mind, I'd have tested you myself."

"I don't think I'd have survived. I'm glad you didn't have it in you to use your wiles against me. You would have wounded me forever."

"You may be right. It's best it played out as it did." Her laughter floated through the room.

Was Gemma flirting with Noah? No, he had to be imagining things again. She wouldn't do that, would she? It saddened him to admit that he didn't know her anymore. If last night was any indication, she no longer wanted him, but perhaps his friend held an appeal to her now. No way would he ever allow it. For a brief moment, Liam was blinded as he saw red flashing behind his eyes. An unknown emotion took root. One he'd never experienced before and had trouble identifying. His pulse raced and his hand shook. Liam clenched his fist at his side and closed his eyes. He took two deep calming breaths and imagined his wife with Noah—and heat fused through his whole body, again. Gemma's amusement brought him back to reality. He needed to get in that room; had to know where things stood with his wife.

He hobbled to the opening and got a glimpse of Gemma. She sat next to Noah on the settee, her hand resting in his. A sparkle shown in her eyes, bright red curls framed her face, and a happy smile beamed on her beautiful face. She looked radiant, and Noah appeared to be the reason.

"I'm not interrupting, am I?" With every ounce of energy he had in him, Liam sauntered into the room. He refused to show any weakness.

"I see you finally decided to crawl out of bed and join the rest of the world." Gemma frowned. "I almost wouldn't be able to guess you had gone out drinking last night. Of course, it probably helped to sleep off most of the nasty effects."

"So much concern for my health, ah... I see now the benefits of having a wife. You must care so much to harp on my actions so elegantly." Liam held his hand over his heart mocking her words. He strolled over and sat down on the chair next to the settee. "What, you didn't think to include me in your visit? No cup for me?"

"I didn't think to ask the servants to bring brandy with the tea, Liam. Forgive me for my oversight. I should correct it immediately." Scorn filled her voice.

"Good, see that you do. It's quite abysmal I don't have something to quench my thirst."

Gemma got up and walked out of the room stomping her feet each step of the way. The anger palpable on her face as her cheeks became as red as the curls framing it.

"Are you always so bloody asinine after drinking so much?" Noah asked raising his eyebrow at Liam. "Cause if so I don't recall you ever acting like an arse before now."

"Go bugger yourself, Noah. I'm not in the mood."

"Got up on the wrong side of the bed, did you?" Noah chuckled. "And here I thought you'd be glad to see me. I did make sure you made it home in one piece."

All of the laughter and amusement started to reverberate through his skull. It added a new layer of pain joining the already steady beat drumming inside his head.

"Not that I'm ungrateful, but I would prefer it if you didn't get too cozy with my wife." Liam scowled.

Noah sat back with shock on his face. "What the hell is that supposed to mean?"

"I heard you talking—flirting with Gemma. Leave her alone." Liam crossed his arms over his chest and stared at Noah with antagonism.

"I'm going to pretend that you are not accusing me of trying something with your wife. You know I wouldn't do that," Noah said baffled.

"Do I?" Liam raised an eyebrow. "You admitted to propositioning her last night."

"Damn it, Liam. Quit while you still can. You know last night wouldn't have happened. I do not want to become your wife's lover."

"Why the hell not?" Liam asked, insulted. "You don't think she's good enough for you?"

"I don't believe you! First you get on my case because you think I'm flirting with Gemma, and now you want to know why I'm not? What the bloody hell is going on in that head of yours?"

"Hell, if I know. Perhaps you should go before I say something else completely insane." Liam scrubbed his hands over his face in disgust. "This is what she is driving me to. I'll be in Bedlam before the day is out."

Gemma walked back in just as Noah stood up to leave.

"You're not leaving, are you? We were just getting to know each other," Gemma said.

Liam noticed Gemma's face light up as she looked at Noah. He had to repress the urge to get up and punch his best friend. Noah couldn't help that his wife liked him. Of course that didn't make him feel any better; the desire to pummel him didn't diminish as he watched her face glow brighter and happier in front of the duke.

"This is your doing, isn't it?" She turned to Liam, anger replacing the joy on her face. "I thought you were close? Why are you chasing him away?"

"He isn't making me leave, I assure you. I have business to take care of. I just wanted to apologize and make sure Liam had survived the night okay. It's time for me to take care of some other pressing matters."

"Oh, perhaps you can dine with us later in the week. I'd like to continue our discussion." Gemma smiled.

"Absolutely. Send a note as to what day and I will make sure I'm here," Noah said.

"Good. I look forward to seeing you again." Gemma grinned. "I'll send a note around later today."

Noah nodded at her and then turned back to Liam. "I will see you later. Perhaps you will be in a better mood."

"I doubt it," Liam grumbled.

"Good day, Lady Marsden," Noah said and left the room.

"What's wrong with you today?" Gemma demanded.

"Not a bloody thing. I'm just perfect. You, on the other hand, seem to like His Grace a little too much. It explains a lot actually."

"Are you still drunk?" She tilted her head to the side and scrunched her eyebrows up in confusion.

"Unfortunately no. Maybe I should be," Liam said. He stood up and walked over to her and stopped in front of her. "Or perhaps I still am, it would explain the lack of control I'm experiencing. Although I believe it's more apt to say you make me this way, dear."

"Don't blame me for your detestable behavior."

"I'm only giving credit where it's due, love."

"I'm not going to stand here and take this. I have better things to do with my time." Gemma started to leave, but Liam grabbed a hold of her hand and prevented her from storming out of the room.

"Like what? Chase after Noah?"

"I don't know where you are getting these delusional ideas from, but I am not interested in the Duke of Huntly."

"I don't believe you," Liam said as he pulled her into his arms. "But that's a matter for another day."

"Let me go."

"I can't. I will never let you go, Gemma."

He lowered his head and with a softness he didn't feel he pressed his lips to hers. She might want Noah now, but she had wanted him first. Liam just needed to remind her that she had loved him once and could again. It might take a while to get her to acknowledge it, but he had faith in his ability to duplicate that emotion within her. Gemma stood there and let him press light, innocent kisses on her lips and cheeks. Her actions made him believe she wasn't going to fight him... or encourage him.

"This isn't a good idea, Liam."

"Possibly not, but I needed to. I will leave you be for now, but Gemma you should be prepared."

"Whatever for?"

"A siege like you've never known before. I don't intend to give up easily. If you think you are going to turn to Noah you are mistaken. You are my wife, and I didn't take those vows lightly. I have never been good at sharing, and I'm not about to start this late in life."

"I told you I don't want the duke. Why can't you believe that? Never mind, I'm not going to argue with you. Believe what you want. I have better things to do."

With those words, Gemma stomped out of the room. Her face still held the red stains of anger on her cheeks or possibly a small amount could be attributed to his kiss. Liam hoped some of it could be accredited to her desire for him. That at least she couldn't fake or deny. The battle lines were clearly drawn and he intended to win the war. Gemma would belong to him in every way. In time, she would realize it too.

CHAPTER 8

Gemma stormed into the library and sat down on a chair and let out a muffled scream. That man infuriated her. How dare he accuse her of wanting the Duke of Huntly! Just because she entertained him while he visited did not mean a thing. She had no designs of being anything other than his friend. After they got past his faux pas, they had gotten along very well. As she spent more time with him, she found him quite charming and personable. For a brief moment, she was able to forget her troubles and just enjoy talking with someone else. The Duke of Huntly made it possible for her to laugh and smile for the first time since she had walked into her new home.

Liam, her husband, had only caused her heartache. How had they come to be in such a place? He didn't want her, but he didn't want anyone else to have her either. He acted like a kid with a new toy. Playing with it when he wanted to and casting it aside after it no longer amused him. Although he hadn't had a chance to entertain himself with her; preventing that last night had taken all the strength she had within her. If Liam had once even pretended to love her, she would have acquiesced to his seduction.

Gemma got up and started to amble around the room. She stopped and looked at the various bookcases. Perhaps she should get a book to read... No, that didn't interest her. She had only retreated to the library to get away from Liam. Restlessness roamed through her, and she knew sitting still to read would prove to be impossible. Too much ran through her mind. She had to find a way to get Liam to agree to annul their marriage.

"Pardon me, but you have a visitor," Pemberly said.

GEMMA TURNED TO LOOK AT THE BUTLER. HE STOOD IN THE doorway awaiting her instructions. Who could be visiting her? The only friend she had in the world lived across the ocean in South Carolina.

"I'm not expecting anyone. Can you tell whoever it is I'm not in?"

"Now dear, I'm not one to be turned away."

Just behind the butler, Viscount Torrington filled the doorway. His dark hair tied at the nape of his neck; his blue eyes sparkled with mischief. He had a very large frame; Liam took after him in height and build. Lily adored her father and often said she took after him in temperament, but Gemma didn't know him all that well. She didn't want to start on that journey now. What she wanted was for them all to leave her be so she could think.

"Viscount Torrington, what can I help you with?" Gemma asked. She only barely kept her annoyance out of her voice. "Pemberly, can you have Janie bring in some refreshments?"

"No need, Pemberly. I won't be here long."

Gemma raised her eyebrow at him. "Maybe I'd like some."

"Do you?"

"No, but it's rude of you to presume I didn't." Gemma shot back at him.

"You've got spirit." He laughed. "I can see why Lily likes you."

"Well the feeling is mutual, I happen to adore your daughter," Gemma said. "I repeat, my lord, what can I help you with?"

"I came to see Liam, but Pemberly informed me I just missed him."

"He left?" Gemma asked surprised. Liam was so bloody rude. She clenched her fists at her side. "I hadn't realized."

Gemma strolled over to the chair she had vacated earlier and sat back down befuddled that he had already left. He didn't believe in letting her know anything. Just decided to leave and didn't care if she might want to know. That man could drive a saint crazy with his carelessness.

"Perhaps you can answer my questions. Liam was supposed to come by and see me last night. He failed to show up."

"What?" Confusion filled her voice. "I assumed he was leaving to go to his club—which he indeed did. He never mentioned going to see you last night."

"Liam went drinking?" Torrington raised his eyebrow. "That's entirely unlike him. What happened when he went to retrieve you yesterday?"

"Oh, that." Gemma snorted. "He lost his mind."

"How so?" the viscount inquired.

"When he got there, Alfie... let's say his hands were roaming in places they didn't belong," Gemma explained. "Liam strolled in, took one look at us, and announced that he hoped my cousin wasn't doing what he thought to his *fiancée*."

"Well, that was part of the plan. He needed a reason to get you away from him. At least that worked well."

Stupid plan—of course, she must be too simpleminded to have been included in on the details of it. Nice to know the big broad gentlemen could take care of the helpless female. If only she could have inherited her funds sooner. Then she wouldn't have needed anyone's aide. Gemma would be in South Carolina with Lily.

"Yes, I gathered that much. I assume the contract was a scheme he concocted to help me leave without much fuss."

Maybe she could get some details out of Viscount Torrington. Liam hadn't been too forthcoming when she asked him questions. Gemma wasn't above getting information from another source.

"I don't know what you mean. The signatures on that contract are completely valid." Torrington smiled.

He was so smug. Gemma wanted to wipe the smile right off his face. She restrained herself from acting on it. Wouldn't be good to strike Viscount Torrington—he might not react well to it.

"Yes, I know. Both you and my father wanted to betroth us several years ago. I assume you didn't fully go through with it, or I'd have known about it. Regardless, it doesn't mean anything now. Your son used the contract to convince Alfie he and I were betrothed, and I left with him."

"Good, at least you don't have to worry about his less than desirable attentions. Anything else I need to know?"

"He also decided my cousin needed to be taught a lesson. I didn't get to witness that. He wouldn't allow it. After I left the room, he took care of it."

"So far I'm not hearing anything to indicate he is going crazy," Torrington said. "I'd have done the same."

"Yeah, I'm sure you don't." Gemma smiled. "But then you didn't get the joy of experiencing it all."

"Too true," Torrington said. "I'm glad he was able to help you. I hate that Lily worried over your safety. So when are you set to sail to South Carolina?"

"I don't know." Gemma shrugged her shoulders. "He did say we'd go there for our wedding trip. He's been… strange since we left the vicarage."

"Wait, the vicarage?" Torrington's eyes widened. His mouth fell open for several seconds. He shook his head, disbelief clouding his eyes. "Are you saying you actually got married yesterday?"

Wait… they weren't supposed to get married? Did she just read him right? Why had Liam married her when that part wasn't included in the plan? A little flutter took root in her heart—hope. Dangerous, but she couldn't stop it from expanding into something full-fledged deep inside her.

"Well, yes. I thought that was the plan? Liam didn't exactly fill me in on all the details. Just said I had to go along with it, or I'd end up unhappily married to Alfie. Don't get me wrong, I am grateful I didn't have to travel down that road, but I didn't exactly want to trade one unhappy marriage for another."

Torrington rubbed his temples with his fingers. Gemma could relate to his frustrations. Liam had deviated from whatever plan they hitched together. She had to wonder what he had been supposed to do. After a few moments and

346

several different plays of emotions crossing his face, he looked at Gemma with a humorous smile on his face.

"You're right." Torrington nodded in agreement.

"Of course I'm right." She pressed her lips together and tilted her head to the side. "But please explain what you think I'm right about."

"That boy has lost his bloody mind." Torrington laughed.

Nice to see one of them found humor in this situation.

"I fail to see why that is so funny."

"You would, dear, you would. This is going to be quite entertaining." Torrington chuckled.

Gemma crossed her arms over her chest and stomped her foot.

"I'm glad that your son going insane amuses you so. I don't share in that sentiment as I have to live with him. Will you please quit laughing! It isn't that funny."

Heat filled Gemma's cheeks as she watched the hilarity take over her father-in-law. The viscount now laughed so hard he had trouble breathing. His face turned red and he held his stomach with his arms.

"I can't wait to tell Pia that her baby boy finally got himself hitched," he said after he gained some composure. "By and by, welcome to the family. I should get home and let my wife in on the good news."

"Hmph, tell her I said hello and to come visit soon. Her company at least is something I can look forward to. The men in this family lack manners."

"We make up for it in other ways. Tell Liam I stopped by and to come see me soon."

Gemma watched as Liam's father left the library. She waited until she could no longer hear his footsteps in the hall and left to return to the sitting room. Her reason for hiding out in the library had left the townhouse. Liam would no doubt return at some point, but for now she had a little breathing room. What she couldn't understand was why his father had found the situation so hilarious. To her, nothing about being married to Liam was amusing. She still had to find a way to get out of it. Perhaps she should just arrange to travel to see Lily. As a married woman, she didn't have quite the same constraints as a young miss. Yes, that idea appealed to her, maybe marrying Liam wasn't an entirely bad thing. She'd look into the requirements and possibilities. Lily would be able to help her sort through the shambles of her life. Maybe she'd also have some insight on how to deal with her unruly brother.

CHAPTER 9

Liam opened the front door to his parents townhouse and walked inside. He traveled down the hallway and stopped just outside his father's study. He had to update him on everything that happened.

He had no idea where to even begin to explain everything.

His father had been the last thing on his mind. Nothing had gone the way he had planned. No, what happened was the world had spiraled out of control, and he didn't have the first clue on how to get it all back on track.

Marrying Gemma was never part of the plan. That part was supposed to be a farce, but he lost his mind when he walked in and saw Alfie's hands all over her. Something snapped inside him, and all he could think about was breaking her cousin's neck.

Once he had her safely tucked away in his carriage his heart had calmed. It made it a little easier to think rationally. It was in those moments he realized the only way he could keep her safe was to marry her. In his mind that course of action made sense because he could ensure no one ever hurt her again.

Liam didn't take into consideration his growing desire. He wanted Gemma in ways he'd never imagined. She made his heart beat faster, and he itched to explore every inch of her. He wanted to see her smile—for him alone. A sultry one that bespoke of pleasure and passion, but also one that sparkled with inner happiness. Liam needed her to be all right with their marriage and to accept every aspect of it.

He should have taken her feelings into consideration—in some ways he was no better than Alfie. Liam had presumed to know what was best for her. The only difference was he'd at least respect her wishes. Liam would never force himself on her. Gemma clearly didn't want him any longer. He had wrongly assumed she would be ecstatic to be his wife.

It was equally apparent what a bloody fool he'd turned into.

"Liam, why are you just standing there?"

He turned to see his mother standing in the hallway. Her pale blond hair twisted into a chignon and her blue eyes filled with concern. Not once had he thought about how he would explain it all to her. She wanted her children to be happy. She would not be pleased to see him all tied up in knots over Gemma.

"Hello mother," Liam strolled over and gave her a quick hug. "I came to see Father. We have some things to discuss."

"Oh well, you missed him. He left a while ago." She studied him for a few moments and nodded . "You will join me for tea and tell me what's troubling you."

Liam gulped as he prepared himself for her interrogation. He wiped his hands on his pants to remove the moisture beading on his palms.

His mother could always see right through him. Escaping was completely out of the question. She didn't ask him to join him, but rather demanded it. Liam didn't want to disappoint her and dreaded the upcoming conversation.

He did the only thing he could in this situation. Liam turned on his heels and followed her to her sitting room. Once inside, she gestured for him to take a seat in one of the chairs as she sat down on the settee.

"I already ordered tea when I heard you walk in the door. I haven't had a chance to visit with you in a while. I wanted to catch up. As soon as I saw you I knew something bothered you, and now you can tell me what is on your mind. Perhaps I can help."

How could he explain to his lovely mother that he had

made a mess of his life and had no clue where to even begin straightening it out? She sat there with her hands folded in her lap, and her face turned towards him with questions radiating from her eyes.

"It's a long story."

"Lucky for you I have plenty of time."

"I don't know where to begin..."

"I'd say you start from where the issue began. Don't leave any details out. If I'm to help, I need to know everything."

Everything? No, he couldn't tell her it all. Not a chance in hell would he tell her about what happened between him and Gemma in his bedroom the night before. Some things one just didn't discuss with their mother.

"I guess it began with Lily's letter."

"I need more than that. Lily writes often. Which letter?"

"She wrote to Father about her concern for Gemma. Are you aware of her situation?" Liam asked.

"Yes. I know that her cousin is trying to force her to marry him."

"Not going to bloody happen—" Liam muttered under his breath. He clenched his fists tight against his legs.

"What was that Liam?"

Liam forced himself to relax and unclenched his fists. He had to be careful before he went off on a tangent. He needed to stick to the facts or he didn't have a chance of getting through this conversation.

"Alfie isn't going to marry Gemma," Liam said.

"Oh, that's good. I know Lily will be relieved. I'm confused though how you can say for sure that will not happen."

Liam sucked in a deep breath and slowly exhaled. Now he needed to tell her that he married the girl himself. He had no idea how she would react to the news. She liked Gemma, at least he believed she did.

"Uh, well, he can't marry her because she is already married to someone else."

"Really? How wonderful for her. When did she get married and what is the lucky gentleman's name?"

Her face glowed with happiness that Gemma had found someone to share her life with. That was a good sign. She did want her to be happy, so he hoped she was also okay with her being his wife. He didn't want to add to Gemma's stress. He already fought an uphill battle where she was concerned.

"Liam, you're not answering me. Is it a bad thing that she is married to a different gentleman? Is this what is bothering you?"

"Yes and no."

"Yes, it's a bad thing or yes it's bothering you. Quit stalling and just tell me what is going on."

His mother's hands flew up in the air. Her lips pursed as her eyes narrowed into slits, studying him.

"No, it's not a bad thing. At least I don't think so. I married her yesterday by special license." Liam got up and paced. He stopped a few feet away and turned back to her. "Yes, it is what is bothering me. I've made a bit of a mess of things with her."

A whoosh of relief flooded him. He returned to his seat and relaxed back into it. There he finally got it all out. Now he just had to sit back and pray his mother reacted well to the news. She was a bit unpredictable at times. He never knew what to expect with her.

"Oh," she said in a quiet tone. She sat back and folded her hands in her lap. Her gaze drifted to the wall behind him. She tilted her head and studied some innocuous object. Her mouth hung open for several seconds and then softened into a half smile, but she didn't say another word.

That's it? All she had to say was oh? That didn't leave him with anything to go by. She said she would help him, and she didn't have anything to say about the situation?

"What? You don't have any other reaction? I expected more than that out of you," Liam said.

"I've never been at a loss for words before. I didn't expect you to say you married her. Yes, I knew how she felt about you, but I also thought you were nowhere near ready to settle down with anyone. You vehemently stated that on more than one occasion. I guess I am a bit shocked and confused."

"You and me both. I can't explain it. I don't quite know how it all happened. It wasn't the plan, and yet it feels so right."

"Tell me how this all came about. I know Lily had

concerns, and your father had an idea about how to extricate Gemma from the situation. He didn't explain it to me, and I didn't think to ask."

"The original plan was to get Gemma on a ship and take her to live with Lily in South Carolina. Father did ask me if I had feelings for her first. He didn't want to ship her off if I wanted her for myself. He suggested I marry her if I wanted her. It was a good solution to save her." Liam paused and took a moment to catch his breath. "At the time I said no. I had no intention of tying our lives together. I didn't want her hurt though, so I agreed to help Gemma and make sure she arrived safely in Lily's care."

"So how did you end up getting married? If you didn't want to be with her why put yourself through so much unnecessary pain. You both deserve better than that."

"I hope it won't all be pain. I want a happy life with, Gemma, but I messed up. I tossed her aside when she expressed her feelings to me two years ago. I was cavalier with her and laughed. I was too young and didn't know what I would ultimately be giving up."

"You love her," his mother said in a soft tone.

Did he? Noah had suggested it, but he had tossed it aside as nonsense. He cared for her. But love? That was an entirely different thing. Liam pictured Gemma. Her gloriously vibrant red hair and her alluring green eyes—he definitely desired her.

"How does one know when they are in love?"

His mother paused and studied him. "That's not an easy question to answer."

"Then how will I know if I love her?"

"Let me ask you this," she tilted her head. "How do you feel when you are not with her?"

The question didn't make any sense to him. What did being away from Gemma have to do with being in love with her? His mother wasn't helping at all. This was just leading to more confusion.

"What do you mean?"

"You're here with me. How do you feel about leaving Gemma alone?" A knowing glint took root in her eyes. "How would you feel if she insisted on going to live with Lily in South Carolina?"

Not bloody happening. Gemma was never leaving him. He clenched his fists again, and his breathing became more ragged. Liam could feel heat filling his cheeks and spreading down his neck.

"Gemma belongs with me."

"Do you feel that way because you see her as one of your possessions?" Her tone was the mask of innocence. She had no expression on her face.

"Of course not," Liam's mouth hung open as he sputtered for words. "Gemma isn't an object. She deserves to be happy.

"She certainly does, but what if that's not with you?"

Liam sat back and considered her words. She had a point. What if Gemma couldn't be happy with him? No, he wouldn't consider that as a possibility. He loved her—Oh God. His heart sped up and beat hard inside his chest. He did love her. Liam could make her happy. He'd just have to find a way to make her see she belonged with him.

"Let me ask you one more question. It might help you to understand your motivations." His mother leaned forward and looked him in the eyes. "If you didn't know you loved her why did you marry her?"

"It was pure instinct. I walked in and saw Alfie with his hands all over her, and I saw red. I reacted and just went with it. It felt right so it had to be the best decision." He paused and scrubbed his hands over his face. This was such a mess. "The problem now is she no longer feels the same way. She doesn't want me, and I'm not much better than Alfie. I forced her to marry me because I thought it was best for her. I refuse to give up though."

"Then you shouldn't."

"I don't know where to even begin..."

"I think you've always had deep feelings for her. You got them all clouded up in that stupid betrothal agreement. Let it all go and just tell her how much you want to be with her."

"You think it's that easy? Just tell her I love her and hope it reminds her she loves me too? I don't think it will work that way." Liam got up and paced again. "What did I do before to make her love me? I need to do that again if I can only figure out what it was."

A laugh rolled through the room and bounced off the walls echoing around him. He looked at his mother and realized the sound came from her. She found his troubles amusing? There was something strangely perverse about her finding his issues entertaining.

"I fail to see why this is so funny," he said.

"Darling you didn't *do* anything to make her fall in love with you. It just is what it is. I doubt she fell out of love with you to begin with. She loved who you are or who she believed you were. Just be yourself and tell her how you feel. Gemma just needs to know you feel the same way. She isn't going to lay her heart on the line again and have it stomped on. You hurt her and she is just protecting herself. It's up to you to make the next move. She isn't going to do it for you."

Was his mother right? Is it really that simple? *Does Gemma still love me?* He had to find out and try it. Maybe he just needed to let her know that she meant the world to him.

"You believe that? I just can't believe it's that easy."

"Life is only as hard as you make it. If you want to make things work in your marriage, you need to open up and talk to your wife. Nothing gets solved by closing yourself off and ignoring the problem. Maybe I'm wrong, but I doubt it."

"All right. I will talk with Gemma. I should be honest with her. It took me long enough to realize I love her. It's only right I am as sincere with her as she was with me in the past. I only hope it's enough."

"It's all you can do. Let me know how things go. Did you still need to talk to your father? I don't know when he will return."

He didn't want to repeat this conversation with his father. The viscount would probably goad him a lot more than his mother did with her laughter. He had an even more wicked attitude than she had. Probably a leftover remnant from his pirating days...

"Could you fill him in on the details? If he still needs to talk to me have him send word and I will return another day."

"I can do that. I can handle your father. I think we need to have a little talk ourselves."

Amusement filled him—it might be interesting to stick around and see their chat. His mother tended to break things when she was mad at his father. If he wasn't mistaken, she seemed a little irritated when she said they needed to talk. He had better things to do though. Gemma was his only concern for the moment.

Liam nodded . "Thank you, mama. I didn't realize how much I needed to talk about this."

"Anytime. Go and talk to Gemma. Straighten out your marriage."

Liam turned and walked out of the room. A new sense of purpose blossomed inside him. He had a lot to do, and he knew just where he would start with Gemma. He should have seen it himself. Why would she open up to him if she still believed he didn't return her feelings? His mother was right. He would plan something special and tell her everything.

CHAPTER 10

The viscount's departure left Gemma with a mix of emotions. Her stomach churned within her. She held her hand over her midsection in an attempt to calm the queasiness setting in. This marriage business didn't sit well with her. She had a father-in-law struck by the hilarity of it and a husband who didn't stick around long enough to be one. Gemma desperately needed something to keep her mind off the last days tumultuous events. The best course of action was to get engrossed in an activity that was both time-consuming and mentally draining. Which gave her an idea... wouldn't it be wonderful to attend a function later that evening? It would give her a reason to be absent and something to keep her mind busy. Maybe if she weren't home, she wouldn't be so painfully aware of her husband's lack of attention.

If she was going to go out, she needed to know what social events were taking place. She remembered Janie had informed her of a stack of neglected invitations. Going through each one would give her something to occupy herself with until later. Gemma sat down at the writing desk in the library to look at those that had arrived over the past week. From the amount of unopened invitations, it seemed rather obvious her husband loathed socializing.

Gemma had taken a liking to attending events when she

became friends with Lily. Prior to that fated meeting she had garnered similar feelings towards interacting with the ton that Liam seemed to have. The ton writhed with gossipmongers and pariahs, but it had also just as many wonderful individuals encased within it. She had learn that lesson the hard way. After her father's sudden death, she had to withdraw from society a bit as the rules of mourning hadn't allowed her to go to many balls or soirees.

Gemma didn't see any reason not to attend a few social events. She didn't need Liam to escort her and had no problem going on her own. There were still a few people that she could socialize with since most of her new friends were married themselves.

She picked up the first invitation. Ironically it was from Lady Silverton. Lily had met her husband, Rand, at the Silverton Ball three years prior. Gemma believed it a fitting occasion to instill her newfound freedom as a matron, instead of a maid. She may not feel married, but that didn't mean she couldn't take advantage of it. The more she thought about it, the more she realized marrying Liam might be the best thing that happened to her. Yes, he was a complete idiot, but she could work with that. She intended to enjoy a few social events and then make plans to visit Lily in South Carolina.

Gemma placed the invitation to the Silverton Ball in the accept pile. The ball was for later that evening, but that didn't matter. It was well-known Lady Silverton expected everyone to be present at her ball and prepared for those that decided to attend at the last minute. After going through each invitation, she decided on three that she would like to attend. Besides the ball she had a garden party and a musical she decided to attend.

She also had her dinner party to plan. With that in mind, she drafted invitations for her own party to Liam's parents, the Viscount and Viscountess Torrington, the Duke of Huntly, and her friend Pearla Montgomery. After Lily had left for South Carolina, she became good friends with Pearla. If not for their friendship she may have become a wallflower once again. In a lot of ways, Pearla reminded her of Lily. She had a dislike of marriage that rivaled Lily's. Lily caved when she met Randall Collins and gave marriage another look because of him. Perhaps Pearla would do the same one day.

"Ma'am, Cook said to let you know dinner will be ready in an hour. Is there any correspondence you need me to post?"

Gemma looked up at the butler as she sealed the last invitation to be delivered.

"Yes, Pemberly. I have three invitations for a dinner party in two nights. Can you make sure they are delivered? Also have Janie come in. I would like to discuss plans for the dinner party with her before we sit down to our meal tonight.

"Very well, ma'am. I shall send her in. If you give me the invitations, I will have a footman deliver them personally."

"Thank you Pemberly." Gemma handed all of the letters to him. "I also have two acceptances to post as well." As for the invitation to the Silverton Ball, she would accept in person later that evening. Thankfully all of her trunks had arrived earlier in the day. Otherwise, she would have had to decline for lack of a ball gown to wear.

Pemberly took all of her notes and left the room. Gemma straightened up the writing desk and pulled out a clean sheet of stationary. She dipped her quill in an ink pot and began making a list for the dinner party. A short time afterward Janie entered.

"Lady Marsden, Pemberly said you required my assistance."

"Yes, Janie. I am having a dinner party in two nights. I have made a list of what I would like for the meal and everything I require. Can you please make sure that all of this is completed?"

"Yes, ma'am." Janie took the list and examined it.

"Do you have any questions?"

"No. This is pretty clear. I will let Cook know what you would like for the meal. If she has any questions I will let you know after I speak with her," Janie said.

"Very well. I shall retire to the sitting room until dinner is served. "

Janie nodded and left the room. Gemma got up and went to the sitting room. As soon as she sat down, Liam walked into the room.

"Ah, there you are."

"I haven't exactly been hiding." Gemma's sarcasm evident in each word she spoke.

"I never said you were. I just couldn't locate you when I first arrived home."

"I was in the library going through invitations. I accepted a couple and wrote out a few for the dinner party I plan on having in a couple of days. You should know I invited your parents, the Duke of Huntly, and my friend Pearla. I hope you will deign to attend, so I have even numbers."

"Of course I will be here. I'd never be so rude."

"Right." Gemma rolled her eyes. Liam rude? Never. That's why he was making sure she was comfortable in her new home and paying a lot of attention to her. "Anyway everything is planned. All you need to do is show up."

"You said you accepted a couple of invitations for social events. Which one did you accept?"

Gemma didn't see any reason not to inform him of her plans. Maybe if he knew what they were, he would leave her be.

"A musical at the Carrington's and a garden party the Duchess of Westland is hosting. I also plan on attending Lady Silverton's ball tonight. Don't worry I can attend on my own. You have no need to come."

She wasn't sure if she wanted him to attend or not. A small part of her hoped he would while the part of her irritated with him just wanted Liam to leave her in peace. What would be the point of escaping to a ball if he were fast on her heels? It was best to dispense with the notion of him attending at once. Gemma didn't want him to feel obligated after all.

"Ridiculous. I can escort my wife to a ball. I will be ready when you are."

Gemma sighed. He couldn't possibly want to attend the ball with her. From what she recalled he hated escorting Lily. She'd rather he just let her go alone. It would give her the opportunity to spend some time with her friends and enjoy herself. She didn't want to worry about the gossip mills or Liam's belligerence. He'd no doubt have an attitude all evening.

"It isn't necessary. I'd prefer to go alone. Do whatever you had planned for the evening. I am perfectly capable of going on my own."

Gemma fidgeted in her seat. Her lips pursed in displeasure as she looked up at him. How to get him to change his mind? It would be damned annoying to have him around all night. If he attended, no doubt he would ruin the whole evening brooding over everything she did. He had reacted badly just by her being nice to his best friend earlier that day. All she did was be polite to him and attempt to get to know him better. The Duke of Huntly appeared to be a charming and caring man.

"I have no other plans this evening. I had hoped to spend it with you. We have a lot we need to discuss."

"As far as I'm concerned we have talked more than I care. Keeping the peace works best if you don't open your mouth too much. I might start to like you a little better if you were mute more often."

Liam opened his mouth to speak and closed it in a tight firm line. His displeasure evident on his face as his eyes narrowed, and his brows bunched together while his forehead crinkled.

It was almost adorable—no, it definitely was. How cute. He wasn't happy. Too bad for him. Gemma hadn't been in the best of moods herself. She couldn't help admiring how absolutely gorgeous he was though. It made it difficult at times to stay mad at him. Why couldn't things have gone differently? All she wanted to do was wrap her arms around him and erase his discontent. She sighed. If his feelings mirrored hers she might just do it. She knew better though.

"Is it necessary to be so rude?" Liam asked.

Yes, it was—it made a fine defense mechanism. She needed as many as she could muster to keep her wits about her. Liam had the ability to leave her brainless, if she allowed it.

"I am only speaking my mind."

Gemma stood up and walked over to the window and looked out at the busy London street. She didn't want to argue with her husband, but she had to put a wall up between them. If she opened herself up to him again, it would lead to her downfall. The more time she spent with him the more it added to her chances of falling for him all over again. Gemma refused to love him any more than she already did.

"I am not allowing you to go to the ball on your own. If you want to attend, then expect me to be your escort."

Gemma turned to him and pinned him with her gaze. He was being mulish on purpose. He couldn't possibly want to attend. Why was he so determined to ruin everything for her? Heat filled her cheeks and spread throughout her body. She clenched the folds of her skirts in her hands. She gritted her teeth and took a few deep breaths.

"If that is the only way I can go, then I will plan on you accompanying me. I don't see why you are being so difficult."

"It's my prerogative. If you will excuse me, I have a few things to take care of before dinner is served."

Liam damn near stomped out of the room. His cheeks were flushed red with his anger. Gemma didn't see any reason why he'd be so upset. She gave him plenty of opportunities to stay home. She certainly wasn't forcing him to go to the ball. She turned on her heels to go sit back down. Her whole body shook after the confrontation. Damn him for unnerving her. Her hand trembled as she brushed it over her hair to smooth it in place. She needed some distance from Liam if she wanted her heart to remain unscathed.

It might prove futile because her heart and mind already headed towards a collision of uncertainty.

One wanted desperately to love him and believe he could love her; the other only wanted to protect the already bruised emotions housed deep inside its depths. At some point, the conflict must be resolved, or an implosion would occur. Gemma didn't know how much longer she could hold off all of her unresolved feelings.

In that moment, she decided to step up her plans to visit Lily. The plan no longer a want, it now upgraded to an urgent necessity to ensure her continued existence. If she stayed in England, she would lose a part of herself and she wanted to hold on to every piece of who she'd grown into over the past three years. Her independence and ability to stand up for herself depended on proving a point to Liam.

The man expected her to bow down to his every command. He had a hard lesson to learn, and Gemma knew how to teach it to him. With a plan hatching in her mind, Gemma smiled for the first time since her husband barged into the sitting room. Liam didn't have a clue what she truly could make happen. He would discover the truth soon enough. She only hoped it would happen before her heart and mind collided.

CHAPTER 11

Liam stomped up the stairs to his room to change for the ball his wife insisted on attending that evening. Gemma had excused herself an hour ago to prepare for the festivities. Liam decided he needed some liquid courage to get through the evening and instead of immediately getting ready for the ball, he went to his study and poured himself a snifter of brandy. He gulped down the first glass and nursed the second one for almost an hour.

Nothing went as he had planned.

When he left his parents' home, his intentions had been to tell Gemma exactly how much he loved and adored her. But, she turned on him as soon as she laid eyes on him. Her scathing retorts had put him on the defensive. Instead of a meaningful conversation they'd had a stilted one. It wasn't even a heated argument. He stood in front of her like a fool issuing proclamations.

She was driving him mad.

How could he possibly tell her what was inside his heart if she didn't even allowed him a chance to speak? So in lieu of a wonderful evening filled with love he was following her to the Silverton Ball. Every step of the way Gemma fought him, and his purpose was constantly thwarted.

Dinner that evening had been a silent affair. She didn't say one word to him through the entire meal. She said very little to the staff serving them. If Liam were to hazard a guess, she pretended he didn't exist while she ate. His state of nerves amounted to a bundle of repressed energy. At any moment, they would explode and leave a wake of devastation in their path. If he didn't gain control of the situation, he would not be held responsible for his actions. They had only been married a couple of days, and he was already ready to collapse from the sheer torture. He knew that not all ton marriages were love matches, far from it, in fact. Marriage in his family was different though.

They married for love even if it didn't appear to be on the outside looking in. The world thought his parents' married because his father had forced his mother to in his pirating days. On a small scale, they were right. He did force her, but not entirely for the revenge everyone believed. He married her because he loved her and couldn't imagine a world without her by his side. That was how Liam saw his marriage to Gemma.

When he looked at her, he saw exactly how their life could be if only she would allow them a fraction of happiness. Instead, she fought him every step of the way. Liam didn't blame her entirely. This path had been created two years prior when he foolishly pushed Gemma away. It was his mistake, and he needed to rectify it. If he couldn't fix things, his life would fracture and he would never again be whole.

He wasn't about to give up on them. She would listen to him. Tonight he would make her hear the words he'd found it difficult to assimilate. Liam loved Gemma. It had just taken him longer to see what was right in front of him. Gemma was *his*. She'd always been the one woman meant for him. It was time to stop being nice and stake his claim in every way possible.

Liam finished dressing without the aid of his valet. With the state of his current mood, he thought it best to not inflict it on anyone else unnecessarily. After he tied his cravat, he walked out of his room and strolled back down the stairs. Gemma hadn't yet emerged from her bedroom, so he found himself fidgeting at the bottom of the stairs awaiting her arrival. He didn't have a whole lot of patience for anything.

Finally, he caught sight of her at the top of the stairs. She was a vision. Her emerald green ball gown fit her curves and cascaded down her hips to her ankles. The bodice was draped in lace and silk organza. Tiny green beads wrapped around her waist in an intricate pattern depicting a belt of flowers that trailed down the side of her overlaying skirt. Gemma's crimson hair were twisted around her head and plaited into a long braid that coiled at the nape of her neck. Tiny ringlets were curled framing her face with a small emerald hair adornment twinkling on the left side of her head.

Watching her descend the stairs Liam was breathless with anticipation. He wanted nothing more than to pull her into his arms and kiss her. The only thing that would be better was to turn her back around and march her upstairs to his room. Once there, he could slowly undress her as he savored every inch of her delectable body.

Why couldn't he kiss her? He should—it would be a start in the direction he hoped to head.

"I hope you haven't been waiting long. I had quite a bit to do to prepare myself for the ball."

Liam stepped toward her and caressed her cheek with the tips of his fingers. Her gaze locked with his. Her breathing became ragged as she gulped in air in short fast bursts.

"What are you doing?"

Liam didn't answer her with words. He leaned down and placed a soft kiss on her lips. Her mouth opened up as she gasped. It gave him an advantage, and he saw no reason not to take it. The tip of his tongue touched hers as he pulled her tighter in is embrace. Liam coaxed her with his mouth—wanting to fill her with every inch of desire coursing through his veins. She needed to be with him every step of the way. This was only the beginning of his fight to own every inch of her soul. Her body relaxed against him, and he took it as a sign. She wasn't as immune to him as she wanted him to believe. Gemma still wanted him. He could use that and he would.

Liam took a step back, pleased with what he saw. Gemma's eyelids were closed, her lips slightly parted and moist, and her cheeks a pretty pink. Her eyelashes fluttered up, and irises of green fire met his—she looked both a little dazed and well pleasured. They could move forward now. He'd managed to get her exactly where he wanted her.

"The carriage awaits us outside. I think it is time for us to depart."

Gemma looked a little dazed, but in a good way. She looked well pleasured. A confident arrogance took root deep inside her. He'd done that—built a craving in her she'd never experienced before. Soon he'd make sure she got a taste of it all.

Gemma cleared her throat and shook her head. She looked up at him and nodded. "Very well."

Liam hooked her arm over his and for the first time that evening believed that they may have a chance. She hadn't once snapped at him since she walked down the stairs.

"You look lovely; by the way. I love the color green on you."

"I didn't dress to please you, Liam. This just happens to be one of my new favorite ball gowns. I haven't had a chance to wear it yet, and this seemed like the perfect time to do so."

Maybe she hadn't—somehow he doubted it though. His lips tilted into a half smile as his gaze traveled over her.

"Doesn't make you any less beautiful to me. I quite enjoy how it looks on you."

Gemma didn't respond to his compliment—just stared at him in silence. He meant every one of his words. The dress enhanced her beauty and made her even more exquisite. Maybe going to this ball wasn't an entirely bad idea. Dancing would give him the chance to hold her in his arms and stare into the depths of her light green eyes. Perhaps it would remind her of the times they danced previously. He needed all the help he could get to help her realize she still loved him.

They exited the townhouse and walked over to the awaiting carriage. Liam helped Gemma inside and hopped in after she took her seat. Once the door closed, the driver nudged the horses into moving and they were on their way to the ball.

"I haven't been to a ball in quite a while. I don't socialize unless I am required to do so," Liam said.

Gemma's gaze was off to the side as she looked out the window of the carriage. She was doing her best to ignore him.

Liam didn't want her to forget the heat between them. He needed to draw her back into his circle of warmth.

"I remember you always hated escorting Lily to all of her social events," she said, still looking outside.

"When did you start attending social occasions again?"

A distance was starting to form again. Liam didn't like it one bit.

She turned to look at him. "You mean after my father died? I just began ordering ball gowns and more appropriate clothing a few months ago. I haven't been out much. Alfie didn't allow it. I had a seamstress visit me at home to prepare the gowns before he could prevent it from happening. Otherwise, I wouldn't have any new gowns at all. He even sequestered me. I couldn't visit my friends or having them visit with me. Although the only person that tried, besides the day you came to retrieve me, was Pearla. No one else realized anything was wrong. I managed to get someone to mail a few letters to Lily, but a lot of my missives got confiscated by my nefarious cousin. I despaired of ever being allowed outside the walls of my former home ever again."

"I hadn't realized that the situation had gotten so dire. At least Lily was able to contact my father."

"Hmmm yes. Speaking of your father, he stopped by while you were out. We had an interesting discussion."

"Really?" Liam raised his eyebrows.

What had his father done? Did he make the situation worse with Gemma? No, that wasn't possible. He messed up all on his own. Still, he'd plan on having a conversation with him to get all of the details of his visit.

"He was under the impression the plan hadn't included us getting married. He agreed with me that you are losing your mind."

"I assure you my mind has all of its faculties intact."

"We will have to agree to disagree. I just haven't seen much evidence to the contrary."

"I admit my behavior… has been less than savory lately. In my defense, you do drive me to the point of insanity at times."

Gemma looked him directly in the eyes. She pursed her lips as anger filled her eyes. Sparks flew out of them as her brows drew closer together, and her forehead crinkled in displeasure.

"You dare blame me for your turbulent moods? I have no control over your emotional state. Don't pretend I do for even a moment. I won't have you hold me responsible for your bad attitude."

That's much better. He enjoyed having her all to himself. All of her emotions steamrolling forward, right in his general direction. Liam tilted his head back and studied her. A half smile filled with cockiness spread across his face.

"Aren't you? I am usually an even-tempered person. Since I married you, I have been one big mess of disturbing outbursts. I can't seem to control what my next action may or may not be. I think you are entirely at fault for my state of being since I first walked in and saw Alfie attacking you."

"I'm not going to argue with you. You are clearly out of your mind. I intend to have fun tonight, and I refuse to allow you to ruin my good mood."

Good mood? Liam restrained from laughing. Who did she think she was fooling? She was most definitely *not* in a good mood.

"Fine. I only have one request."

"And what makes you think I will honor it?"

"Because if you don't I will instruct the driver to turn the carriage around and take us home."

"Oh, all right, you win. What do you want?"

"I want you to put me down for the first waltz of the evening."

Gemma crossed her arms across her chest and glared at him.

"No. I don't want to dance with you."

Liam sighed. Gemma would argue with him about anything. If he said the sun rose in the sky she'd shake her head and tell him that it did not raise, it, in fact, fell each day. Why couldn't she agree to one dance? What made her want to avoid him? The kiss they'd shared seemed to sear right through her. Was she afraid of her feelings? It was time to test her reserve.

"Very well. I shall inform the driver we wish to skip the ball."

"No. I will put you on my dance card. You don't have to be so difficult. I don't even know why we are arguing about this. Never once did you want to dance with me willingly in the past. Lily had to practically force you too."

"Times change, I'm not the same man I was a couple years ago." Liam looked her in the eyes, pleading her to give in, accept him once more. He reached for her hand and rubbed his thumb over her palm. "Just give me a chance to prove it to you."

The green depths of her eyes remained unmoving. She studied him for several seconds. He kept moving the pad of his thumb over her hand, coaxing her into compliance. Her expression softened, her lips parted, and the tension left her body.

"I don't know if I'm willing to take that risk. A dance is more than I want to give to you, but I will acquiesce to your demands. I want to attend the ball, and I'm willing to do whatever is necessary to make that happen."

"I will take whatever you are willing to give me. In time I hope it's everything. For now I will settle for a dance."

Gemma didn't say anything else for the rest of the journey to the Silverton Ball. Liam allowed her to remain silent. He said all he could on the subject for the time being and had meant every word he said. Patience wasn't always one of his strong suits, but for Gemma he would be. Liam played to win because if he didn't he would lose it all.

He refused to allow for that possibility.

Liam clenched his hands open and closed several times. Gemma wouldn't leave him. He needed her. In time, she'd come around. He wouldn't think about the possibility of losing her. It just would not—could not happen. Instead, he'd concentrate on the upcoming ball. At least he'd be able to hold her in his arms as they danced. He'd achieved that goal, and he'd attain them all. Liam looked forward to each battle because in the end they'd both win. They'd have each other always.

After several moments, the carriage came to a halt in front of the Silverton residence. The carriage door opened, and Liam stepped out. He reached in and offered his hand to assist Gemma. With a delicateness ingrained in her she placed her hand in his. He helped her out, and they walked inside to attend the ball.

So far, Liam believed the night progressed towards meeting every one of his expectations. Soon he would be able to hold Gemma in as they danced in the waltz. A tingle of energy flowed through his veins, an awareness of her beside him. His fingers itched to reach out and just touch her, draw her close to him.

In the past, he dreaded the possibility, but now he looked forward to it with a glee he couldn't explain. Happiness bubbled inside him and hope filled him to the brim. Nothing could ruin this night for him.

CHAPTER 12

Gemma walked alongside Liam as they strolled towards the opening of the ballroom. They waited until they were announced and made their entrance for the first time as husband and wife. Gemma found the moment incredibly ironic. At one time, she would have given anything for them to enter on each other's arms as a married couple.

Now all she wanted to do was cringe when the announcement was made.

Small gasps and whispers filled the room. Heads turned to stare at them as they walked into the ballroom. Gemma held back tears from falling. She knew her marriage to Liam would be a shock to the ton—but she'd hoped that it wouldn't cause too much of a stir. A futile endeavor it seemed as eyes followed them throughout the room. Gemma didn't doubt they were all gossiping about them. Instead of letting them see how much it bothered her she held her head high and pasted a smile on her face. Outward appearances would go a long way into making them think they had no power over her.

Pain stabbed her chest as she sucked in a breath of discontentment. No, she would not think of things she couldn't change. Liam may be her husband, but she refused to allow him access to her innermost feelings. He gave up that right and Gemma rejected any possibility of allowing him to know how much she still loved him. Even though a tiny part of herself realized she still hoped for him to love her in return. That forthcoming collision of dueling emotions threatened to surface, and she needed to escape him if she had any chance of getting it under control.

She looked over and spotted Pearla and found the excuse she desperately sought to leave Liam's side. Pearla looked over at her anxiously, and Gemma knew she must have questions. She probably already received her invitation to the schedule dinner party. The time had come for her to explain her newly married state to her second best friend. Lily would always be her first and the one person she told everything to, but Pearla had filled up a hole in her life with Lily's absence.

"If you will excuse me I see a friend I've desperately wanted to talk to for some time," Gemma told Liam.

"I will escort you there."

Why couldn't he just let her go off on her own? She didn't need him to watch over her every move. Gemma needed some space, and Liam's hovering made her feel closed in.

"You don't need to. I can find my own way."

"I insist. I would like to meet your friend."

Gemma opened her mouth and closed it into a pursed, straight line. Her gaze skirted over the crown and the prying eyes. They all seemed to wait for something to erupt between her and Liam. Did they know her marriage was a farce? Gemma refused to give them the show they appeared to be expecting. She didn't want to provide the ton with anything else to gossip about. No doubt they had already wondered about her hasty marriage. That at least she could brush off with the marriage contract Liam had procured miraculously. Gemma nodded in agreement and twined her arm with Liam's. If he wanted to deliver to her friend's side, she'd allow it. Once they reached their destination, she could send him on his way. She led her husband over to where Pearla stood and introduced them.

"Liam, I would like you to meet my dear friend, Miss Pearla Montgomery. She is. I hope, going to join us for dinner in a couple of days." She turned to her friend and smiled brightly. "Pearla, my husband, Liam Marsden."

"It's nice to meet a friend of my wife," Liam said. A

charming smile grew on his face as he bowed to her. "Perhaps you will honor me with a dance later."

"Oh, well. I don't know." Pearla looked up at Gemma. After she had nodded in approval, Pearla looked back at Liam. "I suppose that would be all right. I can fill you in for the second dance. I assume you will want to dance with Gemma first. It is a waltz."

"I do indeed. If you will excuse me, ladies, I see a friend I haven't seen in a while. Gemma, I shall be back soon to dance with you. I would also like you to mark me down for every waltz."

Gemma's mouth hung open. She had closed it quickly before anyone took notice. Every waltz? Liam was most definitely losing his mind. It wouldn't do, and she'd have to make him realize what a mistake that would be. She looked down at her dance card and the dances scheduled for the evening. They had several dances planned—three of them waltzes.

"That's a bit much, Liam. People will talk if we dance that many times. I'm supposed to leave it open for other men to dance with me."

"I don't care. I claim them as my right. I'm your husband, and I refuse to share them all with other men."

Liam's lips were set in a firm line. The color of his eyes darkened to a deep blue. His jaw clenched, locking into place as his eyes became firmer—demanding he be obeyed. Was he jealous? No, he had no reason to be. He was just being his usually overbearing self. Still, it was… nice. Maybe he wanted her, and this was his way of expressing it. Gemma tilted her head and studied him.

Perhaps he did, but the man needed to be disabused of the notion he could dictate to her. She opened her mouth to tell him just that and thought otherwise. It wouldn't do to put him in place with words. Actions spoke volumes, and she'd find a way to get through to him. It was best just to appear to acquiesce to his wishes for now.

He'd learn—the hard way.

"Fine. I will put your name down for them all."

"Good. I will take your leave now."

Gemma glared at his back as he retreated across the room.

Dance every waltz with him? Not going to happen... Someone else was just going to have to dance one of them with her. A man brave enough to stand up to her husband as he could be a little intimidating. All she needed was time to locate a gentleman willing to dance with her. Liam would be angry, but she could deal with it. Gemma would allow her husband to have two of them. He'd just have to accept one had to go to another man. She hated when people gossiped about her.

"Your husband is quite the charming fellow, now please explain to me how you happened to find yourself married to him," Pearla said.

She looked at her friend and admired her golden blonde hair. She had it pulled back into a chignon; tiny tendrils of wispy curls framed her face floating around her ears and neck. Her cerulean blue eyes glowed with anticipation and concern. Her heart-shaped face tilted inquisitively as she waited for Gemma to answer her question.

"It's a long story." Gemma sighed.

"Well lucky for you I have plenty of time. I have lots of questions. It's nice to finally be able to talk to you. I have to admit I was rather surprised by the hand-delivered invitation. I didn't even know you were no longer at the country house of the new Earl of Devon. How did that little weasel react to your marriage? I would have loved to witness that."

Pearla hated Alfie almost, if not more, than Gemma did. They had taken an instant dislike for each other. It probably had something to do with his lecherous nature and her unyielding independence. Pearla was not encumbered with a guardian. The sum of her wealth was inherited from her grandmother without any stipulations. She was the only unmarried female free to do whatever she wished without answering to a male relation.

"Alfie thought to marry me himself."

"I heard he racked up quite a bit of debt and ran through all of the money he inherited with your father's estate."

"Indeed he did. He thought marrying me would help him get out of debt. It probably would have temporarily until he wasted all of my inheritance."

"So how did you get out of marrying him? I assume by

latching on to that handsome devil you married, but how did that go about?"

How to answer that? Did she tell her friend the complete truth or continue to deny what her heart constantly tried to beat into her head?

"Liam is very handsome. Don't let that fool you. He can be just as devious as any man." Gemma sighed and considered her next words. "But he also has a protective streak to go along with it. If not for him I don't know where I'd be right now."

"Oh, I'm sure he can be. Most men are capable of it on some level." Pearla pinned her with her gaze. "You are dodging my question. What don't you want me to know?"

"A lot. I don't want to talk about it. Perhaps I should though. It would probably help to get it all out, and then maybe I can let it go. I'm not sure where to start."

"Try the beginning."

Gemma stopped and looked at the ground. She didn't want to discuss any of it. Unfortunately, she also knew she needed to let it out, or she'd burst. No one was better to converse about it with than her friend. She didn't have an invested interest in the outcome.

"That would take us back to before we met. When I was first introduced to Liam. He is Lily's twin brother."

"I thought they may be related. I was just not sure exactly how. Go on, explain the rest."

A dreamy look came over Gemma as she remembered the first meeting. Liam had been so incredibly handsome. His blond hair glowed in the sunlight, and his blue eyes burnt with unrepressed delight. He and Lily had been laughing over some joke she hadn't been privy too. That first glimpse ruined her for anyone else. She wanted to have him look at her with love and happiness.

"I fell in love with him the moment I met him and yet thought him completely unattainable. I squashed all of those feelings and thought I never had a chance with him. If you had asked me even a week ago, I'd still believe that. I still do if I am being honest. I don't know why he married me. The truth is he didn't have to, and I'm even more confused now that I ever was."

Pearla's eyes squinted with confusion. "I don't understand. He married you to save you from your cousin right?"

"Yes, he did."

"What other option did he have?"

"He could have escorted me to Lily," Gemma explained. "Of course, Alfie might have come after me there. I doubt he'd have let it go, but he wouldn't have been able to make me come back to England, once I was safely with Lily."

"Ah, I see your point. He could have made you miserable though. Alfie's good at that. Maybe Liam has feelings for you."

Gemma shook her head. "No, I don't believe he does."

"Does he know how you feel about him?"

"Yes. Well, he did. I had this attack of conscience a couple years ago and thought of course I will never have a chance if he doesn't know how I feel about him. I confessed my love only for him. His eyes were cold as he looked down, said he didn't feel the same way and had no intention of ever marrying. Words can't express how crushed my heart was. I didn't think I would ever recover. Maybe I never did. I can't allow myself to trust what I feel, and I am even more leery of Liam."

"What a fool." Pearla placed her hand on Gemma's arm, attempting to reassure her. "Maybe he finally realized how much you mean to him."

It took everything she had not to laugh. It was so nice to have Pearla to talk to, someone so completely on her side. She needed this in the worst way.

"No. I think it is some misplaced duty to his sister. Lily asked her father to help me. She knew about Alfie's plans for me and wanted me to come live with her. Liam and the viscount devised a plan to help me escape and go live in America with her. Something changed in Liam's mind when he arrived and saw Alfie attacking me." Gemma shook her head, cleared away the unwanted image of her cousin. "Liam didn't marry me because he has unrequited love for me. He did it to protect me from my horrid cousin. Running away wasn't the answer. Alfie would have chased me to the ends of the Earth."

"Do you still love him?"

Gemma started to fidget. Now was the time to admit how much she did need Liam. She didn't want to, but the time had come to be honest with herself. She had never stopped loving the dratted man. She couldn't breathe without thinking about him and the love still burning inside of her.

"Yes. I know I shouldn't. I am fighting every feeling I have for him. My mind keeps telling my heart to give up, but it still holds hope."

"I'm so sorry, Gemma. I can't be mad at him though. He did save you from that awful cousin of yours. I know you are miserable right now, but I agree with him." Pearla embraced her in a quick hug and stepped back. "Alfie would not have given up on attaining you for his wife if you had merely run away. He needed your money too much to let you go that easily. I wouldn't be surprised if he still had a plan hatching in his greedy mind."

"No doubt he does. I can't worry about that right now. I have more pressing concerns."

"Such as?"

"How am I going to get out of three dances with Liam? I am not going to give the ton any more reason to gossip about me. My hasty marriage is enough fodder for the gossip mills."

Just as she said the words, she spotted the Duke of Huntly arriving at the entrance to the ballroom. He was announced and made his way inside. How serendipitous... The duke wouldn't balk at standing up to her husband, and he'd no doubt readily agree to dance with her. She'd just fail to mention how Liam wanted to dance every waltz with her.

"Never mind I think I have an idea. I need to go speak to His Grace, the Duke of Huntly."

"You know him?" Pearla's mouth hung open with surprise.

"Yes. He is Liam's friend. He will be at dinner as well. You may as well meet him now."

"Really? Who else is going to be at this dinner party?"

"Only his parents. Have you met them?"

"No, I can't say I have. I look forward to it."

Pearla and Gemma walked over to the Duke of Huntly. He stopped before them and bowed. His black hair curled around his neck, and his eyes held a sadness that Gemma wished she could erase.

"Gemma, it's nice to see you here. Is Liam with you this evening?"

"He is. Were you looking for him?"

"I do need to speak with him. I stopped by, and Pemberly said he believed you were both here tonight. I don't like balls or any social occasions, if I'm being honest. I did receive your dinner invitation. I will, of course, attend."

Gemma smiled at him. He was a nice and charming gentleman. She looked over and found Pearla charmed with him and for the first time completely tongue-tied.

"Noah, please excuse my rudeness. This is my friend Miss Pearla Montgomery. Pearla this is His Grace, Noah St. John, Duke of Huntly."

"It's a pleasure to meet you, Miss Montgomery." Noah bowed.

"I'm glad you will be attending the dinner party. Pearla will be there along with Liam's parents."

"A nice intimate affair, good, I detest crowds."

"I hope I can talk you into at least one dance before you leave. I know you have pressing concerns with Liam, but I still have yet to fill up my dance card."

The duke didn't look happy at the idea of dancing. His face paled, and his lips formed a straight grim line. He looked all around the ballroom, everywhere except directly at Gemma. Pearla continued to nod her head at the appropriate times, but not once did she speak in the presence of the duke. Later Gemma would question her unusual silence, but now she had more pressing concerns.

"I suppose I can. Is it too much to ask for the first dance? I would like to leave as soon as possible. I don't want anyone to get any hopes up of my staying."

"You are in luck, Your Grace. I can write your name in for the first dance and it is about to start."

As the words left her mouth, the beginning strands of the waltz reverberated through the room. Noah hooked her hand in his arm to led her onto the dance floor. In the distance, she could see her husband enter the ballroom with a murderous look on his face. She knew she played with fire by dancing with Noah, but she was willing to get burned to get her point across. Liam thought she wanted his friend, and she didn't see any reason to disabuse him of that notion.

Just because she admitted to herself she still loved him didn't mean she shouldn't follow her instincts. Liam flat out told her he didn't have any feelings for her. Why should she believe he'd suddenly had a change of heart? Gemma needed to protect herself before she found herself unwilling to live without Liam. Loving him would only lead to her ruination. She refused to give into those unwanted emotions. All she wanted was a little distance—to be able to think clearly. Liam made her forget who she was, and she got lost in wanting him. If he believed she desired his friend perhaps she'd get some of that much needed space.

As soon as Liam entered the ballroom after leaving his business acquaintance, he saw his best friend leading his wife to the dance floor. Never would he have guessed her intentions – had he known, he'd never have left her side. It was a total surprise to see Noah at the ball. When Noah lost his wife, his need to socialize also vanished. Without Rubina, he had lost hope and any wish to be around people. Especially around anyone that would fawn all over him because they believed he was once again the catch of the season. Liam had never envied his friend his title or properties. They came with adverse side effects.

He loved Noah like a brother, but at that moment all he wanted to do was murder him.

All right maybe that maneuver would be a tad extreme, but Liam had never before had rage coursing through his veins as it now did. He weighed his options and tried to decide what his next move should be. If he marched out onto the dance floor, he would create a scene that would forever be remembered. He didn't want to look like the jealous arse he actually was. He scanned the ballroom and saw Gemma's friend, Pearla on the outskirts watching them dance. With a plan of action in place, he strolled over to her side.

"I need your help."

Pearla jumped up, and her voice squeaked as she said, "What?"

"Dance with me."

"Um no, I don't think that is a good idea. I can tell you are rather angry. Don't be mad at Gemma, she was only trying to prevent a scandal. Dancing with her three times isn't a good idea."

Gemma must have told her that was her reason for wanting to dance with Noah. Pearla didn't realize that his wife had developed an attachment to his friend in a very short period of time. Well, if she believed that he was going to allow her to further along that connection she would soon find out exactly how wrong she was.

"Is that so? Well, it may be a little late to prevent that. I wanted to dance with my wife and I will. Now come dance with me."

"All right, but I want my objections to this to be noted. It is a bad idea."

"Duly noted and also rejected. I don't care if it is a bad idea or not, it's going to happen."

Liam grabbed her hand in his and led her onto the dance floor in the middle of the waltz. He guided her along the floor until they neared Gemma and Noah. He weaved her around the floorboards as fast as he could without knocking into anyone. Once he spotted his intended destination, he did the necessary steps to arrive there.

"Now this is what is going to happen, Pearla. You are going to switch places with Gemma. I need you to dance with Noah so I can dance with my wife. Do you understand?"

"Yes, it is a horrid plan. Please don't make me do this. I beg you," she pleaded.

"Please help me, Pearla. I need to dance with my wife."

She stared at him for several seconds. "Do you love her?"

A lump formed in his throat. God yes he did. Why couldn't he get his wife alone long enough to tell her? He nodded. "Yes"

She smiled. "I still think this is a very bad idea."

"What could you possibly have against switching places with Gemma? Most ladies would kill for a chance to dance with a duke." Liam knew she would do it. She'd have said no outright if she didn't want to help. His lips tilted into a half smile and teased her a bit. "Noah won't bite, I promise. He will be a perfect gentleman. We are almost near them, be prepared to switch."

"I'm not most ladies. I have no wish to dance with any duke; in fact, I really don't want to dance at all."

Liam ignored her protestations and led her to the other side of the dance floor. Once they were next to Gemma and Noah, he twirled Pearla around until she almost collided into them. Both of them looked up in surprise, and Noah nodded in Liam's direction. He understood what his friend was after. They both did some fancy maneuvering and switched partners. Liam finally had Gemma in his arms where she belonged.

Only it hadn't been where she wanted to be.

Liam wasn't entirely sure what her motivations were. When he'd come to find her for their first dance, he hadn't expected to see her being led onto the floor by Noah. It's rocked him to his very core. He'd clenched his fists as spurts of heat spread through him. Now having her in his arms again he could feel that heat turn into something deeper. A longing to drag her closer so he could feel her body rubbing against his own. He wanted to brand her in every way possible. Gemma couldn't possibly just not want to dance with him because it might cause a scandal—Liam had to dig deeper. Whatever was driving her further away had to be eradicated. Letting her go was not an option he would ever entertain.

"What's this about you not wanting to dance with me?"

"I don't know what you mean. Noah offered and I accepted. He said he could only dance the first dance because he didn't like social events and had some things to discuss with you. I didn't think you would mind."

"Don't lie to me, Gemma. Your friend said you thought dancing with me three times would cause the gossip mill to start talking about us." Liam stared into her eyes. He wanted her to understand his position and how he saw the situation. "I don't give a damn what they say. They mean nothing to me. You will not do this again."

"You're taking this all wrong. This isn't something you

should be concerned with. All I did was dance with your friend. That is perfectly acceptable."

Normally it would have been, but he knew how much she had flirted with Noah earlier in the day. He did not believe for a minute she had altruistic intentions. He didn't answer her because he had no words for her. Did she really expect him to believe that nonsense? Liam knew better. He had plenty to be concerned about. His wife was doing her utmost to avoid him. She didn't want to be near him.

All he wanted was to pull her close and breathe in her rose-tinted scent, skim his fingers across her silky smooth skin and feel her tremble with desire. Tell her how much he loved her—adored every inch of her.

Gemma appeared as if she couldn't wait to run in the other direction. She wanted to distance herself from him. Liam would give her anything in the world, except that. At the very idea of never seeing her again, shards of agony stabbed him through the heart. He needed to get her off of the dance floor and take her somewhere private. Tingles of sensation pooled inside him as a plan formed in his head. They needed to talk where ears were not privy to their discussion. Liam also had an unruly craving to kiss her, and that was not something anyone needed to witness. He twirled her around the dance floor until they reached the edge. He pulled her hand in his and led her away from the ballroom. Luckily, he was very familiar with the Silverton House so he knew exactly where to take her to have their conversation.

"Where are you taking me?"

Liam ignored her question. She would see soon enough where they were headed. He pushed open a door and pulled her inside. The door closed behind them with a quiet click. He turned to Gemma and reached for her. Now they could talk in private. She bit her lower lip and shook her head. Fear spilled out of her eyes, and she started to back away from him. Damn her and her need for space. Distance was the last thing they needed between them. Stalking toward her Liam decided what she needed from him at that moment was to know she belonged to him. She'd never belong to anyone else—she was his wife, the woman he loved beyond reason. Liam needed to claim her in the only way he knew how.

"Liam, what are we doing here?"

He stepped forward, grabbed her hand and pulled her into his arms. Once she was securely within his embrace, he fixated his complete attention on her. Gemma licked her lips and let out a breath thick with anticipation.

"You belong to me."

He leaned down and captured her lips with his. Her mouth opened, and he pushed his tongue inside. He licked hers with his as they dueled for control. A fierce heat ignited within him as he tasted her sweetness. Nothing would ever compare to her sweetness and Liam lost himself in the kiss. A soft moan filled the room. He wasn't sure if it came from him or Gemma, but it only encouraged him to seek more of her. His hands roamed over her back as he pulled her tighter into his arms. She leaned her head back and gave him better access to her sleek neck. He began to rain kisses down her throat and stopped just above her lace-encased bosom. He rolled his tongue over the top of the pearly white mounds and this time the moan that echoed through the room was hers.

"Liam, we should stop."

"No, we have only begun. I need more."

He wanted her completely naked, so she knew once and for all who she belonged to. Liam wanted to claim his wife and consummate their marriage, but she was right. This was not the time or the place to do it. Once they arrived home, they could continue where they left off. In the comforts of his bed, he would love her properly. When they were there, he would tell her how much she meant to him and that he couldn't live without her. It would be perfect and the most amazing experience of his life.

"Liam, please. Not now—No, don't stop, I changed my mind. Kiss me again."

Who was he to deny her what he wanted himself? With a newfound softness, he caressed her lips with his. As gentle as he could he showed her that he loved her with a simple kiss. He poured every ounce of what was inside his heart into that action, hoping, praying, and trusting her to realize what it meant. One of her hands roamed across his neck, and the other one rested on his hip as she tried to get closer to him.

He breathed in her scent and memorized every aspect of this moment with her. It promised to be something he wanted to remember for the rest of his life.

As he made love to Gemma with his lips, he could feel her hands move from their positions. She cupped both of his cheeks with her hands and pulled away. She looked into his eyes and stared deep into them for several moments. Liam believed she was seeking an answer to a question that she desperately needed. While he pondered what that question might be something struck him from behind and threw him off balance. He fell to the ground and hit it with a small thud. The room span. Gemma voice called to him, his name echoing in the distance. Her voice seemed so far away, but he could see her blurry image right in front of him. What happened? What had struck him from behind? Who would ruin such a perfect moment? Liam struggled to remain conscious because Gemma could be in danger. In a minute, he would get up, he could do it. Blackness overcame him, and he gave into it.

CHAPTER 14

Gemma watched as Liam crumpled to the floor. One minute she experienced a bliss only Liam could give her and the next she saw blood trickling down his forehead with him falling to the floor. It was the most surreal moment of her life. It couldn't possibly be happening. Gemma took a deep calming breath. She leaned over and brushed one of Liam's blond locks away from his forehead. His breathing seemed to be even. That had to be a good sign. Her hand shook as she caressed him one more time. Tears threatened to fall from her eyes, but she pushed them back. She couldn't give into such a weak and useless emotion.

Liam needed her help. If she was going to be free to get it for him, she had to take care of some unwanted business first. She stood up and clenched her fists at her side. Hatred coursed through her veins as she faced her cousin... She studied him and assessed the situation. How was she to handle Alfie? He didn't seriously think he'd get away with harming Liam. He stood off to the side and watched Gemma with an evil gleam. He held the statue he'd used to hit her husband firmly in his hands. He was tapping his hand with it in an aimless motion. He let it fall to the ground near Liam as he moved toward her. What could he possibly gain by harming Liam? Even if he killed him, that would not guarantee he could gain access to her money.

"Alfie, what are you thinking? You could have killed him!" her voice frantic as she thought about her next move. She took a few slow steps away from Liam's crumpled body. The more distance she put between him and her cousin, the better his chances were.

"I'm thinking, dear, that he does need to die."

"It won't help you to kill him. You must know that. As his widow, I gain complete control over my funds."

"As well as a good number of his too, I assume."

Gemma hadn't thought about what assets she would gain through her marriage. All she thought about was her own and that Alfie wanted her money to pay off his ever-growing debts. Did he see a way to get more than what she had? Of course, he did. If he could somehow coerce her into marrying him up on Liam's death, he would get whatever she inherited from him as well. He was a bloody fool because no way would Liam's father allow that to happen. Gemma continued to back away from Liam and the fool followed her, watching her every move to make sure she couldn't escape. Once she figured enough distance was between them she stopped. Liam lay still on the floor behind them both.

"You're an idiot."

"I don't think so. I am going to win, and you will help me. First, Liam needs to die."

No, Gemma wouldn't allow it. A world without Liam in it? She held her breath as the image took root inside her head. She wouldn't survive. If he died, she'd be lost. Alfie would not take him away from her. She'd just started to think it might be possible for them to have a real marriage. Liam could love her. He at least desired her. When he held her in his arms and showered her with kisses, she'd given in. She was tired of fighting her love for him. Gemma would rather stop breathing altogether than allow her cousin to kill the love of her life.

"No, wait. Think about this, Alfie. He doesn't need to die. I will give you all my money. Just leave with me now and I will make sure you get everything. I will even leave Liam and stay with you if that is what you want."

"I don't bloody want you. I just want your funds. I will take them and his. Rest assured I will enjoy you a bit before I kill you too. I plan on leaving England and never set foot in this rotten hell again."

"England isn't at fault for your foolish mistakes. Only you are. You can't run from yourself."

Alfie had clearly lost his mind. She had joked Liam had lost his when he insisted on marrying her. There wasn't any doubt in her mind her cousin truly was insane. How had she not seen it before? He would do everything he said to get what he wanted. He believed she owed him. If it saved Liam to go with him, she would, but she hoped it wouldn't come to that.

"I don't care what you think. I know what needs to be done. Now quit your babbling and don't move. I am going to kill your husband and then the two of us are going to leave this place as quietly as possible. We leave for France tonight."

Gemma saw a movement in the distance. Liam had started to wake up. She had to find a way to distract Alfie to allow him time to regain all of his faculties. What should she do? He told her to be quiet, but she suspected if she kept talking it would work as a good distraction.

"I don't see why I should go along with you. If you want to kill Liam I don't have a problem with that. You would be doing me a favor actually. I just hadn't thought that through." Gemma shrugged her shoulders, trying to give off the impression she didn't care. A bundle of energy burst through her giving her the strength of will to move forward with her plan. She prayed if Liam heard her words he didn't believe them. All she wanted to do was distract her evil cousin. "My intention had been to get an annulment, but by all means you should make me a widow instead. I won't be going to France with you though."

"You think what you want, Gemma dear, but soon you will realize that fighting the inevitable will prove futile."

Gemma circled around to the other side of the room as they talked. What could she do now? Talking wasn't working as a good enough distraction. A plan—she needed one. Gemma took slow concise steps until she stood near the fireplace and looked down at the nearby toolset. A quick action was needed. Alfie needed to be incapacitated. He'd never leave her and Liam alone if she just let him leave the room. A reasonable discussion was out as a means of getting through to him. Her cousin was insane and beyond reason.

Gemma moved to stand in front of the fireplace toolset and placed her arms behind her back. She reached down and, as slow as she could, grabbed one of the irons. Once she had a firm grasp on it she pulled it up as quietly as possible so that Alfie would be unaware that she had a weapon to use against him. The heavy statue he had used to knock Liam out still lay on the floor where he had dropped it. Gemma hoped he had no other weapon available. She started to move toward him with her hands behind her back while Liam still struggled in the background to get to his feet. He had made a little bit of progress as she gained access to one of the fireplace irons.

"I disagree. I would never willingly go with you anywhere. I would always fight until I had no breath left within me. You sicken me, and it disgusts me that you think I would ever allow you to put your filthy hands on me. You are insane and should be in Bedlam."

"I sicken you?" Alfie laughed. "Well, it's a good thing I don't give a damn how you feel. Women are only good for one thing, and once I have it from you it won't matter anyway."

Alfie reached into his pocket, pulled out a pistol and raised it in Gemma's general direction. She stopped with barely two feet between them. She still had the iron firmly in her hands, but the pistol changed her plan.

"Are you going to shoot me now?" Gemma giggled manically. She couldn't seem to help herself. The panic welling inside her made her react in an odd way. "When you haven't gotten everything you wanted out of me yet? Like I said before you're an idiot."

"Oh, I'm not going to shoot you—yet. If I wanted you dead you would be already. I couldn't very well shoot Liam when he had his hands all over you. I might have accidentally missed and killed you instead." His smile made goosebumps spread all over her. The malicious gleam in his eyes sent shivers down her spine. "No, I had to knock him out first and kill him once I separated the two of you. Enough talking, it is time to say your final goodbye to your husband."

Alfie turned to see Liam had already risen to his feet. He

was still a bit unsteady as he stared into Gemma's eyes. She took advantage of Alfie's back being turned to her and pulled the iron in front of her and raised it up high. Just as she reached it up to swing at him, Alfie raised his pistol toward Liam, ready to shoot.

"Well look who decided to join the party. Are you ready to die, Liam? I owe you for that beating you gave me the other day. Did you really think I'd let that go?"

"I had hoped you wouldn't be so foolish as to try to kill me. Apparently my hope was a bit misplaced."

"Don't worry, you won't live long enough to stress over your own follies."

Just as Alfie pulled the trigger, Gemma swung the iron around hard and hit him in the shoulder. It jerked the pistol to the side forcing the bullet to graze past Liam and lodge in the wall. Liam leaned forward and knocked Alfie to the ground. He wrestled the gun away from him and bashed Alfie unconscious. Gemma raced into his arms and shook visibly. Tears flowed down her cheeks as she sobbed uncontrollably.

"You were so brave. It's okay. Let it all out. I'm here for you." Liam assured her, "If not for your quick thinking he would have hurt us both."

"I couldn't let him hurt you. We need to get out of here. I can't be in the same room as him. Take me home Liam."

"I want to take you home. I need to have you safe there, but first we need to make sure he'll not hurt anyone else ever again. You understand that right?"

"I do. But I can't be in this room." Gemma's arm shook, and she rubbed her hands up and down trying to dispel the tingles. "I will leave and go get someone to help. Stay here and make sure he doesn't wake up and try to escape."

"Yes. That's a good idea. Go see if Noah is still here. He will know what to do."

Gemma nodded and raced out of the room. She entered the ballroom and found Noah talking to another gentleman she didn't know. She hurried over to his side and tapped him anxiously on the shoulder.

"Oh Gemma, there you are. I wondered where you and Liam disappeared to."

"I need your help. Liam, he is in a room." Gemma spoke

rapidly and in short bursts. "The library I think. My cousin attacked us."

"Say no more. Show me where to go."

"No, you need to get the constable. Alfie is subdued for now, but if we let him go this could happen again."

"I will send someone to get them and then we will go back and help Liam. Is that okay with you?" Noah asked.

"Yes, but please hurry."

Noah walked off in the opposite direction and spoke to one of the servants. Gemma watched as the servant nodded and then took off to follow his directions. Noah returned to her side after the servant left to do his bidding.

"All right, Gemma, take me to where your husband is waiting."

"Follow me."

She led him to the room and when they entered, she saw her cousin was still unconscious. Liam held the pistol in his hand and kept a close eye on the fallen man, a grim look on his face.

"Gemma tells me you two were in a spot of trouble and here I thought you were off to a more pleasurable evening."

"It started out that way" Liam smiled. "But then it went to hell pretty fast."

"I sent a servant to get the constable. They should be here shortly to arrest the man. Why did he attack the two of you?"

"He wanted to kill Liam so he could get his hands on my money," Gemma said.

"Greedy bastard," Noah said in a scathing tone.

"Broke. He is bleeding debt and needed it to get solvent again. Before I married Gemma, he planned on marrying her to get his hands on her money. I thwarted his plans, and he decided I needed to die because of it."

"I see. Well, it looks like money is going to be the least of his worries soon."

They sat in that room for almost an hour before the constable arrived. He asked a bunch of questions and determined that Alfie needed to be arrested. After a time, he would go on trial and most likely be sentenced to prison or sent to a penal colony to serve out his sentence. It didn't matter to Gemma as long as she never had to lay eyes on him again. This was one experience she never wanted to live again.

"Can we go home now, Liam?"

"Yes. I think it is time we went home where I know I can keep you safe. At least we know he won't be bothering us ever again."

"That is a small comfort right now. I haven't exactly stopped shaking from the whole experience."

"In time it will get easier. Don't expect it to happen overnight though. I need to go talk to Noah for a quick minute and then we will leave."

Gemma watched as Liam walked over and talked to his friend. Noah nodded and turned back to talk to the constable.

"What did you ask him?"

"If he could take over here so I can take my wife home."

"I take it he said yes."

She certainly hoped she'd read the situation correctly. Gemma didn't ever want to lay eyes on her cousin again. All she wanted was to curl up in Liam's arms and wrap up in his warmth. He made her feel so protected, almost loved. For now it was enough, it had to be. She wouldn't give Liam up without a fight.

"He did indeed. He also said I owed him and to expect to pay up at that dinner party you planned."

Gemma smiled, in all of the chaos she had forgotten about her dinner party. She also made a decision when she saw Liam lying on the floor bleeding from the head wound Alfie had inflicted him. She would tell him she loved him and never stopped. It was time for her heart and mind to quit fighting.

CHAPTER 15

Liam helped Gemma into their carriage. The entire way out of the Silverton Ball Gemma didn't utter a word. Her face was devoid of all color but her green eyes held the luminosity of a dull jewel. Liam didn't know what to do to shake her out of this state of numbness.

When he had regained consciousness and saw Alfie brandishing a pistol in her general direction his heart had stopped beating for a second. It had taken him longer than he would have liked to regain his equilibrium. If not for her quick thinking, he might not have made it out of the situation alive. The bullet had grazed him, leaving a streak of blood on his arm as it passed by and embedded itself into the wall behind him. Gemma had saved his life by striking her cousin with the fireplace iron.

"Everything will be all right. We just need to get you home." Liam tried to reassure her.

Gemma leaned her head against the side of the carriage and closed her eyes. Liam hoped she wasn't closing herself off to him. He needed her now more than ever. This fight for control they battled over, since they married a couple days ago, must end tonight. Gemma didn't trust that he could love her. He saw that now. She believed that he only married her to protect her from her cousin's nefarious intentions. Now that Alfie would never be a problem again she could very well find a reason to bolt. Lily would always welcome her in South Carolina. Liam had to stop her before a plan formulated in her mind. Gemma couldn't leave him—he wouldn't allow it.

If she left, his heart would not recover from the loss. He was such a bloody fool. How could he have not realized sooner how much he loved her? Why had he been so damned stubborn? Gemma was his everything. Without her, his reason for being would be obliterated. He had to fix this mess once and for all. The path that must be taken was clear to him. It had always been obvious what must be done. He had only put off the inevitable. Tonight, once he had her safely in their home, he would make sure he'd tell her he loved her. When she was ready to accept him, he would show her exactly how much.

Once he spilled out all of the emotions welling up inside him, and if then she still wanted to leave him, he'd have to find a way to let her go—wait hell no, he wouldn't let her leave him. Liam couldn't believe he'd even considered giving in and stepping aside. He'd just keep pushing until she admitted she never stopped loving him. Liam refused to believe her love for him didn't still fill her heart. When you truly love a person, it doesn't go away.

The carriage came to a complete stop. Liam looked out the windows and saw the outline of his townhouse directly in front of him. They had finally arrived home. The footman opened the door, and Liam stepped out. He reached his arms back in and picked Gemma up into his arms. She slumped her head on his shoulder and wrapped her arms around his neck. Her skirts dragged on the grown as he carried her up the steps and inside their home. He nodded at Pemberly as he walked inside.

Gemma was way too complacent. Why didn't she argue more? She wasn't acting like her normal self. He had to get her to snap out of whatever world she'd retreated too. He needed his fiery Gemma with him.

"I don't want to be disturbed the rest of the night."

"I will see to it sir," Pemberly replied.

Still carrying his wife in his arms he walked up the stairs to his bedroom. He refused to be separated from her another night. From this night forward they would never be parted again. He pushed open his door and strolled over to his bed. He set her down on top of the bed and with extreme gentleness caressed her cheek.

"Please say something. I need to make sure you are okay," Liam pleaded with her.

Gemma looked into his eyes, and he noticed that at last the glassiness had started to abate and a little life had started to show in their depths. She raised her hands to cup his cheek inside her palm. Green eyes surveyed him while her other hand reached up and skimmed over his superficial wound.

"You could have died," she whispered. Her hands shook as she studied the blood staining his shirt. "Because of me. My cousin was going to murder you to get to me..."

"But I didn't. This is not your fault." Liam touched her cheeks with the palm of his hand, making her focus her eyes on his. "I'm here. I'm safe. Because of you. You're the bravest person I know. You fought him every step of the way."

"No, you're wrong because of me you were a target." Gemma shook her head. "Alfie never would have shot you otherwise. I had to do something to help. I kept him talking as long as I could. I said some things..."

"I know they were not true. You would never wish me dead," Liam reassured her.

"Do you? Really? I haven't exactly been nice to you the past couple of days. My heart hurt so much, and I reacted instead of stopping to think about what my words and actions might do to you. I'm so sorry."

"You have nothing to apologize for. Stop saying you are sorry. I'm not."

Tears fell from her eyes and trailed down her cheeks. Liam wiped them away with his fingertips. "Yes, I wish I could have avoided hurting you, but I wasn't ready for your love. I wish I had been, and we could have avoided this whole mess. If anyone should be sorry, it's me, but I can't be. Do you want to know why?"

"No. Yes. I don't know." Uncertainty shown through her eyes.

Liam laughed. "I will tell you anyway. I'm not sorry because as crazy as this path has been it led me to the exact place I was always meant to be. Right here with you. We will be stronger because of everything we have gone through. This means the rest should be easy or as easy as we make it. No matter what life throws in our path we can get through it as long as we stay together."

"How can you be so certain?"

Liam lifted her hand and placed a small kiss in her palm. He gazed into her eyes, attempting to pour all the emotion he felt into her. She needed to believe in his sincerity.

"Because I love you."

What he didn't say to her was that he believed she could still love him too. In that moment, it didn't matter if she didn't say it back. He needed to let her know how much she meant to him. Her well-being and what she needed to get through this moment was his top priority. The time for them to stop and share how they each loved each other, and how much, could be saved for another day.

Liam cupped her face in both of his hands and placed a light kiss on her lips and stepped back from her. He held his hand out to her, and she looked up at him apprehensively. She appeared to be gauging his reactions and trying to determine if it was all real. Her head tilted to the side, and her lips opened as a small breath released from her lungs. She looked down to his hand and then back up to his face directly into his eyes. A small smile formed on her face as she placed her hand in his. He pulled her off the bed and into his embrace. He leaned down and captured her lips with his once again. Her arms slid up his chest and wrapped around his neck. The kiss deepened as they touched their tongues together, mimicking a dance. The beat of his heart thump faster inside his chest as he continued the kiss. Gemma's hands roamed to his hair as she ran her fingers through them; pulling him closer as they each fought for control.

Liam pulled back and turned her around. With agile grace, he started to unpin her hair and pull it out of the braid so expertly weaved. Once every strand was loose he fanned out her sanguine curls over her back and shoulders. The silky strands were heaven on his fingertips. Pushing the strands aside, he placed small kisses along her shoulder to the base of her neck. With each kiss, he unlatched one of the hooks holding her dress together until it draped open revealing her corset. Liam pushed the dress down, and it pooled at her feet. He yanked at the laces of her corset until it loosened enough for him to remove it. He spun her back around to face him. She stood before him only wearing her chemise. Her face no longer pale, but flushed bright and rosy; her green eyes sparkled with desire and her pink tongue darted out and slid over her plump lips. She reached for him, and he wrapped his arms around her once more, needing to feel her in his arms.

Their lips met in mutual desire. Kissing and touching each other was the only thing that mattered to Liam at that moment. He had waited so long to have her in his arms. It had only been a short amount of time, but to him it had dragged on for an eternity. He lifted her up and her legs circled his waist. He walked them back over to the bed and sat her down on top of it. Gemma untied his cravat and yanked it off his neck, throwing it over his shoulder. With a wicked gleam in her eyes, she pulled his shirt up and ran her fingers across his chest. Liam groaned at the feel of her hands on his bare chest. He pushed her backward so that she lay on the bed and pulled his top over his head. The rest of his clothing followed soon afterward and he returned his attention back to his stunning wife. While he had been divesting himself of his clothing, she had removed hers as well. She lay on his bed in all her wondrous glory. For a brief moment, time stood still as his gaze took in the sight of his beautiful wife.

"You're so alluring," he whispered. "I want to taste every inch of you."

Gemma laughed as he crawled in bed next to her. Her nipples tightened into tiny nubs inviting him to bring them into his mouth. He ran his tongue across one as he pinched the other one between his finger and thumb. A moan of pleasure could be heard throughout the room. Gemma liked having him touch her beautiful bosom. Liam switched over and brought the other tight nipple inside is mouth and licked. He pinched it with his teeth and soothed it again with a gentle sucking of his mouth and lips. Trailing his other hand down across her stomach it rested at the apex of her legs. He caressed the curls he found there with the palm of his hand

and stroked the sensitive nub with his thumb. Gemma's breathing became more ragged, and the sounds of pleasure coming from her encouraged him to explore even more. He slid down the bed and pushed her legs apart. With as much tenderness as he could he licked her core and suck the nub into his mouth. Gemma squirmed and tightened her legs around his shoulders. Liam kept licking and stroking her with his mouth, tongue, and fingers. It didn't take long for her to scream when she found her source of ecstasy.

"That's amazing. We must do that again."

Liam laughed and crawled up to lay next to her on the bed. Her face glowed with a languidness that showed the aftereffects of her orgasm.

"We're not done yet."

"I know, but I liked that. I'm not so sure I will like the next part."

"I'll be gentle. It's only the first time that hurts. After that, it will be nothing but pleasure I promise."

"I trust you, Liam."

Liam kissed her as he stroked her breasts with his hands. He positioned his body over hers and pushed one of her legs up to accommodate his large size. She wrapped the other leg around his hips. One slow inch at a time, he pushed himself inside her. He could feel her begin to stretch and welcome his length. After a few excruciating minutes, he reached the barrier marking her a virgin. He looked down into her trusting eyes and gave her a moment to adjust to what was about to happen. She reached up and twined her hands around his neck and pulled him down for a sweet kiss. Liam decided to distract her with his lips while he pushed all the way inside of her. Gemma stiffened as he broke through, and he placed soft kisses across her face and neck. She needed a little bit of time to adjust to his size. Once she started to move underneath him, he took it as a sign to begin thrusting inside of her. Slow at first, he moved almost all the way out of her and then just as slowly, he went back inside. He had done that for several strokes before she thrashed with wild abandon. Liam lost control and moved at a much faster pace until he felt her channel start to tighten on him with tiny ripples and Gemma screamed as another orgasm wracked through her body. He followed soon after with an equally intense release.

Liam rolled them onto their sides and withdrew himself from her body. He didn't want to leave her because everything had an incredibly right feeling while he was buried deep inside her.

He had finally made love to his wife, and it had surpassed all of his wildest imagination. He couldn't' wait to do it all over again. He pulled a bed sheet over both of them as he snuggled closer to her. Gemma's head rested on his shoulder a contented smile on her face. Liam didn't want to be anywhere else than in that room with her nestled beside him in bed. With that though drifting through his mind, he let himself fall into a deep sleep.

Gemma woke up, warm and comfortable, enclosed within Liam's arms. Lifting her head, she looked outside and saw the sky was still dark. Moonlight beamed through the window and bounced across Liam as she turned to gaze at his sleeping face. She couldn't have been asleep very long before something startled her awake. Her throat closed up tight with an unidentifiable emotion. Shallow, rapid breaths emerged from her mouth. She raised her hand to her chest as sharp pinpricks stabbed her. The panic that shot through her took root at her center and spread throughout her whole body. She needed air and to think. Staying in bed with Liam would not allow her that freedom. No decisions could be made with him sleeping beside her. It didn't make sense, but something had snapped inside her. Gemma needed to get out of this room and gain some distance from Liam...

He almost died because of her. She looked down at her husband's sleeping form. He deserved better than her tumultuous feelings. How could she love him so much it hurt and still need to find some distance from him to think?

Because of what her cousin almost did to him, he was probably better off without her in his life. What if Alfie escaped justice? He'd just keep coming after them. Gemma needed to make sure Liam would never come to harm again because of her. She didn't want to leave him, not really. She just needed to be sure of him and his professed love. If she could establish that once and for all, she'd be able to accept her place at his side.

They needed to have a conversation that didn't involve him kissing her senseless.

Gemma slowly extricated herself from Liam's embrace. A bedsheet tangled between her legs and Liam's arm held her tight against him. First she needed to find a way to unravel the sheet from her legs. Once that small task was accomplished, she could move out of her husband's arms. She twisted her legs until the sheet loosened and then as carefully as possible slid out of bed. Gemma knew that Liam's injury had been minor, but she still didn't want to interrupt any healing sleep.

Perhaps it was a tad ridiculous when the wound hadn't even needed any bandage. The bleeding had stopped before the constable arrived, and it appeared to be no more than a scratch under direct scrutiny. She couldn't help from worrying about possible long-term damage. Any injury could lead to larger and more pressing issues. She didn't want anything to happen to Liam just because she couldn't sleep and developed an enormous case of anxiety.

After crawling out of the bed, Gemma took a minute to assess the situation. Her dress lay in a green pool of satin and lace on the floor next to the bed. Her chemise lay shining like a bright white beacon a few inches next to it. She could put that on and sneak over to her room to grab her wrapper. Everyone in the household probably still slept, but the servants would probably be getting up soon to start their daily chores. She didn't want to give them something to gossip about. Gemma knew she was being unrealistic, but she didn't like anyone talking about her. Her marriage to Liam hadn't started out the best and she couldn't deal with their wagging tongues. In time spending the night in her husband's bed would become commonplace, for now, though it was something she wanted to hold close to her heart. It wasn't the servant's business when her husband made lover to her.

Grabbing her chemise she put it on as quickly as possible, and tiptoed out of the room. She closed the door with a soft click and continued to her room. Once she arrived at her door, she pushed it open and hurried inside. The drapes were spread wide open at the windows in the room allowing the moonlight to highlight areas of the bed. Her wrapper lay on her bed next to her pearly-white silk nightgown. She grabbed both of the items and put them over her chemise. At least on the outside it would appear like she hadn't been sleeping naked for the past couple of hours.

Making love with Liam had surpassed anything she could have anticipated. If she were honest with herself, she hadn't known what to expect, but she knew she loved him and wanted to express that with him. When he had told her he loved her, for a brief moment her heart stopped and her ears rang. Her whole body went numb and then she could feel the echo of her heartbeat against her eardrums.

Liam loves me...

She repeated that over and over inside her head and still didn't quite believe it. The whole thing just didn't feel real. The dreamlike quality forced her to pinch her arm. She squeezed the skin between her fingers, and the small stab of pain ensured her that everything happened.

"Ouch." She let out a small quiet squeak.

Gemma exited her bedroom took quiet steps down the stairs. She needed to find something to occupy herself with. Anything...as long as it wouldn't let her dwell too much on the things that kept her awake; she should be upstairs still asleep in Liam's arms. Gemma couldn't help but think that not everything was as settled as she would like them to be. Something still nagged at her, and she didn't know how to explain what it was.

At the bottom of the stairs she realized she had a tiny problem. She had no clue what to do with herself. She could go to the library, but the light outside and inside wasn't exactly conducive to reading. The past couple of days had been filled with chaos and stress, and it started to affect her ability to reason properly. No matter, she could still relax on the settee in the sitting room and think about what she wanted or rather what she expected from her marriage. She already made her decision. It was not a matter of how to proceed with it. She would worry about the particulars later;

right now, she could go to the library and have a glass of sherry to alleviate her anxiety. As she turned to stroll to the library, she bumped right into someone and knocked them down.

"Oh, I'm so sorry. I didn't know you were there." Gemma apologized.

Janie sat on the floor looking up at her. Her skirt fanned out around her as her legs peeped out from underneath it. Gemma reached down and offered her hand to help her to her feet. Once Janie was standing, she smoothed her skirt and addressed what was on her mind.

"No, the fault is mine, ma'am. I should have made my presence known. I saw you walking down the stairs and thought you might need something," Janie said.

Gemma thought about it and maybe it was a good thing she bumped into Janie. She could help her with a few things. Food being one of them as she suddenly .

"I'm a bit hungry and thirsty. I thought everyone would be asleep still." Gemma bit her lip after the words spilled out of her mouth.

"Everyone has been asleep for hours. I woke up about a half hour past to start my day. Pemberly usually awakes around the same time. He should be rousing soon. What can I get for you?"

"I'd love something light to eat. And some milk? Whatever you can find available is fine."

"Would you like me to bring it up to your room? Or perhaps *another* room?"

Janie no doubt referred to Liam's room. She was too good of a servant to be so indifferent about the situation. What she wanted to know was if the new lovers, her and Liam, wanted a meal to share after their strenuous lovemaking. She was wrong, of course, not about them finally consummating their marriage, but that she wanted something to share with Liam. No, he needed to rest, and she would not disturb him for anything. Maybe she should have thought about his possible health before they fell into bed together, but sadly all she could think about at that moment was how much she needed him. While deep in those incredible moments, her feelings brimmed over the top and she rejoiced being alive. The rest was all second thoughts and worries for a later date.

"My room is fine. When do the servants awaken for the day?"

"Everyone should be up and moving in about a quarter hour."

"Oh really, that soon?"

"Yes. We do get up early to run the house."

"No, that's not what I mean. I just didn't realize how late or early it is depending on how you look at it..."

"Ah, I think I see what you mean. I will have a maid bring you up a tray to your room."

Janie turned to leave to do as Gemma wished. Her back was fully to her when Gemma had an idea.

"No, Janie wait. Can you just send my maid up without the tray? Have something sent to the library in an hour. A light meal like we discussed and plan on joining me. I have a few ideas I want to deal with for the dinner party tomorrow evening. I will need your thoughts on it."

"Very well, ma'am. I shall see you in an hour in the library." Janie turned on her heels and left.

Gemma strolled up the stairs to her room. She wanted to make the dinner party something even more special than she had already planned. It could be the wedding dinner they hadn't had. It was perfect because the most important people in their lives were already going to be there. The only person that wouldn't be in attendance was Liam's sister, her other best friend, Lily.

She wished Lily could be there with them. Gemma missed her a lot. It couldn't be helped though, and she wouldn't dwell on something that could not be changed. Liam promised her a, and she intended on holding him to that promise. With a little help perhaps she could make the arrangements herself.

The door opened, and her maid peeked her head into the room. She looked a little surprised to see Gemma awake at such an early hour.

Her eyes were wide, and her mouth opened up as if to let out a small "oh".

She didn't remark on whatever thought crossed her mind.

The maid fully entered the room and stated her reason for being there.

"Ma'am Janie said you needed me."

"Yes, I need you to help me dress for the day. My hair is a mess, and I will need my maid to help me brush it out so it can be plaited. I have a lot to do today, and I need to get started on it right away."

"All right. Where would you like to start first? Dressing or your hair?"

"Let's work on my hair first. It will take the longest to get through, and I told Janie to meet me in the library in an hour."

Her maid nodded, and Gemma walked over to sit down at her vanity table. Gemma grabbed one of her combs, and the maid grabbed the brush. They both started the long process of untangling her hair. Once all the knots were out, the maid quickly plaited her hair and twirled it into a bun at the nape or her neck. Her hair done Gemma walked over to her armoire and pulled out a dress. She stepped out of her nightgown and threw it on her still made bed along with her wrapper.

"Oh, I left my corset in Liam's room. I am going to go without one today."

Gemma was a bit embarrassed to admit she left clothing in her husband's room but decided to let that go. The servants knew anyway and she had nothing to be uncomfortable about. After her gown was laced up, she dismissed her maid. The maid wasn't needed at the moment for the rest of her plans. Gemma followed her out of the room and headed to the library for her meeting with Janie. As she descended the stairs, she could see the sun starting to rise through one of the hall windows. She smiled to herself knowing that she had a surprise in store for her husband. That is if she managed to pull it off in time for the dinner party. No matter what, she intended to make sure everything would go just right. She needed to tell Liam she still loved him, and this was the first step in making him know that it had never changed. Her heart belonged to him and it always would.

CHAPTER 17

Liam woke up and reached across his bed to locate his wife. As he spread his fingers over the soft sheet, he realized his hands hadn't located what they were in search of. He opened his eyelids to mere slits and looked over to the other side of the bed. Yes, it was empty, and Gemma had once again vacated the bed before he had awakened for the day. Two days in a row, she had managed to sneak out of bed without waking him to her intentions. The first night he made love to her, after the ball, it had been wonderful. She needed to stop this insane habit of waking up at the break of dawn. He wanted her wrapped in his arms so he could love her again in the early morning hours. When he saw her later that day, he would let her know how much this practice of hers disturbed him. Her penchant for early morning hours was not the only thing that bothered him. It had not escaped his notice that she hadn't told him she loved him. Again that is… What she said in the past was irrelevant to the here and now. He didn't know if she *still* loved him. It made him a desperate man and he needed to hear her say the words once again.

He might as well get up and start his day. Rolling over, he disentangled the sheets from around his body and crawled out of bed. He went to his armoire and grabbed the first pair of trousers he could find. After he pulled them on, Liam retrieved a shirt and pulled it over his head. Once he was fully dressed, he walked out of his room and went down the stairs to his study. He had a lot of work to do and a short amount of time to get it done. He had sat there for most of the morning before the overload took its toll on him. A sharp pain beat against his skull, as if a carpenter fast at work hammered away inside his head, making thinking a difficult endeavor. Liam rubbed his temples to dispel the thrumming deep inside his head. The last time this kind of pain visited him was when he'd had the idiotic idea to drink away his problems. He hadn't done that, so he didn't understand why the throbbing insisted on finding a home behind his eyes. Perhaps the stress of his life finally caught up with him and took up permanent residence.

"Looks like something is troubling you."

Liam looked up to see the Duke of Huntly, Noah walk into his study. His dark hair disheveled and his blue eyes twinkling with devilment. A lopsided grin on his face, the duke strolled over and sat down in a chair in front of Liam's desk.

"I have a lot on my mind. What can I do for you?"

"Are you sure you have time to help me. It looks like you have enough here to keep you busy for the next year or so."

"I can make time. If not for your help the other night I would have been stuck at the Silverton Ball far longer than I would have liked. I do owe you a debt of gratitude for wrapping up the Alfie mess."

Liam really did owe Noah quite a bit for dealing with that. If he had had to stay any longer that night, he might have just murdered the new Earl of Devon. It still bothered him the man had the gall to try and kill him to get his hands on Gemma. He broke the quill he held in his hands while thinking about breaking Alfie's neck instead. It snapped in two before he knew what happened.

"A little frustrated still by it all, I see."

"That's quite the understatement."

"How are things with Gemma?"

"Good. I think. Better at least."

"Well, that is an improvement over the other day when you were drinking your troubles away. Have you finally told her that you love her?"

Liam watched as Noah sat back in his chair and crossed his arms over his chest. His blue eyes pierced him with the question. That subject was the very one that troubled him the most.

"I did." His response barely a decibel above a whisper.

Noah raised his eyebrow in query over his response. "It didn't go well?"

"No, it went just fine. The only problem is—she never once said she loved me."

"I thought you believed she does. Did something happen to change your mind about that?"

"No. Yes. I don't know. I have doubts. She may still care about me, but I'm worried that she doesn't love me anymore. I may very well have destroyed my chances two years ago."

"Because when she professed her love you ran away like a scared little school boy?" A rumble of laughter echoed through the room as Noah held his chest while it rumbled.

"Don't make fun of me. You would have too."

"On the contrary, I married the love of my life as soon as I found her." Sadness laced Noah's voice.

"I know. I can't imagine your pain when you lost her. I think my heart stopped beating when I saw Gemma in danger that night. I don't know what I would do if she died. Thank the Lord that didn't happen. I'm sorry I made light of your feelings. I know more than anyone how much you loved Rubina. I hoped you could find someone else, not to replace her, but to at least fill a bit of the hole in your heart."

"I don't think that is possible. She filled it to the brim, and when I lost her she left an empty shell. No one could ever truly fill that gap. I will probably marry again someday, but never again for love. I would like children though so when I think I can stomach it I will attempt to find someone at least bearable to live with."

Liam understood what his friend was feeling more than he wanted to. It just wasn't fair that Rubina died and left him alone. Not entirely alone, but some things just didn't measure up to the person you loved most in the world.

"I hope soon. I'd like our children to grow up as friends."

"I can't make any promises."

"I don't expect you, too. Just expressing my own selfish desires." Liam smiled.

"You are not selfish. I hope things work out with you and Gemma. That is part of the reason I am here."

"I don't understand."

"I just had an extensive meeting with the constable regarding Alfie."

"Really? I didn't know that it all hadn't been settled already. What did you discuss with him? Do I need to go and talk with him as well?"

"We had a lengthy discourse on the merits of stripping him of his title and shipping him off to a penal colony for the rest of his miserable life. The constable agreed. Alfie is no longer known as the Earl of Devon. That honor will befall to your firstborn son."

"My own son is going to outrank me?" Liam asked. "That's as ironic as it is incredible."

"He considered just bestowing the title on you but believed this was a better option. Once you inherit your father's title—hopefully sometime in the very distant future—you can change the succession rules to have it go to your second son. The paperwork is all being drawn up. There is some obscure rule in the line of succession with the Earl's title that allows it. The entailment on your title ends when you inherit it. That allows for you to make the necessary changes."

"What if I only have one son? This seems all a bit crazy."

"Then you don't need to make any changes. You can just let him inherit both. I'm just explaining all of your options. With the Earl of Devon's title, all of the properties entailed come under your control as Gemma's husband. It's not pretty though, as Alfie beggared the estates in a short time. You are going to have to work some miracles to make them profitable again."

"That's astounding. I don't have words for that. Gemma will be relieved her ancestral home is going to remain in her family. I can't wait to tell her the good news."

"You also can move into the country house if you wish to do so. As the guardian of the estate, it's your right to oversee personally all of its operations. That very well could take some personal and immediate attention."

"We may do that after the season is over. It's a busy time of the year for Marsden Shipping. I still need to finalize the merger with RandCo. Speaking of personal attention, I think I'm going to have to travel to South Carolina to meet with him to iron out some of the final details."

"Have you discussed that with Gemma?"

"No, I am not positive I need to go yet. I owe her a wedding trip, perhaps this can double as one. I know she wants to visit Lily so she shouldn't be adverse to the idea. I'm hoping that if she doesn't love me now by the end of the trip she will."

"If you want my opinion, you are overthinking it a bit. Just sit down and ask her. What are you afraid of?"

What was he afraid of? He feared she'd come out and say point blank that she didn't love him anymore. Lust was an equally powerful emotion. Maybe that was all she had left to offer him. Liam's worst fear was losing Gemma before he ever had her. He scrubbed his face with his hands—what a bloody fool he was. How could he ever believe she still loved him? Perhaps she cared. Could that be enough for their marriage to work? Liam didn't know if he wanted to find out the answers to these questions. He might not like what Gemma had to say.

No, talking to her wasn't an option yet. He would give her time to acclimate to her new life and allow her the necessary space to love him freely. When she was ready to tell him of her own love, she would. He just had to pray she would open up to him—express her innermost feelings. Liam trusted her with the truth of his love. He had to trust her to come to him with her own. It would be one of the most difficult things he'd ever done. Gemma deserved the patience to come to terms with her emotions. She'd been brave enough once, and he was the one that ruined it in the beginning. He would give her the time she needed.

"She just needs time. I owe her that much."

"I can see your point. I hope you get the outcome you are looking for. In the meantime, I have a few things I need to do before tonight. I will see you at dinner later this evening."

Liam frowned, how had he let that slip his mind? He had a lot to get done before his parents and their friends descended upon them for dinner.

"All right. Thanks again for the information. I will contact the solicitors to see what needs to be done with the Earl of Devon's estate. I'll see you later tonight." Liam nodded.

Noah left the room, while Liam went back to his stacks of paperwork. He had to make a dent in it before the evening progressed. The amount of work would only double once he got his hands on the necessary information regarding his new responsibilities. Gemma would be happy to have her family estate back under their control. The extra effort needed to make it solvent would be worth all of his time to make her happy.

"Excuse me sir, but you have a missive from your father," Pemberly said as he entered the room.

"Bring it here. I might as well see what he wants."

Pemberly handed him the letter and left the room.

Once alone, Liam opened the note and let out a sigh of irritation. His father demanded his attention immediately. After pondering his instructions for several minutes, he stood up and adjusted his jacket as he strolled out of the room.

"Pemberly I need my horse brought around. I feel like riding and father needs to see me right away."

"It's already been brought around sir. I thought it might be important."

"Very good. Pemberly, I don't know what I would do without you."

"I'm glad to be of service, sir."

Liam walked out his front door. As soon as he descended the steps someone knocked him down from behind and shoved him into an awaiting carriage. All Liam could think before the world went black was: *who the hell is trying to kill me now?*

G emma found it funny how the things least planned for could spring up at the most inopportune time, much like a marriage of convenience, or inconvenience depending on the point of view in question. For Gemma, marrying Liam had been an inconvenience at the time. Her mindset had since changed, but that didn't negate her original feelings.

Switching, rewinding, and rethinking her position did not come easy to her.

Yes, right now, she could be the happiest wife in England and wouldn't change her circumstances for anything. There was only one problem. She still had yet to tell Liam that she never stopped loving him. The time just—well, just didn't feel right. So she had kept her lips sealed tight and left him in the dark. Perhaps it could be perceived as cruel, and Gemma generally didn't have a mean bone in her body. In this instance, maliciousness held no place in her heart. Even though Liam had told her he loved her, she still had doubts.

She wanted everything to work between them, which was why she continued to plan the surprise for the dinner party. In fact, she had a small meeting scheduled with Liam's father in a few minutes to iron out some of the details. Gemma decided that they needed time away to just be with each other. No hassles or stress-inducing activities allowed. It would just be the two of them for six whole weeks.

Gemma currently stood in the middle of the sitting room at Marsden House. She couldn't sit still and had taken her anxiety out on the rug. A path would probably be worn in the carpet from her frequent pacing back and forth in front of the window. It had been a while since she'd been in this particular room—a smile formed on her face at the memory. Ah yes, when Lily plotted to run away from home. She missed her best friend and could benefit from her advice. Gemma had a feeling she was making things much more difficult than then needed to be.

She shouldn't have anything to worry about...

When Gemma had helped Lily, she had not counted on the wrath of her friend's father, Viscount Torrington. She'd never had a reason to meet him much. All she'd know about the man was what Lily had told her. Now he was her father-in-law, and she was seeking him out for his assistance. Gemma did learn one thing from helping her best friend run away. Because of that instance, she both feared the viscount and respected him for the care he demonstrated for his daughter. That didn't stop her from standing up for herself. She didn't let anyone bully her anymore.

"I'm sorry to keep you waiting, Gemma. Would you like to come to my study so we can discuss this in detail?"

Gemma looked over to see Viscount Torrington standing in the doorway of the sitting room. He leaned against the door frame with his hands folded across his chest. His steely blue eyes watched her as he awaited her response.

"Certainly."

The viscount turned on his heels and sauntered out of the room. Gemma picked up the pace and hurried to follow him to his study. Once inside, he took a seat behind his big burgundy desk and leaned back in his chair. She sat down in a chair in front of his desk, her back straight and her posture perfect with her hands folded in her lap. No matter how nervous she was, she refused to let it show in his presence. The viscount reminded her of a predator waiting for its prey to show its weakness. Once that disadvantage was revealed, he would strike the killing blow or, in this instance, get her to cave to his will.

"So I began the arrangements you asked me to do. I have

my ship prepared for you to set sail to South Carolina. I cleared Liam's calendar for the next six weeks. You will be free to go on an extended wedding trip and visit Lily. I do have a few things I want you to take her and my new grandson. I've included a letter which explains everything to her. I will make sure it is loaded on the ship for you to take with you."

"Oh, that is wonderful. Thank you so much for your help. I couldn't have pulled any of this off without your help."

"I did it for Liam. The boy is besotted with you, and I think this time will be good for you both. Not that I don't like you, but I wouldn't have done this if I didn't know he would want it to happen. Plus I was going to ship the stuff to Lily anyway and this is easier. I can rest assured you and Liam will make sure it arrives to her safely."

Gemma tilted her head and studied Viscount Torrington. He acted all tough on the outside and no doubt he was whenever the situation required it, but she suspected he was soft on the inside—at least with anything concerning his family. The rest of them, he would stomp out of existence if necessary. No matter, the man was still a force to be reckoned with.

"I'm glad my plans work well with your own then. It is a mutually beneficial arrangement. When is the ship scheduled to set sail?"

"You will leave in three days. It will give you time to finish packing and have your trunks loaded on the ship. Liam is capable of captaining the ship, so I am going to leave that in his hands. He has sailed enough to learn that area of the business and since he enjoys it, it seemed like a good idea. He doesn't get the chance to sail with the ships anymore."

"Good. Is there anything else we need to discuss?"

"No, that pretty much sums everything up. I sent a letter ahead to Lily, so she knows to expect you. They should be there to meet you when your ship sets anchor in Charleston Harbor."

Gemma nodded. Everything was beginning to fall into place. The only thing that needed to be done was to tell Liam how much she loved him and that they are going to go on that wedding trip he promised her. Probably a bit sooner than he had planned, but that is what made it a surprise, she hoped that he liked it.

"All right, then I will take your leave. I have a few things to do at home before tonight's dinner party."

A half smile formed on his lips as he stared into her eyes. She didn't know what that smile meant, but she didn't think it was necessarily a good one.

"Before you leave Pia wanted to talk to you."

"Oh. I suppose I can wait and talk to her. How long do you think..."

"Okay, I'm here. Sorry it took so long. Did you tell her yet?"

Gemma looked as Lady Torrington came breezing in the room like a strong wind rolling over everything in its path.

"Tell me what?" Gemma asked.

"I've told her about the particulars concerning the ship, Lily's package, and how long they can expect to be gone."

"Oh good, I can tell her the good news then." Lady Torrington smiled.

"Good news?" Gemma asked raising her eyebrows. What were they up to?

"Yes. I'm coming along with you."

That wasn't exactly good news. Gemma adored Lady Torrington, but having her husband's mother along could be a bit of a damper on the wedding trip.

"With us?" The shock was evident in her voice.

"Oh don't worry, I'm not going to get in the way of your personal time, but I thought when Liam is busy captaining the ship we could spend some time together. It's been a long time since you visited here, and I want to get to know you again."

That didn't seem too bad, but still—

"I suppose we can do that."

What else could she say? Gemma couldn't be rude when they helped her out so much.

"I haven't seen Lily in three years. I want to see her and my new grandson." Lady Torrington placed a hand across her chest, a soft smile filler her face. "It's hard to believe my daughter is a mother now."

"You can also see that that package for Lily is safely in her care too," Viscount Torrington demanded.

"Of course. I didn't expect you to deliver it personally." Lady Torrington's gaze flew between Gemma and the viscount. "Oh, I see Thor implied that you would. He didn't want to spoil the news for me. I wanted to tell you myself."

Gemma gulped down a lump in her throat and nodded. It would be an interesting journey, one now she wished she could avoid. She couldn't believe they high jacked her wedding trip.

"Well, I look forward to the trip. I know Lily will be happy to see you. The only thing she would like more is if her father came too… You aren't coming too, are you?"

Viscount Torrington laughed when she looked over at him. He had been sitting quietly at his desk listening to their exchange. He had a very amused look on his face as he studied her. Gemma couldn't help but think they were planning something else. She didn't like the look on his face. He had a devious gleam in his eye that made them twinkle more than usual.

"No, I can't leave right now. Someone has to stay back and take care of the business with Liam taking off. I want at least one family member in England to see to any unforeseen issues. You can relax you won't have to entertain both of us for the journey to South Carolina."

"Oh good."

Torrington's laughter echoed through the room.

"Oh God, did I say that out loud?" Gemma asked.

"I'm afraid you did. Don't worry, we understand how you feel. Now you need to get going. We will see you tonight at your dinner party."

Gemma got up to leave. At the door, she stopped and glanced back at Liam's parents. They watched her, both wearing and identical mask of amusement as they waved goodbye to her. She started to question her idea to travel to see Lily. No, she wouldn't regret that. It would be good for her and Liam even if his mother tagged along for the trip. Plus there would be times when he'd be busy with captaining the ship and it would be nice to have someone to talk to. Gemma smiled as she exited the house and stepped into her awaiting carriage. Yes, everything was going well. Maybe not according to plan but definitely in the right direction.

Tonight's dinner party would be a new beginning for her and Liam. After she talked to him privately, they could entertain their guests and plan for their voyage. Nothing would prevent her from having it all. No one would ever come between her and Liam. She refused to allow anything to stand in the way of her and Liam's bliss. The rest of the trip home, Gemma went over everything she had to complete before the evening's activities. The first thing on her agenda was to locate her husband and finally tell him the truth. All her fears, doubts, and, above all, the love that filled her heart...

CHAPTER 19

Liam woke up in a dark room. Rolling over to his side he could feel the hard exterior next to him and pulled himself up to a sitting position. Leaning his head back against the wall behind him he blinked several time in an attempt to get his eyes to adjust to the darkness. After several minutes, he could make out shadows of objects placed within the room. A desk and chair were located on the far side of the room. Directly underneath him, the surface descended down into softness as he pressed into it. Roaming his hands in front of him he realized he laid on top of a bed.

The room appeared to sway from side to side in a gentle motion. From the little information, he had available he deduced he'd been placed on a ship. What he didn't understand was why. He needed to explore his environment for more clues. The more he knew, the better his chances of extricating himself from these circumstances were. He moved around the bed and stopped when he realized the lump in front of him moved as he placed his hands on top of it. Skimming across the bed he could feel the moderate rise and fall of the person's chest as they breathed.

Who did they throw in here with him?

With as much care as he could muster he checked the person to make sure they were all right and to try to ascertain their identity. He skimmed the surface, and roamed over a person's body, it didn't take him long to realize he had been getting familiar with a woman's body. As a small moan filled the room, he backed away from her to gain some distance. He didn't feel comfortable touching another woman's body other than his wife's.

"Where am I?"

"Gemma?" Liam said, realizing exactly who'd been thrown in the room with him.

"Liam?" Bewilderment in her voice. "Where are we?"

"On a ship I think. I don't know why though."

Who could have put both him and Gemma on board a ship—in a room together? More importantly why? None of this was making any sense to him.

"That can't be a good thing. Who would put us both on a ship?"

"I don't know" Liam shook his head. "I can tell you my first thought was Alfie had escaped, but I don't think that is the issue now. He wouldn't leave you with me."

"No, in his insanity he believes I belong to him. That still begs the question that someone kidnapped us and threw us here together."

"How did you end up here?" Liam asked.

"I don't know. I went to visit your parents and the last thing I remember was getting in the carriage to come home."

As that information processed in his mind, Liam started to wonder what or who might be the culprits of their predicament.

"That's odd. I had been on my way to visit my father when I got jumped from behind."

"Do you suppose they had anything to do with this?"

Liam pulled her into his arms and held her tight, breathing in her scent. At least, no matter what, they were in this together. He placed a light kiss on her forehead and pulled away from her. Having her in his arms was wonderful —but they had other pressing concerns.

"I don't know, but I think we need to get some light in this room and explore a bit."

Liam got out of the bed and began the slow process of discovering every aspect of the room. As he reached the desk, he ran his fingers across the surface until they landed on several items. One of those items was a box of matches, and the other was an oil lamp. With care, he opened the box of matches and struck one to light the lantern. He used the glow of the fire light to guide him in lighting it. Once the lantern was lit, he adjusted it, so a soft flush of light filled the room.

With the room illuminated by the light of the lantern, Liam searched the room for clues. His eyes landed on a parchment folded in half and resting in the middle of the desk. Grabbing it, he opened the note up and read it hoping an explanation would be enclosed. After he had finished examining it, he looked over at Gemma, puzzled about its contents.

"What is it?" She stood up and walked over to him.

"It's addressed to you. Here read it."

Liam handed her the note and watched as she read the words written on the page. He already played them back in his mind and wondered what it all meant.

DEAREST GEMMA,

By now you will have awoken and found yourself on board a ship. Please forgive us for our deception. I know this is not how you planned on making this voyage. It's not our intention to upset you or Liam. After a conversation I had with him a few days ago I realized you two needed help in solving your issues. You were taking a step in the right direction by arranging a surprise for him. Thor and I didn't believe it was enough and began to plan something on our own. Kidnapping you and forcing your hand seemed like a good idea. It worked for us after all. If Thor had never kidnapped me, I wouldn't have fallen madly in love with him. Our methods are a tad—underhanded, but our hearts are in the right place. We just want you both to be happy.

I know you will be devastated to realize I am not going to be joining you on this journey. We will just have to make up for that when you return home. I was sincere in wishing to get to know you better. Take care of my son, give Lily a hug for me, and give Baby Will a kiss. I trust you will still deliver our package to Lily when you arrive. It's why Thor explained how important it was to you in detail. Some things can't be explained in a letter, and some things are better done in writing. We hope in time you will look back on this with fondness and realize we did you a good turn.

You will be locked in the cabin until morning. The necessary items you will need are already in the room with you, including some food. The ship's captain will let you out (if you choose to leave the room) once the sun rises the next day. Use your time wisely.

Tell Liam how much you love him and let the rest take its natural course.

Love Always,

PIA

P.S. DON'T WORRY ABOUT THE DINNER PARTY YOU PLANNED. WE took steps to dismantle it already. Janie and Pemberly were extremely helpful in assisting us with our subterfuge. When you return, we can plan a new one.

"YOUR PARENTS ARE RESPONSIBLE!"

"Yes, that is clear. What I don't understand is this surprise she speaks of."

Gemma nibbled on her bottom lip as she twisted her fingers together.

"I did plan something. It has some similarities to where we are, but no, this is not how I wanted things to go."

"So tell me what you actually planned."

She stopped in front of him and rubbed her hands up his chest. Winding her arms around his neck she leaned back staring into his eyes. Her fingers twirled through the ends of his hair.

"I wanted us to take the wedding trip you promised. I asked your father to arrange it. Of course, I didn't mean for us actually to leave for a few days."

"I like the idea of taking a trip with you" Liam smiled.

"Me too. Even though your parents went about this in a mad fashion, I'm glad they did."

"You are? Please elaborate."

"When I left Marsden House I was coming home to you. I

have been putting something off because of my own fears and doubts. While I was there, I came to a decision to let it go and just be honest with myself and tell you what's on my mind."

"You doubt me? I know I gave you a reason to. I hoped that I put that to rest."

"It's hard to let go of feelings you have been carrying around for a long time. You dismissed my feelings as nonessential. It left me devastated, and it took me a while to crawl out of that despair. The idea of opening myself up to the possibility of revisiting those feelings did not appeal to me. It's the reason I have fought you every step of the way. My instincts screamed to put distance between us."

"I'm not running away now," Liam whispered. "I've been chasing you for days."

"I know. I'm done trying to escape the inevitable."

"Is that so?" Liam raised an eyebrow. "What do you want to do now?"

"It's time to open up and say the things I've been burying deep inside me. I've been the queen of denial for several days. No matter how scared and uncertain I've been, there is one blaring insurmountable truth."

Gemma placed her hands on both sides of Liam's face. She rose on her tiptoes and placed a soft kiss on his lips and took a step back.

"I love you. I never stopped. It's time to quit fighting something I can't control. Trusting you and believing you love me is the only option I have. You have always owned my heart."

Liam smiled when she finished saying the words he'd been longing to hear. This is what his mother's letter alluded to. She knew that Gemma still loved him and was giving her a way to express it—albeit an extreme measure, but he found it endearing his parents' cared about the outcome of his marriage.

"I love you. I don't know how many times I need to say it for you to believe me, but I will keep saying it until it sinks in, and you do."

"I do believe you. Only someone that loves me would put up with the emotional upheavals I've put you through."

"I'm happier than words can express. Since we've

discussed everything, how do you suggest we use the rest of our time locked inside this room?" Liam wiggled his eyebrows.

"I don't know," Gemma took a step back and tapped her chin. "They said we had everything we need here. Do you suppose they left us some cards? Lily taught me how to play whist a few years ago..."

She couldn't be serious? Whist? Liam could think of a million things he'd rather do than play cards. Honestly, there was only one thing he wanted to do at that moment. It involved them getting naked and loving each other all night long. He couldn't wait to strip her of her clothes and love her as he craved to. If she wanted to play cards, perhaps they could make it more interesting... a game of whist where the loser had to forfeit pieces of clothing to the winner. Now that was a game he'd willingly play. Somehow, he doubted Gemma had that in mind when she suggested whist. He stared at her with disbelieving eyes until she finally began to laugh so hard she had to hold her stomach by wrapping her arms tight around the middle.

"You should see the look on your face. I don't think I've ever seen you look more surprised. This even tops when I told you I loved you for the first time."

"I don't find it so funny. You know what I want to do."

"Yes, I do. Which is why I suggested cards. Which maybe we can do later because I want to do exactly what you have on your mind."

"Oh, you can read my mind now?"

"No. I just know we are for once exactly in the same spot wanting the same things, and I want to take advantage of it."

Liam agreed with her. He reached for her and pulled her back into his arms. Gemma tilted her face up towards his and he pressed his lips to hers. Once her mouth opened, he took advantage and tangled her tongue with his. Their passion ignited, and he pulled her as close as possible as their tongues dueled for control. Gemma's fingers trailed across his neck and up to his hair, and she seized strands of it in a tight grip. Liam pulled back and could see a slight blush begin to creep up her cheeks. Leaning down, he traced the red stains with butterfly kisses down to her neck stopping only when he could hear her moan of pleasure. He took a step back so he could look at her flushed with passion.

"I love you, but I absolutely adore looking at you in moments like this. I look forward to loving you for the rest of my life, and I plan on taking my time and savoring each moment."

"That has to be the sweetest thing you have ever said to me."

"I mean every word." Liam's gaze held Gemma's. "My family has a tradition. Well, it started with my parents."

"Kidnapping?"

Liam laughed and pulled her back into his arms, "No. Well yes, there is that, but it's a different tradition I'm speaking of. When we were children, my parents used to tell us a fairy tale. At the time, we didn't know they were telling us their story. I'd like to do something similar with our children."

"That's a lovely tradition. At what point would we start our story? Once upon a time a gentleman saved a lady from a nefarious villain?"

"No, our story goes back even farther than that." Liam shook his head. "I'd start with once upon a time a gentleman foolishly ran away from the only lady he would ever love..."

Gemma's face softened into a delighted smile. Liam never wanted to cause her heartbreak again. From this moment on he would do his best to ensure her happiness. Leaning down, he kissed her again to finish what they started mere moments ago, loving his precious sanguine gem…

**Read further for an excerpt from A Hidden Ruby: A Marsden Romance Book 4: **

A HIDDEN RUBY

DAWN BROWER

Dawn Brower

A Hidden Ruby

PROLOGUE

"I no longer wish to live... Without my love, I have nothing."

Rubina Leone St. John, the Duchess of Huntly meant those words. Without Noah... Her head fell forward hitting the palm of her hands. Tears streamed down her face. How could she go on without the only man she'd ever loved? If Paolo Fonte, Duca d'Sordillo, told the truth, her husband was dead.

"Don't be dramatic, Rubina." He held his hand over his heart. "On my honor, I will always take care of you."

She lifted her head and stared at him through hooded eyes. What a fool. Did he honestly believe she'd willingly stay with him? Her heart would always belong to Noah. No other man would fill the empty void his loss left behind. Slowly, she stood and faced him. With all the strength she had left, she spit in his face.

"You'll never take the place of my Noah." She returned to her seat. Rubina had better things to do with her time than deal with Paolo. He proclaimed to love her, but he'd kept her a prisoner for months in a tiny room. Only coming to visit her so he could stare at her while declaring his love. You don't imprison someone you supposedly love.

Paolo pulled out a handkerchief and wiped his face. "You'll regret that."

"No, I only wish I'd have done it sooner."

He stormed over to her side and lifted her chin, forcing her to look at him.

"*La mia bellezza…*" He stroked his fingers through her hair. "Such beautiful golden-blonde hair—so silky to touch."

Chills ran down her spine and her stomach rolled with queasiness as he touched her. Rubina was not his beauty… She never would be his in any way.

"I don't belong to you. I never have. When will you accept that?" She stared up at him in defiance.

"Never?" He raised an eyebrow. "It is such a very long time, my love. You will learn to love me."

Rubina choked back tears. If Noah was truly dead—it didn't matter. Paolo could do his worst. No matter how hard she tried, her feelings would remain the same. Her heart remained untouched by his false charms…

"*Ti odio.*" She let every ounce of hatred pour out of her. Rubina didn't want there to be any doubt how much she loathed Paolo.

"No, you don't." His sinister laugh filled the tiny room. "My dear, you don't really know what hate is—but you will."

"How did Noah die?"

Rubina needed details to understand how he could really be gone. Her husband was a strong virile man, so full of life. She couldn't truly believe he was—she gulped down a lump in her throat—dead.

"If you must know, someone helped him along to his untimely demise."

"No…" Rubina gasped. "Please—tell me you didn't murder him."

"I'll tell you no such thing. I'm not about to start lying to you my dear." He shoved his hands into his pockets and rocked back on his heels. "It's best you get acclimated to our long life together."

Rubina wanted to die. That would remain true as long as Noah was gone. She had something to take care of before she joined him again. Paolo Fonte's life must end. He would pay for his sins—for hurting Noah. She would live long enough to see it happen. Once she sent him to hell, she'd allow herself to breathe her last breath. She could once again be with her husband. They could spend eternity in each other's arms.

"*Sei un bastardo malvagio*," she exclaimed. Duca d'Sordillo was an evil bastard. "One day your cruelty will leave this world. On that day I will rejoice."

"Say what you want. Your words mean nothing, but you will come around." He grinned. "Until then, please enjoy the accommodations.

He turned to leave. The door shut with a loud thud. Paolo turned the key, locking her once again in her tiny hovel. Such love he showed her. Rubina stared at the door with disgust. It didn't matter. She had a reason to continue living. Once she found a way to end Paolo's life her mission would be complete. He must pay for the atrocity he caused.

❧

RUBINA GREW WEAK. SHE BARELY SUSTAINED ENOUGH STRENGTH to lift up her head. Paolo limited her food to bread and water—barely enough to survive. He was trying to get her to cave—give in to his demands. The evil bastard wanted her to willingly join him in his bed. It would never happen. To betray Noah in such a manner... No, she'd rather die. If she didn't gain strength soon, she'd get her wish.

"Duchessa..."

Her body rocked back and forth, shaking from an unseen force, but she didn't want to open her eyes.

"Please wake up, Duchessa."

Rubina's eyelids fluttered open to gaze into the dark brown eyes of a man she'd never seen before.

"Who are you?" She stared at him, puzzled. Maybe he was a new guard Paolo sent to watch over her.

"I'm here to save you."

Rubina shook and tears streamed down her face. She didn't want to believe it was true. She didn't know how long she'd been a captive in Paolo's home. All she wanted to do was go home—see her father and brother again. They were all she had left in the world. If only Noah...

Rubina cried harder.

"Duchessa, we must hurry."

She tried to swallow a lump in her throat, but it was too

dry. She let her gaze meet his again and voiced her fear. "Are you real?"

He nodded. "I assure you, I am. Can you walk?"

"I'm so weak…"

"We will go slowly. I will carry you if I must."

He helped Rubina to her feet and led her to the open door. She was about to leave her prison. How long had she been locked away from the world?

"Why are you helping me?"

"I work for your brother, Conte Leone." They made their way down the long hallway. He stopped at the top of the stone stairway. "My name is Arturo."

"Damian sent you?"

Her family still believed she lived? Why had it taken them so long to find her? Paolo insisted the world believed her dead—as dead as her husband. No more Duke and Duchess of Huntly—no more beautiful love story.

"I'm afraid not." He lifted her up into his arms. "Everyone believes you are dead. I'm here on a different mission. It's a miracle I learned of your existence."

"Grazie." Rubina hugged him. Her whole body shook with the weight of her emotions. "I feared I'd die locked in that room."

"No need for thanks. I'd do it for anyone." His mouth formed a firm straight line. "What the Duca d'Sordillo was doing to you was wrong."

Rubina didn't want to think about Paolo. She just wanted to get as far away from him as possible. Maybe she'd return to England… She loved her home. Italy still held a special place in her heart, but it also filled her with terror. If she had never argued with Noah, Paolo wouldn't have been able to hold her captive. Her only intent had been to return to Naples and visit her father. As soon as she stepped onto the ship heading toward Italy, Paolo's men had seized her. They took her to his ship and locked her inside. Somehow, he arranged to have the ship she'd been on to sink into the ocean's blue depths—sealing the belief of her death.

"If you're not here to rescue me, then what are you doing in Duca di'Sordillo's home?"

"He is believed to have ties to the Mafioso."

Arturo set her down and scanned the room. He pulled her hand into his and led her outside. They stopped in front of a carriage, and he helped her inside. Once Rubina was safely seated, he flicked the reigns to get the horses moving.

"Somehow it doesn't surprise me. He's an evil man—and evidently a mastermind in the criminal underworld."

Arturo nodded. "That's what we believed. We had no idea the extent of his criminal activities. Conte Leone sent me to investigate. If he'd known you were here, he would have come himself and ripped Duca d'Sordillo apart."

Rubina didn't doubt it for a minute. Damian was ruthless when he needed to be. He had a high power seat in the government. He hated the Mafioso and sought to eradicate them from Italy. It was turning out to be a daunting task. The Mafioso themselves were shrouded in secrecy.

"Where are we going?"

"Do you know where you are, Duchessa?"

"Please, call me Rubina," she offered. "I owe you my life. To answer your question—I have no idea where I am or how long I've been here."

Arturo frowned. "This is not good, Your Grace." He shook his head. "You are in Sicily near Palermo. It's been three years since the Conte and your father believed you drowned aboard that ship."

Rubina gasped. "No, so long..."

"Your family—they will be so relieved to find you still live. Thankfully, your brother awaits me in a nearby port. We can escape with him and travel to Naples."

Damian was near? The fates had finally decided to step in and help her. If only they'd done so sooner—she might have been able to save Noah. Pinpricks of pain shot through her heart as a vision of her beloved floated before her. She missed him so much.

Arturo urged the horses to go faster. The wind blew through Rubina's hair. Soon she'd be with her brother again, and she could plot Duca d'Sordillo's death. He would pay for his sins. First she'd need to regain her strength. She would not be able to defeat him being so weak.

"We'll be to your brother's ship soon, Your Grace."

"Thank you. I'm so tired... Maybe I should sleep a little

bit." Her head fell forward, eyes drifting closed. They flew open as she gazed over at him. "I thought I told you to call me Rubina."

"Yes, Your Grace, but I cannot. Please, stay awake. We will be there soon."

Rubina fought her body's need for sleep. Once they got to the ship and reunited with her brother she could give in. Arturo assured her it was near. Deep breath in, exhale, if she kept reminding herself, it all would still be true. If this was a dream, Rubina never wanted to wake up. Only one thing would make it perfect: Noah—alive and well.

The carriage came to a halt near a small pier. The night sky was dark as pitch with tiny white stars dotting the black canvas.

"Duchessa, we are here." He nudged her forward. "Come, I'll help you board the ship."

"I don't think I can move, Arturo." Her eyes rolled backward, and her eyelids fluttered shut. "I don't have much strength left."

"I will carry you." Arturo lifted her into his brawny arms.

The warmth engulfing her spread throughout her whole body. She'd been cold for so long. He nestled her, letting her head rest on his broad shoulder. It was so nice to be taken care of.

"I don't know if I can ever thank you enough," she muttered.

"Quit thanking me, Your Grace."

Rubina never would. He saved her from a living hell.

"What do you have there, Arturo?"

Damian! His voice was music to Rubina's ears. Arturo hadn't lied. He'd brought her to her brother. Rubina wanted to cry again, but she held it inside.

"I found your sister, Conte."

"What?" Disbelief etched through Damian's voice. "You lie, my sister drowned aboard a ship several years ago."

"No, Conte." Arturo shook his head, jostling Rubina's head forward. "She lives. Duca d'Sordillo has kept her locked in a room for years."

Rubina lifted her head and met eyes that matched her

own. In the moonlight, his silver-gray irises glowed in front of her. Damian gasped. *"Dio mio*, it's true..."

"Hello, brother."

Damian rushed forward and pulled Rubina out of Arturo's arms. His hug so tight breathing became difficult. "I can't believe you're here. If I'd known..."

"I know, please, I can't breathe."

Damian let her go, never once taking his gaze off of her. She understood because it all seemed like a dream to her too.

"Rue, oh God—Noah. How are we going to tell him?" Damian rubbed his hands over his face. "He is about to get the shock of his life. We must get to him fast."

"What?" Rubina gasped. "Noah lives? Paolo told me he murdered him."

"I assure you, your husband is alive and well." Damian nodded. He paced back and forth in front of her. His agitation making her nervous. "There's something you should know... He's set to remarry."

"No..."

Noah was hers. No other woman would lay claim to him. She had to get to London and reclaim her husband. How dare he move on when she suffered so much? She'd believed he was dead, and still she didn't give in to Paolo. When she got there, Noah would rue the day he'd ever thought to replace her.

CHAPTER 1

Noah St. John, the Duke of Huntly took a deep breath and set aside the financial documents he'd been perusing. He rubbed his hands over his face to wipe the exhaustion away. It was already a difficult day, and the sun barely rose in the sky. He'd had trouble sleeping the night before and left his bed while it was still dark outside. Since sleep evaded him, he might as well get some work done.

"You look like hell."

Noah glanced up at his best friend, Liam Marsden, as he strolled into his study.

"I feel like it."

Liam tilted his head to the side. "You're not having second thoughts are you?"

"Of course not. It's the right decision."

It was. Even if it made his insides tighten with dread.

"You don't have to remarry," Liam said softly. "No one knows more than I how much you loved Rubina."

Noah shook his head. "No, it's time. If I want to have children, I need a wife."

He just hoped Pearla knew what she was getting into by marrying him. She said she did, but he doubted she truly understood. Noah had tried being a husband once, and look how it had turned out. Not married a year and his wife fled him in anger, and to her death. If only he'd handled the situation differently...Rubina might still be alive.

"You don't want more?"

"I can't handle it if I lost..." Noah shook his head. "Love has only brought me heartbreak. The ability to love another woman is lost to me."

Pain seared through what was left of his heart. Beautiful and so full of life, Rubina had been his everything. It took him months to begin functioning again. If he let himself love another woman only to lose her—he'd never survive it.

Liam nodded. "I understand. Gemma is my one and only love. I don't know if I could handle losing her."

"You're lucky to have her."

"Is it really fair to Pearla to marry her knowing you will never love her?"

Noah considered Liam's question. Was it fair? No, it wasn't. Pearla understood how he felt about marriage. He hadn't lied to her about anything. She had her own reasons for agreeing to this marriage. Pearla had an inheritance, but lacked the freedom of a matron. She agreed to be his wife and give him a child. Her only requirement was to gain her own freedom. Pearla had dreams of traveling the world, and Noah didn't have a problem letting her. If she wasn't around he was less likely to develop any tender feelings for her.

"Pearla knows what she's getting from me." Bitterness filled his voice as he remembered his first wedding day. This one was sadly lacking and plain miserable. Noah didn't really want to marry anyone, but he had a duty to his title. If he didn't have an heir, the dukedom would revert back to the crown.

"Noah, you look like you are about to walk toward the hangman's noose. This is not a good way to approach your wedding day." Liam frowned. "I don't like seeing you this way."

Noah stood and strolled over to the small bar behind his desk. He grabbed two goblets, filled them with two fingers of brandy, and then placed one in front of Liam. "I assume you would like a drink too."

Liam raised an eyebrow. "It's kind of early isn't it?"

"It's never too bloody early." Noah downed the contents

of his glass and slammed it down on his desk. "Sometimes a man just needs a damned drink."

Noah's heart constricted in his chest—it all seemed so wrong. He'd been justifying his decision for weeks. The day had come, and soon he would be married...again. His whole body repelled the very idea, yet he intended to go through with it.

He glanced up at his best friend. Concern etched his features. Noah had no idea how to explain to him what was going through his mind. Liam had the woman he loved. They were blissfully, adoringly besotted with each other. Gemma was the perfect complement to Liam's broody nature. He couldn't be happier for him, but his own misery seared his soul.

"I think you're making a mistake, but if this is what you want, I will stand by you." Liam's lips formed a thin flat line. "But Pearla is Gemma's friend. If she's unhappy..." Liam shook his head. "I'm not telling you what to do. I want you to be happy, and this doesn't seem the way to get there."

"Right. I don't think I know how to..." Noah patted his chest attempting to rub the ache in his heart. "Without Ruby I'm hollow inside. This is the best I can hope for."

"I don't have words. This pain you feel—I don't have anything to draw on."

Noah ran his fingers across the rim of his glass. Maybe he should have another drink. It might numb him enough to get through the ceremony. Liam was right. Pearla deserved someone far better than him. Rubina's ghost haunted him, and she always would. Bloody hell, maybe he would have that second drink after all. He grabbed the brandy decanter and filled his glass to the top.

He took a swig and tipped the glass toward Liam. "I pray you never know the pain of losing your one true love."

"Is this your convoluted way of toasting to the long life of my marriage?"

Noah nodded. "Don't waste it for a second."

Liam sighed. "Didn't plan on it." He studied Noah for several seconds. "I'm only going to say this one more time, and then I'm going to drop it."

"What's that?"

"There is still time to call off the wedding. I can even do it for you. Just say the word."

"The wedding will happen." Noah looked him in the eyes, letting Liam know, without words, his wishes. "This is what I want."

What a joke. No, this wedding wasn't what Noah wanted. If he had one wish, it would be for Rubina to never have died. For her to walk through the door at any moment with her laughter floating around him. He hadn't felt true happiness since he lost her. In lieu of getting his one true wish, he'd settle for a child of his own. Fate owed him at least that much.

Liam picked up his glass and raised it high. "Then how about a real toast. To my good friend Noah. May he find it in his heart to forgive himself and learn to love again. For, without it, happiness will always be beyond his reach, and more than anything he deserves to find it."

Noah stared at him. "That's the worst toast I've ever heard."

"Well, it is all you're getting. Now drink up." Liam downed his brandy and set his glass down. "Now, let's make our way to the carriage. We have a wedding to rush to."

Noah grumbled. "Don't we have more time?"

"I'm afraid not, my friend. It's time to head to the church. The ladies are awaiting our arrival."

Liam would stand beside him as Noah married Pearla. His wife, Gemma, was standing with his intended. They had been planning the wedding for weeks. The banns having been read for the past three weeks in Westminster Abbey, the church where he was going to marry Pearla Montgomery.

Oh, hell. Noah downed the contents of his glass. He did need the liquid courage to go through with it. It wasn't Pearla. No, it was him. Pearla was a lovely woman with gorgeous blonde hair and cerulean blue eyes. In some ways similar to Rubina, but his deceased wife's hair was a rich golden-blonde while her gray eyes turned silver with desire. Noah shook the image from his head. It didn't matter. Pearla was not Rubina. His dear wife, his one true love, was lost to him forever.

It was time to take a new wife.

"Lead the way." Noah stood up. "I'm right behind you."

Liam stopped and looked him up and down. He shook his head. "I'll be with you every step of the way. Just say the word, and I'll take care of anything you need, no matter what it is."

"I can't change the man I've become, Liam. I'm not sure if I want to." Noah frowned. "Rubina's death made me harder than I ever thought possible. I've lost too much, and I can't afford to lose any more. If anyone else even tries to take what's mine, I won't be able to stop myself from annihilating them."

"Let's pray it doesn't ever come to that."

Noah hoped not because, if it did, he'd lose what was left of his soul.

"How much time do we have to get to the church?"

"We should have been there twenty minutes ago."

"What?" Noah blinked as shock filled him. "Why didn't you say something sooner? I didn't realize what time it was."

Liam shrugged. "I had hoped you'd changed your mind. But, alas, it wasn't to be, so now we need to make haste."

Noah took two quick strides and exited his study. He stopped in the foyer and hollered for Simmons. "I need the carriage brought around. I'm late for my wedding."

"It's already waiting for you, Your Grace."

"Thank you, Simmons. I don't know what I'd do without you."

Simmons nodded and headed for the door, opening it wide for Noah. Liam followed close behind him, and they entered the ducal carriage.

"How did you get here anyway?" Noah asked. "I didn't see your carriage or horse."

"I had our carriage drop me off. Gemma took it to the church to wait for our arrival."

That couldn't be good. Gemma must know on some level how much Noah didn't want to marry her friend. He respected Liam's wife. Having her displeased with him—it didn't sit well. He'd try to make her understand…later.

It didn't take long, or at least it didn't seem like it, before the carriage halted in front of the church. Noah took a deep breath and hopped out of the carriage. He stopped in front of the steps and stared up at the tall cathedral.

"I said I wouldn't ask again."

Noah's sliced his head left and pinned Liam with a glare. "Then don't."

Liam threw his hands up in the air. "Have it your way. I'll stand by your decision."

Noah nodded and opened the doors wide. He walked with purposeful strides to the altar where the clergyman was awaiting their arrival.

"Let's start the ceremony. I have a lot to do today."

All he wanted to do was get it over with. He ignored the guests filling the pews. They expected more from him, but he couldn't give it to them. This wasn't a love match, and he wasn't about to pretend it was on any level. The vicar nodded his agreement. Music filled the church halls as Noah stared down the aisle.

Gemma floated forward first with light steps in tune to the music. Liam's gaze never left his wife's face. Noah looked back and forth between the two. An ache filled his heart. He'd had that once. Gemma kissed Liam and then hugged Noah. She took her spot on the other side of him. They all turned to watch Pearla march down the aisle on her father's arm.

She was so lovely and perfect. Not one golden hair was out of place. The smile on her face—she looked so happy. Noah didn't understand why. What was there to be so bloody happy about? They reached the end of the aisle. Her father kissed her cheek and sat down in the front pew next to his wife.

Noah grabbed Pearla's hand and led her to the front of the altar. He nodded at the vicar to begin. The vows went by in a blur; if asked, he wouldn't be able to recall saying them.

"If anyone has just cause for these two not to be joined in holy matrimony please speak now or forever hold your peace."

The Vicar's words blended into the background. Noah wanted this done.

"I have some objections."

A soft accented voice reverberated through Noah's ears. His gaze shot toward the location it came from. Everyone turned to see who interrupted the ceremony. Loud murmurs filled the church and echoed back at him, but words failed him. Noah's mouth fell open as shock overtook him. He had to be seeing things. He rubbed his eyes and blinked the blurriness away. His heart beat hard against his chest. How much brandy had he poured down his throat before coming to the wedding? He stared for several seconds, but the apparition in maroon silk kept moving toward him. Noah couldn't believe what his eyes were telling him.

Surely the blonde vision in front of him wasn't...

"Rubina?" he croaked out.

CHAPTER 2

"Hello, Noah dear." Rubina moved closer to him at the altar. She batted her eyelashes at him coquettishly. "Have you missed me?"

Her gaze fell on his new bride. So young, innocent, and perfect in her wedding gown, her gold curls fell down to her shoulders and her blue eyes kept going back and forth between Rubina and Noah. Poor thing chose wrong in deigning to marry her husband. She'd learn Noah belonged only to her.

Wait, Noah couldn't belong to her. His life depended on him hating her. Rubina had to stay focused and not make claims she couldn't make.

"I'm not interrupting anything important am I?" Rubina waved her hand dismissively. "Never mind I see. You're about to replace me. How rude of me to object."

"You're really here." Noah just stared at her.

Rubina could tell she'd shocked him. She shouldn't be upset he moved on. If she were truly dead—no, if she were honest, she didn't want him with anyone else. He said he'd love her forever, and he'd moved on far too quickly for her tastes. Noah would pay for that. She couldn't hurt him more than necessary. She had to protect him. His safety came first. It didn't matter in the grand scheme of things as long as she knew he was whole, healthy, and happy. Rubina would not be selfish at the cost of Noah's life. Paolo would come looking for her, and Noah would be the first place he looked.

"Of course I'm here." Rubina moved in close to him and ran her hand across his broad chest. "Where else would I be but at my husband's wedding. It looks like you had a good turn out."

Rubina smiled brightly and waved to all the guests. Their shocked gasps filled the room. She never did much care for English society. They were all stuck-up snobs.

"I don't understand." Noah shook his head.

Poor man. Rubina should take pity on him, but she wouldn't. Couldn't.

She gazed up at him. His chocolate brown eyes were filled with a mixture of confusion and hope. Rubina cupped his cheek with her hand. "It's simple enough, dear."

She dropped her hand and took a few steps back. Being close enough to touch him was almost too much for her to bear. It had been hellish believing him dead. One thing Rubina understood was the pain of losing the person you loved more than yourself. Noah must have gone through that too. The difference was Rubina couldn't move on and Noah had.

"Nothing is simple about this." Noah clenched his jaw. "I don't understand how you could possibly be here, and I have so many questions."

Rubina smiled. "Oh, but it is, you see. Rumors of my death..." She paused for dramatic effect. "How do I put this... have been a bit exaggerated."

"Noah?" his pretty little bride looked at him, questions in her eyes.

"Pearla, I'm sorry. I don't..." His gaze flew back to Rubina's. "I can't explain this. Please, forgive me."

"It's all right. I understand." She smiled sweetly at him.

Rubina wanted to smack the woman. Bitterness filled her as she watched their exchange. How dare he—Rubina wanted to scream at him with every ounce of frustration building up inside of her. How could he have fallen in love with another woman and forget her so easily.

"Maybe we can move this to someplace a bit more

private." A red haired woman suggested. "I'm sure you don't want the ton to know all your personal business."

"I don't mind," Rubina interjected. "What's a little back-from-the-dead experience worth if you can't share it with the world?"

The red-headed tart could bite her damn tongue off for all Rubina cared.

"Rubina," Liam coaxed. "This is a shock. Gemma is right. We should go someplace quieter—at least somewhere you and Noah can figure out what happened. I'm sure you both have many questions."

Rubina tilted her head. "Hello, Liam. I see you're still sticking by your best friend. When I was...away, I thought about you. Considered maybe you shared my grief. Now I see I was the only one who truly grieved."

"It's not like that, Ruby," Liam said.

"Isn't it though?" She raised an eyebrow. "You moved on. Look at each one of you. So happy and content with your picture perfect lives. Who cares what happened to poor Rubina. Life goes on." Rubina couldn't help the anger interwoven through her words. She had a right to it after all—having earned it the hard way.

"Pearla, perhaps we should go," the redheaded woman said to Noah's bride. "I think it's safe to say the wedding is not going on as planned."

A tear fell down Pearla's cheek. Rubina would feel sorry for her, but she couldn't. She knew what it was like to have Noah's love. Jealousy turned her green with envy. Noah was only supposed to love her. For that alone, Rubina hated Pearla.

"You're right, Gemma." She nodded. "Can you take me home?"

Gemma nodded. "Of course." She looked over at Liam. "Are you going to stay, or...?"

Liam looked from Gemma to Noah, and then back to Rubina. He nodded. "I think I might be needed here. See Pearla home. I will call on you later when all of this"—he motioned between Rubina and Noah—"is settled."

"You should go, Liam," Rubina urged. "I think Noah and I can settle this between us without you overseeing anything."

"I'm staying," he said. His jaw tightened in determination.

"Suit yourself." Rubina shrugged.

She was mildly amused by the domesticity Liam showed Gemma. There was an intimacy there. He loved her, and perhaps they were already married. She never thought she'd see the day when Liam Marsden succumbed to love. He'd vowed to never marry. Well, wonders would never cease—even he could fall hopelessly for a woman.

"Ruby?" Noah approached her. "We should go home too. We can talk there."

"What, you don't want to air out our difficulties for the whole world?"

She didn't wish to make things easy for him. Nothing had been easy for her since Paolo kidnapped her three years ago. Rubina wanted him to feel every ounce of pain she experienced in his hands. He didn't know grief, but soon he would.

"Please," he begged.

It was a start. She wanted him on his knees prostrating himself before her. Even then she wasn't sure it would be enough. Her heart broke into a million shards when she found out he was planning on getting married again. Rubina wasn't sure if she'd ever be able to piece them together again. Her love for him was forever altered by his choice.

She needed some distance. Time to cry her heart out without witnesses—after she got what she came for she would find someplace to lick her wounds. As much as she'd like to, she couldn't make Noah beg for anything, Rubina needed him to hate her.

"No." She shook her head. "I don't think I will go anywhere with you ever again."

He reeled back as if she'd slapped her. "Why?"

"I think it's pretty obvious."

"But it isn't." Noah took a step toward her. He raised a hand as if to touch her but let it drop to his side. "You're here. Alive. It's something I never believed possible."

"And yet you were about to take a bride and move on as if I'd never existed."

His face paled. "It's not like that, Ruby."

She tilted her head and studied him. Uncontrollable

laughter spilled out of her lips. It was time to lay things down for Noah to understand. Rubina did not take this lightly. It was all too important for her to do what she came here for. As much as it pained her, it was time for Noah to look at her with the hatred she needed him to feel.

"It's exactly like that, Noah." She smiled at him. "So I'm going to do us both a favor and let you go."

"What?" he asked, confusion filling his eyes once again. "I don't want that."

Rubina had to be harsh. It was the only way to make him see her way was best.

"I want a divorce."

Noah flinched. "No."

"No?"

He shook his head. "Absolutely not. I won't give you one."

"Not even if I was unfaithful?"

His lips tightened at her words. Rubina had hit her mark dead on. It was the only way. She loved him, but he clearly didn't love only her anymore. As much as she believed Noah belonged to her, Rubina knew when to cut her losses and move on. She loved him enough to let him go.

Noah was only holding on because he believed in forever and he'd made her promises. If he'd believed she was still alive, he'd never have stopped looking for her. She wouldn't have found him about to marry another woman. Her Noah was honorable.

"You didn't—couldn't have."

"I'm sorry, Noah, dear." She patted his chest lightly and gazed up at him through hooded eyes. "I don't love you anymore."

He roared loud with denial. Oh, how fierce he looked, a lock of his dark hair falling over his forehead. Rubina resisted the urge to push it back in place.

"I don't believe you."

"Believe what you will." She shrugged. "But it's time to let go. This is good, no? You can marry your perfect fiancée and live happily as if I never existed."

"Stop. Just stop talking." He paced back and forth in front of the altar.

"Noah…"

"I said to be quiet," he seethed. His anger flashing within his eyes.

Rubina did as he asked and watched him in silence. He stopped suddenly and turned toward her. No longer was his gaze filled with shock. He'd overcome it all and had a new emotion ruling him. Pure rage. His cheeks were flushed a bright red. Noah clenched his fists at his sides as he stalked toward her. If he had less control, Rubina had no doubt he'd strike her.

"Why did you come back?" he asked.

"To set you free."

"No, I was already free."

"Were you?" She raised an eyebrow. "Or did I still haunt you even a little bit?"

He flinched. Her words hit another mark. She knew Noah too well. Of course her death paid a toll on him. But still, he'd found another to love.

"Apparently I didn't do the same to you. You appear rather—healthy." He looked her up and down. "For someone presumed dead."

He had no idea what she went through. It'd been three weeks since her rescue. She'd had time to heal and gain a little weight on their passage from Italy to England.

"I've never felt better," she retorted.

He studied her. "A little too thin, but yes definitely glowing and content."

Noah knew her too. He'd notice that while she gained some weight, it had not been nearly enough. Her struggle to survive in order to make Paolo pay, it took everything inside her to get through it. She still had to make sure Paolo never hurt another soul again—soon he'd feel her wrath.

Another reason to let Noah go.

If Paolo believed she no longer wanted Noah, he'd leave her husband be. She had to protect him at all costs. Just because he moved on didn't mean she had. Rubina would always love Noah.

"I don't know. I think my figure is finally perfect." She ran her hands down her waist. "My gowns have never fit so well."

"You were perfect before." He paused. "You still are."

"Damian should be here soon with the divorce papers I had drawn up." She had to distract him before she threw herself at her husband. She loved Noah so much. It hurt to hurt him. "You'll sign them, yes?"

"I said no," he shouted. "I will never divorce you. If you didn't want me, you should have stayed dead."

It was Rubina's turn to flinch.

"I didn't mean that how it sounded."

"I'm sure you didn't," Rubina said softly.

Then Noah did the one thing she didn't expect from him. He lifted her up and threw her over his shoulder. Then with quick, purposeful strides he carried her out of the church. The guests still sitting in their pews watching the show—like predators stalking their prey. The gossip mills would be rolling with the scene by the end of the day.

"Put me down."

Liam called out, "I'll take care of things here, Noah. Go take care of your wife."

"I plan on it," he replied.

CHAPTER 3

Rubina was alive.

Noah still couldn't wrap his head around it. She squirmed in his arms as he carried her out of the church. So full of life and energy and simply amazing. Having her with him had been his greatest wish, and now, by some miracle, it had been granted.

Let her go?

Not a chance in hell would he ever let her ago again. They might have a lot to work through, but suddenly he had a reason to fight. He'd fight anything and anyone—including Rubina herself—to have her with him again, forever.

"Noah, I said put me down."

"And I believe I already told you no."

He carried her all the way to his carriage. Noah opened the door and set her inside, climbing in after her. The carriage jerked forward as the driver flicked the reins, urging the horses to move. Rubina sat across from him, a mulish expression on her face.

She was so bloody lovely.

"Now, how about you start explaining to me where you've been for the past three years."

Rubina stayed silent. Her eyes shot daggers at him. Fine. She wanted to give him the silent treatment. He could work with that for now. Noah knew his wife. It was next to impossible for her to not say a word for long.

"How about I tell you what I've been doing for the past three years instead."

Nothing. She turned her head to look out the carriage window, attempting to ignore him. God, he loved her. He'd almost forgotten what it was like to have her around. She breathed life into him by just sharing the same space.

"When I heard your ship sank in a freak storm it felt like my heart was ripped out of my chest. I stayed drunk for days, weeks, hell, it might have been months."

Her jaw clenched. Good, at least she was listening.

"If not for Liam, I might have drank myself into an early grave. He took to staying with me for weeks on end. He dumped out every ounce of alcohol remaining on my estate. Then, he waited for me to start living again."

A small tear fell down her cheek. Noah took that as a good sign. If he kept talking, explaining, maybe she'd tell him what happened to her. Why she'd stayed gone for so long.

"You seem to be doing that rather well," she replied.

Noah smiled. He knew she couldn't stay silent.

"Looks can be rather deceiving. You know that."

Her gray eyes grew stormy as she studied him. "I do. A wedding is generally a damn good indicator you've moved on."

He had to find a way to make her understand why he'd decided to marry Pearla.

"Maybe on the outside looking in."

"It matters not." Rubina shook her head. "Once you sign the divorce papers we both can move on."

"I'm not saying this again." He glared at her. "There's not a chance in hell you will ever obtain my signature on those papers. Even if you did, it would take a lot for parliament to agree to grant the divorce. I won't even get into how much it would cost."

"I'm not worried about the money. It will be worth it to be free. Pay whatever is necessary. Take it out of my dowry." Rubina's face was devoid of emotion. "Just make it happen."

Why was she so eager to be free of him?

"Ruby, please, talk to me."

He tried to remain calm. Noah learned that lesson the hard way. When they met, he was reckless and so much in love he couldn't hold in his emotions for anything. They were all on the surface. His anger, love, frustrations—there was no reason to hold them back. Until one argument sent her fleeing away from him and he'd lost her. Now, she sat in front of him wanting to leave him again.

"There is nothing to discuss. Grant me the divorce I seek and we'll never need to see each other again."

"Is it really so bad to be with me?"

It hurt to ask, but he had to know. He still couldn't believe she was alive. Had she hidden from him all these years? Did he frighten her?

"I can't be around you."

The words were like a knife to his heart.

"Why?"

Rubina pursed her lips and stared him in the eyes. "I told you. I no longer love you."

Noah couldn't—wouldn't believe it. How could she have suddenly stopped loving him? Then he remembered, it hadn't been sudden. She'd been gone for three years. Maybe she never loved him at all.

"So you want me to believe you love someone else."

"Yes." She nodded.

Another jab right into the pain mass he called his heart. How much more could he take?

"Did you ever love me?"

"Maybe. I don't know. I was a foolish young girl rushing into marriage. What young person truly knows what is in their heart or what love really is."

Noah knew. He loved Rubina more than life. He still did.

Disgust filled him. He was such a bloody fool to keep holding on to her. She'd been his everything and, to her, he'd been nothing more than a passing fancy. Well, she'd made her bed, and she was bloody well going to lie in it.

"I will grant your divorce on one condition."

She studied him and asked, "I thought you were against it."

He had been. Noah didn't want to believe she'd never loved him. He might be a fool, but even he could see through something if he looked at it long enough. Rubina didn't want him. Fine. He'd let her go, but not before she gave him something in return.

"I've had a few moments to assess the situation, and I can see a way for this to be mutually beneficial to us both."

She remained quiet for a few moments. "What are your conditions?"

"I will petition parliament for a divorce and pay all the hefty fees—out of my own pocket. I will even return the full amount of your dowry to you. You only have to agree to one small thing."

"That's a generous offer. What do I have to do in order for you to do all that?"

He smiled. Noah had her reeled in right where he needed her to be. She was interested enough to ask questions. Now he just needed her to agree to his demands.

"Give me an heir."

She gasped. "That's preposterous. You were about to get married. Get your new bride to give you a son."

"I was only marrying Pearla to have a child. I needed a wife for a legitimate heir." He paused and gave her a wicked grin. "Since I still have a wife, I don't see a reason to marry again. Spend a year with me. Bear my child, and only then will I do whatever is necessary to grant you your freedom."

"No"

He shrugged. "Fine. Then be content on being my wife until we both pass on from this world."

"Why are you being so difficult?"

Because he got his greatest wish. His one true love was alive. The only caveat was she appeared hate him. What was it people said? He should've been careful what he'd wished for because the reality was far from what he remembered. This was a cruel joke, but he intended to make the best of it. Liam had a point. It wasn't fair to marry Pearla when he knew he could never love her. Rubina could give him the heir he needed, and he could let her go. It seemed to be what she really wanted. After all, she'd stayed away from him for three years, letting him believe she died. She must despise him to do something so horrible. She only surfaced to gain her freedom to marry another man.

"I like to see it as a win-win situation. You get what you want, and I do too."

Life hardened him. Losing her destroyed him. She made him this way, and she would have to deal with those consequences. Earlier, he'd been drowning himself one final time in his own misery before his wedding. Now, he wondered why he'd bothered.

"You expect me to have a child. To leave and never see him again. What if it's a girl?" She frowned. "What would you tell them about where I am?"

"I suppose you'd better hope we accomplish our goal the first time." Noah shrugged. "As to where you were... I'd tell them you died."

She gasped and held her hand against her heart. "Even though I'd still be alive?"

"You're already dead to me, Rubina. Why should you be alive for our child?"

Harsh words, but Noah couldn't help the disgust filling him. For a brief moment, he'd been happy when he saw her standing in the church. He'd thought God had finally listened to his prayers and gave him back his beloved. Then she'd sat across from him and ripped his heart out over and over again.

She never really loved him.

"What happened to you?" she asked, softly. "This is not the Noah I remember."

"That man died when you did. It's best you acclimate yourself to the person you created when you ran away from me and faked your own death."

"I didn't do that."

"Run away from me or fake your own death?" He waved his hand. "Never mind, it doesn't matter. You made your choice and now you must deal with the consequences. Do you agree to my terms?"

"I can't abandon my own child." Her gaze pleaded with him. "Please, don't do this."

"If you ever want to see your new love again, you will agree to my terms. Or have you already started to share his bed? You're not already enceinte are you?" Noah glared at her. "I will not accept another man's bastard. As long as you are with me, you will be with no one else."

"I've not..." She gulped. " I lied earlier. I've only ever been with you."

He nodded. He wasn't surprised she would attempt a turnabout. "I will take your word. Whatever it's worth these days."

"I'm telling you the truth."

Noah wanted to believe her, but when his own wife didn't want him, it was hard to believe a word she said. She purposely ripped his heart out and made him believe she died. Why say she loved another unless she really did? Was she that cruel? How could he ever trust her again?

"So, do we have an agreement?" he asked.

Rubina turned away from him and stared out the carriage window again. It came to a halt, forcing her forward. She landed in his lap. He picked her up and set her firmly in his arms. The scent of honeysuckle drifted in his nose. His wife smelled exactly as he remembered her. He held back the urge to do what he needed. Noah desperately wanted to kiss her and feel her squirm with desire in his arms.

Rubina's eyes met his. Then, he just knew she'd had the same thoughts he did. His wife was not as unaffected by him as she let him believe. She may claim to love another man, but she still desired him. It was something he could work with. Maybe it could be enough to convince her to give in to his demands.

He pulled her close enough so their breaths mingled together. His hand cupped her breasts and rubbed his palm across it. Her nipples pebbled with the movement. Noah smiled wickedly. Before she could object, he captured her lips with his own. She gasped, giving him the opportunity to deepen the kiss. Her hands flew to his head grasping his hair and pulling him closer. Passion ignited between them, and Noah couldn't get close enough to her. Heat burned through him, and he felt himself harden beneath her.

Oh yes, his wife still wanted him.

He pulled back and looked at her swollen lips. Her eyes were pools of silver and her breathing ragged. Noah had done that to her. Made her forget the other man she claimed to love.

He flashed her a cocky grin. "I take that as a yes?"

Rubina nodded. "Fine. You win. One year." She started to pullback. "And then I will be gone."

"Not so fast, dear." He yanked her back into his arms. "I'm not letting you go so easily. We need to seal this deal once and for all in the only place we can."

"Where's that?" she asked.

He pushed the carriage door open and stepped out in front of his townhouse, not once letting go of her.

"In my bedroom, of course."

CHAPTER 4

Noah set Rubina down just in front of the door step but held on to her hand. It took every ounce of her self control to not yank it free and run. This plan of hers was not going at all how she had envisioned it. He was supposed to be disgusted and willingly give her a divorce. Her husband needed to do whatever it took to distance himself from her.

Now that she wasn't lost in his kiss, she was able to see reason once again. She couldn't stay with him and give him a child. If she did—she'd never leave. In truth, she never wanted to leave him. Until Paolo was taken care of, Noah would not be safe. The man had an unnatural obsession with her. There wasn't a doubt in her mind he'd murder Noah in truth at the first opportunity. Paolo had to believe Noah didn't want her and that she'd moved on to someone else.

"Noah." Rubina set her free hand on his chest and looked up at him. "This isn't a good idea."

He glared down at her. His chocolate brown eyes filled with anger. "Too late. You've already agreed."

He pushed open the door and led her inside their home. It was exactly as she'd remembered it. Noah must not have changed a thing. A lump of emotion welled up inside of her. If only things were different...

"Your Grace..." Simmons stopped short and looked between the two of them. It took a lot to ruffle the proper butler and the return of the duke's wife was a good excuse if ever there was one. He recovered quickly and bowed before them both. "Welcome home."

"Hello, Simmons," Rubina greeted him. "I assume my chamber is prepared."

Simmons blinked, but showed no outward emotion. "Of course, Your Grace."

He didn't mention it had been prepared for a new duchess. That would have been unseemly. Rubina didn't care though. It gave her an avenue for escape. Noah wanted too much from her. Another time and another place she'd have willingly given it to him.

"Excellent. It's been a long day. I think I'll rest for a while. Could you have something light sent up to me? I don't much feel like company."

"I'll let one of the maids know." He nodded and headed down the hall.

Rubina walked toward the stairs, but was jerked back suddenly by Noah.

"Not so fast, dear." A wicked smile greeted her.

"We can talk later." Rubina stared into his eyes. "We have plenty of time to get reacquainted."

He nodded. "You're right."

Relief flooded through her. Maybe he was starting to rethink his demands. Rubina certainly hoped so. She didn't know if she could leave if she spent even one second in her husband's bed. This would give her the time necessary to escape.

"I'm glad you're finally being reasonable."

"Reason has nothing to do with my decision. There are a few matters I need to take care of. We will continue where we left off."

Rubina bit her lip. Part of her was irritated he was running off. This was what she wanted though. Right? In order to keep Noah safe.

"Don't worry about me. I'll be fine on my own."

He smiled, but it didn't reach his eyes. "I didn't intend to. You, my dear, can get by where others fear to tread. I have no doubt you'll come out of anything completely intact."

That hurt. A lot. But Rubina wasn't going to let him know

459

how wrong he was. She was not the same woman he married years ago. She'd been to hell and back. There might not be any physical scars, but the ones deep inside flared up with pain at the slightest provocation.

"That's correct. I'm a survivor. I won't make any apologies for it."

And she wouldn't. She made it to the other side to invoke her revenge. Rubina was patient, and her tormentor would know true pain when she was done with him.

"I didn't ask you to." He raised an eyebrow as he stared down at her. "A little touchy aren't you?"

Damn it. She'd not wanted to give him a reason to question her.

"Not at all. Just reminding you of who I am now."

The muscles in his jaw clenched at her words. "There's not any chance of that happening. Trust me I will never forget how little you care for me. It's a life lesson I didn't think I'd ever live through."

"I'm glad we understand each other."

"Oh, I am all too aware of who you are. A part of me wonders if I never fully saw you. Did you pretend to love me? Was the idea of being a duchess such a grand idea that you pretended to be someone you're not?"

"I never pretended with you."

At least not then. Now, she'd be whoever he needed her to be. As long as it made him send her in the opposite direction. Loving Noah was her greatest joy and her deepest fear. If she'd not caught the attention of a mad man everything would be so different. Perhaps she'd have a child already and they'd still be so blissfully happy. Unfortunately, wishing didn't make it so. They were very far from ever having that again. It had all been ruined by her impetuous decision to flee to Italy to visit her family. She couldn't take back that decision, as much as she'd like to. The life she'd begun with Noah wasn't to be. Soon he'd be free to marry the young woman he'd been set to marry. With her, he could have the family he desired. She'd see it happen.

"I don't believe you."

Rubina wanted to defend herself, but she couldn't. This was good. He doubted her, and that would make it easier for him to set her aside. To grant her divorce, setting them both free. She could pursue Paolo with a clear conscience knowing Noah was safe.

"It matters not. The past is where it belongs. It's best not to rehash something that cannot be changed."

"Truer words have never been spoken." He glared at her. "Don't leave this house, Rubina. I will find you, and you'll not like it when I do."

He spun on his heels and headed in the opposite direction of her. She'd landed a blow to his pride. Noah had always had an abundant amount, and now Rubina had wounded it. It was for the best. She couldn't let him love her anymore. Even if she would always love him.

Rubina sighed. She had to get out of the house and away from Noah despite his warning. Coming home with him had been a huge mistake. It was something she should not have allowed to happen. Paolo had spies everywhere. If he knew she'd become reacquainted with her husband, he could already be making plans to kill him.

She headed to the front door and pulled it open wide. Standing with her hand in mid-knock was the brazen redhead from the wedding.

"Oh, pardon me. I was about to..."

"Knock on the door?" Rubina raised an eyebrow. "That was obvious. How can I help you?"

Her eyebrows scrunched up in puzzlement. "Why were you answering the door? Where's Simmons?"

Rubina glared down at her. Insipid creature. Why did she feel she had a right to question her? What was her involvement with her husband? "This is my home."

"Could have fooled me." She pushed her way inside. "Seeing as you left it several years ago without a second thought."

Rubina saw red. She did not like this woman.

"You have no idea what I've been through."

"Right. I don't know if I care either." She waved her hand dismissively. "I didn't come here to see you regardless. I need to talk to Noah."

She was on a first name basis with her husband? Rubina didn't like that one bit. The jealousy bug hit her hard. When she saw him ready to marry the blonde she'd dismissed it. She didn't realize it until that moment, but he seemed—detached during the ceremony. This woman seemed different somehow.

"He's busy."

"Oh?" She studied Rubina. "With what?"

"Business, I presume."

It killed her to admit that. She had no idea what Noah was taking care of.

"I find it rather odd that his wife comes back from the dead, and he's abandoned her to take care of business."

If it had been a true reunion Noah wouldn't have left her for any reason. She'd goaded him until he'd stormed off. Rubina wouldn't let this woman know that.

"I'm sure it has something to do with dissolving the wedding that didn't happen. Since I'm alive and well, he can't very well wed another woman."

She nodded. "That's why I'm here actually. Is he in his study?"

The odious woman started to head toward Noah's study. Rubina couldn't let her disturb him. She'd finally got him to leave her in peace. Escape would become rather impossible if he came back out. This intruder had to leave—and soon. Otherwise, she'd have a hard time meeting up with Damian. They had a rendezvous point, and it would soon be well past their scheduled time.

"He doesn't want to be disturbed." Rubina grabbed her arm to stop her. "Maybe if you came back at another time."

She shook her head. "No, this can't wait."

"Listen…" What was her name anyway. They'd said at the church. Oh hell, it didn't matter. She needed to leave.

"Gemma, or Lady Marsden for you. I don't know that we'll be close enough to use first names."

"Fine, you can address me as Your Grace."

An evil smile formed on Gemma's face. "That's fine, Your Grace. Now get your bloody hand off of me so I can go talk to Noah."

"I can't do that, Lady Marsden." She clenched her teeth together.

Gemma brought her hand up on top of Rubina's and

threaded her fingers into her. While she smiled sweetly, she yanked Rubina's hand back and twisted her wrist.

"Ouch! Was that really necessary?"

"I don't like to have anyone touching me that I didn't invite to do so."

Rubina glared. "You could have asked me to let go."

She raised an eyebrow. "Would you have?"

Probably not, but she didn't know that.

"I'm starting to see why Liam was drawn to you."

"Thanks." She frowned. "I think."

"It wasn't a compliment."

Rubina never did understand why Noah and Liam remained such good friends. They came from different worlds. Yes, they were both sons of noblemen, but Noah lived a life of isolation where Liam was encased in a loving family. Both were strong, reliable, and stubborn. Rubina believed that was why her husband was drawn to Liam's family. Being around them helped him get over the losses he had been dealt as a boy. They gave him something he craved. Liam helped him in so many ways.

He kept to himself and didn't encourage social interactions. Liam thrived and floated through society, not giving it a care. It came much easier for him. His wife was full of fire and life—a perfect fit for Liam. Rubina wished she'd been around to see their courtship. It must have been fascinating to watch. In another lifetime, maybe they could have been friends. She had a new respect for the woman.

"I will choose to take it as one regardless."

"What is going on here?"

Rubina gazed up into Noah's eyes. "We have a visitor."

"I can see that." He frowned. "Why are you here, Gemma?"

She smiled, reassuringly. "Do you have a moment to talk?" She looked over at Rubina. "In private?"

He nodded. "I always have time for you. Please come to my study."

Noah held his hand out, gesturing the way, letting Gemma walk before him.

He turned to head back in the direction he'd just come from. Noah stopped and pivoted toward Rubina. "Remember what I said earlier." His voice was harsh. "Don't make me come find you."

Gemma stopped and stared between them. She shook her head. Sadness filled her lovely green eyes.

Ruby didn't want her pity.

"Go. Have your visit." She smiled sweetly. "When you're done, by all means, please come find me. I promise you it will be something you'll never forget."

Instead of waiting for his reply, she went up the stairs with every ounce of pride she owned flowing through her. She held her head high and took each step with the poise and grace of a princess on her way to greet her subjects. No one would ever pity Rubina.

From the moment she got free until she'd made herself a promise, never again would she be a victim. She'd die a thousand deaths before she let anyone see her as weak again.

Especially Noah and Gemma Marsden.

Nothing would get her to admit how much it hurt to watch her husband dismiss her so easily. He barely gave her a second thought. Everything should have been so different. A tear traveled down her cheek. She quickly wiped it away. There wasn't time to give into the pain. This was the plan. It had to be this way.

Noah, the only man she would ever love, must always come first.

Only then would revenge be hers.

CHAPTER 5

N oah followed Gemma into his study. He held out a chair for her and then sat behind his desk.

"What can I do for you?"

Gemma took a deep breath and studied him in silence for several seconds. "First, tell me how you're doing."

How did he answer that question? His wife was alive. Something he'd dreamed of happening but never dared wish for. Good thing he hadn't because it was less than ideal.

"Did Liam send you over to check on me?"

Gemma shook her head. "No, of course not...I mean, not that he isn't probably concerned, but I haven't spoken to him since I left the church with Pearla."

"I see."

Noah stared off in space. The church—what a disaster that turned out to be. When he turned to see Rubina walking down the aisle... He stopped breathing for a second, sure he'd been seeing some apparition sent to play tricks on him. Then reality came crashing in, and it was all too real. Rubina was not only alive, but she claimed to no longer love him.

"Don't think I didn't notice how you failed to answer my question." Gemma smiled. "Nice try, but I'm not leaving until I am sure you're doing all right."

Noah sighed. "How do you think I'm doing?"

She raised an eyebrow. "I wouldn't presume to know. But

if I were forced to guess, I'd say you're not doing well at all. Something isn't right because I'd have thought you'd be ecstatic to have your wife back."

"Under normal circumstances I would be." He ran his hand through his hair. "Let's be honest, nothing is normal about this situation. I can't make sense of any of it."

Gemma nodded. "I expect that is the only thing normal about this situation."

"I need a drink."

Noah stood and grabbed the nearly empty brandy decanter near his desk. That's right. He'd drank quite a bit of it in the morning before his wedding. Drinking hadn't helped that situation any more than it would help the one he currently found himself in. There was nothing that would help it.

Rubina was alive.

Maybe if he said it enough he'd truly believe it. The problem was she wasn't anything like he remembered. Oh, she was still as beautiful as the day he met her, but her eyes told a different story. She was harder and less forgiving. The loving woman he married didn't look back at him. Instead, a stranger had taken her place.

He set the decanter back down, rethinking his idea for a drink.

"Good choice," Gemma said.

"I feel like my whole world tipped upside down in the matter of minutes."

"Because it has."

"Drinking isn't going to make that right." He shook his head. "It will probably make it inherently worse."

She nodded. "Probably a good assumption."

Noah jerked his head around and asked, "How is Pearla doing?"

Gemma sighed. "That's why I'm here. She asked me to return this to you."

She set a ring down on his desk. It was an alabaster pearl flanked by brilliant diamonds. He'd purchased it for her specifically.

"No. I meant that for her. Give it back."

"I'm afraid I can't do that."

"Why the hell not?"

Noah clenched his fists at his side as anger seized his heart. Why couldn't anything go right in his life? Ever since his parents died, his whole existence was nothing but loneliness. If not for Liam and his family, he'd probably never go out and socialize. Everyone left him eventually. He felt...unlovable.

"Pearl has decided she can't stay in England." Gemma frowned. "She believes the stigma of what happened at the church makes her...undesirable."

"That's ridiculous." Noah glared at Gemma. "It's not her fault my wife pretended to be dead for years."

She cleared her throat. "She said to tell you she doesn't blame you for any of it. If you'd known Rubina was alive, you'd never have put her in that situation."

"Of course not. I'd have hunted her down and brought her home."

At least long enough to obtain his heir. Which he fully intended to get from her before she disappeared again. She may not love him anymore, but she owed him.

"Yes. As I was saying, she thinks you are very honorable and deserve far more than what's been dealt you." She took a breath. "Which is why she can't keep the ring. She says it's not fair to keep a token of your affection when she knows you are very much in love with your wife. She doesn't want anything to remind her of what could have been."

Noah's eyes whipped upward. As he stared into Gemma's, he asked, "Come again?"

"She believed herself to be in love with you. This wasn't a business deal for her."

Noah scrubbed his hands over his face. Could this day get any worse? He'd thought she knew—understood—he was incapable of loving anyone else. Rubina took it all with her when she died—no, she still had it. She may be a deceptive witch, but he still loved the illusion.

"I'm so sorry. I didn't know..."

"Don't feel guilty. She wouldn't want you to." Gemma reached across the desk and placed her hand on his arm. "It was her choice. One she thought she could live with. Now it's time for her to accept a different path. Just as you must. Your wife is alive and upstairs waiting to start your lives together again."

"No, she isn't." Noah frowned. "She can't wait to be rid of me."

"No? Why would she come back if she doesn't want to be with you? There must be some other explanation. I don't believe for a minute she doesn't still love you."

"You're wrong." Noah swept his arms across his desk, knocking everything to the floor. The brandy glass from earlier shattered on impact. "She wants a divorce. Ruby stated her wishes clearly before the entire guest list at my failed wedding."

He stood and started to pace. Noah turned to look at her and stopped in place.

Gemma's face had lost all color.

From the look on her face, he'd frightened her. He'd make it up to her later. When he got his feelings under control.

"There must be some mistake," Gemma said.

Noah's hand shook as he covered his face. That's what he kept telling himself. It was all a grievous mistake. Rubina didn't love him anymore. He'd heard wrong. It was all some bizarre nightmare he'd wake up from at any moment.

"I'm afraid not."

"I don't understand."

He shook his head and fought tears. Men didn't cry. Noah wanted to give in, but he wouldn't, not with Gemma still in the room. "That makes two of us."

"Why is she still here if she wants a divorce?"

A bark of laughter escaped his mouth. "Because I made a deal with her."

Gemma stood up and approached him. "What did you do?"

He'd bargained with one of the devil's servants. It was the only thing he could think to do when she'd cornered him with her insane request. There was no way parliament was going to grant him a divorce. No matter how much he paid them to get out of it. There was only way to end a marriage—one of them had to die.

They were stuck together whether she liked it or not.

"I agreed to her terms if she agreed to mine."

"What did you ask for?"

Noah looked down at her and replied, "I asked for a child."

"Oh, Noah."

Sadness filled her eyes. He didn't like the way she was staring at him. Gemma meant well, but she didn't know what it was like to live inside his skin. To know love and then have it ripped from him—nothing hurt more than that. Even though both his parents died while he was a child, this was so much more painful. His heart was ripped to shreds with no hope of being repaired.

"Don't look at me like that."

"I'm sorry."

He frowned. "What for? You didn't do it. You've always been a good friend to me. Without you and Liam I'd be alone."

At least he wouldn't inflict himself upon Pearla. She may think she loved him, but in time, she'd probably get over that. She escaped a bad fate by escaping marriage to him. He was a bad bet.

"You're a good friend too. Don't sell yourself short." She stepped up to him and wrapped her arms around his waist, hugging him. Her head lay upon his chest. "Rubina doesn't know what she's missing by not staying with you forever. It's her loss, not yours."

"Then why does it feel like I've lost a piece of myself?" He wrapped his arms around her, returning the hug. "Everything I thought was up is down and vice versa."

She took a step back. A lone tear fell down her cheek. He reached up and wiped it away. "It won't always be that way. One day you'll wake up and realize you're going to be just fine. The ache that takes over your heart won't be quite as painful and breathing will come a little easier. It only feels so devastating because it's all fresh and new."

"How do you know?"

"I was you once. When I first told Liam I loved him he practically ran in the other direction. It wasn't a grand love story like you and Rubina—but it was very real to me. It took a while for me to move on with my life. It helps to have something else to focus on."

He shook his head. "Liam was an ass."

She smiled. "He was then, yes. And he certainly can be still, but I love him regardless."

Noah nodded. "He's lucky."

"Rubina is too." She placed a hand on his arm. "She will realize it eventually. I'm sure she has reasons for what she's doing."

"She does. She claims to love another and wants to be free to be with them."

She shook her head. "She's lying."

"I don't think she is."

Gemma smiled. "I'm willing to bet she still loves you very much. You should ask her about her time apart from you. There's something she's not telling you."

Noah didn't think there was. He didn't really want to listen to tales of her new love. It would hurt too much. No, it was much better not knowing all the gory details. He was afraid of what they were and what they would tell him about his wife. All of his illusions had already been shattered. Why make it even more difficult that it already was? Maybe after he calmed down he'd demand answers. For the moment, he was all right without them.

"I'd rather not know."

"That's your choice to make, but Noah..." He looked down at her. "She does still love you. You can count on it."

"How could you possibly know that?"

She smiled. "Because you didn't see how she looked at you when you weren't looking."

He shook his head. "That means nothing. So what if she still desires me? That does not equate love by any means."

It didn't. Rubina may still own his heart, but she took hers back. She wanted to give it completely to another man. Noah couldn't stomach the idea.

"It's not the same thing."

"No. Lust burns out a lot faster. Love is supposed to be forever."

"I wouldn't know." She shook her head. "I do know what a woman in love looks like, and your wife never stopped loving you."

She held up her hand when he started to speak, stopping him.

"Let me finish. You can do what you want with that information, but I think if you try hard enough, in time, she'll admit the truth to you."

"I don't know." He frowned.

"I do." She smiled. "Take this little bit of advice. Don't toss what you had aside. Try to see things from her point of view. Maybe dig a little deeper so you can see things from her side. Don't throw your marriage away without at least trying."

Noah sighed. "I'm not making any promises."

"I'm not asking you to," she said. "Now, I need to get home to my husband. If you need someone to talk to, come see me or Liam. We'll always be here for you."

Gemma headed toward the door to leave.

"Wait," he called out to her.

"Yes?"

"You never did say where Pearla was going."

She smiled. "I don't know. She didn't want me to slip and tell you."

Great. Women seemed to be in a hurry to run away from him, and they didn't want him to be able to track them down. Gemma meant well, but he didn't think she saw things as they were. Rubina would give him a child. That's all he needed from her. Then she could run away and never come back. Noah would find a way to be content with that.

Even if he had to become even more closed off than he already was.

CHAPTER 6

Rubina rushed through Piccadilly and headed toward The Albany. Damian had a set of rooms there. It was a bachelor residence he kept so he had his own place when he visited London. He'd acquired them when Rubina married Noah. Her brother hadn't wanted to intrude on her new marriage, but he still wanted to be able to visit her. She didn't know why he'd kept them upon her supposed death, but the rooms would be their meeting point now. Luckily, they allowed her entrance. There was a time when a woman hadn't been allowed to even enter the prestigious bachelor residence.

Rubina looked over her shoulder. A niggling feeling someone was watching her crawled over her skin. She didn't know where it came from, but she couldn't shake the sensation. No one seemed to be around. Still, she'd have to be careful. Just because she couldn't see anyone didn't mean they weren't there.

Rubina shook it off and lifted her skirts, rushing toward the entrance of The Albany. She headed straight to Damian's set of rooms and knocked on the door. It flew open after a few seconds. Damian looked up and down the hall and yanked her inside.

"You're late."

Rubina peeled off her gloves and tossed them on a nearby

table. "I know. It couldn't be helped." She strolled over to a chaise and sat, letting out the breath she'd not realized she'd been holding. "Do you have news?"

He nodded. "Nothing specific. Just a rumbling."

"Tell me."

"In all due time." Damian walked to a nearby window and peered outside. "What happened with Noah?"

"He's being difficult."

Damian let the curtain slide closed. He laughed. "What did you expect?"

Rubina frowned. "I'd hoped he would be so disgusted with me he wouldn't question my request."

Damian frowned. "He loves you, Rue. When you died— when he thought you were gone—he shattered. I can't imagine how it must have been for him to see you alive in front of him. It must have been quite a shock."

Rubina looked away. Her brother had no idea how hard it was to stick to the plan when she saw Noah in the church. The look on his face... It tore her apart. But in order for Noah to live, she had to break him even more.

"Indeed."

"So why did it take you so long to get back here?"

Rubina sighed. "Noah absconded with me and took me home."

"That had to be difficult." He shook his head and laughed again. "Though I'm not at all surprised he did. I'd have done the same."

"I'm sure you would." She bit her lip. "He's not going to go along with the divorce so easily—he wants more than I can give him."

She couldn't help wanting to give in to his demands. To make love with her husband and create a child together... Rubina would give anything to have it all. Fate had other ideas for what she could have though.

"So what does he require to see the divorce through."

She waved a hand. "It matters not. I can't give it to him. We'll have to find another way."

"There is no other way. We already discussed this in length. Paolo has to believe you've severed all ties, or else he will go after Noah."

"I know," she exclaimed. "If only we could put an end to this…"

The crafty bastard was in hiding. They couldn't locate him anywhere. When Arturo had brought her to Damian, he hadn't known why Paolo couldn't be found. He was on a secret mission that no one had all the details for. Rubina was partially glad he'd disappeared. It made her rescue possible. The downside was no one knew exactly where he was—which put Noah in danger.

"My sources all point to London. He has to be here." Damian frowned. "If he isn't he will be soon."

"That's what I'm afraid of." Rubina shook her head. "Why couldn't he be on the other side of the world and far away from my husband?" She sighed. "I think I was followed here."

"Did you see anyone?" He skimmed the curtains with his hands and looked outside again. "We can't be too careful with your safety. Perhaps I should accompany you when you leave."

"It was more of a sensation of being watched." She didn't need Damian to go into protector mode. Rubina suffocated enough under Paolo's control. "Let the evil bastard make his move. It will give me the opportunity to finish this. Noah will come around and grant me a divorce. It's his only option. For now I will take up residence in the townhouse we've rented for my stay in London."

"Noah is the key to all of this. I can feel it in my gut." Damian paced around the room. "I think you need to go back."

"What?" Her eyes widened in shock. "If I go back, he'll never let me out of his sight again. I'm lucky to have gotten away without him following me."

"How did you manage that?"

Rubina hadn't wanted to leave. If she'd been given a choice, she'd never leave her husband again. Especially with a beautiful woman keeping him company. She gritted her teeth and clenched her hands into tight fists when he left her alone to speak to Gemma in private. The only way she had been able to allow the slight was to remind herself over and over again the other woman was married to Liam Marsden.

The one thing she knew for certain was Liam would never stand for his wife to stray—especially with his best friend. He was no cuckold.

"He had a visitor. I took advantage and slipped out while he was occupied."

Damian's eyebrow rose. "I'm surprised he let you out of his sight. Noah doesn't seem like the type to allow you to take advantage of a situation."

He was correct. Under normal circumstances Noah wouldn't have been so easily duped. Her husband had his whole world turned upside down in a short time. He wasn't at his best—which Rubina took advantage of. When he had time to stop and think, he'd know exactly where she could be found. He'd warned her after all. Which meant she'd have to wrap up her meeting with Damian soon and make herself scarce...

"He isn't. It's been a hard day—I expect he'll be by soon in a full fury."

"Really?" He smiled. "I suppose you're correct. I look forward to the visit. Now go home to your husband."

"No. You know I can't."

"I know you want to protect Noah, but I think the time for that has passed."

"You don't know that for certain."

Damian folded his arms across his chest and stared down at her. "I do."

"How?"

He crossed the room and pulled out a slip of paper from a drawer. Damian looked back at her and frowned, then walked to her side. "I received this coded message just before you arrived. Take a look at it."

Rubina opened the folded note and scanned the contents. "Arturo can verify this?"

Damian nodded. "We may not have located Paolo, but we have discovered his mission."

She shot to her feet and paced the room. Rubina didn't say a word for several minutes. Her mind whirled at what Arturo had discovered. How could Noah have been so reckless? He'd unwittingly put himself in far graver danger than she'd realized. There was no protecting him with distance now.

She'd have to stay. Her heart leapt with joy at the prospect. Leaving him had never been her wish—but how much could she tell him.

Damian nodded. "Noah invested in some orchards along the coast of Sicily near Palermo. If I were to hazard a guess, it was something to remind him of you and where he met you."

"Oh hell…"

"The Mafioso doesn't like usurpers. They want control of that property. Paolo is all too glad to deal with it, knowing how important he is to you. He'd gladly end Noah's life."

"I'm too late." She threw up her hands. "I broke him even further for nothing."

Tears fell from her eyes. She wiped them away. They wouldn't help the situation. A new plan had to be formed. Noah would not die because of his ties to her and her family.

"So what am I to do now?"

Damian pulled her into his arms. He hugged her tight. "Don't worry, Rue. I won't let them kill Noah. Paolo will pay for what he's done to you and our family."

Rubina pulled back and steeled herself for their next move. "He will pay. I'll gladly be the one to end his life. Paolo is an evil man and shouldn't be allowed to inflict any more pain on another soul."

"I can't let you do that. You already have too much to deal with." He shook his head. "First and foremost, you need to go home to your husband. Watch everyone around him. Anyone and everyone is suspect. Paolo could take the opportunity to instill someone in Noah's house to spy on him. We can't take a chance someone might start feeding him crucial information. You need to be there to prevent any potential danger to your husband."

Rubina nodded. "You're right. Of course, he would try to plant a spy there. Paolo is nothing if not efficient."

And smart. Rubina intended to be smarter. She would have to be to defeat him.

"When I know more, I'll come by."

"What am I to tell Noah?"

Damian shrugged. "Tell him you went for a walk. Whatever you can to distract him. I'm not so sure it's a good idea he knows everything yet. He can be—hardheaded."

Rubina snorted. Damian didn't have to tell her how stubborn her husband could be. She knew all too well how he could dig his heels in when a notion came over him. In those times, up was down and vise versa. No one could persuade him when he got an idea about something.

"At some point we will have to tell him everything."

Damian nodded. "I know. Just not yet. Play along with whatever he wants for now. It shouldn't be much longer, and then you can unburden yourself."

The truth shall set her free…

Hopefully Noah wouldn't hate her too much when that time came.

"All right." She picked up her gloves off the table and slid them back on. "I'll return to Noah. I won't say anything for now. But Damian…" She stared him in the eyes. "Find Paolo. End this. I don't know how long I can keep up this pretense without breaking."

"I am working as hard and as fast as I can." He ran his hands through his chestnut hair. His silver eyes filled with worry. "There are only so many places he could be, and I will find him."

Rubina nodded. "I hope so."

A thunderous boom filled the room. It echoed throughout the entire residence. The earsplitting racket repeated over and over again. They both stopped and turned toward the entrance. A very unhappy person appeared to be knocking on Damian's door. There really could only be one person who would come by and hit his door with such force.

Noah had come looking for her.

He'd promised he would find her, after all. Where else would she have gone but to her brother. Her husband knew her better than he realized. She might be playing a game of illusions with him—making him doubt her—but at her core she hadn't changed. Rubina always ran to Damian for help. The only exception was Noah. When she met him and fallen in love, that dynamic changed slightly. She'd run to her husband first—unless her problem was about him.

"I think it's safe to say your husband is here."

Rubina glared at him. "Oh?" Sarcasm filled her voice. "What was your first clue?"

Another deafening boom filled the room.

Damian laughed. "I suppose I should let him in before he breaks down the door."

Her brother headed toward the door. He took his time. No reason to rush or anything. Noah was just about to do some serious damage to the entrance to his rooms. Why ever wouldn't he hurry to let him in? Rubina sometimes thought her brother had a death wish.

He eased the door open and greeted her husband. "Noah, how good to see you? What can I help you with?"

Noah raised an eyebrow in derision. "Don't treat me like an idiot. Give me my wife. Now."

Damian opened the door all the way allowing Noah to see Rubina.

Noah's smile was so full of wickedness it her caused her heart to speed up. She raised her hand across her chest and her mouth fell open in anticipation.

Oh my…

"Hello, dear. I told you I'd come for you."

CHAPTER 7

"I wasn't exactly hiding." Rubina shrugged. "If you'd waited a little bit longer, I'd have returned home all on my own."

Noah stalked toward Rubina. When he'd discovered her missing, his vision went red. How dare she run off again. After what happened the last time…

He shook the image from his mind. She was alive. Something he had to constantly remind himself of. What had happened before was an elaborate ruse. He had no idea what her end game was, but he intended to find out. It was time for him to face the truth. He wanted answers, and he intended to make her start to doling them out. At least she'd been easy to find. Unlike before…

Of course she'd run to her brother. Damian had always been the one person she'd turn to when she was mad at him. It was the first place he thought to look—even though he'd not been certain Damian was in London. But he was—where else would he be? How much did her brother know, and when did he find out? Noah wasn't happy with either one of them, and he planned on letting them both feel every ounce of his rage.

He raised an eyebrow. "I somehow doubt the validity of your statement."

"It's true." Damian jumped in. "Rue was just about to leave."

Noah jerked his head in his brother-in-law's direction. "How long have you known she was alive?" He seethed.

"Not as long as your look implies."

He tilted his head, crossed his arms, and studied Damian. "I'm willing to bet it's still longer than I've known. Tell me what you know."

Damian shrugged. "Not a whole lot. Rue found me near Palermo. One of my men showed her where to find me. I was shocked to see her alive."

Noah bet he was. Damian wasn't telling him everything. No doubt that little bit information was the truth—but he knew him well. There were details he was purposely holding back. In time, Noah would have them all. For now, he'd settle for dragging his wayward wife home where she belonged.

She owed him far more than her brother did. It was Rubina who had betrayed their love.

"Since you were leaving, my dear,"—he turned toward her—"I will escort you home."

Rubina smiled. "Why of course. Give me a moment to say goodbye to my brother."

She sashayed over to Damian and hugged him tight. "I will see you again soon, yes?"

"I promise."

She stepped out of Damian's arms and walked over to Noah. She looped her arm in his, tilted her head, and studied him through her lashes. "I believe you were taking me home…"

Her lips tilted into an enticing smile. It was an invitation Noah could not mistake. His wife intended to seduce him. He hardened at the thought. What game was she playing now?

He choked back the lump in his throat. Rubina would not get the best of him. It was time to take control and play things the way he wanted.

"Damian." He tore his gaze from his wife's plump lips. "I will speak to you later about this whole ordeal. I want more details. For now, we are leaving."

Damian nodded. "Absolutely. I will stop by and speak with you in a few days. I'm sure you have many questions."

His gaze landed on Rubina's and held it for several seconds—something unsaid passing between them.

Noah didn't know what they were hiding, but he would find out. It disgusted and irritated him that they went to such lengths to hold back the truth.

"I look forward to your visit. When you come by, make sure to leave some time for me." Rubina pouted prettily at her brother.

"I already said I'd visit you, Rue." He grinned. "How many promises do I need to make?"

"As many as I require." She flashed him a gamine smile.

"Enough. It's time to depart," Noah said roughly. This nonsense must come to an end.

"Goodbye, Damian." Rubina waved as Noah escorted her out of the room.

They walked outside to his awaiting carriage. His ducal crest emblazoned upon the door. He gritted his teeth so he didn't give her any more biting replies. She was fast driving him insane—though not in the way he wanted.

His every dream had come true when she boldly strolled down the church aisle, interrupting his wedding. Unfortunately, it fast turned into his worst nightmare. What difference did it make if his wife lived when she clearly despised him? What other reason would she have for staying away from him for so long? Well, she was in for a rude awakening. She wouldn't be able to get rid of him as easily as she wanted.

He helped her inside the carriage and joined her, sitting across from her. She looked out the window, apparently refusing to meet his gaze.

"Don't worry. We will be home soon enough."

She whipped her head to meet his gaze. Fury shot out of her eyes. Her fists clenched in her lap, but she quickly eased them into a relaxed state. "I wasn't worried about arriving home."

"No?" he asked, studying her beautiful face. "What could you possibly be fretting over?"

"It doesn't matter." She brushed it aside with the wave of her hand. "Nothing but trivial concerns. It isn't anything you need to bother yourself with."

"If it concerns you, it does me as well. Tell me what is on your mind."

Rubina bit her lip and looked back out the window. "It's just I don't have anything to wear."

Of course. His fashion conscious wife would be concerned about her lack of wardrobe. "If you wanted to purchase new gowns, all you had to do was ask. No reason to pout in silence."

Her smile brightened. "You were always so generous with me. Can we go to Madame Roussard's now?"

Noah frowned. "It's getting rather late in the day…"

"Please," she begged prettily. "I do so need some new gowns. If I'm to stay in England, I will need them to go out in society. The world needs to know your wife has returned."

"I know… but—"

"You don't want them doubting our child is yours do you?" She raised an eyebrow. "We must give them a united front, and show them how very much in love we still are."

"So you want me to lie?"

She tilted her head and studied him. "You're saying you no longer love me?"

Noah clenched his jaw as her words hit him where it hurt. She spoke the truth. He never stopped loving her, but he refused to admit it to her. He'd be damned before he gave her the satisfaction.

"Why don't you tell me why you really want new gowns, Ruby?" He leaned back against the of the seat, acting as relaxed as he possibly could.

"I already told you…"

He held up a hand. "Quit playing your silly games and tell me the truth."

She sighed. "I don't have but the gown I'm wearing and the one in my valise. I haven't gotten any new gowns since I left England three years ago. I've had to make do with a couple second-hand gowns."

Noah frowned. She was telling the truth. He could see it in her eyes. It didn't make any sense to him. If she'd been so destitute, why had she stayed away? He would have gladly bought her anything she wanted. Rubina had been his everything, and there was nothing he wouldn't have done for her. Did she really need to get away from him that bad? To live without any of the amenities she'd been used to?

"Why this pretense?"

"I don't know what your mean?" She frowned. "I am telling you the truth."

He believed her. That didn't mean he understood any of it.

"No." He shook his head. "With Damian and your father. Why not tell them you were alive? If you didn't want to be with me, they would have supported you. What were you thinking, Ruby?"

"I couldn't." She returned her gaze to the window.

"Bloody hell. Why not?"

"So, are we going to go to Madam Roussard's?"

She didn't meet his eyes. His wife didn't even bother to answer his question. Instead, she changed the subject. He could respect that a little bit. It was evasion at its best. He'd deflected her question about loving her just as easily. What a pair the two of them made.

"No, we are not going to the dress shop today."

Finally, she turned to look at him. Her silver eyes reflected sadness. "You never were cruel Noah. What happened to you?"

"My wife died."

She tilted her head. "But I am very much alive."

"You're not my wife." He stared her in the eyes. "You're an imposter living inside her body. The Rubina Leone I married loved me and would never have put me through the hell you have."

Rubina gasped. Her hand flew to her chest. Her gaze held resignation. "I deserve that."

She deserved so much more than mere words could inflict upon her. Noah held back all the anger building up inside of him. This wasn't the time nor the place to unleash it all on her. They would be home soon enough. Once they were there, he'd drag her to his room. Then he'd seduce all the information she held inside out of her treacherous body.

"I couldn't agree more."

"So I'm not to get new dresses?"

Rubina was not going to let the idea of new gowns go. He'd have to give into her desire at some point. But for the moment, what he wanted came first. She'd already played fast and loose with his emotions. She promised him she'd remain with him and give him an heir. He was afraid she'd run away before they could beget one. His greater fear would be she'd become enceinte and disappear again. Then he'd lose his wife and his unborn child.

Still, it was a risk he was willing to take.

Surely she wouldn't be as cruel as she appeared and deny him his one request. His gut churned at the idea. He was fast learning that anything was possible where his wife was concerned. Perhaps it was time to hire someone to watch out for her—or more apt to watch her period. He didn't trust her to not disappear again. He'd just fail to mention to her that she'd have a constant tail for as long as she remained in his house.

It was the only reassurance he could give himself.

"Not today. Perhaps I will gift you with some at a later date." He smiled wickedly. "For now, you won't be in much need of clothing of any kind. I plan on keeping you in bed for the next several days."

Her hand flew to her chest. "Caro, you can be positively decadent."

Darling? She'd not called him such since she'd returned. Was she falling into old habits? He refused to acknowledge the endearment. His treacherous wife was not to be trusted, and Noah would not be lured into her web again. There was only one thing he wanted from her, and he'd enjoy every minute of it.

He'd not had a woman in years. The only one who aroused him was the deceitful bitch sitting across from him. So creating a child with her would be such torturous sweet pleasure.

The carriage stopped in front of their townhouse. Noah looked out the window. It was time to show her exactly what he expected from her. Rubina would be so well pleasured she'd be too limp from exhaustion to leave him for a while.

He kept his wicked grin in place, never once taking his eyes off of her. It was time for her to see exactly what he expected from her. He didn't hold back any of the desire flowing through him. The heat, the need, and the unwavering longing that had built up inside him while he believed she was dead.

"Darling," he enunciated the word, filling it with every sinful implication he felt. "I promise you, over the next several days, you will know exactly how wicked I can be."

CHAPTER 8

Rubina held her breath as she stared into Noah's heat-filled gaze. God help her, but she wanted everything they promised. She wouldn't fight him. He must know on some level that she wanted him just as much.

"I look forward to your,"—she tilted her lips into an enticing smile—"efforts…"

"Good, because we are going to start now."

"In the carriage?" She patted the seat next to her. "Oh, Noah, I didn't know you had it in you." She beckoned him with her finger. "Please, join me, and let's find out how wicked my husband has become."

Noah stared shocked for a second, then practically leaped at her. He pulled her into his arms and found her lips with his. The heat was instant and glorious as it spread through her. This is what she had been craving. The all consuming desire she could never resist—this is what she'd missed most when she'd lain awake in her lonely room. Heat was something she didn't feel a lot of in her prison.

Noah radiated enough to keep her warm for several years.

He trailed kisses down her neck as she entwined her fingers in his midnight hair. Every touch even more delicious than the last one—until he abruptly stopped.

Her eyelids flew open, and she met his lust filled gaze.

"As much as I'd like to follow you into carnal bliss, this is not the place to do it."

She raised an eyebrow. "Where's your sense of adventure?"

He laughed. "I will not be enticed into getting naked in the carriage with you, Ruby."

"Why not?" She pouted.

Just then, the door opened. A footman stood outside, holding it in place. "Do you need assistance, Your Grace?"

"No, Dobbins." Noah grinned. "We are ready to go inside." He leaned down and whispered in her ear," Is that reason enough?"

Her cheeks filled with heat. Noah had a point. This was not the place to fully reunite with her husband. "Yes, it is."

Noah stepped out of the carriage and turned to assist her out. He tucked her arm into his and led her into the townhouse. Simmons stood inside the foyer and nodded to them. He shut the door behind him. Rubina looked back at him after they had passed. She caught him with a huge grin on his face—like a cat enjoying the canary he'd caught. What did the normally stodgy butler have to smile about?

Noah didn't lead her to the sitting room. Instead, he turned down the hall to the staircase—leading to their bedrooms.

"Deciding to pick up where we left off in the carriage?"

Rubina couldn't wait to get him naked and at her mercy. The need to touch every inch of him welled up inside of her. It had been way too long since her husband made love to her. Her desire for him hadn't eased one bit.

"I already told you that I plan on keeping you in bed for days."

"Don't be ridiculous." She flashed him a smile. "That would be nearly impossible to do."

"And yet I intend to do just that." His gaze held so much promise. "I wouldn't want to shirk on my duty to get you with child. The sooner my heir is born the quicker you can run off to your new love."

Rubina held her breath at his words. Slowly, she let it out. It would do her no good to stop breathing now. There was much she still needed to do. Shock had filled her—why, she didn't know. He only spoke the things she'd wanted him to believe. If only Paolo... No, Rubina wouldn't harp on what she couldn't control. Soon the man would pay for his treachery. Then she could tell Noah the truth and start to rebuild their relationship. For now—for his protection—she'd have to keep her secrets. When it was safe for him to know everything, only then would she unburden herself.

For the moment, she'd gladly take every ounce of what he offered her. It would have to be enough. It wasn't his fault she'd deliberately deceived him. This was her cross to bear.

"You're right, of course. The sooner I'm carrying your child the better."

She swallowed back the bile that filled her mouth at her lie. Part of her hoped she didn't conceive at all. What if she did and somehow Paolo got a hold of her again? Then he'd have her and Noah's heir.

He looked down at her with such derision it made her heart skip a beat. The hate in his eyes hurt to see reflected back at her.

"Don't worry, dear. I will do everything in my power to make it happen as soon as possible. Once you're carrying my heir you won't have to stomach my attentions again."

Rubina bit her lip. Another reason for her to not want to conceive right away. She wanted to be with him in every way possible for the rest of her life. If she couldn't have his love, she at least wanted everything else. The idea of never feeling his arms wrapped around her again—it was almost too much to bear.

"Then, for your sake, I hope I conceive quickly. It must be difficult for you to have to make love to me knowing I no longer love you."

This pretense was killing her. The paleness of Noah's face at her words struck her heart with thousands of pinpricks. She didn't want to hurt him, yet she must. Soon, she'd let him know what was going on. After they located Paolo and made sure he'd never harm anyone she loved again. Then, and only then, would Noah know how much she still loved him. There would never be anyone else for her.

Noah dropped her hand and studied her a second. Then he started walking down the hall. Rubina followed closely behind him, unsure what he intended. He stopped just outside his bedroom door and turned to her. "It's a chore that will be worth it in the end."

He grabbed her hand and led her inside the room. Then he shut the door with a click and turned the lock.

"Don't want anyone disturbing us."

Rubina shook her head. "No, we have a reunion that must not be interrupted."

Noah frowned. "This is not a reunion. It's a necessity."

"However you wish to see it is fine with me." Rubina shrugged.

"Good. As long as we understand each other."

"I understand perfectly," Rubina said quietly.

Noah circled her as he studied every inch of her. Then he stopped behind her and started the long process of unlatching all the buttons of her dress. He pushed it down to the floor leaving her in her shift and corset. Soon, it too fell to the floor. The thin linen of her chemise was all that stood between her and complete nudity. Noah was still fully dressed.

"Aren't you going to remove your clothing too?"

"Are you in a hurry?" His gaze traveled over her.

Wetness pooled between her thighs. She wanted to feel him sliding inside her, bringing her to ecstasy. She needed it more than words could say.

"Yes." She nodded.

"Too bad. I want to savor this moment."

"I thought you couldn't stand me."

Noah's actions were baffling her. What game was he playing with her? He didn't really want her, did he? He kept saying it was only to get an heir. This didn't require more than the actual act of intercourse.

"Some things need to be done, even when every part of you screams to run. I want you, Ruby, and I intend to have you..." He paused as he let his eyes roam over her again. "My way and in every way. You belong to me, and you will know it when I'm done with you."

Oh yes, she did belong to him. If he wanted to exert that control... She'd gladly let him. He loosened his cravat and pulled it free from his neck and tossed it on the bed. Next came his jacket, which he laid on a nearby chair. He opened a drawer and pulled out another cravat and tossed it on the bed next to the other one. He yanked the coverlet down enough to expose the sheet.

"What are you planning?"

"Not now..." He grinned wickedly. "But soon you will see."

He rolled the sleeves of his white shirt and stalked forward. He stopped in front of her. His fingers grazed her chemise so lightly she almost didn't feel his touch. Then he yanked her chemise off her body, leaving her completely naked in front of him.

"You're so damned beautiful."

He leaned down and licked one tight nipple. Rubina groaned with each sweep of his tongue over her sensitive flesh. Before she had time to react, he lifted her up and carried her over to the bed and lay her across the top. The cravats he'd tossed on the bed earlier were laying next to her head. Noah picked up one and wound it around her wrist and tied it to the bedpost—then did the other one.

"Have you learned a few tricks since we last saw each other?" She raised an eyebrow.

"For you, I learned many things."

Noah stood and stared at her for several seconds. It made her body heat up even more. If she reacted this way with just a gaze, she'd explode when he finally got around to touching her.

"Are you going to stare at me all day, or are you going to actually touch me anytime soon?"

She squirmed with need—resisting the urge to beg him.

"Perhaps it would help if you were blindfolded as well..."

He went over to his drawers again and pulled out another cravat. He tied it around her head, blinding her. This was a side of him she'd never seen before...and she liked it very much.

Since she couldn't see, the anticipation grew even more inside of her. So when she finally did feel him touch her, she groaned with the pleasure of it. The palm of his hand cupped her breast. He kneaded it, making her groan even louder.

"Do you like this?"

"Yes. Give me more."

Silence.

"No. You've been a very bad girl. You don't reward wickedness. You need to be punished first."

Oh, God. He was going to torture her with pleasure.

"I have been very, very bad. Perhaps you should spank me for my impudence."

"You'd like that, I think."

Noah pushed her legs open wide. Her knees were bent forward over her stomach. When his tongue touched the sensitive nub between her thighs, she nearly jumped from the intense pleasure. He kept licking over and over until she thought she couldn't bear it any more. Soon she'd explode around his sinful tongue. Then he stopped—leaving her unfulfilled.

"You were about to find your release. We can't have that yet."

Rubina cursed in Italian.

Noah laughed.

"You can't explode until I am buried deep inside of you, dear. It's the only way. Should we continue with your punishment?"

Sweat trickled down her forehead. He was killing her—it was glorious.

"Do your worst." She laughed. "I look forward to it."

"No, I don't think so." He joined her on the bed. The heat of his skin touched hers—the only indication she had that he was as naked as she was. "It's time we found bliss with each other."

Noah pushed her legs forward again. Slowly he pushed himself inside her tight channel. It stretched and burned, but it was the most wonderful thing she'd had happen to her in a long time. He stopped when he filled her completely.

"Wrap your legs around me," he demanded.

Rubina didn't need to be told twice. This was the only concession he'd given to her. He stroked in and out of her. Rubina moaned with each new thrust. Just when she thought she'd explode, he'd stop and suck one of her nipples into his warm mouth.

"Noah, please," she begged.

It seemed like forever. This constant battle of wills. He'd

bring her close only to deny her the pleasure she sought. It was driving her mad.

"How much do you want me?"

"I want it all, Noah. Give it to me now."

"No, tell me you want only what I can give you."

"Caro, only you can bring me such pleasure. I need you. Make me explode in your arms."

Rubina would say anything he wanted to make him continue.

"All you had to do was ask."

Noah pumped inside of her in rapid strokes. The need built up inside of her again. She tensed, waiting for him to stop again. He didn't, and she saw stars burst apart behind her eyes. Rubina screamed as it hit her. Noah stopped as he found his own release and groaned in pleasure. It had never been so intense before...

"Grazie..."

Noah rolled off of her. He untied her hands and removed her blindfold. Rubina was so weak she couldn't move a muscle. That had been the best...well...ever.

"You can return to your own room now."

He turned and walked into his dressing room, leaving her stunned.

What had just happened?

CHAPTER 9

Noah dipped his pen in the ink pot and wrote a few words into his account book. The words blurred in front of him. He tossed the pen down on his desk with frustration.

He couldn't stop thinking about Rubina.

Over the past month, they'd met in her bed chamber. He'd make love to her—leaving her weak and satisfied. As soon as they were done, he'd jump out of her bed as fast as he could. If he stayed, he would start begging her for things he knew she wouldn't give him.

He wanted her to stay—to love him like she used to.

This whole idea to have a child with her was slowly killing him. To have a small part of her wasn't nearly enough. If she didn't conceive soon, he'd be at her feet pleading with her. She already owned his heart. All he had left was his pride. Noah refused to give in completely to her. Surely she'd know if she were pregnant by now…

He'd ask her when he saw her again.

"For someone who prayed every day, for years, his wife would come back to him, you sure don't look like a happy man."

Noah looked up as Liam strolled into his study. For the first time in week he smiled.

"Where have you been?"

"At home." Liam's eyebrow rose. "You could have stopped by any time."

Noah sighed. "I've been busy."

Liam picked up a document and read it over. "Doesn't look too important. What's going on?"

"Rubina doesn't want to stay with me."

"I see." Liam sat down in front of Noah's desk. "Why?"

This was the hard part. The real reason he'd been avoiding visiting his best friend. How do you explain that the woman you married fell out of love with you? To make matters worse, she'd disappeared and let him believe she was dead for years. Only to return when she wanted to sever ties to be with someone else—a new man she claimed to love.

Even if she screamed his name each night as he made love to her. Noah had doubts she could possibly love the other man all that much. She crumbled at a mere touch from him. A woman in love with another man wouldn't be so ready to go to bed with someone else. Something wasn't adding up, but Noah had yet to figure out Rubina's game.

"She claims to love another."

"So why come back at all?"

Noah shrugged. "Hell if I know. She hasn't left the house the past month. I was going to hire someone to follow her, but she's stayed inside the entire time. It's baffling me."

"That doesn't sound like Rubina at all." Liam frowned. "Perhaps Gemma and Lily can get her to go out."

"Gemma and Lily?"

"Yes. Lily and Rand arrived a couple of days ago for a visit. Little William is a cute little tyke. Which reminds me..." Liam's lips twitched upward. "I'm going to be a father. Gemma just informed me she's pregnant."

Rubina might be pregnant... Part of him dreaded finding out. Then he'd have no reason to visit her bed again. It was the only thing she gave to him willingly. He both coveted and despaired the moment she'd inform him he'd be a father. If only he could look forward to it as Liam did.

"Congratulations." Noah smiled. "Now that's a reason to celebrate. I will get the brandy."

"No." Liam waved his hand. "I came by for a reason."

"Oh?"

"Gemma is having a dinner party. She's excited to have Lily around for a visit."

Noah didn't know if he wanted to drag Rubina over to Liam's for dinner. It might prove too much to have to pretend they were happy. Plus, he never did arrange to take her to a dressmaker. He'd have to rectify that as soon as possible. How was he to entice her to stay when he was being an abysmal husband?

"I see," he said. "When is this occasion to take place?"

"A few days' time." Liam smirked. "She'd have it tonight if she could make it happen. As it is, she'll be driving me mad for the next few days making all the arrangements."

"Who all is going to be in attendance?"

"My parents, you and Rubina, and of course Lily and Rand," Liam explained. "It shouldn't be too bad. I know how little you like to socialize."

No. Dinner with Liam's family would be wonderful. They had always been a second family to him. He'd yet to meet Lily's husband, and he looked forward to it. She apparently was rather happy living in South Carolina and running the plantation. These visits were few and far between. Her son, William, would only be around a year old. Noah was a little surprised she'd decided to travel with him still being so young.

"Why did Lily decide to visit?"

"My parents haven't been able to visit. They meant to after Gemma and I returned, but the business has been busy, and Father hasn't found time to travel. Lily, being the headstrong woman we all know her to be, took matters into her own hands. She says her son needs to know both his grandfathers and made the trip over. Rand has his hands full with her."

Noah remembered how happy he had been when he brought Ruby home. He'd been so happy. No doubt Lily's husband was equally so. "I'm sure he doesn't mind."

"No, he loves her. The poor bastard." Liam grinned. "I love her, but I kind of have to. She's my sister and all."

Noah wished he had a family as close as Liam. Some of the best memories he had were spending the holidays with him. The marriage of the Viscount and Viscountess of

Torrington was wonderful to see. It was the kind he'd hoped to have some day—one he thought he'd found with Rubina.

How wrong he'd been.

So wrong it hurt to think about. There wasn't anything he could do to change it. The energy it took to hold all the tears inside was excruciating. It was a battle he'd been fighting his whole life. The only difference between his childhood and now was he'd made this choice. His parents hadn't decided to leave. They'd been taken away from him.

Rubina chose to leave.

"He's lucky to have your sister."

"Damn right he is. He knows it too," Liam said. "All in all, he's a good man. Lily chose well. It's a good thing she has him. Running that plantation is hard work. From everything they've told me, it's an uphill battle. There is a lot of tension still after the War Between the States ended. I wouldn't want to deal with it."

"Right." Noah tried to focus on what Liam was saying, but it was getting hard to follow him. Something about Lily's home… "Is Gemma sending formal invitations?"

He had a lot on his mind. After Liam left he would arrange for the dressmaker to visit Rubina. She needed new gowns and one done fast. He didn't want her to feel out of place at the dinner party in one of her old dresses. She hadn't asked again, and he'd forgotten. It wasn't an excuse, but it's what happened.

"If I know my wife—and I do—she will. This is a heads up so you can prepare yourself. I know she's been wanting to come by and formally meet Rubina. Now that Lily is here, don't be surprised if she drops by one day."

Great, just what he needed to look forward to. Gemma had tact—Lilliana lacked it. She would blurt out what everyone else dared not. Noah had found it charming in the past. Now though, he dreaded it. He didn't want his life dissected. Was it too much to hope Lillian had mellowed since she married?

"How is your sister these days?" Noah asked. "I mean really. You said she's happy to be married and living with the heathens…"

"Yes?"

"Is she still the same spirited woman we always knew?"

"Did you miss the whole headstrong part of why she's here?"

"Right…" So he missed some important information while he'd been lost in thought. "I mean, is she as…blunt as she's always been?"

"I see. You want to know if she'd going to interrogate you or Rubina?"

Noah nodded. "I want to be prepared for anything. We all know how your sister can be."

"Well, then I'd prepare for her to storm the front lines, so to speak." Liam frowned. "She mentioned something about becoming reacquainted with Rubina. It didn't sound…good."

That was what Noah feared. Lily wouldn't let them get by with any deflection. When she asked a question she demanded an answer. Noah and Rubina had been getting along by not asking the hard questions. Perhaps it was time they were asked and answered. This impasse had been nice, but it was always doomed to crumble.

Noah sighed. "Duly noted." He scrubbed his hands over his face. What a mess.

"How are you doing really?"

"I'm not…" Noah didn't know how to answer it. "No matter what I say I'm not over her. I want to be. But for me… time didn't erase my feeling. I don't know if I can convince her to stay."

"Do you want her to?"

Yes. He did. But not if she wasn't happy. The past month opened his eyes in a lot of ways. She went willingly to his bed, and he loved her in every way possible. He couldn't hold back while he held her in his arms. If showing her how he felt wasn't enough, nothing would be.

"It doesn't matter what I want."

"Don't be ridiculous." Liam crossed his arms across his chest. "If you want her to stay, fight for her. Don't give in just because she says she loves another."

"It's not that easy."

Liam didn't understand. You couldn't fight for someone who didn't want to be fought for. Rubina made her choice. Noah would let her go. If she wasn't already pregnant, he'd let her go sooner than he had planned. He wouldn't hold her to a promise he'd demanded in anger.

"Nothing ever worth fighting for is," Liam stated. "If you love her, then tell her. Show her that this is the place she belongs. She should never have left. Make her want to be with you so much she lives and breathes it."

Was it possible? No, Noah wouldn't give in to false hope. It had already bit him in the arse hard. He shook his head. "Maybe you're right, but…"

Liam held up his hand. "No buts. Fight for her."

Noah let his mind roam to what it would be like if Rubina stayed. If she learned to love him again—to have children with her. Their lives so intertwined he couldn't see where she began and he ended. It was something he'd always wanted. He only dared to dream he could have it when he'd met her on his grand tour. When he first saw her… He knew she was the one for him. She'd been so beautiful in the moonlight. Their courtship had been fast, and he'd married her before he left. It wasn't until they got back to England that they'd started to fight. The realty of their life together hadn't been all sunshine and roses. Then, one day, she'd had enough and ran away.

He couldn't blame her. She'd been miserable.

"I don't know how to even begin to fight for her."

"You know Rubina better than anyone. Start there and woo her again. Show her that your love for her is enduring. You asked her for forever, and it's time she paid up."

Noah laughed. "You're right."

"You bet I am." Liam grinned. "I'm always right."

"Really?" Noah raised an eyebrow. "I'll have to ask Gemma about that when I see her again."

"Please don't." Liam shuddered. "I rather like sleeping with my wife each night. And with that, I really need to go home." Liam stood up. "Before I forget, I saw some strange man lingering across the street staring at your townhouse. Didn't like the looks of him. You might want to check him out."

"I will look into it." Noah frowned. Why would some ruffian be interested in his home? Were they thinking of robbing him? He would look into it later and order the house on full alert. "Thanks for coming by. I didn't realize how much I needed to talk to someone until you strolled through my door."

"Anytime." Liam waved as he left the room.

Noah sat back in his chair and steepled his fingers together. He had a lot of plans to make. His wife wouldn't know what hit her. Woo her? Oh, he intended to…

A siege of epic proportions was about to be enacted upon his wife—he couldn't wait to see her reaction.

For the first time in a month, Noah smiled. This was going to be fun.

CHAPTER 10

Rubina lay on top of her bed. The room spun as soon as she'd lifted her head. Whatever caused the vertigo to hit her, she wished it would go away. Becoming incapacitated was not conducive to her plans. She needed to know what was going on with the search for Paolo. Damian had not come by, and she was nervous. It couldn't be a good sign. What if something nefarious had happened to him? She swallowed back her fear. Her brother knew how to take care of himself. She couldn't worry about him.

"Pardon me, Your Grace…"

Rubina turned her head, slowly. She winced with the effort. Damned nuisance this was.

"Yes, Abby?"

"There are two ladies here to see you. Should I tell them you're not available?"

Who could possibly be coming to see her? She had no friends—sad but true. No one came to visit her. It was usually busybodies or someone Noah knew. Although, this could be a way for Damian to reach her—he probably didn't want to get questioned further by her husband.

"No. I will come down. I can't lay about in bed all day."

She could—but she wouldn't. There was far too much at stake.

"Yes, Your Grace." Abby turned to go.

"Wait," Rubina called to her. "Please have some refreshments brought into the sitting room, and tell our guests I will be with them shortly."

She took a deep breath and rolled off the bed. First, she'd have to make herself presentable. Rubina sat at her vanity and gasped. She looked like death warmed over... She must be coming down with something. Perhaps she shouldn't visit with anyone—no it might be important. Whatever malady had overcome her, she'd take the risk. This social call could very well be a life or death situation.

Rubina pinched her cheeks in an effort to bring color to her porcelain skin. She sighed when it didn't seem to do much good. Hopefully her guests weren't so rude as to comment upon it. Hard to say—depending on who it was. If it was some busybody—God help them. Rubina didn't have the patience for them.

She quickly discarded her dressing robe and put on her burgundy gown. It was a good thing she'd gotten used to so little clothing choices over her years locked away or she'd have been highly irritated with Noah's refusal to visit the dressmaker. Suggesting it had been an excuse for why she'd been so distracted. What she'd actually been doing was scanning the streets for any unsavory individuals. Paolo's men could be lurking anywhere...

Time to go face the music...

Rubina descended the stairs and entered the sitting room. She held back her reaction to the visitors awaiting her.

"Oh, good. We were thinking you were intentionally avoiding us." Lilliana strolled across the room and pulled her into a hug. "I don't want you to think that we're cross with you. I'm glad to see you alive—even if you do look rather pale. Are you feeling all right?"

"Lily." Gemma gasped. "No need to be rude."

Lilliana shrugged. "It's the truth, so why not speak it?"

"I'm fine really," Rubina reassured them. The last thing she needed was for them to start asking questions. It would lead to places she didn't want to go. "I was resting."

"Why didn't you tell your maid you weren't feeling up to company?" Lilliana asked.

Gemma glared at Lilliana.

"Don't start, Gemma. It's a reasonable question."

Ruby laughed. She could tell the two women were the best of friends. She wished she could have had something similar, but it hadn't been her fate. Lilliana had always been outspoken, and she'd liked that about her. Too bad she didn't still live in England. It would be nice to call her a friend—if she got past her supposed betrayal of Noah.

"I thought it might be important. No one stops in to see me," Rubina interrupted them.

Gemma stopped to stare at her. Her mouth fell open as shock filled her green eyes. "Are you saying you've locked yourself away in this mausoleum and haven't gone out to socialize once since you returned?"

Rubina paused. How to answer that? With the truth? "I went out to visit my brother."

"That is just...wrong." Lilliana frowned. "What is going on inside of Noah's head?"

"Don't be hard on him. It's not been an easy month."

Rubina didn't want them to think badly of Noah. None of the tension between them was his fault. He was only reacting to what she wanted him to believe.

One of the maids pushed in a cart with tea and little cakes. The smell filled Rubina's nose, and she swallowed back bile that rose up her throat. She quickly covered her nose to block the offending odor... What the hell had they put in those foul cakes?

"Will there be anything else, Your Grace?"

She shook her head. The maid curtsied and left the room.

Rubina wanted to order the cakes removed, but Lilliana was already picking one up and popping it in her mouth. Gemma looked over at them warily.

"I think I will pass on the cake," she said. "Just tea for me."

"More for me," Lilliana piped in. "They are delicious." She turned to Rubina and asked, "You want one."

She waved it around in her vicinity just enough for he to get a good whiff of it—and send Rubina running in the opposite direction. She stopped by a nearby vase and lost what little contents remained in her stomach. The cake smelled so sickeningly sweet...

"Oh dear," Gemma stated. "How far along are you dear?"

Sweat dripped down her forehead. What was wrong with her?

"What?"

Gemma didn't make sense. Far along for what?

She tilted her head and studied Rubina.

"These things happen you know. There is no reason to be embarrassed. They say it only happens in the mornings, but they are wrong. It has hit me at all times of the day and sometimes the most innocent smells hit me hard." She turned toward Lilliana. "Why don't you carry the tray of cakes out of the room? They are a bit much for her weak stomach at the moment."

Yes. Yes, they were. How did she know? They were horrid little pieces of square monstrosities. She'd have to order cook to never make them again. Her stomach didn't react well to them at all.

"Oh, you poor thing. Why didn't you say something? I'd never have put them anywhere near you. When I was pregnant with William, I couldn't stand to be around eggs. I had to make cook promise not to make any for months." Lilliana picked up the tray and left the room.

"What is she talking about?" Rubina asked Gemma.

They were talking nonsense. What did eggs have to do with anything she wasn't pregnant...was she?

"Oh, you didn't know did you?" Gemma patted her on the arm. "Have you noticed any other signs?"

"Signs?"

This was all so confusing. They had to be wrong. She couldn't be pregnant. All right, she could—but it was unlikely. She never once conceived the whole first six months of her marriage. She'd begun to wonder if she was perhaps barren...

"Do you feel tender?" Gemma leaned in and whispered, "You know, on your bosom?"

Rubina jerked back in horror. This was not something she wanted to discuss, but now that she thought about it...

"I can't be..."

"Are you sure?" Gemma asked. "You and Noah haven't..."

"No, no, no. We are not going there." Rubina paced. "Yes, of course we have, but this just..." She stopped as a horrified thought entered her mind. Noah would have no reason to make love to her again. He'd achieved his goal—and in record time.

Lilliana came back in the room. The tray was no longer in her hands. She stopped suddenly and stared at Rubina. "What's wrong?"

"She's a bit in shock. I don't think she realized she was you know...enceinte." Gemma gestured toward Rubina with her head.

"You can't tell him," Rubina said as panic seized her. "Promise me you won't say anything."

"It's not our place to tell Noah anything." Gemma frowned. "This is news that should come from you, but why don't you want him to know?"

Noah would distance himself even further from her if he knew she was carrying his child. This was what he wanted. He didn't really want her anymore. It was her fault—she'd made him hate her. After he made love to her, he practically ran away from her. He no longer held her afterward—it was an act of procreation. Even if it was hotter and more wild than it had ever been... She didn't want to give up the only reason she had to hold or touch her husband. He couldn't know yet. She'd tell him when she had no other choice.

"It's too soon..." What could she tell them that would get them to agree? "I don't want to..." She waved her hands wildly. "You know..."

Gemma smiled. "I think I understand. Nothing is guaranteed, and you want to be sure before you tell him."

Rubina nodded. "Yes. That's it."

Noah would have expectations, and he'd get even worse with his dictations too. This baby—or the idea of it—was the only thing he clung to. She'd destroyed his love for her. It had been a difficult thing to do. No one—except maybe Liam—knew how he felt about family. He'd lost everyone he loved far too young. This child would be his only remaining link to having that back. Rubina was just the vessel to give it to him.

"Don't worry, your secret is safe with us," Lilliana reassured her. Gemma nodded in agreement.

"What secret?"

Rubina froze. How much had Noah overheard?

Gemma turned and smiled. "Noah, how good of you to come and see us while we're here. I thought you'd be too busy to bother."

Noah frowned. "I was just coming in to tell Ruby I have some things to take care of and I wouldn't be home for dinner. I had no idea you or Lilliana were here."

Lilliana pouted. "So you're going to run away and not even visit for a little while?"

These two were a tag team of distraction. Rubina had never been so grateful in her life. They had effectively changed the subject of any kind of secret. Maybe Noah hadn't heard what they'd been discussing. She could only hope...

He shook his head. "No. Now tell me what you three are hiding?"

No such luck.

Lilliana sighed. "If you must know, Rubina was telling us how you haven't allowed her to socialize at all. I mean look at her? Has she even seen sun in days? Do you keep her locked up in her room all the time?"

If she'd been talking about Paolo that would have hit the mark.

"Don't be ridiculous. Rubina can come and go as she pleases."

It was time for Rubina to steer him in a different direction. "In these rags?' She held up the skirt of her burgundy gown. "I wouldn't want the ton to think you mistreat me."

Gemma turned and studied her dress and continued where Rubina left off. "She does have a point. Why haven't you taken her to Madame Roussard's?"

"Ah, the secret isn't much of one now is it?" Noah smiled. "That is the other thing I came to tell you. I've arranged for Madame and her assistant to come by today and fit you for a brand new trousseau. Perhaps Lilliana and Gemma can help you choose some new gowns. Get whatever you want. Don't worry about the expense."

"Truly?" Rubina raised an eyebrow. "You're not saying that because we've guilted you into it?"

Noah grinned. "I would have done it sooner, but it slipped my mind."

Rubina didn't know what to make of his attitude—he was pleasant. Perhaps it was because his friends were visiting. Maybe he didn't want them to know how strained their relationship had become. If so, she'd willingly play the game for him. She didn't want to cause him any more undo heartache.

"Oh, this is going to be wonderful." Lilliana clapped her hands together. "I haven't gotten any new gowns in forever. Do you think she'd measure us all?"

Noah tilted his head and frowned. "Tell her to charge whatever the cost to my account—for the inconvenience. Tell her your own husbands can pay for your gowns. They can very well afford it."

"I'm going to pass for now. I'm going to need larger gowns soon. I might as well wait," Gemma said.

Noah smiled. "Liam told me your good news. Congratulations." He leaned down and kissed her cheek. "You will make a wonderful mother."

Rubina turned and stared at her. That is what she'd meant earlier. She'd not put two and two together. Her mind wasn't functioning as it normally did.

"Thank you." Gemma smiled. "One day you'll make a wonderful father too."

Noah's eyes grew distant at her words. Maybe he was remembering that she'd be the child's mother—or he believed he'd be raising their child on his own. Whatever the reason, Rubina didn't like it. She would never abandon her child. Her hand hovered above her stomach—Noah couldn't know yet. If she gave him any signs, she'd lose him entirely. She wasn't ready to let him go. Rubina let her hand fall back to her side.

"One day I may be lucky enough to have a child. For now, I will leave parenthood to you and Liam." He smiled, but it didn't reach his eyes. "Now I must say goodbye. Enjoy your time with the dressmaker."

He turned on his heels and left the room.

He took her heart with him.

"All right, spill it. What is really going on between you two?" Gemma demanded.

Rubina turned to stare at her. "I'm afraid my husband no longer loves me, and I'm afraid it's very much my fault."

She burst into tears and ran from the room. Gemma and Lilliana could deal with Madame Roussard when she arrived. Rubina just couldn't handle any more company.

CHAPTER 11

The women were acting strange. Noah couldn't think about what that little scene had meant. He'd started the process; he needed to court his wife. He hoped his actions wouldn't prove foolish. Love shouldn't be so damned hard.

He scrubbed his hand over his face.

Thinking about the difficulties life had thrown him wouldn't get him anywhere. There were plans to be made. If he had any hope of winning Rubina's love again, he had to stop letting his thoughts drift down paths it shouldn't. Whatever had driven her away before—he'd do everything in his power to prevent it this time around. It was time to start considering it the gift it was. He had his wife back. For now, that was enough. Time was finally on his side. She wouldn't be running off until she gave him an heir.

Arranging for Madame Roussard to do a fitting in the comfort of their home was just the beginning. Maybe, with new dresses, he could coax her out of the townhouse and attend a few social functions. The first would be Gemma's dinner party. They appeared to be getting along, so Rubina would be less likely to object to attending. Then, after a while, they could start accepting offers to balls and soirees. Rubina used to be a social butterfly. Something was—different. Noah couldn't pinpoint it, but she seemed to be more content staying inside. The only time she'd willingly left was to go see her brother.

Another thing he must deal with. Damian hadn't been by. This secrecy between Rubina and her brother was irritating him. He had to know what they were hiding. So he had one very important errand on his list—someone who could help him get to the bottom of it all.

The carriage stopped outside a jewelry shop. Noah stepped out and walked inside. One of the first errands on his list—ladies loved jewelry right?

"Hello, Your Grace. May I help you."

Noah nodded at the jeweler. He knew him rather well. It was the establishment he'd purchased all of Rubina's gifts before. The benefit of having a standing account with them gave him superior service. As long as he paid his bills, the jeweler's eyes lit up when he walked in. The last item he'd purchased was Pearla's engagement ring. He hadn't expected to return to purchase gifts for Rubina. It was odd, but good.

"I need to commission something special for my wife."

Noah could almost see the excitement twinkle from his eyes. A special commission would garner a hefty sum, but his wife was worth it. Nothing was too good for her.

"What did you have in mind?"

Noah explained what he wanted for Rubina. It was part of his big surprise. One that would take a lot of secrecy and planning—but he hoped in the end it would prove worth it. This was his whole life he was fighting for. He loved Rubina more than words could explain.

"Do you think it is possible?"

"Yes. It is very much possible. How soon would you require it?"

Noah thought about it. How to put a time limit on winning his wife back? This could tip the scales in his favor, but it was hard to tell. He could only hope.

"Can you have it ready in two weeks?"

"Certainly, Your Grace."

"Good." Noah smiled. "Now I'd like to look at your selection of necklaces."

"Did you have something in mind?"

"Rubies."

"I have just the thing." The man walked over to a safe, pulled out a black box, and then brought it back to Noah. "These were recently finished."

Inside, lying against black velvet, was a ruby pendant shaped like a teardrop. It was flanked by brilliant white diamonds trailing all the way to the clasp, a matching pair of ear bobs were nestled next to it.

"It's perfect." Noah gestured toward it. "Wrap it up. I would like to take it with me today."

"Certainly." The jeweler nodded.

Noah picked up the wrapped package and tucked it under his arm for safe keeping. "Let me know when my other item is ready."

"Yes, Your Grace."

Noah nodded and stepped out of the shop. One of his stops wasn't going to be as pleasant. It would take place in a seedier part of the town. Not a good idea to bring an expensive necklace with him. He went to his carriage and told his drive to take him to his club. He could put it in the lockbox there until he was ready to go home.

It didn't seem to take long before the carriage was stopping once again. Noah hopped out of the carriage and headed into Whites. He was immediately greeted by one of the club owners.

"A pleasure to see you, Your Grace. It's been a while."

"I've been busy. Can you put this in your lockbox until I'm ready to leave?"

"Yes, Your Grace."

Noah handed him the package and strolled into a private room. A waiter came by and took his drink order.

Liam strolled into the room. "I thought I saw you come in."

"Just a quick stop. I have a meeting in an hour."

"What for?"

"I'm going to hire an investigator. I need to know what happened to Rubina three years ago."

Liam frowned. "Don't you think it would be easier to ask her?"

Nothing about his wife's return had been easy. She didn't seem to want to talk about her time away—other than to tell him she no longer loved him. Something was driving her. Noah needed to know what that was.

"Not at all."

The waiter set his drink in front of him. Noah picked it up and swallowed the contents.

"So you decided not to woo her?"

Noah shook his head. "I didn't say that. I've already started the plans to do that. Which reminds me—I need your help."

He explained to him what he had in mind. Liam would be instrumental in helping him pull a lot of it off.

Liam whistled. "When you decide to court a woman, you go big."

"If you're not going to do it right, why bother?"

"You make a valid point." Liam nodded. "Do you think it will work?"

It better. He was banking everything on it.

"I will do some little things to lead up to it. If she's willing to stay with me forever, then she will know in a couple of weeks." Noah could only hope it all worked as he foresaw it. "I have a plan, and I intend to have everything I want— including my wife."

"You think two weeks is enough time?"

Noah smiled. "She agreed to marry me in two days the first time I courted her. I think two weeks is plenty of time."

Rubina had shined brighter than the stars the first time he saw her. No other woman ever compared or ever would. Once she owned his heart, he knew he would never feel the same way about anyone else. He didn't give his heart to her lightly. Once Noah loved, it was forever. Now he needed her to see she still loved him too. He believed with everything he was that she still did.

"For your sake, I hope you're right. I know how miserable you were without her."

Liam only saw a little of how much he hurt after Rubina supposedly died. He'd lost himself for so long without her. His best friend picked up the pieces and put him back together—at least as much as Noah had allowed him to. He was never completely whole again. Rubina was his other half. Now he had her back, and he'd be damned before he lost her again. For a little bit, all he saw was his own injured pride. No more. It was time to do something instead of wallow in self pity.

"This will work. Tell me you can pull off your end."

"I can, but I don't know if I will be able to hide it from Gemma."

Noah smiled. "She can keep a secret. If I know your wife, she'll want to help. So tell her and enlist her planning abilities to my cause."

"Gemma does have a romantic heart—all right, I will tell her when I get home."

Noah laughed. "About that..."

Liam scrunched his eyebrows together. "Why don't I like the sound of that?"

"When I left, Lily and Gemma were about to help Ruby with a dress fitting. Don't be surprised if you get a bill from the seamstress."

Liam waved his hand. "That's fine. She'll probably need new dresses soon anyway and I don't mind the expense."

Noah understood. He'd buy Rubina the world if she'd take it. Whatever made her stay with him...

"I hate to cut this short, but I have a meeting to get to."

"Why don't I come along." Liam stood. "I don't have anything pressing to do."

Noah nodded. "I'm walking over. I will have to stop back here to pick up a package before I go home."

"Lead the way."

They exited the club and headed to a tavern down the street. The establishment they entered was a bit seedier than the one they'd left. It had a lot of commoners inside and bar maids that moonlighted as doxies.

"Can I help you guv'nor?" One of the maids approached them. She had stringy black hair and a very generous bosom —fully on display.

"I'm looking for Marcus Shepard."

"What you wanting him for?" Her lips pursed in displeasure. "He's not a fun fellow." She skimmed the back of her hand down his arm. "I can promise you pleasure you'll never forget."

Noah repressed a shudder. He only wanted one woman —his wife.

"Just tell me where he is."

"What about you?" She turned to Liam. "You like pleasure?" She wiggled her eyebrows suggestively.

Liam coughed and covered his mouth with his hand. After he got control over his laughter, he said, "I'm not looking for any amusements. Can you tell us where the gentleman is?"

The barmaid pouted. "Suit yourself. You don't know what you're missing. Marcus is over there at the corner table sitting by hisself. He don't much like company."

She walked way in a huff—clearly disappointed neither of them wanted the charms she offered.

"She's a character," Liam said.

"Not my type." Noah headed to the table Marcus was sitting at. "Hello, Mr. Shepard."

He glanced up—his gaze sharp and piercing as he studied Noah. "The Duke of Huntly, I presume?"

Noah nodded. "Yes."

"You brought company." He gestured toward Liam.

"This is Liam Marsden."

Marcus Shepard stared at Liam and smiled.

"The son of Viscount Torrington?"

Liam scowled. "You know my father?"

"We've—how do I put this—had business dealings in the past."

Liam held up his hand. "I don't want to know."

The man grinned. "Probably best you don't."

Noah didn't much care what Viscount Torrington hired him to do as long as he did his job well. "You come highly recommended. How good are you at tracking down information?"

"I'm the best." He tilted his head toward Liam. "Ask his father."

"I don't have to," Noah informed him. "He's the one that told me to seek you out."

It was Liam's turn to be shocked. He turned toward Noah and asked, "When did you see my father?"

Noah shrugged. "He stopped by a couple weeks ago. I

told him about my concerns and he gave me a name to help me out. I'm just now using the information."

Viscount Torrington didn't ask for details. He'd taken one look at Noah and wrote down Marcus Shepard's name and handed it to him. Said when he wanted answers to seek him out. Now, it was time to finally find out what happened to his wife three years ago. It wasn't as simple as she made it all seem.

"What you need me to do?" Marcus leaned on the table. "I don't kill people, so we get that straight. I try to do things honorably—even if others in the company do some shady business from time to time—we all draw a line at killing people."

"I need you to investigate my wife's disappearance—three years ago. She returned suddenly, and it is all a bit—strange."

"I can do that." He frowned. "It will take some time. The trail is probably a bit cold at this point."

"You have two weeks," Noah explained. "I'm working on a timeline."

"That might be impossible—all I can do is try."

Noah nodded. "I also need someone trustworthy that can watch her when she leaves the house. I think she might be in danger." The man Liam had mentioned outside Noah's townhouse made him uneasy. He didn't know for sure if he meant them harm, but he had to be careful where his wife was concerned.

Marcus tilted his head and studied Noah. "I have a couple colleagues that will welcome the blunt. They are good at what they do. She won't even know they are there."

"Perfect." Noah stood. "One more thing. I don't want her to know any of this. So be careful when you send communications."

"I can be discreet." Marcus smiled. "It's what makes me so good at what I do."

"I look forward to your report." Noah tilted his head. "Until we meet again."

Liam got up and followed him out of the establishment.

"You really think Rubina is in danger?"

Noah didn't know why he felt it—but the niggling feeling wouldn't go away. It festered deep inside his gut whenever she was around. She was always nervous. Not once since she returned had she actually relaxed. His wife was so jumpy; even the smallest noise startled her. That spoke volumes to him.

"Yes. I don't know what's going on, but I will find out." He frowned. "I think this supposed lover of hers is a ruse. She's afraid of something, but I just don't know what it is."

They stopped off at Whites, and he grabbed his gift for Rubina.

"I hope it's not as serious as you think. When Gemma's cousin Alfie attacked me, the thought of losing my wife scared me. I don't know what I would do without her. I know you went through hell when you thought Rubina died."

They exited Whites and headed toward Noah's carriage.

"I know. I'm glad that all turned out well. You and Gemma are good together."

Liam smiled. "I have never been happier."

"Now I must return home to my wife." Noah stopped in front of his carriage. "I will see you in a couple of days at the dinner party."

Liam waved goodbye as Noah entered the carriage.

It had been a long and productive day. He couldn't wait to get home. The drive seemed longer than usual, but they were stopping outside his townhouse before he knew it. He hopped down and entered.

"Your Grace," Madame Roussard greeted him with a curtsy. She pulled on her gloves in preparation to leave. "I've gotten all the measurements I need for your wife's trousseau."

"Did it go well?"

"It did—I have to say the ladies with Her Grace were very helpful. It took a lot of coaxing to get her to do the fitting." Madame Roussard's lips formed a very thin line. "I was sad to see them leave. They had other appointments to get to."

Noah frowned. Rubina said she wanted dresses. Why would she refuse a fitting?

"But you were able to complete it?"

She nodded. "Indeed. I did say I got all the measurements. She was—rather weepy, but that doesn't matter for measuring."

"Can you have a gown ready in two days?"

She nodded. "I will send the first one over right away. I know she needs something for the dinner party. The rest will require some time to complete."

Noah didn't like knowing she didn't have the attire befitting her station. He should have done something sooner. His pride had made him into a terrible husband.

"Spare no expense. I want her to have some new gowns as soon as possible."

"Yes, Your Grace."

"The special dress…"

"Will be ready in time. You have my word."

Noah nodded. "Thank you."

Madame Roussard smiled. "No. Thank you, Your Grace. Your generosity will keep me in business for years."

She nodded and left the townhouse.

Noah stared down the hall. It was time to see what mood his wife was in and if she'd be receptive to the surprise he bought her. He'd never been so nervous in his life—even when he'd proposed to her. Back then Rubina had been a sure thing. Now she was anything but.

CHAPTER 12

Rubina paced her bedchamber.

The seamstress and her assistant had left several hours ago. She hadn't been brave enough to leave her room and demanded a light meal sent to her. The idea of facing her husband—terrified her. How could she keep her pregnancy from him? All he wanted was to be a father. She destroyed any possibility of having a life with him. This was the one thing she could give him... But Rubina couldn't help the selfishness filling her heart. She wanted to feel his arms wrapped around her and the sweetness of him loving her each night.

If he knew she'd conceived it would be lost to her.

So, for a little while longer, she'd hold back the truth. Until she had no choice but to tell him she carried his child. Rubina rubbed her hand over her still flat stomach. It wouldn't take long before the evidence would be clear. She'd not be able to hide her growing belly. Their child nestled in her womb growing more each day—it was truly a miracle. Part of her was so happy her heart burst with excitement...

The other part of her feared the day she'd be forced to once again abandon her heart.

Paolo had to die. It was the only way she could have a chance with Noah and their child. She had to go see Damian. His absence was starting to make her nervous. What if Paolo had gotten to him? After Noah left her for the night, she'd sneak out to visit him. It was the only way she could ensure her husband wouldn't trail after her.

It was the first time she was grateful he left after he made love to her. There was a time when Noah couldn't leave her for even a moment—before she destroyed the love he had for her. Then, he'd hold her through the night, wake up, and make love to her all over again. These days he couldn't get away from her fast enough.

A light knock on her bedroom door startled her out of her thoughts. Noah had come to make love to her again.

It was their nightly ritual. He'd pleasure her until she didn't think she could take any more, and then, he'd jump out of her bed as if scalded. Nothing hurt as much as seeing him run from her. It was her cross to bear. She'd made this choice, and she had to live with the consequences.

"Rubina?"

"Come in," she called out.

The door opened slowly. Noah peeked his head inside. "Are you all right?"

Rubina frowned. "Of course. Why wouldn't I be?"

Noah entered the room and shut the door with a soft click.

"The seamstress said you hadn't wanted to do the fitting."

Stupid Madame Roussard and her wagging tongue. Why did she have to go and tell him that she'd almost turned her away? At least Lily and Gemma had still been around to talk sense into her. Noah would have been suspicious if she hadn't ordered some new gowns. Now he was asking her questions she didn't want to answer.

"I was in a mood earlier. It has passed."

He studied her. "Why were you crying?"

Rubina struggled with the urge to look at herself in her mirror. How did he know? Were her eyes still red and puffy? "I don't know what you mean." Denial might still work if she played it well.

"Don't lie to me, Ruby."

Drat it. How was she going to distract him from this line of questioning? Maybe seduction was all she had left. She sashayed over to him and trailed her fingers down his chest.

"Me, lie?" She batted her eyelashes at him coquettishly. "Why would I?"

"Ruby…"

She palmed his manhood. He hissed with pleasure under her ministrations.

"Yes, *caro*?"

"Don't think I'm letting this go." He wrapped his fingers around her wrist, halting her progress. She looked up into his eyes and saw the fire burning in within them. "I know what you're trying to do."

"I'm trying to entice you into my bed." She raised an eyebrow. "That should be rather obvious."

He lifted her hand and kissed her fingers. "We have time. We don't need to rush. Tell me what upset you."

Noah wasn't going to be so easily distracted. Why couldn't he let it go? She would have to try a different tactic to get him off this topic. She couldn't—wouldn't—tell him why she was so weepy.

"Don't we?" she asked, disgust filling her voice. "You seem to run away rather quickly once you finish with me each night."

He nodded. "I understand."

It was Rubina's turn to be confused. What did he understand? Rubina sure didn't. He was almost—nice. Her husband had been so indifferent toward her for weeks. Now he wanted to talk and show concern? Something changed; she just didn't know what it was.

She tilted her head and studied him. Compassion filled his warm brown eyes. She gulped back a lump in her throat. "Well then, please…" She flipped her hand backward. "Do explain this epiphany you've had."

"It's my fault."

Rubina frowned. What did he think was his fault? He wasn't to blame for the choices she'd made. He'd been wonderful considering…

"I must be daft because I have no clue what you're talking about."

He cupped her face in the palm of his hand. "I've been dreadful to you. I'm sorry."

Rubina stepped back out of his reach. Her heart broke into

a million pieces. She'd done this to him. He didn't know which way was up and what was down any more. This whole charade had made him doubt everything in his life. He hadn't hurt her—not intentionally any way. This was her doing. He'd never have put her through any of this misery if not for her lies.

"I don't blame you," she said softly. "The last several weeks have been trying on us both."

"No." He shook his head. "I won't let you absolve me of this guilt. I made you cry, and I have to make it up to you. I always did hate seeing you so sad."

"Noah, stop," Rubina demanded. "You are not the reason I was crying."

At least not directly…

He smiled. "So you admit it. You were crying earlier?"

Oh, drat—her husband was a clever man. How had she forgotten that? Rubina sighed. "Yes, I was crying, but it had nothing to do with you."

"So are you going to tell me what brought tears to your eyes?"

Rubina bit her lip. There was no getting out of this interrogation. How did she ever think she could? "No."

His head jerked back, startled. "No?"

"I'm not going to tell you. I don't care to discuss it."

Rubina had a stubborn streak, and she fully intended to lean on it. It was the only recourse left to her. Noah could take it or leave it—either way, she wasn't about to explain to him why her life was falling apart. She had to protect him and their unborn child. When the time was right, she'd tell him everything. Now was not that time.

He rocked back on his heels. "I see."

Did he? Rubina was afraid he saw far too much. "Good. Now do you want to do something more pleasant?"

"No."

It was her turn to jerk back. His words were like a slap to the face. "I don't understand."

"You don't need to." Noah sighed. "It's time we did things a little different. Somewhere along the way we lost sight of what we meant to each other."

Rubina nodded. She understood that much. The years

apart—years they'd lost because of Paolo—had destroyed something between them. Her lies held the distance in place.

"I know."

"This whole time I've been trying not to love you—to need you—but I don't think it's possible. It's tearing me apart." Noah reached for her and pulled her into his arms. "It's making me need you—want you—so much more. It's not enough though."

"What do you want from me?"

Rubina was growing more and more confused with each word he uttered. This was a side of her husband she hadn't seen, well, since they married. They'd fought so much when they left Italy. England had bridged a gap between them—like a city divided upon itself. They were both stubborn and believed they were right. They had failed to compromise. Maybe this was the silver lining she'd been hoping for. If he was able to forgive her when he didn't have all the facts... There could be hope for them once they found themselves on the other side of the mess Paolo had made of their lives. Noah didn't know they had another battle to get through yet.

He pleaded with her. "I want a chance."

"A chance for what?"

"To win you back to have the life we originally planned." He started to unpin her hair. It fell down in blonde waves down her back. "To make you love me again."

Rubina gasped. "That's not possible."

Because she never stopped loving him—he couldn't make her feel something she'd never lost.

"It is, and I intend to make it happen."

"No..."

"Yes. This is a war I intend to win." He trailed kisses down her face and neck. "Trying not to love you isn't working for me—it only makes me love you more."

Her eyes watered, and tears trailed down her cheeks. She couldn't tell him she still loved him. Not yet. Still her heart soared to hear him say the words.

"Please, don't say these things."

They broke her. How could she keep her resolve when he tore down her walls with such sweet words? It would make it even more difficult to let him go if she couldn't find Paolo.

"I will say them every day until they sink in." Noah lifted her chin. Rubina refused to meet his gaze. "Look at me."

His voice was harsh. Rubina lifted her eyes to meet his. They were full of heat and a storm of need.

"Two weeks."

"What is in two weeks?" she asked.

"Give me two weeks. If I can't win your love back by then, I will let you go."

This didn't make any sense to her. What had changed? "What about your desire for an heir."

Noah let her go and took a step back. "We haven't conceived by now. I think it's for the best. If you decide to stay, we can try again. For now, I think it is best we abstain from that part of our marriage. It was foolish of me to think to bring a child into a marriage on the brink of falling apart."

Rubina choked back a lump in her throat. He didn't want to make love to her anymore. This was all wrong… She should tell him, but what good would that do. Her husband now believed a child was the wrong thing to bring into their marriage. Stupid—so, so stupid—how could she have messed this all up so horribly?

"So what will you require of me then?" Rubina was almost afraid to ask. "If you no longer require a child from me, I'd like to know what this two weeks is for?"

Noah smiled. "Oh, we will share a bed. We will remain chaste for now."

"You need to explain what you want, Noah. This doesn't make sense to me."

"The simple answer is I'm going to court you."

Rubina frowned. "You don't share a bed with a woman you are courting."

"I realize that, but I have my reasons."

"I don't like this." Rubina paced the room. "What happens at the end?"

"If you still want to leave, I won't stand in your way."

"And if I want to stay?"

This was all rather—strange.

"Then I will do everything and anything to ensure you are the happiest woman for the rest of our life together." He stalked forward. Rubina took a step back. "And when I make love to you that night, it will be so good." He smiled wickedly, "…You'll beg me to give you more."

"What if I don't want to give you this time?"

"On this, I must insist. Two weeks isn't a long time. You were going to give me months before." He grabbed her again and pulled her back into his arms. "Say yes, Ruby."

How could she say no?

"You sure you don't want to make love?"

He laughed. "I think you're worth waiting for."

"So tonight we are just going to sleep together?"

He kissed her lightly. "I look forward to holding you all night. I've been denying myself the pleasure for way too long."

How had she gotten so lucky? Surely she had the best husband in the world. Rubina didn't deserve him, but she wasn't going to turn him down. Maybe this was for the best. At least she'd still have him with her each night. It would give her a little more time to deal with the Paolo situation. There was only one problem: she couldn't sneak away to meet Damian. She'd have to find another way to meet with her brother. It was time to deal with her nemesis once and for all. This was all driving her crazy.

As to Noah's request… She could at least give him the answer he sought.

"All right," she agreed. "I will give you your two weeks."

"I never doubted you'd say yes."

CHAPTER 13

Noah stared blankly down at the report Marcus had sent him. His wife had left the house in the early morning hour and went to visit her brother. She hadn't been inside long enough for a visit though. It appeared as if Damian had been out.

Noah couldn't help wondering where he was, but that wasn't his biggest concern.

Rubina had sneaked out of bed. Falling asleep with her nestled in his arms had been a little piece of heaven. Noah had been sound asleep when she decided to pay her brother a visit. It made him wonder how long she'd been planning to go to see Damian. Why was it necessary to go so early in the morning—well before regular visiting hours. Social calls happened in the late morning hours. The Albany didn't encourage female visitors before then. Noah was rather surprised she gained entrance at all.

This all had to do with whatever secret she kept from him. Marcus had better find some answers soon. He needed to know the truth. This pretending game his wife had going on was going to break them soon if he didn't. He scrubbed his hands over his face. This was becoming an obsession. Jealousy was an ugly emotion, and Noah had it flowing through him in waves. The problem was he didn't know exactly what he had to be jealous of. As the days went by, he firmly believed his wife didn't love another man.

At least not the way a lover did.

The strong bond she shared with her brother though—this secret had to do with him. Noah would bet his entire estate on it. Damian was at the center of it all. Whatever they were hiding was the reason Rubina closed herself off to him. It might not be entirely about her brother, but he did know the truth. It was that knowledge that drove his jealousy. She turned to her family—instead of him. For Noah, Rubina was his family. She was the one person he'd go through the fires of hell for.

They deserved to find happiness. Whatever tore them apart before had to be put behind them. Noah planned to see that happen one way or another. Rubina was his wife, and he intended on loving her for the rest of his days. No other woman would ever hold his heart. He didn't believe, for one second, she'd stopped loving him either. Whatever her reasons were for her lies had to be strong. She was too willing to walk into his arms and let him make love to her. A woman in love with another man would find a way to run in the opposite direction.

His wife practically begged him to love her—without saying the actual words.

That spoke loudly to him. What she wanted was perfectly in line with his own wishes. It was time he listened to the truth. This courtship idea was a way for her to see his words matched what he wanted for them. When Noah made a promise he kept it.

Now, as for her morning visit—she'd have to answer some questions. Her safety was his highest priority. He didn't want her sneaking out on a regular basis. There was always a chance the men he hired might miss her. Noah couldn't take a chance she'd slip away and some kind of harm come to her. He'd lost her once, and he refused to let something nefarious happen again. He folded the missive and put it in his desk drawer. It was time to have a conversation with Rubina.

Noah found her in the sitting room. Her face was rather pale. That seemed to be her usual hue lately. A momentary concern came over him as he observed her. What could be ailing her?

"Hello, dear," he said as he entered the room. "How was your morning?"

Rubina glanced up. "It was splendid. I paid Gemma a visit. I know we are going to be dining there this evening, but I wanted to get out for a little while."

The truth—but not the whole truth. Rubina had gone to see Gemma Marsden. She just made another stop first. He found it interesting she neglected to tell him about visiting Damian. It was one more reason he knew there was something big she hid from him. He would find out what it was soon enough. Noah wouldn't press her—yet. Part of him hoped she'd come to him with the information on her own.

"I trust you found her well?"

She smiled. "As well as a woman who is enceinte can be. She was a little green when I dropped in. The babe is making her ill in the morning hours."

"I'm surprised she felt well enough to visit." Noah frowned. "If she was feeling out of sorts, she should have rested instead of entertaining."

"Gemma is perfectly capable of sitting down and having a conversation." Rubina glared at him, her voice filled with disapproval. "A woman doesn't become an invalid because she is carrying a child."

Noah rocked back on his heels. "I didn't mean to imply she was…"

Rubina interrupted him, "Furthermore, we are more resilient than you think we are. Women are capable of doing a great many things. We do not need to be coddled."

"I see."

And he did.

Noah saw things very clear. His wife was making a big deal over Gemma's pregnancy. It made him wonder if she wasn't telling him something… It would explain her pale complexion. Though he hadn't witnessed any other signs, it could be he was hoping for something that wasn't actually true. He wanted a child. More importantly he wanted one with his wife.

She nodded. "It's best you do."

"Oh, I assure you, I understand perfectly."

Rubina narrowed her eyes into tiny slits and studied him. "What exactly do you think you understand?"

Bloody hell... He might have gone too far. It was time to distract her. "I noticed you left our bed rather early this morning."

She waved her hand dismissively. "I had trouble sleeping."

"You could have woken me up. I would have kept you company."

"No." She shook her head. "You slept so soundly. I didn't want to disturb your rest. I'm capable of seeing to myself."

Noah frowned. It sounded reasonable. Perhaps he was not seeing things as clearly as he'd thought. She seemed fine. Even the color was returning to her cheeks. Sometimes he just saw what he wanted to see. In this case maybe he was only hoping his wife carried his child... She seemed as resilient as she claimed.

"Did you go anywhere else this morning?"

"No."

She lied. Why would she hide her visit to her brother? It didn't make sense.

"Damian hasn't been by. I thought he said he would come for a visit."

Her head jerked up. Fear filled her eyes—she quickly hid it. Not before he saw the flash of it fill them though. Rubina was worried. When he responded to Marcus's missive he'd add another assignment. Damian needed to be found.

"I'm sure he found something to keep him busy."

She hid it well, but Noah knew her. Her lower lip quivered a tiny bit before she answered him. Rubina was worried something had happened to her brother. What though—Noah could only guess. Maybe it was time to push her to give him the answers.

No. She would close up even more. It had to be her idea.

"You're right. Damian always did follow his own path. No doubt he's found something amusing to keep him busy over the past several weeks." He bowed his head toward her. "If you'll excuse me, I'm going to change for dinner."

"Yes. I should retire to my chambers as well." She stood

up next to him. "My new gown was delivered this morning. It's beautiful—the color of rubies. Madame Roussard is a genius with the needle."

"I'm glad you liked it." Noah smiled. She would like his other gift to. He intended to fasten it around her neck himself after she was dressed.

"It's lovely." She smiled. "Perhaps the prettiest gown I've ever owned."

"Come, I'll escort you up to your room." Noah held out his arm to her.

Rubina smiled. "I'd like that."

They strolled up the stairs. He stopped just outside her room. She glanced up at him through a hooded gaze. She seemed to be waiting for something from him.

"I'll meet you downstairs when it's time to depart."

Disappointment filled her eyes as he took a step back.

"Yes." She toyed with her hands, anxiety filled her voice. "I…"

Noah pulled her into his arms. A small gasp escaped her lovely mouth. He took the opportunity to press his lips against hers. Her fingers quickly wound around his neck, allowing him to pull her further into his embrace. The kiss was filled with so much passion it burned inside of him. If he pushed it, they'd be making love in her room in mere seconds. He wanted to strip her and kiss every inch of her.

But he had to be strong. This was a courtship. It didn't matter if they were married. He had to show her respect. Make her realize she could trust him and that he would always keep his word. They would have nothing if she couldn't learn to believe he'd always protect her.

So he took a step back. It was the hardest thing he'd ever done.

"Why did you stop?"

Her breathing was ragged and desire shone brightly in her eyes.

Noah smiled. "I can't very well ravish the woman I am courting. It wouldn't be proper."

Rubina pouted. She ran her fingers down his chest. "I wouldn't mind. I like it when you're not entirely proper."

Noah laughed. He leaned down and placed a quick kiss on her forehead. "Not tonight, dear. We made a deal, and I am sticking to it. Now, be good and I'll bring you a present in a little while."

Her lips tilted into a coy smile. "Does it involve you giving me something I really want?"

"Please," he begged. "I'm only a man—flesh and bone. I can only take so much temptation before I give in."

"One would certainly hope so." She cupped his cheek in the palm of her hand. "You know you want to kiss me again. Just one little kiss... What could it hurt?" She blinked her eyelashes at him as she flirted. "Kiss me like you mean it, Noah."

How could he say no?

So he swooped down and kissed her as if his life depended on it. The truth was it very well might. He could stop at any time. She was his drug—one he willingly succumbed to. How did he think he could survive two whole weeks without making love to her? Somewhere along the way he'd lost his bloody mind.

He tore himself away from her. Her lips were plump from his kisses... It made her even more beautiful to him. Noah shook his head and took several steps back. If he didn't, he'd pull her back into his arms, and then there would be no turning back.

"Love me, Noah."

He jerked his head up and met her gaze. It was filled with such decadent promises. Ones he knew she could and would fulfill if he took her up on them. He couldn't though. This had to go the way he planned. It did not include him giving in a little more than a day.

"Always..."

"Then join me. Show me how much."

"No," he croaked, his voice raw with emotion. "Don't ask me again."

Noah spun on his heels and headed toward his room. One more second and he'd have been stripping every piece of clothing off of Rubina. Then they'd never make it to Liam and Gemma's dinner party. The tether he had on his control was slipping each moment he spent in her company. Soon he'd be on his knees begging her to love him. When that day came he hoped she took pity on him.

If Rubina refused to admit she loved him... Noah would be lost for good.

CHAPTER 14

Rubina sat in front of her vanity staring blankly at her reflection. She would have to move soon. Noah was probably already waiting for her... The dinner party should be something she looked forward to. It was meant to be a light evening amongst family and friends. Instead, she had other worries.

Noah was being rather lovely. Every moment she loved even more than the one before, but she still couldn't bring herself to tell him everything. A decision had to be made. Damian wasn't in his rooms. She'd checked when she attempted to visit him.

Where could he be?

"Trust me, you couldn't be more beautiful if you tried." Noah leaned down and kissed the top of her head. "What's troubling you?"

She had been so lost in her own thoughts that she hadn't heard him approach. Rubina bit her bottom lip. The truth on the tip of her tongue—she swallowed it back. This wasn't the time. Without all of the facts, she couldn't spill her innermost fears.

"I'm not sure I'm up to company tonight."

Truth... The idea of spending time laughing with friends was the last thing she needed. Damian's whereabouts was her biggest concern. She should have gone looking for him sooner. If she had…

"Maybe my gift will help lighten your spirits."

Rubina turned. He held a black velvet box in his hands. "What is it?"

She could guess. It must be jewelry of some sort.

"Open it up and see." He handed her the box.

Her husband shouldn't be giving her gifts. She didn't deserve them… With hesitation she opened the lid. Inside was a brilliant diamond and ruby necklace—matching her gown to perfection. How had he known?

"It's beautiful…" Her hand flew to her throat. "How?"

Noah's smile lit up his whole face. Rubina sucked in a breath. He was so handsome and he looked…happy. She hadn't seen a true smile on his face since she returned. Her heart lightened a little at the joy in his eyes. It might not solve all of her problems, but for the moment it was enough. She could give him this night. Tomorrow was soon enough to worry about her brother. Damian could be deep undercover. He'd surface when he had information. These were the things she told herself to get through the hard moments.

"You have your secrets," he replied. "Let me have my own."

Rubina's lips tilted into coy grin. "All right. For now, *caro*."

She touched the necklace lightly. It was so beautiful.

"Here, let me put it on you."

Noah lifted it off the crushed black velvet and placed it around her neck. The ruby teardrop nestled above her chest. Her husband didn't know how appropriate his gift was. The teardrop was a good representation of all the pain she suffered without him. She'd have to look at it for the present it was. There would be no more tears filled with pain—instead, they'd be full of joy. The ruby would be her reminder of all the good things to come.

"Thank you," Rubina whispered.

Noah kissed her cheek. "I would do anything for you, Ruby. Remember that when you look at this." He let his fingers roam across the diamonds and rested briefly on the ruby. "Our future holds so much promise. I look forward to spending it with you."

Rubina fought back the tears that threatened to spill from her eyes. She stood and turned toward Noah. She wrapped her arms around his waist, rested her head against his broad chest, and held on tight.

"Are you all right, Ruby?"

"I'm fine. I just wanted to hold you for a moment."

She started to step back, but he wrapped his arms around her. He brushed her back with the palm of his hand. "I could get used to this.

She lifted her head and stared into his warm brown eyes. "What?"

"These impromptu moments of affection." He smiled. "Keep this up and we won't need a whole two weeks."

Rubina wished she could end the charade now. She didn't need two weeks to know what she wanted. She'd always wanted Noah. Stupid Paolo… This would end—and soon.

"We should go, or we'll be late."

Rubina stepped out of his arms and headed down the stairs. She didn't turn to see if her husband followed. Noah wouldn't be far behind. He'd been open and honest with her since he made his deal. He wanted her, and he'd follow her wherever she led. Soon she'd be doing the same.

"Is the carriage ready?" Noah asked the butler.

"Yes, Your Grace."

Noah nodded and helped Rubina into her pelisse. They exited the townhouse and stepped into the carriage. Liam and Gemma didn't live to far away. Soon the carriage stopped to drop them off. Rubina took a deep breath. She'd need all the help she could get to make it through the evening. Tomorrow, she'd figure out what happened to her brother. Tonight was all for Noah.

"What's on your mind?" Noah asked as they approached the entrance.

"I was wishing for a wonderful evening. It's been a while since I've had a pleasant one."

Understatement… Paolo had made her life miserable. She loved Noah, but since her return, their relationship had been quite strained. Not his fault—but it was still the truth.

"Everyone should be here. I know Lily and Gemma will do everything they can to make it enjoyable."

The door swung open. "What are you two doing standing on the door step. Come in already."

Viscount Torrington held the door open. Noah's mouth hung open in surprise.

"Why are you answering the door?"

His eyebrow rose mockingly. "Are you giving me lip, boy?"

"I would never." Noah smiled. "Where's Pemberly?"

"There's been some disaster in the kitchen... Gemma is having fits. He's following Liam around, intervening where he can." Torrington laughed. "My son has turned into an idiot since he found out she's carrying his child. It's rather amusing to watch."

"Liam is in the kitchen?"

"He is wherever Gemma is." Viscount Torrington motioned for them to come inside. "Hello, Rubina. It's lovely to see you again."

They stepped inside as he shut the door behind them.

Rubina smiled. "It's been too long."

"Oh, there you are." Lady Torrington strolled into the foyer. "I thought you were going to get Liam."

"Soon enough, dear." He kissed her cheek. "Someone had to answer the door."

Rubina watched their interaction. That is what she wanted with Noah. The love they held for each other filled the room. No one would doubt the affection they had for each other. They were a lovely contrast. Pia, Lady Torrington, stood next to her husband with such grace. Her blonde hair so fair it was almost white and her husband's as dark as sin. Thor, Viscount Torrington, only had eyes for her. Someday, when people looked at her and Noah, they would see something similar.

"I apologize." Lady Torrington approached them. "Liam can't seem to let Gemma handle anything on her own these days. Please, join us in the sitting room. Lily and Rand are already inside."

Noah nodded. "I can go and find Liam if it will help."

Torrington patted him on the back. "Not at all. I will go and get him."

"Come with me." Pia gestured to them. "Lily has been waiting for you to arrive."

The viscount went in the opposite direction.

"Finally," Lily exclaimed. "I thought you'd never get here."

She grabbed Rubina's hand and led her over to the settee. "So have you told him yet?"

Her gaze shot up to her husband. He was in a deep conversation with a dark haired gentleman. "Is that your husband?"

Rubina had never met Lily's husband, Rand.

She glanced over her shoulder and smiled. "Handsome devil, isn't he?"

"I…"

How did she answer that? He was indeed handsome, but to her, Noah would always be the best looking man in the room.

"Oh, I know that look. You love your husband, but surely you can appreciate a fine piece of male flesh still." She waved her hand. "Rand was such a gentleman when we met. Wouldn't make love to me until we said our vows. It was so frustrating." She smiled, her eyes glazing over for a few seconds. "It was worth it in the end. His patience is what made me love him even more."

Rubina bit her lip. She understood, more than she was willing to admit. She was going through something similar with Noah. Why he felt the need to have this moratorium on making love she didn't know, but she respected him even more for it.

"Rand is rather handsome," Rubina admitted. "But you're right. Noah is the only one for me."

"So, have you told him?"

"What?" She tilted her head. What was Lily asking?

"About the baby?"

"Oh…" She shook her head. "No. I told you it's too soon."

"When we left, you were so sad. You said that you were losing him." Lily glanced at Noah. "From what I can see that man only has eyes for you. Are you going to tell me what's going on?"

Could she trust Lily?

"I can't speak of it." It wasn't a good place to divulge secrets. "There are too many ears here."

"I understand." She nodded. "I will pay you a call tomorrow. We can speak them. I will bring Gemma."

"Did I hear my name?" Gemma sat down on a chair near the settee. "Liam is driving me mad. Someone put him out of his misery."

Lily laughed. "Men are such babies. He doesn't know what to do with himself. Have pity on him. He can't help it."

Ruby didn't have experience with this...bonding. She'd only begun to get to know Lily before Paolo abducted her. Gemma was a mere acquaintance.

"What is he doing?" Rubina asked.

She should know what to expect once she told Noah she carried his child.

"What isn't he doing?" Gemma blew out an exasperated breath. "He hovers, he orders, he tells me he loves me every day."

"That...doesn't sound too bad."

"Just wait. When Noah realizes you are carrying his child you will understand. It's almost as if Liam thinks if I breathe too hard I'll break. I'm pregnant not an invalid."

Lily patted Gemma's hand. "It will get better. Wait and see what happens after the baby is born. He'll have something else to focus his attention on."

"One can only hope." Gemma rolled her eyes. "In the meantime, if Liam doesn't stop, he might find himself tied to the bed for the rest of my pregnancy."

"Gemma, love." Liam leaned down and kissed her lips. "If you wanted to get creative, all you had to do was ask. I'm open to suggestions."

Gemma glared at her husband. "Be careful where you tread. I'm still mad at you."

"Don't stay mad long." He grinned wickedly. "What fun would that be?"

"Hmmph..." But no one was fooled by it. She loved her husband too much.

Rand and Noah joined them. Rubina's gaze met her husband's. She wanted this. All of it and everything that came with it. Noah smiled at her. It was almost as if he'd read her mind. He was saying so much with that look. Say yes, Rubina. If she gave in and admitted it all she could have him and friends too.

"Dinner is served," Pemberly announced.

Noah helped Rubina up. Everyone headed toward the dining room. He leaned down behind her and whispered in her ear, "Has the evening met your expectations so far?"

His breath was warm against her ear. She shivered as tingles of energy flowed over her body. Yes. Yes, it had… But Rubina was selfish. She wanted so much more than this. She wanted to turn into his arms and beg him to take her home. Noah was hers, and she wanted to claim him once and for all. If only…

"I can think of only one thing that would make this better."

"What?"

"Another time, *caro*." She smiled. "I will tell you in explicit detail what I want to do at the end of an evening such as this." Rubina turned in his arms and spread her hands across his chest. "But you don't want to do anything close to what I have in mind for several days." She let her hands slide under his dinner jacket. Just a little tug and she could roam her hands against his warm skin—she held back the urge. She stared up at him and licked her lips.

His breathing was ragged. "You're correct."

"You know where to find me when you change your mind." She stepped out of his arms. "Dinner's waiting."

She left him standing in the middle of the sitting room. Rubina didn't look back as she headed toward the exit. If she did, she'd be dragging him out of Liam and Gemma's townhouse, demanding he take her home. They both wanted each other. Why they fought it… Rubina still didn't fully understand her husband's motives.

"Rubina," he called after her.

She turned around and sucked in a deep breath. He looked so…decadent.

"Yes?"

He strolled to her side and looped her arm through his. "This isn't over." Her husband leaned down and whispered in her ear. "I will have you again, and when I do…"

She looked up into his eyes again. A mistake—heat flooded through her.

"I will know all your secrets," he promised. "What's more, you will willingly give them all to me."

Rubina was afraid he was right.

CHAPTER 15

Sunlight streamed through the window of his study outlining the parchment on his desk. He cupped his mouth with his hand as worry filled him. Noah picked up the note that Marcus had sent him and read it over again.

Your Grace,

We need to meet in person. I know what happened to your wife. I will be in the tavern awaiting your arrival. Come with all due haste. It could be a life or death situation. There is some serious criminal activity afoot.

Don't waste time,

Marcus

Noah folded the missive and put it in his pocket. He walked out of his study and ran into Liam, almost knocking him to the ground.

"What's the rush?" Liam grabbed onto the wall to steady himself.

"I need to go meet Marcus. He has news."

Liam nodded. "I will go with you. I'm admit to being rather curious. By the way—I did ask my father about him. He was closed mouth. Makes me wonder now what the man did for him."

"I don't know if I want to know." Noah shook his head. "But I trust your father's instincts about people. He hasn't survived this long dealing with fools."

"You're right about that." Liam grinned. "I'm sure his years as a pirate served him well."

"Let's go. Marcus's note indicated it was important I meet him. I don't want to waste any time chatting here. Not with my wife's life at stake."

Liam nodded and followed him out the door. "My carriage is out front. We can take it and save some time."

"Good idea."

Noah gave the driver instructions where to take them. They got inside for the quick trip to the tavern they previously met Marcus at.

"Did he tell you anything in the note?"

Noah shook his head. "Not much."

He pulled it out of his pocket and handed it to Liam, who whistled.

"This doesn't sound good at all."

Noah was worried. A sick feeling filled his gut after reading Marcus's words. What could Rubina and Damian be involved in? It had to be bad for the man he hired to be concerned. He didn't seem to get stressed out about much. This had to be incredibly serious.

Noah clenched his hands into tight fists. No one was taking Rubina away from him ever again—he would not live in that hell for the rest of his days. He was finally starting to feel alive again.

Rubina was his.

"Whatever it is, I will face it. If it means keeping my wife safe, I will kill the devil himself." Noah's lips were a firm tight line. "Nothing and no one will ever take her away from me again.

Liam nodded. "I will help you in any way I can."

"I know." Noah tilted his head. "I appreciate it."

The carriage came to a stop. They got out and headed toward the tavern. They saw the same buxom waitress that flirted with them the first time.

"Did you two have a change of heart?" she asked. "I'd be willing to take you both on at the same time. Just say the word." Her lower lip lifted into a sexy pout.

"No, we're here for Marcus again." Noah dismissed her.

"He isn't here."

Noah's head whipped around. "What? Where did he go?"

She shrugged. "He hasn't been by in days."

"That seems...odd." Liam stared at Noah. "What do you want to do?"

Panic settled into his gut. Why would he send him the missive and not show up to their meeting? Something was wrong...

"Let's go back to my place. We can figure out what to do from there."

They turned to leave as Marcus stumbled into the door. He held his side as he limped over to them. He gasped for breath and almost fell at their feet. Liam reached out and steadied him.

"What happened to you?"

"Duca d'Sordillo." He groaned. "He means business."

"Who is that?" Liam asked. "It sounds familiar."

Noah paled. Damian had mentioned his name on one of his visits—before Rubina returned home. He had been courting her before she met Noah. The man had offered for her, but Ruby turned him down. She never said why. Damian mentioned her father wouldn't have approved either way. He had some nasty business dealings, and there were a lot of rumors surrounding him. If he was involved it couldn't be good, and it might explain why Rubina was so afraid. It had never occurred to him that he might be. Why would it? Noah had won her hand and married her. How obsessed was the duca with his wife?

"Is he in London?"

Marcus nodded. "He is here to take Rubina back to Italy."

"I don't understand..." Noah looked around the room. "Perhaps this isn't the best place to talk. You need medical attention. We can go back to my townhouse, and I will send for a doctor."

"Brilliant idea, Your Grace." He shook his head. "Only one problem with that. Rubina is at your house and every person the Duca d'Sordillo wants to get his hands on will be in one place." He coughed hard and a drop of blood fell on his lips. "No, take me to a room upstairs. I keep one here. I will tell you everything there. Don't worry about your wife. My men are still keeping an eye on her. No one will get to her inside your home."

Noah and Liam helped him up to this room and laid him on his bed.

"Your wife—as you know—did not go down with the ship she supposedly died on."

Noah frowned. "Tell me something I don't know. What is going on."

"D'Sordillo has been obsessed with her for years. He meant to marry her himself."

"Again, tell me something I do not already know. This is all old news."

The man grimaced and clutched his side again. "If you knew that much, why didn't you tell me. Would have saved me a lot of time and maybe prevented the knife to my gut."

Noah waved his hands in the air with frustration. "I didn't know the man was crazy or obsessed. I figured he'd moved on."

Marcus kept shaking his head back and forth, remaining silent for several seconds. "I thought you were a lot smarter— forgive me for assuming too much."

"I don't have time for this. Tell me what you found out," Noah demanded.

"Give the man some space," Liam urged. "He is bleeding a bit there."

Noah opened and closed his mouth. "You're right. I apologize, but all of this is making me insane with worry."

"Yeah and to think it's only going to get worse now that Rubina is carrying your child." Liam frowned. "Trust me, I know. Gemma is about to pummel me for hovering over her."

"What?" Noah turned, shock filling him. "Ruby isn't pregnant."

"Oh, you didn't know?" Liam's mouth fell open in surprise. "I would have thought... Gemma knew... I just assumed. I'm sorry. That shouldn't be news you heard from me."

Why wouldn't Rubina tell him?

"Sounds like you have even more reason to keep your wife safe." Marcus sat up. "D'Sordillo is going to try and kill you—and he will take her again."

"Again?" Noah asked. "Is he the reason she's been gone for so long?"

"Yes," he replied. "She escaped by chance. Damian had men watching him for different reasons. When one of his men discovered that Rubina was being held captive, he helped her get away. That was when her brother found out she was alive."

"How long ago?" Noah asked, swallowing a lump forming in his throat.

His wife was pregnant, and danger loomed over her head.

"A couple of months..." Marcus paused. "I'd estimate a few weeks before you were about to remarry she managed to find Damian. They sailed to Florence first and then headed straight here. From that point I'm sure you know the rest."

"I'm still confused." Noah paced the room. "Why would she want to divorce me."

The man laughed and then grimaced in pain. "I suspect it was because she loves you."

Noah turned and shouted, "You don't divorce someone you are in love with."

"You do if you're trying to protect them," Liam said softly. "Duca d'Sordillo means to kill Noah as long as he's married to Rubina, doesn't he?"

Marcus nodded. "He might not have if Rubina hadn't escaped, but now that she's home with her husband—yes, that is indeed his plan."

Noah rubbed his hand over his mouth and let their words sink in. It made sense. He wanted to wring her neck. How could she not have told him all of this? She knew how much he loved her. They could have dealt with this together. Instead, she kept it all to herself and left him blind to the situation. At least he had Marcus to thank for filling him into what was really going on with his wife. Otherwise, he'd still be left in the dark.

He started to laugh manically.

"Are you all right?" Liam asked.

"She does still love me." He grinned. "She's got a strange way of showing it, but she never stopped. This is all insane—she might even be a little mad. But you know what? It doesn't matter because she's all mine."

"What are you going to do?"

"I'm going to go home and have a little chat with my well-meaning wife and explain to her why she shouldn't lie to her husband." Noah started to leave.

"Wait, Your Grace," Marcus called out. "There is something else you need to know."

Noah stopped in his tracks and turned. "What?"

"d'Sordillo has Damian." Marcus grimaced. "It's why I was stabbed. I got too close. The good news is I know where they stashed him."

"What's the bad news?"

"It's guarded so well it might as well be a fortress."

Noah cursed. This had gone from bad to worse. How was he going to get Damian out of this mess? They should not have kept him in the dark for so long. What was d'Sordillo involved in that made Damian think he needed to keep an eye on him anyway?

"What is inside that they need so many guards?" Noah asked. "Surely it isn't just to watch over one man."

"I'm not entirely sure what they are guarding." Marcus swung his legs over the side of the bed and sat up. "I suspect it's more for protection than anything. Paolo Fonte, Duca d'Sordillo is high up in the Italian mafia."

"Bloody hell." Noah paced the room again. "This is damned mess."

"Where do we even begin to rescue Damian?" Liam asked.

"I'm not sure you can." Marcus shook his head. "He might be lost to you."

"I refuse to believe that," Noah said.

Rubina would be devastated if anything happened to her brother. Noah knew that Damian was high up in the Italian government—but, at the heart of it, he was protecting his sister. It might have started as an investigation into his criminal activities—that would have all changed when his sister found him. It was now up to Noah to finish what he started.

"One more thing, Your Grace," Marcus said. "The orchard you purchased in Sicily."

"What about it?"

"D'Sordillo wants it. I don't know how, but it's key to whatever plans he has."

"He bloody well can't have it or my wife." Noah growled.

No one took what was his. It was time Paolo Fonte realized that.

"Let's go. I need to check on Rubina."

Liam nodded. "Right behind you."

Noah stopped, turned toward Marcus, and said, "Thank you for finding out everything I needed to know. I will make sure a doctor comes to help you."

"Don't worry about me." Marcus grinned. "I have my own saw bones that sees to my needs. One of my men has already gone to get him. Go look after your duchess."

Noah nodded and headed out the door.

It was time to raise some hell—starting with his wife.

CHAPTER 16

"Pardon me, Your Grace." Simmons entered the sitting room. "This arrived for you."

"What is it?" Rubina asked.

"I'm not at liberty to say." Simmons shrugged. "I don't read my employer's missives."

Rubina rolled her eyes. "All you had to say was someone sent me a note. It's probably from Lily. She was supposed to pay a call today. Give it to me."

She broke the wax seal and read over the contents.

Duchessa,

Paolo has your brother. Meet me at the Albany. I will explain everything. Don't tell your husband—he is still in grave danger.

Arturo

Rubina gasped and clutched it to her chest.

"Is everything all right?" Simmons asked.

"It's fine." Rubina forced a smile on her face. "I need to visit Gemma and Lily. Gemma isn't feeling well enough for travel."

"Would you like me to have the carriage brought around?"

"No need. I think I will walk. I could use the fresh air, and it's not too far away. Tell Noah, if he should return before I do, I look forward to dinner this evening. He said he had a something to talk to me about."

"Very well, Your Grace." He bowed and left the room.

Rubina folded up Arturo's note and rushed out of the room. She didn't even stop to grab her pelisse. There was no time. Paolo had her brother. She needed to know what happened. The sooner she reached Arturo the quicker she would get the information she needed.

When she exited the townhouse she ran into Lily and almost knocked her down the steps. Gemma blocked her fall.

"Where are you off to in a hurry?" Lily asked.

Drat. There went her excuse to leave the house. Simmons would question why Gemma was visiting when Rubina was supposedly off to see her.

"I need to get to the Albany." She might as well go for some version of the truth. "Damian needs me."

"Is he ill?" Gemma asked. "We can come with you."

That was a very bad idea.

"No." Rubina shook her head. "I don't think he would be up for company."

"Nonsense," Lily interrupted her. "We can't let you travel on your own. It wouldn't be right. We will escort you over there."

Gemma nibbled on her lip. "Noah wouldn't like it. He's rather protective of you since, you know—you're not dead as he believed you to be."

There was no getting out of it. She'd have to tell them the truth. They were not going to leave her alone and Damian was in trouble. Rubina sighed and handed the note to Lily.

"Read that and let's get moving. This very well could be life and death."

Lily opened the note and frowned. "Who is Paolo, and why does he have Damian?"

"It's a long story?"

"Why don't you start with Arturo and why he sent you this note." Lily waved the missive in front of her.

Rubina nodded. "I will tell you everything, but please, we need to get to the Albany, so follow me."

Gemma raised her hand. "Why don't we take my carriage? It would save time and we can talk in comfort."

Rubina's gaze flew to the carriage. Gemma did have a point. The only reason she hadn't ordered her own was because it would take too long. Having one already available though…

"Yes, that's a good idea." Rubina headed to the carriage and hopped inside. Gemma and Lily followed her. "To answer one of your questions… Arturo is one of Damian's employees—and I owe him my life."

Lily and Gemma looked at each other and then back to Rubina. "I think we need more details."

Rubina sighed. "When I left Noah, I fully intended to come home to him. I never wanted to leave him."

"Go on," Lily encouraged.

"I was set to board a ship to Florence to visit my father. Noah and I had an argument…"

Rubina held back tears. Her voice cracked as she spoke.

"I know it's hard," Gemma said in a soft voice. "But it will help tell us everything. It must be hard keeping all your secrets buried inside."

Rubina wiped her eyes. "Paolo had his men grab me before I got on board. He took me to his home in Sicily and kept me captive there…" She paused and stared off in space. "He wanted me, but I'd refused him. I married Noah and never regretted that decision. He's the only man I've ever loved." She stared at Gemma and Lily. "Arturo rescued me and took me to my brother's ship. It was there I found out how truly evil Paolo is and that Noah was going to marry another woman. I had to return."

"So all this time…" Gemma's voice trailed off.

"I lived in a locked room, held prisoner by a mad man."

"Now he has your brother?" Lily's voice hardened. "That is wrong."

"I have to find a way to save Damian." Rubina struggled to control her emotions. She straightened her spine and said with conviction, "But above all, Paolo must die."

"Rubina…" Gemma's voice trailed off.

"No. Don't tell me it will be a black stain on my soul.

Allowing him to live would be an error of the greatest multitude. He will never stop coming after me and those I love. The only way to ensure that we are all safe is for him to cease to be. That man belongs in hell, and I will send him there."

"We will help you," Lily blurted out.

Gemma's gaze flew to hers. "Are you sure?"

"Yes. You saw how Noah was when he believed Rubina died. For that alone, this man must pay."

Gemma turned toward Rubina and nodded. "She's right, but we must at least try to be careful. Liam will be so mad if something happens…"

Lily's lips curved into a gamine smile. "My brother will get over it."

"I don't think this is a good idea. You should both drop me off at the Albany and return home. I'd never forgive myself if something happened to you to." Rubina wanted them all safe.

"Too late." Lily said and jumped out of the carriage when it came to a stop. "Meet you inside."

"Lily has always been rather—impetuous," Gemma offered.

"I know." Rubina sighed. "I suppose we should follow her."

The both got out of the carriage and gasped as someone grabbed a hold of them. Lily was being held by a burly man with black curly hair and mean eyes.

"You weren't supposed to bring friends, *la mia bellezza*." Paolo cooed in her ear. "You're as beautiful as I remember. You were a bad girl though, running off with that man. I'll have to make you pay for that."

She was not his beauty.

Rubina spit in his face. "What have you done with my brother?"

"He's safe—for now." He wiped his face. "If you do as I tell you, I may even allow him to live."

"Let Gemma and Lily go," Rubina demanded. "They mean nothing to you."

He shook his head. "I'm afraid I can't do that. They are very much a part of this now. You shouldn't have brought them if you were concerned for their safety. They can keep you company for a while…"

"Then what?" Rubina was almost afraid to ask.

"Depends on their attitude." He laughed evilly. "If they are cooperative, I might let my men have a go at them… If not, well, they can be easily disposed of."

Bile rose in her throat. This was all her fault. How could she have allowed this to happen. Maybe there was still hope. If Arturo was in her brother's rooms… Her gaze flew to the entrance of the Albany.

"If you're wondering about Arturo, he isn't going to come and save you."

Had he read her mind? "How can you be so certain?"

"Because he didn't send you that note, *cara*." He caressed her cheek with the back of his hand. "It was all a ruse to get you out of the house. I'm afraid Arturo is very much dead."

"No…"

"He had to pay for his insolence. If not for his actions, you'd still be where you belong."

Lily bit the man's finger that held her. "Ouch, you bitch."

"You won't get away with this. Our husbands will hunt you down and kill you like the rabid dog you are."

Paolo laughed. "Such fire. Maybe I will keep you for myself after all."

Lily struggled to get free.

"Restrain the spitfire and put her in the carriage." He then gestured toward Gemma. "Put her in there too and take care of the men that were following them. Make sure they don't live to tell tales."

Paolo dragged Rubina along with him, separating her from Gemma and Lily.

"Where are you taking me?"

"Those two have a few lessons to learn." He grinned. "You, my dear, have a much harsher one to finally grasp. We are going to arrive at our destination separate from your friends."

"Please, let them go."

She had to try one last time. Her heart was breaking into pieces. If she could save them…

"I said no. They are part of the price you need to pay for leaving me."

Rubina grimaced. Paolo had grown crazier since the last time she'd seen him.

"I am not yours to keep."

"You are," he bellowed. "You will finally understand that you belong to me."

"I will never be yours." Rubina elbowed him in his side. She attempted to wrench herself free, but it was a futile endeavor.

"Yes. You are mine." He pulled her into his arms. "Look at me."

Rubina let her gaze fall down. She didn't want to look into his fanatical eyes. A huge part of her was afraid of what she might see in them.

"I said look at me," he demanded, lifting her chin. "That's better. I want you to know who it is that holds you. Who will always hold you from this point on."

Paolo leaned down and touched his lips to hers. Rubina fought him, but he held on tight. He forced her mouth open and pushed his tongue inside of her mouth. Rubina bit it as hard as she could until she tasted blood.

"You bitch" He slapped her face. "That's one more thing you will pay for. I am no longer going to be a gentleman with you. I mean to have you tonight. Finally, you will belong to me in every way."

Rubina held back a shudder—barely. She had to do something to save herself, and those she loved. The idea of Paolo... No, she refused to even picture the heinous things he had planned.

Paolo shoved her into a nearby carriage and tapped the roof. Wherever he was taking her...they were well on their way. She would have to get inside his head a little bit and make him start to doubt this foolhardy plan of his.

She grinned, evilly. "When will you understand that there is not a chance in hell of you ever having me in any way. My heart, body, and soul belong to my husband. When he finds me—and he will find me, Paolo—you will finally burn in the fires of hell for what you have done to us."

Noah said he would always come for her. So if she

couldn't find a way to save herself, her only hope was that her husband would tear the world apart looking for her.

Not to mention, Liam was as much of an alpha male as Noah. They wouldn't allow their wives to be held hostage by a mad man. Rubina didn't know Rand well...but she did know Lily. That woman wouldn't go for a weak man. There would be a reckoning.

Rubina couldn't wait to see Paolo torn to shreds.

"That is where you are wrong." Paolo's grin sent fear into her heart. "Soon your husband will be as dead as I originally claimed. I am leaving nothing to chance this time."

Bloody hell...he had to be lying. Right?

Now Rubina had one more thing to stress about. Paolo would not win.

Even if she had to take her last breath to see him dead—he would go to hell where he belonged.

CHAPTER 17

N oah hopped the steps two at a time and swung open the door to his townhouse.

"Rubina," he bellowed.

He was met with complete silence.

Bloody hell. Where was his wife?

"Her Grace went to visit Lady Marsden." Simmons entered the foyer. "She left at the beginning of the hour. She bade me to tell you she was looking forward to dinner this evening."

Noah frowned.

"We could just get back in the carriage and go to see her." Liam stood in the open doorway. "Luckily my townhouse isn't too far from yours. It wouldn't take long to get there."

Liam did have a point. Did he really want to have it out with Rubina in front of Gemma—and possibly Lily? That wasn't a good idea at all. It would put her even more on the defensive.

"No," he shook his head. "I can be patient a little while longer. I'm sure she's perfectly safe at your place."

"Why are you standing in an open doorway?" Rand stood behind Liam. "Is Lily inside? I need her to come back to Marsden house. William is driving the staff mad. When he gets like this, the only one that can subdue him is her."

Liam frowned. "Why would Lily be here?"

"Because she came with Gemma to visit Rubina." Rand rolled his eyes. "Lily had this harebrained idea Rubina needed cheering up about something."

A sick feeling took root in Noah's gut. None of the ladies were inside…

"Lily and Gemma are not here." Noah's hand shook. "Rubina isn't here either."

Liam's normally dark complexion paled. "You don't think…"

"Did someone fail to send me an invitation to this party?"

They all turned to see Marcus stumble toward the entrance of the town house. He winced with each step, but he no longer held on to his side.

"Why in tarnation are you here?" Noah asked.

"One of my men managed to get away…" He paused and shook his head. "The details don't matter. I had to let you know d'Sordillo has your wife and the other two women traveling with her."

Liam cursed and punched the door. "That evil bastard has my wife."

"Someone want to fill me in?" Rand glanced back and forth between all three men. "Who took them?"

None of them volunteered the information.

Noah clenched his jaw struggling to get a hold of his emotions. This was all his worst fears wrapped neatly into one nightmarish package. "I need the location of his hidey hole."

"I'm coming with you," Liam demanded.

"I didn't expect you would want to stay behind."

Rand started to wave his hands. "Hello? Someone better start telling me what is going on before I start hitting one of you to get it."

Marcus shook his head. "I will have to take you there. The place is too secluded to give you directions."

Noah nodded. "Well, as luck would have it Liam's carriage is still available. I suggest we all get inside and go rescue our wives from a man who has unmistakably lost his mind."

Rand folded his arms across his chest and glared at Noah.

"I'm still waiting for you to tell me what the hell has you all fired up."

"Not now, man. We don't have time for this." Liam smacked him on the shoulder. "Get in the bloody carriage, and we can fill you in on the way."

Noah remained silent. He was afraid if he said too much he'd break down and crumble. All the lies and secrets—none of it mattered anymore. His only concern was finding Rubina and bringing her home safely...

"You two whoresons are going to get an earful from me on the way to wherever we are headed to retrieve the women." Rand glared at them both before he hopped inside the carriage.

Noah couldn't fault the man. He'd be cussing too. Hell, he wanted to do a lot more than that. He wanted to pummel something until it was torn to shreds.

Paolo would make a good target for all that pent up angst.

Marcus rattled off directions to the driver and hopped inside the carriage with them.

"Start talking," Rand demanded. "What in the dickens is happening to our wives?"

Noah took a deep breath and steeled himself for Rand's displeasure. "Rubina was kidnapped."

"I gathered that," Rand interrupted him. "Along with Gemma and Lily. Who would do that?"

"That was what I was trying to tell you." Noah shook his head. "This dates back to when Rubina went missing the first time."

If only he'd known she'd been held captive for so many years. She must have lost faith in him. No wonder she wanted to leave him. Why would she want a husband who didn't protect her? Noah had been set to reprimand her for keeping it all a secret. The reasons why didn't matter anymore. She could keep any bloody thing she wanted to herself—as long as she was safe. He loved her too much to try to cage her in. It was time he let her be as free as she wanted.

Rand nodded. "I remember you believed she died, but she just came home recently. Did she tell you what happened to her?"

If only she had...

"No." Rand frowned. Noah continued, "I hired Marcus here to look into the matter. He was injured gathering the information for me and explained all the details earlier. When we arrived at my townhouse, the women were already missing."

"I suppose that is where I come in," Marcus interrupted. "My men were keeping an eye on the duchess. All I know for sure is they got in Lady Marsden's carriage and went to visit Her Grace's brother. Outside of the Albany, they were snatched. Duca d'Sordillo took Rubina, and the other two were taken in a different carriage."

Liam's mouth fell open. He closed it and clenched his jaw. Then after a few more seconds said, "Lily and Gemma were taken to a separate location?"

"I don't even know if Rubina is being taken to where we are headed. This is the only place that I know they could've been taken. It's a starting point."

Bollocks... What a bloody mess this was all turning into.

"How long until we arrive?" Rand asked quietly.

Noah was getting a little worried about the man. He had grown silent with each bit of information they departed on him. It appeared as if his sole focus was on what needed to be done. At least one of them remained calm and collected. It would come in handy when they reached their destination.

"We're not far behind them." Marcus gestured toward Noah. "Shortly after you left, my man stumbled in. As luck would have it, the doctor got two for the price of one. He was still patching him up when I left." He turned to Rand. "To answer your question, we should arrive soon. It isn't far outside of the city—it's well hidden."

They all kept their thoughts to themselves from that point on. Each man focused on their own concerns. Noah ran his hands over his face. This was his fault. He should have demanded answers from Rubina sooner. If he had... His jaw tightened. Noah hit the side of the carriage with his hand.

"Easy now. That's not going to solve anything," Liam reminded him.

Noah glared. "Like hitting the door helped you."

"Fair enough." He frowned. "Now isn't the time for anger.

We need to remain as calm as possible. After they are safe, we can unleash it on the bastard that took them."

"I'm going to rip him to pieces."

They all focused on Rand—each man's mouth hung open in surprise. He'd been so quiet and calm. His statement was unexpected.

"I think you might have to stand in line and wait your turn." Liam shook his head. "It's always the quiet ones that surprise you."

The carriage came to a halt.

Noah stared at each man and nodded. "It's time."

They all got out and made their way to the place Paolo stashed the women—or at least where they hoped he had. If they were in another location...

Noah wouldn't think about it. They had to be inside.

"Do you know anything about this place?" Noah asked Marcus.

He shook his head. "Not much. There are guards at each entrance. There are at least six men inside. At the top of the hour patrols go out and do a perimeter check."

"No pressure at all..." Liam shook his head. "The good news is that it's past their hourly checkpoint. If we can get past a couple of the guards at the back entrance, we might be able to break in and rescue the women without too much fuss."

It was probably the best chance they were going to get to make it happen.

"Once we're inside, we will split up and search. Liam, come with me and Rand go with Marcus." He nodded to each man. "Let's do this."

They sneaked their way across the lawn. Two men patrolled the perimeter. Noah gestured to Liam and he nodded. They each circled around to deal with them and efficiently knocked out the two guards. One hurdle down, many more to go, until the women were safe. They remained as silent as possible as they entered the house.

It was time to divide and conquer, Noah looked toward the stairs gesturing to Liam to follow him. Rand and Marcus went left down the first hall. Liam and Noah made their way to the second story. They moved their way down the hallway at a slow pace. Careful to not make any noise and check each room they passed. A shrill voice filled his ears and he stopped to listen. Noah heard shouting as he crept toward a door at the end of the path.

"I told you." A woman's laugh filled the room. "You didn't listen to me."

"Cara," the male voice coaxed. "Put the pistol down. You don't really want to shoot me."

"I assure you," the woman said with conviction. "Not only do I want to, but I will."

Rubina…

Noah pushed open the door and found his wife holding a pistol in her hands. Her golden blonde hair fell down her back in waves. Her eyes were the color of melted silver.

"Don't be so hasty, Ruby dear. If you kill me, you will never find your brother."

Rubina raised the pistol higher, aiming for Paolo's head. "You implied he's already dead. Now you want to change your story?"

"I may have exaggerated a bit." His grin was filled with menace. "He was a thorn in my side. I had to take him or he'd have caused problems. He could be alive." Paolo shrugged. "He could be dead. I don't know for sure. If you put the gun down, I can tell you how to find out for certain."

Her hand shook. "I don't believe you."

"You need to stop her," Liam said. "Killing him would be a mistake, at least for now. Lily and Gemma are still unaccounted for. We can always end him later."

"I know," Noah agreed.

He eased his way inside, getting a little closer to Rubina. He had to get the gun from her before she did something she would regret. Taking person's life, even someone as evil as Paolo, would haunt her.

"Ruby?" Noah approached her. "Give me the gun. You don't want to kill him."

She shook her head. "I do. You don't know what he's put me through. He needs to die."

A tear fell from the corner of her eye and trailed down her cheek.

"Rubina," Liam's voice was filled with panic. "Where are Gemma and Lily?"

She shook her head. "I don't know…"

"Well, I do have some use left then." The man laughed with malevolence. "You may not care for Damian, but those two women are important enough to stay my execution."

"There is no reason to allow you to keep breathing. We will find Gemma and Lily without your help." Rubina held the gun up higher. "I am going to send you to hell today, Paolo."

Liam paled at her words. His hand raised as if itching to take the gun away from Rubina. His jerky movements raised Noah's anxiety. He needed a new task before he tried to wrestle Rubina for control of the gun. Liam's concern for Gemma was warring with his good sense.

"Liam, go help Rand and Marcus search the rest of the house. I will take care of this." Noah turned to Rubina. "Please, Ruby. Give it to me."

Liam stilled and stared at Noah. He didn't want to leave. Noah understood. If it were his wife, he'd want more information too. Him being in the room wasn't helping though. He could go do something productive, such as actually trying to find the women. Perhaps they were still inside, and he could aid them in exiting the premises. After several seconds, he nodded and left. Noah breathed a sigh of relief. Only one more pressing problem to get through before he could let go of his own anxiety.

Rubina's hand shook. If he didn't take the pistol from her soon, she might hurt herself.

Noah eased over to her side and wrapped his hand around hers. The hilt of the pistol was encased in both of their hands. "Let me do it."

She shook her head. "No. It's my vengeance to take." Rubina shook his hand free of hers. They were both distracted and took their eyes off of their enemy for a few precious seconds.

Paolo rushed forward. Rubina flinched, causing her to squeeze the trigger. A loud boom filled the room as the gun went off.

The look of shock on the man's face—he really believed

he'd make it out of the situation alive. His body crumpled and hit the floor with a loud thump. Rubina's hand shook and the pistol fell from her hand, landing on the hard surface with a sharp thud. Tears fell in a rush from her eyes.

"Is he really dead?"

Noah only had eyes for his wife. He pulled her into his arms and held her as tight as he could. "I've never been so scared in my life. Don't do that to me ever again."

"I'm so sorry." Her tears fell harder with each breath she took. "Please forgive me."

"Shhh." He kept his voice as soothing as possible. Noah reined in his emotions. Rubina needed him to be strong. "No one will hurt you I won't let them."

It was a promise he intended to keep.

"I love you," Rubina whispered. "I never stopped."

"I know," he reassured her.

A part of him had always known. It had taken him a little while to get over his anger. A love like theirs didn't just go away. They were meant to be together forever, and now they wouldn't have anything to stand in their way.

"There is something else." She stared up into his eyes. "I wanted to tell you everything, but I was so afraid. There is nothing preventing me now."

Noah ran his fingers through her hair relishing in the silkiness of her curls. "You can tell me anything. Don't ever feel like you need to keep secrets from me. Nothing you could say would ever change how I feel about you."

He wiped the tears from her eyes. A small smile formed on her face.

"This is good news."

"You're carrying our child," he finished for her.

She glanced up with surprise. "You knew?"

He laughed. For the first time, his heart didn't constrict with pain—instead only joy filled it.

"I suspected." He kissed her lips lightly.

She bit her lip. "Are you happy?"

"More than words can say." He wrapped his arms around her once again. "But it's not all settled. Lily and Gemma need to be found."

"All taken care of." Marcus stepped into the room. "They

are headed toward the carriage to go home with their husbands."

"How are we going to get back?"

"Paolo took Gemma's carriage. It's probably still here," Rubina explained.

"Her Grace is correct." He nodded. "I will drive it back since the driver didn't make it here with it."

Marcus left to go prepare the carriage for their journey.

Noah smiled. "Everything worked out how it was supposed to."

Rubina frowned. "Not entirely. We still don't know what happened to Damian."

He could see the concern in her eyes. She'd been so brave facing down Paolo. Her brother meant so much to her. How could he make it better? Damian could still be alive. Paolo never confirmed one way or the other.

"We will find him."

"I don't know if that is possible." She nibbled on her bottom lip. "The duca was an evil man. I shudder to think what he did to my brother. Perhaps death would be kinder."

Noah feared Rubina would never be able to fully recover from the atrocities she endured. "I will have Marcus investigate. If anyone can locate your brother, he can. Try not to worry overmuch. We will have answers. It might just take a while to get them."

Once they found Damian, everything would be right in their world. Rubina's happiness was all that mattered to him. They had a life to build together. The only blight on that was Damian's predicament.

"Yes, *caro*." Rubina cupped his cheek in the palm of her hand. A hint of sadness still lingered in her eyes. "Are you ready to go home?"

"I'm already home." He kissed her cheek. "My home is wherever you are. But yes, let's leave this place behind us and go somewhere inherently more pleasant."

EPILOGUE

Rubina caressed his cheek. It was soft and beautiful. He was the most beautiful child in all of creation. Perhaps all mothers believed that of their children, but she couldn't stop looking at him.

It gave her a small amount of joy through a difficult time. Knowing her son was alive and well while her brother...

She didn't want to think about Damian. They had been grieving him for months. There seemed to be no reason to believe Paolo hadn't murdered him. Throughout her entire pregnancy they had searched for any sign he might be alive. Whatever Paolo had done... They couldn't find any answers. When Lucien was born, they were forced to give up the search. The family went into mourning. Now that her son was a year old, it was time to let her brother go. They had much to live for.

"Are you staring at Lucien again?" Noah entered the nursery. "Let the poor boy nap."

She pouted. "But he is so lovely when he's sleeping. When he's awake, he often gets in touch with his impish side."

Noah leaned downed and gave her a quick kiss on the lips. "This surprises you? The Marsden twins are his playmates."

"You make it sound as if Alexander and Andrew have the ear of the devil himself."

"No, but I don't know how Liam and Gemma keep up with them. Once they started walking…"

Rubina laughed. "They are adorable."

"Come with me," he urged. "I have a surprise for you."

Rubina looked down one last time at her son. He had his father's dark brown hair and her silver eyes. He was the perfect mixture of both of them. It was hard to believe he was going to be a year old in less than a week.

"What do you have for me?" She turned toward her husband. "You give me the best gifts."

The best one being their son…

He led her down the hall to her bedroom—turned dressing room. She never slept in it. Not when she could sleep encased in her husband's loving arms.

"Why are we here?" She asked.

"Go inside."

She stared at him, puzzled, but did as he bid.

Inside, lying on top of her bed, was one of the most beautiful gowns she'd ever seen. It was pure white with silver lace embellishments. Tiny seed pearls were sewn into the bodice and shined against the lace.

"What is this?"

He grinned. "Do you remember our two week deal?"

Rubina nodded. It had been when he believed he needed to court her again. Foolish man—she never stopped loving him.

"I had this elaborate plan. It all fell apart—well, you know why. I put it on hold, but I think today is a good time to see it through."

He pulled a ring out of his pocket and held it before her. It was a ruby flanked by diamonds on each side.

"Noah?"

"Will you marry me again?" He lifted her hand and kissed it. "I promise to love you forever. I even had it engraved inside. I know that Paolo took your wedding ring—I want you to wear this one as a symbol of how much I will always love you."

Rubina took the ring from him and looked inside. Ruby, my heart beats for you—Noah

Tears fell from her eyes.

"So, is that a yes?"

She rushed into his arms and kissed him. "Did you think I'd be foolish enough to say no?"

Noah grinned. "Ruby, love—life wouldn't be interesting if you became predictable."

"This is true." She laughed.

"A maid will be up in a minute to help you put on your new gown."

"Today?" She asked surprised.

"Did you think I'd wait more than a few moments to make you mine?" He raised an eyebrow. "I can't let the world believe, even for a second, that you are not my wife."

Rubina laughed. "We wouldn't want that."

It didn't matter that they were already married. This was the fresh started that had been denied to them. This was one thing she would do over and over again if it kept their love where it belonged.

Noah left the room and allowed her time to change.

When she came down the stairs, she had to choke back tears. Her father stood at the bottom to escort her to her groom.

"Papa." She hugged him. "How long have you known about this?"

He cupped her cheeks in the palm of his hands and kissed her forehead. "Long enough to sail across the ocean to be here with you."

"Thank you."

"I wouldn't be anywhere else." His eyes were full of warmth as he looked down at her. "You're my only daughter, and I thank God that you are still with us."

Noah stood next to a vicar, waiting for Rubina to join him. Their friends and family all sat in chairs, watching for her arrival. Lily and Rand had even made another trip from America to attend. Her eyes narrowed into tiny slits at one of the guests—Pearla Montgomery. What was she doing there? Rubina hadn't seen her since that fateful day she'd interrupted her wedding to Noah. She sat next to Gemma and Liam. Maybe this was some torturous closure she was putting herself through. Rubina didn't care. She could be generous after all—she had Noah. Maybe if Pearla was lucky enough, she would find someone as equally wonderful. It was the least she could wish for. The woman had lost a wonderful man—she deserved to move on and find her own happiness.

They all turned to see her walk toward her husband.

This was so very different than the wedding she interrupted.

It was all about her and Noah.

Her husband's smile grew wider with each step she took toward him.

She moved forward to meet him. "Hello, *caro*."

"I was beginning to think I'd have to come find you."

Rubina smiled. "You will never have to come find me ever again. I will always be right here by your side…"

They said their vows. Emotions welled up inside her as she spoke them. Hearing them reaffirmed everything she wanted with Noah. They had been through so much. Going through the ceremony again helped them take back what belonged to them. Nothing would separate them again. They had their whole lives to look forward to.

"You may now kiss your bride."

Noah stared down into her eyes. "You don't have to tell me twice."

"Pardon me for interrupting—I always did show up late for important events."

Noah and Rubina glanced across the room. A gasp of surprise fell from Rubina's lips. Her brother strutted in—as if he didn't have a care in the world. Never mind they believed him dead. This must be how her family felt when they thought she'd died. His hair was a little longer than she remembered. It fell to his shoulders in long black waves, but his silver eyes held something she couldn't identify. He'd changed. Rubina didn't know what it was, but it looked good on him.

Rubina ran to him and hugged him tight. "I'm so glad to see you. Where the bloody hell have you been all this time?"

Damian hugged her tight in his embrace. He kissed the top of her head.

"Easy now, Rue." He eased back. "I rather like breathing."

"Are you going to answer my question?" She raised an eyebrow.

"I will explain it all at another time." He scanned the guests. "I came for another reason."

Rubina pursed her lips in displeasure. She was happy to see her brother but... She stopped and looked at him. Then she turned in the direction that held him riveted.

Pearla stood up. Her blue eyes shot daggers at Damian. Her hand flew to her chest; her mouth hung open with shock. She shook her head several times as if not believing what she saw in front of her. Rubina could relate to what she appeared to be going through.

She turned to her brother and asked, "Do you two know each other?"

"I think a man would know his wife when he sees her." Damian's eyes never left Pearla.

Rubina stared back and forth between them. Even more questions entered her mind. When had these two met? All she knew about Pearla was she was gone for more than a year nursing a broken heart—who could blame her? She'd have been devastated if she'd lost Noah to another woman too.

"I am not your wife," Pearla said with disdain.

Pearla pushed her way past everyone. She left the house in a huff, with Damian not far behind her. Rubina shook her head. It was their mess to straighten. They would work it out —or wouldn't. She just hoped her brother found happiness. He could explain what happened when he settled things with Pearla. Rubina liked to think she learned patience over the past several years. Damian deserved happiness, and if that was with Pearla she wouldn't stand in the way.

Liam strolled over to stand next to her. "I will say one thing about you and weddings—never a dull moment."

He laughed and walked away.

Blasted man did have a point. Although, their first wedding was uneventful...

"Don't listen to my brother," Lily interrupted. "This was the best wedding ever. Think of the stories you can tell you children. Noah's an honorary Marsden, you know. So he should have a tale like the rest of us."

"What do you mean?" Rubina asked.

Noah laughed. "The bedtime story your parents told you two?"

"Yes." Lily nodded excitedly. "I know, yours can start with: once upon a time, a woman objected to a wedding…"

Rubina and Noah laughed. It wasn't how they actually began, but it did tell how they found each other again. Perhaps this was a tradition she could get behind.

The following is an unedited excerpt from A Discarded Pearl: A Marsden Romance 5.

A DISCARDED PEARL

DAWN BROWER

Dawn Brower

A Discarded Pearl

ACKNOWLEDGMENTS

Thanks to all my readers for reading everything I write, and those that have been patiently waiting for me to finish writing the Marsden books. This is the final one, and I hope you love it.

Thank you to Victoria who has put up with me on the edits of these last two books. You have some amazing skills, and patience. These books are better because of your due diligence.

Finally thanks to Elizabeth, my original beta reader and amazing proofreader. You're awesome.

CHAPTER 1

Heat filled her cheeks as she rushed across the dock toward the ship she'd secured passage on. Pearla Montgomery wanted as much distance between her and England as she could possibly get. Had anyone ever experienced such monumental embarrassment?

"No. That honor only goes to me," she muttered under her breath.

She had been so close to marrying Noah St. John, the Duke of Huntly. She'd fallen in love with him the moment she saw him. The hurt spilling out of his chocolate brown eyes...all she wanted to do was wrap him up in her arms and ease the pain away. Noah didn't or, to be more accurate, *couldn't* love her. She knew that, but she hoped in time he would at least come to care for her.

Unfortunately, his not-so-dead wife had crashed their wedding. *Had it only been that morning?* Rubina had waltzed into the church without a by-your-leave. Not that the woman needed permission. Her husband had been about to marry another woman. In her position, Pearla would have done the same. If only she'd come home sooner and prevented the resulting embarrassment. For that alone, Pearla resented her intrusion.

No one had known Rubina lived. Noah believed he lost her to a watery gave when a ship she'd been sailing on capsized in a storm. Pearla believed if he'd been aware Rubina was alive he'd have searched for her. The duke hadn't said much about his wife, but it was clear he loved her. The tone in his voice changed whenever he said her name. When she'd appeared at the church, it had become clear the duchess's resurrection was the end of Pearla's relationship with Noah. It was a combination of sadness and happiness that filled her heart at the sight of Rubina. She was ecstatic for him, and morose that she had to relinquish the connection they'd shared. Rubina was the woman he loved; Pearla was the usurper in their relationship.

"Just my luck." Pearla sighed and marched toward the ship.

She'd rushed home, demanded her maid to remove her wedding attire, and ordered her trunks packed for a different trip. If she never laid eyes on the bloody dress ever again, it'd be too soon. At the day's start, she'd thought she would be moving into Noah's townhouse. The staff had been given instructions to send the trunks to his home later in the day. Pearla was no longer going to be his duchess, and never would be. Not that she wanted the title; it'd been the man she craved. Sadly, she had to let go of that desire. Now, here she was, hours later, preparing to embark on an alternate excursion. The sun would be setting on all her hopes and dreams in a few hours. This was a day she'd not soon forget, but not for the reasons she originally thought.

"Can I help you, missy?"

Pearla turned and held in a breath. She cringed at the sight of the burly man before her. His demeanor was menacing, and he was covered in dirt and grime. By the smell of him he'd not deigned to bathe in several days—perhaps weeks. He stood near the gangway to board the ship, blocking her path. She lifted her chin and glared at him as haughtily as she could manage.

"I am Miss Pearla Montgomery. I have passage on this ship."

"Do you now?" His eyes leered across her bosom. "Why don't you wait here while I go and find the Captain."

It took everything she had to not visibly shake under his lewd gaze. This was just a means to an end. It wouldn't do to

574

stay in England and watch Noah being blissfully happy with his wife. No one expected Pearla to stay and witness their reunion. Her best friend, Gemma Marsden supported her decision. She was happy for Noah. Truly, she was.

However, she wasn't in the least joyful at her own circumstances. Running away from the problems life had thrown at her wasn't an ideal situation. Everything she'd done since her wedding had ended in failure screamed of desperation. It was a sad fact. She'd loved a man who wasn't available. If only she'd known before she'd suffered the shame of loving him. Losing him and what they could have had... She shook her head and cleared her thoughts. Noah wasn't hers. That unfortunate outcome was for the best. Marriage hadn't been in her plans until he waltzed into her life. It was time to do what she'd originally intended. Travel the world and see what it had to offer. The morning's disaster prompted what should have been her path all along.

"Miss Montgomery?"

Pearla's gaze shot upward and landed on a tall man with a scruffy beard. "Yes."

"My bosun tells me you've secured passage aboard my ship."

She played with her lip between her teeth. There better not be some mistake. It would be awful if she'd been played a fool and some thief, under the guise of booking her passage, stole her funds. She had to be on this ship. "I spoke to someone named Paolo about an hour ago."

He narrowed his eyes and studied her. He nodded. "I am Captain Blythe. I do recall Paolo saying we would have a couple passengers. Please, follow me."

A couple of passengers? She didn't bring a lady's maid. The idea of having anyone with her...made her uneasy. It was not something she wanted to deal with. As far as she was concerned, she didn't have a reputation to salvage. Why put up with someone that would only get in her way. Still, she couldn't help wondering who else was supposed to board the ship. She hoped the captain didn't expect them to share a cabin. Pearla wanted to be alone, and having a cabin mate would be too annoying.

The captain led her below deck to a small room with one

narrow bunk. She breathed a sigh of relief. With only one bunk, surely that meant she would be alone as she wished.

"Do you have trunks that needed to be brought aboard the ship?"

The captain's words snapped her out of her own mind. "Yes. They are in my carriage. Do you have someone that can retrieve them? If not, I can have the footmen bring them aboard."

He nodded. "I will have my men secure them below deck."

Pearla set her valise and reticule on the bunk. The only things she expected to have on the long journey were inside her traveling bags. The rest she'd worry over later. She didn't even have any idea where this particular ship was heading. It had the only thing she required when looking for passage: it left immediately.

"Captain," the burly man from earlier interrupted. "Our other passenger has arrived."

The captain turned toward him and said, "Perfect. Then we can set sail as soon as the anchor is hoisted."

The man stared lewdly at Pearla. She gulped back unease that pooled at the bottom of her stomach. She would lock her door after they left. The way the man looked at her made her skin crawl.

"Are you wishing me to keep you company?" The disgusting man licked his lips suggestively. Pearla lifted her hand and held a finger under her nose. The captain needed to control his men better. This one in particular needed to understand his place better.

Pearla shook her head and stumbled back into the room. "No. I'm fine. Honestly. Perhaps you should help with the new passenger." She gestured toward the captain.

"Leave the young lady alone, Perry," the captain ordered. "She's right. I do need your help with our new guest. Besides, the boss gave express instructions to make sure we keep Miss Montgomery safe on her journey."

Perry? She wrinkled her nose. Even his name was distasteful. The captain's smile made her feel even more uneasy. Paolo must be his boss. He did seem overly concerned for her welfare. Maybe she had lucked out in that regard. She certainly hoped so because she didn't like how Perry was ogling her. He smacked his lips as if anticipating his favorite sweet treat would touch his tongue. It wasn't something she particularly liked seeing. He was a combination of scary and disgusting. Did he believe in bathing at all? She wanted to cover her nose and mouth again. It took every ounce of etiquette instilled in her to refrain from doing so. He could leave the cabin and his offending odor would still linger.

"Too bad. We could have had some fun, you and I." He wiggled his eyebrows. "Let me know if you be changing your mind."

"While I appreciate your, um…" She paused, considered her words, "offer, I must decline."

"We will leave you to make yourself comfortable." The captain turned to leave. "Please stay in your cabin for now. You will be in the way as we set sail. I will let you know when it's safe to come on deck."

Pearla nodded. She didn't have a problem with the request. She was more than happy to wallow in self pity in her cabin. It would give her time to properly grieve what she lost. The man of her dreams… How does a woman get over that?

The captain closed the door with a *click*. A key turned in the lock. *What the hell?* She said she would stay in the cabin. Why would the captain lock her inside? She walked over to the door and yanked at the door knob, hoping she'd been wrong. Unfortunately, she wasn't. The damned man had made it impossible for her to leave.

That uneasy feeling turned into angry knots pounding through her whole body. Her breathing became frantic. There was very little light in the cabin. The small porthole only allowed a tiny stream of sunlight into the room. Was she to suffer in the dark? She scanned the room to see if perhaps there was a lantern she could light. Nothing.

She stormed back to the door and pounded on it with her fists. "Let me out. Let me out now. I can't breathe."

No one came to her rescue. She was truly stuck. What had she gotten herself into?

Pearla crumpled against the wall underneath the porthole.

Letting the sun bathe her in what little light the hole allowed. She let her face drop into her palms as tears fell from her eyes. In everything that happened, she hadn't allowed herself the time to cry. She'd lost so much, and apparently she was about to lose much more before the day was done. It served her right for acting so foolhardy.

Stupid. Stupid. Stupid.

Pearla wasn't sure how much time passed as she gave into her misery, but it seemed like ages. She glanced at the porthole. There was still some sunlight, so night hadn't fallen yet. When she arrived on the dock it had been early evening. The setting sun gave her something to work with time-wise. With the onset of warm weather, they gained more daylight hours, which meant she'd been locked in the cabin at least a couple hours. The door creaked open, and Pearla shot to her feet. Finally, someone was coming to let her out. They had heard her. *Thank God.*

A body was shoved inside. Whoever it was tumbled to the ground with a loud *thud*. Just as fast as the door opened, it was closed again. She hopped over the unconscious figure and pounded on the door.

"You can't leave him in here with me. Come back," she shouted. "There isn't room enough for one person, let alone two."

They ignored her. Bloody rotten bastards, the lot of them. She would get even with them for being so inconsiderate. Her fists clenched tight against her side as her cheeks flushed with heat. It might take time, but they would regret treating her like common baggage.

A small groan filled the silence. Perhaps she should check on her cabin mate. Who knows what they did to the poor soul. Pearla kneeled down beside him and rolled him over onto his back. Sunlight spilled across his face, and she sucked in a breath. He had an angry knot swelling across his forehead, but everything else about him was perfect. Inky black hair curled around his shoulder, and his face was almost too pretty to be considered handsome. She brushed back his hair to get a better look at his injuries. He moaned with her ministrations. His eyes flew open and she once again had the breath knocked out of her. His eyes were so beautiful.

They were a silver gray that sparkled in the tiny sliver of sunlight sliding through the porthole.

"Who are you?" His voice reminded her of warmed brandy. She'd only consumed the amber liquor once; it'd been enough to know she'd been playing with fire. When this man spoke, his rich timber was similar to that blaze engulfing her from the inside out.

"I should be asking you the same. Why would Captain Blythe toss you in a cabin with me and lock the door?" Pearla shook her head. "What did you do to anger him?"

More importantly what had she done to deserve such ill treatment? At least they didn't shove a malodorous beast into the cabin with her. She'd not have been able to suffer through such torture. Perry's stench had been rotten. This man almost smelled—nice. If she was forced to share her space with a disreputable man, she could be thankful he wasn't disgusting to gaze upon either. There could be worse fates...

"I had the audacity to disagree with his boss's treatment of my sister." His eyes narrowed. "What did you do to anger him?"

She chewed on her bottom lip. "I don't have any idea."

"What is your name?" he asked.

She shook her head. "You first."

He chuckled and then winced with pain. His hand flew to his forehead. "Fair enough. But have pity on me. I have one bloody hell of a headache."

A smile twitched on her face. "I reserve the right to make life as difficult as possible, sir. I do not know you."

"I think I like you." A cocky grin filled his face. "I am Damian Leone or Conte Leone if you prefer formality." He lifted his hand and traced his fingers across her cheek. "If I get a choice, I'd have you call me Damian."

She raised an eyebrow. "Just Damian?"

"Yes. I have a feeling you and I are going to be spending a lot of time together."

Pearla frowned. "I hope not."

"Does my company displease you that much?"

How was she to explain it had nothing to do with him. This whole mess was not his fault at all. He was quite charming and beautiful to behold. She would have been entranced with him under other circumstances.

"You don't figure into my consideration. I am not familiar with you enough to ascertain if you're likeable or not." She shrugged. "However, I do have to find a way out of this cabin."

"I hate to tell you," he paused and sat up. "But we are not obtaining our freedom for some time. The ship is already sailing out of the harbor."

Pearla cursed and stood. She headed to the porthole and looked outside. The blasted man was right. They were already well on their way. How long had she been in the cabin before they tossed him inside with her? It didn't matter. They were stuck together. She'd have to make the best of it.

"Come, *cara,* and tell me how you found yourself in the company of such disreputable ruffians as those in the employ of Paolo, the Duca d'Sordillo."

"Who?" Pearla sat down on the bunk and huffed out a breath. "I'm not familiar with that name."

"No?" Damian frowned. "That doesn't make sense. Why would they stick you with me? Tell me your story; maybe I can figure it out once I have all the information. Why are you on this ship?"

"It's kind of a long story." How to explain her failed wedding to a stranger? It wasn't something Pearla looked forward to. She didn't even want to think about it let alone put voice to it.

"I have nothing but time, *cara.*" He waved his hand toward the porthole. "I think it's accurate to assume we will be confined to each other's company for the foreseeable future."

"Quit saying that," she demanded.

"What?" he asked, confused.

"I am not your darling."

"Ah." His lips tilted into one of his half-cocky smiles. "You have yet to tell me your name. What else am I to call you?"

Why did he have to have a valid point? More importantly, why did she still refuse to tell him her name? Maybe it was the fantasy of it. There was a certain romanticism to it all. Instead of telling him her name, she told him her story. This was exactly what she needed upon further reflection. A stranger was much easier to talk to then friends. Gemma had meant well, but she could see the pity mixed with concern in her friend's eyes.

"Today was supposed to be my wedding day," she began. When she finished, a loud whistle filled the room, and then he cursed more colorfully than she had.

"Bloody hell, you're Miss Pearla Montgomery." He scrubbed his hands over his face. "It all makes sense now."

"Well, I'm glad you understand what is going on." She crossed her arms across her chest and glared at him. "I sure don't. I'm as confused as ever." Like how the hell did he know who she was? She hadn't mentioned names. All she told him was her fiancé's presumed dead wife interrupted her wedding. The desire to leave England had made her jump on the first ship available. Had rumors spread that fast already?

His next words made her heart almost stop.

"Rubina is my sister."

She had the worst luck of anyone alive. Only she would have the misfortune of being stuck in a room with the brother of the woman who'd ruined her life. Someone out there truly hated her.

CHAPTER 2

"Ignoring me isn't going to solve all of your problems."
Damian stared at Pearla. The sun was low in the sky,
illuminating her golden blonde hair. He could see why Noah
had been attracted to the beauty. She'd been bloody obstinate
for weeks. They'd managed small talk when it was required.
Nothing personal or what they needed to discuss. She was
pouting because he'd tried once again to broach the subject.
"We *are* going to be stuck with each other for a while, so we
might as well get to know each other.

When Rubina showed up at his ship near Palermo, he'd
been overjoyed to find out she was alive. After he'd gotten
over his shock he couldn't stop hugging her. They rushed
back to England to stop her husband's wedding. Not once on
their race to get there had they stopped to think how it would
affect Noah's fiancée. It saddened him that his sister's
happiness caused Pearla misery. When she'd told him her
story, he wanted to hug her for different reasons. The lost and
lonely look in her eyes called out to him. He wanted to erase
all of her worries and make the world a better place for her.
She was a headstrong woman though and refused to talk to
him. How was he to ease her concerns if she wouldn't
share them?

If he was correct, Paolo had brought them together for a
reason. Whatever nefarious scheme the evil man hatched

could be their undoing. Paolo hated him, but hated Noah more. Pearla had been set to marry the duke. Hurting her only meant one thing: it was a way to get even with Noah for obtaining Rubina's love. He'd gone over every detail in depth, and there was no other reason for Paolo to kidnap Pearla.

"I'd rather not." She leaned against the cabin wall and folded her arms across her generous bosom. "If it's all the same to you, please pretend I'm not here."

Damian chuckled. Stubborn chit. "Let's talk this over a bit."

She turned toward him, her eyes a blue flame sparkling in the light. "I already told you I don't want to speak to you. Why are you being so relentless?"

She needed him. Why couldn't she see that? Damian would get through to her. He'd never been able to resist a woman in distress. Pearla put on a good show, but he recognized the fear she tried to suppress. He made her uncomfortable. It was up to him to put her at ease. She didn't realize how fortunate she was to have him locked in the cabin with her. Any other man would have taken advantage of the situation. Honor prevented him from preying on innocents.

"Because we are in a bind, and you may not like it, but you and I are in this mess together."

They'd been on the ship for days—no weeks. Damian had no idea how long she stewed in silence. She even ate their meager meals without complaint. What woman could hold back their disdain with such ease? Their captors didn't make life easy for them. Each day had begun to blur into the next. It had to have been at least a fortnight, probably longer. It was time for her to stop being so bloody stubborn. They'd no doubt be reaching their destination soon.

"When we reach port, I will find a way out of this cabin and put as much distance between us as possible." She lifted her hand and ran her fingers through her mess of curls. She cursed as they got stuck in a knot. They'd not been allowed baths, but they'd been provided with a pitcher of water, a small basin, and a bar of soap. Pearla had used the water and soap to wash her face and hair. He'd offered to help her, but she'd refused. Her hair dried into the mess of curls she fought to run her hands through.

"Do you have a brush in your reticule?" he asked.

Earlier, her eyes had been pure fire—the gaze she now threw him was pure ice. How she could go from one emotion to the next, Damian didn't know, but he wanted to find out.

"Why do you ask?"

When would she give in and stop being so difficult? He'd let her use most of the water for bathing. He'd only had enough for a quick wash. Surely she'd start to see, at some point, he wasn't a bad person and could be trusted. Damian sighed. "I can brush out the knots if you'll let me."

Pearla stared at him as if he'd grown three heads. Was it so odd for him to offer to help her? He wanted to make her as comfortable as possible. Noah had cared about her, and if something happened to his former fiancée he'd blame himself. His sister finally had her husband back. They didn't need any unnecessary guilt from whatever Paolo had in store for them. He was a devious bastard and was capable of anything. Besides, Damian rather liked her. She appealed to him. The little details she did impart only wetted his appetite for more. Miss Montgomery was willful, brave, and full of surprises. All traits he found intriguing, and it didn't hurt she was gorgeous.

"I don't think that's a good idea."

Damian shrugged. "Suit yourself."

He wasn't going to force her to allow him to help. There would come a time he would need her to trust him. When they did reach a port, they would have to rely on each other to escape. If he pushed now, she'd be less likely to follow him to their own mutual safety. In the short time they'd been locked in the cabin together, she'd come to mean something to him. When given the opportunity he'd like to explore what was between them. Their situation was complicated and wrought with emotional overload.

Pearla dug through her reticule and pulled out a brush with a polished silver handle. With a sigh she picked up the brush and tried to run it through her golden strands. A bit of sunlight hit the handle of her brush and blinded him. Damian cursed and shielded his eyes. He couldn't watch her with the sun daring to get in his way. *Blasted sunlight.* He wasn't lost on the irony. He craved to be outside enjoying the sun's warmth, but it was preventing him from enjoying the only lovely view available to him.

Pearla winced. Damian couldn't stand watching her torture herself. "When are you going to give in and let me help you?"

He wanted to know if her hair was a silky soft as it looked. But he also wanted to help her, and she was refusing something so simple. He could brush her luscious locks better since he had easier access to the long tresses. They were so long that they fell past her waist in waves.

Damian clenched his fists at his side. These were not thoughts he should entertain. He needed the lady to trust him. It would do no good for her to know exactly how much he desired her. If she'd allow it.

No, he wouldn't go there. She was not for him. His life was far too dangerous for a wife and children. He couldn't risk a family when they'd only be at constant risk.

Another wince filled the room. Bloody hell, when would she give in? He thought Rubina was stubborn—Pearla took it to all new levels.

"Fine." She threw the brush at him. "See if you can do a better job."

"Why, *cara*, you beg so sweetly." The corner of his mouth twitched. He fought the smile that wanted to form. "Since you asked so eloquently…"

Finally, permission to touch her. Yes, it was to brush her hair, but it was something he craved. One concession would lead to another, and before long he'd have everything he desired. He wanted to be deep in all she had to offer. One taste or one touch would not be enough. All he knew for certain was that she was the one woman he desired more than any other. Maybe it was because he believed her to be forbidden.

She glared at him. "Don't make this even more difficult than it already is."

He winced as he stood and walked over to her. Pain shot through his side with each movement. Paolo's men had done a number on him. He'd begun to heal, but it would still take several more days for him to be at full strength.

"Turn your face away from me." He sat down on the bed beside her. "I will be able to get the knots untangled better with full access to your lovely hair."

"Quit trying to be charming. I am immune to the likes of you." She threw the words at him as she turned her body.

Damian wanted to see if she was as immune as she claimed to be. He doubted it. Noah had told him that he was only marrying Pearla so he could have children. The Duke of Huntly needed heirs. His brother-in-law believed he was incapable of loving any woman other than his sister, Rubina. Seeing his former fiancée in the flesh, he found it hard to believe he wouldn't have fallen in love with her eventually. Hell, he was half in love with her already, and he'd only been in her company for a short time. He shook his head. What was this nonsense he was thinking? He didn't love her. Lust? Definitely. Love was an entirely different thing.

"Your hair is as silky as I thought it would be." He picked up a few strands and ran the brush through them. "You shouldn't have let them get so tangled. We could have avoided this if you had tried to brush it hours ago."

"Forgive me for having more pressing matters on my mind," she spat out. "My hair was the last thing I thought to take care of."

Damian chuckled quietly. It wouldn't do for her to know how her anger amused him. "Rightly so. This is a precarious situation we are in."

She sighed. "Tell me why they put us together."

"Why are you suddenly interested in your fate?" He raised an eyebrow. "You seemed perfectly content to ignore my existence for days now."

He couldn't help needling her. It was about bloody time she started to get on board with what was happening to them. She needed to know everything if she was going to be fully armed for the battle they were going to face. They'd wasted too much time with her stubbornness. He'd tried to tell her what happened with his sister several times. Paolo was an evil man and his deeds shouldn't be taken lightly. They were on the ship together for a reason. Damian hadn't ascertained what that was yet, but he had a feeling they'd find out soon. Whatever the duca's plans were, Damian was sure of one thing—they wouldn't end well. His sister's tale was one of torture, both emotional and physical. He wanted to spare Pearla such a fate if possible. Their own predicament already bordered on it.

"I wasn't ready to admit I needed to know. When Rubina…" She paused and took a deep breath. "It was more than I could deal with. I had to get away. You wouldn't understand."

"So you loved him?" Damian asked softly. He cursed inwardly. Of course she did. From what he understood, many women had coveted the title of Duchess of Huntly. It would have taken someone extra special to catch Noah's eye. The duke had standards. He wouldn't have chosen Pearla lightly, especially since she would've been the mother of his future heirs. So he'd wooed her without giving her his heart—Pearla apparently hadn't been so lucky.

Damian hadn't begrudged Noah any happiness. His sister loved him, and for that he'd wanted to see him happy. It'd been clear to him that Noah hadn't been without her. The duke went through the motions, put on a good show, but the sadness never left him. When Noah believed Rubina died, a part of him had too. It was something Damian could appreciate, in a way. He loved his sister, but romantic love was something he'd never experienced. He had no idea how he'd react if he'd lost the love of his life. If he ever experienced such pain, he hoped he could live through it with as much grace as his brother-in-law. How Noah managed to survive it, he would never understand.

"I thought I did. Maybe I was in love with the idea of love." She turned her head slightly. A tiny tear fell from the corner of her eyes. "I had plans. I wanted to heal his heart. Oh, I know he didn't love me… But I thought, in time, he'd at least come to care for me. It's taken me the days I've spent in this cabin with you to come to terms with what I've lost."

Damian paused, holding the brush against her hair. He could understand that a little bit. It wasn't easy to lose a dream. Noah wasn't the love of her life, but that didn't make the plans she'd made any less important. He resumed brushing and inhaled her scent—a whisper of lilies mingled with vanilla.

"I suppose we should start at the beginning." Damian needed a distraction and talking was the best one he could come up with. "Paolo is obsessed with my sister. She didn't leave Noah willingly. He held her captive and arranged for everyone to believe she died." Rubina's supposed death had nearly destroyed Damian, and he'd thrown himself into his work with the government to bury his grief.

Pearla gasped and jerked around to look at him. "That's terrible. How did she manage to get away from him?"

"It was pure luck." He sighed. "We've been watching Paolo for different reasons. He's an evil man and has ties to the Sicilian mafia. We don't know how deep he's in…"

"So you rescued her?"

He shook his head. "No, my man Arturo did. He discovered her presence by accident. He'd been working undercover as their gardener. When Paolo left for business one night, Arturo brought Rubina to me."

Damian hadn't believed it was her at first. He wanted to, but the shock of it… Anger at the unnecessary grief came crashing down on him all at once. Paolo had to pay for the injury he caused his family. Rubina came first. They left Palermo immediately to see to her care. On the journey to Naples, they made plans and discovered Noah was in danger. He still was if Rubina hadn't eradicated the problem. His only choice was to have faith in his sister, and her husband. Noah wouldn't stay in the dark for long. He'd made his suspicions clear when he came to Damian's room to collect Rubina. That had been one of the longest days of Damian's life. Noah and Pearla's failed wedding day would be forever ingrained in his memory. Now, he was stuck on a ship and couldn't help his sister. All he could do was pray she was able to eradicate Paolo and keep her husband safe. He had a new objective; Pearla's safety was his utmost concern.

"That must have been quite a shock for you. I remember the look on Noah's face when she showed up to the wedding… Everyone else disappeared for him. I knew then that he never would have loved me, at least not the way he loved her." Her voice was tinged with sadness. It broke as she spoke. "It hurt to see it."

He found himself wanting to console her. No one should

have their heart broken in such a manner. It was too late to prevent it, but maybe he could ease her pain in other ways. Loving a man shouldn't be a hardship. It should be a joy to be reveled in. Noah unwittingly destroyed a part of her. The reason for it didn't matter. The fact it happened was all that counted.

"You deserve to have that kind of love. Don't sell yourself short."

"You're right. I needed time and distance to see that for myself." She turned her head slightly; a tiny wistful smile filled her face. "Are you almost done brushing my hair?"

Damian stared at her lips. He wanted to kiss her. The desire flooded him to his depths and he fought for control. "Almost, *cara*."

"When are you going to cease calling me that?"

"Never," he replied.

"I wish you would. That is a lover's term." She frowned. "We are not lovers."

Not yet anyway… Damian had no doubt they would be someday. It was no longer a matter of if, but a matter of when. Something about her made him want things he shouldn't. This might not end well. Perhaps he should give into his desires and take what they both wanted. He wasn't ignorant to the little looks she kept throwing him. She had a bit of desire growing inside her too.

Instead, he finished his story. "To make a long story short we knew Paolo was in England. We were hoping to find him before he did something to Noah or my sister. It looks like we were too late. There is no better way to hurt both of them than to kidnap us both."

Pearla gasped. "But, I don't mean that much to Noah. That's ridiculous."

"You keep telling yourself that if it makes you feel better. He may not have been in love with you, but Noah did care about you."

Damian was glad his sister was alive for more reasons than one. It freed Pearla to find someone who would appreciate her. Noah cared for her, but not enough. He'd never have gotten over his sister. Pearla was better off, and soon she'd realize it.

Her mouth fell open at his words. "I..."

"It's all right to accept that you meant something to him. You were going to be married after all."

Damian was rather glad that wedding didn't actually happen. The lust flowing through his blood wouldn't have boded well with his relationship with Noah. The man would have killed him if he'd touched his wife. Lucky for him, she was unencumbered and he could let his desires run free.

"You're right. You're damn near perfect. Why wouldn't you be?" She bit her lip. "Of course you are. It's a lot to let sink in. What does this mean for us?"

Paolo was determined to make him pay. It wasn't only because the duca was obsessed with his sister. He had other reasons for hating Damian. Pearla was caught up in a mess he'd made. If he could change things... He shook his head. The time for regrets had passed. He owned his mistakes, and it was time to explain his part in the mess they were in.

"I've never claimed to be perfect." He lifted his hand and ran his fingertips over the top of her head. "Mistakes are a part of life, and I've made my fair share of them."

"Do tell." She goaded him. "What was the one mistake you regret the most?"

Believing his sister had died. No, that wasn't his mistake. It was something someone forced upon him. "I seduced a woman for information. It didn't sit well with me, but I believed at the time the end justified the means. I was wrong, and it hurt her terribly."

Paolo's sister had been that woman. She'd been innocent of any wrong doing. She'd been forever altered from that transgression. He'd broken her heart after he deserted her. Damian couldn't change what he'd done, but from that moment on he'd vowed to never do anything so malicious ever again.

"You used a woman and you expect me to have faith in you?"

He had to be honest with her. Telling her had been a risk, but he'd hoped she would see it as him being open. Damian didn't want to hide anything from her.

"I will understand if you don't. It's a lot to ask." He frowned. "I hate for you to think badly of me, but it's necessary for you to have all the information. He finished brushing her hair. It shimmered in the fading sunlight. "You and I have to rely on each other to get out of this mess. You have to trust me and let that stubborn streak you are so fond of go."

"I'm not making any promises." She sighed and glared at him. "I am not stubborn."

He laughed. "*Cara*, trust me. You are by far the most obstinate woman I have ever met." He leaned down and kissed the tip of her nose. "But don't worry; I rather like that side of you."

She folded her arms across her chest. "Stop that."

"What?" His eyebrow rose. "I've done nothing."

She stomped her foot and glowered at him. "Quit making me like you."

Women. Would he ever understand them? "Maybe you should accept what is between us and make things easier on yourself."

"I wouldn't know what you could possibly mean."

"Perhaps it would be better to show you…"

Damian pulled her into his arms and found her lips with his. A small gasp fell between her lips allowing him to take advantage of her open mouth. He touched her tongue with his. She tentatively touched his in return.

That's it, cara. *Let me in.*

Damian deepened the kiss. He cupped her breasts in his palms. She moaned as he continued his ministrations. If he pushed a little bit he could have her—but he didn't want her like this. They may be living on borrowed time, but he would rather her not regret being with him. Pearla deserved to be wooed.

With every ounce of control he could muster, he pulled back. He groaned at the sight of her. Her lips were plump from his kiss and her cheeks were flushed a bright pink.

"Why did you stop?" Her breaths were ragged as she spoke. It made him want to pull her back into his arms all over again. Every inch of her screamed her desire at him. His self control was close to toppling over the edge.

"You deserve better than a quick tumble on a tiny cot in a dark musty cabin. When I make love to you, *cara*—and I will be on a soft bed with at least a hundred candles lit so I can look my fill."

Damian had to remind himself over and over again why it was not a good idea to give in to their mutual desire. Pearla was so damned pretty and delectable. He closed his eyes and took a deep breath. When he opened them again, he had to clench his hands into tight fists or he'd have pulled her back into his arms again. Being a gentleman was so bloody difficult at times.

Her eyes softened. "Maybe one day I will let you do that too. But you were right to stop this now. I want so much more than to lose my innocence in a hasty act of foolishness."

"Oh, *cara*, trust me, there would have been nothing hasty involved."

She smiled. "If it makes you feel better to think so."

Damian cursed. It was as if she was baiting him to give in and make love to her. He couldn't allow her to gain the upper hand. He meant what he said. Pearla should be loved properly. He still wasn't sure he was that man, but he wanted to be.

"*Cara...*"

The door swung open, and they both turned to see who was barging in on them. Damian frowned.

A dirty man with a full black beard filled the doorway. "Oh, good, you're both awake. The captain has something planned for you both tonight. Come with me. You both are about to witness something you will never forget."

Damian cursed. Whatever it was, it couldn't be good.

CHAPTER 3

The dirty-bearded bosun who'd leered at her when she boarded the ship gripped Pearla's arm and yanked her forward.

"Let me go," she demanded.

"Sorry, missy, captain's orders. You're coming with me."

Pearla wrenched her arm free and stumbled backward. Her backside hit the floor. She winced as pain shot through her. Damian helped her to her feet.

"It'll be all right, I promise," he whispered in her ear.

Pearla didn't believe anything would ever be all right again. She wasn't about to start giving herself false hope. No doubt Damian sought to give her some kind of comfort, but she knew better. Whatever the captain had planned was not good. She wanted to delay it as long as possible. If it meant she had to scratch the eyes out of the disgusting man in front of her, she would. It was quite clear what he wanted from her. If he got his way, he'd happily debauch her. There wasn't a chance in hell she'd go anywhere with him willingly.

"Having some problems, Perry?"

Pearla's gaze shot upward at the sound of a new voice joining the bosun. It appeared their luck was running out—if they ever had any to start with. The burly man had friends to help force them on deck.

"I can handle the chit. I like my women a bit feisty."

"Hurt her and you will die." The tone of Damian's voice was a combination of rigid and lethal. Pearla swung around to gaze into his silver eyes. She believed he was capable of murdering them all, if only he was at full strength. Unfortunately, he was still healing from the beating he'd taken a few weeks ago. Their time locked in the cabin had allowed him some time to heal, but she didn't believe it was enough.

"Don't worry, Conte. Your time will come soon enough." The bosun leered at them both. "You two, help him topside." He gestured toward two sailors standing nearby. "The missy and I will follow shortly behind you."

Pearla shuffled her feet backward. She couldn't let the evil man anywhere near her. If she did, he'd get his way. The very idea of having him touch her in any way made her skin crawl. Disgust wrapped itself around her stomach as she fought dry heaves. He stalked toward her, preparing once again to grab her. He took two steps, his gaze filled with licentious intent.

The bosun made one fatal mistake. He hadn't allowed the other two men to help Damian topside before he made advances on Pearla. Without any hint of his intent, Damian's fist flew through the air and landed square between the bosun's eyes. Perry's eyes rolled back, and he crumpled to the ground with a loud *thud*.

"Bloody hell." One of the sailors scratched his beard as he studied the bosun's unconscious body. "I suppose we'll have to leave him here for the time being. Someone else can drag his stupid arse out of the room. I'm not doing it"

His co-conspirator nodded at him and then at Damian. They both lunged and grabbed him. One held his arms around his neck in a chokehold. The other held a knife to his gut. "Make one wrong move, and you will bleed like a stuck pig."

Damian held his body completely still. What a mess. How were they going to get out of this now? Pearla bit her lip as she studied the two ruffians. They looked like they'd studied at the school of pirate comportment. There wasn't a doubt in her mind they would kill them both if they believed them to be a threat.

"Now, missy, don't be getting ideas. We don't particularly

want to upset the plans the captain be having, but don't make the mistake of thinking we won't kill you and throw your body overboard. If you want your friend here to live to actually see the deck, then you best follow behind us all nice like."

All the warmth she had in her body seemed to drain right out of her. If she were to look in a mirror, she'd probably be as pale as the white clouds floating in the sky. She nodded her head at them. Now was not the time to put up a fight. Besides it was the bosun who'd meant to ruin her. These men wanted them to go meet with the captain. Whatever he had planned couldn't be as bad as what the bosun had meant to do to her.

"I'll do as you ask." Her lips wobbled as she spoke. No. That wouldn't do. They couldn't know how much their actions struck terror in her soul. She squared her shoulders and tried to show no fear. "Please be careful where you stick that blade. You might accidentally poke a hole in Damian, and that would be quite a bloody mess."

Damian's lips twitched as he fought a smile. He rolled his eyes. "Nice of you to show such concern for my well-being."

She snorted. "Who said anything about caring what happens to you?" She raised an eyebrow. "I rather not deal with the repercussions of your imminent demise. I only have one dress, and it wouldn't do to walk around in my chemise the rest of the journey."

The bosun already had issues keeping his hands to himself. She didn't need to give him any more ideas. She didn't want Damian hurt—truly—but she also had to think of what would happen to her if something nefarious happened to him. He appeared to be the only man on board concerned about her welfare. He was also all that stood between her and the evil intentions some of the sailors directed at her. As much as she hated to admit it, she needed him. They were stuck together, and she depended on him.

"You wound me." His eyes sparkled with mischief. "If we were alone, I'd remind you how much you would care if something happened to me."

The charming rogue had a valid point. She'd desired him more than she wanted to admit. She'd enjoyed his kisses and wanted to see where they would lead. If he hadn't stopped, they'd have gone a lot further in their exploration of each other. A fire had ignited within her that she'd never experienced before. Damian's touch only made her crave more. He was too handsome, and alluring for her poor female heart to withstand. He didn't need to know the full extent of the temptation he presented.

"But we aren't alone, are we?" She tilted her head and held back the smile that threatened to form on her face. What was it about this man that amused her so? "Gentleman I believe you were leading us up to the deck. What does the captain have planned to entertain us? Remind me to lodge some complaints about the accommodations. When I secured passage aboard this ship, I thought I'd have a cabin to myself. It's completely unacceptable that he not only stuffed me in a room with another passenger, but a male one at that. It's going to ruin my impeccable reputation."

Both men's mouths fell open in shock. Good. If she kept them guessing, they wouldn't have time to think about what they might or might not do. She didn't even know exactly where they were. Somewhere in the massive ocean—they could only hope they were somewhere near land.

"Where exactly are we heading anyway?" Both men stared at her blankly. She snapped her fingers and waved in front of their faces. "Can you hear me?"

"I don't understand your question," one of them finally answered her.

She rolled her eyes. "Are you two imbeciles? What port?"

"Oh...um..."

Damian started laughing. One of them punched him in the gut, resulting in some harsh coughs. Pearla wanted to smack some sense into him. Why was he acting like such a bloody idiot? Surely he knew what he provoked with his projected amusement. He must be insane. It was the only explanation for his behavior. If he kept up his current demeanor, they'd murder them and toss them overboard.

"Do you have a death wish?" Pearla stomped her foot. "Do you not at least feel the pointy object in the vicinity of your gut?"

"Oh, I feel it," he wheezed out. "If you don't want me to laugh, then quit making jests."

"I didn't think that was a joke. I truly want to know where we are headed."

Information was power. She wanted to gain all the advantages she could. It was the only way they would have any chance of escaping. She would not spend years imprisoned as Damian's sister Rubina had. There was too much life in her to be stifled in such a way.

"Quit your jabbering and walk in front of us." The man gestured with his head.

"But I don't know where I'm going…" These two were actually idiots. How was she to lead when she didn't know the ship?

"Start walking. We will give you directions as we go."

"Hmmph. Fine." Still didn't make sense to her. What did they think she'd do if she followed? Walk into a different room below deck and disappear? What good would that do? Someone would find her eventually and stuff her back in the room with Damian. If she were being honest with herself, she was glad she had him for company. He made her feel…safe.

Pearla stepped out of the door and eased her way down the dark passage. There had been only one way to turn outside of the door. She had forgotten the cabin was at the end of the passageway. How long had they been locked in that cabin? She'd stopped counting days a while ago. She knew it was weeks…but what if it had been longer.

"Keep going straight."

"Where else am I going to go?" How bloody stupid were they? "It's not as if there are any other passages I could accidentally go down."

"Keep your trap shut and move."

They got irritated rather easy. Maybe she should talk more and put them further on edge. No. If they got too mad they might stick Damian with that knife just because they could. She couldn't risk it. Chatting for the sake of ticking them off wouldn't do them any favors.

"Turn left and follow the ramp up."

Pearla did what he told her to and followed the ramp all the way until they hit the deck. The sun was low on the horizon. If only they could have been topside to see it high in the sky. The little bit of light that came through the porthole wasn't nearly enough. They had very little, and when the sun fell each night the moonlight was a poor comparison.

She stopped in front of the ship's railing. Surely they didn't expect her to walk right overboard. Pearla peeked over her shoulder. They dragged Damian over and shoved him next to her.

"Don't even think of doing something stupid, Conte. Captain Blythe will be here shortly to deal with you both." The crew members kept close eye on them, not leaving their side.

Where did they think they could possibly go? "Is he going to make us walk the plank?" Pearla asked.

"*Cara*, please don't give them ideas."

She turned and glared at Damian. "I told you not to call me that."

He shrugged. "I doubt I will stop any time. You might as well get used to it."

"Nice to see you both getting along." Captain Blythe strolled over to join them. "It will go well with what I have planned."

Damian's lips formed a firm, straight line. His eyes appeared to shoot daggers at the captain. It was evident he wanted to let loose every ounce of fury inside of him on the wretched man. Pearla wouldn't stand in his way. She wanted to push him overboard herself.

"What, no questions?" Captain Blythe's eyebrow rose. "As chatty as you two were before, I thought at least one of you would ask what tonight's festivities were going to be."

Oh, hell. From the tone of his voice something bad was about to take place. What *did* he have planned? For the life of her, she couldn't figure the captain out. Nothing made sense to her since she'd been locked inside the cabin. She needed answers. This debacle had to end.

Damian's chin jutted out with defiance. He wouldn't be asking anytime soon. So that meant Pearla would have to do it.

She studied her fingernails, acting as blasé as possible. Her head shot up and a smile of feigned joy lit her face. They had no idea what she was capable of. If she had to act helpless and stupid, she would. "Are we having a party?" She clapped her hands with false excitement. "Wonderful. Why didn't you two oafs say so? I'd have skipped happily up here. Do you have musicians? I'd love to dance and have some food and champagne." Pearla shot the words off in a rapid succession, only barely stopping to take a breath. She paused and surveyed the deck. "What, no decorations?"

Captain Blythe's laugh was full of menace. "Conte Leone, I'm going to enjoy tying you to this birdwit for the rest of your lives."

How dare that odious man insult her! She was not the moron in their situation.

He was for not seeing she was playacting. One she had to continue. It wouldn't do to let him see her for who she really was. She squeezed her eyes together with contrived confusion. "Who's a birdwit? Can you bring my trunks up? And maybe a bath too. If we're having a party, I'd like to get ready. It's been so long since I was able to do something fashionable with my hair."

Captain Blythe shook his head, and his laugh echoed loudly on the wind.

"What do you mean by tie me to her for the rest of my days?" Damian finally asked, his tone harsh. His face was devoid of emotion. The charming rogue was gone and replaced with a man who faced danger on a regular basis. Pearla repressed a shiver. What was he thinking?

"Oh, it's simple enough. You two are getting married —tonight."

Her mouth fell open at the captain's words. Surely he was jesting… Marry Damian? *No. Not. Happening.* She gritted her teeth together. How were they going to get out of this debacle?

CHAPTER 4

"I must have heard you wrong." Damian paused to let the captain's word sink in. "I swear you said something about getting married."

Damian didn't intend to ever get married. He liked Pearla well enough, but he didn't want or need a wife. Was this the nefarious plan Paolo hatched to ruin Damian? How was an unwanted marriage supposed to destroy him? None of it made sense. Captain Blythe played with his beard and laughed. Damian fought the urge to punch him in the face. Maybe if he broke his nose it would improve his visage. No. Nothing would make the dirty bastard look any better. Acting rashly wouldn't get them out of whatever the captain had planned.

"You heard correctly, Conte Leone." The captain's grin grew ever wider. "I get the honor of performing the ceremony."

Damian gritted his teeth. "On whose authority?"

"You know who. Don't worry, it will be relatively painless."

Pearla waved her hand. "Excuse me." Her voice was pure ice, as she glared at them all. "Don't I have a say in this?"

"Not at all, missy. Best be prepared to get hitched to the man you've spent weeks locked away with. Your reputation is in tatters. We're doing you a favor."

She snorted. "Please don't. I'd rather not get married today—or any day."

Damian's thought process mirrored hers. A wedding was not something he'd foreseen or even wanted. He still couldn't figure out why Paolo of Captain Blythe thought it would hurt them. Well, besides the fact neither one of them wished to enter into a union of any sort. As much as it pained him to admit it though, the captain had a valid point. Pearla was indeed ruined, and while he'd not intended it, his presence was a direct result of it. He had to help repair the damage. A wedding was the only option they had left to them.

"Too bad. You're going to get married whether you like it or not." The captain growled. "Now prepare to become blissfully wed."

"I decline." Pearla replied, her tone dripping with disdain. "I think I will return to those wonderful accommodations you have prepared for us."

Pearla turned to head below deck. Damian grabbed her wrist and held her in place. "Don't push your luck, *cara*."

A bad feeling festered in his gut. Damian didn't want to find out what would happen if they didn't go along with the captain—and Paolo's—reprehensible plans. A marriage could be undone, but dead was dead. You didn't come back from that. Pearla must be made to see reason. Their marriage would benefit her. They didn't have to act on it, but for appearances sake it would help her. One day they could find a way to dissolve it and move on with their lives. For now though, it had to happen if they would have any future at all.

"Let me go." She yanked at her wrist. "I'm not marrying you, and they can't make me."

Damian stared down at her and considered his options. They didn't have many.

"But I can," the captain interjected.

"How?" Pearla asked mulishly.

"It's simple. Either you marry him or you die?"

Pearla folded her arms across her chest and glared at the captain. "Kill me then. I will not bend to any man's will."

Damian groaned. "Don't give the man permission to end your life. Would it be so bad to marry me?"

He knew he wasn't a duke, but surely being tied to him

couldn't be all bad. He could provide for her and give her a life she was accustomed to. There were plenty of woman who'd found him attractive. Pearla wasn't immune to his charms. She'd fallen willingly into his arms not too long ago. Her moans told him a different story than her current objections. Why was she putting up such a bloody fight over a wedding?

"Yes." She didn't even turn to look at him. Her gaze was unwavering as she shot daggers at the captain. "I made up my mind; I will never marry. One humiliation in my lifetime was quite enough."

"If you don't value your life, perhaps you value his." The captain nodded to one of his men standing next to Damian.

"What do you…" Pearla gasped as one of the men held her arms at her side. "This is outrageous. What could us marrying have to do with you or your despicable boss?"

"It matters not. He wished to see it done, and it's my job to see it through." The captain replied, his voice harsh. "Don't worry your pretty little head about it. In time, you will understand everything."

One guy held Damian and the other held a knife at his throat. "Say the word, Captain, and I'll slit his throat."

Pearla gulped, her face whitening as she stared at Damian.

"Don't worry about me, *cara*. Do what you feel is best."

"You expect me to watch them kill you?" Her lips trembled. "What kind of person do you think I am?"

Damian didn't want her to feel responsible for him. He'd prefer not to die, but he didn't want to see her hurt any further. What Noah had done…Was unavoidable. He didn't know his wife still lived. That didn't erase the pain Pearla felt because of it.

"If you don't want to get married, we won't," Damian said firmly. Even if he believed it would be for the best. He'd never forced a woman to do anything she was unwilling to do. He wasn't about to start because a mad man held a knife at his throat.

The captain walked over to stand in front of them. "The little lady still seems to be reluctant. Perhaps something worse than death would persuade her to go along with the ceremony."

Pearla's gaze flew to the captain. "What do you mean?"

"I can arrange for my men to each have a turn with you. They've been itching to see what it's like to have a go between your lily white thighs. One word from me, and it will happen. I'll even force Conte Leone to watch."

Damian didn't think Pearla could get any whiter—he'd been wrong. With his fists clenched tight against his sides, he took a deep calming breath. The captain needed someone to break his face in more than one spot. Death would improve his disposition.

"I will decline your generous offer to watch your men debauch Miss Montgomery." Heat fused through his face. "Go ahead with your wedding. I think you've made our positions quite clear."

"You're both willing?" Captain Blythe asked. "I want to make sure we all understand what is at stake."

"We understand," Pearla muttered.

"Get on with it, man. I would like to return to the pleasant cabin you have been keeping us in." Damian's voice reverberated with barely contained fury.

This day was not one he'd soon forget. After all, it wasn't every day a wedding was forced upon him. He wanted it over with. When he was free, he'd enact his revenge. Now wasn't the time to see it through.

The captain laughed. "In a hurry to enjoy your wedding night? Say no more." He winked. "I know how much you've been looking forward to this. I will keep things simple."

What nonsense was the captain spouting now? Looking forward to his wedding night? He almost acted as if they'd planned this farce of a wedding together.

"Are you ready to become a wife?" He turned to Pearla.

She remained mute. A puzzled expression filled her face. "What has Damian been looking forward to?"

"Don't listen to him, *cara*." Damian shook his head. "He's clearly inebriated or has lost his mind."

Whatever game they were playing had taken a different turn. Damian was as confused as Pearla was. He just wanted to be done with them all.

"Oh, you know what I'm referring to conte." He shielded

his mouth with his hand, and in a loud whisper said, "Don't worry. Your secret is safe with me."

Damian scrubbed his hand over his face. "Can we move on? I'm not even going to pretend I understand what you're doing."

"Never let it be said I won't help a friend in need." The captain laughed, and gazed at Pearla. "Do you take Conte Leone as your husband?"

Right. Friend. He rolled his eyes, and waited for Pearla to answer the captain. Damian took a deep breath. If she didn't agree to the wedding, he didn't know what he would do. He couldn't watch the crew violate her. She had to say yes. It was the only answer that was acceptable. He understood her reservations. Honestly, he did, but in light of their choices, she had to let them go. They had no choice.

"It's a simple yes or no Miss Montgomery, or would you like to revisit the other options?" the captain asked.

"No."

"No, you won't marry him?"

She shook her head. "I don't need to go over what will happen if I don't marry him."

Damian let out a breath he hadn't realized he'd been holding. For a minute there he thought he'd become witness to a tragedy. Thank God she'd come to her senses.

"Then let's begin again. Release the conte so he can stand beside his bride."

The captain motioned to the man holding the knife to Damian's throat. He stepped next to Pearla and brushed her cheek with the back of his hand. Her skin was cold against his warmth.

"It'll be all right. I promise," he whispered.

Pearla shook her head, shifting her gaze away from his. It broke his heart in two. They could have had something. He saw it clearly now. If they'd been allowed to explore what was happening with them without interference, their life would have taken a different direction. Now he didn't think she'd ever be able to trust in him—in the blossoming desire building between them.

"Isn't he sweet, Miss Montgomery?" The captain laughed.

"See, he will be a devoted husband. You won't have to worry for *anything*."

"Please, keep your opinions to yourself. I've agreed to this farce of a wedding. Let's not add anymore." Damian glared at the captain. "I've had enough of your drivel for a lifetime."

"Since you're in a hurry, we will continue." The captain turned toward Pearla and asked. "Will you take Conte Leone as your husband?"

"I will." Her voice was barely above a whisper.

Time stood still as Damian stared down at his soon-to-be wife. Her gaze met his. It was filled with resignation and a tinge of defeat. Her mouth fell with a hint of sadness. He vowed to find a way to erase all her pain. The breeze blew her blonde hair around her shoulders. He reached over and brushed one of the curls with his hand. There were worse fates than to be tied to a beautiful woman. They'd figure out what it all meant later.

"Good. Now, Conte. Do you take Pearla as your wife?"

Damian closed his eyes and realized he actually did want to marry her. It shouldn't have gone this way, but this was a gift in a time of total bleakness. Sadly, it would take time to get his bride around to his way of thinking.

"I will." His voice was clear, concise, and full of conviction.

"Then, by the power granted to me as captain of this vessel, before God and these witnesses, I now declare you man and wife. I'd say you may kiss the bride, but I don't think that's a good idea at the moment. I don't want to get the boys all randy by watching you claim your woman." He nodded to the men holding the two of them in place. "Escort the Conte and Contessa to their room."

A rumble of thunder boomed overhead. Damian's gaze shot upward as a torrential downpour descended from the sky. He cursed. The look of the clouds above him told him they'd better prepare for a hell of a storm. The sooner they got below deck the better. He hoped Captain Blythe and his crew were prepared to battle the sea and sky.

The men pushed them down the ramp leading toward their cabin. When they reached the room Damian went in willingly, Pearla close behind him. The door shut with a *thud*, the key turning in the lock.

There was little light in the room. Damian could barely make out Pearla's silhouette in the darkness. The sounds of her crying devastated him. He made his way to her side and pulled her into his arms.

"Sshhh, *cara*." He soothed her with tenderness. "It's going to be all right. I promise."

Her fists beat against his chest as her quiet weeping turned to howling. "No, it won't. It will never be right ever again. We. Are. Married. How are you not as angry as I am?"

At first he had been. He didn't like being forced to do anything against his will. Now...it seemed right. He knew it would take time and gentle coaxing to convince her it was for the best. Luckily, he was a patient man. He would woo her, and one day maybe they could have a real marriage. For now, they had bigger problems. The largest being how they were going to escape from the ship. They had to be nearing land soon. With the storm raging above them, it couldn't happen soon enough.

"I fail to see why you are so upset." He shrugged. "Marriage isn't a fatal wound."

Her chin tilted up. Probably in defiance. His wife was a stubborn chit.

"No, it is much worse than that. It is a lifetime of torture." She pushed back on his chest to get out of his embrace. "I didn't want this."

Damian sighed. "*Cara*, we were both forced into this marriage. The difference between you and me is I'm willing to let it go and move forward. You keep harping on what can't be undone."

"This night can never be undone, but our marriage can. I will see to it as soon as I escape this hell ship." Pearla seethed. "If you think you are getting a wedding night, you are sadly mistaken."

He shook his head. "I never asked for one."

"Good because you will never touch me again." Her teeth chattered as she shivered.

The ship swayed violently, causing her to tumble forward, landing squarely in his arms. Damian's mouth twitched into a smile. He sent up a silent thanks to the storm for forcing her to be where he needed her. Her safety was his priority, especially now that they were wed. The rain splattering loudly against the ship told him the storm was in full force. They should bunker down for the night to ride it out. If she were to stay by his side, it would make his job much easier, as well as help keep her warm. Her body shook inside his arms. "We're going to die tonight, aren't we?"

"No, we have too much to live for. We should remove some of this wet clothing and get warm under the blankets." He motioned to her. "Come, *cara*, let's take cover on the bunk."

"I told you, I am not letting you make love to me." Her voice was full of scorn. "I will not be your wife in truth."

"You *are* my wife in truth." He frowned. "But to ease your fears, I will not make any demands of you. I don't want you in my bed out of obligation." He rather liked it when the women he bedded enjoyed it as much as he did. He looked forward to experiencing desire with her. She may have been willing to marry Noah and provide him an heir for a sense of duty, but Damian wanted more from a wife. Especially one he never expected to have.

Damian hoped to ease her fears. He spoke the truth. When —and there would be a when—he made love to Pearla, she would be a willing participant. He did not force himself on reluctant women. He didn't need to. There were more than enough women who desired to join him in his bed. It should irk him that the only woman he now desired didn't want him, but he never backed down from a challenge. Everything his pretty little wife did was exactly that. They would live a very interesting life together, provided they got the chance to live it.

"I mean it." She reminded him. "I will not lay with you."

Damian smirked. She might believe what she was spouting off, but he knew it wouldn't take much to change her mind. His wife had conveniently forgotten how she'd gotten lost in his kiss previously.

"This whole situation is far from proper." She nodded. "But you're right. We'll catch our death if we stay in wet clothing."

"True" His mood lightened. "But not everything is out of our control. Whether or not we enjoy each other is totally up to us. If you don't want to know what it is like to feel true pleasure, then that is your choice."

Pearla turned her back to him. "As long as we understand each other. Please unlace my dress."

He moved behind her, and kissed her shoulder. "When you're ready all you have to do is say the word. For now, we will only seek the warmth our bodies need to survive."

Damian slowly undid her laces, leaving them gaping open. She slid the dress off letting it pool into a pile on the floor, her delectable body only covered by a thin chemise. He stood rooted in one spot, clenching his fists against his side as he fought his desire. He'd promised he wouldn't act on his impulses, and he intended to keep his word. Pearla picked up her dress and draped it over a chair. She turned toward him. Her gaze met his and she gasped. The sun had fallen and they had almost no light, but the desire in her eyes was a flame that called to him. He must resist.

"Are you going to remove your wet clothing?"

Damian groaned. He was doomed to fail. "Yes," he croaked. He quickly removed his wet clothes, leaving his underclothes on, and set him near hers to dry. Each movement designed to keep his hands from seeking her delectable body.

"I'm getting chilly. I think you're correct. We need to seek warmth before we freeze." Pearla rubbed her shoulders.

Damian closed his eyes and took a deep breath. He could do this.

"Come. Let's get comfortable. The storm might last for hours, even days."

He led her to the bed and sat down. She remained quiet, but sat down beside him. Damian's lips tilted into a half-smile. He'd given her something to think about. The kiss they'd shared had been more than pleasant. Perhaps he should remind her—no he would respect her wishes. If she wanted to kiss him, he wouldn't stop her though.

"I will know pleasure one day." She blurted. "It just won't be with you."

The hell it won't. "If you say so *cara.*"

"I do. You will never know any kind of pleasure with me." Her voice was firm.

The shipped rocked violently causing them to fall backward on the bed. Pearla crawled on top of him and hid her head against his shoulder. He wrapped his arms around her hugging her tight.

"What were you saying?"

"This isn't delight at being in your arms, you oaf." She muttered against his chest. "This is me fearing for my life."

He laughed. "Where I am sitting, this is the greatest pleasure a man could ever have. I get to hold my wife and comfort her."

"Don't get used to it."

"I make no promises, *cara*."

If he got his way, they'd be spending many nights in the exact position they were in—only with far less clothing. Not that they were wearing much now. There was still enough preventing him from having her naked in his arms. Damian groaned. His wife had no clue where his mind was wandering. It was for the best. If she knew, she'd move away from him, and that would defeat his purposes. One day she would willingly fall into his arms. It was one promise to himself he intended to keep.

"Oh, be quiet, Damian. I like you much better when you don't open your mouth."

He chuckled lightly. "Settle in and get comfortable. I have a feeling this storm is going to last all night."

Damian wanted to tell her he could do a lot of things with his mouth she'd enjoy quite a bit, but he knew when to hedge his bets. This was not an argument he would win at that moment. For now, he'd gladly settle for holding her in his arms throughout the night.

CHAPTER 5

Warmth flowed over Pearla, and she snuggled closer into the epicenter of it. She'd never been able to get this warm in her bed before. It was so cozy and solid—wait… Her eyes flew open and met Damian's silver ones. Light danced against them making them sparkle.

She jerked out of his arms and wiped the drool off of her chin. How embarrassing. Damian didn't appear to be ruffled in the slightest. Her eyes narrowed as she studied him in the low light and frowned. How could he look even better than before? For that alone, she could learn to hate him. No one should look that good considering all they'd been through. Damian was too damned sexy.

"Good morning, *cara*…or rather, I think it is morning. The sky is still rather dark and brooding."

The storm had raged forever. Pearla didn't know how many days it went on. The ship rocked and rolled through the furious waves and torrential rain. For a while, though she'd never openly admit it, it seemed as if they were headed toward certain death.

"How long have I been asleep?" Sleep had been nearly impossible, so she was surprised she slept at all. "My body is one big ache." Pearla stretched her arms high above her head and relief filled her sore muscles.

The whole time the ship rocked, she'd been fighting the

urge to lose the contents of her stomach. How Damian managed to not get even slightly queasy she'd never understand. On the way home, and she *would* return to London at some point, she'd book passage on a steamship. These stupid clipper ships were not pleasant to sail on. She'd only booked passage on one because she wanted out of England as quick as possible.

"A few hours at most." Damian stared at her. "You didn't miss anything important. You needed the rest."

His gaze never left her. A tingly sensation filled her belly and a different kind of ache throbbed between her legs. Why him? What did he want from her? She didn't care if they were technically married. They couldn't have a real marriage. Maybe she'd been hasty in saying she'd never allow him to touch her. Why not? She didn't plan on marrying anyone else, and she was his wife. It was something to think about anyway.

She shook her head to clear away her train of thought. Damian would want more than she was willing to give. If she went that route. Ground rules and expectations would have to be laid out and fully understood. She wouldn't have him claiming her and thinking he could dictate to her. After the debacle of her failed wedding, she didn't want to take chances on marriage ever again.

"Did you sleep at all?"

Their clothing had mostly dried hours ago. Pearla didn't feel comfortable in just her camisole and pantaloons. She'd dressed as soon as she believed her dress wasn't damp. Damian had followed her lead and donned his own clothes. She'd breathed a sigh of relief when he had. His naked chest was too tempting.

He turned his head and stared out the porthole. "No."

She frowned. "You should rest. We both need our strength to get through this."

"Are you worried about me, *cara*?"

Damn him and his insistence on calling her his darling. Why wouldn't he stop? This was beginning to become a bit ridiculous. How many times would she have to ask him to cease before he honored her wishes?

"Of course not." She huffed and turned her nose up.

"Why would I concern myself with your welfare?" She rolled her eyes. Hardheaded males didn't deserve to be worried about, but she was lying. It did concern her that he hadn't rested. They had an escape to plan.

"You want to know what I think?"

"No." *Yes*.

"You want to come back here and lay your head on my shoulder." He leaned toward her. "Give in, *cara*. You don't need to be afraid of finding comfort in my arms. It's my pleasure to ease all of your worries."

"I'd rather not." The idea did tempt her, but she was made of stronger stuff. She could resist Damian. She hoped. She pictured Noah for a moment. Not too long ago she'd been willing to marry him and all it entailed. Now she was Damian's wife. They were so different. The circumstances and the men, Noah had been the man of her dreams. Only it had turned into a nightmare of her own making. She had to be careful she didn't make the same mistake twice. Damian could shatter what was left of her bruised heart. He filled it in ways Noah never had.

He grinned. The tilt of his lips was a lure filled with decadent wickedness. Pearla sucked in a breath and held it. Damn him for being so handsome and sinful. She was a weak woman to want to throw herself in his arms and beg for mercy. Breathe—she reminded herself, and a whoosh of air left her lungs.

"I don't believe you."

Drat it. "Doesn't matter if you do."

He grabbed her wrist and pulled her back into his arms. "I can prove you wrong."

Damian caressed her cheek with the back of his hand. It sent tiny sensations down her face and spread throughout her whole body. Maybe he was right. She should find out what this making love stuff was all about. He did make her feel things she never felt in her entire life. That had to be a good thing right?

"Please don't." *Oh, yes, please do*.

Why was she a jumbled mess of contradictions? *Make up your mind, you silly girl*. These wanton feelings were filling her belly for a reason. Damian's eyes held such promises. She wanted to know what they were, but the proper Pearla put her foot down and prevented it from happening.

He sighed. "I would never force you to do something you didn't want to do."

"Will you make love to me?" The words were out of her mouth before she knew what she was saying. *Damn it.* Had she asked him to... No. That wasn't her voice filling the room. Pearla was imagining things.

His gaze found hers. Damian remained quiet for a long time. At least it seemed like forever. Hell, had she read him wrong? What man would take this long when offered the opportunity love a woman proper?

"I'm sorry, I shouldn't have asked," Pearla stammered through the words and scooted to the edge of the cot. She turned away from him. This was so...humiliating. The idea of finding pity reflecting from his gaze was too much to bear.

"*Cara...*" He reached for her, but she pulled away.

The more distance the better. Pearla knew when she wasn't wanted. She wouldn't beg a man to love her. Self respect was a good thing, and she would keep hers, damn it.

"Forget I asked and leave me alone. It was a moment of insanity." Truly it had been. What was she thinking?

"Hell, if it was." He spun her around their gazes locking together. His voice was hoarse and thick with an emotion she couldn't identify. "I wanted to make sure you knew what you were asking from me."

"I knew. I changed my mind. Too late. I don't want you anymore." Lies. She might always want this man, but she needed to be stronger than her base urges.

He studied her again. It was disconcerting. What was he hoping to find in the depths of her eyes? Would he know her deepest desires by staring into them long enough? He appeared to find something he liked because a smile grew on his face.

"All right, *cara*. Let me know when you change it back." He kissed her lips lightly and let her go. "I can wait."

Arrogant bastard.

Sunlight streamed through the widow almost blinding her. When had the sun decided to come out and play? The waves were no longer crashing against the ship's hull. She'd been so wrapped up in Damian she hadn't noticed.

"The storm has finally passed," she muttered.

"Three days were too damn long to be at sea in that mess. Thankfully, it is over."

Had it been three days? It seemed like much longer. The crew had given them limited provisions when it first hit and left them alone for the duration. They had other concerns—like keeping the ship afloat. That they thought of them at all was a blessing.

"How long do you think until we reach port?"

Damian shrugged. "I don't know. It's hard to say where Paolo wants us taken."

Pearla crawled next to him and leaned her head on his shoulder. Whatever comfort he offered, she needed it. Their future looked so bleak. As far as she could see from their porthole, the ocean surrounded them. Escaping seemed impossible. How were they supposed to build a life together when they didn't have their freedom? Damian wrapped his arm around her and pulled her close to him, his head tilted against her head.

The door to their cabin flung wide open and slammed alongside the wall with a deafening *thud*. "Don't you two look rather cozy." The bosun came into the cabin followed by his partners in crime. "The conte is needed on deck."

Damian lifted his head but didn't move off of the cot. "I will have to decline. Tell Captain Blythe to go to hell."

"Is that any way to treat your benefactor?"

He snorted. "Benefactor? Have you been dipping into the rum casks? I think your brain is pickled if you believe that."

The bosun picked his teeth with his fingernails and spit on the floor. Pearla cringed. How charming. Why wouldn't they leave her and Damian alone?

"Damian would rather stay here with me. Run along now. We don't have time for your nonsense." Pearl shooed him with her hand.

"You don't give the orders, missy. Perhaps you need a lesson in respect."

Pearla raised an eyebrow. Did this ruffian think to school her on something as ingrained as respect? He didn't respect anyone, and he wouldn't be teaching her a lesson regarding it. "No, thank you."

He spread his legs apart, evenly balanced and crossed his arms over his chest. "Conte, we can do this the easy way or the hard way. Please choose the hard way. I owe you for knocking me out the other day."

Damian sighed. "What does the captain want now?"

The bosun laughed. "You've had your fun with your wife. Just as you wanted. It's time to go. We've reached port."

His eyebrows scrunched up. He appeared confused by the bosun's words. Pearla didn't know what to make of it. What fun? They had been dealing with the storm's raging winds and waves on the boat the same as the crew. They didn't get any enjoyment out of it. Did he mean... Pearla started laughing uncontrollable. The wretches believed her and Damian had been rolling around and getting to know each other intimately this whole time. How laughable. The bosun implied Damian had asked for it too.

"I fail to understand your logic." Damian frowned. "Oh, stop laughing, Pearla. It isn't that funny."

"But he thinks..." Laughter spilled even harder out of her. "I'm so sorry." She wiped tears out of the corner of her eyes. "It's ridiculous really."

The euphoria of her laugher was shattered with the bosun's words. "Grab the conte. Captain didn't think he'd leave the lady willingly."

The two ruffians pushed her aside and grabbed Damian yanking him toward the exit. He fought against their efforts every step of the way. One of them lifted his arms and let his fist fly into Damian's face. It stunned Damian, temporarily giving them the momentum to get him out of the door.

"Enjoy your accommodations, Miss Montgomery. You haven't reached your destination yet, but Conte has met his final one."

They meant to kill Damian. She couldn't allow it to happen.

"Where are you taking him?" Pearla jumped off the cot and stormed over to the bosun.

"Don't worry your pretty head about it. Conte Leone is getting exactly what he wanted." He leered down at her breasts. "Maybe you will consider my offer now that you know what a man feels like sliding between your thighs."

Pearla slapped him. An angry red handprint spread across his cheek. "You will pay for that."

"Not today, Perry. Leave Miss Montgomery be." The Captain stepped inside the cabin. "You know what will happen if the duca finds out you harmed her."

The bosun's face paled. Whoever the duca was—Paolo, Damian had called him—scared these men. She gulped. What did he have planned of her?

"Yes, Captain. I understand."

"Good. Go back up deck and help them with the conte's departure."

Perry rushed out of the room, leaving her alone with Captain Blythe.

"What are you doing with Damian?"

Please, don't let him be hurt. He'd come to mean something to her in a short time. They hadn't gotten to know each other under the best of circumstances. She'd hate it if he met a bad end.

He smirked. "You're not worried about yourself? How touching. Things must have progressed rather well between you and the conte."

"What happened between us is not your concern."

The captain could go to the devil for all she cared. He meant nothing to her. Damian did. She still didn't understand her feelings fully. One day she'd like to explore them.

"Isn't it though? I did marry you after all. I'd like to think I did one good deed." His smile was pure evil.

Good deed? He didn't do anything out of the pureness of his heart.

"What do you want?" Pearla asked.

"Nothing at all, my dear. I thought you might want to know that your little escapade was not fully orchestrated by the duca. The conte...Damian as you are calling him, played his part rather well."

Confusion filled her. What was he talking about? What had Damian done?

"I don't understand." None of it made sense.

An even wider grin spread across his face. The captain

leaned against the cabin wall and leered down at her. "Then let me enlighten you. Conte Leone paid my crew to beat him up and hold him in here with you. He thought it was a bit of sport to play the hostage."

Damian wasn't the evil one. He wouldn't hurt anyone. It wasn't in his nature. She paused her line of thinking and gazed at Captain Blythe. How well did she know any of these men? She'd never met any of them before she'd embarked on her excursion. Running away from her problems had led her down this path. It was time she faced things head on and got some clear answers.

"You're lying." He had to be. Damian wouldn't do that to her. Would he? He had made it a point to tell her he wasn't perfect, and had used a woman previously. Was that his way of warning her?

"No? How about if I tell you that your marriage isn't real?" Pure enjoyment sparkled out of his eyes.

Rage boiled up inside of her. She clenched her fists against her side. The more he spoke the more she wanted to hit him. The entire farce of a marriage was fake? To what end? "Then why bother with it?"

The captain spoke nothing but nonsense. It was all...wrong.

"So he could have you willingly in his bed. If you were his wife, then why not give yourself to him. He knew it was the only way you'd let him touch you. You are, or rather *were*, a virginal lady, were you not."

That showed what he knew or thought he did anyway. Damian didn't take her virginity. He had been the perfect gentleman, considering. This was all one huge lie, but she didn't know how much of it was. Maybe Damian had planned it all and then changed his mind. Still they weren't married, so she didn't have to worry about dissolving it. If she could get away from Captain Blythe and his crew, she could continue on her sabbatical. She would still need the time to think and figure it all out.

"Again, not your business." Pearla seethed. "This is all rather convenient when Damian isn't here to back up your story."

"He's done with you. Do I need to remind you of the wedding ceremony?"

What was he spouting now?

"I'm not following what you're saying."

"Don't you recall?" He grinned. "I hinted toward his intentions before I asked if you agreed to be his wife."

Wait... He'd mentioned something about helping a friend. That he'd only done what Damian asked of him. Was what he said true? Did Damian intend to use her? Pearla's heart shattered as she recalled their exchange. She'd been so confused, and Damian had appeared equally so. Was he that good of an actor? Could she really trust what she believed him to be?

The captain shrugged. "I've done my duty and told you everything. Now you are free to roam around the ship once we set sail. When we dock again, you are free to leave. We will help you with your trunks at that time."

He turned to leave.

"Wait" Pearla grabbed his arm, attempting to stop him from leaving.

"Yes?" he asked.

"Where are we going?" Why are they doing this?

"You will find out when we get there."

Awful man, why couldn't she know now? It didn't matter. She'd find out when they arrived and deal with it when she had no other choice.

"And Damian?" she asked.

He shook his head. "Is no longer your concern. You're a free woman, Miss Montgomery. Don't squander it."

Pearla wasn't sure what to make of it all, but Captain Blythe was right. Damian wasn't her concern. They weren't married. He'd left her. Maybe not of his own free will, but he was gone just the same. She couldn't think about what happened to him because she couldn't do anything to help him. Perhaps the captain was telling some of the truth too.

Maybe Damian hadn't really wanted her after all.

And that was what she couldn't let go of. No one truly loved her. Pearla was easily discarded as if without value—forgettable. Why should Damian be any different? It was time to focus on something she *could* do. Pearla was so tired of being left behind. Why did everyone think it was all right to abandon her, break her heart, and toss her aside? She was done being a victim. From that moment on, she'd do everything necessary to protect herself from pain. Agony engulfed her heart for the last time. No man would ever hold the power to destroy her again.

Pearla needed to know what she wanted out of life. Without a man or love.

CHAPTER 6

Eighteen months later

The hot sun poured over his sweat soaked skin. Damian wiped his forehead with his sleeve. Today was the day. He would escape the island of hell Captain Blythe had sentenced him to. Then he would find Pearla.

"Why have you stopped working?" The overseer sneered at him. "No one said you could take a break."

Damian bit back the curse that wanted to spill from his mouth. He needed to be patient for a little bit longer. This island he'd lived on for over a year had a stark beauty to it. It was too bad he couldn't have found it under better circumstances. Paolo's revenge was ultimate. He'd seen Damian as a threat. Instead of killing him, he'd arranged for him to become and indentured servant in Fiji. An archaic system that hadn't seemed to have died yet on the island. They worked him from sunup until sundown. He had no choice and no way to escape. Although, under the laws of his indenture, he'd be free soon. They *had* to let him go.

He didn't know if they actually would. Damian feared they would kill him before allowing him to return to his former life.

"Yes sir." He nodded and returned to pulling weeds strangling the sugar cane growing on the island. It grated him he'd been subjected to becoming nothing more than a servant. This was not how his life was supposed to go. "It won't happen again."

He swallowed the lump in his throat. This whole situation sickened him.

"See that it doesn't."

Damian didn't look up at the overseer again. Their workday was almost over, and he needed whatever strength he could muster to escape. He should be able to walk away free and clear. Paolo would have arranged something dire to happen to him. Deep in his gut he knew he wouldn't make it alive if he tried to leave openly. It had taken him many months to organize a way off the island.

"Pss."

Damian glanced beside him to the man working the field nearby him. His naturally dark skin a couple shades darker than normal from working under the hot sun. Hian had been brought from India to work as an indentured servant. He missed his home and longed to return to the freedom he'd once enjoyed. "What?"

"Is everything set?"

Damian forced a smile away. Hian had become a friend in a place he desperately needed one. They were going to leave Fiji together. A ship awaited them in the harbor. Once they had the cover of darkness, they would board it. His men were waiting for him. The message he'd smuggled off the island finally reached them. Someone had slipped him news of their arrival an hour ago. Relief flooded him with the information he'd be able to see the last of the cursed island he'd been forced to call home for months.

"It is. Now we just need this cursed sun to lower from the sky and allow us to make our own fate."

Hian nodded. "Good. I will be ready."

They worked tirelessly until dusk. It seemed like the minutes dragged on even more now that he knew he'd soon regain his freedom. Damian had started to believe he'd die on the island and never see Pearla again. He dreaded finding out what happened to her. What evil scheme had Paolo had in store for her? His plans for Damian had been horrible, but they could have been so much worse for her.

His wife.

Did she know he still lived? Had this been Paolo's plan all along? Their forced marriage had made little sense to him. Did he want to ensure both Damian and Pearla suffered in a similar fashion as Noah and Rubina had? If so, he was succeeding. Being away from Pearla, and not knowing her fate, was agonizing. He couldn't wait to locate her and ensure for himself she was all right. Would seeing him be a welcome sight? He had so many questions and none of them had any answers. Soon he would get them.

The bell sounded for the end of the day.

"*Grazie al cielo.*" Damian hoped someone up in heaven was listening to all his prayers. He had to thank someone for finally allowing him to escape. Heaven seemed like a good start. He nodded at Hian. "It's time."

Soon they would be enveloped in darkness and using it to escape the plantation. They pretended to follow the rest of the indentured servants toward their little huts to retire for the evening. Most of them would partake in a meager meal and fall asleep soon after. Their work schedule didn't allow for any free time. It was eat, sleep, work, and then repeat each day.

Damian turned his head left and then right. No one was giving them any mind. He gestured toward Hian. They exited to the far left and hid behind some bushes as the rest of the workers walked past them. They used the foliage for cover as they left the plantation. So far no one seemed to have noticed they were gone.

"Where are you two going?" An irritated man called out to them.

Damian cursed. He'd gotten lax. He slowly turned to see the hateful gaze of the overseer. "We thought we could go to the beach and bathe in the ocean."

"You know you're not allowed without supervision."

Of course not. If they were allowed freedom, they might escape. The plantation owners couldn't have that now could they? Damian would not stay on this island another day. He had a life to get back to. A family that missed him, and more importantly a wife he had to retrieve from whatever hell his enemy had sent her to.

"My indenture is over. I am free to do as I please."

"Are you now? I wasn't informed of this." He let his thumbs rest on the inseam of his pants and smirked. "Go back to your hut."

The bloody fool believed because Damian had followed his orders without question he would continue to do so. He didn't know Damian had a reason to fight back. No, that wasn't true. He always had a reason. Now he had the means to travel to his reason for living. Pearla needed him, and he would be there for her.

Damian glanced over at Hian. The man gave a quick, jerky nod. He was ready to assist Damian if needed. With a slow, easy gait, he ambled toward the overseer, giving the appearance he was meekly doing his bidding. When he was beside him, he wrapped his arm around the overseer's neck and squeezed with all his strength. The overseer struggled as Damian held on tight. Hian picked up a large rock and knocked their tormenter on the head. He slumped forward and Damian let him go. His body hit the ground with a soft thud, his breathing slow and even. Good. At least they hadn't killed him.

"Let's get off this damned island." Damian stood and headed toward the harbor.

"You won't hear me arguing with that." Hian smiled. "I've been on this island far too long.

They kept a steady pace, and once the sun had set and the moon shone over head they made it to the harbor. His ship sat docked nearby. They had to board it and set sail.

"Conte Leone."

Damian turned toward the sound of his name and smiled for the first time in days. "Arturo, it's so good to see you. I thought you were dead."

He'd seen Arturo fall before taking his own beating from Paulo's men. They'd bragged about killing him, and Damian mourned his friend. He was relieved to see his Arturo alive and well.

The man grinned. "They tried, but I have a hard head. Makes it even more difficult to kill me."

He pulled Arturo into a firm hug. Damian stepped back and placed a hand on Arturo's shoulder. "I've never been so glad to see someone in my life. It seems you have found your calling. First you rescue my sister, and now me."

"I'm only sorry it took us so long to find you. We had no idea where Paolo sent you or if he'd murdered you. We never stopped looking."

Damian sighed. "Sometimes it might have been easier if he had. It's been hell on this island. I am more than ready to leave. Hian here is coming with us." He gestured toward his new friend.

"They are waiting for us. Let's get you home, Conte."

"No. I have something more important I need to do."

He missed home, or more aptly the comforts it offered. He could do without those for a while longer. The desire to find Pearla was much stronger, and he wouldn't be able to go home without checking on his sister.

Arturo studied him for a few seconds. "What could be more important than returning to Naples?"

"I have to retrieve my wife."

That stopped Arturo short. He opened his mouth, but no sound came out, and then shook his head. "I wasn't aware you'd married."

Damian laughed. "It's a long story. Neither one of us planned on our impromptu ceremony. Come, let's get aboard the ship and I will tell you my tale, and you can tell me yours. I'm curious how you managed to survive."

They crossed the dock until they reached their destination. Damian told him about Pearla and Captain Blythe's forced wedding. He believed the wedding was only one of the means they'd devised to torture him. His worry over Pearla's welfare had nearly driven him insane.

"Pearla was going to let them kill her before marrying me." Damian shook his head with disbelief still coursing through him. "I still don't fully understand her."

"It's my experience that women are creatures men will never understand." Hian stated. "It's best you don't try. It will only lead to a massive head pain."

Damian chuckled. "You're quite right my friend."

"Conte!" The captain of the ship came beside them on deck. "We are ready to set sail. Give me the word."

"Consider it given," Damian replied. "Could you have

someone see Hian to where he'll be staying for our journey? I'm sure he would like to rest." They'd worked hard all day, and Damian was surprised they were both still standing.

"The bosun can show him where to go." The captain nodded at the man by his side.

"Come this way, sir."

Hian nodded and followed the bosun below deck. "I will see you later, my friend."

The captain spun on his heels and ordered the crew to set sail. Damian turned toward his Arturo giving him his full attention. "So, Arturo, how did you survive?"

"I was gravely injured." His voice held a morose tone, as he stared into the dark sky. "In truth, I should not have survived. A woman took pity on me and nursed me to health. I've only been healthy enough to aid in the search for you this past month. I didn't have much strength." He lowered his head. "I'm sorry I failed you."

"You did not fail me Arturo." Damian shook his head. "I'm glad you are alive and well. Maybe later you can tell me a little about the woman who saved you."

Damian did not fault him. Arturo had almost given his life in his service. How could he blame him? Still he needed answers. He couldn't go blindly back into the world. When he found Pearla, he'd need to be able to protect her. When it was just him, he'd been careless. He couldn't continue to carry on in that fashion. His wife would have to come first.

"She's amazing. I think you'll like her." Arturo grinned sheepishly. "I plan on asking for her hand in marriage upon our return."

"Good." Damian smiled. "You deserve happiness." They'd all been through a lot at the hands of the duca. It was time to set it all aside and live their lives unencumbered. "Do you have news of my sister or Paolo?"

"I have not seen the Duchessa, but I do know she is well."

That was good at least. His sister was the only other woman who meant anything to him. His mother died shortly after Rubina was born. He barely knew her. He'd focused all his love and adoration on his baby sister.

"Did she and Noah work through their problems?"

Arturo nodded. "My informant tells me that they are very

much in love. I thought it best not to approach her until I had news of what happened to you."

"That's probably best." Damian nodded. He knew Rue would be worried about him. They were close, and he'd never come to see her. She would be relieved to see him, but first he must find his wife. If she wasn't already in danger, she could be now that he was free. "And Paolo?"

"He is dead. Your sister shot him with his own pistol."

Relief flooded him. Thank heaven for taking that evil out. He wished it had been him and not his sister, but at least he knew that was one person he wouldn't have to worry about.

"I'm glad he's dead."

"He was an evil man," Arturo agreed. "But just because he's gone doesn't mean that the evil is gone."

Was it too much to ask to have some peace? What new evil had sprung up to ruin all the plans he had for his life? When would they catch a break? Damian was tired of all the drama life kept throwing at him. All he wanted was to find his wife and start a family.

"What do you know?"

"Someone has taken up where he left off." Arturo sighed. "The only difference is they are not obsessed with your sister —they are fixated on you."

Damian whipped his gaze toward him and asked, "Who is it?"

"Your former paramour, Camellia."

He cursed. Damian should never have gotten involved with her. She was only supposed to be a means to an end. The Duca's sister had become infatuated with him. Damian hadn't seen any reason not to court her for information on her brother. It'd been a disaster, and the one mistake he regretted the most.

"What has she done?"

"Nothing as yet. She's been trying to locate you." Arturo looked out across the ocean. "I believe, if we had not rescued you today, she'd have found you within a fortnight. Her brother had made it impossible to find you. Captain Blythe is currently her guest. It won't be long before he tells her all she wants to know."

Captain Blythe was becoming a thorn in his side. He was

almost as irritating as Paolo. Why was he suddenly keeping Camellia company? He rubbed his temples as pain shot through his head. Would any of it ever end?

Damian shook his head and sighed. "It might not be as bad as you think."

"No, it is much much worse." Arturo's gaze filled with anxiety. "She wants you. I think the insanity gene has spread through that family. But she is a wicked woman in ways her brother never was. She has strange proclivities…"

He opened his mouth to start asking for details, but changed his mind. He didn't really want to know what Camellia was planning. It was something that could wait until later. When he saw her again he'd deal with her. Maybe if he apologized for his misdeeds she'd let it go. Of course, that would only work if she wasn't crazy like Paolo. He could hope Arturo was wrong in his assessment of her.

"I can't be worried about her. She can obsess over me all she wants. I am taken and do not want her." Damian frowned. "I have bigger concerns than what Camellia wants or desires."

"Your wife?"

Damian nodded. "Yes. She comes first always."

When he closed his eyes he could picture her. He wanted to reach out and stroke her beautiful golden curls and reassure himself she was all right. Once he found her, he'd pull her into his arms and never let go. At least until her stubborn streak found a way to make things difficult. It was one of the things he adored about her. He missed her.

"Then we will find her. Camellia can wait for now," Arturo agreed. "But, Conte, don't think she will forget about you. She will find you, and when she does I fear it won't be a pleasant experience."

Damian didn't doubt Arturo was right. Camellia had always been an odd person. He didn't know what she was fully capable of doing. When he saw her again, he'd discover what her plan was. For now, he wouldn't worry about it. He must locate his wife. Wherever she was, he would find her, and then they would work through this marriage of theirs. They had so much they still didn't know about each other.

"Pearla first, and then I will deal with Camellia."

"I only pray you are not too late... For your wife or handling your former paramour."

Damian stopped and turned his gaze toward Arturo. His words gave him an idea. "Maybe the fastest way to find Pearla is to seek out Camellia. Didn't you say Captain Blythe was keeping her company?"

Arturo nodded. "He is."

"Good. The Captain and I have some things to settle. He will tell me what he did with my wife." Damian grinned. He couldn't wait to see the good captain again and show him how much he'd enjoyed his stay on Fiji. Perhaps he should experience a similar excursion. "Where is Camellia calling home these days?"

"She has been in London since you disappeared. I suspect she knows you will return there before Naples. You have ties there again with Rubina finally returning to her husband." Arturo shook his head. "I don't like any of this, Conte. I have a bad feeling."

Damian shook it off. He couldn't be worried about Arturo's foreboding feelings. If he wavered every time something bad might happen he'd never find Pearla again. "Nevertheless, we will sail to London. Inform the captain of our new destination. I am going to retire to my cabin. It's been a bloody long day."

Arturo nodded. "I will do as you instructed, Conte. I only hope this goes how you want it to." He turned on his heels and headed toward the captain, leaving Damian to his own musings. Going to London was the only lead he had to finding Pearla. Camellia would make things inherently more difficult. But it was worth every risk he would take. Nothing would stand in his way. Pearla would be with him again, and they would find out what was between them. Their time together had been too short. Arturo's concerns be damned.

Damian sighed. "I'm coming for you, *cara*..."

CHAPTER 7

Pearla stared across the horizon. The sun had begun its ascent, and glowed brightly as it rose in the sky. She'd be in London soon. The harbor glistened in the distance. She'd been gone from home for so long. A part of her was happy to finally be returning home, but the other part of her dreaded it. What would she find when she stepped back into society?

Hopefully the ton forgot about her botched wedding.

She didn't want to look into the eyes of all her friends and still see pity raining out of them. Pearla had been through a lot in the past year and a half. All of the difficulties life had thrown at her had made her stronger. It was time to return home and face her biggest fear.

Seeing Noah with his wife.

She wanted him to be happy. Truly. But it would still hurt something deep inside to witness it. Pearla had given up on finding that kind of happiness for herself. For a brief moment, she'd thought she could maybe have it with Damian, but he too abandoned her. If Captain Blythe was to be believed, it had all been a ruse. To what end she still didn't know.

"Are you prepared for your return home?"

Pearla turned to the sound of Mason Tennick, The Earl of Addison's voice. His pale blond hair blew in the breeze. His gaze left hers momentarily as he turned to look in the direction that had caught her attention. He had been courting her on the journey. She wasn't a fool. It didn't take much to surmise that he thought she was wife material. What he didn't know was she never intended to marry. She'd tried it once—no…twice, if her fake wedding to Damian counted.

"As much as I can be." She forced a smile on her face.

He turned toward her. Lord Addison did have lovely green eyes. If only she found him attractive enough to marry… Maybe she didn't like blond men. Her track record surely spoke for that thus far. Both Damian and Noah had dark hair. She found that Noah had begun to pale in comparison though. Her thoughts wandered far more to Conte Leone. She often wondered what he was doing, where he was, and why he'd left her. It didn't help she'd been attracted to him. It appeared he wasn't worth her attention, but she couldn't stop picturing him.

"Don't worry about what all the gossipmongers will say," he encouraged. "You're lovely and what happened at your wedding was unavoidable. No one knew the Duke of Huntly's wife was still alive. Not even he did. They can't hold it against either of you. It was an unavoidable transgression."

Dratted man had to remind her of the one thing she didn't want to think about… Besides Damian anyway. Both Noah and Damian had a lot to answer for in regards to her bruised heart. She never should have let herself fall in love with Noah. Damian had *bad idea* written all over him. He'd been in full rake mode when he was locked in that cabin with her. She should be glad that nothing more had happened between them. A part of her wished she'd experienced what he'd offered her, the other part was thankful she'd never given into that dark desire. The mixed emotions engulfed her every day when Damian crossed her mind. Why couldn't she forget him?

"I'm no longer concerned about what anyone in the ton has to say about me. I've had time and distance from the situation. It doesn't matter to me any longer." Lies. It all mattered, but she refused to let the world see it.

He smiled. "I'm glad to hear that."

Pearla squashed the desire to roll her eyes. Lord Addison was so tedious to converse with. "Are you happy to be returning to London?"

"I am." He lifted her hand into his own. "But more importantly, I'm hoping to spend more time with you now that we are both back in England."

Pearla wanted to jerk her hand out of his. Why did he think he had the right to touch her at all? She didn't desire any man's attention. She took a deep calming breath and slowly removed her hand from his grasp. She was overreacting. Lord Addison hadn't meant to make her uncomfortable. It wasn't his fault she detested his touch.

"If I attend any social events, please do seek me out." *Please don't. Just forget I exist.* "It will be a pleasure to see you again."

Why did she have to remain polite? This was all an exercise in futility. She had no plans to go out much in society. Pearla would only attend functions to see her closest of friends. Lord Addison didn't even make the list let alone the short one that contained people she liked.

"May I call upon you?"

Pearla's mouth fell open, but she couldn't come up with a reason to deny him. "It is going to take me some time to get my affairs in order. Perhaps after I've settled in…"

"I understand. I will give you some time. Is a fortnight too soon?" Lord Addison brushed a lock of her hair behind her ear. "I hope we will have a chance to know each other much better."

Pearla gritted her teeth. She wanted to smack his hand for his presumed familiarity. Did he think she would fall into his arms because Noah set her aside for Rubina? Perhaps she shouldn't think badly of his intentions, but she couldn't help it. No one was going to consider her so easily discarded ever again.

"Yes. I see." She bit her lip. "Why don't we wait and see if I'm up to receiving then. I'm not sure how long it will take to prepare my house for visitors."

Another lie. Her townhouse was already prepared for her. She'd sent notice to her housekeeper before she even thought about when she'd return home for good. It had been on her mind for some time. The desire to see England and her friends. So she'd asked Mrs. Hopsen to ready her home for her. Not too long after she booked passage on a passenger ship to return. It was time, after all.

Lord Addison smiled. "I hope it is sooner rather than later. You'll send notice if it is?"

Pearla sighed. "If I remember to..." She'd forget on purpose. There was something about him she didn't like. Perhaps because he was a male and breathed. He seemed nice enough to be around, but Pearla didn't want to garner any man's attention.

"Please, say you won't forget about me."

If she had her way he'd already be a distant memory.

She feigned a bright smile. "Of course not... But you know how busy it is to run a household. I might not have time to stop and consider anyone else. You do understand, don't you?" It was getting rather tiresome to continue forged happiness around Lord Addison.

He lifted her hand and kissed her palm. Pearla resisted the urge to shudder. At least she was wearing gloves. It would have been so much worse if his lips had touched her bare skin. She'd had enough of men and their licentious intentions. Lord Addison meant to court and marry her. He'd made his desires known. When she thought of him, pictured his face, or even spent any time with him her insides were nothing but an icy void. She had not one good emotion regarding him.

"I do." His lips tilted into a cocky grin. "Rest assured I'm willing to wait however long it takes for you to allow me to call upon you. You, my dear, are worth it."

Pearla looked away from him and rolled her eyes. Some much needed distance from Lord Addison would be in her future. He'd been a thorn in her side too long already. She sighed and turned toward him. Maybe she should be a little less polite with him. If only she wasn't so well mannered.

"I appreciate your attention, but you should know I don't plan on entertaining much for a while. Being in the company of others is too taxing."

"Surely you can make an exception for me?" He raised an eyebrow. "I'm not just anyone."

His arrogance knew no bounds. She mentally sighed. He wouldn't be so easily persuaded to leave her alone.

She shook her head. "There is a select few I plan on

allowing into my life. Friends and family I've not seen for over a year. For now, that will be all I have time for."

"I see." He stared off into the distance.

"Pardon me, Miss Montgomery." Mary Alice, a young maid Pearla hired as a chaperone on her journey approached them. "The captain said we're entering the harbor. Do you still wish me to accompany you?"

Pearla smiled. "Of course. Did the captain indicate how long until we dock?"

"He said within the hour."

Lord Addison interrupted them, "Don't you have duties you need to see to then?"

"I…" Mary Alice muttered. Fear filled her eyes as she glanced over at Lord Addison.

Pearla glanced back and forth between them. What reason would her maid have to fear the earl? Her face had paled considerably when Lord Addison addressed her. Perhaps she was intimidated by a lord, or any man's presence. She was more concerned why Lord Addison felt the need or even the right to order her staff about.

"Mary Alice, go down to our cabin. I will join you in a few moments. We will rest a bit until we dock together." She smiled, reassuringly. "It won't be long before we're safe in my townhouse."

Mary Alice bobbed her head and scampered off. She'd question her maid later. For now, she'd put Lord Addison in his place. He would understand why he couldn't step in and order her maid. He wasn't anything to Pearla. No man could dictate to her. She was in full possession of her inheritance, and as far as she was concerned fully on the shelf. Marriage was not something she wanted for herself —ever.

"Lord Addison, do *not* order anyone in my employ or question them again. They know what my wants and desires are. I do not need you, or anyone else, to step up and handle my affairs."

He opened his mouth and closed it again. His lips formed a thin white line, the displeasure in his eyes evident as he gazed down upon her. He hadn't liked being dressed down one bit. *Too bad*. Pearla didn't care what he thought of her.

Maybe it would give him a reason to quit pursuing her hand in marriage.

"Pardon me," he began, "I was unaware I was overstepping. It won't happen again."

Pretty words, but she didn't believe them. He was saying what he believed she wanted to hear. What he didn't know was it didn't matter if he apologized or not. Lord Addison meant nothing to her. It irritated her that he thought he had a right to step into her life in any way. After they docked, she would go home and not give him another thought. In fact, if she never saw him again it would be too soon.

"It's all right." It wasn't, but polite Pearla was coming back out again. "Now that you know, I'm sure it won't happen again." She almost snorted at those words. Lord Addison was an overbearing arse. Of course he'd try to dictate to her again. Pearla was beginning to know his type rather well. She'd been living around his type all her life. Her father, Viscount Redding, was a man like him. At least she didn't have to live under his roof any longer. Thanks to her inheritance from her grandmother, she could live on her own and not worry about answering to anyone.

"Of course not." He smiled. "Would you like me to escort you to your cabin?"

The man was persistent. Was he obtuse or did he just not care? Pearla wanted to extricate herself from his company. Allowing him to escort her anywhere would be defeating her purpose. She shook her head. "I can find my own way. Good day, Lord Addison."

He bowed. "Until I see you again, Miss Montgomery."

Pearla smiled and turned away from him. Only then did she let her smile fall. She watched another ship across the harbor head toward the docks. In the distance, the old clipper coasted through the water. She'd never sail on one of those blasted ships again. The steamer she'd secured passage on was not only faster, but it didn't carry memories she'd like to forget—like the type of ship she'd been held hostage on.

She shook her head as a man with long dark hair filled her mind. Pearla glanced back at the ship. It was a good distance away, but she could almost make out some of the individuals on deck. If Damian was amongst them, she'd never know, but a part of her had to wonder. Would he come back to London? At some point he would. His sister lived there.

She couldn't think about what could or would happen when he turned up again. It wasn't a question of if, but when. On that day, Damian would realize he no longer meant anything to her.

If only she could convince herself of that notion.

CHAPTER 8

Damian stepped into his set of rooms at the Albany and sighed. It had been a bloody long day. They docked several days ago, and he had immediately begun figuring out where Camellia and Captain Blythe were. They hadn't been in residence when he'd paid a call. He'd been away from London for so long he had no clue what entertainments were being offered. The season was in full swing, and no doubt if anyone knew he was in town he'd soon have undesired guests pouring in. Perhaps he should pay his sister a visit. She could spread word of his arrival and speed up the process.

A boom rattled the room, shaking throughout. He jumped at the sound. He brought his hand up and rubbed his chest to ease his rapidly beating heart. "Who the hell is visiting?" He marched toward the door and swung it pen and frowned. "Arturo, do you have any news?"

He brushed past Damian and entered his residence. "I do."

"What have you discovered?" A rush of emotion spread through him. "Have you located Camellia or Captain Blythe?"

"I can tell you that they are not currently in London. My contacts confirmed they left the city a few days ago." Arturo headed over to the liquor cabinet and poured brandy into two glasses, handing one to Damian. He took a swift drink and nodded. "The good news is they are still in England. The bad news is they have headed to Somerset for a few days. Camellia had a need to explore Bath."

Damian snorted. "Did she want to take in the waters? Or was it the theater district that appealed to her—she'd make a good actress for them to acquire."

"I wouldn't presume to understand the inner workings of Camellia Fonte." Arturo swallowed the rest of his drink and set it down. "They are expected to return at the week's end. So you just have to sit back and await their return. Perhaps we can use this time to form a strategy on how to best handle the situation."

What was the best way to deal with a former lover? Camellia had gotten rather possessive, so he'd had to break things off with her. It had been a blow to his investigation of her brother to do so, but she'd been too difficult to handle any longer. She was a beautiful woman with inky black hair and sapphire eyes that made it rather easy to fall into bed with her. Damian never saw her as anything but a source in his quest to rid the world of Paolo Fonte. He had done her a disservice.

Maybe the best way to approach her was to apologize for being the rake that ruined her... Somehow, he didn't think it would go over well. Camellia wanted him—what she expected to do with him once she managed to trap him, he didn't know. The element of surprise was their best bet. Damian didn't want to be the fly to her spider.

"Do you have someone working inside her townhouse?" A staff member in their employ would be a useful tool— making it easier to access her home when she least expected it. He knew Camellia well enough to anticipate her moves once he was inside. It was giving her time to plan that would be his downfall.

"One of our people was hired as a footman and another as a maid. It is the maid who gave me the information on their whereabouts. The footman is traveling with them to Bath. He should be able to give us more information about her sudden trip when they return."

"Good. When they return we will act. I need to know

where Pearla is. The sooner we can question Captain Blythe the better. Waiting is going to be hard…"

"You will have the information you need to find her. We have to be patient." Arturo walked to the window, and glanced outside. "The past couple of years have been difficult for us. They have not been without good tidings though. Perhaps you should use this time to visit your sister. I believe she's had some happy events you will be interested in."

He raised an eyebrow, questioningly. "What have you learned about Rubina?"

Arturo turned toward him. A small smile was on his face. "Her and her duke are doing well. Though you should realize she has mourned you. It's rather ironic that at one time, albeit different instances, the world believed you both dead, don't you think?"

"They believed I was dead? I thought everyone believed I was merely missing…" Damian frowned. Why hadn't he asked more questions? He'd been consumed with his own needs and never stopped to think about how his indenture may have impacted his family. "You're right I should go and see her. I wasn't in a hurry with my priorities being focused on finding Pearla. Rubina will be relieved to see me again— much like I was when you brought her to me. It would be selfish to let her to continue to believe I've stopped breathing."

What a mess. Damn Paolo Fonte for playing God with their lives. He had taken Rubina from them for years and had somehow managed to do the same with him. His father probably believed him dead as well. What it must have done to the older man. First his daughter and then his son…

"It's a wise decision to pay a call on her. You should go to her now. Give her my regards when you see her."

Damian nodded. "We will meet later and discuss how to handle Camellia. Captain Blythe isn't going to be happy to see me. He *will* give me the information I need and then we can see about turning him over to the authorities for his crimes." Kidnapping two people shouldn't go unaccounted for. "In the meantime, we will wait patiently and I'll head over to see Rubina. It's past time I inform my family I am very much alive."

"Of course," Arturo agreed. "I will walk out with you."

They left his rooms and strolled toward the building's exit. Once they were outside, they parted ways. Damian decided to walk to Rubina's. He needed the exercise to clear his mind. Finding Pearla had been his sole focus since he'd been rescued. Never once had he thought about his family. His absence probably would have been missed from the start. Rubina had been in danger and expected him to help her. Why had he not considered they might believe him gone for good? Damian had always put Rubina first in the past. Meeting Pearla had switched his focus entirely. He would have to apologize profusely to Rubina when he saw her. He'd been a horrible brother to her.

At least he could be reassured that she was all right and Paolo would never hurt her again. He wished his sister hadn't been the one to send the evil bastard to hell. Damian wanted that privilege. If he could resurrect him and kill him all over again he would. The harm the duca had caused his family... He shook his head to clear his thoughts away. All that mattered was they'd survived and would continue to do so. Paolo hadn't won. His family was stronger than the malice that pursued them.

Damian rounded the corner and headed toward the Huntly townhouse. He stopped short of it and stared at the entrance. There was a bustle of activity surrounding his sister's home. Carriages being moved away as not to block the street and the door opening and closing allowing people to enter...

Was she throwing a party? Maybe it wasn't a good time to visit.

He almost turned around and left. Until he caught sight of the blonde vision he'd been searching for since his escape. Pearla...

She was going into Rubina's house! How long had she been in London? When had Captain Blythe let her go? He breathed a sigh of relief to know she was free. At least that was one less thing he would have to worry about. Now he had to go inside and claim his wife. Explaining his absence to his family could wait. They would understand.

He stalked forward intending to gather Pearla into his

arms. He'd missed her and couldn't wait to breathe in her scent again. What she must have gone through after they were separated—he didn't want to think heavily about it. The important thing was she was safe and they could pick up where they left off.

When he reached the entrance, the door flew open. "Good evening," the butler greeted him. "The wedding has already started. His Grace asked that late arrivals wait outside the room as to not disturb the ceremony. After it concludes you may go inside."

Wedding? Who was getting married? It didn't matter. He could be patient for a little while longer. He didn't want to disturb another couple's nuptials. Pearla wasn't going to sneak away on him in the middle of the ceremony.

"That's fine. I can wait."

Damian rushed past him and headed toward the sound of voices. He stopped outside the doorway and watched his sister walk toward Noah. Rubina raised her hand toward her husband. He lifted her hand to his lips, kissing the back of it. They stared at each other for a few moments before they turned their attention to the vicar. It looked as if they were going to renew their wedding vows. Good for them. He was glad they'd found a way back to each other. His sister deserved to be happy.

He tore his gaze away from their exchange of vows and searched for the woman he needed to see the most. Damian found her sitting serenely, watching the ceremony. He had to wonder if it bothered her to see Noah marrying Rubina again. At one time she thought she would marry Noah herself. It must bring back memories observing them now. They glowed with happiness and only had eyes for each other. Pearla didn't look away from them once.

His attention returned back the wedding.

"You may now kiss your bride," the vicar announced.

Noah's gaze never left Rubina. "You don't have to tell me twice." The duke kissed his wife as if he'd never get the chance again.

Now would be a good time to interrupt. Damian's patience had come to an end. He needed to talk to Pearla, and he couldn't wait for Noah to stop kissing Rubina.

"Pardon me for interrupting—I always did show up late for important events."

Noah and Rubina glanced across the room. A gasp of surprise fell from Rubina's lips. Damian strutted into the room with large purposeful strides.

Rubina ran to him and hugged him tight. "I'm so glad to see you. Where the bloody hell have you been all this time?"

Damian hugged her tight in his embrace. He kissed the top of her head. "Easy now, Rue." He eased back. "I rather like breathing."

"Are you going to answer my question?" She raised an eyebrow.

"I will explain it all at another time." He scanned the guests, locking his gaze on Pearla. "I came for another reason."

Rubina pursed her lips in displeasure. She opened her mouth to speak and then paused to study him. Then she turned in the direction that held him riveted. Damian could tell she was curious and wanted to ask questions. He would tell her about everything later—much later. He needed to wrap Pearla in his embrace and reassure himself she was indeed all right.

Pearla stood up. She glared at Damian. Her hand flew to her chest; her mouth hung open with shock. She shook her head several times as if not believing what she saw in front of her. Damian could relate to what she appeared to be going through. Finally, he'd found her, and they could be together again.

Rubina turned and asked, "Do you two know each other?"

"I think a man would know his wife when he sees her." Damian's gaze never left Pearla.

Pearla's blue eyes were filled with fire as she stared back at him. She was angry... He couldn't blame her. She probably blamed him for deserting her. When he got her alone, he would explain what Captain Blythe had done. He would never have left her willingly. She'd come to mean the world to him in a very short time.

"I am not your wife," Pearla said with disdain.

Pearla pushed her way past everyone. Bloody hell, he'd

have to chase after her. It wasn't going to be as easy as he'd thought. Why would it have been? Pearla was a headstrong woman and wouldn't cave without giving him hell first. If she wanted a fight, she'd get one. Damian was never letting her go again.

CHAPTER 9

Pearla pushed open the front door and flew down the steps. She rushed past one of the footmen and headed toward her carriage. Her heart beat rapidly against her chest, threatening to push right out of body. Her breathing became tapered as she struggled to control her wayward emotions. How could this happen to her? The sooner she put some distance between her and the Duke of Huntly's townhouse, the better. Only then would she be able to breathe and control her racing heart.

She waved toward her driver and stepped inside the carriage. "Take me home now," she demanded.

Damian had shown up. She knew at some point he would. It never occurred to her it would happen almost immediately upon her return to London. Although she *should* have known... She had the worst luck of anyone alive. It didn't matter. She leaned her head against the back of her carriage and breathed a sigh of relief as the carriage began to move. Seeing Damian had put her on edge, but she'd made it out without too much trouble. Soon there would be enough distance between them to alleviate the worst of her wayward nerves.

The door to her carriage jolted open, startling her already rampant heart. Her hand flew to her chest to steady the rush flowing through her.

"You didn't think you'd get away so easily did you love?" Damian closed the carriage door and sat across from her. "We have some things to discuss."

Her mouth fell open as her entire body seized in shock. When would she learn? Nothing was ever a given—Damian was set to prove her wrong at every turn. Why did the world seem to hate her? All she'd wanted was some distance to think before having to deal with this man before her. Was that really too much to ask? Apparently so, because now she was being forced to spend time with one of the men she'd hoped to avoid. She should have stayed abroad. Things were much simpler, and peaceful, when she was on her own.

She pursed her lips in displeasure as she studied him. "Why are you here?"

"I believe I already said why." His smile was cocky, and he seemed so sure of himself.

As far as she was concerned they had nothing to discuss. He said it all when he left her alone on that ship. Whatever the reasons were for him leaving—she didn't care. All she wanted now was to be left alone. They were nothing to each other.

"I beg to differ. I'd be perfectly fine to never speak to you ever again." Ever. He could just hop out of the moving carriage and leave her be. "I'd be much happier if you left me alone."

"We're married—"

She held up her hand. "Let's stop right there. I believe I already told you I am not your wife. So if you're feeling some obligation toward me under that false assumption let me disabuse you of that notion immediately. I don't need you. You are not my husband, and you never will be."

He stared at her. The muscles in his cheeks flexed. His eyes turned to a molten silver as he studied her. She didn't know what it meant or why he wasn't saying anything. She closed her eyes and sighed, gaining the strength to continue dealing with him. Being in Damian's presence affected her on an intimate level. She was drawn to him in ways she'd never been to Noah. Her whole body craved to move closer to him and bask in his warmth. She couldn't, wouldn't, give into that desire—sadly she knew what a disaster it would be to fall into his arms again.

"Explain why you believe we are not married."

Pearla looked up into his eyes. He seemed—resigned. No that wasn't it either... Determined was more like it. Damian seemed to have a single-minded pursuit in mind, and lucky her, she appeared to be the object of his sole focus. She needed to get his train of thought on something other than her.

"Captain Blythe said it was all a ruse." She shrugged. "You can rest easy. We're not, and never have been, legally wed. You're free, Damian. Go find someone else to bother."

She meant what she said. Didn't she? Maybe if he put up more of a fight she'd believe he really wanted her. It was so hard to decipher what was true and what wasn't. Her heart had leapt with joy when she'd laid eyes upon him. Followed by fear—why was he in London now? She'd just decided to return. There must be some other reason.

"You never thought to check to see if he was telling the truth? The man does like playing havoc with other people's lives." He raised an eyebrow. "You do recall our time together locked in a cabin on his ship, correct?"

How could she forget? It had been one of the worst and best times of her life. She had begun to feel wanted, even important to someone else. Until Captain Blythe added to her already growing self-doubt... Damian didn't want her. He never did. "I remember it in vivid detail."

"So tell me, word for word, what the good captain told you."

She shook her head. "It doesn't matter. None of it does. I am home and free to do anything I want. If you're so concerned about what the captain has done, or did, go find out from him. I'm satisfied knowing I'm not tied to you for the rest of my life."

A sharp sting of pain stabbed through her unsteady heart. That wasn't entirely true. She'd wanted him. Hope had coursed through her body at the idea of him as her husband. Then it all crashed down around her. Why did everyone want to discard her? Damian wouldn't have the power to hurt her ever again. She couldn't let him in only to lose him. It hurt too much the first time. If she opened herself up only to lose him—it would destroy her. She couldn't afford to let herself love him. They'd been doomed from the start.

"It bloody hell does matter." His voice was harsh. "You matter. Don't sell yourself short. We need to know the facts. If we're not legally wed, that can be rectified."

What nonsense was he spouting now? "We're not wed. I have already stated that several times. Nothing needs to be fixed. All I need from you is space. What are you not understanding?"

"We belong together, *cara*." His grin was wicked as his gaze raked over her. "We were inevitable from the start. It's only a matter of time until you're fully mine."

She snorted. He was ridiculous. They were not inevitable. Nothing ever was. This discussion had gone off course and derailed into a subject she didn't want to take part of any longer. Damian needed to find someone else to harass.

"I will never be yours. That ship sailed." In more ways than one. She leaned forward and stated firmly, "I'm not, nor will I ever, belong to you. Get acclimated to that now. You do not have any thing I need or want."

His lips formed a grim white line as anger flashed through his silver eyes. "I refuse to accept that."

"That's your problem, not mine. I've accepted we were not meant to be together months ago. I'm only surprised you haven't reached the same conclusion." This had reached beyond tedious. She waved her hand with frustration. "I deserve better. You're not the man for me."

He stayed silent again. How could he hold his anger in? His body remained completely still as he studied her. He must want to lash out. She had not been nice, and held nothing back from him. She had not lied. She did deserve better. Damian had already proved she couldn't depend on him. He only wanted her because he believed she belonged to him. Pearla belonged to no one, and especially not to a man who would readily abandon her for his own selfish pursuits.

"I understand," his voice was eerily quiet and firm. "You wish to be courted."

No. She wanted to scream at him, but she held it back. Her voice shook with raw emotion as she explained, "You understand nothing at all."

"Oh, I think I do." His smile grew on his face as he continued to stare at her. "You think no one could ever truly want you. Your answer is to push me away so your already bruised heart doesn't suffer further." He yanked her across the carriage and onto his lap. "But, *cara*, you need to know I've never wanted anyone as much as I want you. If you need time to accept what I already know, I can give it to you."

His announcement terrified her. Could she have faith he meant what he said? She wanted to believe him. Give in to the desire, the deep seated need, to belong to him. The idea of it though—if he left her again, she'd never recover. It was too big of a risk. She couldn't trust him with her heart.

"I don't want anything from you." She wiggled in his arms. "Let me go."

"I can promise you forever." He caressed her cheek and brushed a wayward curl behind her ear. "Letting you go is not an option I can entertain."

"Nothing is forever, including this sudden desire to have me."

She had to get out of his arms. The feelings he created inside of her—she wouldn't be able to control her desires if she remained on his lap. He made her want—no, need—him and only him. Damian couldn't know how much she craved his love. Only he made her feel this deep yearning for more.

"What I feel for you, *cara*, is so far from sudden it is ridiculous to even suggest it."

"Then where have you been?" She raised an eyebrow. "Not here with me. So don't attempt to make me believe you've been fighting your feelings and desires for me. I'm not a fool."

"It couldn't be helped—I..."

She shook her head, and interrupted him, "It don't want to hear your excuses." She placed her hands on his chest to push him away, but got lost in the sensation of feeling his warmth beneath them. "Stay away from me. It's all I need from you. I can't say it enough to make you understand."

"I will give you anything you want, anything but that." His gaze softened as he stared into her eyes. "I need you too much. When you're ready to know why I've been away, I'll explain it. In the meantime, I think I should remind you exactly what is between us."

He pulled her closer and placed his lips softly upon hers. Pearla started to pull away but then lost herself in the sensation of his lips against her, and the passion she'd been trying to hold in. His caresses soothed her wounded soul. She wanted to believe everything he was trying to put into that one kiss, but it was all too much. She was on an emotional overload that threatened to burst her at the seams. The kiss went on forever and wrecked her from the inside out. She shook with a need she couldn't describe. Fear took a hold of her and she yanked her head back.

"You shouldn't have done that." Her breathing was ragged. "Release me."

He complied with her request. His arms slackened and he set her on the seat next to him. The carriage came to an abrupt halt, causing her to fall back into his arms once again. She peeked up at him through hooded eyes. She could see retrained desire deep in his silver pools.

"I believe we've reached our destination, *cara*." He smoothed another loose curl behind her ear. "This is where we part—for now. I'll call upon you in a few days. I think you need some time to think." He smiled, softly. "But rest assured, this is not over."

He caressed her cheek once more and left her alone in the carriage. Her hand flew to where the warmth from his hand was still imprinted upon her cheek. She couldn't help the need to absorb it all deep inside of her. Damian was a force that was hard to resist.

How was she supposed to argue against him when he left her an emotional wreck? Already he was beginning to break down every one of her walls of defense. If he came at her full force, it wouldn't take long to crumble them all to the ground. Damian had thrown the first volley in their war, and it looked like he planned a siege that would outlast any resistance she had to offer.

The only question she had was—why was she fighting at all?

CHAPTER 10

Damian scanned the room, looking for the only person he wanted to socialize with. When he didn't see her pretty blonde head he decided to head toward the card room. He would find entertainment elsewhere while he waited for Pearla to arrive. He had it on good authority she planned on attending the Silverton ball. Arturo had someone installed in her household to garner the information he needed to court her properly.

Pearla was being difficult.

She had managed to evade him for a whole fortnight. When she'd claimed to want him to leave her be, she'd not been lying. He hadn't believed for a moment that was what she truly wanted or needed. The way she reacted to their kiss suggested she desired him as much as he did her.

She was afraid. If he was patient enough, he would get her to agree to be his wife in truth. He still thought of her as his. At first, he balked at the idea of taking a wife, but now that he'd gotten over his initial reservations he saw that only Pearla would do for him. She was his equal in every way. He couldn't wait for her to see it as clearly as he did.

"Didn't expect to run into you here," a voice said from behind him.

"Hello, Noah." Damian smiled. "I didn't think I'd see you not permanently attached to my sister's side."

Noah laughed and clapped his hand against Damian's shoulder. "As much as I'd enjoy that, she'd kill me if I tried. She demands her space. Gemma and Lily currently have her full attention. I expect Liam and Rand to join me in here shortly. Once the ladies get talking, they tend to ignore us."

The other two men could provide a decent distraction for him while he awaited Pearla's arrival. She was the only reason he'd ventured to the ball at all. They were not his usual scene. Thanks to his sister's social status, he got invited to all the big social events of the season, but most of the time he declined them. There were too many mamas seeking to marry their daughters to him. As far as he was concerned, he was officially off the market—if he'd ever been on it at all. It was Pearla or none.

"Then we have enough for our own game." Damian grinned. "Why don't we make it interesting."

"I'm all for something interesting?" Liam asked.

Rand followed in close behind him and said, "Please, nothing too exciting. The last time you kept things from me we had to rescue our wives from a mad man. I'd like something a little less stimulating."

There was a story there. Damian would ask about it later. If he were to guess, it probably had something to do with Paolo. Why would he have kidnapped all three women? There were some things Arturo hadn't told him.

Liam rolled his eyes. "We didn't intend for them to be taken. How many times do we have to apologize for that mess?"

"For the rest of your miserable life," Rand quipped. "If you'd let me know what was going on, maybe I could have kept Lily home."

Noah snorted. "What delusional world are you living in? You do know your wife is one of the stubbornest women to ever been born, right?"

Damian hid a smile. He missed this. He didn't know Rand well, but he hoped to become good friends with him. Liam and Noah were best friends, and included him whenever he visited his sister. Rubina marrying Noah had been one of the best things to happen to her—and him. It gave them more of a family. They had their father, but no one else.

Rand narrowed his eyes and glared at Noah. "Watch how you're speaking about Lily. She'd the epitome of everything that is wonderful, and I'll not have you impugning upon her sparkling reputation."

Liam laughed and clutched his chest. "I love Lily. I do. She is my sister after all... But, Rand, you are being a bit blind to her faults."

"No more than you or Noah regarding your own wives."

"He does have a point, gentleman," Damian interrupted. "How do you feel about a game of cards?"

They all turned toward him and nodded. Each of them pulled a chair out and sat around the table. Damian was glad he'd ventured out of his rooms. The evening looked to be entertaining already. Once Pearla came, he could claim a dance—or three, and begin to convince her they belonged together. In the meantime, a rowdy good card game would hold his attention.

Liam shuffled the cards and dealt them to each player. He looked across the table and asked Damian, "So, are you going to finally get around to telling us where you've been for the past couple of years?"

Damian sighed. He knew at some point he would have to explain what Paolo had to done him. He didn't want to relive the experience. It had been hell for too long. He was finally free, and all he wanted to do was forget the horror he'd endured. It was time to move forward with his life. Living in the past was not on his agenda.

"I hadn't planned on talking about it at all," he explained.

"Rubina isn't going to let you get away with that. You might as well practice with us. Tell us the gruesome details so we can keep them from our wives' innocent ears." Noah picked up his cards and sorted them. "You know you can tell us anything. We won't judge."

Noah, Rand, and Liam were not going to allow him keep his secrets. If he let them, they'd pull every single one. Maybe he should talk about it. Then the men would leave him alone.

"There isn't much to tell." He didn't glance up from his cards. Damian knew if he did, he'd see their gazes trained on him, awaiting his response. He didn't want to see pity in their eyes. "Paolo arranged for me to serve an indenture on an island of hell."

Dead silence.

He glanced up and didn't quite observe what he thought he would. No sympathy for what had happened to him. What he saw was more on the brink of intense rage about to explode.

"What exactly did you have to do on this island?" Liam asked, quietly.

"I don't really want to discuss it. The good news is I'm no longer there. I have a friend that helped me escape. He's on his way home to his family in India. If not for Hian, I might not have survived. I owe him my life."

"Fair enough," Noah agreed. "Why don't you explain what Pearla had to do with any of it." This was something different entirely. Damian expected Noah to be protective of her. It only surprised him it had taken him this long to broach the subject.

"Pearla had nothing to do with my indenture." Damian flipped a card onto the table. "She is the only good thing that has happened to me in the past couple of years."

Noah set his cards down and studied him. He didn't say a word for several seconds. They seemed to tick off in his head with a steady beat of uncertainty. He had no clue what was going on through the duke's head.

"How did you two meet?" He folded his arms across his chest. "I wasn't aware you two had been introduced."

Damian tossed his cards on the table. This game had taken a different turn. The men had lost interest as they sought details on his misfortune. The only way to get them to leave it be was to tell them everything. He scrubbed his hands across his face and took a deep breath. "It's a long story, and you're not going to like any of it."

"Start from the beginning," Noah offered. "It's usually a good place for a story to unfold from."

Damian nodded. He told him about Captain Blythe—what Pearla believed was their phony wedding ceremony, and finished with his indenture. He left out some details. Like the hot sun, his often burned skin, along with the bruises and cuts he suffered daily. The long hours and the malnourishment topped the list of evil he had to endure, but were not the worst for him. The belief that Pearla needed him is what kept him going. He'd had to find the strength to survive and find her. Now that he had, she didn't want him around. A part of him was devastated to hear her harsh words. He wouldn't give up on her. Thinking of her every night saved his life, and he believed they were meant to be together. It would take a little longer to convince her of it as well.

"What are you going to do?" Rand asked. "Speaking from experience—a stubborn woman is going to run fast and as far as possible before she admits she wants to be with you."

Liam snorted. "I thought my sister was the epitome of all that as wonderful in the world."

"And she is." He grinned. "But despite what you think, I am aware of every one of her faults. If we'd not been forced to spend time on a ship for weeks, she would have never sat still long enough for me to court her. Damian here is at a disadvantage. Pearla isn't afraid to travel the world to flee his presence."

"Thanks, man. That is all the encouragement I needed," Damian said, blandly. "I'm so glad we took the time to discuss this. It's been extraordinarily useful."

Noah shook his head. "Rand has a point. Our women, and yeah, I'm including Pearla because I have no doubt you'll be able to convince her you two belong together, are incredibly obstinate. You need a plan, and lucky for you we are willing to help you devise one."

Damian smiled. These men were allies he never thought he would have in his life. He was blessed to have them, and soon he would have Pearla too. His patience was running thin. He hadn't seen her in far too long. It was time to seek her out and start his campaign to win her. Her retreat was about to end for good. You couldn't win a war if you didn't have any battles to fight.

"Thanks for the offer, but I already have one I've put into motion." Damian tapped his fingers together. "Although I might need your assistance with one thing, Noah."

"Tell me what you need and it's yours." Noah sat back in his chair and folded his arms across his chest. "I'd like to see Pearla happy, and there isn't much I wouldn't do for her."

Everything was starting to fall into place, except for the minor detail of Pearla ignoring him. He had every bit of faith he'd see her come around to his way of thinking though. He needed a bit of time to convince her that she could trust him. He had no doubts and soon neither would she.

Liam grinned. "Pearla doesn't know what's about fall at her feet, does she?"

No, she didn't, but she was about to find out. He pushed his chair back and stood. "This game has been fun, but I have a lady I need to seek out. We should do this again soon."

"Good luck," Noah replied. "You're going to need it."

"I don't need luck." Damian wiggled his eyebrows. "I have my charm, and she's already succumbed to it on more than one occasion. It's only a matter of time before she caves for good."

Their laughter followed him as he exited the card room. He needed to locate the blonde goddess that had snared his attention two years ago. She was about to realize Damian fought for what he wanted, and Pearla was a woman worth fighting for.

He weeded his way through the haute ton and stopped when he saw her. She stood with her friends: Lily, Gemma, and his sister, Rubina. She was stunning. Her golden hair was wound on her head into a perfect chignon, a few curls falling loose around her shoulders. Her gown was a sapphire blue that matched her eyes. He could close his eyes and picture the jewel tone gazing up at him. Now he had to convince her she wanted to dance the next waltz with him. He narrowed the distance between them and stopped in front of her. Her gaze met his as a weary smile formed on her face.

"Damian," Rubina said, excitedly, "I'm so glad to see you. I expected you would come by and tell me where you've been all this time."

Damian hugged his sister. "I'm sorry I've been so remiss. I've been occupied with getting my affairs in order. I will pay call soon."

She pouted. "Is that your way of saying this isn't the place to discuss it?"

Damian barely held back a smile. His sister was relentless. He would have to make sure to visit her, or she'd come looking for him.

"Yes, Rue, it is."

"Have you seen my husband?" Gemma asked, clutching her stomach with one of her hands. "I need to leave."

"I have," Damian said. "He is in the card room with Noah and Rand."

She nodded and headed toward the room he'd just left. Gemma Marsden didn't look well. Her face was devoid of all color. Liam would take care of her. Damian wouldn't worry about her welfare. There was another lady that had his full attention.

"I think we should follow after her," Lily stated. "It might be a good time for us all to leave."

"I agree." Rubina nodded. "Damian, don't forget to come see me."

Lily and Rubina followed after Gemma. Pearla had been doing her best to pretend he wasn't near. Her face was soft pink, and her eyes darted in every direction—avoiding looking at him directly. Damian wasn't fooled. Her cheeks were rosy with desire. When she started to follow after the other ladies, he stepped in front of her.

"Hello, *cara*. Dance with me." He didn't give her a chance to decline. He led her to the dance floor as the strands of the waltz filled his ears. It was perfect.

CHAPTER 11

Pearla basked in the warmth of Damian's arms. She'd tried to escape before he'd led her out to the dance floor, but he was faster than she was. The last thing she wanted was to give the ton something else to talk about. If she'd outright snubbed him, it would have been food for the gossipmongers. Just a dance might be overlooked—though even that took things further than she wished to go. She wouldn't even be at the Silverton ball if Gemma hadn't insisted. Her friend meant well.

She sighed. "What game are you playing now?"

"I promise you, *cara*, you are nothing I would trifle with. You're important to me."

She couldn't trust he meant it. Her bruised heart wouldn't survive another blow. He made her weak, and she never wanted to be weak for another man again. His transgressions were perhaps worse than Noah's had been. She could forgive the duke. How was he to know the love of his life was still alive? Now she could look back and be happy for them. They had a wonderful family and Noah smiled frequently. It was a side of him she'd not seen before.

"I wish I could believe you." She truly did. "But I can't."

Damian led her though the steps of the dance. Each one brought them a little closer together. He was maneuvering her where he wanted her to be, fully encased in his arms. The small distance the dance allowed apparently wasn't enough for him. She couldn't fault him, at least not completely. There was a part of her that wanted to be as close to him as possible and breathe his alluring scent. To be lost in everything that was this man—could be intoxicating.

Her heart beat faster as she stared up into his silver eyes. It warred with many varied emotions, many of which she didn't know if she'd be able to continue denying him. She wanted to cave and let him lead her down the decadent path his gaze promised her. Just once she wanted to lose herself and not think about what consequences lay ahead of her. If only she was a different person, in a different place, she'd fall into his arms and not look back. Sadly, she couldn't allow any of it. She'd drown in the emotional overload and crash into a mess of denial afterward.

"What will it take to convince you we belong together?" He rubbed his thumb across her hand leaving a trail of heat in its wake. "I'll do anything. Tell me what you need from me, and it's yours."

His gaze pleaded with her—twin pools of molten silver. Her resolve was beginning to shatter. Soon all the walls she erected would tumble down around her. She needed fortification. Something, anything, to keep her from falling all over again for this charismatic man...

"I can't..." She was at a loss for words.

The strands of the waltz came to a winding halt. He smiled down at her and led her off the dance floor. Damian let go of her arm at the edge of the ballroom, near the balcony. He bowed to her. "Perhaps you would consider a stroll outside."

She could use a breath of fresh air. The cool air might also help her overheated skin. Being near Damian always warmed her from the inside out. He made her feel...more than anyone ever had.

"Damian, love, it's so good to see you."

Pearla turned. A woman with midnight hair and emerald eyes approached them. Her gown was the same jewel tone as her stunning eyes. She kept moving forward until she was almost on top of Damian. An exaggeration, but Pearla wanted to push her away. She was too close, too beautiful, too everything, and it made her feel inferior in comparison. Who was she and why was she overly familiar with him?

Damian's jaw clenched. "Camellia, it's been a while."

"Too long." She pouted. "Where have you been? I've missed you so."

Camellia rubbed his forearm with her ungloved hand and batted her eyelashes at him. Damian gazed down at her through hooded eyes. "I think you know exactly where I've been. When did you get back? I heard you'd made an unexpected trip."

"If I'd know you were looking for me, I'd have stayed in London." She licked her plump lips and smiled coyly. "Now that I've returned, you can pay a call whenever you like. For you, I'm always available."

Pearla clenched her teeth. This is what he did with his spare time? He visited this…this…harlot? To think she'd been about to give in and tell him she wanted him too. Thank heavens she'd not said those words. He could keep company with his mistress. Pearla was done with him. Tears threatened to spill from the corner of her eyes. She had to put some distance between her and Damian before they fell down her cheeks in truth. She would not let him know how much he hurt her. As far as she was concerned, he could go to hell.

"Pardon me," she said, sarcastically. "I'll let you two get reacquainted."

"Pearla, wait…"

She spun on her heels to leave. She could hear Damian call out to her, but she ignored him. The Devil belonged with his lover. Pearla was just a challenge. A woman who denied him and he couldn't have that. Too bad. She wasn't a prize for him to add to his conquests.

The balcony called to her. She needed the cool night air for an entirely different reason. Heat coursed through her body, different than what she felt in Damian's arms. This heat was full of anger and humiliation.

"I thought I saw you inside," a voice called to her. "I was beginning to think I'd never see you again."

Pearla turned. Lord Addison was heading toward her. She frowned and shook her head. When she left Damian, she'd wanted peace, but mostly she wanted to be alone. Lord

Addison was the last person she'd expected to see. She'd been avoiding him with as much fervor as she'd ignored Damian. Neither man wanted what was best for her. They both saw her as something they needed to acquire. A trophy to put on a shelf and admire, but not really know or understand.

She curtsied. "Lord Addison. It's good to see you." It wasn't, and she stopped short of rolling her eyes. "I trust you're well?"

"I am." He nodded. "Who was that gentleman I saw you dancing with."

His mouth formed a flat, white line. He didn't like the idea of her dancing with Damian. She looked away so he wouldn't see the disdain in her eyes. Lord Addison didn't have a right to be upset she danced with another man. He had no claims on her other than the ones in his own mind. She belonged to no one and could dance with whomever she pleased.

"Conte Leone is well respected."

"Is he?" He sounded uncertain. "I don't know him."

She spun around and smiled. "He's the Duchess of Huntly's brother."

"Isn't she…" He turned toward the ballroom and then back to her. "I mean to say, weren't you engaged to the Duke of Huntly?"

Why did he have to sound so intrigued at the connection? More importantly, why couldn't the blasted man leave her alone? She had to get away from him. Only then would she obtain the peace she desired. Pearla gazed up at him and fixed a serene smile on her face. She could get through this. She needed to remember to breathe. "Yes, I was."

His frown was one of disapproval. It was all over his face in the moonlight. "Why are you associating with them? They are not worthy of you. He left you at the altar."

Was he serious? She rolled her eyes. He had to be the most ridiculous man she'd ever met. "He didn't have a choice. Rubina is his wife. Do you think he should have married me when he already was? Tell me how that makes sense?"

"Of course not," his voice was full of disdain. "It doesn't discount the fact he dishonored you."

Pearla blew out a breath of frustration. There was no reasoning with Lord Addison, so she wasn't going to waste her time. She'd much rather go home and curl up in her warm bed. Maybe she should get a pet. They were at least loyal and didn't feel the need to dictate to her. First thing in the morning, she'd look into acquiring a dog.

"Right, of course." She paused and smiled brightly. Her cheeks burned with the effort of holding the false grin in place. "But I quite like spending time with my friends, so I've chosen to let the past go. Since *I* am the one that was slighted, I feel it is within my power to forgive and openly socialize with whomever I wish to."

She hoped she'd gotten the message across loud and clear. There wasn't a chance in hell she'd stop calling on her friends because Lord Addison disapproved. She'd rather poke her eyes out with a hot needle than try to please him. He seemed like a nice enough man, even if he was rather bossy... That didn't mean she wanted to spend the rest of her days in his company.

He moved closer to her and bent his head to stare into her eyes. "You're correct. It is the sign of a graceful and generous person to forgive."

She mentally rolled her eyes. So glad he approved. "It was nice to see you again, but I am going to go home. It's been a rather tedious evening, and I feel a megrim coming on."

Pearla moved around him to head back inside. He grabbed her wrist, halting her progress.

"Wait," he demanded. "I wasn't done speaking with you."

She stared up at him, anger spiking through her once again. "That may be, but I was finished with our conversation. Let me go."

His grip tightened around her arm causing a sharp pain to travel through her hand. She winced as the pain increased as he continued to squeeze her wrist. Lord Addison yanked her closer to him. "Why are you always in a hurry to leave me? Don't you understand I hold you in the highest esteem?"

"You're hurting me." Pearla tried to wrench her wrist from within his firm hold.

He lifted his other arm and skimmed his fingers across her hair. She shuddered and jerked her head. "You're so beautiful, Miss Montgomery."

"Am I interrupting?" Damian strolled out to the balcony.

His gait was elegant and unaffected. He appeared to not have a care in the world.

"Yes, you are." Lord Addison seethed.

"I don't think I am." Damian studied him. "Pearla, would you like to go back inside with me?"

She yanked her arm free at last and rubbed her tender wrist. "Indeed, I would. Good evening, Lord Addison," Pearla said with disdain. She spun on her heels and let Damian lead her back inside.

"Was he forcing his intentions on you?"

She was glad Damian had come to her rescue. That didn't mean she was going to encourage him. It hadn't been that long since she was trying to escape him and his arranged tryst with the lovely Camellia. Instead of answering him, she remained silent for their entire trek inside. She nodded to members of the ton as she passed them, leaving a smile on her face as she walked. When they reached the far end of the ballroom near the exit she stopped in her tracks and turned to him. "Thank you for the escort, but I'm going to have to bid you farewell now."

"Don't be so quick to run away, *cara*." He rubbed her tender wrist with intense gentleness. A red welt appeared where Lord Addison had gripped it. "I know he hurt you. He will pay for that."

Anger spiked her blood hot. "I don't need you to fight all my battles for me, Damian. Go find your mistress and spend the evening with her. I will be fine. I'm more than capable of seeing myself home."

He smiled. Why did he have to be so devastatingly handsome? Damn man. She wanted to smack the cocky grin right off his perfect face. That was what bothered her the most. He had looked even better standing next to the flawless Camellia. She ached deep down to the edge of her soul and feared a part of her would forever want this man.

"I assure you, I do not have, nor do I want, a mistress."

She raised an eyebrow and considered throwing the woman and their little tête-à-tête back at him, but held back the retort. Throwing insults and trading innuendos with Daman was counterproductive to what she wanted.

"It matters not. I am going home." She shrugged. "What you do with your time is your business."

He chuckled. "Sweetness, I do believe you're jealous."

She opened her mouth as shock filled her. He was *right*. She *was*. Not that she would ever admit to such a lowly emotion. Damian didn't deserve to know how she felt about him. It was bad enough she was privy to it on a daily basis.

"I wouldn't deign to give you the pleasure."

"Oh, darling," he coaxed. "I promise you one day I will show you so much bliss you won't doubt where my affection lies."

He was trying to tempt her again. She couldn't give in. This conversation had to end before she did the unthinkable and fell willingly into his embrace. She had to be strong and remember who he really was. Damian was not the man for her—no man was.

"Good bye, Damian."

She turned on her heels and took slow steady steps to put distance between them. It wouldn't do for him to realize she was running away from him, and as fast as possible to save face.

"You can run, Pearla." His laugher floated up to her ears. "But you can't hide. We will be seeing each other again soon. And, *cara*, that's a promise you can count on."

She gritted her teeth. So much for pretending she wasn't trying to escape him and the allure he held for her... It was silly of her to think she'd fooled him for even a second. Damian appeared to have the ability to see right through her —and it scared her senseless.

CHAPTER 12

Damian watched Pearla as she left the ball. He was willing to let her leave because he knew one of his men would follow her and ensure she made it home safely. With her gone, he could take care of some other important matters. They were not more important that Pearla, but still had to be dealt with. First, he had to track down Lord Addison and inform him he was never to go near her again. Pearla had played it down, but the man had hurt her. What Lord Addison had hoped to accomplish, Damian did not know. Before he left the Silverton Ball, he would beat the answers out of him, if necessary. He really hoped the man proved difficult. He was bloody pissed off anyone had dared to hurt the woman he loved.

He stalked toward the last place he'd saw the cur. After scanning the area, his gaze landed on Lord Addison as he left the ballroom. Where was he going? It didn't matter. It gave him the opportunity to have a conversation with him in private. He didn't want word to get back to Pearla he'd pummeled the man after she departed. That was one thing he would keep to himself. He didn't want to worry her. This was something he'd gladly handle. Lord Addison would not bother her ever again.

"A word if you will, Lord Addison." He followed him inside the library and shut the door with a soft click. He stalked forward until he was directly in front of him. "I believe we have a few things to discuss."

Lord Addison turned his nose up at him. "I can't fathom what."

The more he was around the man, he liked him even less. "No?" He raised an eyebrow. "Why don't we being with your intentions toward Miss Montgomery."

As in, he wouldn't have any after he was done with him. The bastard was going to forget she existed. His jaw tightened as he studied Lord Addison. The man appeared completely unruffled in his presence. Did he really believe he was safe? Did he not know what Damian was capable of?

"My intentions are honorable of course," he replied. "Though I fail to see how it is any concern of yours, but I intend to marry her."

Never mind beating him senseless. Lord Addison needed to die. The sooner he stopped breathing, the easier it would be for Damian to relax.

"She's not interested." He clenched his teeth together into a snarl. "You're to leave her alone and not bother her any further with unwanted attention."

Lord Addison laughed. "That's a good one. You're playing a joke on me, correct?" He paused and stared at Damian. "Oh, I see. You're serious. Why would I cease to court her? Miss Montgomery has not indicated she was averse to my suit."

Damian clenched his fists against his side. It wasn't time yet. Just a little bit longer and he could wipe the satisfied smirk off of Lord Addison's face. When he was done with the lord, he would know exactly who Pearla belonged to.

"You don't need to hear anything from Miss Montgomery. She wasn't too happy with you outside on the balcony. You left bruises on her wrist." Damian took two even steps closer to him. "A man with honorable intentions doesn't hurt a woman in his care." He'd pay it back tenfold. He'd be throbbing with pain much stronger than Pearla currently was.

Lord Addison stared at Damian and gulped. He finally realized he was in a room alone with an enraged beast. If he didn't tread carefully, he would be shredded. Damian grinned evilly. It was about time he realized the danger he courted by hurting Pearla.

Damian took two more steps. Lord Addison retreated.

"Can we remain civilized?"

"No," Damian replied. "I believe we've passed the very idea of it the moment you thought you had the right to touch her."

He yanked him by his cravat and lifted him off the ground. A little swine of a man, barely worth the effort to warn off, but for Pearla, Damian would do anything. Even send Lord Addison to hell where he belonged. Maybe that was even too good for him. Perhaps he should put the sod on ship to visit a different kind of hell.

"Tell me, Lord Addison, have you ever had the opportunity to travel?"

"Um, I had a world tour…" He was shaking in his grasp. "And I returned from France a short time ago."

Damian laughed. "What about Fiji?" The living hell he'd left might be a good place to send Lord Addison.

"I—I," he stuttered. "Please, release me."

"You mean the same way you were going to let go of Pearla's wrist earlier?" He tilted his head and studied the man. "You're right, I should give you the same consideration."

Damian squeezed his neck until he started to turn purple, and then punched him in his stomach. After he let him go, Lord Addison fell to the floor with a loud thud. He gasped for breath and tore his cravat off.

"You—why—I don't understand," he gasped out.

"I don't intend to kill you. I never did, and as much as I'd like to send you to hell so you'll never bother my intended again, I can't do that. It would make me no better than you." Damian leaned down and said with conviction, "But rest assured if you ever go near her again, I will, and I won't think twice about it. She is mine to protect now."

He scooted backward. "I didn't know—Miss Montgomery never said…"

That didn't surprise him. He had yet to win her over. Soon the whole world would know she was his. He could be patient for her to accept it. This man didn't need to know more than she belonged to him.

"She shouldn't have to say anything to be respected. Leave before I change my mind."

Lord Addison raced out of the library. Damian scanned the room. His eyes locked onto a brandy decanter and decided he needed—no, deserved—a drink. He understood Pearla's reluctance, but it was playing havoc on him. What he needed was to be able to shout from the rooftops she was his. This cloak and dagger routine was getting old. He poured brandy into a glass and then downed the contents in one gulp. It burned as it traveled down his throat.

Clapping echoed through the room. "That was quite the performance. I must thank you for the entertainment."

Damian spun and locked gazes with Captain Blythe. It appeared to be his lucky night. The other man he needed to have words with had walked back into his life.

"Ah, Captain, good to see you. I've been looking for you."

"I heard," he replied. "I have my own spies too."

Damian poured another glass of brandy and took a slow drink. "I wouldn't expect less from someone employed by the late Duca d'Sordillo. I'm only surprised it's taken you this long to track me down."

"Be a good sport and pour me a glass of that brandy. I think we have a few things we must iron out."

Damian didn't want to have a lengthy conversation with the man. He wanted a few quick answers. The fight had left him when Lord Addison scurried out of the room. Now, he wanted to go home and plot how to win Pearla's heart for good.

"Pour your own brandy. I'm not your servant." Damian gestured toward the decanter. "As far as working through a few things... Tell me one thing, and we can be done with each other."

He raised an eyebrow. "What is it you want to know?"

"Why did you marry us?"

He didn't ask if the marriage was valid. It didn't matter anymore. Damian had no problem going through another ceremony. Pearla would never believe that the marriage was real without one. If it alleviated her concerns, then he'd do it a thousand times—as long as the end result was the same. She'd be his forever.

"I assume you're speaking about Miss Montgomery." He grinned. "I did enjoy watching, or rather hearing, you defending her honor."

Damian took a deep breath and glared at the Captain. "Are you going to explain what your master plan was?"

He shrugged and headed toward the brandy decanter. The Captain poured himself a glass and took a sip. He took his time before he turned back to Damian.

"It seemed like a good idea at the time."

That was it? Damian didn't buy it. There had to be more to his motivation than a spur of the moment idea. "I don't believe you."

He laughed and explained, "Conte, I'm not obsessed with you like the Fonte family is. I was—bored. The two of you amused me. I thought if I married you, it would prove to be rather entertaining. I admit that the duca thought that it would be good fun to ruin Miss Montgomery and you be the one who accomplished the task." The captain shrugged. "He believed the Duke of Huntly would never forgive you for ruining his former intended."

Damian clenched his jaw. "He would have destroyed an innocent woman's life to tamper with my relationship with Noah?"

"There isn't anything that the duca wouldn't have done." He swallowed the contents of his glass and set it down. "You were a pawn in a much larger scheme."

What Captain Blythe was telling him proved interesting, but it didn't really answer his questions. He needed to understand it fully in order to move forward. "Care to explain what his plans entailed?"

"No," he paused and studied Damian, "As fun as this has been, I think I've told you all I can."

"You haven't told me anything at all. This conversation is leaving me with even more questions and no answers to speak of."

Captain Blythe shrugged and headed toward the door. He paused before exiting and turned back to Damian. "There's not much I can do about that. The duca was only one boss in a crowd of many, and I rather like my head attached to my body. If I say any more, I might not keep it there."

Damian gritted his teeth and clenched his hand into a tight fist. The more he talked, the more he wanted to plant a fist into his face. If he wasn't going to depart with useful information regarding Paolo and his cohorts, then he could at least tell him something else of import.

"Before you scamper off," Damian said. "Why does Pearla believe we are not actually married?"

His laugh filled the room, making Damian want to act on his impulses. "I'm afraid that is my fault." He shrugged. "I told you I was suffering from ennui. After we took you away and deposited you on that infernal island, I decided she didn't need to mourn your loss. I gave her a reason to be angry with you instead —after all, no one intended for you to leave Fiji and see her ever again. She needed to move on with her life. Perhaps find someone worthy of her. She is a rather lovely woman."

Damian enunciated each word, barely holding in his rage. "What. Did. You. Tell. Her."

"I simply explained how you were only using her." He shrugged. "That you hoped to entice her into your bed and help her lose her virtue along the way."

"What does that have to do with our marriage?" No wonder she was so reluctant to be with him. The Captain had done them a tremendous disservice.

"Oh, that. I explained how it wasn't valid, and only a tool to get you what you really desired from her." He grinned. "There was also the little bit about how you were in on the plan from the start. The lady wasn't amused."

Damian cursed. "So it's true. Our wedding was a hoax to entertain you on the voyage to rid the world of me?"

"Yes," Captain Blythe said and left the room.

Damian threw his half-filled glass and watched it shatter against the wall. The amber liquid dripped down and hit the floor. It still didn't assuage the rage burning inside , so he turned and punched the wall, cursing from the pain shooting through him. How was he going to win Pearla back when she believed the worst of him? At least he knew what poison Captain Blythe had filled her head with. He would have to show her with his actions how much she meant to him. No matter how much he told her he wanted her, she wouldn't truly believe it. Not when he'd been forced to leave her before and she'd felt abandoned, as well as used.

He had an uphill battle from the moment he'd been torn from her side. In the end, he would prevail. The beginnings of love had been stamped in her heart. All he had to do was remind her of the man she'd trusted with her tender heart.

Damian smiled. *Soon, cara, soon I will begin to unlock your deepest desires.*

Pearla sat across from Gemma and Lily in the carriage as they headed to the Huntly townhouse. She'd stopped by, and her friends had talked her into a visit with Rubina. The last time she'd called upon the duchess—if it could be called that—was when she'd renewed her wedding vows with Noah. She still didn't know why she had attended the ceremony. Gemma thought it would be a good idea. What had she called it? Oh yeah, closure. It had been good for her to see how much in love the couple was. Though it made her ache for something similar.

"What is going on inside that head of yours?" Gemma asked.

"Hmmm," Pearla said absently.

"Pearla," Lily exclaimed.

She turned toward them and stared, baffled. What had they been saying? She'd been lost in her own world. There was too much on her mind and she had no idea how to deal with it all. When she'd seen Damian with Camellia the night before, her heart had hurt even more than before. It shouldn't matter that he had a mistress. They were nothing to each other. As much as she pushed him away, she couldn't help how much she desired him. Pushing him away was the only way she could continue to protect herself.

"Yes?" she asked, raising an eyebrow. "What?"

Lily and Gemma exchanged a look. What did that mean?

"I told you," Gemma said.

Lily chuckled. "You did."

Pearla rolled her eyes. "All right, I'll ask. What did you tell her?"

She didn't have the patience to play guessing games with her two friends. In fact, she lacked any tolerance what-so-ever. Her temper was at an all-time high, and she'd been snapping for no reason at all. The staff tiptoed around her.

Lily smiled. "You have something, or should I say someone, on your mind. Do you care to share?"

"I have nothing on my mind." Only one handsomely wicked conte that wouldn't leave her thoughts no matter how much she tried. "Nothing of import. I was thinking perhaps it would be lovely to have a dinner party. Would you two be willing to come?"

The last thing she wanted was a dinner party, but she needed to distract them in some way. She could get through an entire evening of their company if it halted the current conversation.

Gemma shook her head. "You're not getting off that easy."

Lily nodded. "We know something is bothering you, and you're going to tell us. If you want to discuss dinner plans, we will do so afterward."

"Why are you two being so difficult?" Pearla sighed. "I don't wish to discuss it."

"Don't you think it's time?" Gemma asked, softly.

Pearla resisted the urge to stomp her foot and throw a tantrum that would put a two-year-old to shame. How many times must she tell them? She only had one wish—to forget Damian Leone existed. All he'd done was destroy any chance she'd love another man. She'd thought she loved Noah. She hadn't realized how bland her emotions were for the duke until she met the conte. Now when she closed her eyes all she saw was his silver eyes alight with passion.

"I rather not." She turned her head away so they couldn't see the fear in her eyes.

"Tell us what happened with Damian," Lily insisted. "We know there is a story there. He claimed you were his wife when he interrupted the wedding."

The carriage came to a screeching halt, giving her a reprieve. Pearla took the opportunity to exit the carriage and head to the front door. Surely they wouldn't discuss the duchess's brother in her presence. She could pretend the conversation hadn't turned around and cornered her.

"Don't think this is over with," Gemma said from behind her. "It's only paused for a few moments."

Drat. So much for thinking they'd drop it around Rubina. Pearla sighed. "Why won't you leave it be?"

"Because we can see your heart in your eyes whenever he's around. It's time to face your problems head-on. If you want him, and we think you do, we are going to do whatever we can to make sure you get him." Lily patted her on the hand. "I have experience here. So does Gemma. Let us do this for you."

They walked into the townhouse and into Rubina's sitting room. She was already waiting for them. "Good, you're here. Did you ask her?"

"Yes, we did," Gemma answered her. "And no, we don't have answers yet."

The duchess stared at them for a brief moment, and then shook her head. Pearla didn't want to know what was going through her thoughts. She was very much afraid she wouldn't like it one bit.

Rubina waved them in. "Come sit, refreshments will be here shortly."

"Did you plan this?" Pearla asked as she looked back and forth between the three women. How could they do this to her? She thought they were her friends.

"We had planned on confronting you…" Gemma began.

"But we were not going to ask you yet. You happened to make it easier for us by stopping by to see Gemma today. All we did was take advantage of the situation," Lily finished.

"They're right. I wasn't expecting you. Lily and Gemma, yes, but it is a surprise." Rubina smiled. "A welcome one, but I apologize if I've made you uncomfortable."

Pearla gulped down a lump that formed in her throat. She wanted to run away from them. Perhaps they were right and it was time to face her fears. What if she *could* have Damian? If they were aware of something that she wasn't…

Perhaps he'd shared something with his sister. Did she dare ask?

She paced the room as anxiety filled her. Where should she start? "After the wedding…" She paused and took a deep breath and turned toward them. "I left."

"We know that." Lily waved her hand. "Tell us how you ended up with Damian."

Pearla glanced at each of their faces. They appeared a little too eager to hear the details. Why were they so interested in what happened? Rubina must not know much if they were all interrogating Pearla.

"I'm getting to that." Such impatience. "I booked passage on a ship. It seemed like fate, and I could get out of England and away from the embarrassment."

Rubina blushed. "I'm sorry about that—if I could have returned sooner, I would have."

Pearla waved her hand. She no longer blamed the woman. How could she? It wasn't as if she planned to hurt her. An evil man had held her captive in his home for years. She had suffered more than Pearla ever had. "I know, and there is nothing to forgive. Damian explained what happened to you. I'm sorry you had to go through so much pain. You and Noah shouldn't have been put through that because a mad man had been obsessed with you. It's clear to see how much you two love each other. I'm happy for you."

"Thank you," Rubina said quietly. Her tone was soft, yet demanding. "This would be a good place to tell us about your relationship with my brother."

"Don't skip the good parts," Lily interjected. Gemma smacked her on the shoulder. "What? Don't tell me you're not curious. I'll call you a liar."

Pearla smiled. This was a good thing. They *were* her friends, and she *could* trust them. "The Duca d'Sordillo kidnapped Damian and arranged for him to be on the ship I booked passage on."

"He implied as much, but we couldn't find the evidence we needed to confirm it. Paolo is an evil man." Rubina sighed. "We feared Damian died at his hands."

"Did you help rescue him?" Lily prodded. Gemma glared at her. "Quit giving me that look, Gemma Marsden. We've been waiting long enough to hear this story, and I don't want her to get distracted."

Gemma sighed and shook her head. "Please continue, Pearla."

Pearla laughed. "Thank you."

"For what?" Rubina asked.

Warmth spread through her. She didn't know how much she'd needed this…time with these three women to help her put it into perspective.

"For forcing me to talk about it."

She told them everything. Explained how she'd been locked in a cabin with Damian for weeks. The wedding Captain Blythe had forced on them, and then the finale when Damian had left. When she found out the wedding had been nothing but a sham, and then the captain's claims Damian had orchestrated it.

Rubina shook her head. "I don't know what happened to my brother. He hasn't bothered to explain any of it to me yet. That tells me it isn't good, or he'd have spilled all of the details already. He's always been protective of me." She frowned. "I do know this: he cares for you, and he wouldn't have left you willingly. I bet my life Captain Blythe lied to you. Talk to him and let him explain what happened."

Pearla bit her lip and considered her words. Rubina would know Damian better than anyone. Could she trust him again? She wanted to. Her heart belonged to him in a way it never had to anyone else. If he loved her—she could have everything. But what if she did as Rubina suggested and he broke her all over again. Could she take a chance and lose everything?

"I don't know if I can…" She looked away from them. "I thought I loved Noah. I know now I didn't have a clue what love is. If I go to Damian and lay my heart before him, I don't know if I'd survive it if he tossed it aside."

"Why do you have reservations?" Gemma asked. "Has he done something to make you believe he'd hurt you?"

"Other than the lies that Captain Blythe told you," Lily said. "Because it's clear he had his own agenda."

Pearla glanced at Rubina. "Do you know a Camellia?"

Rubina's face lost all color. Her voice was high-pitched as she demanded, "How do you know *her*?"

Pearla sighed. She knew that woman was trouble. "I saw her last night at the Silverton ball. She was awfully friendly with Damian. Her words implied that they were—involved."

Please let me be wrong. She didn't like to think of Damian with another woman.

Rubina took a deep breath. "Camellia is Paolo's younger sister." She waved her hand. "Which isn't important... Damian and Camellia were—courting I guess is the word. I know now that it was much deeper than that."

Pearla's heart broke. It was as she feared. He did have a past with the stunning woman. "I see." She fought tears. This was not the time to give into the pain.

"No, you don't," Rubina said softly. "Damian never loved her. She was a tool. He knew if he got close to her, he'd be able to find out more about Paolo's organization." She frowned. "I hate to admit this, but he used her. He knew she wanted him, and he saw it as a way to end Paolo's criminal activity."

Camellia was the mistake he'd referred to when they were being held captive together. He'd said he regretted it. Pearla tilted her head and considered the information Rubina imparted. "He doesn't love her?"

"He never did." She smiled. "I do believe he loves you. I know my brother, and he's never looked at a woman the way he does you. He may have not said it out loud, but I believe you own his heart."

How was she to use this new information? It could change everything for her—she needed to talk to Damian and figure out what future they had.

"Sometimes the biggest leap you make can give you the best rewards," Gemma explained. "If I'd given up on Liam, we wouldn't be where we are now. Trust yourself and actually listen to what he has to say."

Lily smiled at Gemma. "My brother is an arse. He never should have run from you to begin with. It's the Marsden stubbornness."

Pearla knew a little about the urge to runaway. She'd been doing it for months. Her friends were right. It was time to face her fears and talk to Damian. Making assumptions was not getting her anywhere. If he loved her... Gemma was right; the rewards would be enormous. She could finally fall into his arms and feel all that pleasure he kept promising her.

"I believe it's time I acted on your advice." Pearla smiled. "I have a lot to think about, some preparation to do."

"Maybe now is the time to organize that dinner party you mentioned earlier," Lily reminded her.

"Dinner party?" Rubina's eyebrow rose. "Did I miss something."

Gemma tapped her chin. "Perhaps it would be better if Rubina planned one instead."

They all looked at Gemma. She explained her idea and they all agreed. As Damian's sister, she could invite him and give Pearla the perfect opportunity to find some quiet time with him. It would be both proper and private. Pearla couldn't wait now that she'd decided to give him a chance. She smiled at the thought of seeing him again. A weight lifted off her shoulders she hadn't realized she'd been carrying around. For the first time in as long as she could remember the future looked bright. All she had to do was let go of all her doubts and she could have everything she wanted.

Soon, Damian. Soon.

Damian knocked on the door to his sister's home. She'd effectively demanded he attend a dinner party she planned in the invitation she'd sent to his room. He didn't doubt it was an excuse to interrogate him. Subtlety wasn't one of Rubina's strong suits. When she wanted something she asked plainly, and it appeared as if she was done waiting for him to come to her. He didn't even know why he avoided the conversation.

She wouldn't look badly upon him. If anyone knew what an evil man Paolo was it was her. There was no reason he shouldn't have explained everything to her. He had a lot on his mind, and honestly didn't have the time. His conversation with Captain Blythe had given him a lot to think about. Now he could tie up loose ends and begin to pursue Pearla in truth. He knew what she believed, and now it was up to him to alleviate every one of her misgivings.

"Good evening, Conte Leone," the butler greeted him after he opened the door. "Everyone is meeting in the sitting room until dinner is served."

"Thank you, Simmons." Damian nodded. "How many people did my sister invite to this little party of hers?"

"It's an intimate affair," he replied. "Only close friends and family."

That could mean any number of people his sister viewed

as a friend—perhaps he'd get lucky and Pearla was among her guests. She had been at their renewal ceremony. It was possible. Damian nodded at Simmons and headed to the sitting room. He found his sister engrossed in a quiet conversation with the object of his desire. No one else was in the room.

"Am I early?" he asked.

He usually was one of the last to arrive. By all appearances, he wasn't though. Who were they waiting for? A small part of him hoped no one else would be in attendance. He could easily squire Pearla away for a little heart-to-heart and finally convince her she belonged with him.

Rubina smiled brightly. "You're right on time. Come in and join us." She patted the settee. "We've much to discuss."

Dread began to pool inside of him. What had his sister planned? He raised an eyebrow. "We do?"

They'd had their heads together whispering when he'd entered. He had an uneasy feeling they were up to something. The demand for him to attend should have been a warning. His sister had no problems hatching a scheme to get what she wanted. He dreaded finding out what she was up to.

Rubina nodded. "Absolutely."

Pearla had yet to acknowledge his presence. She did great at pretending he didn't exist. Why did he think that would have changed? When he spoke to her directly, she lit up from the inside out. He forced her to admit what was between them. If he let her, she'd go on ignoring the fire burning deep inside them both.

Damian sat down next to his sister and glanced between Pearla and Rubina. Their wide grins were not very comforting; they only made him more uneasy. "Where is everyone?"

Pearla remained quiet. It was enough to give a man a complex. How could she find it so easy to ignore him? He was exceptionally aware of her whenever she was in his presence. What would it take to stir her emotions to the surface?

"Never mind about the guest list." Rubina waved her

hand. "I've been talking to Pearla, and I think you have a few things to explain."

Damian glanced at Pearla again. She met his gaze with determination. He looked at his sister and encountered the same expression from her. They'd effectively lured him to a dressing down as if he was an errant school boy. He wanted to laugh, but he knew they were serious. He would play their game, and then he'd have his own private time with Pearla. He was done with the chase, and he wanted to claim her as his.

"What is it you think I need to enlighten you both with?" He leaned back into the settee and watched them both carefully.

"I have been waiting patiently for you to tell me what happened to you." Rubina glared at him. "I've been forced to ask Pearla to fill in some of the blanks. You interrupted my wedding and claimed she was your wife. Then nothing..." She waved her hand.

He could almost feel Pearla's stare burning through him. He turned and gazed into twin blue flames. She wanted to cut in but held back. This was Rubina's show, and Pearla was waiting for her turn to pounce. He wanted her to. It was about bloody time she sought him out. It was a nice turn of events.

He tapped his fingers together. "At the time, I believed that to be true. I've since realized I was duped by someone in the employ of Paolo."

Rubina tilted her head. "There is more to it than that. What happened to you after you left Pearla on that ship with Captain Blythe?"

Ah...so Pearla had filled her in on the details she was aware of. That made things a little simpler. He still didn't want to get into the fine details of his horror as an indentured slave. No one needed to know how bad it had been. He still had nightmares about it. In time, he'd be able to let it go, but he wasn't going to subject the two most important women in his life to the atrocities he suffered. He didn't need to share his ordeal and add to their pain.

"Paolo arranged for me to spend some time on a secluded island near Australia."

Pearla's head snapped toward him. "Don't do that."

Finally, she spoke. It took her long enough. "Do what?"

"Make it seem like you were on holiday when we both know it was far more than that."

Did they? Was she finally able to see past Captain Blythe's lies? Things might have progressed far more than he realized. She seemed—open, almost trusting as she gazed at him. What caused her to finally see clearly? Still...he didn't plan on giving all the details.

He shrugged. "A lot happened, *cara*, but none of which matters. If it's all the same to you both, I'd rather forget about my time on that horrid island."

Pearla tilted her head and studied him. She was quiet for a few moments as she contemplated his words. Then, with a firm voice, she confirmed, "Captain Blythe did lie to me."

He studied her. "About some things, yes he did."

"What was a lie and what was the truth?" Pearla asked.

Rubina stood and said, "I need to check on dinner." She left the room. Damian didn't once glance in her direction. His gaze never left Pearla's. His sister had given them privacy to discuss what happened. He would thank her later for the gift.

Pearla fidgeted in her seat. She looked down at her lap. Damian wanted to ease her discomfort. The only way he knew how to do that was to tell her how much he needed her.

"I would never have willingly left you." He lifted her hand and caressed it with the pad of his thumb. "But that wasn't his biggest lie. The one that played the most havoc on our lives was letting us both believe we'd married. It was a shock to be forced into the ceremony, but it had felt right. Now that I know it was false, all I want to do is rectify it. Please, *cara*, consent to be my wife in truth."

A soft gasp left her lips. He was afraid she might say no, so he pulled her into his arms and kissed her until he couldn't tell where she began and he ended. Not once did she try to pull away. She lifted her arms and wound them around his neck, entwining her hands in his hair. He couldn't get close enough to her. To finally have her in his arms again...no words could describe how wondrous it was. He pulled back and saw his own passion reflected back at him in her fiery gaze. This is what he'd missed and craved all the months they'd been separated. How it would be between them.

"You didn't give me a chance to answer you." Pearla cupped his cheeks. "Do you always leap without looking?"

"For you, I'd walk through hell and back."

She smiled at him. "I'm starting to believe that might be true."

His heart filled with hope. When he'd left his rooms, he never thought he'd find all his dreams waiting for him at his sister's home. Now he might finally have everything he'd been longing for. Was she telling him what he thought she was?

"Are you agreeing to marry me?" *Please say yes.* "If so, I'd like to have the ceremony as soon as possible."

"I'm still considering all my options."

His heart fell. Not the answer he'd hoped for, but still an improvement.

"What is there to consider?" He let his smile show all the pleasure he could give her. "You know what the right answer is, *cara.* Say yes, and I'll make you the happiest, most satisfied, woman in the world."

"You still haven't told me everything." She frowned. "How am I to trust you when you won't share with me what really happened to you? I know by your evasiveness it isn't good."

Not this again. Why was she being so persistent? It didn't matter the horrors he suffered. All he needed was for her to agree to spend the rest of her life in his arms. Her softness would erase the atrocities he suffered and ease his soul. "I don't wish to speak of it." He set her down on the settee and paced the room. "It isn't worth speaking about."

"Damian, please," she begged. "Make me undersand."

He ran his fingers through his hair with frustration coursing through his veins. "I was an indentured slave," he spat out. "They made me do things...I can't do this. Don't make me."

Tears trailed down her cheeks. She walked over to him and wrapped her arms around his waist, leaned her head against his chest. He closed his eyes, basking in her warmth, and held onto her with all he had inside.

"All right, you win," she muttered. "I won't push. When and if you want to talk about what you went through, I will listen."

Thank God. He enjoyed holding her. This was what he needed. To feel her wrapped in his arms. She was what he'd lived for and fought to return to. If he could keep her warmth near him forever, it would erase all the things he'd suffered on that island. None of it mattered as long as she agreed to be his. "When will you give me an answer to my question?"

She glanced up at him through hooded eyes. "I haven't made a decision."

He smiled. She was being coy now. He lifted his hand and trailed his fingers through her silky blonde hair. He pulled the pins out and let them drop to the floor one by one until her curls flowed down her back. "Perhaps I can convince you."

"Oh?" She licked her lips. "What did you have in mind?"

He kissed her forehead. "A little bit of this." He trailed kisses down her cheeks and the base of her neck. "Some more of this." His lips hovered above hers. "A whole lot of this."

He pressed his lips to hers and tasted her sweetness. Their tongues dueled for control as he pulled her tighter in his embrace. The burning flame between them threatened to set them ablaze with pleasure. Damian would never get enough of her. She was his everything.

"Dinner is..." Rubina's voice filled his ears. "Oh, um, perhaps I should come back."

Damian stepped away from Pearla and smiled. "Don't go, Rue."

"Did you two settle everything?" she asked.

"No." His gaze never left Pearla's. "I'm still waiting for her to give me an answer to my question."

"What question is that?" Noah asked as he entered the room. "What did I miss? Simmons said dinner is ready. Why are we still in the sitting room?"

Pearla's laughter filled the room. It was music to his ears.

"Please, *cara*, say the word that I have been waiting forever for you to say."

"Yes." She paused and placed a soft quick kiss on his lips. "I will marry you."

Damian hugged her tightly against him, and then glanced

over his shoulder to meet Noah's gaze. He nodded, understanding what Damian was asking without words. Pearla stepped out of his embrace. A huge smile lit up her beautiful face.

Noah clapped his hands. "Great, so that special license you had me obtain will be used after all."

Pearla's gaze whipped toward Noah and back at him. She raised an eyebrow and said, "What is he talking about? You knew I'd say yes?"

"I'd never presume to know what you will or will not do, *cara*." He caressed her cheek with the palm of his hand. "I was only hoping you'd agree. On the lucky day you said yes, I wanted to be ready to say our vows all over again."

She smiled. "You were always too charming for you own good." She sighed. "So when do you want to have the ceremony?"

"After dinner."

She laughed lightheartedly. "I'm serious."

"So am I."

Pearla tilted her head and studied him. Her gaze softened. He missed her so much and hoped she agreed to an impromptu wedding. He didn't want to give her a chance to change her mind. The sooner they had the ceremony, the happier he would be.

She shook her head and chuckled lightly. "Fine. Noah, do your magic and make it happen."

"Consider it done," he said and left the room.

Damian would owe the duke a great debt for making all his dreams come true. Soon, Pearla would be his wife, and nothing would stand in the way of their happiness.

CHAPTER 15

Dinner flew by in a blur. Pearla ate, but the food had no taste. Nerves filled her as she went through the motions. A vicar would be arriving soon to marry her and Damian. This time the wedding would be real.

Was she really ready to tie herself to him?

She glanced across the table, her gaze locking with his. A sense of rightness overflowed through her. *Yes.* She wanted him like she'd never wanted anything in her life. Her wedding to Noah had been planned down to the last detail, and it ended up being cancelled. This time she wasn't going to wait. Damian was hers. It was time the world knew what she already did inside her heart.

Noah sighed. "Is the food that bad?"

Pearla heard his voice, but the words hadn't registered in her mind. All she could do was stare at Damian. Waiting was killing her. She wanted to marry him and start their life together. He'd made her promises she fully intended to ensure he kept. She needed to experience the passion he guaranteed she would find in his arms.

"What?" Pearla asked absentmindedly.

Damian chuckled. "The food is fine. We're anxious to get to…*dessert.*"

Pearla blushed. When he said dessert, heat permeated

inside her. He hadn't meant a sweet confection when he said the word. It was much more decadent than that.

She wiped her mouth with a napkin. "Right. I am done."

"Let's retire to the sitting room." Rubina stood up. "The vicar should be here soon."

"We'll stay behind and discuss a few things." Noah gestured toward Damian. "Let us know when he arrives."

"I will." Rubina nodded. She leaned down and quickly kissed Noah. Then she wrapped her arm through Pearla's, leading her out of the room. "I'm so glad you're going to marry my brother. I've always wanted a sister."

Pearla was baffled. "Don't you find it strange?"

"What?" she asked.

"Two years ago, I was standing in a church ready to marry Noah, your husband, and now I'm about to marry your brother." Pearla didn't understand how Rubina could be so accepting of her. She didn't know if she would've been able to return the favor if their roles were reversed.

"No," Rubina said. "Everything happens for a reason. I think you were meant to be in that church so it could lead you to the one place you were destined to be."

Perhaps she was right. If she'd never fled London, she might not have fallen so quickly into Damian's arms. He'd been there when she needed someone to lean on. She'd been prickly and he'd remained charming and kind. She didn't know the full details of what happened to him when he had been torn away from her, but she hoped he would feel comfortable enough to tell her eventually. Secrets had a way of driving a wedge between people, and she didn't want to lose Damian ever again. Prying wouldn't give her the answers she sought. Only patience would do that.

"I understand." Pearla smiled. "Noah is yours, and Damian is mine. That is how it was always supposed to be, and losing Noah led me to where I really belonged."

Rubina nodded, her lips tilting into a soft smile. "These things work themselves out. I'm so glad Damian has found a woman worthy of his love."

"How do you know I am?"

Pearla bit her lip. Did he love her? He never said. Maybe that was something she should have asked him before she agreed to be his wife. They were doing everything backward. Rubina had such faith, and Pearla questioned everything. How could she believe they belonged together and would make it when Pearla constantly doubted him? One second she was sure and wouldn't change anything for any reason. Then a niggling feeling deep in her gut made her want to run away and not look back. How was such indecisiveness worthy of Damian's affection? His sister should be telling her to stay away and not break his heart.

"Now you're being silly." Rubina laughed. "You're worthy for several reasons, but the easiest and most obvious is because he loves you. That's enough for me."

There was that word again. *Love*. Rubina believed he loved Pearla. He certainly desired her and believed they belonged together. He was so gentle and possessive... *Enough*. She wasn't going to debate the merits of marrying him anymore. She'd agreed to marry him. The time for thinking about it had past.

"Pardon me, Your Grace," Simmons said. "The vicar has arrived."

"Very good. Show him in, and please let my husband and brother know to join us in the sitting room." She clapped her hands. "We have a wedding about to commence."

"That we do," Damian agreed as he entered the room. "One I've been waiting far too long for."

Pearla glanced at him with a sheepish smile. "Seems like we already had one wedding...not my fault it wasn't valid."

Damian chucked and hugged her tight in his embrace. He leaned down and kissed the top of her head. "That is true, but it is your fault for keeping me waiting for a wedding we both know *will* be valid."

Pearla held onto him and breathed in his scent. With him near, every one of her doubts and fears melted away. He always made her forget why she'd ever had a reason to object to being with him. She belonged in his arms. When they were wrapped up in each other, she couldn't help wondering why she fought him at every turn. He was right. They were inevitable.

"I know, and I can't apologize enough." She stepped back and gazed into his eyes. "I had these doubts and fears. I couldn't let them go. I've been let down too many times and didn't believe I could trust my own instincts with you."

"What changed your mind?" he asked.

"The truth?"

He nodded. She took a deep breath.

"No matter what I said or did, I couldn't get over you. You were always there at the back of my mind and when I saw you again…" She closed her eyes and took a deep breath. "I was so angry and betrayed. You left me when I needed you the most and had just begun to accept we could have something good. How could I not believe you would do it again? I had to protect my heart because no one has ever put me first."

His gaze softened. "Oh, *cara*…" He lifted his hand and caressed her cheek. "I didn't leave you. I was torn from you when all I wanted to do was stay with you forever. It was the worst thing that happened to me, and trust me, there have been some horrible things I've had to endure. Being away from you nearly devastated me. Knowing one day I'd be with you again gave me a reason to push on and fight."

Her insides turned to mush at his words. He may not have said the one word she hoped to hear, but how could he not love her when she gave him a reason to go on living? That was enough for now.

"Are you two ready to exchange your vows?" The vicar asked.

"Yes," they both said in unison.

The ceremony was fast and simple. They recited their vows, and before she knew it she was Damian's wife and the vicar announced that he could kiss the bride.

"My pleasure," Damian said and leaned down. Once his lips touched hers, sparks ignited into full-blown flames. Every time he touched her, she lit up with a need she couldn't describe. Only he had ever had that affect on her. He lifted his head and gazed down at her. She knew he had the same need pouring out of him by the color of his eyes. They always turned to molten silver when passion ruled him.

The vicar cleared his throat. "I guess I will be going now."

"Thank you again for coming on such a short notice," Noah said. "Let me see you out."

687

Damian looked up and watched them exit. "Rue, I think it's time that Pearla and I left as well." He hugged his sister. "Thank you for everything. We will come by again soon."

"You better." She laughed. "I've missed you. Besides you've yet to meet your nephew. Lucian needs to know his Uncle Damian."

He laughed. "I look forward to it."

Damian reached down and lifted her hand with his. He kissed the palm of her hand. "Are you ready to go home, *cara*?"

She frowned. "Where exactly is home now?"

He opened his mouth and then shut it again. "You're right. I have a bachelor residence."

A wide grin grew on Pearla's face. "The good news is I have a perfectly good townhouse. You can work on selling your rooms at the Albany tomorrow."

Damian laughed and escorted her out of the townhouse. "Do you have a carriage?" he asked.

"I do."

"Good. I walked over. I had a lot on my mind, and it gave me time to think." He kissed her lips. "Now I find I'm in a hurry to take you home."

Pearla smiled. "I am too."

They headed toward her carriage. She nodded at the driver. When they reached the side, Damian leaned over to open the door—he crumpled to the ground before he could unfasten the latch. Pearla's gaze shot up. A man she'd hoped never to see again stood in front of her.

"Captain Blythe," she exclaimed. "What are you doing?"

"It's a pleasure to see you again, Miss Montgomery," he said. "I have to apologize for rudely interrupting your time with the conte, but I'm under orders to take you two to see my employer."

Pearla gulped down a lump that had become lodged in her throat. Who was he working for now? When he held her captive before, he'd worked for the Duca d'Sordillo. She'd been informed that the evil man was now dead. Who would wish her and Damian harm? As far as she knew they had no enemies to speak of. They were supposed to go home and bask in the glory of their finally being together. They were finally married, and their lives were once again thrown into tatters at the whim of a mad person.

"What if I don't cooperate?" she asked mulishly.

"If you'd rather I end Conte Leone's life now, I'd be happy to oblige." He shrugged. "Or you could come with me, and maybe you will both make it out of this alive."

"There's a chance we won't?"

A sick feeling settled down into the pit of her stomach. The dinner she'd consumed threatened to come back up. Why did these things continue to happen to her? She glanced down at Damian's unconscious body and made a snap decision. She couldn't take a risk with his life. He needed her to keep calm and make rational decisions. It was her turn to protect him and make sure nothing horrid happened to him again. If it meant going to meet the person who'd hired Captain Blythe, she'd do it. Then she would make them pay for interrupting her wedding night and threatening their lives.

She lifted her chin and said with conviction, "Take us to your leader. I have a few words they need to hear."

"Good girl." He laughed. "I knew you had some grit in you."

He gestured to someone behind her. They lifted Damian's body and tossed him in her carriage. Then Captain Blythe helped her inside. She sat next to her husband and caressed his hair. It comforted her more than it helped him. As the carriage rocked forward she formed a plan.

She was so done with insane people playing havoc with her life. It was time to let go of polite Pearla and let them feel the strength of her wrath.

First, she would have to make sure Damian was safe; although, she had no clue how she would be able to. Their fate didn't look good...

CHAPTER 16

An ache slid up his neck and traveled up to his head. A little hammer seemed to be beating a steady rhythm against it, causing pinpricks of pain to shoot behind his eyes. The idea of lifting his eyelids to check his surroundings didn't seem like a good idea. What the hell had happened to him? Last thing he remembered—Pearla.

His eyes flew open and he shuddered from the weight of them. Damian tried to sit up, but he couldn't move. He looked down and his hands were tied securely in front of him. His legs were secured to the sides of the chair he currently found himself in. There had to be a way to gain his freedom. His wife needed him. Who had hit him and taken him captive? This was starting to get old. He was on his way to his new home…to finally make love to Pearla.

"I see you're awake," a feminine voice filled his ears. He recognized it…where had he heard…

"Camellia," he replied scathingly. "Untie me, now." He jerked his legs and hands against the rope.

"Why would I do something as silly as that?" She sashayed over to his side. "I finally have you where I want you."

She was as crazy as her brother. How had he never seen it in her before? Was she as obsessed with him as Paolo had been with Rubina? Would he suffer a similar fate? Perhaps Camellia could be reasoned with.

"You have to know this is not a good idea. I will be missed."

She tilted her head and studied him. Her hair fell down her back in black waves. "I don't plan on keeping you here forever." She laughed. "I'm not my brother."

Damian stared at her, not saying a word.

"Oh, I see you are comparing us." She flicked her wrist nonchalantly. "I'm not crazy, Damian. Once were officially wed, you'll be free to go."

And she thought to convince him she hadn't lost her mind? Insanity clearly ran far and wide in the branches of that family tree. Reasoning with her might not work, but he still had to try.

"I can't marry you, Melia," he said softly. He really couldn't. He already had a wife.

"Sure you can." She smiled serenely. "The vicar will be here soon to perform the ceremony."

He hadn't really believed she was in the same league as her brother. Perhaps he should try reasoning with her again. It might help if he pled his case with her. She appeared rather calm about the entire situation. It scared him a little. It wasn't normal to hold the groom hostage before a wedding, and Camellia was acting like it was.

"You don't think he'll have issue with the groom being tied up for the ceremony?"

She strolled around the room and laughed. "Why would he?" She clapped her hands with manic happiness. "I've paid him well not to think at all."

He took a deep breath and studied her. There had to be a way to get through to her. She must care about him on some level if she wanted to marry him. Crazy, sure—but there must be a soft spot inside of her for him. He could try to play on that a little bit to get her to let him go.

"Melia," he coaxed. "I can't be your husband. It's the truth."

"Don't be ridiculous I told you already that you could."

He tried again, "I can't marry you because I'm already married to someone else."

Please don't ask who. He didn't know where Pearla was. He had to protect her, and he had no clue how far Camellia's insanity ran through her mind. She might get the notion to kill his wife so she could have him. What was it about his family attracting the mad people of the world? This one he could blame himself for. If he hadn't pursued Camellia for information on Paolo she might never have latched on to him.

She narrowed her eyes on him and glared. "Don't lie to me, Conte Leone. I won't be made a fool of."

He closed his eyes and prayed for patience. "I'm not lying."

"But...you love me," she said. "I know you do. The way you looked at me—it warmed me from the inside out. I was so sure..."

He shook his head. "I only love one woman, and I'm sorry, Melia." —He paused and looked into her stormy green eyes — "I owe you so many apologies for what I did to you. I used you in the worst possible way, but I never loved you."

She stalked toward him and leaned into him. Her face mere inches from his and demanded, "Is it the blonde you were following around at the ball? Is she the woman you love?"

He gulped but held back from saying it.

"Never mind, I can see it in your eyes. You care for her." Her lips tilted into a half smile. "What was her name again? Pearla Montgomery if my memory serves me." She tapped her fingers together her smile growing bigger on her face as she stared at him. "You'll be happy to know I have her here. Captain Blythe is keeping her company while we prepare for our wedding."

Did she still believe they were going to get married? He'd already explained... She better not hurt Pearla. What would he do if she harmed his wife? There was nothing he wouldn't do for Pearla—even give his own life. "What are you going to do?"

"Wouldn't you like to know?" She strolled over to his side and raised her hand to cup his chin. She lifted her other hand and ran her fingers through his hair. "Don't you worry about a thing. I will make sure your wife is disposed of before the wedding."

She let go of his chin and took a few steps back. Damian jerked against the ropes, and they started to dig into his flesh with each attempt to free himself.

"Don't hurt her." He roared with frustration. "Please, I'm begging you."

Tears burned around the edges of his eyes, one escaping and trailing down his cheek. He'd fought so hard to get back to her. The hell he survived—it would be nothing without her. She was everything to him. If Camellia ended her life, she might as well take a dagger and stab him through the heart. He wouldn't be able to live without her.

Pearla had endured so much because of him. If not for the Fonte's obsession with his family, she'd be safe. She'd never have been kidnapped, either time. There was so much they hadn't discussed yet. He didn't deserve her love, but he wanted it. His selfishness had brought this upon them. All he'd wanted to do was protect her. He'd failed. Now Pearla would pay for all his past mistakes.

"You really do love her, don't you?"

He glanced up at her. His vision was blurry from the tears threatening to flood his cheeks. "If she dies, do me a favor and kill me too."

"You poor, poor man." She smiled. "You're a besotted fool."

He blinked several times. "I have never loved a woman the way I do Pearla. She is my everything, always will be. If I don't have her, I have nothing. I would rather die than spend my life without her. So either kill me or let me go. If she's dead, I will find a way to leave this world on my own."

Camellia shook her head and laughed. "I never took you for the dramatic type. Relax, your wife is fine. I told you Captain Blythe was keeping her company. In fact, she's in the next room." She waved toward a nearby door. "She can hear everything we're saying."

His mouth opened and closed. Word failed to find their way out. "I don't understand."

What game was she playing now?

She sighed. "It was never my intention to hurt you, Damian. I thought I was doing you a favor."

693

"Tying me up and planning to marry me is your way of helping?"

He was oblivious to how her mind worked. Damian wasn't sure he wanted to know.

"Yes," she replied. "I was under the impression you were having difficulty getting Miss Montgomery to believe you really loved her. This was my way of alleviating every one of her doubts once and for all."

"What?" His vision blurred. "If you mean me no harm, then untie me."

"All in good time." She paced back and forth in front of him. "Before I let you go, I need your assurance you won't hurt me." She shrugged. "There are also a few things I need to tell you."

"I won't hurt you." As long as Pearla was not harmed. "Loosen the ropes."

Camellia ignored him. "I have been searching for you for some time. I knew Paolo had done something to you." She sighed as she strolled around the room, and then stopped in front of him glancing down. She took a breath and continued her tone full of conviction. "I know how evil he is—was, and I wanted to make sure he hadn't done something irreparable to you. What he did to your sister was unforgivable. He wasn't any easier on me. He had me on a tight leash. His death freed me in so many ways. I owe your family a great debt."

"Untie. Me. Now."

"I will in a few moments," she replied. "I went to Bath because there was supposed to be someone with more information on how to find you. Captain Blythe wasn't being as forthcoming as I would have liked. I'd been informed Paolo had him do something to you. The captain refused to impart with the necessary information." She smiled. "Seems there are men worse than my brother. Can you believe that?" She raised an eyebrow, and then waved her hand dismissively. "He's said on several occasions he rather likes his head attached to his body. He's been most irritating. The blasted man has been following me in a misguided attempt to protect me. Imagine my relief to see you at that ball. I have been searching forever, and you seemed happy and contented with this little slip of a woman."

"She is more than that." Pearla was the only woman he'd ever love. If he managed to untangle them from their current mess, he'd make sure she knew how much he loved her. Camellia's insanity had taken a different direction than her brother's. Damian wasn't sure he appreciated her shaky moral code.

"I know she's the woman who captured your heart." She smiled at him. "I did some investigating and hatched this little plot of mine. I'm not crazy; I truly only want to see you happy, and I think I did help you. My methods might be a little...high-handed and a tiny bit extreme, but they are effective."

She snapped her fingers and the door opened. Pearla came rushing in with Captain Blythe fast on her heels.

"Oh, Damian, I'm so sorry. He wouldn't let me in until he got the signal from her." She glared at Camellia. "Give me something to get these ropes off of him."

Captain Blythe shook his head and took several steps forward. He pulled a dagger out of a sheath and cut the ropes at his feet first. Then he slid it under the ropes around his wrists and cut them clean through. Damian rubbed his wrists and glared. How dare they put them through all the unnecessary torture? His fist connected with Captain Blythe's nose before he'd realized he had clenched his hand. The captain's bones cracked beneath his knuckles. It was by far the most satisfying act of violence he'd ever embarked upon. It would be gratifying if he could break more than his nose.

"Easy now," the captain said. "None of that is necessary."

"I beg to differ." Damian glared. "I've wanted to do that for too long now. You know you deserved it."

"You're both free to go," Camellia interjected. She turned her gaze toward Pearla. "I hope you can trust that he loves you now. There's no reason to doubt him."

Pearla nodded.

Damian stood and wrapped her in his arms. As stressful as it had been to wake up tied to a chair, he was relieved it had all been a farce on the part of Camellia.

"Camellia, if I don't see you for a long time—don't come looking for me." He glared. "Your way of helping doesn't work for me."

She laughed. "Conte, it's been a pleasure seeing you, but it's time for me to return to Naples. I have more messes of my brother's to clean up." She nodded toward Captain Blythe. "Are you coming?"

They both exited the room, leaving Damian and Pearla alone.

"I'm so sorry you had to go through that," Damian lifted his hands and cupped her cheeks. "I will spend the rest of my life making sure only joyful things fill your life."

"I'm sorry I ever doubted you."

"*Cara*, after all we have been through, I'd have been surprised if you hadn't." He loved her so much.

"Thank you for being patient with me." She leaned into him. "I love you too, even though I think I probably don't deserve you."

"I promise you, it's I who doesn't deserve you." He pressed his lips against hers. "I'm the lucky one. Before you, I only saw darkness. You are the light that gives me a reason to live and find pleasure in life."

"Why don't we agree that we are both blessed to have each other?" She hugged him closer. "Now take me home." She wiggled her eyebrows suggestively. "I believe you made me a promise or two you haven't fulfilled yet."

Damian chuckled. "We will work on rectifying those."

He wrapped her arm through his and led them out of the door. They had their whole lives together. Nothing but good things from now on—they'd already had enough excitement for two lifetimes. Damian was looking forward to easy going days and starting a family with his wife.

"I will say this much—this will be an interesting tale we can tell our children when they ask how we met."

Pearla laughed. "Once upon a time a man kidnapped us…"

"And we lived happily ever after."

Damian leaned down and kissed her, basking in the paradise of finding her love.

"Good morning, beautiful…"

Damian pulled her into his arms and trailed kisses down her neck. He dipped his head lower and ran his tongue across one of her breasts. He cupped the other one in the palm of his hand and pinched her nipple.

Need flooded through her. This is how every woman should wake up in the morning. Damian loved her thoroughly and left her breathless. Their desire for each other never wavered, even after being together for years and having three unruly children.

Pearla sighed as her body tingled with her husband's ministrations. "Damian, I need…"

"I know exactly what you need, *cara*." And he proceeded to give it to her. He always kept his promises until she screamed from the pleasure of them.

This time was no different.

She basked in the glow of his loving. "I could lie here all day."

"Me too," he agreed. "Unfortunately, we must leave the warmth of our bed at some point."

Did they? Their bed was her favorite place, and when she was enclosed within his arms she didn't see any reason to leave it. Regrettably, they had responsibilities to see to outside of their bedroom.

Pearla sighed. "I know. I promised Gemma I would be down early to help her set up for the Viscount and Viscountess Torrington's surprise." She rolled out of bed and dressed. Damian languished behind and watched her. "Are you not going to come with me?"

"I was enjoying the view." He winked. "I will be down shortly. I have something I need to discuss with Noah and Liam."

She nodded and exited their room. They were at Huntly Manor, Noah's country estate. They were planning an intimate gathering to celebrate Liam and Lily's parents' anniversary. Forty years ago, they embarked on their own adventure together. Pearla hoped she would be as lucky as they were.

Their love had, thus far, stood the test of time. She and Damian had celebrated their fifteenth a few months ago. Their oldest child, Rafael, was born a year after they were married. Sofia and Gabrielle followed a few years after him, a year barely separating their births. All three of them kept her and Damian busy. They were full of life and too curious for their own good.

"Oh, good, I'm so glad you're here," Gemma exclaimed as Pearla walked into the sitting room. "I was afraid I'd have to come looking for you."

Pearla laughed. "I promised I'd help. What can I do?"

Four boys came running into the room. Liam and Gemma's twins, Alexander and Andrew headed the group. They were followed by Noah and Rubina's son, Lucian, and her own son.

"Mother, can you tell Angeline to quit following us everywhere we go?" Andrew demanded.

Gemma pinched the bridge of her nose. "Be nice to your sister."

Angeline was Gemma's youngest child, and her only daughter. She reminded Pearla of Lily. She took after her aunt a little too much. She was sure to drive Gemma and Liam mad as she grew up. She fully understood Andrew and Alexander's frustration with their little sister.

"But..."

"No, Drew. You are her older brother. You should be used

to having her follow you around. One day it will be your job to protect her."

"I told you." Alex folded his arms across his chest, glaring at his twin brother. "Next thing you know, Emilia will be joining her."

Emilia was Noah and Rubina's daughter. She was the spitting image of her mother. She had silvery blonde hair and beautiful gray eyes. Her beauty was going to cause Noah problems once suitors began clamoring for her attention. At least they had several years before they had to worry about it.

"I can assure you my sister has better taste." Lucian turned up his nose. "She would rather be a lady."

All four boys left the room, resigned to dealing with their younger sisters.

Pearla shook her head and laughed. Had they ever been that young? The years seemed to fly by, and before they knew it their children would be having families of their own. She wished she could bottle them up and keep them small forever.

"I'm sorry I'm late," Lily rushed into the room. "Brianne had a crisis with one of her dresses and was in a fit of tears. Sometimes I wonder how she could possibly be my daughter. If I hadn't given birth to her, I'd think someone was playing a trick on me."

Pearla glanced at Lily and laughed lightly. Her friend and been through a lot. They all had. After the birth of her son, William, Lily had been afraid she would never get pregnant again. She and Rand had tried to no avail. Pearla was so happy for them when they'd been blissfully surprised to be expecting again. Brianne was the blessing Lily never thought she'd receive. Although, she often remarked that her blessing was as opposite from her as she could get. Lily lamented often how her niece was more like her than her own daughter.

Gemma hugged her and laughed. "Where is she now?"

"She was trying to coerce William to play dolls with her. He tried to tell her he is a grown man now and doesn't play with dolls." Lily shook her head. "She's ten years old and doesn't understand why her big brother would rather do anything but play with her."

"She'll grow out of it, and he'll be an overprotective brother before long." Pearla turned toward Lily and asked, "Now that we're gathered tell me what we have left to do before your parents arrive?"

Lily was probably a general in a previous life. She barked orders and devised plans that would put some to shame. She lifted her hand and started checking off items on the list on her fingers. "Rubina is dealing with the menus and has the staff doing last minute decorations. Everyone that was invited, except my parents, is here. Noah and Liam arranged for them to arrive later this afternoon."

"It sounds like you have everything covered."

She grinned. "Planning has always been one of my strong suits."

"That's putting things mildly," her husband Rand said as he walked into the room. He pulled her into his arms and placed a quick kiss on her lips. "What do you need me to do?"

"Go rescue our son from Brianne. I'm afraid he might murder her if left with her too long."

He laughed. "Consider it done." He strolled out of the room, leaving the ladies to wrap up the festivities.

"Why did I get out of bed again?" Pearla asked. "I was rather warm and content there."

"I bet you were," Lily laughed. "Quit thinking of your husband and keep your mind on task."

"Why should I?" Pearla pouted. "You haven't given me anything to do."

They all enjoyed their husband's attentions. It was one of the things they discussed when they had nothing better to do. There were no blushes between them anymore. They were all well loved by the men in their lives.

"They're here," Rubina exclaimed as she rushed into the room. "They're early. I gave those two men one task and they seemed to have bungled it."

Pearla tilted her head and studied Rubina. She appeared to be stressed out about something. Who had arrived?

"No," Lily muttered. "Leave it to them to come early. I should have known they'd do something like this."

"Who's here?" Pearla asked.

She really should go back to bed. Her brain couldn't think past the pleasure of Damian's arms. It didn't seem as if they needed her help either way. Why not enjoy her day in other ways? The viscount and viscountess weren't supposed...she mentally groaned. How could she be so dense?

"I hear you're having a party for us," Thor bellowed as he entered the room. "When is it supposed to start?"

Pearla jumped from the boom of his voice. She'd met Viscount Torrington on several occasions. It was hard not to when she was so close to his children. He seemed sincere, but a small part of her remained terrified of him. He *had* been a pirate, after all. An endeavor that surely taught him how to give off a dangerous allure as natural as breathing.

Lily threw her arms up in the air. "I don't even know why I try. No one gets anything by him ever since I ran away and married Rand. Now he has spies watching us all the time."

"Princess, if I don't who will?" Lily's father kissed her forehead.

"You do have a valid point." Lily grinned up at her father.

Pia, Lily's mother, rolled her eyes. "Don't encourage him. He's already difficult to live with."

Thor, Viscount Torrington, glanced down at his wife; a hint of wickedness gleamed within his eyes. "You love every minute of it."

Pia, Lady Torrington, actually blushed from the heat of her husband's stare. Pearla didn't think it was possible to make the other woman's cheeks tinge with red.

"Grandfather, I thought I was your princess," a little girl asked as she tugged on his sleeve.

Rand followed behind her. He looked at Lily and shrugged, as if to say nothing could've stopped her. Brianne was a force to be reckoned with—much like her mother. That was the only thing they apparently had in common. Headstrong and determined to get their way.

Lily sighed. Pearla could relate. Her own daughters could be terrors on two feet.

"You're my other princess." He picked her up into his arms and hugged her. "Your mommy was the first princess to capture my heart. I think I have room for both of you."

"Will you play with me?" She pushed her bottom lip out. "William says he's too old to play with dolls."

"Did he?" her grandfather asked. "Don't worry I will have a talk with him later. Why don't you show me these dolls of yours? Are they as pretty as you are?"

"Of course not," she replied and pushed her chin out. "I'm much prettier. Daddy told me so."

Viscount Torrington glanced over at Brianne's father.

"Well she is," Rand replied.

Thor laughed and escorted his granddaughter out of the room. Pearla thought she heard him say, "This once I'll have to agree with your daddy. I didn't usually do it on principle." Pearla's heart melted watching them. She wished her own father had been this way with her. At least her children had Damian's father to dote on them. They didn't miss out the way she had growing up.

Damian, Noah, and Liam entered the room. Liam stared at his mother and shrugged. He too appeared to accept the inevitable and wasn't surprised to see his parents. Noah headed toward Rubina, and Liam joined Gemma. Damian strolled to her side and stood behind her, wrapping his arms around her. Pearla leaned into him and watched their friends and family. They were so blessed to have each other. As chaotic as their lives were, she wouldn't trade it for anything.

"Any regrets?" Damian asked.

It was a question he asked often. His way of checking to make sure she was happy with their life together. They didn't keep anything from each other. Their open communication was a gift they had received the hard way—at the hands of Camellia Fonte. One they never thanked her for, or intended to. It was a harsh way for them to begin to open up to each other fully. That night, after they made love for the first time, Damian finally told her everything that he endured on the island. She shuddered whenever she thought about what he had been through, but she kept his secrets close to her heart. If he wanted to share them, it was up to him. It was his past and his to keep to himself.

"Never." And she meant it. There was no reason to regret the choices they made. They had so many good memories already and many more they would make.

"I love you, *cara*."

"I love you too."

Words that had become easier to say the more she uttered them. Her heart overflowed with happiness. Damian and their family was all she needed. The rest were just details. They could survive anything as long as they had each other. Damian would always hold her heart, and she trusted him to keep it safe always.

He kissed the top of her head. All her doubts were left in the past where they belonged. This was the life they were meant to have. One day their children would arrange such an event to celebrate their love and marriage. Their future was bright, and they had so much to look forward to. More importantly, they had all the blessings in the world to keep them content at that moment and for years to come. She'd once said nothing was forever. Now she knew better. Her luck had changed when she met Damian. It might have taken them a while to find their way to each other, but the struggle had only strengthened their bond.

Their love was all encompassing.

It was all she could ever ask for...

Read further for an excerpt from Saved by My Blackguard: Linked Across Time1

EXCERPT: ALL THE LADIES LOVE COVENTRY

BLUESTOCKINGS DEFYING ROGUES

USA TODAY
BESTSELLING AUTHOR

Dawn Brower

All the Ladies
Love Coventry

PROLOGUE

April 1794

C harles Lindsay, the Earl of Coventry surveyed the building he was hoping to purchase. The structure was sound and would work splendidly for what he had in mind for it. The street it was located on was also ideal. A secret gentleman's club would be well hidden in the neighborhood, and its residents wouldn't question the constant comings and goings that would be involved. He had a lot of plans and this townhouse was only the beginning.

"The owner is willing to part with it?" He turned toward the solicitor in charge of the sale. Charles didn't want to seem too eager. It might give the solicitor a reason to raise the price. He wouldn't pay a penny more than it was worth.

"He is, my lord," he answered. His salt and pepper hair was sprinkled around his ears and the back of his head, but the top was completely bald. The solicitor had beady eyes that made him appear untrustworthy. Not a good look on someone that should invoke that particular feeling. "Would you like to make an offer?"

"No," he answered. "It needs major renovations and I'm not sure it'll work for what I have in mind." That was a lie, but he didn't want to make the man aware of his complete interest. "The entire bottom floor would need to be stripped and the walls rebuilt. Your employer is asking too much."

"I see…" The solicitor swallowed hard. Charles wished he could recall his name, but as it hadn't been important to him he'd dismissed it upon hearing it. He fumbled with some parchments and then glanced up. "Is there anything that will convince you to purchase it."

Charles held back a grin. It wouldn't work in his favor and he did want the property. He tapped his chin and tried to act as if he was considering his options. The truth was he knew exactly what his next move would be. That was the benefit of being several steps ahead of his opponent. He had a gift of seeing the larger picture and how all the pieces around him could fit together. This project of his was going to be big and he had to do everything right for it to work. "I might consider it if the owner will take off a thousand pounds from the selling price. I won't pay a shilling more than that."

He shuffled his feet and then met Charles gaze. "That sounds reasonable, my lord. I'll inform the owner that you're willing to purchase it."

Charles lifted a brow. "Is that all?" He shrugged and headed to the exit. As far as he was concerned their business had been concluded. If the owner took the offer the solicitor could send him a missive about it. He had a good feeling though. Soon he'd have the building necessary to start his club.

He hadn't reached the exit before the solicitor called out to him. "Lord Coventry."

He turned toward him and said, "Yes?"

"I have the authority to approve the sale within a certain amount. If you want the property it's yours."

This time he did allow the smile to form on his face. The Coventry Club was now one step closer to becoming a reality. He couldn't wait to tell his good friend the George, the Earl of Harrington about it. They could plan the development and reconstruction of the townhouse together.

"Wonderful," he told the solicitor. "I'll let my solicitor know and you two can handle the details." Charles nodded at him. "Thank you for your assistance." With those words he did exit the building and headed home. He had an appointment later with George and they could make their final plans then.

~

CHARLES TAPPED HIS FINGER ON HIS DESK IMPATIENTLY. WHERE the bloody hell was George? He was supposed to arrive several hours ago. He sighed and poured a glass of brandy from the decanter on his desk. They would have to discuss his plans for Coventry Club later. He sipped on his brandy and wondered what could have held his friend up. For the life of him he couldn't discern a reason for George to stay away. His friend never missed an appointment. He was the most reliable man of Charles acquaintance.

He set his glass down and peered at the deed to his new property. He'd already sent out missives to start the repairs and renovations. In a matter of months, no more than a year, his dream would be a reality. A safe haven for men who had no place else, a den of iniquity for those that needed it, but mostly a place where loyalty would prevail more than anything else.

The door to his study flew open and George stepped inside. His face lit up with a huge grin as he exclaimed, "I'm a father Charles."

He'd forgotten George's wife was enceinte. That was a damn good reason for his friend to be late. Now that he realized why he felt like a right arse. Charles reached for a glass and poured two fingers of brandy into it, then handed it to his friend. He lifted his own glass and toasted, "To fatherhood." He sipped his brandy, and then asked. "I must ask—an heir or a daughter?"

"It's a boy," George answered. "The most perfect little bundle of joy I've ever held. We named him Jonas after my maternal great grandfather. It'll make my mum happy."

Charles knew he should look for a wife and carry on his line, but the idea of tying himself to one woman for the rest of his life didn't appeal to him. He hadn't met a woman that inspired that kind of commitment. George had married his wife because of his father's demands. The Duke of Southington was a difficult man to say no to. Charles didn't envy his friend's situation in that regard. "I'm sure she'll be ecstatic to just have a grandchild to dote on. I hear women like that sort of thing."

"You're probably correct in that assumption. Either way I'm grateful it's a boy. The birth was hard on Sarah. I don't think she could handle another pregnancy." He sighed. "Jonas is a blessing for us both. My father will finally leave us alone about carrying on the family line."

"Your father is brutal." He was an overbearing arse who browbeat George whenever he could. Charles wished he could find a way to remove the Duke of Southington from his friend's life. Unfortunately, it wasn't up to him to extricate George from the control of his father. His friend had to find the bollocks to do it himself. It was the only way he would ever know what it felt like to be free to make his own decisions.

"I have news," Charles began. "I've purchased the building I need for Coventry Club."

"You did?" His face lit up with happiness. "That's wonderful. Now you can achieve your goals and we'll all have a place to escape the realities of life."

"I'll have to discern the rules of the club before we invite new members. I'd like you to be the first head of the club if you're willing." He wanted George to have the responsibility so he felt included, and it would give him something else to focus on other than the terror his father was.

"Me?" George asked surprised. "You don't want to run your own club?"

"I'd much rather enjoy it at first. One day I'll take over the duties, but I'd like the time to experience it first. You're much more level headed than I am and will be able to enforce whatever rules we put in place. I think the first one will be— the leader of the club is the only one that can be married. I don't want a bunch of cheating husbands to take their mistresses to the club."

"So once they marry they have to hand in their key?" George asked. "That's not a bad idea. So you're not going to take over until you find a bride? That's going to be a long ways off isn't it?"

Charles smiled. "I know one day I'll have to marry

someone, but you're correct, I don't plan on finding a lady to wed for some years to come. I'm going to depend upon you to keep things running smoothly until then. But there isn't a requirement to wed to hold the position. If you find it is too difficult I can take over. If I marry before that...I'll have to take over is all."

"Yes," George agreed. "That makes sense." He nodded at Charles. "All right I'll run your club." His lips tilted upward into another grin. "I can't wait to get started."

Charles picked up his glass and tipped it at his friend. "I already have my friend. Now let's drink to that new son of yours."

"That is a fabulous idea," George replied. He picked up his glass and clinked it with Charles's. "And to your future club. It'll be as successful as you imagined it would be."

They both drank the contents of their glasses, and then Charles filled them again with brandy. They drank several glasses before George left. They had all the rules of the club in place by then and the future of his Coventry Club would be a reality before long. Charles loved when a good plan came to fruition.

ALSO BY DAWN BROWER

Broken Pearl

Deadly Benevolence

A Wallflower's Christmas Kiss

A Gypsy's Christmas Kiss

Snowflake Kisses

Begin Again

There You'll Be

Better as a Memory

Won't Let Go

Enduring Legacy

The Legacy's Origin

Charming Her Rogue

Scandal Meets Love

Love Only Me (Amanda Mariel)

Find Me Love (Dawn Brower)

If It's Love (Amanda Mariel)

Odds of Love (Dawn Brower)

Bluestockings Defying Rogues

When An Earl Turns Wicked

A Lady Hoyden's Secret

One Wicked Kiss

Earl In Trouble

All the Ladies Love Coventry

Marsden Descendants

Rebellious Angel

Tempting An American Princess

Heart in Waiting

Broken Curses
The Enchanted Princess
The Bespelled Knight
The Magical Hunt

Ever Beloved
Forever My Earl
Always My Viscount
Infinitely My Marquess

Kismet Bay
Once Upon a Christmas
New Year Revelation
All Things Valentine
Luck At First Sight
Coming Soon
Endless Summer Days

ABOUT THE AUTHOR

USA TODAY Bestselling author, DAWN BROWER writes both historical and contemporary romance. There are always stories inside her head; she just never thought she could make them come to life. That creativity has finally found an outlet.

Growing up she was the only girl out of six children. She is a single mother of two teenage boys; there is never a dull moment in her life. Reading books is her favorite hobby and she loves all genres.

bookbub.com/authors/dawn-brower

facebook.com/AuthorDawnBrower

twitter.com/1DawnBrower

instagram.com/1DawnBrower

AFTERWORD

Thank you so much for taking the time to read my book.
Your opinion matters!
Please take a moment to review this book on your favorite
review site and share your opinion with fellow readers.

USA TODAY
BESTSELLING AUTHOR
Dawn Brower

CAPTIVATING ROMANCES THAT TRANSCEND TIME

www.authordawnbrower.com